Ornamen

6

1761 – 1804

Chris Fogg is a creative producer, writer, director and dramaturg, who has written and directed for the theatre for many years, as well as collaborating artistically with choreographers and contemporary dance companies.

Ornaments of Grace is a chronicle of eleven novels. *Kettle* is the sixth in the sequence.

He has previously written more than thirty works for the stage as well as four collections of poems, stories and essays. These are*: Special Relationships, Northern Songs, Painting by Numbers* and *Dawn Chorus* (with woodcut illustrations by Chris Waters), all published by Mudlark Press.

Several of Chris's poems have appeared in International Psychoanalysis (IP), a US online journal, as well as *in Climate of Opinion*, a selection of verse in response to the work of Sigmund Freud edited by Irene Willis, and *What They Bring: The Poetry of Migration & Immigration*, co-edited by Irene Willis and Jim Haba, each published by IP, in 2017 and 2020.

Ornaments of Grace

(or *Unhistoric Acts*)

6

Laurel

Vol. 1: Kettle

by

Chris Fogg

flaxbooks

First published 2020
© Chris Fogg 2020

Chris Fogg has asserted his rights under Copyright Designs & Patents Act 1988 to be identified as the author of this book

ISBN Number: 9781708151447

Cover and design by: Kama Glover

Cover Image: Dalton Collecting Marsh Fire Gas, one of the Manchester Murals by Ford Madox Brown, reprinted by kind permission of Manchester Libraries, Information & Archives

This book is sold subject to the condition that it shall not, by way of trade or otherwise be lent, resold, hired out, or otherwise circulated without the publisher's prior consent in any form of binding or cover other than that in which it is published and without a similar condition, including this condition, being imposed upon the subsequent purchaser.

Printed in Poland by Amazon

Although some of the people featured in this book are real, and several of the events depicted actually happened, *Ornaments of Grace* remains a work of fiction.

For Amanda and Tim

dedicated to the memory

of my parents and grandparents

Ornaments of Grace (*or Unhistoric Acts*) is a sequence of eleven novels set in Manchester between 1760 and 2020. Collectively they tell the story of a city in four elements.

All the Fowls of the Air is the tenth book in the sequence.

The full list of titles is:

1. Pomona (Water)

2. Tulip (Earth)
    Vol 1: **Enclave**
    Vol 2: **Nymphs & Shepherds**
    Vol 3: **The Spindle Tree**
    Vol 4: **Return**

3. Laurel (Air)
    Vol 1: **Kettle**
    Vol 2: **Victor**
    Vol 3: **Victrix**
      part 1: **A Grain of Mustard Seed**
      part 2: **The Waxing of a Great Tree**
      part 3: **All the Fowls of the Air**

4. Moth (Fire)

Each book can be read independently or as part of the sequence.

"It's always too soon to go home. And it's always too soon to calculate effect... Cause-and-effect assumes that history marches forward, but history is not an army. It is a crab scuttling sideways, a drip of soft water wearing away stone, an earthquake breaking centuries of tension."

Rebecca Solnit: Hope in the Dark
(Untold Histories, Wild Possibilities)

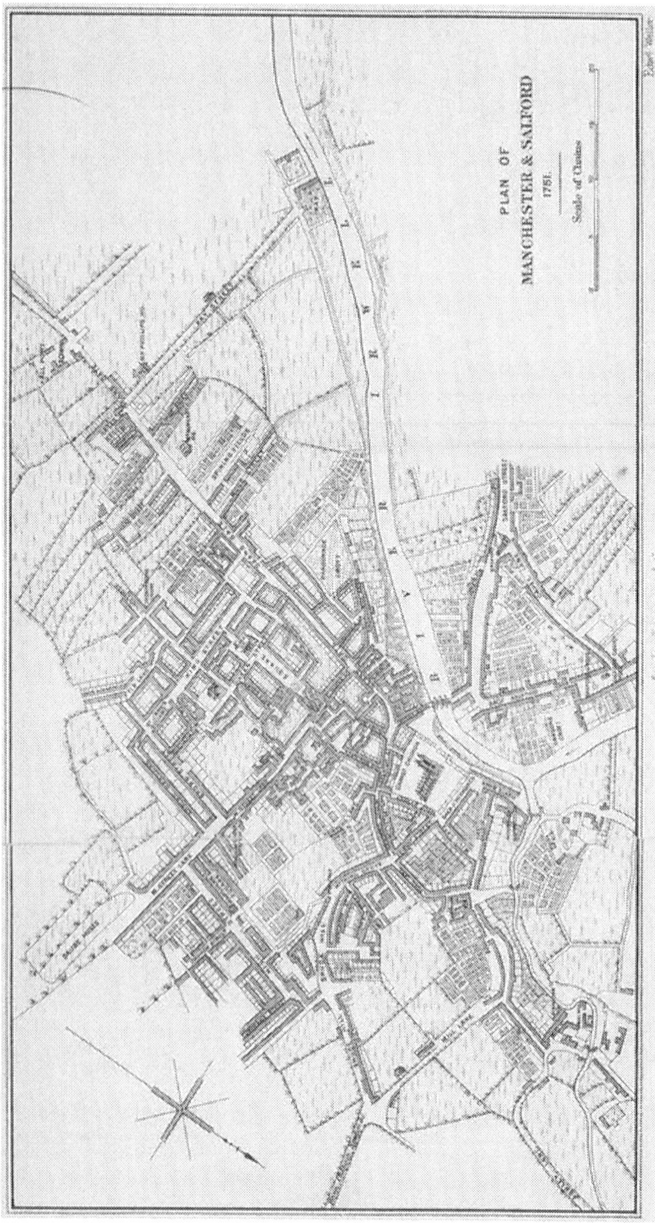
PLAN OF
MANCHESTER & SALFORD
1751.
Scale of Chains
RIVER IRWELL

Contents

PROLOGUE
1761

in which a piece of raw cotton is transformed into a singular and much sought after article

19

ONE
Earthquake

1777

in which an earthquake strikes – a swarm of flies escapes – a literary club is formed – twin boys are born – and church bells ring unaided

Chapter 1:	21st September	31
Chapter 2:	14th September	34
Chapter 3:	15th September	100
Chapter 4:	10th October	115

TWO
Flight

1785

in which two balloons take to the skies – a new cotton mill is opened – a proposal of marriage is offered – a naked cross country race is run – a young man joins the army – fourteen families arrive from overseas – a daring escape is made from a first storey window – we learn more about the piece of cloth, a brief history of its owners during the first years of its existence – and a new settlement is built

Chapter 5: 6th – 13th May
    Sunday 6th   125
    Monday 7th   142
    Tuesday 8th   159
    Wednesday 9th   183
    Thursday 10th   211
    Friday 11th   219
    Saturday 12th   234
    Sunday 13th   361

Chapter 6:   1761 – 1777   376
Chapter 7:   17th October 1785   422

THREE
The Lot

1798

in which a lecture is given on aspects of colour
wherein not everything is black and white –
a kaleidoscope is made – a game of cat's cradle is played –
some places and people are given new names –
a lot is cast – three young men come of age –
one discovers his calling, one resists his fate, one experiences
an epiphany –
and a new use is found for some old bricks

Chapter 8:   29th September   437
Chapter 9:   15th October   457
Chapter 10: 31st October   479

FOUR
Weights & Measures

1804

*in which an early atomic theory is expounded – a duel is fought
– an eminent French ambassador visits Manchester –
a person is placed under house arrest –
a painting is commissioned – a play is given –
a bequest is used to bring light into darkness –
and a balancing act is attempted one last time*

Chapter 11:	2nd February – Candlemas	511
Chapter 12:	1st August – Lammas	524
Chapter 13:	29th September – Michaelmas	570
Chapter 14:	25th December – Christmas	658

Map, Manchester: 1750	10
Engraving, Manchester SW Prospect	18
Dramatis Personae	670
Acknowledgements	682
Biography	685

Ornaments of Grace

"Wisdom is the principal thing. Therefore get wisdom and within all thy getting get understanding. Exalt her and she shall promote thee. She shall bring thee to honour when thou dost embrace her. She shall give to thine head an ornament of grace. A crown of glory shall she deliver to thee."

Proverbs: 4, verses 7 – 9

written around the domed ceiling of the Great Hall Reading Room Central Reference Library, St Peter's Square, Manchester

"Fecisti patriam diversis de gentibus unam…"
"From differing peoples you have made one homeland…"

Rutilius Claudius Namatianus:
De Redito Suo, verse 63

"To be hopeful in bad times is not just foolishly romantic. It is based on the fact that human history is a history not only of cruelty, but also of compassion, sacrifice, courage, kindness. What we choose to emphasise in this complex history will determine our lives. If we see only the worst, it destroys our capacity to do something. If we remember those times and places—and there are so many—where people have behaved magnificently, this gives us the energy to act, and at least the possibility of sending this spinning top of a world in a different direction. And if we do act, in however small a way, we don't have to wait for some grand utopian future. The future is an infinite succession of presents, and to live now as we think human beings should live, in defiance of all that is bad around us, is itself a marvellous victory."

Howard Zinn: A Power Governments Cannot Suppress

Laurel (i)

A heavy numbness seized her limbs, thin bark closed over her breast,
Her hair turned into leaves, her arms into branches,
Her feet so swift a moment ago stuck fast in slow-growing roots,
Her face lost in the canopy –
Only her shining beauty was left...

(Ovid: Metamorphosis, Book 1)

Air (i)

"This castle hath a pleasant seat. The air
Nimbly and sweetly recommends itself
Unto our nobler senses..."

"Whither are they vanished?
Into the air, and what seemed corporal melted
As breath into the wind..."

"Fair is foul and foul is fair
Hover through the fog and filthy air..."

(Shakespeare: Macbeth)

Kettle

– noun

a container, having a lid, a handle and spout, in which water is boiled and converted into steam

a semi-spherical drum, traditionally made of copper with a calf skin covering, originally used as a military drum, its sound resembling thunder

of fish: a completely different kind of person or thing from the one previously thought

an awkward state of affairs

of birds: collective noun for a flight of birds, such as kites or hawks

– verb

to confine a group of protesters to a small area, as a method of crowd control during a demonstration

(Oxford English Dictionary)

R. Whitworth: Manchester, South West Prospect circa 1750

"The greatest mere village in England…"

Daniel Defoe: *A Tour through the Whole Island of Great Britain*

Prologue

in which a piece of raw cotton is transformed into a singular and much sought after article

1761

Manchester is neither Borough nor Corporation, but a spacious, rich and populous Inland Town in the Hundred of Salford and South East portion of Lancashire.

Situate upon a Rocky Cliff, at the confluence of the Rivers Irk and Irwell, which add much pleasure to its healthfull soil, which is most part gravelly, it is a Mannour with Courts Leet and Barony; which at the decease of the present Lady Dowager Bland will devolve to Sir Oswald Mosley, Baronet. 'Tis governed by two Constables, annually chosen in the Court Leet at Michaelmas. 'Tis famous for the Woollen, Linnen and Cotton Manufactories, whereby it is immensely enriched and many a hundred poor families employed therein from several Counties.

The Town is adorned with many noted Buildings and with handsom broad Streets both New and Old; and a large Bridge over the River Irwell which joyneth Salford, a populous, Beautiful Town, giving name to the Hundred, and seemeth as a Suburb thereto. The Exchange now building by Sir Oswald and the River Irwell falling into the Mersey, the Town communicateth with Liverpool which, by its expence and labour, hath gained a considerable progress and is soon expected to be made navigable.

Inscription beneath An Engraving of
The South West Prospect of Manchester
County Palatine of Lancaster by S & N Buck

On an unexpectedly warm March afternoon, just at that point when spring shifts from being a distant hope to a definite promise, like a moth emerging from the entombment of its chrysalis, Gabriel Locke was driving his cart the twelve miles from Manchester to Rochdale, laden with goods collected from the Castlefield Basin, where the soon-to-be-opened Duke's Cut, the 3rd Earl of Bridgewater's much lauded canal, would flow into the River Medlock, but which for now still marked the end of the Mersey-Irwell Navigation – although *weaving* would perhaps be a more accurate term than *driving* to describe Gabriel's somewhat erratic forward momentum. He wove thus, not because the contents of his cart consisted solely of bales of cotton, though that would have been almost poetically apt, but because he had been imbibing at regular intervals from a hip flask of rum he always carried with him when making this journey. To those who asked, he would say that these small but frequent infusions were necessary to stave off the cold, but he could not use such an excuse to justify his over-indulgence on as warm a day as this. Perhaps it was the very heat of the day which exacerbated the effect of the rum, for on this particular day he quite literally lurched from one side of the track to the other. He was sober enough still to comprehend that if he continued along his present course, he could well end up in one of the many ditches that lured the unwary traveller along both sides of the road, but not so sober as to prevent it from happening if he were not to take the utmost care.

Somehow he arrived at his final dropping point, in the hamlet of Bagslate Moor, a stone's throw from the village of Norden, just three miles to the west of Rochdale, where an excited Edwin Stone awaited him.

"What took thee so long, Gabriel?" asked Edwin, at once helping to unload the bales he had been so impatiently anticipating.

"I've got a touch o' the wavy eye," confided Gabriel in a whisper. "The world just won't keep still. It insists on tilting first this way, then that, as though its very axis might keel over and not get up again. 'Tis a sign for sure, Edwin." He pointed to where Edwin was not, for Gabriel was by now seeing twin versions of everything.

"It's a sign tha's been drinking too much too early," said Edwin with a grin. He held up a half-eaten apple to Gabriel's patient old horse. "It's a good job Old Ned knows his way home, for I'm as certain as the shadow that'll follow thee whichever way tha' takes, that tha's as lost as if tha' were in a maze."

"I am, Edwin, and that's the truth," sighed Gabriel helplessly. "How will I ever find my way?"

"Put tha' faith in t' Lord, Gabriel. Amos, Chapter three, Verse seven: *'The Lord God will do nothing but revealeth his secrets unto his servants, the prophets'*."

"I'm no prophet, Gabriel."

"Then put tha' faith in Old Ned." And he slapped the rear of the faithful nag, who at once began to trot his much travelled way back towards home.

The raw cotton had travelled from the Tappahannock Plantation in Virginia, owned by the merchant Thomas Hibbert, down the James River to the port city of Manchester, close by the state capital Richmond on the opposite bank, where it was loaded onto *The Aurora*, a three-masted brigantine barque, for its passage across the Atlantic. After a reasonable, if at times choppy crossing, it landed in Liverpool. There the cotton was transferred to a fully-rigged Mersey Flat, which conveyed it the fifteen hours it took to travel down the Mersey-Irwell Navigation as far as Water Street in that other Manchester, where Thomas Hibbert's brother, Robert, who headed the English side of the family business from his office on King Street, signed for delivery, before dispatching it to Gabriel, who was waiting at the quayside with Ned and his cart. From one Manchester to the other had taken just eight weeks.

The day after Edwin had taken possession of the raw cotton he and his family began their systematic and diligent work upon it. It was of the Native American species *gossypium barbadense*, which naturally produced longer, stronger fibres. This made it perfect for the production of high quality cloth, which was precisely why Edwin had ordered it.

First they had to check that all of the seeds had been fully removed. This was a time-consuming, often painful process because of the sharp edges or stickers the boll might have. Most of this would have been carried out by slaves on the plantation before shipment, where they would have had to wait until the bolls turned brown and began to open. Then they would have removed them from the plant and placed them into large wooden bowls, from where they would have been taken one at a time and the loose cotton picked from them. The seeds would then have been stored in separate containers to be pressed later into oil for burning in lamps. Sometimes a few stray seeds would be left behind and Edwin wanted to make absolutely certain none remained before they embarked upon the next stage of the process – the roving.

Once the seeds had been fully extracted the fibres needed to be combed, or carded, to untangle the threads to produce a slender rope of parallel strands in order to make the next stage – the spinning – possible. There were different ways of doing this. The rope was beaten with sticks and teased between the metal teeth of small hand combs. This work was carried out by Edwin's children, while he supervised the older men, who combed the longer fibres with outsized, warmed needles. There were two basic types of carded fibre – woollen or worsted. The latter produced a smoother, stronger yarn and was extremely fine. This was what Edwin required for the job he had in mind. As soon as the fibre was carded to Edwin's satisfaction, it was semi-spun into long slivers, or slubs, which were then ready for the spinning proper.

The spinning was the women's domain, overseen by Edwin's wife, Joan, on large wheels with a sharp projecting needle – hence the fairy story. It was done standing up and required a large space about them. Joan was renowned for miles around for her proficiency in being able to spin the finest yarn, gossamer thin, perfect for this most special of items, such as the one which Edwin had now been tasked to produce.

There was talk everywhere these days of new machines being tested that might replace the likes of Joan. Men such as James Hargreaves of Oswaldtwistle, Richard Arkwright a few miles away in Preston, and Samuel Crompton in nearby Bolton, were taking out patents for a jenny, or engine, which might drive eight, fifty, even a hundred spindles simultaneously. Edwin heard such talk and was troubled. Recently it had grown, like the rumble he would hear coming from under the ground sometimes, when the quarrymen were blasting for stone at Tong End a couple of miles away. Change was coming. He could feel it. The miners thought little of cutting away the earth to a depth of twenty or, even, thirty feet, leaving great scars upon the surface of the moors. If they were not careful, he thought, the whole land would slip from under them.

Edwin was not against change *per se*. It was in the nature of humankind to want to secure a better, more comfortable life for itself and its children. But in this instance Edwin distrusted the motives behind it. These machines were designed to put the likes of Joan and all the other spinners out of work. It was more about cutting corners and costs, for the betterment of the few, at the expense of the many. But no machine in Edwin's opinion would ever spin yarn half so fine as Joan did on her own individual wheel. And if the minds of men with an eye only for profit were seeking ways of eliminating the need for Joan and her ilk, how long before his own particular craft came under threat? What did the future hold for handloom weavers such as himself? Or his son, Henry, not yet fourteen, but who was already showing signs of impatience.

He took Joan's exquisitely spun yarn – perfect for a delicate, fine muslin – and threaded it onto his loom. Some looms had four shafts, others eight. Edwin's had sixteen. Suspended from these shafts were the heddles – small hooked strings through which the cotton was threaded – not to be confused with the pedals, which were situated beneath the loom and operated by the weaver's feet. The threads that passed from the back of the loom, those that had been threaded through the heddles to the front, were known as the warp. These had also to pass through something called the reed or beater, which secured and tightened them. As Edwin pressed one or more of the pedals, one set of warp threads were raised while the rest were lowered. In this way he created a shed, through which he passed the shuttle on which the weft thread was wound. Edwin then changed the pedals, creating a different shed. The shuttle was now able to be passed back through that new shed and so a piece of cloth began to be fashioned, consisting of two sets of threads, one set the warp, the other the weft.

Between the pedals and the shafts was a series of horizontal rods known as lambs. The whole contraption – heddles, shafts, pedals and lambs – was suspended from the main frame of the loom, which was known as the castle, by pulleys, which in turn had further small rods known as horses. The whole edifice appeared to Edwin as something quite magnificent, a castle indeed, protecting him from the buffeting forces of the world beyond it.

The order in which the warp threads were raised and lowered was crucial in determining the pattern. This was where Edwin truly came into his own. He could envisage the whole design in his mind and transfer that to the cloth as it grew inch by inch before his eyes simply by touch, a skill he had acquired over many years, passed down to him by his father and grandfather, and generations of weavers before them.

To watch Edwin at work, rhythmically adapting his body to the clickety-clack of the loom, was like witnessing a dance, of which Edwin was both performer and choreographer, his actions completed by the inclusion of the one modern innovation he approved of – John Kay's flying shuttle, invented less than thirty years before, just down the road from Edwin, in Walmersley, near Bury, but which now he would not be without. Instead of having to pass the shuttle through the shed manually, as his father and grandfather had had to, all he had to do now, with a practised, almost nonchalant flick of the wrist, was simply to pull a cord. This enabled the shuttle to fly through on a sort of spring mechanism. It was this spring that produced the familiar, reassuring sound of the loom, the clickety-clack, which provided the pulse and rhythm for his dance.

The idea for the design for the item he was now working on came to him through his son, Henry, who as a rule could barely keep still for a minute. Edwin smiled as he recalled the occasion, not three months before, when he had first received the confirmation of the order from Mr Robert Hibbert in King Street. An excited Henry came running in from outside.

"Quickly, Father. Look. Tha' must come, see. I've never seen t' like of it."

Indulgently Edwin set down his pipe and followed his son to the back of the cottage. Over the years several laurel bushes had grown and spread there, forming a kind of hedge sheltering them from the winds that would blow down from the moors up above Red Lumb, a prominent outcrop of millstone grit, under whose shadow they lived. Just as they neared the hedge, Henry turned to his father and put his finger to his lips, so that the two of them crept the last few yards. Once they had reached it, Henry silently pointed. At first Edwin could not think what it was that his son was trying to show him. Then he saw it. A succession of tiny wings, opening and closing, like the sails on a fleet of miniature ships. There, basking in the last of the afternoon sun, lay a whisper of moths. Father and son stood transfixed, watching their display for many minutes until a sudden gust riffled the laurel leaves, and the moths took flight as one – a luminous cloud of them – before dispersing along the line of bushes, where they once again proceeded to open and close their wings until, at last, they settled.

Edwin did not forget this sight, as much for the effect it produced on his son, as for the inherent beauty of it. When he received this special order through Mr Hibbert, the memory of it returned to him. It would make the perfect design. A repeating pattern of moths caught in the web of laurel, in the most delicate of fine muslins, to match both the fragility and strength of their wings. White on white on white.

He set about a complex, precise order of threading and pedalling in order to create the repeating pattern, completed afterwards with hand stitching and over-darning of the more subtle details, such as the striated markings on the moths' wings' backs.

Edwin was now ready for the final stage of the process – the finishing. For such a special cloth as this, he would do it by hand. He carefully cut the cotton from the loom in such a way as to prevent any fraying or loose ends. The straightness of the long edges of the cloth, known as the selvages, was a sure sign of quality to the connoisseurs of such matters, and such was the accuracy of Edwin's work with this piece that it could have been held up against a surveyor's ruler and judged the truer.

Finally the cloth was washed in cold water, then stretched to ensure it did not shrink and remained even throughout. When it was finally finished, Edwin held it up to the light to inspect it. Yes. It was as good a piece as he had ever made. Almost perfect. Fit for a King. Or, as in this case, a Queen. For the item had been requested as a gift for Queen Charlotte on the Coronation of her husband King George III in a few weeks' time. Edwin sighed with a deep sense of relief and pleasure.

This would establish his reputation once and for all. It would make both his name and his fortune.

Just at that moment he felt a growing vibration beneath his feet. The whole house shook with it. The windows and doors rattled. A slate fell from the roof and smashed as it landed outside.

"What is it?" asked Henry in a mixture of alarm and excitement.

"It's another explosion in the quarry," replied his father.

"What does it mean?"

Edwin thought a while before he answered. He remembered the talk of the new machines he had heard folk mention at *Owd Betts*, the inn up at Ashworth Moor, out along the Edenfield Road. He picked up his pipe and tried to relight it.

"Summat's coming," he said.

"What?"

"I don't know, son. Summat big…"

The match struck and flared.

ONE

Earthquake

1777

*in which an earthquake strikes –
a swarm of flies escapes – a literary club is formed –
twin boys are born –
and church bells ring unaided*

1

1777

21st September

Afterwards they would all be able to recall precisely where they were the moment the tremors began.

"I was upstairs in the Function Room of *The Bull's Head Inn* at Shude Hill," said Charles White, founding doctor of Manchester's new Infirmary.

"As were we," chimed the three Thomases – Barnes, Henry and Perceval – pouring themselves a stiff brandy each. "We had invited anyone who might be interested in forming an illustrious club, something we hoped might become a significant contributor to the artistic and scientific debates of the day. Now, at least, we have a suitable topic for our first full meeting."

"I was having supper with my good friend John Wesley," said Andrew Oldham, felt maker and resident of Newton Lane. "We were discussing the possibility of building a new chapel on some adjoining land. I happened to be looking out of the window at the several small fires that had been lit by squatters in the unfinished houses beyond the hedgerow opposite."

"I was just on my way to those same small fires," cut in Mrs Elizabeth Raffald, wife of the publican at *The Bull's Head*. "I remember acknowledging Dr White as he arrived for the meeting upstairs. I'd been called to attend to one of the squatters who was about to give birth out there in the open, beside one of the fires. It half crossed my mind to ask Dr White to come with me, but I was certain he would have trusted me to manage on my own."

"That's quite correct," said Dr White. "Mrs Raffald is a most competent midwife. If there had been complications, she would most certainly have sent for me. But no word came."

"I was a guest of Mr Joseph Saxon and his family," said Brother John Swertner, a follower of the Moravian doctrine, "in their modest town house in Spring Gardens, on a visit from Fulneck in Yorkshire. Brother La Trobe was there, Brother Worthington too, as well as Mr John Lees of Clarkesfield in Oldham, together with a number of Brethren and Sisters from the congregations in Shakerley and Manchester, along with several from Dukinfield. After a plain but wholesome supper of mutton broth, at which we discussed plans being put forward by Mr Lees for the establishment of a new settlement at Fairfield, Brother La Trobe offered up a fervent prayer for success in our enterprise. I then retired to my chamber, where I worked by candlelight upon my picture of a Great Vine, with its spreading clusters, upon which I have been labouring these many years."

"Whereas I had just begun to show Sir Ashton Lever my collection of live insects," cried sixteen-year-old Leigh Philips.

"That he had," rejoined Sir Ashton, "much to my delight, after what had been the dullest of dull evenings."

"Quite so," agreed his wife, "but it was far duller for me, I can assure you, for I did not have the benefit of being distracted by twelve different varieties of fruit fly."

"Seventeen, to be precise. But needs must, my dear, in these straitened times, when even gentry must go cap in hand to captains of industry if one's debts are to be repaid."

"Or one's extravagances curtailed?"

They each exchanged a ruefully raised eyebrow.

"The tremor provided some much needed excitement."

"Yes. We may disagree on many things, but in that we are of one mind. Come – I believe our horses have been recovered and we may at last begin our journey home…"

"My collection was scattered to the four winds. Almost as if it had never been."

"When I got there, I was too late. The poor woman had died."

"Something is beginning here. Something new."

"And where better than here, in England's fastest growing metropolis."

"We have to provide more shelter."

"More beds."

"An exclusive club. Members only."

"A growing vine."

"I shall start on a new collection."

2

14th September

One week earlier.

It was a cold, unseasonably cheerless night. Saturday the 14th of September, 1777. The sun had not shone all day, and a low, heavy blanket of cloud lay across the town. The air felt uncomfortably thick, and the light, as it drained from the evening sky, was a sulphurous yellow.

A mischief of rats huddled for warmth in the corner of the stable at the back of Lever's Row on the edge of the Daub Holes, a series of open clay pits in the centre of Manchester. Sir Ashton Lever, the son of Sir James Darcy Lever, former High Sheriff of Lancashire, after whom the Row had been named, was guest of honour at the home of Mr John Philips and his brothers Nathaniel and Thomas, arguably the largest manufacturers of textiles in the town, certainly the most influential, for John was Deputy Lieutenant for Cheshire, Nathaniel a Justice of the Peace for Lancashire, and Thomas the Chairman of Magistrates for Stockport. The stable had only recently been installed and at this moment it housed a fine pair of nut brown Cleveland Bays, which had conveyed Sir Ashton Lever the five and three quarter miles there from his home in Alkrington Hall, and which now munched contentedly on a truss of hay, beneath which the rats had hunkered down.

As had become his practice ever since he first founded the Manchester Infirmary just twenty-five years before with his colleague, the industrialist Joseph Bancroft, in 1752, Dr Charles White was making his nightly patrol of the wards.

Although the scientific evidence for his belief that cleanliness, if not exactly the bedfellow of Godliness, was nevertheless a close companion, as well as a cure-all for many of the various devilries visited upon the hospital by cleanliness's so-called counterpart, the scurvies and scrofulas, dropsies and diphtherias, was not yet forthcoming, he still insisted on the highest possible standards of hygiene to be in place throughout, which was not, he was sorry to observe, the case with other similar establishments he had visited, especially those in London, where he had recently been invited to deliver a lecture to the Royal Society on his various breakthroughs and discoveries. Sir Oswald Mosley, Lord of the Manor of Manchester, had granted Dr White a nine hundred and ninety-nine year lease on the section of land known as the Daub Holes, those aforementioned open clay pits filled with stagnant, mosquito-ridden water, for an annual rent of just six pounds. In less than five years it had become necessary to add further wings and outbuildings – an asylum for lunatics, a laundry, a public baths and a wash house. Dr White was an ardent advocate of the benefits obtained from the regular use of the various amenities on offer. Cold water baths could be purchased for sixpence, a warm bath for ninepence, and a Buxton bath – hot water mixed with edifying herbal salts – for a shilling. Prices were doubled for Sundays, but proved extremely popular nevertheless, though people with venereal diseases were excluded from the Buxton baths, which were heated to a temperature of ninety-two degrees Fahrenheit and could house more than six thousand two hundred in a single dip.

Dr White also forbade those who suffered from the more contagious diseases, such as typhoid and cholera, from admission anywhere in the Infirmary, where they might spread their infections unchecked. Instead, each day would see scores, if not hundreds, of such poor unfortunates huddling together on the steps outside, pitifully crying out for cures instead of coins, neither of which would be forthcoming. He daily dispatched the nurses on a quick check of those queuing up outside, instructing them to pinch the backs of their hands. Loss of elasticity of the skin, its failure to return quickly to its original position, was a sure sign of the early onset of those unwelcome putrid fevers. The appearance of a flat, rose-coloured rash on the body of any of those clamouring to be admitted would lead to their immediate expulsion from the site, accompanied by the gift of a bag of apples and the kind but unambiguous command to stay away until all instances of vomiting and diarrhoea had ceased.

Andrew Oldham, felt maker and Methodist, looked out of his first floor drawing room window in his recently built house on the corner of the street which would in a few years' time bear his name, but which for the moment was still known locally as Newton Lane, an unkept, muddy track bordered by wild hedgerows which formed a cut-through between Lever's Row and Shude Hill, out towards the ramshackle of unregulated, unfinished Hulks of other new houses, which sprouted all around him. Where once he could enjoy an unbroken view of fields and orchards stretching as far away as Ardwick Green, now he was becoming increasingly hemmed in by these constant new uprisings.

His guest for the evening, his long time friend John Wesley, was haranguing him on the subject with all the force and passion of one of his outdoor sermons, in a voice more accustomed to booming across open tracts of land peopled by crowds in their thousands, rather than an audience of just one in a modestly apportioned drawing room. Even so his companion's voice was frequently drowned out by the sound of the steam hammers and excavating machinery digging up the heavy clay earth before sinking the foundation piles for the rash of new homes and bonded warehouses mushrooming all around, even as he and Oldham progressed from the soup to the fish, a plate of pitch-cocked eels, which was a speciality of Mrs Oldham's.

"One of Mrs Raffald's recipes," said Oldham between mouthfuls. "She swears by them, don't you, dear?"

"They are indeed delicious, Mrs Oldham. What is the secret? So I might pass it on to Mrs Wesley?"

"No secret, sir. Make sure they're fresh…"

"I can vouch for that," her husband interrupted, "having watched them being plucked from the Tib just this afternoon, a veritable cauldron of them seething in the waters just below Tinker's Hollow…"

Mr Wesley pursed his lips and knitted his formidable brow. "I had not taken you for a frequenter of Pleasure Gardens, Mrs Oldham. I understand the Angel Meadow is adjacent to the stream of which you speak, is it not?"

Mrs Oldham blushed, while her husband looked away in discomfort.

"The Irk, yes, into which the Tib does flow. But adjacent only," she demurred.

"Indeed, John," interjected Oldham. "Adjacent only. Neither my wife nor I attend the notorious earthly delights which nightly take place on the Meadow.

"I'm most relieved to hear it."

"Hieronymous Bosch himself could not depict a more depraved licentiousness."

"I do not doubt it, sir. Pray continue, Mrs Oldham, do, with your account of how we came by this most excellent repast you have so kindly placed before us."

Mrs Oldham inclined her head. "First you must skin, gut and take the blood out of them," she continued with a certain relish. "Once you're satisfied that they're clean enough, you cut off their heads, dry them with a cloth, sprinkle them with pepper, salt and a little dried sage, turn them backward and forward, then skewer them. Rub your grid iron with beef suet, broil them a good brown with the yolk of an egg, put them on your dish with some melted butter, and lay around some fried parsley."

"Excellent," declared a very satisfied Wesley, depositing his knife and fork noisily on his plate as he finished.

Upstairs, in the Function Room above the public saloon of *The Bull's Head Inn*, Dr Thomas Perceval tapped the side of his glass with a spoon, calling for order.

"Gentlemen," he said. His voice was famously quiet, yet immediately the room fell silent, all eyes and ears turned towards him. "Thank you very much for braving the muddy lanes of the town, side-stepping the myriad pot holes which assail us on every side just now, as our burgeoning community swells and grows before our sight, to join us here this evening. Our thanks as ever to Mr John Raffald for his hospitality, and so, if your glasses are well charged, let us proceed with the business of the day.

"On behalf of my fellow Thomases – the estimable Messrs Barnes and Henry – may I welcome you to what we hope will become the first of many such regular meetings."

"Hear, hear!"

"We should like you to consider the possibility of the formation of a special society, an exclusive club, where members comprising like-minded individuals of the town might meet to discuss the important issues of the day, to debate the latest discoveries in the arts and sciences. This club, which we propose to call *'The Manchester Literary & Philosophical Society'*, would be the first of its kind anywhere in Great Britain, and would so demonstrate to all that here in Manchester we are not only the driving force of the country's manufacturing industries, but that we lead the way in cultural and intellectual discourse also."

"Agreed!"

"Splendid!"

"Furthermore, our Memorandum of Articles would seek to ensure that, as well as its members wielding a certain economic influence, they might also strive to promote the advancement of education and the widening of public interest in the appreciation of literature, philosophy, science, the arts and public affairs."

This final remark was greeted with a prolonged and resounding drumming of hands upon the tops of the table around which the assembled gentlemen sat.

Having made his money in calico in Middleton, a mere hop, skip and a jump from the park lands of Alkrington Hall, whose horizons had been too narrow for a man with the cultural aspirations he had possessed when young, Sir Ashton Lever had removed himself to London, where he founded the Inner Circle of The Archers' Company in Regent's Park, but his principal passion lay in collecting. He began while in Middleton by accumulating every known variety of mollusc. To these he added all manner of fauna, including many purchased from the voyages of Captain Cook. These he initially kept at Alkrington. Sightseers flocked in their thousands to gawp in wonder at the reptiles, fish, exotic animals, birds and insects he had acquired, so much so that he was forced to place guards around the perimeter of his estate, restricting admission only to those who arrived by carriage and who could afford the high entrance fee he deemed necessary to impose. In 1775 he opened his celebrated *Holophusicon* in Leicester House, a palace built originally by Henry VIII, where later George II had lived, while still Prince of Wales, after having been evicted from St James's Palace following that notorious quarrel with his father, where the young Prince Frederick had died having been hit in the throat by a cricket ball, and where now Sir Ashton Lever housed more than twenty-eight thousand of his specimens, a mere fraction of his entire collection, across fifty-six rooms, which was on the cusp of bankrupting him.

But on this cheerless September night in 1777 Lever kept such troubles to himself. Back in Manchester to lick his wounds, he had accepted this invitation for supper at the home of John Philips with an eye to the future. If he were forced to re-integrate himself back among the town's rising meritocracy, there was no more promising place to start than here in the fashionable row of houses which bore his family's name.

"A most excellent pie, Mrs Philips," remarked Sir Ashton as the plates were being cleared away.

"There's none finer to be had in Lancashire," said John, beaming towards his wife, who lowered her eyes, her cheeks reddening in the candle light.

"Will you not impart your secret?" urged Sir Ashton, "so that I might impress it upon my own cook back in Alkrington?"

"Yes, Josephine. Please. Enlighten us for our guest's sake."

"It's no secret, sir. Merely a recipe passed on to me by my own mother, God rest her soul, and one which I am happy to share. Simply take three or four brace of woodcock, according as how you have them in bigness. Dress and skewer them as you would for roasting. Keep the heads on and tuck each beak under the wing. Draw them, and season the inside with a little pepper, salt and mace, but don't wash them. Put the trales back into the belly, but nothing else, for there is something in them that gives a more bitterish taste in the baking than in the roasting. When you put them in the dish, lay them with the breast downwards. Beat them upon the breast as flat as you can first. Remember also to season them on the outside just as you did on the inside, with perhaps a pinch more mace. Bake them in puff paste, but lay none in the bottom of the dish. Put to them a jill of gravy and a little butter. Be careful not to bake the pie overmuch. Then, when you serve it, take off the lid and turn the woodcocks with the breasts upwards."

The assembled company, led by Sir Ashton, applauded resoundingly. Josephine, now hotter and redder than ever, turned an imploring eye towards her husband, who gave a barely perceptible nod of his thickly silvered head. With palpable relief she stood away from the table and said, "Well, ladies, I think it may be time for us to leave the gentlemen to their brandies and cigars and whatever it is they would prefer to talk about, for I cannot believe they are really interested in the finer points of a baked woodcock pie, while we take our ease in the music room."

It was back in 1760 when Dr White first presented one of his many groundbreaking papers to the Royal Society outlining his pioneering treatment of a fractured arm by reuniting the ends of the broken bone, which earned him admission two years later to the College of Surgeons, to whom he gave a notable lecture on the use of dry sponges for the purpose of *haemostasis*, the successful arrest of serious, external blood flow.

He had first risen to prominence some two years before. At that time he was the family physician present at the funeral of one John Beswick, a neighbour of his in Sale, just six miles to the south of Manchester. A mourner thought he saw one of Beswick's eyelids flicker, just as the coffin lid was about to be nailed shut. Alerting the gathering with a cry, White was able to confirm that the corpse was indeed still alive. A few days later the resurrected man regained consciousness and went on to live a healthy life for several more years. The revived corpse's sister, Miss Hannah Beswick, was so fearful of the same fate befalling her that she left strict instructions with White that, in the event of her own death, she was to be kept above ground until it was completely certain she was dead. As if tempting Providence, Miss Beswick did indeed pass away shortly afterwards, and White, maintaining his promise, had her embalmed, keeping the mummified body in a room in his home in Sale, where he stored it in an old grandfather clock case, which nevertheless managed to keep excellent time for several years afterwards.

But his most influential contribution to medicine was to be found in his abiding interest in obstetrics, which became the main focus of his study in Manchester once the Infirmary had been opened and had established itself as a beacon for modern practice. In 1773 his *Treatise on the Management of Pregnant & Lying-In Women* was to revolutionise the experience of giving birth for thousands of northern women, laying the foundations for the country's first specialist hospital for them, known as the Lying-In Hospital, housed first on Old Bridge Street in Salford, later taking over the premises of *The Bath Inn* on Stanley Street, where the bar was converted into an apothecary's shop and accommodation provided for eighty patients at a time, including widows and deserted wives. Among many innovations brought in by Dr White was the insistence on midwifery training for women, encouraging them to enable mothers-to-be to give birth naturally, not to be assisted before the baby's shoulders had been expelled, an insistence on fresh air and ventilation, with the expectation that they should vacate their beds as soon as possible.

He was greatly supported in this work by the remarkable Elizabeth Raffald, who served as his assistant for more than a decade. For fifteen years before, she was employed as a housekeeper for the Warburton Baronetcy in Arley Hall, Cheshire, where she met her future husband, John, who was Head Gardener. In 1763 they left for Manchester, where John sold flowers on market stalls, while Elizabeth ran a successful confectionery business. In 1769 she wrote *The Experienced English Housekeeper*. This was so successful that it went through thirteen authorised reprints as well as many more unlicensed ones. Among the dozens of recipes catalogued within its pages was the world's first recorded Eccles cake and the woodcock pie served up for Sir Ashton Lever at the home of Mr John Philips and his wife that very evening. Eventually she sold the copyright for fourteen hundred pounds, in order to clear the debts accrued by her husband, and to open *The Bull's Head*, a successful coaching inn on Shude Hill, where this very evening the nascent *Manchester Literary & Philosophical Society* was holding its inaugural meeting, and from where she had written, under the guidance of Dr White, a highly regarded book on midwifery. In 1772 she compiled the first Trade Directory for Manchester and Salford, in which the factories of the three Philips brothers all featured prominently.

In the wood-panelled dining room of Brother Joseph Saxton and his family in Spring Gardens, Brother LaTrobe had just called the assembled company there together in a prayer of thanks for their safe arrival in the town. Now, as they all remained seated around the plain, unadorned oak trestle, he began to warm to his theme.

"Tonight is indeed a happy occasion," he began. "Barely thirty years have passed since a band of just twenty-six brave and faithful Moravians alighted in Lightcliffe, near Halifax, eager to spread the Word of the Lord, like John the Baptist before them. '*Behold the Lamb of God*,' he proclaimed, '*who takes away the sin of the world*'."

"Amen," came the reply.

"Bishop Spangenberg was with them then, having responded to the urgent request of a young curate, Benjamin Ingham, an Anglican who had seen the error of his ways and who looked for deeper understanding. He had begun to work among the people of Lightcliffe and knew in his heart that they would respond to the fervour of the Bishop, who at once left his lodgings in London, where he had been meeting to study and pray with men and women from many walks of life, all of them wishing to see the true spirit of Christianity revived in this land, among whom were John and Charles Wesley, George Whitfield and the Countess of Huntingdon. But what did our esteemed Bishop care for public renown and celebrity when there were souls to be saved? When he reached Lightcliffe, with his twenty-six followers, crowds flocked to hear him in their hundreds, swarming like hungry bees, all turning their shining faces towards the radiant Light of the Lamb."

"Amen."

"Soon their work spread. The Yorkshire Settlement, renamed 'Fulneck' in honour of the sanctuary first afforded our movement by our great Ecumenical Pioneer, Count Zindendorf of Saxony, attracted the likes of James Taylor and John Wood, a pair of impassioned preachers from Cheshire, ignited by their faith in the Lamb of Christ, both suffering and triumphant, who lit new fires in Dukinfield and here in Manchester, and whose influence continues to grow, for more and more seekers of salvation are now come a-knocking at our doors, in search of new pastures, which is the reason for our meeting here this evening. Brother Lees?"

A tall, gaunt, but nevertheless rather hunched gentleman now stood. He had extreme difficulty in straightening his long limbs, which uncurled slowly and reluctantly, rather like a fiddleneck fern when exposed to unaccustomed sunlight. His skin was pale, almost grey, as if it had spent most of its life underground, which was true, for Brother Lees was a miner, a mine owner to be precise, but who had begun as a humble trapper, when he was just six years old, opening and closing the wooden trap doors to allow fresher air to flow through the mine, often crouching alone in total darkness for up to twelve hours a day. After that he had become a hurrier, hauling the full tubs of coal on hands and knees to the surface, then a thruster, pushing those same tubs from behind. As he grew taller and stronger, he was put to being a getter, hacking at the coal face with a heavy pick axe by the light of a candle, through which he learned to read which seams were likeliest to produce the most profitable yield. Swiftly he had worked himself through the various jobs below ground, excelling in every one of them, until he had progressed to more overseeing and managerial positions on the surface. He was thrifty – some might say parsimonious – he saved, invested shrewdly, and by the time he turned thirty he had amassed sufficient capital to purchase a small mine of his own. He applied the same diligence to his new role as owner, as he had first as collier, next as master, so that one mine became two, and two soon became three. He was an avid reader. His father had chastised this habit in him as a boy, begrudging him the cost of candles. "Books are a dear pastime," he'd say, chidingly, accompanying each word with a cuff about the ears, but Brother John had persevered. He read everything he could lay his hands on – account sheets, poetry, broadsides and the Bible – as clearly and as easily as he had read the coal seams, and he remembered every word of all of them, extracting detail and meaning that other, less assiduous readers, might miss. Now, as each separate vertebra in his spine clicked in turn while he stood to address the rest of the brothers and sisters, and as he flexed and cracked every joint of every finger, he perched a pair of half moon spectacles upon the bridge of his nose, the frameless lenses slipping immediately into their well-worn grooves on either side of that gnarled and veined proboscis, holding up several sheets of paper in his left hand, which he proceeded to lay upon the table before the assembled company. As he smoothed out the creases of this well-thumbed document, his fingers resembled the talons of a carrion crow, an impression amplified further by the way his shoulders hunched about his ears, his elbows stretched wide, the frayed patches at the much-stitched seams of his coat's sleeves, splayed like ragged feathers.

"The settlement at Dukinfield is too small," he pronounced.

"Ay," chorused his listeners.

"We need to expand," he continued.

"Ay," again.

"And here, I believe," he said, smoothing out the last of the creases on the document before him, "are the means by which we might go about it."

A deep and interested murmur ran around the room.

"Broad Oaks Farm," he declared. "The present owner is a Mrs Greaves of Droylsden. She is, if I understand her correctly, prepared to listen to reasonable offers. There is land adjacent, already held by Brother Saxon…" Here he deferred to their host, who was sitting opposite him, vainly trying to suppress the smile that was forming upon his lips.

"Is this true?" asked one of the sisters fervently, her eyes shining.

Brother Saxon modestly nodded, replying that it was.

"The Good Lord be praised," cried the sister.

"A hidden seed," said Brother Swertner quietly. The entire company turned as one towards him. He was another with that rare ability to command a room without ever needing to raise his voice. "Did not our great benefactor Bishop Comenius, in the final days of the Thirty Years War, say that one day our faith, which we had been long forced to bury in darkness and conceal from the light, would again rise and bear fruit?"

"Ay!"

"A new Herrnhut is at hand, a new Church, the Lord's Watch."

"Amen!"

"But how are we to make acquisition of this Broad Oaks Farm?" asked Brother Saxon, frowning. "We do not have the funds for such a purchase."

They all turned as one back towards Brother Lees, who removed his half-moon spectacles, folded them back into their leather case, took out a white handkerchief from the top pocket of his jacket, blew his long, thin nose somewhat noisily and smiled broadly. At once the carrion crow was transformed to a bird of an altogether brighter demeanour, a thrush perhaps, on account of his flecked waistcoat.

"Once you have worked down a mine, as I have, no matter how many years may have passed since you last went underground, the black dust never quite leaves the back of your throat. It catches your every breath. It leaves an irritating speck of grit in your eye. It settles like a second skin. Now I believe I can finally shake off this patina of years. Now I understand why God has tested me in all this time. Now I can do a service unto Him."

"Are you saying what I think you are…?" asked an incredulous Brother Saxon.

"What I am saying is that I have shed my old skin, like a hermit crab when his carapace is outgrown and no longer fits him. I am born again in the adoration of the Lamb. In short, Brothers and Sisters, I am decided this night to sell two of my mines in Dukinfield and, with the proceeds accrued thereby, purchase the farm of Mrs Greaves in Fairfield."

A great cry of joy rang out in the dining room on Spring Gardens, so that nobody sensed the slight tremor in the ground below them, nobody, that is, save Brother Swertner.

"Did you not feel it?" he asked.

Silent, they turned towards him.

"Look," he said and pointed towards the sash-windows, which hummed and rattled in the silence that had now fallen upon them. "It is a sign," he whispered.

"Would you care for a second helping, John?"

"Thank you, but no. Moderation in all things, eh Andrew? For does not Peter urge us ever to be sober? *'Be vigilant, for our adversary is the devil, who, as a roaring lion, walketh the land, seeking whom he may devour'*."

"Indeed, John, but I understand the common man's need to take succour where he can, especially in these afflicted times. Come," he said, "take a look at humanity before us." He walked to the window, beckoning Wesley to join him there, and gestured below, where small fires were springing up within the confines of each of the unfinished Hulks of houses creeping along Newton Lane. "No sooner do the workmen leave for the day than these empty husks are descended upon by the desperate, in search of shelter and warmth. And, like rats displaced at every turn, they are driven out as the sun comes up, only to return again the next night."

"We must cater for their spiritual wants even more assiduously, I warrant. As more mills and factories are built, so more labourers will be needed to work their machines. More dwellings must then be built to house these labourers, but unless we provide this work force and their families with profitable and instructive activities for when they are not at the loom, they will continue to haunt the taverns and inns of the town, before returning, like those rats you speak of, to their rude, uncared for homes."

"What are you suggesting I do, John?"

"You have land still, do you not, adjoining this house?"

"Ay. I do."

"Then build a chapel there, large enough to accommodate three thousand souls, with side rooms for Sunday Schools, where the people may learn their letters and look to better themselves. Remember what Paul said to the people of Philippi. *'I can do all things through Him who strengtheneth me'.*"

"Quite so, John. But these we see before us now huddling together for warmth by mean fires in unfinished buildings with neither roof nor walls do not enjoy the same advantages bestowed on Paul."

"Perhaps not, but did he not also say, in his second letter to Timothy, *'All scripture is breathed out by God and profitable for teaching, for reproof, for correction, and for instruction in righteousness, whereby the man of God may be perfect, thoroughly furnished unto all good works'?*"

*

Among the colony of homeless who huddled for warmth in the expanse of partly-built dwellings below Andrew Oldham's window was a young woman, extremely heavy with child, who was the most recent to arrive. Exhausted, she settled herself in a corner, leaning against the half-completed lower wall of 'the Hulks', as she had learned these unfinished houses were called. She was furthest away from the fire but had the benefit of shelter against the wind, which continued to pick up.

Septimus Swain, or The Old Retainer, as he liked to be known, on account of having been the first to arrive in the Hulks shortly after they began to be constructed, studied her with serious misgivings. She looked perilously near her time, and so the chances of any of them getting much sleep that night appeared slim. If they'd had their way, the others would have refused her entry when she dragged herself into their company, barely able to stand, but Septimus had for some reason taken pity on her, and silently nodded his approval to her request to stay.

"Just till the baby is born," she'd gasped.

Now, as he watched her breathing, lying like a beached whale, he asked himself why. He was not normally known for his tender heart. He had the rest of the encampment to consider. None of the squatters stayed long, a week or two at most, but they all recognised his authority and quickly conformed to his few simple tenets – no stealing, at least from one another; any unexpected bounties to be shared; a small gift, no more than a token, to be silently deposited within his old cracked palm upon arrival as an acknowledgement of his seniority. These tokens rarely had any monetary value, it was the gesture itself that counted, the act of giving, which mattered. Sometimes it might be an apple, occasionally – though rarely – a farthing; he had quite a collection of old keys, symbols of former lives now abandoned, which he wore like a necklace, and one or two more valuable items – a locket with a likeness or snip of hair, a regular supply of old boots, a ring. The young pregnant woman had given him a piece of cloth, white cotton delicately worked, embroidered with a pattern of moths caught among laurel leaves. It might have been a family heirloom, intended perhaps as a Christening shawl for the baby she carried, before circumstances had forced her on to the roads and led her finally to the Hulks.

The nature of Manchester's rapid, unregulated growth meant that there were always half-finished buildings the hulk-dwellers could find and colonise for temporary shelter. Sometimes a building would go up so swiftly they'd be forced to move on, but sometimes an enterprise might run out of money and all work on whatever the building was intended to be – a house, a mill, a warehouse – would cease at once. These were the ones Septimus favoured, naturally, and he always had his ear to the ground, listening to the talk among the architects, foremen, carpenters and roofers for any sign of impending misfortune about to befall them. He had lived this way for more than ten years now, and he found that he enjoyed the seniority and respect bestowed upon him. He did not lack for food, for warmth, for shelter, while the prospect of suddenly having to up sticks and move to a new situation, far from being a source of anxiety, was, he discovered, quite the opposite. He found the uncertainty quite liberating, freed from the shackles of responsibility which had so bedevilled his former life before the Great Panic of 1772, the credit crisis caused by the collapse of the bank of Neal, James, Fordyce and Down, after Alexander Fordyce had fled to France to avoid the debt collectors following the loss of more than £300,000 of East India Company stock. Septimus had been an investor and he had lost everything – his wife, his home, his position, as well as his money. Now he felt himself float on the air, like the smoke rising from the fires burning in their temporary shelter, dancing on the wind in the darkening night sky.

The other squatters came from a variety of sources. Some, like himself, were once successful merchants who had fallen on hard times. Many of these, when they first arrived, railed against the forces of the world who they blamed for their current impecunious misfortune – the banks, the courts, God – and their talk was all bitterness and revenge. Others retreated into a fantasy world, trying to convince Septimus, but mostly themselves, that their current situation was, though inconvenient, almost certain to be temporary, and refused to accept their new reality. Neither of these types, Septimus noted, lasted for long. But most of the squatters were already experienced in the school of life's hard knocks, having lived on the streets since before they were grown and so quite used to having to fend for themselves, seizing what opportunities they could. It was these Septimus had to watch most closely, for some saw, in Septimus's role, a chance to carve a niche for themselves, to foster or exploit, depending upon their temperament, and he had always to be on his guard for any possible usurper.

The current occupants, however, were all well known to him, and as a consequence knew their place. Only the young woman was new, and she was too far retreated into a world of pain and survival to offer any kind of threat. They did not often accommodate young female guests. There were older women, to be sure, toothless and drunk, most of them, and young girls who were still little more than children – skinny, feral types, who could slip between the narrowest gap when filching from a market stall or picking a pocket, who could shin up a drainpipe if necessary, and who could deliver a bite as sharp as a rat's if you happened to catch hold of their tiny wrists – but as they grew older, more often than not, they would find themselves on the game, selling favours for food. Young women of the type like the one Septimus continued to watch now were rare. Usually they were victims of abandonment, disowned by their wealthy family for some kind of romantic indiscretion, or the cast-offs of some aristocrat, who'd grown tired of his once shiny play thing, particularly if she had inconveniently conceived and was tiresomely pressing for some kind of commitment.

Septimus looked at her again. Which was *her* story, he speculated? Whatever it was, of one thing he was certain. There would be no return to her former life now. Would she, he wondered, be able to embrace her new situation? Like he had done. He sighed heavily. It was, he understood, completely different for a woman than it had been for him. She would need someone to afford her protection. Might that be something he would be prepared to consider? Whenever he felt the need for company, there were always women to be found, who, for a price, could be depended upon to scratch that particular itch, but he was not getting any younger. He may not be that much of a catch himself any longer, but as long as he was able to cling on to his position as The Old Retainer, there was security enough in that to make him more of an attractive proposition than outward appearances might otherwise suggest. And lately he had found his thoughts turning towards who he might pass on his role to when he was no longer able to hold on to it himself. He had idly speculated that he might spot some likely young fellow who viewed the world as he did, who he might train up, teach the tricks of the trade to, so to speak, but what if he were to adopt this young woman's baby once it had been born? Offer both her and it his protection and guidance? Lay down the foundations of a new dynasty? In his old life he had ended up spat upon and rejected, the bottom of the pile. Here he was king of the heap. And every king needs his queen and his prince...

It was to *The Bull's Head* where Dr White was heading as soon as he had finished his evening rounds at the Infirmary to attend the meeting called by the three illustrious Thomases – Barnes, Henry and Perceval, the last of whom, the highly regarded physician and health reformer, had issued the invitation to Dr

White specifically – to discuss the possibility of forming a cultural society in the town to rival any to be found in London or elsewhere in the kingdom. Dr White was particularly looking forward once again to crossing swords with Dr Perceval who, although he admired him greatly, he frequently disagreed with, and who had recently compiled a draft volume on medical ethics, several tenets of which Dr White took serious issue with.

Just as he reached *The Bull's Head*, he paused at its threshold. Fleetingly he felt the earth shift slightly beneath his feet as he lifted one of his boots to scrape the mud from its leather sole. A pewter tankard fell from its hook immediately above the lintel, which Dr White caught deftly in his left hand, replacing it as he stepped inside, where all was noise and commotion, so much so that no one but he appeared to have noticed the tremor. He shrugged. Perhaps he had been mistaken. Elizabeth Raffald caught sight of him from behind the bar and beckoned him across.

"The other gentlemen are all upstairs, Doctor," she said. "Please go up directly. I'll be along presently, tell them, with some supper."

Dr White tipped the rim of his hat and took the wooden stairs two at a time, flinging open the door to the private room above as soon as he reached the top.

"My apologies, gentlemen. My duties at the Infirmary detained me longer than I anticipated. You may have seen for yourselves the recent rise in the numbers of Putrescents waiting vainly on the steps outside?"

The gentlemen in Lever's Row duly stood, while the ladies all retired, before settling into armchairs or standing to warm their backsides before a welcome fire.

"Where do you source your coal?" asked Sir Ashton, carelessly tapping ash from his almost spent cigar into the hearth. "The Duke's Cut?"

John Philips inclined his head. "Sometimes," he said. "More often by cart from nearby Bradford."

'There's s-some talk," interjected his brother, Nathaniel, pausing to control the slight stammer he had whenever he was confronted by somebody unfamiliar, "of a n-n-new canal from Ashton."

"Ay," said Thomas, the youngest of the three, "and another from Rochdale."

"We are beset with Canal Mania," observed John.

"All of them linking here in Manchester," added Thomas. "We'll soon be able to transport our goods anywhere we choose. You could not have returned at a more opportune moment, Sir Ashton."

Sir Ashton took in the three brothers, each gazing up at him in anxious expectation, and raised his glass.

"You say nothing, Sir Ashton?" remarked John.

"No, but I listen, gentlemen, and most attentively."

"Forgive me if what I am about to say appears in any way impertinent. That is not my intention. Although you are titled, Sir Ashton, with land and a heritage, while we are but tradesmen, you are, if I may say so, cut from the same northern cloth. We speak our minds here in Manchester, and while some may call us blunt, rough even, I prefer to think of it as plain speaking, down to earth honesty. We call a spade a spade in these parts, in what Mr Defoe chooses to call 'the largest village in England', do we not, Sir Ashton? I hope you do not take offence, Sir?"

"Not at all, gentlemen. I am your guest this evening."

"And a most honoured one," rejoined the three brothers separately.

John, warming to his theme, picked up the thread of his argument once more. "The Earl of Ellesmere has already led the way by demonstrating so wholeheartedly with his Bridgewater Canal, his Duke's Cut as you so adroitly described it, Sir Ashton, that the modern aristocrat need not be averse to the advantages of commerce. The Earl has had the foresight to recognise that this largest village in England has the potential to grow and expand into something much, much larger."

Outside a wind was picking up. The doors to the stable were flung open. The windows in the dining room where the men now stood imagining a different future rattled. Nathaniel strode across to secure its fastenings.

"That wind," continued John, "is a sign that change is on its way, Sir Ashton. Even now, Mr Arkwright is contemplating a new factory on a patch of land adjacent to Miller Street, not a half mile from where we are standing, larger than anything previously built, steam powered, with more than a thousand spindles and several hundred workers. And he will not stop there. More mills will rise. Where Mr Arkwright walks today, dozens more will follow tomorrow. We are blessed with three rivers, the Irk, the Medlock and the Irwell, each providing endless supplies of fresh water. We have land currently standing idle, waiting to be built upon, not just with mills to spin the cotton, but dying factories and bleaching works, warehouses to store the textiles we can then manufacture into garments to export right across the globe. London may be the seat of Government, gentlemen, but Manchester can be the engine of the nation, a northern powerhouse if you will, where goods can be produced more cheaply, more quickly, and in greater quantities than ever before."

"Leading to greater profits too, no doubt?" quipped Sir Ashton, one side of his mouth curling into a smile.

"Bringing greater prosperity to all," added John, returning his guest's smile.

The wind outside whipped up with an added ferocity. A lump of coal leapt from the hearth onto the rug, causing the gentlemen to scurry aside. Thomas rushed forward, seized a pair of tongs and hastily returned the hot coal back to the fire, where it sizzled and roared.

"To the future, gentlemen," said Sir Ashton, raising his brandy glass.

"To the future," the brothers immediately chorused back.

"And how is this club to operate?" asked one of the gentlemen present in the upstairs Function Room of *The Bull's Head*.

"To answer that more specifically," replied Dr Perceval, "I shall refer you to my colleague Mr Barnes."

"Thank you, Thomas," said Barnes, taking the floor. "The club shall be for members only, whose individual applications will be considered on merit by a representative committee – currently the three of us – which is to be re-elected annually. The members would then decide on a programme of events, some of which would be for members only, while some, the lectures on particular topics, for example, would be open to the public."

At this moment, a tall, rake-thin gentlemen in plain Quaker-like clothes stood up. "Excuse me, Thomas," he said. "Do you have a venue in mind for these public lectures?"

"No, Robert, we do not."

"I think I know most people present here this evening, but for those of you to whom I am unfamiliar, please allow me to introduce myself. I am Robert Gore, Minister for the Unitarian Chapel on Cross Street, a duty I currently share with my colleague Mr Ralph Harrison, who sends his apologies this evening. He was most anxious to attend but unfortunately his wife is unwell and he has stayed at home to attend to her."

"We are sorry to hear that, Robert," said Dr White. "Would Mr Harrison wish me to call round after we have finished this evening?"

"Thank you, Doctor. That is most kind of you, but it is nothing serious, I believe."

"Then please be good enough to pass on to him and his lady wife the best wishes of all present here this evening."

"Hear, hear!"

"I shall indeed. Thank you once again. Now – to the matter in hand. If, Thomas, you do not yet have a venue for your proposed public lectures, might I offer the club, once it has been formally brought into life, the use of the Cross Street Chapel for this purpose?"

"That is a most generous offer, Robert. Our aim in time of course will be to have premises of our own, but until they become available, we should be delighted to meet at Cross Street."

"On one condition…"

Everyone's eyes turned back towards the Minister.

"And that would be…?" enquired Mr Barnes.

"That those lectures which are to be open to the public, you say, and quite distinct from members-only activities, should be free, so as to encourage this 'advancement of education', as you have termed it in your articles."

"Do I hear any objection?" asked Barnes, looking around the room. "There being none forthcoming, I take that as an agreement. Thank you, Robert. You may consider your condition to be met *nem con*."

A further drumming of fingers upon the table greeted this announcement, as Barnes yielded the floor to the third Thomas – Mr Henry.

"Thank you, gentlemen. This is a most encouraging beginning. There may be fewer than twenty of us gathered in this room this evening, but from tiny acorns do mighty oaks grow. If each of you can interest four of your associates, we shall reach a hundred members, from which we may be able to garner sufficient funds to begin saving for a building of our own, notwithstanding Minister Gore's beneficent gesture of the temporary use of the Cross Street Chapel. Who knows? With luck, gentlemen, we may be able to open our society in two, perhaps three, years, which should also provide us with sufficient time to commence the planning of a putative programme of speakers for the regular lectures in the interim."

At this point Dr White once more stood up. "Precisely. I was wondering when we might move towards a discussion of possible topics."

"Do you have any suggestions, Doctor?" asked the first of the Thomases – Dr Perceval. The two physicians had been known to cross swords before, especially on ethical matters, and the assembled company metaphorically rubbed their palms with glee at the prospect of another disagreement that evening.

"Yes," replied White, still on his feet, "as a matter of fact I do."

Just at the moment, interrupting the reverie of Septimus Swain, The Old Retainer, there came a sudden rumbling beneath the ground. At first he was not concerned. These unfinished Hulks frequently creaked and rocked in the wind, before their foundations became fixed, but then the earth shook again. A part of the roof above them crashed to the ground. The pregnant woman awoke from her inward concentration, opened her eyes and began to scream.

Immediately her panic and fear spread like a fever through the rest of the squatters, who all began to scurry like rats towards the safety of the fire, away from the threat of any further falling masonry. Septimus realised at once that he must act, swiftly and decisively, to re-establish calm and control. The others all looked towards him. This is what they expected of him.

"Move to the open ground," he commanded in a loud and clear voice, which sounded much calmer than he felt. "You," he said, pointing to one of the feral girls, "Whelp. Run to *The Bull's Head*. Fetch Lizzie Raffald. Tell her she's needed here. There's a ha'penny for you, and another when you return."

Behind the house on Lever's Row, Tom, Sir Ashton's groom, who had been enjoying a tot of brandy himself, smuggled out to him at the scullery door by Nancy, the kitchen maid, with whom the groom had been hoping to engage in something more than polite conversation, was roused into action by the startled noise of the horses, rearing and bucking as the stable doors flew open.

Tom reluctantly prised himself away from Nancy's charms and attended to the horses, calming them at once with a soothing word. They knew his voice, recognised the touch of his hand upon their flanks, and quickly settled down once more to resume their munching of hay. Tom made sure the stable doors were securely fastened, then turned back. The wind had died as suddenly as it had risen. He looked up at the dark sky. The cloud was thick and low, but for a fleeting instant a crack appeared, through which a gibbous moon tried vainly to peer. In its weak half-light Tom briefly made out the mischief of rats cowering in the far corner of the yard. One of them appeared about to give birth to a litter and had made a small nest of hay in which she burrowed as deeply as she could. Then the cloud covered the moon once more and Tom lost sight of her.

He thought he felt the ground vibrate a little beneath his feet. At first he simply put it down to too much brandy, but then he felt it again. Something odd was happening tonight, he felt, some great change was coming, but what? He had no inkling. He shrugged, tipped the flask once more to his lips, only to realise it was empty. He strode back towards the scullery to ask Nancy if he might have a refill, only to find the door shut and bolted, and Nancy nowhere in sight.

The particular feral girl to whom Old Septimus Swain had just now given instruction was used to being called any number of names. Usually something in the tone of her interrogator would make her realise that it was she who was being spoken to directly and she would rise up from whatever hole she was sheltering in, eyes and ears alert, skin prickling with attentiveness. She'd learned to be always on her guard from the first moment she could remember, a condition that was as natural as breathing. Even when snatching a half hour's sleep, she'd keep at least one eye open. She no longer recalled what her real name was, or if she'd ever had one. Whelp was a new one. It was good as any, she decided, and the prospect of a ha'penny was motive enough.

She caught the coin with her teeth and bolted into the dark, slipping between the shadows as deftly as an eel in a ditch.

"Pray, enlighten us," said Perceval, spreading his hands and sitting back down himself.

"Polygenism," said White.

An audible gasp from Perceval resonated around the room.

"I'm afraid you will have to elaborate," interjected Minister Gore. "It is not a term I am familiar with. Nor, I suspect, are many of our companions here this evening either."

"It is a most foul and heinous conceit," Perceval almost spat out, "not in any way fitting for a society with the noble aims we have unanimously approved but moments ago."

"I understood," remarked White, attempting to maintain his temper, "that we also approved its name. The Manchester Literary *and Philosophical* Society. Polygenism is a philosophy upheld by men of letters across the civilised world and deserves its right to be debated alongside any other."

"A philosophy," countered Perceval, "which has been rejected and ridiculed in equal measure."

"But what exactly *is* it?" demanded Gore. "Will one of you not tell me?"

"It's an abomination," said Perceval, banging his fist on the table, "that is what it is."

"I believe," said White, "I might be allowed to defend it, since it is I who has raised it as a possible subject for discussion."

"The Doctor has a point, Thomas," said Barnes, attempting to restore calm.

"Very well," said Perceval, sitting back down. "Let him be judged by his own words."

Dr White held his rival's gaze until the latter looked away, then turned his attention to the rest of the company, whose faces were all upturned towards him in expectation. "Polygenism," he said, "is a scientifically held opinion empirically affirming a hierarchy of the races within humans."

An uncomfortable silence fell upon the assembled company. Taking this as an encouragement to continue, White proceeded to expound his theory.

Back in the dining room at Lever's Row, more cigars were being lit and passed around.

"And now, I believe we must conclude our business discussions for the time being," announced Sir Ashton, "for we are in danger of boring our youngest guest." He turned his attention to John's son, Leigh, a young man of just sixteen summers, who had been up till this moment standing almost invisibly in a corner of the room. "I understand from your father that you too have an interest in natural history?"

"Yes, sir. I should dearly like to hear more about your *Holophusicon*."

"Ah, but I would much rather hear about your own collection."

"Mine, sir?" stammered Leigh.

"Of course. Your mother let slip over her excellent woodcock pie that you have built a small *vivarium*."

"Yes, sir. It is only small, but..."

"As all things must be at their beginning."

"Yes, sir."

"So tell me – what was the first thing you ever collected?"

Leigh looked across to his father, who nodded and smiled.

"It was this," said the young man, leading the way out of the dining room down a hallway where, mounted on the wall, was a mahogany butterfly case.

"Ah yes," said Sir Ashton, bringing his face close up to the glass. "A white peppered moth. Very fine. But why this particular specimen? What was it about this quite common *Lepidoptera* that so drew your attention?"

"Actually, sir, they are becoming rarer. As a small boy I used to see them in flocks, grazing upon the plants that grew in the Daub Holes, but lately they are not nearly so numerous."

"Perhaps they have found more abundant pastures elsewhere?"

"Yes, sir. Perhaps. But I miss them, and so I have this example here, my first, to remind me."

"Quite so. Now – perhaps we might see your *vivarium*?"

"If you're sure, Sir Ashton…?"

"I would not have asked if I weren't."

"Thank you, sir. Then if you'll just follow me. Through here, gentlemen…"

Whelp reached *The Bull's Head* just as a second tremor threatened to throw her known world off kilter and she had to grab a nearby leg to catch her balance. The man to whom the leg was attached became faintly aware of something rodent-like clutching his ankle and he irritably shook it off as he made his way back towards the bar for a refill of his rapidly emptying tankard. Whelp darted between the myriad other legs which confronted her until she reached the staircase leading up to the Function Room above, just as Mrs Raffald was descending it with a tray stacked with pewter plates. Not seeing the girl, she tripped over her, the pewter plates spinning in slow motion before her eyes, only for Whelp to stretch out a spindly arm and catch them before they hit the floor.

"A stitch in time," cried Lizze with admiring gratitude. Then, looking more closely at the stick of a girl in front of her, she added, "and you're little more than a scrap yourself. Be off with you," and she aimed a casual cuff at the back of the girl's head.

Undeterred, Whelp tugged at the woman's sleeve and pointed in the direction of outside. "Come," she said. "You're wanted." Not used to speaking, Whelp's voice had the timbre of a rusty nail scraping an old kettle, uncertain of pitch or inflection.

Realising what was meant, Mrs Raffald bent down so that her face was at a level with the skinny girl's. "Is it Septimus who sent you?"

Whelp nodded.

"Some poor woman near her time in the Hulks?"

Whelp nodded again.

"Tell him I'll be along directly," she said and jerked her thumb in the direction of the staircase. "I've important guests up above."

"No," said Whelp fiercely, still tugging at Lizzie's sleeve. "Now," she uttered, the words expelled as a cat might a fur ball.

Something in the feral girl's punkish demeanour struck Lizzie forcibly. She would brook no deferral and would not budge until she, Lizzie, had decided to follow her.

"Very well," she said, "show me."

"Just as Man is the apogee of creation," began White, "at the head of the great chain of being, so within Man there are further natural gradations and classes."

Everyone shifted awkwardly in their seats, except for Minister Gore, who responded quietly and calmly.

"But does not the Good Book tell us that God created Man in His own image?"

"Yes, but..."

"And does it not also encourage us to be glad and sing for joy, for God rules the peoples of this world with equity?"

"Possibly, but..."

"Do we not all have but one God? Did not one God create us? Therefore *'why do we profane the covenant of our ancestors by being unfaithful to one another?'*"

"My point exactly, but when Malachi preached such sentiments, he did not have the benefits of the advanced science and learning we have now at our disposal. My many pathological specimens irrefutably demonstrate these racial differences..."

"Differences, possibly, but where are your grounds for the kind of supremacy you would have us all adhere to?"

"Well, I would say that..."

"For God does not show favouritism. As no less a disciple than Peter learned to his cost. *'Of a truth I perceive,'* did he not say, *'that God is no respecter of persons'*?"

"If you would but permit me to explain..."

But Mr Gore continued undeterred. " *'Here there is no Gentile or Jew, circumcised or uncircumsized, Barbarian, Scythian, slave or free, but Christ is all, and is in all'.*"

"It may interest you to know, gentlemen," retorted White, now distinctly hot under the collar, his cheeks flushing with more than the wine he had been liberally drinking while attempting to defend his position before the immovable object that was the Unitarian Minister Robert Gore, "that our good hostess for this evening, the highly esteemed Mrs Raffald, has recently compiled Manchester's first ever Directory of Trades and Businesses. Many of you here can find yourselves listed there. One of the more disturbing statistics contained within its pages is the recent rapid rise of merchants from overseas – from Spain, Portugal, Turkey, the Levant, not to mention Jews and

Chinese – and that this influx is completely unregulated. Do we want to risk the potential for greatness we all of us here believe our municipality is capable of by so diluting its blood stock through the prospect of inter-breeding such new arrivals will inevitably lead us towards?"

"Now we come to it," shouted Dr Perceval, unable to contain himself a second longer, and pointing an accusatory finger towards his rival. "Did you not sign the Hippocratic Oath, sir?"

The two doctors then flung themselves at each other's throats and for a brief moment there was the serious risk of injury to either or both, only for the swift intervening actions of the other two Thomases to prise them apart.

"Gentlemen, please," said one. "We must allow ourselves to disagree with civility."

"Behaviour of this sort," added the second, "will simply not be tolerated within the walls of *The Manchester Literary & Philosophical Society*. Let us at least attempt to proceed by the standards of decency we intend to uphold once our Memorandum of Articles has been formally approved."

"I apologise," said White, straightening his attire and holding out his hand.

"I accept your apology," replied Perceval, "but I fear I cannot shake your hand, sir."

Minister Gore stood once more between them. "Let us be counselled by Leviticus, gentlemen. '*The stranger that dwelleth now with you shall be unto you as one born among you, and thou shalt love him as thyself, for ye were once strangers likewise in the land of Egypt*'."

In the silence which followed, as everyone pondered the verses for themselves, the floor of the Function Room appeared suddenly to tilt beneath them. The glass in the windows rattled and shook, then one by one they cracked and shattered.

"What the Devil…?" cried Henry.

"I do believe this may be an earthquake," said Barnes.

"Meeting adjourned," added Henry hastily. "Let us each repair to our homes, observing this phenomenon as we go, bringing aid and succour to any who need it."

The would-be members of the *Literary & Philosophical Society* dispersed at once without further word. For the moment the floor was still. Downstairs in the public bar of *The Bull's Head*, such was the Saturday night commotion, nobody appeared to have noticed the earth's recent convulsion. Minister Gore's words trailed after them as they made their separate ways.

" '*When thou makest a feast, call the poor, the maimed, the lame, the blind; and thou shalt be blessed…*' "

Young Master Leigh unlocked the door onto a completely empty room, devoid of all furnishings or decoration, tucked away at the back of the house. There were bare boards, unplastered walls and curtainless windows. No sooner had he ushered everybody in than he swiftly locked the doors behind them.

"As a precaution, you understand. If any of the insects were to escape, my mother would not be best pleased."

"No indeed," laughed John.

Leigh spread his hands wide. On more than a dozen trestle tables positioned around the edges of the room was a series of glass *terraria* of different shapes and sizes. They were so designed as to allow air to enter them through an ingenious arrangement of small holes, which were then covered with a fine muslin mesh in order to ensure that none of the specimens could escape. Inside each one were to be found literally thousands of different species of fly.

"*Diptera*," declared Leigh proudly. "Here we have examples of *sphaeroceridae, stratiomyidae, conopidae, empididae, hybotidae, clusiidae, therevidae, tachinidae, tabanidae,* my favourite the *rhagionidae,* and of course the *muscidae...*"

"For heaven's sake, speak in English, Leigh," said John, covering his nose and mouth with his hand, while trying to raise his voice at the same time above the incessant buzz and drone, which threatened to overwhelm them.

"Sorry, Father. Stiletto flies, dagger flies, druid flies, all manner of soldier flies – colonels, majors, centurions – horse flies, dance flies, my favourites the snipe flies, with their large translucent wings, bluebottles, fruit and house flies." Leigh, bursting with pride, addressed his remarks entirely towards Sir Ashton.

"Capital," the latter replied enthusiastically approaching the different glass cases, while the three brothers kept as far away as they could. "A gentleman needs a hobby, something to stretch his intellect, as well as providing diversion for his hours away from business. I regard such a man much more seriously."

"Thank you, Sir."

"Tell me, from where do you obtain such splendid specimens?"

"The same Daub Holes beyond the house, sir."

"And you remove merely a male and a female of each, then let Nature take its course?"

"Yes, sir."

"Behold, gentlemen, how populations increase when conditions are favourable." The three brothers remained at a distance, their faces screwed with discomfort. "Pray, do not be so squeamish. Approach. Observe more closely. Is not this a very microcosm of our community? With representatives of the military, the church, labourers in agriculture, workers in houses and factories. See how they prosper and thrive. Less than sixty years ago returns made to the Diocesan Bishop suggested a population of just twelve and a half thousand in Manchester and Salford combined. Twenty years ago, as a result of the dispute concerning manorial corn-mill rights, a further enumeration claimed seventeen thousand in Manchester alone, and just five years ago, according to the good Dr Thomas Perceval, the renowned natural philosopher whom I have the great honour of describing as my friend, and someone whom I should be most pleased to introduce you, Master Leigh, there were twenty-four thousand, three hundred and eighty-six persons housed in Manchester in five thousand, six hundred and seventy-eight families. This figure does not take into account the great number of houses built since the recovery from the financial crisis of that year, nor to the rapid influx of new arrivals into our midst who have yet to find accommodation."

"Indeed, sir," declared Thomas, briefly removing his sleeve from his face, "we are in danger of becoming over-run."

"Come, come, man. This increase will supply greater demand for your products."

"I suppose, sir."

"Not to mention an inexhaustible supply of new recruits for your work force."

"But w-where are w-we to h-house them all?" interjected Nathaniel.

"Ay, that is the question, gentlemen."

"S-see how overcrowded they are," continued Nathaniel anxiously. "There is b-barely room for them to b-breathe in there."

"And yet," said Sir Ashton, "still there is beauty to be found there. What did you say your favourite species were, Master Leigh?"

"The *hybotidae* and *rhagionidae*."

"Those with the large translucent wings which dance?"

"Yes, sir."

"We may learn much from young Master Leigh's collection, gentlemen. If we are to transform ourselves from what Mr Defoe so quaintly describes us as the country's largest village into becoming its first industrial city, which is an ambition I believe all of us here share…"

"Indeed."

"… then we must recognise that there is much to be done to create the necessary corporate identity, along with the municipal underpinning which must inevitably accompany that, if we are to successfully manage this rapid increase in industry and population. Our current institutions are oligarchical and corrupt and totally inadequate to address our pressing needs."

"What are you recommending, Sir Ashton? Reform? Such talk is highly dangerous. I hope you are not suggesting sedition, sir? Not in *my* house?"

"I suggest nothing, my good man," said Sir Ashton, a wry smile forming across his lips. "I merely observe. True flies – more properly termed what, Master Leigh…?"

"*Diptera*, sir."

"*Diptera*, yes… they are an immense group with untold numbers of known species. They all have their hind pairs of wings reduced to inhibit the range and height of their flight, pin-shaped structures known as *halteres*, which act as gyroscopes to enable them to maintain balance while in movement. Most feed on liquids, including nectar and blood."

A silence fell upon the speakers, or would have done but for the continuous, unbroken, rising roar of the insects trapped inside their glass cases.

Mr John Philips inclined his head. "More brandy, Sir?"

"No, thank you. It's rather late, I fear, and Lady Ashton will be fretting. It's time we bid you a good night."

"As you wish, Sir Ashton. I shall instruct the groom to ready your horses."

"Must we, Father?"

"Come, Leigh," said Thomas, ruffling his nephew's hair. "Sixteen is not yet an age at which you should be arguing with your father."

"Not in p-public at least," rejoined Nathaniel.

"I'm sorry, Father, but I was so very much taken with what Sir Ashton had to say about my collection."

"Then I must come again to look at it," said Sir Ashton, hastily throwing an enquiring look in John's direction, "at a more civilised hour. A veritable cabinet of curiosities indeed."

In an instant the feral girl bounded off, leaping over the prostrate bodies of those customers who had already drunk themselves into horizontal oblivion, down the narrow Newton Lane in the direction of the Daub Holes. Mrs Raffald followed as best she could. She too was increasingly aware of the tremors now shifting the ground beneath her as she tried her best to keep pace with Whelp who, every few yards, was forced to wait impatiently till the publican's wife had caught her up, puffing and panting in her agitation.

She's too fat, thought Whelp dismissively. That's what comes of eating too much. She herself was always hungry, but if ever there was a windfall, a market stall crashing beneath the weight of all its produce, or a wagon overturning in the muddy ruts of Mosley Street, Whelp had learned to her cost not to stuff herself, nor to try and make off with more than she could easily carry. Feeling hungry gave her an edge, kept her on her toes, needfully vigilant, in case anyone tried to rob her. She only ever took what she needed, the smallest amount possible to stave off the worst of her stomach cramps. That way she could remain fleet of foot. There'd always be another bounty.

Eventually the fat publican's wife, her face red with sweat, caught her up and Whelp pointed. Not that she needed to, for by now the young woman had started to give birth and was screaming. Lizzie followed the sound of the noise, dropped down beside the woman, noted with relief the fire that was burning still close by, and set to with her work.

"Hush now, dearie. What you're going through now a thousand women have done before you. It'll all be over soon.

Scream and curse as much as you like. There's nothing I won't have heard before…"

Just then, at the home of Mr John Philips and his wife, the ground shifted once more beneath their feet. A sudden crack split the shuttered glass in the skylight above their heads. The flies, for the briefest of instants, ceased their murmuration, only to resume it again almost immediately, but with greater agitation.

The five inhabitants of the room regarded each other with a puzzled expression.

"What the Devil…?"

They hastily left the *vivarium* and proceeded along the hallway back towards the dining room, where they were met by the frightened and flustered ladies. Everyone began speaking at once.

"Husband!"

"Come quickly!"

"What's happening?"

"Is this truly the end of the world?"

As they collided into one another jolting and churning like whipped up particles of water coming too quickly to the boil in a rocking steam pan, there was no longer room for doubt. The ground tipped and bucked beneath them, throwing them into an undignified heap on the floor, scrabbling for traction on one another's clothing, kicking and trampling as they tried to regain their equilibrium. The air around them quivered in a high-pitched, nerve-shredding hum, torquing bones and joints tighter and tighter till they threatened to snap. Throughout the house, windows began to split and crack. A look of horror suddenly swept across sixteen-year-old Master Leigh's face. He turned on his heels and fled, back in the direction of the *vivarium*, knowing already he would be too late. In the initial stampede when they left, he had, he was certain, neglected to bolt the door behind him.

*

Mrs Oldham burst in upon her husband and Mr Wesley just as the vibrations from the latest tremor had blown out the candle she was carrying and the dining room was plunged into immediate darkness. She emitted an involuntary shriek as she clung tightly to Andrew's elbow.

"What is happening?"

"I do believe it is a minor earthquake," replied her husband, sounding calmer than he felt.

"Minor? Do you mean it could get stronger?"

"Who knows?"

"Only God," boomed John, " *'who moves in a mysterious way His wonders to perform'*."

"I do not know this maxim, John. It is not from the Bible I am thinking…?"

"No indeed, though it sounds as though it might be, I agree. It is from a hymn written by an acquaintance of mine, Mr William Cowper. He is more a follower of Mr Whitfield's Calvinism than our own Arminian branch of theology, but a kindred spirit none the less. *'He plants His footsteps in the sea and rides upon the storm'*."

"We seem to be in the very eye of the storm just now, John," answered Andrew as another tremor rattled the window. "What are we to do?"

" *'Judge not the Lord by feeble sense,*
But trust him for his grace.
Behind a frowning providence
He hides a smiling face'."

"If we survive this trial, John, I shall build your chapel. You have my word."

" *'His purpose sure will ripen fast,*
Unfolding every hour.

The bud may have a bitter taste,
But sweet will be the flower'."

And with that John Wesley threw on his coat and hat, flung open the window and called out to the fleeing crowds below.

" *'Fear not for I am with you, saith the Lord. Be not dismayed, for I am your God. He will strengthen you, yea he will help you. He will uphold you with His righteous Hand'."*

He swept from the room, while Andrew pulled down the window, drawing his trembling wife closer to him.

Outside in the yard, the pair of Cleveland Bays had kicked down the stable door and fled, nostrils flaring, black flanks white with sweat and fear. They headed straight for the Daub Holes, careening through the line of the sick and the dying, coughing with putrid fever, the most severe form of typhus, who, being nightly refused admittance to the Infirmary, were left to fend for themselves within the oozing slime of their decomposing discharges.

While these unfortunate, abandoned souls clamoured desperately to be let in, on the far side of the Infirmary, in an adjacent wing, where the country's first lunatic asylum and public baths were housed, the inmates there were by contrast intent on trying to get out. Bars were loosened from walls as a score of shrieking, naked men leapt from the upper storey windows directly into the Daub Holes themselves, those clay pits whose normally stagnant pools of festering water now boiled and seethed.

The carriage horses bucked and reared in panic as they swerved between these nightmarish figures, whose emaciated flesh was licked by the dancing shadows of flames thrown by the rocking motion of the lanterns carried by the asylum's wardens who pursued them, the Bedlam Boys, who sang to the sky as the ground tipped beneath them.

"Still we sing bonny boys, bonny brave boys
Bedlam Boys are bonny
For we all go bare
And we live by the air
And we want nor drink nor money…"

Down among the Daub Holes strode Wesley, roaring his comfort to the Bedlam Boys.
" *'I was naked and ye clothed me. I was sick and ye visited me. I was in prison and ye came unto me'…"*

Before he had gone but a few yards, Leigh was engulfed by the full force of the swarm. They penetrated his clothes, his skin, his hair. The entire world was fly. He could feel them crawling across his eyelids, burrowing in his ears, prising open his clamped-shut mouth. He swatted impotently with his arms as he whirligigged his way out of the house, a buzzing cauldron of *squama*, *ocelli* and *pulvilus*, a convulsion of antennae, thorax and abdomen, tarsal claw and pincer, a blind thrashing of compound eyes. In a moment he was gone, taking the swarm with him.

A moment of sudden stillness descended on the house in Lever's Row before John, Nathaniel and Thomas rushed headlong out into the night, in pursuit of the drowning Leigh, pursued by their wailing wives.

"One last push," urged Lizzie Raffald.

The young woman was exhausted. Somehow she summoned the last scrap of strength she had left in her, screwed up her face with the effort and bore down for a final time.

"Here he comes," said the midwife. "That's it, dearie. A lovely little boy. And just listen to him roar. He's a fine pair of lungs on him, and no mistake. You'll always be able to tell when this one's hungry."

She went to hand the screaming infant back to its mother, only to realise that she no longer appeared to breathing.

"Dearie," she said, then again more urgently, "Dearie!" She slapped the young woman's face a few times, but still she did not stir. Lizzie Raffald looked down at her pale, still, broken body and shook her head. This was no place for babies to be born. Dr White was right. Women should be encouraged to go to the Infirmary as soon as the first contractions started. But there'd been no time with this one. She gathered up the squirming, wriggling infant and headed in the direction of the Daub Holes and the Infirmary. It was only then she noticed the Bedlam Boys, who by now were armed with sticks, which they had lit from the many fires that had broken out all around and which they were brandishing before them, the flames licking their emaciated, naked bodies, barring the way to any and all. Lizzie turned tail and hurried back the way she'd come, holding the whimpering child under her coat. With luck, she was thinking, Mrs Clamp, the wet nurse, would be in her usual corner in the snug of *The Bull's Head*. But she would have to hurry. The skeleton of the Hulks creaked, rattling its bones with a shudder as another convulsion shook the earth, so that Mrs Raffald almost lost her footing and stumbled.

Whelp retreated back towards her hole.

She wasn't interested in watching the birth. She'd seen enough already in her short life and she was determined that it was an ordeal she herself would never succumb to. Instead she found out Septimus, tugged the end of his tattered frock coat till he gave her the second promised ha'penny, after which she withdrew to her favoured hole, near an angle of two half built walls, where she was out of the wind. The ground shook again.

While the others in the Hulks continued to panic and flee, Whelp hunkered down.

She liked this sudden tilting of the earth, this unpredictable seismic shift, and allowed herself the luxury of an apple she'd filched a couple of days before, which she'd been saving for later. Now, she thought, later had come.

Septimus felt the ground shift beneath him once more. He watched the rest of the squatters rise up in panic, like startled pigeons, unable to remain airborne for long, so unused had they become to exercising their wings, preferring instead to scavenge for what scraps might be found among the street's detritus, so that now they felt awkward and heavy. They careered into one another, pecking and scratching with beak and claw, tapping their frightened heads like imaginary hammers into thin air.

He himself chose to remain where he was. After all, where else was there to go? Instead he looked towards where the young pregnant woman lay completely still, seemingly not breathing. He fingered the piece of white cotton she had given him in lieu of payment. Well, he thought, with a certain sadness, she'll not be needing it back, not now, and he wrapped it around his shoulders as the cool night wind continued to pick up. His fingers closed over one of the stitched moths, caught up in the web of laurel leaves, and he brought it up towards his face for a closer inspection.

In the instant that he did so, he momentarily let down his usual guard. At once, one of the Young Pretenders, a Spaniard with black curly hair which fell in unkempt tendrils from beneath his acquired continental tri-corn hat, wearing a frayed and dusty frock coat which had once been a fine crimson but which now was a mottled mosaic of mud and clay, leapt upon him and began to beat him across his back with a stolen nephrite-handled cane, its top shaped like the head of a snake, its mouth opened wide to reveal sharp fangs and a flicking tongue.

"This *terremoto* is a sign, I think, *Señor, no lo es*? Time for an *auto da fe*. An act of faith. *El Rey esta muerto. Larga vida al Rey*. The King is dead, *Señor*. Long live the King."

He accompanied each phrase with a blow from his cane. Septimus sank to his knees, covering his face with the white cotton shawl. Just as he thought his time had come, the earth took another sudden tilt. The Spaniard momentarily lost his footing. He slipped and put out a hand to steady himself into the hole where the feral girl was quietly eating her apple, savouring each tiny mouthful with a zealot's fervour. She transferred her attention in less than a heartbeat, the snap of a twig, the click of two fingers, from the fruit to his hand, which she sank her teeth into with the same dispassionate relish that she had previously bestowed upon her systematically stripped and gnawed apple core, which she now tossed to one side, where a column of rats fell upon it. The Spaniard howled and leapt in pain, turning away just long enough for Septimus to snatch the nephrite-handled cane and smartly rap his attacker twice across his pate, causing him to flee while still he could.

Lizzie Raffald slithered her way along the narrow Newton Lane, dodging between the nests of jays and toms, dollymops and molls, all of them doing a brisk trade. A hellfire preacher was standing on an orange crate by the entrance to Shude Hill.

"Where will *you* spend eternity?" he called out to the panicking crowds who surged past him from all directions.

"In the arms of Paradise," replied one of the molls.

Lizzie forced her way through the press of flesh till she reached *The Bull's Head*, where inside a different roaring trade was to be had, with the scores of customers raucously singing.

"There is a thorn bush in our cale yard
There is a thorn bush in our cale yard

*At the back o' t' thorn bush there lies a lad and lass
A-busy, busy faring at the cuckoo's nest..."*

The ale was freely flowing and the clientele were either blissfully unaware of the tremors and convulsions rocking the town that night, or had drunk themselves into oblivion so as not to care.

*"It is thorn and it is prickle and it's compassed all around
It is thorn and it is prickle and it isn't easy found
I said, 'Young man, you blunder,' but he said, 'It isn't true'
Then he left me with the makings of young cuckoo..."*

Lizzie held the young cuckoo she carried closely even tighter to her chest as she scrambled over the sprawling legs and bodies of the drunken crowds in search of Mrs Clamp, the wet nurse, wondering just who it might have been who abandoned the poor young woman she had left for dead not half an hour before in the Hulks with the makings of this cuckoo, who was bawling loud and angry with hunger. Lizzie looked down into his furious, purple, scrunched up face. Against the riotous din of *The Bull's Head* his cries went unheard.

Eventually she found Mrs Clamp, or rather, trod upon her, where she lay blissfully unconscious, while all around, inside and out, the world bucked and roared.

*"Hi the cuckoo, ho the cuckoo, hi the cuckoo's nest
Hi the cuckoo, ho the cuckoo, hi the cuckoo's nest
I'll give anybody a shilling and a bottle of the best
That will rumple up the feathers in the cuckoo's nest..."*

There was nothing for it, thought Lizzie. She must try for the Prison. As yet Manchester had no Workhouse, but an impoverished wing of the New Bailey Prison carried out many of the functions of one, and that was where Lizzie knew she must now make for. But extricating herself from the melee in the inn was no easy matter. Tankards were being flung across the room, plates and dishes were being smashed against the walls and ceiling. Her husband, John, catching her eye in the eye of the storm, saw the baby in her arms and at once had assessed the urgency of the situation. As the singing was reaching its raucous climax – "*I'll give anybody a shilling…*" – he tossed a coin of that value towards her above the heads of his brawling customers. As one they froze, each catching sight of the coin in turn as it spun in near slow motion in a perfect arc. As one they held their breath, a split second's silence in what had previously been a cacophony, and as one they simultaneously leapt towards it, each of them sprawling and tumbling over one another in a vainglorious scrum. Lizzie lifted one hand from the mewling baby, plucked the shilling out of the air, and was back out into the tumultuous night and away to the Prison before any of the crowd could follow her, all of whom were now gleefully throwing each other across the inn floor, knocking over tables and smashing chairs over backs of heads.

Without a backward glance Lizzie was running headlong in the direction of the Collegiate Church of St Mary, St Denys and St George.

*

Sir Ashton delicately allowed one of the last remaining airborne stragglers to alight upon his finger, which he lifted close to his face where he might examine it more closely. He smiled.

"I'm glad someone is pleased," remarked his wife, somewhat ruefully, as she brushed the sleeves of her gown with the backs of each hand and shuddered. "Though I should have thought," she continued, "that after what has just happened, even you might have had your fill of flies for one evening."

"One can never have enough, my dear." He transferred the fly from one finger to another and slowly stretched it across towards his wife, who turned away with disgust.

"You were so long examining that poor boy's wretched collection, while I was stuck all by myself with the three Mrs Philipses, each one duller than the next, I thought I might be trapped there for ever, like one of your revolting specimens. Their only topic of conversation seems to be the weather. I kept wishing I could be with all of you instead."

"But you dislike all such collections."

"It's true. I do. All those insects pinned and trapped behind glass. Ugh. But even they would have been preferable company to the Mrs Philipses."

"You're tired, Frances."

"Yes, I am. And is it any wonder?"

"*Rhagonidae*," mused Sir Ashton, returning his attention fully back to the fly. "The boy's favourite. He admired its large translucent wings." He held it up again for her to inspect. "Not unlike the diaphanous material on the sleeves of your gown, my dear."

"Charming. My husband is comparing me to an insect."

"The highest compliment I can think of."

"That makes me want to tear one of the damned creature's wings off."

"Which would have only the most temporary effect. The fly would learn to adapt its flight."

She batted away her husband's hand and together they watched the fly hover before heading off in pursuit of its fellow escapees.

"Seriously, Ashton, will the boy recover?"

Lever nodded. "All that need be done is to place something sticky and glutinous that will tempt the swarm away from him."

"The remains of Mrs Philips's woodcock pie perhaps."

The earth's tremors had abated and Sir Ashton and Lady Lever stepped out into the night, laughing arm in arm.

There was no sanctuary to be had within the Collegiate Church this night. Its doors were locked and were not for opening, despite the desperate pounding on them by dozens of frightened parishioners.

From within the angle of the Irwell and the Irk, to the south of the Church and the College, Lizzie Raffald, midwife and gazetteer, hastened past in the direction of the Market Place, in the centre of which stood the Booths, tolls which guarded the entrance to the town, clustered around the Conduit, erected almost a century before through the munificence of Mrs Isabella Beck, a fountain piping water from the well a quarter of a mile away in Spring Gardens.

Hurrying down Penniless Hill, past the site of the Old Exchange on the corner of Acresfield, she made her way north to the Shambles, a warren of narrow passageways, rank with the stench of rotting meat. East of the flesh boards stood the Market Cross, with the pillory and stocks close by. In the latter a loudly snoring drunk slept unperturbed by the tumultuous events of the night. Lizzie was faced with two exits. The one to her right would take her back along the old Mealgate, away from where she needed to go. The baby had stopped crying now – a bad sign. Lizzie turned left, through Smithy Door, down a shallow but slippery flight of steps to the Irwell and to the Salford Bridge, which would take her across the river. The normally still waters were boiling. She tried not to think about what might be causing this, concentrating instead on making sure the tiny scrap of life she held in her arms was still breathing. She gently pinched its cheeks and was heartened to see them pinking up. Just beyond the bridge, emptying into the Irwell from Shude Hill was the Hanging Ditch, little more than an open sewer.

She had thought the less populous far bank of the Irwell would provide her with a swifter passage towards the Prison, avoiding the warren of lanes and cellars on the Manchester side, but fires had been lit just beyond the bridge, around which demonic figures were dancing and trying to leap the flames. Cursing, she doubled back along the Dean's Gate, past the lower entrance to Acresfield, where the remnants of the Annual September Fair lay broken and abandoned. A few of the cattle, which had been grazing the enclosed common between the square of fine town houses only recently built on either side of St Ann's Church, had become untethered and roamed wild and bellowing through the smoke from the fires. She ducked into St Mary's Parsonage, wove between the tenements and burgage gardens that lay between Market Street Lane and St Peter's Field, and headed out along the old Roman road that stretched all the way to Chester, until she reached the Bailey Bridge and the Prison, where this apology for a workhouse was housed in a makeshift lean-to at the back.

Mrs Philips found her son shortly after the last tremors had ceased and the thick blanket of cloud which had covered Manchester for the last week had at last begun to disperse. A defiant half moon poked its way clear and shone down upon the scene of devastation which lay around the Daub Holes.

A few of the Bedlam Boys still cavorted nakedly in the sediment-encrusted water, but most lay still, whimpering and shivering. As Mrs Philips approached one of them, pity overcoming fear and disgust, he pointed a straightened, gnarled finger. She followed the direction of his gaze. A dozen yards distant, lying on his back, nestled between two of the clay pits, was her son.

"Leigh," she called, running heedless across the pitted ground, strewn with the bodies of the broken and the wounded, like a scavenger in a battlefield, checking the corpses for one she recognised. But none of those she passed were corpses. They were simply the dazed, uncomprehending survivors of the now finished quake.

Eventually she found him. His eyes were wide open and staring up at the sky. Above his head the last few stragglers of flies desultorily buzzed. The remnants of his clothes, which he had stripped away from him in a desperate attempt to rid his body of the swarm, lay about him in shreds and tatters. His teeth were chattering. A wide, mirthless smile had spread across his lips. If she had not known him, his mother might easily have mistaken him for another of the Bedlam Boys.

John Wesley roared away from the Daub Holes towards Market Street Lane like a winged apocalypse. Eschewing the narrow eighteen inch pavements that bordered each side, he strode down the centre of the King's Highway, his coat flying out behind him. Pausing only to harangue the drinkers from their stupor outside the doors of the town's inns and coaching houses, each a series of outer rings until he reached his intended bull's eye, the centre of *The Bull's Head* itself, on Shude Hill.

Once there, he flung open its doors and, ignoring the mayhem and wreckage around him, proceeded to unleash the full force of his formidable tonsils on all within. Accustomed as he was to addressing thousands in open air meetings on hill top and valley bottom, a few dozen brawling, carousing taverners were of little consequence if they thought they might quell his ardour.

"*Woe to that wreath of pride,*" he bellowed, like a bull himself, "*that pride of Ephraim's drunkards, that fading flower, which is God's glorious beauty, set at the head of this fertile valley! 'Behold,' saith Isaiah, 'the Lord sends One who is powerful and strong'. Like a hailstorm and a destructive wind, like a driving rain and a flooding downpour, yea, like a very earthquake which will rock the place where we walk, He will cast it forcefully to the ground.*"

By now he had the attention of all and continued like a river in full spate.

"*That wreath, that pride of Ephraim's drunkards, will be trampled underfoot. That fading flower, His glorious beauty, set at the head of this fertile valley, will be like figs ripe before the harvest...*"

The gentlemen from the upstairs Function Room, having adjourned their meeting to discuss the founding of their *Literary and Philosophical Society* once the first tremors had occurred, roused by the preacher's thundering voice, had entered the now silent inn below and took note of the rapt faces all turned as one towards Wesley, a man they all either knew or recognised, though not all with the same approbation and favour. Wesley espied them as they approached him, fixing them with his boldest stare, addressing his next words to them directly.

"*... as soon as people see them and take them in hand, they will swallow them whole, not heeding their true provenance.*"

Dr White attempted to brush past the preacher, who stayed his arm.

"*In that day the Lord Almighty will be a glorious crown, a garlanded wreath for the remnants of His People...*"

"If you will excuse me, Mr Wesley, for it is to those remnants which you describe to whom I must now repair." He removed Wesley's hand from his arm, put back his hat upon his head and strode out into the blazing night.

Wesley continued. "*He will be a spirit of justice to those who sit in judgement. A source of strength to those who turn back the battle at the gate.*"

At this point Minister Gore stepped quietly forward. "Do you mean the good Doctor, John, or do you speak only of yourself?"

Methodist and Unitarian eyed each other warily across the tavern.

"I hope," said Wesley, "that I speak for every man and woman here present, for do we not all seek to turn back the battle at the gate?"

"Perhaps," replied Gore, "But does not Isaiah go on to say, '*Priests and prophets reel when befuddled with wine*'?"

"Not I, Richard."

" '*They stagger when seeing visions. They stumble when rendering decisions*'. I have always found comfort in those words, a warning against our own hubris."

"The hubris of sinners, Richard, not those who are true to the spirit of the Lord."

"Gentlemen," called out Thomas Perceval, who had become increasingly impatient as the two Non-Conformists butted heads like rutting stags, "I do not believe that now is the time for a theological discussion, not when the earth rocks beneath our feet."

But Wesley was back in full flow. "*Are not all the tables covered in vomit? There is not a spot that is without filth.*"

"That's as mebbe," cried out John Raffald, "but tell us what we must do."

"Ay," chorused a large contingent of frightened customers.

"Who is it he is trying to teach?" asked Perceval. "Oh yes, Mr Wesley, I too know my Isaiah. '*To whom is he explaining his message? To children scarce weaned from their mothers' milk? To those just taken from the breast?*' What? '*Do this, do that*'?"

"*A rule for this, a rule for that.*"

"*A little here, a little there?*"

"*I am the Lord, thy God, and thou shalt have no other gods but me.*"

"Very well then, '*with foreign lips and strange tongues God will speak to His people...*'"

"*Thou shalt not make unto me any graven image...*"

"This is the resting place, let the weary rest. This is the place of repose," and he swept his arm around the stupefied inn.

"But they would not listen'," cried Wesley, addressing himself now directly to Perceval and the other would-be members of the *Manchester Literary & Philosophical Society*. *"Therefore hear the Word of the Lord, you Doubters who rule here in Jerusalem. You boast that you have entered into a covenant with Death, with the realm of the dead have you made an agreement. When an overwhelming scourge sweeps by, you say, 'It cannot touch us for we have made lies our refuge, and falsehoods our hiding place'."*

Another tremor shook the foundations of *The Bull's Head*, pitching the room violently. Panic at once ensued and people began rushing for the door, trampling anyone in their way underfoot in their haste to reach the streets outside.

Wesley remained unmoved. Undeterred he continued to rage against what he saw as the weakness and folly, the greed and selfishness he perceived around him, heedless of the buffeting he received by all those trying to make their safe passage beyond him.

" *'I lay a stone in Zion, a tested stone, a precious cornerstone for a sure foundation. The one who relies on it will never be stricken with panic. I will make justice the measuring line and righteousness the plumb line. Hail will sweep away your refuge, the lie, and water will overflow your hiding place. The bed is too short to stretch out on, the blanket too narrow to wrap around you. The Lord will rise up as he did at Mount Perazim. He will rouse himself as in the Valley of Gibeon. Listen and hear my voice. Pay attention and hear what I say. When a farmer ploughs for planting, does he plough continually? Does he keep on breaking up and working the soil? When he has levelled the surface, does he not sow caraway and scatter cumin? Does he not plant wheat in its place, barley in its plot, and spelt in its field? God instructs him and teaches him the right way. Caraway is not threshed with a sledge, nor is the wheel of a cart rolled over cumin. Caraway is beaten out with a rod, and cumin with a stick. Grain must be ground to make bread, so one does not go on threshing it forever. The wheels of a threshing cart may be rolled over it, but one does not use horses to grind grain'.* All this comes from the Lord Almighty, whose plan is wonderful, whose wisdom is magnificent."

But by now the inn had emptied and Wesley spoke only to overturned tables and upended chairs, to half-drained tankards, which rolled unsteadily on the tilting floor.

A small iron grille was pulled back, at which a yellow-eyed face appeared, a drool of spit flecking the corners of a mouth which held just a few remaining stained stumps of teeth. He held up a lantern to look out, which only served to accentuate his nightmarish appearance still further.

"Quick," cried Lizzie. "He's fading fast."

Muttering under his breath, the owner of the sickly yellow face pushed back the grille, then swung open the heavy outer prison gate. Lizzie was a frequent caller and the gatekeeper swung his lantern in the vague direction of an imposing studded door across the cobbled courtyard.

Lizzie did not need to wait to be shown the way. She ran on ahead, pushing open the door which led inside the low, mean dwelling that served as a sorry substitute for a workhouse, which was still under construction elsewhere in the town on New Bridge Street. The Beadle was already waiting for her, hastily removing a napkin from the front of his waistcoat, which bore the stains of beef broth, accompanied by a surfeit of claret.

"Another charge for our already overstretched service," he said, more a statement than a question. "It's lucky old Mrs H died this morning, otherwise we might not have had room."

"Always room for a newborn, Alfred," she replied.

"I daresay," he replied, somewhat lugubriously, though not untenderly, looking down upon the sleeping infant. "No mother, I suppose?" he asked, raising his protuberant eyebrows.

"No," said Lizzie, squeezing past him. "He's in urgent need of a wet nurse."

"Maud," he said. "Follow me."

They hurried together down the unlit stone passageway. The Beadle took out a bunch of heavy keys from his waistcoat pocket and opened a door into a large, bare dormitory, which housed upward of forty females. One of these he roused roughly. "Maud," he whispered, *sotto voce*, "your services are required."

Lizzie handed the babe quickly towards a thin, exhausted-looking woman, her eyes blinking as she stirred herself awake. Like an automated doll she placed the barely moving child to her sore and leaking nipple, where, after falling off it a couple of times, it eventually latched on and sucked greedily and noisily.

Lizzie sat down on the edge of the iron cot and allowed all of the tension she'd been holding in her body for the past hour to drain from her. The Beadle looked down upon this modern *pieta* and allowed himself the briefest of smiles.

"Amos," he pronounced. "That's what we'll call him. "Amos."

Lizzie nodded, then, satisfied that her work was now done, stood up and, with a final look down on the clearly reviving Amos, thanked Alfred, placed the shilling coin silently within the Beadle's huge ham paw, before striding back across the dormitory, along the passageway and out once more into the night.

There had not, she realised with a certain grim satisfaction, been a tremor for several minutes. Alfred, the Beadle, opening his folded fist, noted the coin gleaming in a pale shaft of moonlight dropping through the dormitory's single window high up near the ceiling. He picked it up with the thumb and forefinger of his other hand and testingly bit on it hard.

From her sheltered hole in the corner of the Hulks, Whelp cautiously emerged. She had not felt the earth tilt or shift for almost half an hour and wondered if it might have stopped altogether now, so that she risked raising her head above the parapet of wood and stone she had earlier surrounded herself with.

The Hulks were deserted. Except for Septimus, who sat holding his head from when the Spaniard had struck him earlier. He rocked repeatedly back and forth, groaning. Whelp could see naked figures still dancing around the makeshift fires among the Daub Holes, but they were some way off. She crept fully from her hole and made her way towards the young woman who had given birth to the child. She was not the first dead person Whelp had seen. The thought of her still, lifeless body did not distress her especially. She was simply curious. Birth and death jostling like playmates side by side. Whelp stood over her, looking down. The eyes were closed. The expression on the face strangely calm, serene almost. The skin was beginning to acquire that grey patina Whelp had noticed on the dead before. Like stone. Like a statue.

Whelp felt an overwhelming urge to touch the woman's cheek. She knelt beside her and reached out her hand. As her fingers lightly brushed against her face, which was still warm, Whelp noted, the eyes suddenly sprang open. A hand shot up and grabbed Whelp's wrist. The head turned towards her, then twisted in a spasm of pain, the eyes clamping shut once more. She was alive. Whelp tried to stand back, gasping aloud with the shock, but the woman's grip on her wrist was a vice which would not let go. Mesmerised, Whelp watched as the woman pulled her knees back towards her and began to moan, an eerie keening that did not sound human to Whelp's young ears. She followed the woman's gaze down towards her belly and realised in a sudden panic that she was about to give birth once more.

Whelp may have witnessed death before, but she had not been so physically close to birth until this moment. Instinctively she reached with her free hand for a branch from one of the fires nearby and held it lower, so that she could better see what was happening. The baby slid out from between the woman's legs like an uncoiled eel. Whelp managed to extricate her hand from the woman's grip and was just able to catch it as it flopped out of her. A boy, bloodied and bruised, with the cord still attached. Whelp held it up towards the woman, who smiled thinly, before laying her head back down onto the ground, with a last, shuddering breath that emptied her. There was no mistaking this time. She was unreachably dead.

Whelp placed her wet fingers over the woman's eyelids and closed them. She looked at the squirming, wriggling infant in her hands. A kind of instinct took over. She brought it up closer towards her face, fastened her teeth around the cord and bit until the baby was free.

Wheeling round she ran across to where Septimus was still rocking and groaning, her eyes darting rapidly till they alighted on what she had been seeking. Yes. It was still there. The piece of white cotton, the shawl, which the young woman had offered to Septimus as payment for letting her settle in the Hulks for the night. Before the quake had struck.

"Give," she demanded of the old man. "Need."

Septimus, who had never before heard Whelp speak, despite knowing her for more than two years, instantly stopped his rocking and groaning, took in the sight of her, holding the baby in one thin arm, stretching the other bonily towards him. Without a word he removed the shawl from around his shoulders, where he had worn it ever since the Spaniard had first attempted to seize it, and handed it towards her. Solemnly she took it from him and quickly wrapped it around the now howling child.

She knew what she would do. She knew every house which was inhabited in nearby Newton Lane and who lived in each. In the grandest of them, on the corner, where Newton Lane joined the London Road, lived the felt maker. She had seen him often. He had a kind disposition. Sometimes he had dropped a coin into the lap of her skirt if he had passed her while she sat by the roadside. He had a kindly-looking wife, who once or twice had smiled at her on her way back from Market Street Lane. What was more, they had no children, she had noticed. Surely they wanted one? Was that not what every marriage desired?

She climbed up out of the Hulks and made her way carefully towards their house. She placed the baby, now wrapped neatly in the white cotton sheet, carefully on the front step, its starfish fingers flailing from its nest of laurel leaves, another moth trying to disentangle itself from the web, reaching towards a spark of flame. Whelp lifted the brass knocker and rapped the door sharply three times, before darting back towards the Hulks, where she melted into the shadows, and from where she watched and waited. The baby continued to cry lustily and loud.

*

As the tremors ceased and the riots ebbed, as the flames from fires that blazed across the town, from Angel Meadow in the north to St Peter's Field in the south, from Kersal Moor in the west to Ardwick Green in the east, began at last to settle and die back, an unearthly quiet fell upon the stunned inhabitants.

Stepping boldly from their host Brother Saxon's residence on Spring Gardens, the party of Moravians processed through the streets, carrying lit torches, singing one of Brother Swertner's recently composed hymns. The light from their lanterns bounced off buildings, danced on earth and water alike, rendering them indivisible, their voices tentatively taking to the air around them, gradually growing in strength, carrying a stillness with them, which they imparted to all they passed.

"How precious is the Book divine
By inspiration given
Bright as a lamp its doctrines shine
To guide our souls to Heaven

Its light descending from above
Our gloomy world to cheer
Displays a Saviour's boundless love
And brings His glories near..."

Even the Bedlam Boys broke from their manic dance to pause and listen, scratching their itching bodies as they squatted low between the Daub Holes, dazed and exhausted. The Brothers and Sisters continued to sing while they walked their measured progress.

"It sweetly cheers our drooping hearts
In this dark vale of tears
Life, light and joy it still imparts
And quells our rising fears

This Lamp through all the tedious night
Of life shall guide our way
Till we behold the clearer light
Of an eternal day..."

Eventually they faded from sight, leaving nothing behind but the echo of their voices hanging on the wind, the drip of water from a leaking gutter, the last cracking of twigs in a dying fire, the drone of flies dispersing.

"Did you see them, Mother?" asked a tremulous Leigh Philips, not looking at her as she knelt beside his feverish body, vainly trying to restore some decency to him. His teeth chattered but his head was hot.

"Who, darling?"

"My collection."

"No, darling, I didn't."

"Weren't they magnificent?"

Mrs Philips said nothing.

By now her husband and brothers-in-law had reached them.

"He's in shock," she said simply to them. "We must get him home. We must get him warm."

John nodded grimly. "Thomas, you go on ahead. Tell Nancy to light a fire in the boy's bedroom. Nathaniel, you and I will carry him between us."

The two brothers hoisted Leigh to his feet, placing one arm each across their shoulders.

"Thank you, Father," said Leigh meekly. "As soon as I am well again, I shall start a new collection..."

Whelp held her breath as the lantern procession of singers passed by the big house on the corner of Newton Lane, their voices drowning out the questing cries of the baby she had placed on the front step there.

Within a few more minutes they had receded into the night, no longer visible or audible, their absence now lingering like a half buried memory of a home she once had known. Her eyes fell upon a shard of brightly coloured glass winking at her from the mud below where she crouched. She picked it up and brought it nearer to her, so she might examine it more closely. It was a colour to which she could give no name, somewhere between a deep blue and dark green, like a river in certain casts of light, constantly changing, the kind of light that might have tempted her ancestors to first crawl out of the primeval slime, a birth canal. The baby, Whelp realised, had fallen worryingly silent.

In that moment the door to the big house opened. Whelp placed the coloured glass into a fold in her skirt. A servant girl glanced out from behind the door nervously. She was just about to go back indoors, when her attention was caught by a sudden reawakening of the baby's hungry cry, weaker now than it had been, broken and pitiful. The servant girl looked down, then covered her mouth in shock.

"Mistress," she cried, over her shoulder and back into the house, before stooping instinctively to pick up the child, which she held close to her, rocking and shushing it.

Mrs Oldham appeared on the step within seconds. Whelp strained to catch what might next transpire.

The servant girl handed the baby to her mistress, whose face broke instantly into wreaths of tears and smiles conjoined.

"Look," she whispered to her husband, who had now joined her in the doorway. "It's a sign, Andrew. It must be."

"Now, Catherine," he said, putting his arm around his wife. "Let us not be presumptuous, nor jump to any unwarranted conclusions...."

"Can we keep him? Please. He's been left here. As an offering. By someone who can't look after him herself."

"We don't know that, Catherine. We don't know anything. We must make enquiries."

"I suppose you are right, Andrew, but while you do, may we not keep him till then?"

"That cloth he is wrapped in is uncommonly fine cotton."

"Yes," she replied, noticing it for the first time. "Moths fluttering among laurel."

The baby continued to cry more urgently.

"Begging your pardon, Mistress – Sir – right now the little one needs feeding. Who knows how long the poor mite's been out here? He doesn't look like he's more than a few minutes old..."

"Yes, of course. You are right, Fanny. Gently warm some milk for him. As quick as you can."

Fanny bobbed a curtsey and hurried indoors. Andrew stepped out into the lane, raising the candle he was carrying as if in search of enlightenment. Whelp withdrew further into the shadow of the wall she leant beside. "Whatever must have befallen the poor unfortunate mother…?" he whispered.

"Matthew," pronounced Mrs Oldham suddenly. "I shall call him Matthew, for he is like a deliverance to us, a gift, a promise withheld these many years."

Andrew shook his head sadly, turned back to his wife and ushered her and the defiantly crying Matthew into their house. Whelp exhaled deeply, then headed back to the Hulks.

In the lean-to behind the Prison, Maud had scarcely laid the infant Amos down beside her when it seemed he was in need of feeding again.

Tom, Sir Ashton's groom, eventually found the runaway Cleveland Bays grazing indiscriminately among the bushes and hedges which lined the gardens of the grand houses on Mosley Street on the far side of the Daub Holes. They were skittish and easily spooked, rearing up on their hind legs as he approached them. Steam was rising from their flanks, which were soaked with gleaming patches of white sweat. They shook their manes and pawed the ground with their enormous hooves, some of which, Tom saw, were cut and bleeding.

He spread the palms of his hands, which he raised in a conciliatory gesture in front of him, edging tentatively towards them. Eventually they were sufficiently calm for him to be able to grasp their bridles, one in each hand, before walking them slowly back towards Lever's Row.

Once he reached the sanctuary of the stables he examined them more closely. The eyes of one of them were rolling slightly. Its muzzle was flecked with foam and spittle. It was as he feared. There was laurel in the hedges on Mosley Road and this bay must have inadvertently eaten some of it, while grazing on the more palatable blackthorn. Judging from their condition – they could still stand and their skin was not burning up – they could only have ingested a small amount. Added to that, they were large animals, both more than seventeen hands in height, and so they would have had to have eaten a considerable amount for the effects to be fatal. Even so, Tom was taking no chances. He scooped several beakers full of charcoal powder stored in a large metal bin in the corner of the yard, which he mixed into a mash. After he had stirred it thoroughly he needed to let it stand for half an hour to allow the charcoal to do its work. While he waited, he led the two bays to the water troughs, which he encouraged them to drain, before refilling them with buckets from the well. That they were eager to keep drinking in this way was a good sign.

It was just as they had begun to eat the charcoal mash that Sir Ashton and his wife joined him, enquiring after their horses' welfare.

"I think I got to them just in time, sir," explained Tom. "But they'll not be fit for taking you back to Alkrington till the morning at the earliest, sir. You can never be too careful with laurel."

"Quite so," acknowledged Sir Ashton.

"Thank you, Tom," said Lady Lever, stepping in on behalf of her husband, who had stomped out of the yard, clearly displeased at this new turn of events. "My husband is most fond of these bays. They mean a great deal to him. He bred them, you understand, and it distresses him to see them so agitated."

"Yes, Ma'am," said Tom, reaching his hand to his forelock.

"Castor and Pollux, he calls them. After the stars. Gemini. The twins."

"Yes, Ma'am."

"Well, Tom, I'll leave you to your ministrations."

"Yes, Ma'am. Thank you, Ma'am."

"Damn and blast," hissed her husband as soon as she rejoined him.

"Tom is doing his best, Ashton. In fact, you owe him a great favour. Lord knows what we'd have done if he hadn't rescued them."

"Yes, I know. I'll see him right in the morning."

"I should think so."

"I just hate the thought of having to spend a whole night under the roof of this upstart, John Philips, that's all."

"An upstart to whom you are now financially beholden, Ashton…"

"Yes, yes," he sighed wearily.

"One must learn to accommodate the times as one lives them."

Husband and wife eyed each other closely in the night air. It was the husband who looked away first.

The Moravian Choir continued to walk in darkness the eight miles across open country, field and moorland, past Clayton Vale and Failsworth, skirting Boggart Hole Clough and the base of Tandle Hill, until, in a little under three hours, they reached the home of Brother Lees' father in Clarkesfield on the edge of Oldham, where those from the Fulneck community had been invited to stay before making their way back across the Pennines the following day. After they had said their final prayers, thanking the Lord for keeping them safe in this tumultuous night, they each settled themselves to sleep.

Only Brother Swertner remained awake. He took out pen and paper from the bag he always carried and opened out a single, well worn sheet, already covered with the drawing of a great vine, which he had been labouring over for many years. The fruit of this vine, which hung in rich clusters, were the names of Moravian Churches across the world. The early Greek Missionary Movement of Cyril and Methodius from 890 AD was depicted at the top, below the inscription *Unitas Fratrum*, the Founding Church at Kunwald in Bohemia underneath, then all of their resting places ever since, in Germany, Holland, London, then further afield to Greenland, America, the Indies. Lightcliffe, Fulneck, Dukinfield, each had their own cluster, and now Brother Swertner tentatively dared to outline in pencil 'Fairfield', alongside a drawing of the Moravian emblem of the Lamb and the Flag.

"Can you not sleep, Brother?" asked a concerned Brother Lees. "Is there anything I can get you?"

Brother Swertner put down his pencil and shook his head. "Our Lamb has conquered," he said, smiling. "Let us follow him."

Whelp too found sleep elusive that night. She picked up the shard of coloured glass once more and studied it. An idea began to form in her mind. If anyone had come across her just at the moment, they might almost have thought a smile was trying to form its unaccustomed shape across her pinched, starved face.

Instead a column of rats ran silently over her unshod feet. Whelp paid them no heed. She stood up, resolved. She knew what she must do.

*

The rat can breed throughout the year if conditions are favourable, with each female producing up to five litters a year. This particular dam, who was now in the throes of giving birth, was in the twenty-first and last day of its gestation.

In the sudden turmoil following the escape of Sir Ashton's Cleveland Bays, several rats from the colony had instinctively sought shelter in the warren of underground burrows which had been dug by generations of their forebears, while a number of male bucks remained behind to mate with the dam the moment she had completed delivery of her litter of seven pups. They each ejaculated multiple times in a rapid instinctive sequence, thereby increasing the likelihood of future pregnancy while decreasing the risk of stillborns.

The lactating dam suckled each of the seven pups in turn. In three weeks she would once again be giving birth. In five weeks the females from these new-born pups would themselves be fertile, and in fifteen weeks the population would be growing by a factor of ten.

In less than a year this single dam would be dead, but she would have been responsible for the birth of fifteen thousand additions to the colony, in which, on this particularly momentous Saturday night, there were already a further thousand more gestating females, many of whom would not survive the convulsions of the quake. But whatever catastrophe befell them this night, they burrowed deeper, confident that their colony would survive.

3

15th September

The next morning the clouds had lifted slightly, but it was still grey and dreary. Smoke hung in wreaths above the town, not moving. Few people ventured out of doors, and those who did stumbled through the streets silent and uncomprehending.

Tom gave the all clear for the Cleveland Bays at first light. The charcoal mash had done its work. Two hours later they set off from Lever's Row, drawing Sir Ashton and his wife in their Clarence, with the family crest of a pelican painted in decorative gilt on the mahogany door. The leather hood was pulled down, so that they were hidden from any eyes that might be tempted to pry, but the few people who were abroad at that early hour had their eyes firmly cast down, as if seeking some evidence of where the earth had shaken the previous night. Of cracks and fissures there were none, however, and so Tom, sitting out in the open air at the front of the carriage, was able to steer the Clarence along the Middleton Road with only the customary obstacles of pot holes to be navigated. Into one of these he unavoidably plunged the carriage's rear right wheel, throwing up a fountain of red mud, which covered a small child hunched up by the roadside.

The small child was Whelp. She barely noticed the sprays of clay and mud which now lay spattered about her face and hair, as well as her threadbare clothes, for she was already generously streaked with clay from her night time's exertions.

As soon as the Oldhams had taken the baby indoors, which she had placed instinctively on their front step, Whelp had roused Old Septimus and led him to where the young dead mother lay among the wreckage of the birth. She pointed. He nodded. He knew without further words what it was she wanted him to do.

Over the next several hours they had done their best to give the poor woman as decent a burial as they could between them. First they had dragged the body towards a shallow outflow of Shooter's Brook, little more than a stagnant ditch at that point, seeping its sluggish way from the Medlock to the Tib, without ever reaching it. The ditch lay some three feet below the level of the small tract of open ground between the Daub Holes and Newton Lane, by one of the lime pits, which made it relatively easy for Whelp and Septimus, once they had placed the body there, to anchor it with stones before covering it over with mud. Next they carried more stones from the piles which lay abandoned around the edge of the Hulks, from when construction had ceased after the money ran out. These they heaped up in a small cairn, almost to the lip of the ditch. Finally they smeared a last layer of wet earth from the clay banks in the Daub Holes, until they were satisfied the body would not be dug up by dogs in the coming days and weeks, while it slowly sank into the pit of lime.

Just as they were laying on the last fistfuls of mud, Whelp noticed another piece of coloured glass, winking at her in the dawn's grey light. Whereas the first one she had found had been somewhere between blue and green, this second shard was blood red. She placed it inside the small hessian purse which she wore at all times around her scrawny chicken neck, knowing that the two pieces, knocking gently against each other unseen, made a myriad of new colours.

From this quiet corner of the Brook, Whelp could just make out the back of the Oldhams' house. It seemed right somehow that the grave where the mother lay was in sight of where her second son was for now protected. She resolved, if she could, to come and visit this spot at first light every day and watch for any signs of the rescued child. She looked now. Fanny, the servant girl, was hanging out the white cotton shawl on a line. She must have been up early washing away the blood and dirt.

Now it fluttered in the wind. The moths, caught in the fine weft, danced in the morning air, straining for release.

Someone else who had not had much sleep during the night was Dr White. After the cut and thrust and badinage of his argument with Thomas Perceval, he had left *The Bull's Head* in a high temper. So caught up was he by playing and replaying the scene in his head, going over what he had said, and what he might have said if he had been better prepared, he barely noticed the fires and panic on the streets. It was only as he reached the Infirmary, a route his feet had taken him without his consciously directing them, did the full extent of the quake's impact strike him. The first thing he noticed were the escaped Bedlam Boys, rampaging naked across the Daub Holes. Then he saw that the huddle of Putrescents always to be found clamouring at the entrance to the Dispensary was nowhere to be seen. That could only mean one thing. Somehow they must have forced their way inside. At once his attention was arrested by the sound of breaking glass. The windows in the Infirmary were being smashed.

Now, as the grey morning light began to climb the sky, a quiet calm had descended. The Putrescents had all been ejected and once more slunk in a desultory fashion on the steps outside. Most, though not all, of the Bedlam Boys had been recaptured and confined to their cells. A local joiner was boarding up the broken windows and a glazier, even though it was a Sunday, was busy measuring the windowless frames. The nurses had already cleaned up all the damage and mess inflicted by the incursion of the previous night, and were now on hands and knees scrubbing every inch of the walls and corridors, and every other surface. Hygiene was something of a fetish with Dr White, and he was finally able to breathe more deeply and easily, now that order and cleanliness were being restored. Cheered by the progress he was witnessing all around him, he fetched from the Dispensary some bottles of diluted red wine, two parts wine to one part water, and went to offer what succour he could to those afflicted still gathered outside.

He had been greatly influenced by the recent pronouncements of William Cullen, an Edinburgh physician, who, unlike most taxonomists of the time, had divided fevers on clinical grounds, 'according to how they show an inflammatory irritation or some weaker reaction'. True inflammatory fevers he labelled *synocha*, or continuous, unabating, while the slow nervous fever he renamed *typhus*, from the Greek, meaning smoke or mist, an epithet favoured by Dr White, for they summoned up exactly the nature of the unfortunate wretches who feebly stretched their painful fingers towards him now as he walked among them. They were like ghosts, wraiths, neither living nor dead. He might treat these poor souls pitifully gathered on the Infirmary steps today, but next week, next month, next year, hundreds more would rise up like smoke from the Daub Holes, creeping across the town in a low, icy mist, infecting the very air that all must breathe. One of the more prominent symptoms displayed by those afflicted with the disease was a certain mental impairment in the form of delirium or stupor. Both of these manifestations presented themselves to the Doctor now as he set about corralling them into an orderly queue.

He was familiar, both from reading and from direct personal observations, with the disease's progress, beginning with insidious malaise, severe headaches, loss of appetite and little heat, as judged by the touching of the patient's skin, who then began to experience increased prostration, a slow weak pulse, accompanied by an insidious dry cough, followed by the appearance of more nervous symptoms, such as restlessness, drowsiness, muscular pains and tremors, eventually producing a high fever. Instead of reaching an immediate crisis, the illness had a tendency to go into a brief period of remission. Dr Cullen had, as a result, referred to it as 'the remitting disease', but this pause did not endure for long. All too soon it would return, with renewed bouts of fever and delirium, the appearance of a petechial rash on the chest or abdomen, red and purple spots caused by bleeding from broken capillary vessels, followed by gangrenous sores erupting on the patient's fingers, toes and other pressure points within the joints. This later complication was typically described as the 'transformation' stage of the disease, when it metamorphosed from the nervous to the putrid, due to the progressive dissolution of bodily fluids, from which no patient recovered. Any treatment administered to these would only ease, not cure, these symptoms, and then but temporarily.

The ghosts Dr White walked through now had all reached this terminal stage. They were termed 'putrescent' as soon as the sickly sweet, fetid smell of their breath was detectable, followed by the cadaverous stench that emanated from their infection-ridden, sore-pocked bodies, together with the uncontrolled emission of loose green stools.

White had seen at first hand the conditions which both bred and spread the disease. In less than a generation, Manchester's population had trebled, with new arrivals entering the town every week. Affordable, available housing was becoming increasingly scarce, so these multitudes of newcomers were crammed indiscriminately into narrow, windowless rooms, damp, verminous cellars, or the dark, festering 'workhouse' wing of the New Bailey Prison. White, like other attentive physicians, quickly realised that the conditions in these overcrowded urban slums were not dissimilar to those encountered in the enclosed, confined communities to be found in prisons, barracks, or on board ships. Once the disease took hold it spread unstoppably, until every inhabitant was affected. To explain the sudden appearance of typhoid fever among these institutions and dwellings, White postulated that the explosive generation of such poisons arose spontaneously within the stale air of cramped spaces saturated with the exhalations of too many unwashed bodies crowded into single, unventilated rooms. Another key agent in spreading the disease so rapidly must, he concluded, be perspiration. This, combined with the vapour rising from decaying foodstuffs and the accumulated filth on walls, floor and ceilings, only served to exacerbate the condition. This invisible contagion, White argued, could be inhaled, ingested, or otherwise transmitted, directly by skin contact, but only within a limited radius from its source. If he could have his way, White would have every citizen of Manchester forcibly stripped naked and every square inch of their skin scrubbed with scalding water and carbolic soap, and for this to be repeated in regular doses. Consequently, while he had a doctor's Hippocratic sympathy with these foul, rank specimens he walked among, dispensing wine and water, he nevertheless held an unshakeable view that on no account should any suspected typhoid cases be allowed to cross the threshold of the Infirmary and enter its wards, for fear of spreading the disease among the nurses and patients already admitted. In this stance, effectively barring entry for the largest contingent of sufferers, he regularly crossed swords with certain members of the Infirmary's trustees, who, they would frequently point out, were the stewards and guardians of the Hospital Board's stated and avowed charitable aims of providing help and care for those not able to provide it for themselves, namely the poor and the destitute. On the contrary, White would counter, allowing possible typhus cases to enter the Infirmary threatened these same 'benevolent designs' so prized by the charity's trustees, since a hospital-based epidemic could only lead to an increased mortality among patients already admitted. The ensuing negative publicity that such an epidemic would inevitably create, White argued, would deter prospective future patients and – here he played his trump card – lead to the possible reductions in public subscriptions, on which the trustees depended for keeping the Infirmary open.

"There cannot surely be a greater contradiction in the nature of things," he concluded, "than a disease produced by a hospital."

For now he had won the argument – he had insisted in the building's original design of large floor-to-ceiling windows on either side of the main wards for greater cross-ventilation, implemented a daily routine of fumigation using tar water to mop all tiled floors, and arranged for the periodic whitewashing of the walls with lime – but as he walked among the putrescent ghosts rising up from the Daub Holes all around him, some of them too weak even to lift their heads from the wet clay, he felt more and more that he resembled Canute, unable to turn back the unstoppable tide of disease carried in with each successive wave of newcomers.

For the first time in his professional life, he began to experience doubt.

Another experiencing doubt that Sunday morning was Mr Andrew Oldham.

He was making his way to Chapel along the Withingreave. Some of the town's more recent arrivals had taken to calling it Withy Grove. He heard Fanny describing it thus only yesterday – before the Earthquake struck, before the world turned upside down, before they had found the child.

"Withy Grove," she had said, then smiled, shaking her head at the puzzled expression on his face. "You know the place, sir. Through the Mealgate, or Mill Gate as Fanny pronounced it, across Hanging Ditch, then right towards Shude Hill."

He had nodded. The town was changing so rapidly he could scarcely keep up. Yet he himself knew that he was in part responsible for some of these changes, and others like him, the Philipses, Mosleys, Arkwrights and Wrigleys, each of them opening a new mill or factory, tannery or dye works every week, it seemed. Less than a decade ago willows still grew all along the Withingreave, some still did by Hanging Ditch, and Shude Hill was bordered with green hawthorn hedges, covered in white May blossom each spring.

He was so completely lost in thought, deeply ruminating on his own perpetually vacillating feelings with regard to the nature of these changes, and how they affected him, and all those whose lives appertained to him, that he almost missed his way. He had reached Fennel Street before he realised his mistake and had to double his way back, almost to where he had started from. Change. He both embraced and reviled it equally. Unquestionably it brought benefits, not just for him and his family, but for everyone. But with each new change that occurred, he recognised, something was lost. Something irrevocable. He walked steadfastly, his eyes firmly fixed on the boots on his feet, not noticing where they were taking him. Until recently he had always walked with his head held high, looking about him, stopping to pass the time of day with whomever he might meet, the other merchants by the Old Exchange, the stall holders on Market Street Lane, even the beggars on Penniless Hill. They all of them breathed the same air.

But this morning he was troubled, his mind preoccupied, his thoughts uncertain. It was his custom, whenever he found himself in such a quandary, to seek comfort in his bible, but even that was offering him little solace as he made his now circuitous way to Sunday Matins. Instead every verse that jumped into his mind seemed to contradict the preceding one, so that by the time he had at last retraced his steps to Hanging Ditch, he was mired in confusion.

'I the Lord do not change,' reminded Malachi. *'So you, the descendants of Jacob, are not destroyed.'*

'And that is what some of you were,' consoled Corinthians. *'But you were washed. You were sanctified. You were justified by the Spirit of God.'*

But Andrew did not feel especially justified.

'*Look,*' said Isaiah, '*I am doing a new thing. Now it springs up, do you not perceive it? I am making a way in the wilderness and streams in the waste land.*'

A new thing, thought, Andrew. Yes, that is what I am doing. But are these green hedges, these withy groves, really such a wilderness that I should be tearing them down?

'*Have I not commanded thee?*' rebuked Joshua. '*Be strong and courageous. Do not be afraid. Do not be discouraged. For the Lord thy God will be with thee wherever thou goest.*'

'*Every good and perfect thing,*' agreed James, '*is sent from above. It cometh from the Father of Heaven, who doth not change like shifting shadows.*'

Andrew shook his head. "But every good and perfect thing," he said aloud as he walked, "brings with it all manner of change, not all of it good, not all of it perfect. How are we to know which is which?"

A young couple, walking in the opposite direction, gave him a wide berth, almost causing Andrew to slip from the narrow raised causeway down into the waters of the ditch below. He paused to collect himself. His breathing was short and ragged. I really must take a hold of myself, he thought. Such outward manifestations of my troubled conscience must not be allowed to be voiced upon the air like this.

'*Do not be anxious,*' he recalled from Philippians, '*but in every situation, by prayer and petition, with thanksgiving, present your requests to God.*'

But what might those requests be? What form or shape might they take? '*Do not conform to the pattern of this world,*' said Paul in his Letter to the Romans, remembered Andrew. Do I conform to this pattern? Or do I myself design it? And if the latter, who guides me?

'*I know the plans I have for you,*" declared Jeremiah, "*plans to prosper you and not to harm you, plans to give you hope and a future.*'

Hope and a future.

Andrew looked down from the balustrade of the Hanging Bridge, the precarious wooden rail, which prevented pedestrians from sliding into the sluggish channel of the Irk below, where eels, fattened on the grease and other effluents daily deposited there, gulped for air. A wheeled wagon, pulled by a pair of oxen, flies settling on their noses and lips, clouding their eyes, made its slow, determined way along the ditch towards the centre of the town. For all its clogged narrowness, this was still the King's Highway, and it was the oxen's right to travel on it. The driver of the cart flicked his whip idly. He looked up towards Andrew on the raised causeway above and nodded. If any eels did not escape in time, the wheels would roll unseeingly over them.

This child, thought Andrew for the thousandth time that morning, has been sent as a test. Perhaps Catherine had been right after all in her instinct to name him Matthew. A gift. A deliverance.

'We have this hope as an anchor to the soul,' he remembered from Hebrews, *'firm and secure. It enters the inner sanctuary behind the curtain.'*

Someone who *did* sleep that morning was sixteen-year-old Master Leigh Philips in Lever's Row.

After he had been found the previous night, delirious but serene, out among the Daub Holes, his mother and aunts had brought him back home. Exhausted almost to the point of oblivion, he was quite content merely to lie on his back in his bedroom, after he had been carried upstairs, while his torn and dirty clothes were removed and the myriad of sores from the swarm of flies that had covered him were individually and painstakingly washed clean. His mother then gently applied a home-made lotion of oatmeal and calamine to soothe the inflammation and depress the itchiness, so that Leigh felt no desire or need to scratch. Within minutes of the mixture being applied, he slipped into a calm, peaceful, though not entirely dreamless sleep.

His mother stayed by her son's side throughout the night, watching an expression of pure joy settling on his lips. Occasionally his eyelids would flutter, but his brow never creased. Leigh dreamed he was walking along the banks of all of the Manchester rivers – the Irk and the Irwell; the Medlock and the Mersey; the Tib, the Tonge, the Tame; the Beal, the Bollin, the Croal; the Glaze and the Goyt; the Roch and the Spodden. Then, when he had explored each of these, he took himself beside each of the smaller brooks – the Bradshaw, the Brearley, the Butterworth; the Boggart Hole and the Langdon End; the Kirklees, the Micker, the Naden; the Parr, the Piethorn, the Red; the Dean and the Tack; the Chorlton, the Wrigley; and Shooter's, which was close to where they had found him. By every watercourse he lingered, to gaze in wonder at the clusters of flies that gathered there, waiting for him, or so it seemed in his dream, to reclaim his place among them.

By half past ten the streets began to fill. People from all classes stepped out into the morning air. Not merely to survey the damage wrought by the previous night's tremors, which was surprisingly little considering the violence of the convulsions, most of it being caused by the ensuing panic, the fires, the looting, the smashed windows, but to make their way to the main Sunday services at the various churches spread across the growing metropolis, the outlying villages and neighbouring small towns. Mostly they walked in silence, reflecting on the fragility of existence when set against the raw power of nature and marvelling at their own particular good fortune to have survived. Manchester had endured catastrophe before – floods and fire, famine and plague – and would do so again.

Crows gathered on slateless roofs and scorched trees, patrolling the ravaged patches of waste ground, scavenging for scraps, untouched by these silent processions, not only here in the centre of the town, but along the lanes and across the fields in Newton Heath and Ardwick Green, in Rusholme, Birch, Withington and Didsbury, and through the silent streets of Stockport and Stretford, Cheadle and Chorlton, in Worsley and Wigan, Walkden and Warburton, north to Bolton and Bury, Heywood and Rochdale, Whitworth, Syke, Royton and Oldham. The whole of south-east Lancashire, it seemed, was on the move. The day felt unnaturally still. Not a breath of wind troubled the air. Not a leaf stirred on tree or hedge. By the time Tom guided the Clarence carriage of Sir Ashton Lever along the final approach to Alkrington Hall, the estate was empty, persuading even the Lord and his Lady to summon the priest for a service of deliverance in their own private chapel.

Parishioners across the land knelt on the stone floors of all the various churches to offer up their own personal thanks for their safe passage this grey Sunday morning in September. Priests and vicars, canons and curates led their congregations in the Lord's Prayer. Protestant and Catholic, Anglican and Dissenter. Methodist and Moravian, Baptist and Unitarian. For ever and ever. Amen.

In the heart of the silence that followed the end of each prayer, in that final moment before the people rose up from their knees, there came a low deep rumble from beneath their feet. There had not been a tremor felt for twelve hours, but now the earth was giving them one last reminder of the power of its voice, the merest hint of the forces it could unleash if it so desired. The ground gave a sudden, single, violent shudder and tilt.

Each congregation uttered a collective, convulsive gasp. Neighbour clung to neighbour. Ministers gripped the sides of their pulpits till their knuckles turned white.

Then, almost as quickly as it had started, it stopped, and somehow they all knew. This would be the last of them, this final after-shock.

The air in all the naves and choirs, aisles and apses, chancels and chapels trembled and quivered, like a haze in summer, except that it was cold, and in that mirage that was no mirage, they heard a humming. The humming grew to a ringing. Everyone looked up. The bells in the towers were swaying, though no hand pulled a single rope.

All across the land they rang.

In the Collegiate Church of St Mary, St George and St Denys they rang. In St Ann's in Acresfield they rang. In St John's in Byrom Street, St Mary's in Parsonage Street. In all the St Marys – Cheadle, Prestwich, Radcliffe and Eccles. St Matthew's in Wigan, St Mark's in Worsley. Holy Trinity in Birch by Rusholme, All Saints by May Street, Newton Heath. St James's on Stenner Lane in Didsbury, St Paul's in Little Hulton, Peel. St George's on Carrington Moss, St Thomas's at Friarmere, Delph. St Wilfrid's in Standish, St Werburgh's in Warburton, and Old St Chrysostom's in Chorlton-on-Medlock.

The whole of Manchester vibrated with the sound. Not the rounds and changes of custom. Not the Plain Bobs or Grand Sires. Not the doubles or triples, caters or cinques. But instead a random, unknowable Aeolian sighing.

Locked up in their cells, back in the asylum on the Daub Holes, the Bedlam Boys heard them too. They lifted their faces rapt in delight. They climbed up to the bars on their windows and stretched out their hands into the outer air as far as they could reach, almost as if they were trying to imbibe the sound through the pores of their skin deep into the fibres of their being, feeling the vibrations of the ringing seeping through the soles of their feet, the tips of their fingers, through every bone in their skulls, the frontal and temporal, parietal, occipital, the sphenoid and ethmoid, the lacrimal and zygomatic, until they felt the sound flow right through them.

A pulse, a rhythm.

One by one they began to dance. They heard words, tumbling from this celestial music of the spheres that only they, it seemed, heard, and slowly they started to sing.

"Welcome, all comers
Say the bells of St Thomas
To join in the dance
Say the bells of St Ann's
Pay me five guineas
Say the bells of St Denys

The world is contrary
Say the bells of St Mary
Tax, excise and customs
Say Old St Chrysostom's
Mill, loom and forge
Say the bells of St George

Your sons are begotten
From the loins of King Cotton
Scrawling their names
Say the bells of St James
On factory walls
Say the bells of St Paul's

Don't stray after dark
Say the bells of St Mark
Lest your pockets be pilfered
Say the bells of St Wilfred
Mayhem and murder
Cry the bells of St Werburgh

Gargoyles and statues
Snarl the bells of St Matthews
Will make you to faint
Chime the bells of All Saints

Now tis all done
Toll the bells of St John

Entertain strangers who knock at your door
For they may be angels though they be so poor…"

4

10th October

A LETTER TO THE INHABITANTS OF MANCHESTER FROM THE MOST REVEREND BEILBY PORTEOUS, BISHOP OF CHESTER ON OCCASION OF THE LATE EARTHQUAKE IN THOSE PLACES

My Dear Friends and Brethren,

The great dangers to which you have been so lately exposed, and which you have so providentially escaped, are of too important a nature for me, who stand to you in the near relation of diocesan, to pass over in total silence. Notwithstanding the recent date of that relation, I could not resist so powerful a call upon me to discharge my own duty and remind you of yours. The occasion, I hope, will justify me.

The first impressions which the Earthquake made upon you were most sufficient strong, but by this time, perhaps, they may, in some of you at least, be entirely erased, and you may be going on in the very same unremitted round of business or of pleasure, as if nothing in the world extraordinary had ever happened to you. If this be the case, it is but the more necessary that I should bring back this awakening incident to your thoughts again, and endeavour to imprint a due sense of it upon your minds.

When your first terrifying alarm was over, and gave place to more sober and cool reflection, to what did this naturally lead your thoughts? Did it not immediately direct them to the great Governor of the World? Were not your eyes and your hands – I may safely add your hearts too – almost involuntarily raised up to Him, as having just given a most awful display of His almighty power? Let the sceptic, if he pleases, call this superstition. A name, I hope, that cannot be applied to you, who read this now.

What the immediate causes of earthquakes are, I shall not here stay to enquire. Notwithstanding several plausible and ingenious theories concerning them, these disorders of our globe, like many diseases of our bodies, do still in large measure remain among the mysteries of nature, and that for a very obvious reason: because we can neither look into the bowels of the earth, nor yet of the human frame. But whatever these causes may be, they must still be referred to the First Great Author of All. Those laws of nature, as they are called, which He has Himself established, must be ever under His overruling influence and control. Could they be for one moment interrupted, or suspended, without His knowledge or permission, He would no longer be the Sovereign of the Universe, a possibility not to be countenanced, for even those things which appear to us the most contingent and fortuitous, and which we therefore call accidents, are all under the direction of His Supreme Intelligence. 'The lot is cast into the lap,' says Proverbs 16, 'but the whole disposing thereof is of the Lord.'

Nor is this all. Since He is not only the Preserver of the Material, but the Governor also of the Moral world, is it not highly reasonable to suppose that He may render the former subservient to the greater purposes of the latter; and since He evidently designed the regular course and order of nature for the support and comfort of man, must we not therefore seem authorised to conclude that He will apply its irregularities and disorders to His punishment, correction, and admonition of those among us who transgress His law? The sun, the moon, and all the other celestial bodies, have their stations appointed, and their motions regulated by Him.

The thunder is His voice, and the lightning He dispatches is His messenger to the ends of the earth. The sword, the pestilence and famine are instruments of His displeasure. Fire and hail, snow and vapours, wind and storm, all fulfil His word.

All these things He causes to come, whether for correction or for mercy. And when these judgements of His are in the Earth, we are expressly told that He expects the inhabitants of the World will learn righteousness.

Surely then such convulsions of the Globe as you have felt must be amongst the means He makes use of for the same important purposes? As Job tells us, 'He, without whose knowledge not a sparrow falls to the ground, will not suffer those pillars of the earth, which He himself bears up, to be shaken, and the inhabitants of it to be filled with terror and consternation, but for great and weighty reasons.'

Let me not, however, be understood to infer from hence that, because the Earthquake was principally felt in your towns and neighbourhood, you are therefore more wicked than the rest of your countrymen. Such a conclusion would be un-Christian. Luke tells us that even those 'upon whom the Great Tower of Siloam fell in Galilee' were not sinners above all others. But we are all of us, God knows, sinners great enough to stand in need of frequent corrections. It behoves you therefore very seriously to consider whether your present situation may, or may not, have particularly required such dreadful warnings as you have lately had.

By the flourishing state of your trade and manufactures,

you have for many years been advancing rapidly in wealth and population. Your towns are every day growing in size and splendour. Many of the higher ranks among you live in no small degree of opulence, some of their inferiors in ease and plenty. What the usual fruits of such affluence as this are is but too well known. Intemperance and licentiousness of manners; a wanton and foolish extravagance in dress, in equipage, in furniture, in entertainments; a passion for luxurious indulgences and frivolous amusements; a gay, thoughtless indifference about a future life, and every act connected with it; a neglect of divine worship, a profanation of the day peculiarly set apart for it, and perhaps, to crown all, a disbelief and contempt of the Gospel.

These are the vices and the follies which riches too often engender, and which, I am sorry to add, have with a fatal profusion been disseminated over this kingdom. What proportion of these may have fallen to your share, I have hitherto had no opportunity of knowing, and it would therefore be as unjust, as I am sure it would be painful, for me to become your accuser.

Let me rather, with the sincerity of a friend, and the tenderness of a guardian over you, entreat you to be your own judges in this important question. You have had a loud call to recollection.

'For with whatever judgement you judge,' Matthew tells us, 'so you too will be judged. With whatever measure you measure, thus will it be measured unto you.'

Examine your own hearts thoroughly. Look well, extremely well, if there be any way of wickedness in you, that if there be, you may turn from it into the way everlasting.

It is possible that, notwithstanding the unhappy state of our national morals, you may have escaped the general contagion. You may have been able to separate the advantages of wealth from its dangers and temptations, and to enjoy the one without being corrupted by the other. Should this appear to be the case, you have been highly favoured of Heaven indeed, and have reason to thank God most devoutly for so rare a felicity.

'But when thou hast eaten and art full,' as Deuteronomy asks us, 'and when thou hast built goodly houses and dwelt therein; and when thy herds and thy flocks multiply, and thy silver and thy gold is multiplied, and all that thou hast is multiplied, hast thou forgotten thy Saviour? Hast thou sayest instead in thine heart that it has been thy *power and the might of* thy *hand which hath gotten thee this wealth, rather than the Lord thy God's?*

How were your thoughts employed at that very moment when the ground shook beneath you, and the walls of your churches trembled around you?

If you have indeed preserved a due sense of piety in your own minds, have you endeavoured to transfuse it into those of your children, your servants, your manufacturers? Their souls, as well as their bodies, are to a great degree, in your hands. Have you been faithful to this trust, and consulted equally the welfare of both? Have you made them early acquainted with their Maker and their Redeemer, and explained to them the connection they have with another world? Is it on that world you have taught them to fix their hearts and affections, and have you been more anxious to instruct them in the means of securing an inheritance there, *rather than in the arts of amassing wealth, and acquiring distinction* here?

What is it that has been principal in your intentions, and the ruling passion of your souls? For what purpose have you, as Psalm 127 asks us so fervently, 'risen early and taken rest late, and eaten the bread of carefulness'?

Has it been solely to extend your trade, to accumulate fortunes, to multiply houses and villas, and to join field to field? Or have you carried your views still farther, and entertained ideas of a far more noble and exalted nature? And if God has blessed your honest labours with success, have you paid, with cheerfulness and liberality, that tribute of beneficence which He requires of your hands for the relief and comfort of your more necessitous brethren?

Had He permitted the shocks you felt to have continued a few minutes longer, you might have been involved in the same destruction which some years ago overwhelmed the unhappy city of Lisbon, and a greater part of its inhabitants. Compare your own deliverance with that dreadful catastrophe, and then forbear if you can, to bless God from the bottom of your souls, for chastising and admonishing you with so gentle a hand.

Deuteronomy tells us that 'as a man chasteneth his son, so has the Lord chastened you', not to consume, but only 'to humble and prove you, and to do you good at your latter end'.

'His anger endureth but a moment,' Psalm 30 reminds us, 'and in His favour is life', a sentiment echoed by Isaiah. 'In a little wrath I hid my face from thee for a moment, but with everlasting kindness will I have mercy on thee, saith the Lord'.

Let not this kindness, I beseech you, be lost upon you. Your first terrors and apprehensions will gradually die away, and the little temporary reformation which they might possibly have produced at the time, will vanish with them. But if the warmest sentiments of gratitude for your preservation do not remain deeply impressed upon your souls, and produce the most salutary effects on your hearts and lives, you will shew yourselves to be utterly unworthy of the mercies you have received, and can have no reason to expect a repetition of them on any future occasion. If this forbearance of God is despised, and this lenity abused, He may think it necessary to visit you with yet severer judgements.

Take then the best, the only, rational method to avert His future displeasure: 'by acting justly,' as Micah says, and 'keeping yourselves unspotted from the world'.

I do not say that no misfortune will then ever befall you. For even the most righteous of men must expect to taste sometimes the bitter cup of affliction. But you will have the very best security against the evils of life, and if they do overtake you, the best support under them that either this world or the next can give. You will be under the immediate inspection and care of that Almighty Being, who, in Isaiah's words again, 'has the whole creation at His command, who measures the waters in the hollow of His hand, and metes out the heavens with a span, and comprehends the dust of the earth in a measure, and weighs the mountains in scales, and the hills in a balance, and takes up the isles as a very little thing'.

To His gracious protection I earnestly recommend you, and remain

Your affectionate brother, and servant in Christ,
Beilby Porteus, CHESTER

This 10th Day of October in the Year of Our Lord, 1777

TWO

Flight

1785

in which a balloon takes to the skies –
a new cotton mill is opened –
a proposal of marriage is offered –
a naked cross-country race is run –
a young man joins the army –
fourteen families arrive from overseas –
a daring escape is made from a first storey window –
we learn more about the piece of cloth, a brief history of
its owners during the first years of its existence –
and a new settlement is built

5

1785

6th – 13th May

WONDER OF THE AGE

The celebrated aeronaut, Mr James Sadler, the first Englishman ever to fly, will, on this the 12th day of May, a Saturday, in the Year of our Lord 1785, undertake the first manned balloon ascent to take place here in Manchester from Haworth Gardens, situated between the Long Millgate and Shude Hill.

*

Sunday 6th

Eight years have passed.

Amos lives a life apart. An orphan, friendless, in the recently built House of Correction on New Bridge Street, which now serves as Manchester's Workhouse, for the Court Leet has still not passed the necessary laws to construct one.

Half a mile away, in the Manse adjoining the Unitarian Chapel on Cross Street, the Reverend Richard Gore, Joint Minister to his flock, wrestles with the problem presented by Amos and hundreds like him, nameless, faceless, locked away from sight, unregistered, unregulated, unknown. In his congregation each Sunday morning, the faces of many of the borough's wealthiest and most influential merchants stare up to him as he stands in his pulpit about to deliver his weekly sermon. They are men of action, who will not shirk from taking steps to fill the current moral and civic vacuum that sits in the heart of Manchester, thinks Gore, if I can but stir their consciences.

"In this great manufacturing town," he begins, "the preservation of parochial records has been almost wholly and woefully neglected. Information is scant and unreliable in all areas, but in matters appertaining to the Poor it is practically non-existent. Manchester is much divided into several parties respecting the administration of such concerns and strong charges have been made against many of the persons vested with the management of the Poor, not without just cause, for it would seem to be their sole intent to render them invisible. Yet the evidence of our senses tells us that this is not so. Every day our eyes are stricken with the sight of those less fortunate than ourselves living destitute on our doorsteps, while our ears are assailed by their most piteous cries for help. Sir Edward Knatchbull's Act, passed more than sixty years ago, stated that..."

Here he pauses to place a pair of half moon spectacles upon the bridge of his nose and read from a paper he fetches from his pocket.

" '... *the Church Wardens and Overseers of the Poor of any Parish, with the Consent of the Major Part of the Parishioners, in Vestry or other Public Meeting for that purpose assembled, upon usual notice given, may purchase or hire any House or Houses in the Parish, and Contract with Persons for the Lodging, Keeping and Employing of Poor Persons; and there they are to keep them, and take from them the Benefit of their Work and Labour, for the Better Maintenance and Relief of such persons'.*"

He pauses once again and looks out over his flock to see what, if any, effect his words are having upon them. They appear held, their faces rapt in concentration. They are not, outwardly at any rate, wishing themselves elsewhere, their thoughts turning to the matters of business they may wish to discuss once they are released back into the outside air. He removes his spectacles and delivers the final extract from Knatchbull's Act from memory, holding their collective gaze.

" '*And in case any Poor Person shall refuse to be thus Lodged, Kept and Maintained in such Houses, such Person shall be put out of the Parish Books and be not entitled to any Relief. No Poor Persons, or their Apprentices, Children or likewise other Family Members shall receive a Settlement in the Parish, Town, or Place to which they shall be removed by Virtue of this Act*'. Yet every day more and more people arrive at our gates, seeking to make a better life for themselves in our mills and factories. Some of these succeed, but many, as we know, do not, but the workhouses cannot accommodate them, for they are victims of this punitive Act, which *de facto* prohibits the free movement of people. As far as I am able to ascertain, for as I have said, the keeping of records concerning the Poor is so scandalously incomplete, there are at present approximately three hundred and twenty persons resident in the House of Correction on New Bridge Street, principally old women and young children. They are chiefly employed in the winding of yarn. Particulars of their current welfare and diet I have not been able to obtain, for a malignant fever currently rages within the premises, rendering it unsafe to enter. Out of sight, but not, I hope, out of mind. We may close our eyes and ears to what we find uncomfortable, but God will open them. He forces us to look, He urges us to listen. For did He not tell us that the last shall be first…?"

Afterwards, outside, standing on the Chapel steps in the warm spring air, a world away from the choleric damp reigning in the New Bridge Street House of Correction, the Reverend Gore's flock disperses into smaller knots of conversation, a few still musing on his sermon's call to arms, but more already turning their thoughts to Sunday lunch and the prospect of a walk in the afternoon, on Angel Meadow, or St Peter's Field, while others are eagerly anticipating the Balloon Ascent due to take place from Haworth Gardens in just a few days' time, about which ballad singers are now regaling the people parading up and down the streets and squares of the town as church services everywhere are ending.

"It will mount up on high, almost touching the sky
You may peep if you please in the moon
All mathematicians and deep politicians
Admire Mr Sadler's Balloon…"

Several hawkers are doing a brisk trade in selling toy balloons for the children. One of these children, an eight-year-old boy in white knee-breeches and a blue silk waistcoat, is clamouring to have one. The servant girl, whose hand he is holding in the press of crowds at the corner of Cross Street and King Street, appears harassed and looks around. "You'll have to ask your father," she says.

"But he'll say no," says the boy, pouting sulkily.

"I can't help that," says the servant girl.

"Yes you can. You can buy one for me, then my father will have to agree."

"That's not how it works, Matthew, you know that."

"I hate you," he cries.

"No you don't, Mattie."

"Yes I do. I'll tell Mother. I'll say you were mean and unkind."

Fanny wavers fractionally, but it is just long enough for the boy to observe and seize upon.

"Please," he wheedles.

"No," she says, gathering her resolve once more. "You can ask your father like I said. Look – he's finished talking with the other gentlemen and he's just on his way."

"I hate you," he shouts, even louder this time, and kicks Fanny hard on the shin. She yelps in pain and momentarily lets go of Mattie's hand. Taking advantage of being thus unexpectedly released, he bolts from her like a ferret diving down a rabbit hole as he plunges into the thickening crowd. In less than a second she has lost him.

"Matthew!" she cries. "Matthew, come back!"

The boy ignores her. He charges off as fast as he can, making a bee-line for one of the balloon sellers, weaving his way in and out and between the throngs of taller people, until finally he reaches him.

"Hello, young Master," says the hawker. "Want to buy a balloon?"

Matthew nods.

"That'll be a penny then."

Matthew looks around, then back to the man.

"What's the matter? Cat got tha' tongue?"

Matthew points to the one he likes best. The hawker holds it towards him.

"Penny first," he says.

Now that he can see it close up, Matthew finds that he no longer wants it. It's a pig bladder. Something about its bloated shape disgusts him. The way its veins appear to pulsate as the hawker waves it in front of his face makes him want to be sick. But now that he has come so far, he will not back down. He can't lose face. Fanny and his parents think he's still a baby, but he'll show them. With a sudden lunge he snatches the balloon from the hawker and runs off back into the crowd, the cries of "Stop! Thief!" quickly becoming swallowed up by all the other street sounds.

He runs till he has no breath left. He looks around him. He does not recognise where he is. He's lost. He wants to cry out, so that Fanny might hear him and find him. But he won't do that. Not now. Not ever. He sits on a low stone wall and stares at the bloated pig's bladder dancing on the stick. He dares himself to touch it. It feels slippery and alive. He brings it closer towards him. He looks deeper into it. He can just make out, reflected back, the twisted, grotesque outlines of his own face.

Just then he hears Fanny calling his name. Then his mother and his father. He's in a square, where part of the Pentecost Fair is being set up. Traders are putting up stalls. Cows and sheep are being led into the middle and rounded up into pens. Pigs are rooting among rotten fruit and vegetables that have been tipped from carts. One of them comes very close to Matthew, sniffing the bladder on the stick. He gets up and runs towards a church in the opposite corner of the square. Up above he sees a benchmark, a set of deep, scored lines carved with a chisel, etched into the stone over the tower door, through which a man now walks, climbs a ladder and places an angle-iron into the benchmark to form a levelling rod from which he appears to be calculating something. The man notices Matthew and nods.

"Are you lost, young Master?" he says.

"No," says Matthew too quickly. "I was just wondering what you were doing."

The man regards him with a dry smile.

"Surveying," he says, then adds, when he sees the puzzled look on the boy's face, "measuring."

"What?"

"Height."

"What of?"

"Something which hasn't been built yet?"

"But will be?"

The man nods. "Ay."

"Where?"

"Over there," he says, squinting through an eyepiece he is holding, and points.

"Then why aren't you measuring it there?"

"Because this," he says, tapping the carved mark in the stone, "is a known height. It never changes. But things that haven't been built yet might change."

"What do you mean?"

"They might be higher, they might be lower."

"I don't understand."

"It all depends."

"On what?"

"Whether they run out of money."

"I ran out of money," says Matthew, looking once more at the pig's bladder.

"Did you now?" says the man, climbing down the ladder now to join him. "And why's that?"

"Because I'm too small."

"But you'll grow."

"Yes. I will."

"Which is why I can't use you as a benchmark," he jokes, resting the angle iron on the top of Matthew's head.

"What's a benchmark?"

"Something you can rely on."

"Can I rely on you?"

"You ask a lot of questions."

"How else do you learn? That's what my father says."

"Does he now? And where might he be?"

Matthew looks away.

"Does he know where you are?"

"Can you keep a secret?"

"That depends on what it is. Why don't you tell me what it is, then I'll let you know whether I can keep it or not."

Matthew puzzles over this. Although it seems reasonable, he's not sure he likes the sound of it. But before he can think how to answer, he sees Fanny, his mother and his father, each entering the square from three different corners. Apologising to the man with the benchmark he makes a quick dash towards a narrow entry he can see opposite him – the Ackers Gate – into which he dives headlong.

Whelp, who has been watching all of this from the moment Matthew first stepped out of the Chapel with his parents, and who has been eyeing him from a distance ever since, immediately follows after him. Once inside Matthew is trapped. An overturned cart blocks his progress, shutting out much of the light from the far end of the alley. Figures step out from the darker recesses of its damp walls. Hands thrust towards him, fingering his shiny blue waistcoat. Faces loom from the shadows, red-eyed, with sour breath. A foot stretches out and trips him. The pig's bladder escapes his grasp as he hits the ground, the breath knocked out of him. But before bony fingers can strip him bare, he feels himself grabbed from behind. A hand grips his arm and drags him back into the square, Acresfield. Whelp has rescued him. Emerging from the shadows of the Ackers Gate, she thrusts him straight into the arms of Fanny, who was just on the point of entering herself.

Immediately, she holds him to her closely, scolding and kissing him in equal measure. Andrew and Catherine Oldham arrive moments later. Matthew is passed with joy and relief between them.

"We thought we'd lost you," says one.

"What on earth possessed you?" says a second.

"The Lord be praised," says the third.

Whelp, invisible once more, which is how she likes it, slinks back against the wall. She holds out the balloon on its stick, the pig's bladder, straining to reach it to Matthew, but the gap is just too far. At the last second she lets it go. Matthew watches it fly slowly past him and up into the sky. Hoisted high upon his father's shoulders he makes a last grab for it, but in his haste he fumbles and drops it. The stick punctures the swollen bladder which bursts, showering him with shreds of pig skin.

"Let that be a lesson to you," whispers Fanny to Matthew, quietly in his ear, so that his parents don't hear.

A dry-eyed Matthew says nothing.

The man with the benchmark is back up his ladder, peering through his eyepiece. He appears to be surveying them all, but his gaze lingers on the young woman handing the boy back to who he presumes must be his parents. Briefly she appears to be looking directly at him, so that he has to remove the eyepiece so as not to seem as though he is spying on her, which he would have to admit to her he was if challenged. He raises his right hand in a tentative wave, but she has already turned away. She must not have been aware of him after all. He lifts the eyepiece once more and watches her as she leaves the square. He wonders if, in this city of strangers, he will ever see her again.

Back at Cross Street, as the last of the congregation leaves, Minister Gore is about to retreat back into the cool shade of the Chapel when his attention is caught by Dr Perceval raising his cane.

"A word, Reverend, if I may?"

"Of course."

"I was much taken by your words this morning."

"I'm glad someone was."

"Oh, I think most people were – in their way, you know?"

"Thank you. But fine words, Perceval…"

"… butter no parsnips."

"Quite."

"It's action we need."

"I agree, but what kind of action?"

"There's the rub."

"Precisely."

"Perhaps," ventures Perceval, "it might be a topic for discussion at next month's *Lit & Phil*?"

"I fear our members may regard the problem as one that falls not within their orbit."

"Too worldly?"

"Too real."

"But its philosophical significance is beyond question."

"How we are to deal with our fellow man."

"Specifically those less fortunate than ourselves."

"A moral imperative, but I fear it would merely lead to yet more fine words, and none of the actions you so rightly crave."

"The problem is as much a political one."

"Explain."

"While Manchester retains its current inadequate status…"

"Not even a municipal borough…"

"Still within the Hundred of Salford…"

"Whom she has long outstripped…"

"Merely a collection of small parishes…"

"While daily the number of people grows…"

"Surpassing much smaller settlements…"

"Which nevertheless are classed as cities…"

"With all that such recognition bestows…"

"A legislature…"

"Judicial system…"

"Devolved authority…"

"In short, representation…"

"Representation, yes…"

"While rotten boroughs up and down the land…"

"With less than a tenth of our population…"

"Have not just one…"

"But two…

"Members of Parliament…"

"While we have none..."

"Scandalous..."

"Careful, Doctor," says Gore, lowering his voice and ushering the two of them further inside the Chapel, "such talk could be regarded as seditious."

"I care not," says Perceval, wheeling around as if to face any who may dare to challenge him."

"Walls have ears, they say," remarks Gore, smiling at his passionate friend. "Here at least," he adds, shutting the door behind them, "we may have sanctuary."

"Which is more than is being currently offered to those poor unfortunates you described in your sermon this morning, Reverend."

"Indeed."

"As I said, while Manchester retains its current inadequate status – that is to say, no status at all – such actions that we may carry out can have little effectiveness, for they will be but the actions of a few."

"True, Thomas. But the man who moves a mountain begins by carrying away small stones."

"No doubt, but today we have machines, driven by the power of steam, which can move mountains in a matter of hours, and replace them with canals, by which many thousands more flock towards us here to be a part of this great enterprise. Are we meant merely to exploit them and then cast them aside when they are no longer of any use to us?"

"When Queen Elizabeth visited Cambridge in 1564, ostensibly to encourage greater conformity among the many different Protestant scholars there, but actually to honour those celebrated bishops Cambridge had educated which Oxford later had burned, she urged caution. Caution and patience."

"She was a monarch. Power was already hers."

"She spoke to them in Latin..."

"... as some of our more dyed-in-the-wool members would have us do at the *Lit & Phil*, flying in the face of the needs of the common man."

"*Romam uno die non fuisse conditam.*"

"Rome wasn't built in a day."

"A most fitting comparison – wouldn't you agree?"

"Manchester has a Roman name."

"Mamucium."

"But built on two, rather than seven, hills."

"Point taken."

"And the Irwell is hardly the Tiber."

"No."

"But Queen Elizabeth…?"

"Yes. She then went on to say…"

"In English please."

"Very well, in English. '… that this common saying has given me a certain amount of comfort. A saying which cannot take away, but can at least lessen, the grief that I feel'."

Perceval pauses, reflecting on these words from more than two centuries before, thinking how this city he loves – and yes, a city it is, even if it is not yet recognised as such – was first built as an outpost of Rome, on a site of two hills and at the confluence of three rivers, and which now stood poised to become a city just as great, with its trade reaching out to all corners of the world, yet was doing so by trampling underfoot another wretched underclass whose lives were no better than the slaves who had reputedly built Rome.

"We can't wait," he says. "We mustn't. You're right, Richard. We may only be few in number but our actions can matter. Those small stones we carry, we might cast into the rivers and see what ripples they may spread."

Gore nods. "No more talk of sedition then?"

Perceval smiles. "Sedition, no. But reform, most definitely."

They shake hands.

Perceval turns to go, but on reaching the door, he pauses, then walks back towards his friend.

"First, let us do away with the badging. It is iniquitous. It does not behove a civilised society to act in such a manner, to force those who refuse the shame of entering a Workhouse and are thus evicted from their Parish to wear the letter 'P' upon their persons, like a branded animal."

"I agree, Thomas, though I think you'll find most who are badged tear it from themselves before they enter a new Parish."

"As would we all. Next, let us address the law on Bastardy. Currently, as the law stands, a woman pregnant with an illegitimate child is required to declare the fact and name the father."

"The father should face up to his responsibility, Thomas."

"Of course he must, and if, once so named, he fails to do so, he can face the prospect of imprisonment. I have no quarrel with that."

"What then?"

"When the father is *not* named – and there could be a thousand different reasons for that – the law turns its wrath upon the woman, whom it should succour not punish. A bastard born to a woman convicted of vagrancy – and many women in such circumstances have little alternative but to become vagrants – is to have the settlement of its mother, regardless of where the child is actually born, and the woman is to be publicly whipped."

"Preposterous, I agree, Thomas, but it is the law."

"A bad law, and one which should not be enforced."

"Now you are preaching sedition again."

"Here in Manchester we have an opportunity, Richard."

"An opportunity?"

"While our status remains…"

"… inadequate?"

"Uncertain…"

"Very well…"

"... we can use that uncertainty to our advantage."

"How?"

"We Non-Conformists, Dissenters, call us what you will, outnumber the Anglican Establishment by two to one."

"We do."

"Let us therefore infiltrate that establishment by appointing ourselves to the Borough Reeve, the Board of Magistrates, the Court Leet, the High Sheriff's Office."

"They are all Royal or Church appointments. It's not as if they are put to a public vote."

"But those who make the appointments, are they not open to a little persuasion?"

"I will not listen to talk of bribery, Thomas, or worse. If we are to work to change the law, we cannot put ourselves above or beyond its reach."

"Then what do you suggest?"

"We must simply work to exert our influence in those spheres in which we already legitimately operate – in our Chapels, our Sunday Schools, our factories, our mills, our newspapers, our hospitals and, yes, our Workhouses. Get ourselves on their Boards of Trustees and Guardians. Far better to try and reform from within, than to tear ourselves apart."

"Or pull up our drawbridges and live in our ivory towers."

"However tempting."

"No. Better to swim in the stream, even if it's against the current, than to stand on the bank and do nothing."

Standing on the bank at that very moment, or rather overlooking it through the barred windows of the House of Correction, which continued to serve as the Manchester Workhouse, eight-year-old Amos watches the steady flow of boats plying up and down the Irwell either side of the Ducie Bridge.

There are always boats on the river. On Sunday afternoons, like today, they are mostly row boats, taken by wealthy families for pleasure, pulling in at Angel Meadow for picnics, or, for those who are a little more adventurous, for longer trips to the Pomona Botanical Gardens at Trafford Park, where wild animals are kept in cages for the public to marvel at. Lions and tigers, elephants and apes.

Amos has never seen such sights. But he has heard tales from those who claim they have. One day, he thinks, perhaps he too might see them. He *has* seen bears, muzzled and chained, being walked across the Bridge by their handlers, swaying their mighty heads from side to side, their fur mangy and fly-blown.

There is always traffic crossing the Bridge, ceaselessly, from morning till night, carts laden with fruit and vegetables coming in from the farms and orchards on the edge of the town, returning empty later, cattle and sheep being led to the slaughterhouses in Smithfield, live chickens crammed in wicker baskets, geese with iron collars around their long necks waiting to be wrung, smaller birds squawking in cages, the smell of fish being gutted on the roadside, the boats and barges, bringing in goods from Liverpool, and always, always, people, new arrivals, seeking their fortune.

All of them arriving from somewhere else, thinks Amos. He has no idea of where these other places might be, only that he longs to travel to one of them, any, it does not matter which, just so long as the boat he imagines himself jumping aboard, unseen, then hiding himself away beneath whatever cargo they are transporting, grain perhaps or cotton, is taking him as far away as possible from the House of Correction.

He looks away from the window. Facing him on the far wall is a large notice. He cannot read what it says, but he knows every syllable of it by heart, for every day, before their breakfast of thin, watery gruel, the Matron reads it out, commanding all of those who live within the House's walls to recite it after her.

THE POOR IN THE HOUSE
are required
TO OBSERVE THE FOLLOWING RULES

I. *That they obey the Governor and the Matron in all their reasonable commands.*

II. *That they demean themselves orderly and peaceably, with decency and cleanliness.*

III. *That they never drink to excess.*

IV. *That they be diligent at their work.*

V. *That they work from six o'clock in the morning until six o'clock at night in the summer; and from seven o'clock in the morning until such hours in the evening as the Governor shall appoint in the winter; except Saturday afternoons from four o'clock; and on Good Friday, Christmas Day, and the two days following, and Monday and Tuesday in the Easter and Whitsun weeks, which are to be regarded as Holidays.*

VI. *That they do not pretend sickness, or other excuses to avoid their work.*

VII. *That they do no wilful damage, but that they execute their work to the best of their abilities. Such rewards and gratuities shall be distributed to the industrious and skilful in proportion to the quantity and perfection of their work, as to the Church Wardens and Overseers shall seem reasonable.*

VIII. *That they regularly attend divine service on Sundays, and prayers before breakfast and supper every day.*

IX. *That they go to breakfast, and to supper, in the Dining Hall, when summoned by the ringing of the bell.*

X. *That they be allowed half an hour each at breakfast and an hour at supper.*

XI. *That no strong or spirituous liquors be allowed in the House, except by order of the Physician or Apothecary.*

XII. *That they do not curse, or swear, or lie.*

XIII. *That they do not steal, sell their provisions, or sell or pawn their clothing, nor be guilty of any other breach of trust.*

XIV. *That they never go out during working hours, nor at any other time, without leave.*

XV. *That when permitted to go out, they do not stay longer than the hour appointed.*

Amos has never yet been permitted to 'go out'. Despite being only eight years old, it is not because he is deemed too young. It is more as a result of hardly *any* of the inmates being allowed to leave the premises, on account of the near constant state of fever which pervades them. Amos's head has been shaved for lice. He is daily dosed with tar water. An ointment of mercury is roughly rubbed onto the skin of his arms and legs by the Matron or, more commonly, one of her assistants. None of the children in the House have died from the typhus yet, though many of the older men and women have. Amos knows this, for he has seen their bodies being carried out of the exercise yard at night, then slopped into the Irwell.

At supper, while he is queuing up for the Apothecary to administer him his tar water, he overhears him talking to the Matron about the Balloon Flight scheduled for the following Saturday. The whole of Manchester, it seems, is agog with excitement. The people talk of nothing else. Thousands are expected to attend, with visitors travelling in from the outlying smaller towns and villages. The Matron, pinching the nose of the boy in front of Amos, then tipping back his head before pouring a spoonful of the foul tasting substance past his not tightly enough clamped lips, complains that such an act is not natural.

"What is this aeronaut trying to do?" she asks. "Strike the face of God?"

"Does not Luke tell us to '*strive to enter in at the narrow gate, for many will seek to enter, and few shall be able*'?"

"But does not Luke also tell us," responds the Matron, stirring the pine tar vigorously into the pan of slimy water in front of her, "that '*whosoever exalteth himself shall be abased, while he that humbleth himself shall be exalted*'?"

"I hear," replies the Apothecary with a scarcely suppressed, mirthless smile, "that he does indeed come from humble origins. A pastry cook. And yet he is the first Englishman ever to soar into the heavens. And now he is coming to Manchester. Another sure sign that our fame continues to spread abroad."

The Matron says nothing.

"Well," concludes the Apothecary, staring down at Amos, who is standing there, mouth obediently open for the tar water to be spooned into it, his shaved head like a featherless sparrow not yet ready to leave the nest, "what are you waiting for? Back to your place."

Amos scurries back to join the others, thankful that in their wrangling they have omitted to pour any of the noxious mixture down his throat. Maybe that, too, is a sign that things are looking up. Maybe he may yet contrive a way to go and watch the balloonist himself.

*

Monday 7th

But such an opportunity seems as remote as ever the following morning as he is set to treading the felt in the enclosed courtyard at the back of the House of Correction.

Amos, along with a dozen other young boys, is lifted into one of six large vats, which occupy most of the yard, two boys per vat. Each vat is filled with water fetched straight from the Irwell just beyond the outer walls. A thick scum of sludge floats on the surface. This is then mixed with human urine. All the chamber pots from the House are emptied into the river water, and each of the boys is then encouraged to piss into the vat they are now standing in, before bundles of sheep wool, mixed with dog, rat and human hair, including the inmates' own hair, which, as Amos knows only too well, is regularly shaved to protect them from lice and other vermin, are tipped in by the cart-load to bulk up the sheep wool. The fibres of these hairs are covered in thousands of tiny scales. The scales are split by the action of the boys treading through the fibres and the resulting agitation of the liquid passing through them. This agitation causes the fibres to latch onto each other and is the first stage in the process of making felt.

When the boys have been treading the contents of each vat for an hour, the fibres are sufficiently bonded to be hauled out, hung over ropes to dry, while they wait to be collected by one of the town's many fullers, who will cleanse the oils, dirt and other impurities from this rough cast felt, roll it and smooth it, before sending it to the larger manufacturers, who will refine it further to produce all manner of items – padding for parts of machinery to prevent wear and tear, the hammers which strike piano keys, the lining of muzzles in breech-loading firearms, and for articles of clothing, especially hats.

One such manufacturer is Andrew Oldham, who arrives at the House at around eleven o'clock, by which time an exhausted Amos has already been treading the felt for more than three hours. Mr Oldham wears a particularly fine example of a top hat made in his own factory on Dale Street. It is made principally from imported beaver skin, transported to Manchester via the Mersey, Irwell and now bustling Bridgewater Canal, the loaded barges arriving at the Castlefield Basin at the southern end of the Dean's Gate, from where it is conveyed to Mr Oldham's warehouse by wagon. Once there, it is added to the bonded fibres which have been purified by the fuller and subjected to a diluted solution of mercury compound. These are then dried in a hot oven, causing the beaver hair to turn orange, a process known as 'carroting', which gives the hat its distinctive colouring. The pelts are stretched over a bar in a cutting machine, which slices away the skin in thin shreds, so that the remaining fleece will separate in its entirety. This fur is then shaped into a cone over a large colander, treated with hot water to consolidate it, then peeled off and passed through wet rollers to cause the fur to felt. This is then dyed and blocked to make the finished hats. The toxic vapours from the mercury compounds used in the latter stages of the process are themselves foul-smelling, but as nothing compared to the stench created by the House of Correction boys treading the untreated animal and human hairs in river effluent and urine. So overpowering is the smell that Mr Oldham is forced to place a handkerchief over his mouth to avoid breathing in too much of it, while Matthew, who has accompanied his father on this particular morning, finds that his eyes are streaming within seconds of their arrival.

"Pfooh, Father, what is it?"

"Now then, Matthew, let us have no fuss from you. The smell may be unpleasant but it derives from natural waste, and it would be neglectful of us not to make use of that which we discard. What is it my grandmother used to say?"

"Waste not, want not, Father."

"Or more precisely, 'wilful waste leads to woeful want'."

"Yes, Father."

"Good boy." He looks down on his son's narrow frame, trying not to shrink further in the face of the admittedly malodorous air, and takes pity on him. "If you would prefer, you may step outside and watch the boats."

"Yes please, Father," says Matthew his expression brightening.

"Off you go then."

"Thank you, Father."

"Take care not to stray too close to the water's edge."

"No, Father."

"Meet me on the New Bailey Bridge in half an hour."

"Yes, Father."

As Matthew runs towards the gate which leads into the outer courtyard and thence to the street, his direction takes him within a few feet of Amos, still treading bare foot knee-deep in one of the vats, but he does not see him, is not even aware of him, just one more piece of human filth he cannot wait to leave behind.

But Amos notices Matthew. There are no mirrors in the House of Correction. The only reflections Amos has ever seen of himself are here, sloshing in his own urine where now he walks. The glimpse he catches of Matthew, as he hurries past in his desperation to leave, is barely a second, but is enough for him to see at once a likeness. He sees a boy roughly the same size and age as himself, but a world away in the life he leads. He pauses momentarily from his treading to watch Matthew disappear, a black dot against the outside sun that dances like a spinning silver coin towards which Matthew runs, hands outstretched. Amos shields his eyes from this sudden hot intrusion of light, sharp as a dagger against his skin, until Matthew has disappeared and the outer gate is slammed shut. He tries to imagine the world that waits there on the other side and is rewarded for his efforts with a sharp cuff to the side of the head and a warning that "there'll be more where that came from" if he continues to idle. His thin shoulders stoop as he starts once more to tread the felt.

Andrew Oldham winces with the blow he witnesses being administered to the waif-like boy whose face is hidden from him by the dark shadows of the low beams, over which are hung the drying bonded fibres, which are now being loaded up in stacks upon the back of the cart that will carry them to his factory on Dale Street. He makes a mental note to enquire as to the whereabouts of an alternative source of his raw materials, one which does not rely on such medieval methods as those still employed here in the House of Correction.

"A word if I may, Mr Overseer?"

"Yes, sir?"

"Are the children taught their letters here?"

"We try, sir, but they show no appetite for learning, sir."

"Indeed?"

"No, sir. And you know what they say, sir?"

"No, Mr Overseer, what *do* they say?"

"A little learning is a dangerous thing."

"Is it now?"

"Oh yes, sir."

"And why is that?"

"It gives them hope, sir, hope that they might rise above the station God has seen fit to place them in, sir."

"You're saying then that everyone should know their place and be thankful for it?"

"Indeed I am, sir. To talk otherwise is treason."

"In which case, I must be a very treasonous fellow, for my father was a fuller, and his father before him a poor farm labourer."

"You misunderstand me, sir. I'm not implying anything against you, sir. You've done well for yourself by dint of your own hard work, sir."

"Yes. I've worked hard, but that alone would not have been enough."

"Sir?"

"There's something else that has been even more important."

The Overseer looks blank.

"Education. Learning to read helped me to see other possibilities. I don't hold with your fixed view of the world, Overseer, with everyone fixed in their place. We're all equal in the eyes of God, and so we all of us have within us the potential to make something of ourselves, to climb out of these barrels of piss these boys must daily wade through."

"If you say so, sir."

"I do say so, but to do this we need a little help sometimes."

"And that's what we provide, sir, for those who are unfortunate enough to have to come to us for succour." He spreads his arm expansively around the stinking courtyard.

"And does that succour you provide extend to teaching these children to read?"

"As I say, sir, they don't show the appetite for it, but even if they did, we wouldn't have the time. There are only twenty four hours in a day, sir, and gentlemen like yourself, sir, would be disappointed if they came here and found their raw materials were not ready for them, sir, because these wretches had been idling away the time learning to read instead of working as God intended them to."

The Overseer, not normally so voluble, sits down on a bench beneath one of the racks of drying fibres, exhausted.

"Well," replies Andrew Oldham, "this is one customer who shall not be returning to do business with this establishment any longer."

"I'm sorry to hear that, sir," says the Overseer, hastening wheezily to his feet once more."

"And what's more, I shall be encouraging my fellow manufacturers to follow my lead. In addition, I shall be writing to your Board of Governors to explain my reasons for doing so. Good day to you."

The Overseer watches him leave and shakes his head. Change is coming, there can be no doubting it. Manchester used to be such a quiet place, he thinks. He can remember when willow trees still grew along Withy Grove, by the banks of the Irk, but they have all gone now, as have the rooks that used to roost in their branches. Now they screech and croak their complaints along the rooftops of all the buildings that are constantly springing up where the old trees used to stand. He turns back to see all the boys, standing in their stagnant vats looking at him. He clips the ears of several of those he passes as he makes his way from the courtyard. Amos is the last of these boys, and so he hits Amos twice. Amos hardly feels either blow. The words of the fine gentleman, the father of the boy who bore a striking resemblance to himself, have stayed with him. He must find a way to learn his letters. The Overseer staggers towards the kitchen, where he hopes the Cook will have some hot coffee on the stove, to which he might add a thimbleful or two of gin from the flask he keeps in a cupboard there for emergencies such as these.

Amos watches him go. His ears are ringing, not just with the force of the beating they have just received, but from the words spoken by the rich gentleman and his finely dressed son, the boy he thinks he might have been, had circumstances been different. Learn to read, the gentleman had said. Amos cannot read. The letters swirl in front of him, no more comprehensible than the reflections that ripple before his eyes in the mixture of piss and sludge he wades through now. They keep changing, dancing before his eyes, tormenting him with the secrets they hold.

In the yard some of the older boys are helping the carter to stack the dried fibres onto the back of the wagon, which, Amos knows, will be parked just outside the House's gates. He pictures the horse patiently waiting, grazing absently on a patch of nettle. He imagines this from other horses he has occasionally glimpsed through the barred windows of the cold, high-ceilinged dormitory where he sleeps with forty other boys, some of whom are carrying the bales of rolled felt now. They hoist them onto their shoulders. Flakes of fibre, motes of dried hair, shower into the air, tiny acrobats caught in the hard-edged chink of light that falls through the crack of the not-quite-shut outer gate. The edge of this light strikes the far wall, where the House Rules are hung, these rules which Amos cannot read, but which he knows by heart through hearing them recited every day. It illuminates the last two of these rules:

"*That they never go out during working hours, nor at any other time, without leave.*"

Amos has never been outside, with or without such leave.

"*That when permitted to go out, they do not stay longer than the hour appointed.*"

If he were ever to find himself on the other side of the gate, he would want, he is certain, to stay for much longer than the hour appointed.

He looks again at the way the shaft of sunlight strikes the words. For one infinitesimal moment he believes he can detect a pattern in the dancing hieroglyphs, a hint of meaning in the chaos, but then a speck of fibre falls in his eye. He blinks and the letters all swim formlessly before him again. He looks back at the shard of light, traces its flight from the notice back to the gate, which still stands tantalisingly half open. One of the boys carrying the stacks of dried felt stumbles and trips. Another of them puts down his own burden and goes to the aid of the one who has fallen.

Amos sees, in the confusion of the moment, the chance he has been waiting for and makes a sudden, instinctive dash for the chink of light. Keeping low to the ground he scatters a coil of rats foraging among the fibres. He dives between the legs of one of the Overseer's assistants, evades the flailing fist of another and squeezes through the gate just before a third can swing it shut. Outside the full glare of the sun blinds him. Fixing his eyes on the ground immediately in front of him he runs past the carter's horse, who is indeed comfortably grazing, startling him so that he kicks out one of his back legs, which catches Amos a glancing blow that sends him skidding into Walker's Croft, a narrow lane at the back of the House of Correction, close to the Irk, which he crosses via the crowded Scotland Bridge, into Red Bank, where he is knocked to the ground by a surge of people making their way back towards the river to reach the markets of Shude Hill. He doubles back, is carried with the flow till he reaches Miller Street, where a great number of wagons are unloading raw cotton at Arkwright's Mill. Amos is forced to stop running by the sheer press of people, jostling like bees in a crowded hive. They all, it seems, know their business, have their allotted task, are aware of which direction they should take, all, that is, except Amos, who freezes. He has never been beyond the House's walls before and now that they are no longer in his sight he is overwhelmed. He is also completely lost. He has no idea which direction he should take. He hesitates – fatefully – and in that moment he is shoved into the path of oncoming traffic. The instinct to survive takes immediate hold. He swerves just in time from the hooves of heavy horses. He rolls underneath a passing cart, making himself as small as he possibly can, narrowly avoiding the wheels as they trundle either side of him. He views this brave new world through their revolving spokes, watching the army of feet marching past. When the cart has gone, he picks himself up and tries to weave his way through the throng of people to the other side of the street. It is like threading a needle. He needs several attempts before he can manage it. He manoeuvres his way, without knowing how, down the Long Mealgate, along Toad Lane, across Fennel Street, towards the Apple Market, ranged along the Irwell, the river he has dreamed of in the bleak nights inside the House of Correction, and he sees the sail boats, skiffs and barges he has so many times imagined himself stowing himself away upon in order to make his escape, tying up alongside.

But these vessels are all coming *in* to Manchester, not going out. He must wait till nightfall if he is to try and effect his plan. He looks up. The sun is directly overhead. There are many hours to kill between now and then. For the first time since he darted through that chink of light in the House's courtyard, he allows himself to stop. He looks around. Nobody, he realises, is taking any notice of him. They are all too busy getting on with whatever it is they are doing, carrying sacks and depositing them into large wicker baskets which are then hauled on ropes to the top of tall warehouses, pushing handcarts through the rutted mud of lanes and alleys threaded between these warehouses to the shopkeepers around the Market Cross, behind the Collegiate Church of St Mary, St George and St Denys, and down towards Penniless Hill, where the merchants are pouring out of the Cotton Exchange after a morning's brisk trading, the rumble of machines from the riverside mills and factories constantly vibrating the ground and air. Amos notices a pile of straw heaped against the low wall by the narrow Ring O' Bells passageway leading down to the Actors' Bridge. He sees potato and vegetable peelings being tipped indiscriminately into the straw, along with discarded apple cores. Pigs are noisily rooting through them, their hides caked with dried mud, their snouts unerringly burrowing through the detritus. Amos, furtively looking over each shoulder, slowly backs his way towards them, squats down low among the heaped straw and rubbish and joins the pigs with a tentative forage of his own.

Looking down on this scene from the nearby New Bailey Bridge, Matthew waits patiently for his father to join him. Unlike Amos he feels quite at home among the market day crowds. He is quite familiar with the busy traffic of goods and people, could find his way back home along Lever's Row to Newton Lane quite easily if he had to. Or Oldham Street, as he must now learn to call it, for it has recently been widened and renamed.

"After your father," his mother proudly informs him.

"No, no, no," retorts Andrew. "Don't listen to her."

"Then why else would they change it?"

"You know very well, my dear. Because it takes you in the direction of Oldham."

"That may be so, but that's not the reason they renamed it, as you know full well."

"I've done nothing to deserve such an honour," he says, sitting down to supper.

Catherine shakes her head, smiling fondly at her husband as Fanny brings in their soup and bread.

"Remember, Matthew," says his father, putting his hands together in readiness for grace, "humility in all things."

"Yes, Father."

"O Lord, we thank Thee for the food we are about to eat and remain Thy ever humble servants. Amen."

Matthew remembers this again now as his gaze falls upon a small boy he sees trying to wrestle a crust of mouldy bread from a pig down below him in the Apple Market close to the water's edge. The pig nips the boy's elbow sharply and the boy yelps in pain, dropping the crust, which the pig immediately snatches up and wolfs down. The boy, Matthew notes, is dressed in the garb of those foul-smelling wretches he witnessed in the House of Correction not thirty minutes ago and wonders how he has come to be there. Perhaps he has run away, he thinks. He knows that that is what he would try to do if fate had somehow flung him within those cheerless walls and abandoned him there. The boy's head is shaved, but is turned away, so that Matthew cannot see his face. The scalp is a raw and livid pink, covered with cuts, sores and dried scabs. He wrinkles his nose with revulsion and instinctively scratches his own head. As he does so, he sees a woman open a window high up in *The Bull's Head Inn* and tip out a bucket of slops with a cursory shout of "Beware below!" The shaven-headed boy looks up just in time to receive the full force of the slop's contents all over him. He leaps to his feet, too late, only to trip over the pig, who grunts complainingly before trampling over him on his way to a new patch to forage. The boy tries to pick himself back up again, clutching his ribs, a grimace of pain creasing his face, only for him to step backwards in the direction of the Ring O' Bells entry, miss his footing on the slippery steps leading down to the Actors' Bridge, fall and hit his head against the low stone wall. Matthew temporarily loses sight of him, then sees a shape moving in the mud, moaning, curling itself up into a ball, where it remains while passers-by step over him, spit upon him, kick him, empty the contents of their buckets over him, until he has completely merged with all the rest of the market's offal and waste.

Matthew is reminded again of his father's words in the House of Correction.

"Wilful waste leads to woeful want."

He closes his eyes. Just at that moment, he feels a hand on his shoulder. "There you are, Matthew." It is his father. "I am later than I intended. You have been enjoying the sights and sounds, I trust?"

Matthew opens his eyes and nods. His father has another gentleman with him. Another merchant from the Exchange, Matthew presumes.

"Do you know what these sights and sounds represent, my boy?"

"No, sir," Matthew replies.

"Shall you tell him, or shall I, Oldham?" the gentleman asks

"Be my guest, Mr Haworth."

"Money, my young fellow. Money. And there's lots of it to be made. It's like walking through the orchards in my garden. One simply has to reach out one's hand and pluck it from the tree."

Matthew thinks of the boy wrestling with the pig for a thrown-away apple core.

"Till Saturday then, Oldham?"

"Till Saturday."

"Bring your boy with you."

Matthew looks questioningly towards his father.

"Mr Haworth is hosting Mr Sadler's Balloon Flight in his Gardens on Saturday. Would you like to see it?"

"Yes please, Father," Matthew replies immediately, the memory of the boy and the apple core receding at once.

Mr Oldham raises his eyebrows meaningfully and Matthew turns back to Mr Haworth. "Thank you, sir. You are most kind."

Haworth laughs and takes his leave. He mimes plucking another apple from a tree and winks.

"What a most disagreeable man," says Andrew as soon as he is out of earshot.

"What makes you say that, Father?"

"All that talk of money. He makes it sound so easy, when the making of it should be by dint of one's hard work."

"Yes, Father."

"And with the making of it comes a certain responsibility."

"Father?"

"Helping those less fortunate than ourselves, rather than wasting it on fripperies like balloon rides."

"Does that mean we shan't be going to see the balloon after all?"

Andrew Oldham looks down on his adopted son, who looks up at him now with such a desperate hope. "Yes, Matthew. We shall go. We'll make a picnic of it, shall we?"

"Oh yes, Father. I should enjoy that."

"Flying balloons is a serious matter. That's what Haworth fails to understand. He sees it as merely another way of making money."

"How will he do that, Father?"

"By charging people admission to see it."

"But people will be able to see it from anywhere, won't they, Father, once it is up in the sky?"

"Quite right, my boy," chuckles Andrew, ruffling his son's hair. "Quite right."

He removes his beaver top hat and polishes its brim on his sleeve. His hand, he notes, with grim satisfaction, is perfectly steady, unlike his hatter's, which shakes quite uncontrollably when he attempts to measure the circumference of his head. It is a symptom he has observed in all hatters who have been working in the trade for several years. It troubles him to think, however unwittingly, his business practices are bringing pain as well as profit, and his mind casts back to that most distressing scene in the House of Correction earlier this morning. He had not realised that such medieval practices of the boys being required to tread the animal fibres in their own urine were still being pursued.

"Father?" asks Matthew, sensing that his mind has drifted elsewhere.

"Forgive me, I was distracted. What was I saying?"

"Ballooning, Father."

"What of it?"

"That it's a serious matter."

"Indeed it is. If we are really intended to take to the skies like the birds, for what purpose do we do so?"

Matthew shakes his head, frowning. "Because we can?"

"That's a very wise answer, Matthew. Perhaps there will be no need for you to go to school next year after all."

"Oh no, Father. I should very much like to go to school."

"And so you shall. I was speaking in jest. Though not about the wisdom of your reply. Man has always pushed against the boundaries of knowledge. Right from when Eve first bit the apple, or Prometheus stole fire from the Gods."

"But weren't they punished for doing so, Father?"

"They were. But it has not stopped us from continuing to strive towards new horizons, has it? When Columbus sailed across the Atlantic, some people were certain that the world was flat and so he would surely fall off the edge. But he didn't, and now our ships sail right around the world to bring us the raw cotton from America, so that I might carry out my business here in Manchester and export our wares back there, as well as to many other countries."

"Yes, Father."

"When William Harvey demonstrated the way that blood circulates around our bodies, proving that it was the heart, not the liver, which was responsible for this, many at the time felt that his theories were tantamount to heresy, but now, because of his discoveries, Doctors no longer indulge in the barbaric practice of blood letting to treat diseases."

"Even here?"

"Especially here. Dr White at the Infirmary is known throughout the kingdom for his modern methods."

"I'm glad of it, Father. I would hate for my own blood to be let."

"Then, when James Watt watched the lid of his mother's kettle be lifted by the force of the steam, he had an idea to harness that power to drive great machines, and now, just two years ago, Mr Arkwright opened his new mill on the corner of Shude Hill and Miller Street in which a combination of steam and water power can turn machines that operate more than two thousand spindles, which not twenty years ago, would have required two thousand individuals each working at their own spinning wheel in a cellar or room where they lived, while now we can house dozens of these mighty machines on each of the several storeys of these giant mills which are proliferating weekly along the banks of our rivers, so that I predict, Matthew, that by the time you are one and twenty, Manchester will be the centre of the largest cotton empire the world has ever seen, and you will be at the heart of it."

Matthew likes the way that all sounds.

"But this ballooning business, my boy, that is an entirely different matter, for I cannot see where the benefits lie for the rest of us. Yes, it is exciting to think that Man may finally conquer the skies, but to what end? I fear I share the sentiments some are expressing in those songs the ballad singers are hawking round the town ahead of Mr Sadler's flight on Saturday."

"What fears are those, Father?"

"*Should War again break out as people say's no doubt*
With some it may happen quite soon
The French will invade us, their troops all parade us
Brought o'er in the Hot Air Balloon…"

"Oh? Is that what you think, Father? That in the future countries may make war with each other not just by land or by sea, but by air?"

"Very possibly, Matthew, but not in our lifetimes. If reports are to be believed, these balloons struggle to carry just one person, let alone whole armies, and nor have they yet discovered a reliable way of steering them, relying solely on whichever direction the wind may be blowing them in, if indeed it is blowing at all."

"I should still like to go up in one, Father."

"And why is that?"

"I should like to be able to look down upon the earth from a great height, to see the pattern of the fields with the sheep and cows grazing in them like toys, and the way the streets are all laid out in the towns, with all the people coming and going, no larger than a column of ants. I should like to be able to see where we live, Father, to see Fanny hanging out the washing behind the house, and you and Mother seeing me float by, all of you waving up at me. It would be like being the king of all I survey."

Andrew looks down on his son's shining face, lit up by this vision he has of himself, and smiles. He cannot help but think at once of Matthew, chapter four, verse eight. *'And again, the Devil taketh Him up into an exceedingly high mountain, and sheweth him all the kingdoms of the world, and the glory of them...'*

He half opens his mouth to speak, but decides against it. Instead, he says simply, "I heard on my way over to find you that one of the boys from the House of Correction had escaped..."

Matthew jerks his head involuntarily back towards where he last saw the beleaguered boy. At first he cannot find him, but then he sees him, a pale shape against the darker pile of rubbish he lies among. He has not, Matthew realises, regained consciousness from when he banged his head in his fall. Or if he has, he is preferring instead to lie low until there are fewer people around. Matthew wonders what he would do if their situations were reversed, but his imagination fails him. He finds he cannot envisage not having a home to return to at night.

Just at that moment a number of the Overseer's assistants from the House of Correction enter the square, but their efforts to find the runaway are half-hearted at best. Clearly they have been sent against their wishes and are showing more interest in one of the young girls selling fruit from a stall nearby. Matthew wonders if he should do his civic duty and alert them to the boy's whereabouts. Wouldn't that be the proper thing to do? If he was returned to the House of Correction, he would have a safer place to sleep than to risk what might happen to him unprotected on the streets throughout the night. If he went back, perhaps someone would take pity on him there, dress his wounds and sit with him until he falls asleep. But deep down he knows that this will not happen. And so he says nothing. He stands by his father and the two of them survey the scene from above, not quite from the dizzying heights that are promised to be afforded by Mr Sadler's balloon, but sufficiently removed to be able to see clearly the interplay of light and shadow, the way the many scores of people slip from one to the other as St Michael's Church strikes midday. They watch until the Overseer's assistants grow bored with their futile efforts to win the attention of the pretty fruit seller and drift away.

"And time too that we were on our way, Matthew," says his father.

Matthew wonders if he should now inform his father that he knows where the escapee is hiding. His father would, he knows, take pity on the boy and insist they take him with them back to their house, where Fanny will wash his foul-smelling body, dress his wounds, while Dr White is summoned and a treatment diagnosed. Matthew imagines a future where the boy recovers, the two of them make friends and become firm companions, but then a voice in the farthest recesses of his mind whispers to him ingratiatingly, asking him if that is truly what he desires, to share the affections of his parents, the attentions of Fanny, with this young stranger whom he has never clapped eyes on till earlier this morning. He finds himself answering no, he does not want to share his advantages with this ragamuffin, who he doesn't know the first thing about, and so he says nothing. He and his father make their way back along Market Street Lane, past the Daub Holes, along Lever's Row, to their comfortable house on the newly renamed Oldham Street, in honour of Matthew's father, where Fanny fetches in their warm fresh soup, just as his father had predicted, and that Matthew can barely wait to finish saying grace before greedily and gratefully requesting a second helping which, for once, his father consents to. By evening time, Matthew has all but forgotten the prostrate heap lying alone in the muck and straw by the steps leading down to the Actors' Bridge, his thoughts instead all turned towards the anticipation of seeing Mr Sadler's balloon ascend the heavens from the close proximity of Mr Haworth's Gardens, away from the press of undesirable common people.

*

Tuesday 8th

Whelp does not know her age, has never known it.

If asked, she would answer, "Seventeen."

She thinks this is what she would say, but she is not certain. Two years ago – she guesses it was two years ago, though she finds it difficult to be certain – she told the man at the mill she was fifteen. On Miller Street, close to where the Irk meets the Irwell.

Both rivers still flowed smoothly then. It was why they built so many mills there in the first place. The abundance of fresh water to turn the wheels to power the machines. As well as a source for washing and bleaching. But Arkwright's new factory on Miller Street changed the rules of the game. He brought all the processes under one enormous roof. Carding, rolling, spinning, dyeing. Starting out as a wig maker he became interested in cotton while living in Derbyshire. First he patented the water frame, a refinement of Hargreaves' Spinning Jenny, which produced a yarn that was suitable for warp, as well as weft. Next he invented a Carding Machine, which could transform raw cotton into lap. Then he developed the Factory System. Two thirteen hour shifts, including an hour's overlap at the start and finish of each. A bell was rung at 5am and 5pm and the gates were shut at precisely 6am and 6pm. Anyone who was late was locked out. Not only could they not work on that day, but they lost an additional day's pay as a penalty.

Now, in 1785, he owns mills in Cromford, Wirksworth, Chorley, Matlock, Nottingham, New Lanark, as well as Manchester. He is worth half a million pounds and he employs more than five thousand people, two thousand of these in Manchester, of which fifteen hundred are women and children. One of these is Whelp.

But which of these is she? When she tells the man who is hiring on Miller Street, in answer to his question, how old are you, "Fifteen," he looks up. He is evidently surprised.

"Tha's quite small," he says.

And it's true. She is. Stunted. She still lives in the Hulks, but their location is not the same as on the night of the Earthquake. It has moved several times since then. New buildings are sprouting up like weeds everywhere in the town. Along Lever's Row, down Oldham Street, in Stevenson Square – even Sir Oswald Mosley has sold off stretches of his estate for the construction of large warehouses between the Daub Holes and St Peter's Field. Cotton Palaces. Some of these remain uncompleted for want of funds, while others are abandoned altogether. Any single one of these might be referred to as the Hulks, until a new entrepreneur comes in, with new money and a new scheme. Then Whelp will move on.

She has tried to stay as close as she can to the old Newton Lane. She likes to keep an eye out for sightings of the baby she rescued – Matthew, she now knows his name is, or Mattie, she hears people call him – and she is often rewarded. When she sees him, it can stop her in her tracks, and she loses focus. Other, newer arrivals in the Hulks take advantage of this and snatch the food from her hands, suspended as it can be then between her fingers and her lips. Sometimes, when she has been following him home from the Market Cross or the Fair in Acresfield, she has returned to find her usual spot by the Old Retainer's fire has been taken. Septimus Swain has long gone. Whelp woke one morning to find his stiff, cold body lying face up next to the untended fire, which had long gone out, his pockets being rifled by some of the newcomers, a party of jays circling the corpse with interest. The role of Old Retainer has now been taken up by someone else. Whelp doesn't know him. The Great Usurper, she hears some of the old lags call him, but not to his face. He runs a tighter ship than Septimus did. Symbolic tokens of respect are no longer sufficient to ingratiate oneself with him. He demands coins. Whelp rarely has coins. But she still collects shiny coloured glass she sometimes finds in the mud, which she places in the hessian purse looped on the string around her scrawny neck. Sometimes she is forced to offer one of these to the Great Usurper, but never the two she found on the body of the boy's dead mother, the sea green and the blood red. These she keeps, will always keep.

That is why she seeks this job at the new mill. She needs coins to make sure she can bunker down in the Hulks each night.

"Name?" asks the man at the front gate.

Whelp says nothing. She rarely speaks. Only when she is forced to. It takes her some time to realise that now is one of those occasions.

"Name?" the man demands again, more impatiently this time.

She is not good with names. They mean very little to her. She does not speak to anyone unless she has to. At such times she is usually facing that person directly, so that she can see their face. A name is then not necessary. In her mind she refers to people as they present themselves to her. The tall man. The taller man. The old woman. The older woman. The one with no teeth. The one who limps. The hare lip. The hook for a hand. And so she does not know her own name, has never known it. She answers, though, to Whelp. She has learned to do so. When people bark it, like a dog to a bitch, she responds.

This man, who is now looking at her with barely concealed dislike, appears to need a name he can write on his piece of paper. She recognises that she must furnish him with one, so that she might be given this job, for which she will then be paid with the coins she needs for her place in the Hulks.

"Whelp," she says at last.

"Whelp? What kind of name is that?"

She shrugs.

He shakes his head and writes it down. "What about your first name? I can't just call you 'Whelp'."

She shrugs again.

People must, he supposes, and he leaves that space blank. "Very well, Whelp," he says.

She does not move. She remains standing where she is. The man looks at her with irritation. "Fifteen, you say?"

She nods.

"Tha's quite small for fifteen," he says again, looking down at her. "Tha' can start as a piecer."

She turns to go, when he whistles to her sharply. She stops and turns. It is a command she has learned to obey.

"Whelp," he says and tosses her a piece of string. "Tha'll need to tie back thy hair if tha's to be a piecer."

She picks up the string and fastens up her hair. The man regards her with a mixture of curiosity and distaste. He walks towards her. She holds up her hair for him to inspect. It is coiled and matted, like hanks of rope, and crawling with lice. She feels the man looking at her, wrinkling his nose with repugnance, but somehow unable to tear his eyes away from her.

"Tha' can start tomorrow morning. Five o'clock."

She feels his breath linger a moment on the back of her neck, then she bolts back into the ceaseless flow of human traffic, keeping low to the ground, as if she is following a new scent, and is lost from his sight.

Life as a piecer is something she slots into more easily than some. She spends most of each day scuttling on the floor beneath the mechanical spinning mules, twisting the pieces of snagged thread, which sometimes snap and break, back onto the ends of the machines. There are five storeys in the giant mill, whose brick chimney is the tallest structure in Manchester. Each of the storeys is two hundred yards long, with no partitions, stretching the entire length of the mill, connected by an outside wooden staircase. Inside, the ceilings are low, the beams of solid oak fixed with iron pins designed to spring against their own weight to resist the pressure from the floors above. Two rows of twenty-five spinning mules are housed on each floor, which run continuously, day and night, stopping only for an hour each day when fresh bobbins are attached to the ends of each one. Though the man who first employed Whelp, who she learns is called Jem, is apt to turn a blind eye if the little piecers are encouraged to oil and clean the mules and change their bobbins while they remain switched on. For when the machines are stopped, so are the workers' wages.

Whelp, who has lived all her life barefoot, finds the splinters underneath the mules of little discomfort, though her soles and ankles are frequently pitted with fine cuts. She quickly becomes adept at what Jem calls "fettlin' under". This requires her to crawl on her stomach beneath the constantly turning wheels of the mules, to scavenge for loose bits of fluff that might have got caught in them, remove them with a wire brush, then sweep the accumulation of dust and broken cotton from the floor. She usually does this each day during what is supposed to be her dinner hour.

The other piecers are much younger than Whelp, some only five years old, and they cry sometimes if they're asked to do the fettlin' under. They are frightened they will get their fingers trapped in the machines, maybe lose one, maybe even a whole hand. Whelp has seen this happen, so if she sees one of the children shaking as they crawl underneath, she tries to intervene and do the job for them. They adore her for it. But Whelp just shrugs. A shaking hand is a prelude to a lost or broken hand. And a broken hand will mean the mule will have to be stopped while they remove it, and that will mean she may lose an hour's pay, something she prefers not to happen.

Jem watches all this as he patrols each floor. He finds himself drawn more and more to this strange, silent, feral creature. After just a few weeks he promotes her. He asks her to supervise the other children in their other tasks – helping the blenders to mix the cotton from the bales, fetching baskets of bobbins up the outside wooden staircase, carrying pails of water from the river to the spinning rooms to keep the floors damp to inhibit the threads from drying and snapping. Manchester's rainy climate helps keep the air moist, which is another reason, along with the access to the water from the three rivers, why the town is so suited to the manufacture of cotton, but it does little to prevent each of the mill's five storeys from becoming hotter and stuffier, especially on the top storey, where Whelp now mostly works. The air is thick with tiny cotton fibres and filaments that rise and dance and settle on her like a second skin, covering every inch of her.

Jem. Always Jem. Never his full name. Jeremiah. Just Jem. Because of his surname. Stone. A childish nickname – Jem Stone – that has stuck. He can't remember the last time anyone called him Jeremiah, not since his father died, when he was just twelve, and then only if he was in trouble. He's twenty-seven now. Even Mr Arkwright calls him Jem. Once, in the first few weeks after the mill opened, when they regularly experienced teething problems with the combining of water with steam power, and they had to keep shutting off the machines, Mr Arkwright began to address him as 'Mr Stone', not out of respect, but frustration, and swiftly reverted to calling him Jem again, like everyone else, once the machines were working once more.

Now it is too noisy to call him anything else. Nobody speaks much in the mill. Their voices cannot be heard above the din and clatter of the mules. People take to reading each other's lips, or using simple signs. The girl called Whelp prefers this. Jem can see that she has never been one for talking. Now she has a ready made excuse not to have to engage with other people any more than she has to. She can read their lips easily enough, but she finds it is not expected that she should mouth or sign a reply back, unless she absolutely has to.

After six months Jem promotes her from being a piecer and a fettler to being one of the riders, operating the spinning machines with girls her own age and older. She proves just as quick and adept there, but the other women object to her working with them. They go in a body to Jem to complain. She stinks, they tell him, her smell so rank that she is making them ill. Jem duly returns her to being a piecer again. Whelp does not care either way. Scuttling on the floor beneath the machines reminds her of her life on the streets, scavenging in the gutters for what gets thrown away. The younger children are happy to have her back with them again, protecting them. Looking out for them. They do not appear to notice how she smells.

Even so Jem is unsettled. He feels a certain responsibility towards her. More than that. A kind of parental concern. He calls her over after a shift. Her matted, lice-infested hair and her grey dirt-encrusted skin is flecked and feathered in white filaments of cotton.

"Where dost tha' live?" he asks her.

She shrugs.

He suspects by this that she means where she can.

"Come wi' me," he says and turns to go.

She remains where she is.

He turns and extends his arm. "Come," he says again. "Follow. I'd like thee to meet my family."

Whelp considers this. She is no longer afraid of Jem, knows that he watches out for her, not in the way she has seen other men cast their eyes over her, on the streets, late at night, in the Hulks.

When it comes to sex, the Hulks operate their own brand of morality. It was the Old Retainer's role to enforce this, now the Great Usurper's, and in this one thing he does not differ from his predecessor. Bedding down beside someone for warmth is quite the norm in the Hulks, as close to one of the fires as people can get. Whelp sees nightly these animal couplings, the mounting and bucking, the fierce fumblings, the biting and scratching, the wordless moaning. The lusts and passions that spark and sputter in a moment. She does not see love in any of these, but she recognises need. But children are off limits. She knows what might take place in the dark, windowless cellars that are now proliferating beneath the rotting banks of the Irk, but here in the Hulks she's been safe.

So – as she follows Jem down the labyrinth of alleyways that twist and turn and double back on themselves below the Hanging Ditch, she considers the risk. She would not wander these cobbles after dark alone, but with Jem she feels protected. For all his bluntness, he is looking out for her. She knows this.

They reach a place called Fogg's Yard.

Fogg's Yard, Omega Place, Commercial Street. Proprietor: Mr Samuel Sparks. Jem lives in one of the dwellings there with his mother and five siblings, which he rents from Mr Sparks. Across the way is a brick factory. Jem's father worked there until he died the previous year in an accident, buried beneath a ton of bricks following a gas explosion. The factory has lain in a heap of rubble ever since, while a dispute over who owns the land is lying under an even greater pile of papers in the office of the Court Leet. Jem's father's body has never been found, but it is known for certain he was working in the factory when the explosion occurred, along with more than a hundred and fifty other men. The remains of a few of these were unearthed, but not many. Sometimes, at night, Jem would fancy he heard the screams of some of them, his father included, calling out to be rescued. But not any more. Now he can walk past the scene without giving it a second glance.

As he does this evening. Though Whelp's eyes are drawn towards it. It would make a good location for the Hulks, she is thinking, when it next comes round for them to make a move. Instinct is already prompting her to scout out where she might find herself a safe spot. She pictures where she might light a fire, notices the pump in the corner of the yard, from where she might draw water, an almost unimagined luxury. A farrow of pigs roots among the hill of bricks.

Jem taps her lightly on the shoulder and nods towards one of the dwellings. "Wait here," he says, while he goes inside. She looks around while she waits as instructed. There are sixteen cottages, with as many again in the process of being built. She wonders how many people live there altogether. Later she will learn that there are more than ninety, at least sixty of whom comprise litters of orphaned children.

From inside one of them now she hears raised voices.

"No, Jem, we've no room." A woman's voice, fractious and tired.

"Just for one night," Jem asks.

A baby cries.

"No," says the woman. "I know what you're like. One night would become a week, then she'd never leave."

Jem says nothing. He heads back to the doorway, looks out into the yard, checks that Whelp is still there, smiles at her, nods, holds up his hand. "I won't be long," he says.

"Try one o' t' cellars," the woman relents. His mother. "Try Ada Briggs."

Jem goes back to Whelp, then leads her across the yard to a flight of stone steps leading down to one of the cellars. There are more than a dozen cellars. Little more than kennels dug out of the earth below the level of the Irk, each comprising two windowless rooms. Whelp follows Jem down the slippery steps. Heaps of rubbish are piled in the doorway where a husk of rats forages undisturbed. She steps across the threshold. She becomes aware of several pairs of eyes staring listlessly from the dark. Both human and animal. Whelp is not concerned. She has seen such places many times. One of the pairs of eyes blinks. Beneath it a mouth opens. A slurred voice begins to speak. It belongs to Ada Briggs.

"I suppose," the voice says. "If she can find herself a space. How tall is she?"

Jen thrusts Whelp towards the eyes. A match is struck. It flares briefly in the dark, illuminating for a second the face of Ada Briggs. Whelp sees a veined, bulbous nose, red rheumy eyes, three black stumps of teeth, before the match putters and goes out.

The mouth breaks out into mirthless laughter. "She's nobbut a runt. There's room for ten of her."

Jem thanks her, then leads Whelp back up into the slightly less malodorous air of Fogg's Yard. The light is fading. Jem's mother carries a small child over towards the one privy which serves for the whole of Omega Place. Whelp un-self consciously takes herself off towards the pile of bricks and squats behind it. One of the pigs approaches her curiously. Jem tosses a stick at it, so that it retreats, grunting a few feet further off.

When Whelp returns, Jem says, "Tha' can stay here if tha' likes," and he points back towards the steps leading down to where Ada Briggs presides over her squirming brood. "Meantime I'll work on Mother. She'll come round."

Whelp looks up at him. She is frowning. Jem can see she is working out whether she wants to.

"The rent's two shillings a week," he says. "Normally water's extra," he adds, pointing to the pump, "but I'll square that wi' Sparks."

Whelp frowns again.

"Well?" he asks. "It'll be dark soon. I'll need to go in and help Mother."

Eventually she shakes her head.

Jem's shoulders slump. "Where will tha' go?"

She looks back at him. Her lips part in what for her is almost a smile. She points. He follows the line of her grimy finger. It is signalling a point among the ruin of the brick works. She skips towards it, clambers skilfully across it, lighter and more nimbly than the pigs, who are too heavy to climb its delicately weighted structure and lumber away from her. Jem watches as she clears away some bricks without causing the entire edifice to collapse and carve herself a kind of nest within them. She does all this in just a few seconds. Jem smiles, then nods.

"Alright," he says. "I'll clear it wi' Sparks."

Whelp shakes her head.

"I suppose not," adds Jem with a smile. "The brickworks don't belong to 'im." The thought of her perched perhaps directly above where his father's bones may still be buried somehow comforts him. He makes his way towards her, as close as he dares without actually risking disturbing the concertina of bricks. "Wait till after it's dark," he whispers, "before tha' uses t' pump."

She looks at him again with that same frown creasing her forehead.

"Tha' needs a wash," he says. "Why else dost tha' think I brought thee back 'ere? The women in t' mill won't work wi' thee till tha's cleaned tha'self up a bit."

He winks and then is gone.

Whelp watches him head back across the yard, meet his mother and baby sister coming out of the privy, hoist the baby onto his shoulders and then carry her indoors. His mother pauses on the step, wipes her hands down the front of her apron and looks back towards the heaped ruin. Whelp ducks down into the nest she has made for herself and so she does not see Jem's mother smile with a grim resignation before following her son indoors.

Whelp watches the moon climb the sky until it is directly overhead. It shines down on Commercial Street, into Omega Place and from there into the heart of Fogg's Yard. She hears the different sounds emanating from the cellars underneath her, the animal throated lusts, the whimpering children, the babies' howls of rage, the snores of the bone weary. She could not have survived among them. She knows this. She belongs in the upper air, unconfined by damp walls or closed doors. The pigs ignore her, bent on other rootings. The rats graze and nuzzle her toes. She does not mind this, never has, so long as she can see them, flick them aside if they are tempted to nibble or gnaw.

She waits till the yard has grown as quiet as she thinks it is likely to get, then creeps out of her nest, edges slowly down from brick to untoppled brick, till her feet reach the flagstoned paving. She scuttles lightly towards the pump, a mouse taking its chance while the cat sleeps, and, looking round, quickly removes all of her clothes, which she places in a small pile beside her. Her skin goose-pimples, forcing her to tense her bony shoulders. She releases the water from the pump into a bucket she finds lying close by. Once this is filled she begins to scoop handfuls of it, which she splashes onto her face and neck, before tentatively rubbing each arm.

Jem hears the sound. He has not been asleep. He is at the door almost at once. He spies her crouching by the bucket. The moon picks out her scabbed and grimy body, pitilessly exposing just how paper thin she is. He can make out her ribs, her elbows, her shoulder blades, her knees. Her body is all sharp edges. In the moonlight she appears quite brittle, yet he knows from having watched her at work in Arkwright's Mill that this is deceptive. She's stronger than she looks, but it is clear that she has little idea of how she might wash herself properly. She flinches with each drop of water as it makes contact with her unguarded skin, patches of which he suspects have not felt the caress of light or air in years.

He finds himself approaching her, his feet taking him towards her before his brain has registered the fact. For once, her senses so attuned to the alien touch of water, she does not hear him come until he is right upon her. She freezes, a hare caught in the death stare of a greyhound, instinctively covering herself with her arms.

"Shh," he whispers and reaches a hand to her shoulder. He lets it rest there a long time until she grows used to its presence there and starts to relax. Then he holds up in his other hand a rough cake of lye soap he has brought with him. He lets her sniff it. It smells of wood ash and animal fat, and it is not unpleasant. She nods and hands it back to him. He wets the soap in the water, froths it into a lather, then proceeds to rub it gently all over her body. He starts with her arms, lifting each above her head in turn, washing above and below, then down into her hands, one finger at a time. He washes the sides of her body, taking care to be as careful as he can as he encounters the various sores there. He turns her to face him. She crosses her arms in front of her. Gently he uncrosses them. Her breasts are just buds. He hands the soap to her and gestures for her to continue, which she does. When she has finished, she allows

Jem to continue, soaping her back, her hips, behind her knees, scrubbing her feet and toes, before handing the soap back to her to finish between her legs. She has stopped shivering now. She is completely absorbed in this strange new activity. The water, whose touch so alarmed her at first, she now luxuriates in.

While she is thus engrossed Jem picks up the bucket and tips it completely over her head. She gasps, almost emitting a scream, then smiles. For the first time her face seems to Jem to be completely unguarded, and he is captivated by her.

He rubs his hands vigorously through her matted hair. She squirms and wriggles, flinches as his fingers drag through every knot and tangle but stands her ground, allowing him to finish. He refills the bucket with more cold water from the pump, which he then invites her to dip her head completely into. She does, then shakes herself all over him like a wet mongrel.

"Wait a moment," he whispers. He hurries back into his cottage, returning almost at once with a long piece of grey cloth. "Dry yourself," he says, "then get dressed."

While she does so, he collects a few bits of wood and dried straw and lights a small fire at the edge of her nest among the bricks.

"Come and get warm," he says.

She clambers back up the bricks to join him. As she warms herself in front of the fire, he takes out a comb and gently pulls it through her hair, removing any remaining knots, along with the lice trapped within them. Although it snags and hurts, she allows him to do this. A faint memory stirs in her brain, but is then carried up to the sky by the embers of the fire.

Back inside the cottage Jem's mother lies hard awake, listening to the kindling crack and split in the growing flames.

Whelp does not return to the Hulks.

Nor has she gravitated to the inside of Jem's cottage.

A year later she is still to be found among the brick heaps in Fogg's Yard. She prefers the outside air. She feels hemmed in by walls and ceilings. She is a recognised figure by all who dwell in Omega Place now. Even Jem's mother acknowledges her with a brusque "Good e'en" each night when she arrives back from her shift at Arkwright's. She no longer needs Jem to escort her to and fro. But there is a closeness between them that both of them feel, even if they never speak of it. Whelp has washed herself a number of times over the past months. Late at night when the rest of the Yard is asleep. She has even washed her hair too once or twice. But Jem has not joined her by the fire to comb it through again, though she has sensed him watching her sometimes from the shadow of his half-open door.

The summer crawls by. The dog days, the dysentery days. Flies gather in swarms over the Irk. Eels flap and flounder in the shallows. Fogg's Yard is a cauldron. It sweats, it swelters. The mud is dried and caked on the pigs' sunburnt hides. They seek out what little shade there is and pant wheezily. The troglodytic children have emerged blinking from the cellars. Jem arrives back late from a shift and finds them basking on the bricks around Whelp like beached seal pups. She stretches out her rag of a skirt as far as it will go. She spreads her arms out wide. She gathers the children to her. They open and close their hands like starfish.

No, thinks Jem, not seal pups, but a farrow of newly spawned pigs, a litter of unwanted runts. He wants to swat them aside, but he hasn't the heart, for secretly he wants to join them – no, not join them, usurp them. She stretches out a hand towards him, but he walks straight past, towards his cottage, where his mother sits in the doorway peeling potatoes. He steps across her and goes inside. She watches him curiously, then returns Whelp's wave with one of her own.

Jem's mother. She refuses to accept what has happened. "He'll be back," she says, "you'll see." It takes Whelp some time to realise she's talking about her dead husband. Jem's father. Every night she waits on the doorstep watching for his return. She no longer permits herself to sleep. At every sound she starts, every footfall sets her senses on high alert, certain that this time it will be his, returning to her at last. Weeks pass. Months. Years. She ceases to count the days. They all merge into one endless night. She never ventures further than the doorway out of her house, which lies in permanent shadow in the farthest corner of Omega Place, from where, some nights, she sings, darkly to herself.

"*Fine laurel, fine floral*
You proved all unkind..."

"Jem's father were a weaver," she says, to no one in particular. "Like his father before him. Edwin. They named him Henry. After King Henry, the Plantagenet, who formed the Worshipful Company of Weavers more than six hundred year ago. It were a noble calling. They lived in a stone cottage in Bagslate Moor, between Norden and Rochdale. His father's loom took up most o' t' front room. There were a small kitchen at t' back. They could fetch water straight from Sudden Brook, which flows direct into th' Irwell. Cold an' clear. They reckon it used to be like that 'ere in Manchester once upon a time, but tha'd never know it now, would thee?" She smiles grimly, a smile which quickly turns into a wince, and she places her hand to her side, just below her ribs, to ease the hurt.

" 'E 'ated it 'ere. 'E felt 'emmed in. I wish tha' could've seen 'im afore. 'E were full o' such hope… 'E'd tramp about t' moors, carryin' 'is tools on 'is back, an t' samples o' 'is work for t' folk to see." She drifts away again into bitter memories of the part she played in his demise, singing to the night sky.

"When I was a tailor I carried my bodkin and shears
When I was a weaver I carried my roods and my gear
My temples also, my small clothes and reed in my hand
And wherever I go, here's the jolly bold weaver again…"

"That's when I first met 'im," she says and begins to laugh. " 'E cut quite the romantic figure back then. 'E knew who 'e were…Then 'e'd go back whoam an' make up all th' orders his feyther 'ad left for 'im, those 'e reckon'd 'e could manage… 'E made me a lace collar once, to stitch to my Sunday blouse. I'd wear it when us went out walkin'… I worked in t' new mill in Ramsbottom then. Peel's Mill… I've still got it somewhere. I'll show thee if tha'd like me to…"

She trails off, lost again, and wanders back indoors.

Whelp hears her start to sing once more, and the whole sad story plays out before her.

"I'm a hand weaver to my trade
I fell in love with a factory maid
And if I could but her favour win
I'd stand beside her and weave by steam…"

Jem's mother is speaking to herself indoors. " 'Enry could see t' writing were on t' wall for weavin', even back then. Far too many of 'em chasing far too little work. 'E'd 'ave to tramp further an' further across t' moors, as far away as Bacup an' Rawtenstall sometimes, beyond th' Irwell's source, to where it were nobbut a ruined shack an' a hard scrabble, just to get t' meanest of orders. Where once 'e'd been pullin' in wages o' sixty shillin' a week, 'e were now bringin' in less than twelve. 'It's no use', 'e told 'is feyther, 'I'm jackin' it in. I'm for t' mill now'. 'E were just seventeen. One day, while Edwin were away, deliverin' a special item that 'e'd entrust to no one but hisself, Henry just upped an' left. It broke 'is feyther's heart. Edwin. 'Is own too if tha' wants t' truth…"

"My father to me scornful said
'How could you fancy a factory maid
When there are local girls fine and gay
Dressed like unto the Queen of May...?'

"As for your fine girls I don't care
If I could but enjoy my dear
I'd stand in the factory all the day
And she and I'd keep our shuttles in play..."

She comes back out into the yard carrying a small basket through which she is rummaging, still trying to lay her fingers on the lace collar. "It's 'ere somewhere, I know it," she says and continues to sort through the various scraps and keepsakes she holds there, some snags of threads, a thimble, a needle, a child's sampler. Cross patch, draw the latch, sit by the fire and spin. She stops. Her eyes light on what she's been looking for. The lace collar. She holds it up to the fading light. She places it against her throat. She is lost. Over the hills and far away...

"I went to my love's bedroom door
Where oftentimes I had been before
But I could not speak nor yet get in
The pleasant bed that my love lay in

'How can you say it's a pleasant bed
When nowt lies there but a factory maid...?'
A factory maid although she be
Blessed is the man who enjoys she..."

Jem returns to the yard. The sight which greets him is so tender it stops him in mid-stride. Whelp is sitting next to his mother. Tentatively she is reaching a hand towards her. His mother seems unaware of her presence. She is holding up the lace collar. Whelp gently lays her hand upon her shoulder. His mother leaps away, a cat whose skin has been scalded. She thinks Whelp means to take the lace from her. Whelp looks up towards him. He hurries between them, tries to settle his mother, but she is far away. She looks at him, strokes his hair, smiles. He does not know whether it is him she sees in front of her, or his father. She continues to sing.

"Oh, pleasant thoughts come to my mind
As I turn down the sheets so fine
And I seen her two breasts standing so
Like two white hills all covered with snow…"

Jem turns away. He can hardly bear to watch her when she's like this. His eyes fall on Whelp, who holds his gaze. His mother sees this and is at once brought back to the present. "It's startin' again," she hisses. She lunges at Whelp, grabs her roughly by the wrist and jerks her towards her, so that their two faces are very close. Whelp can feel her hot breath on her skin. " 'Is feyther slipped when 'e courted me, from one rung down to t' next, till 'e were buried beneath t' weight of it all." She twists Whelp's face until it is staring in the direction of the collapsed bricks, where every night she sleeps, where every night Jem goes out to look down upon her. "Don't think I don't know," she snarls towards her son. "I've seen thee there."

Jem's face reddens. "Come, mother," he says as gently as he can, his voice shaking with a mixture of sadness and guilt. He prises the fingers of her right hand, one by one, from Whelp's wrist, then carefully removes her left hand from Whelp's face. "I never really knew my feyther," he says to Whelp. "Not properly. 'E died inside when I were just a lad." Jem jabs his chest with his fist. "But I do remember this. 'Is body were broke long before t' gas explosion brought t' brick factory down on top of 'im…"

His mother is singing again, stretching out her arms wide, taking in the whole of Fogg's Yard, trying to encompass the thin rectangle of light entering from above, down into the sunless court of Omega Place.

> *"The loom goes click and the loom goes clack*
> *The shuttle flies forward and then flies back*
> *The weaver's so bent that he's like to crack*
> *Such a wearisome trade is the weaver…"*

She holds up the lace collar to her neck once more and dances round the fallen bricks.

> *"The yarn is made into cloth at last*
> *The ends of the weft they are made quite fast*
> *The weaver's labours are now all past*
> *Such a wearisome trade is the weaver…"*

Jem catches both her hands in his, enfolds her to him, then leads her gently down the steps into their cottage.

The bell for the start of the 5am shift begins to ring. Whelp picks herself up, gathers the other children who have all risen up from the cellars to watch what has been happening to her, and together they make their way, back up the Hanging Ditch towards Red Bank and Arkwright's Mill. All the streets around resound with the march of a thousand pairs of clogs striking on the cobbled flagstones, matching their rhythm to the ceaseless roar of the machines.

> *"Where are the girls, I will tell you plain*
> *They have all gone to weave by steam*
> *And if you'd find 'em you must rise at dawn*
> *And trudge to the mill in the early morn…"*

In the tiny space between stepping from the external wooden staircase as she enters the Carding Room and the heavy door shutting out the light behind her, Whelp hears the faint echo of Jem's mother's voice receding until it is no more than the rusty croak of a jackdaw pecking out some masonry from the factory chimney, trying to find purchase for its makeshift nest.

"When I was a tailor I carried my bodkin and shears
When I was a weaver I carried my roods and my gear
My temples also, my small clothes and reed in my hand
And wherever I go it's the jolly bold weaver again…"

"Do you know what your name means, son? Why your father chose it for you?"

"Yes, Mother. You've told me many times."

" 'Jeremiah'," she says, raising her head. " *'The Lord will lift you up'*."

Jem shakes his head wearily.

The next night, when he has finally settled his mother, Jem steps back outside into Fogg's Yard. He puts his hands in the small of his back on either side, tips back his head, closes, then opens his eyes. He takes a deep breath then wanders across to the ruin of bricks, where Whelp has been expecting him. She says nothing. Instead she waits for him to speak, which she knows he will given time.

"Me feyther hated this place," he says at last. "Mother knew that of course, so she always blamed herself for what happened. She still does."

Jem looks past the crumbling edifice of clay and mortar, beneath which, for all he knows, the decaying body of his father still lies buried. But he doubts it. The force of the explosion was so strong that few remains of anyone working inside at the time have ever been found. It blew out the windows in several of the buildings on Commercial Street. Those in Omega Place, specifically those in Fogg's Yard, have never been replaced. Mr Sparks promises he will get round to it, but it's been years now and nothing's been done. Meanwhile rival claimants continue to wrangle in the Court Leet, which only meets when it feels like it and has yet to consider what to do with the now vacant lot in Fogg's Yard.

"Handloom weavers regard 'emselves as th' aristocracy o' t' cotton trade," he says, "an' me feyther were a Crown Prince. All set to inherit the kingdom from 'is own feyther, Edwin. 'E were a real master so they say, there were none to rival 'im." Jem takes out a pipe and taps it on the corner of one of the bricks to empty it. "This were 'is," he says, sitting next to Whelp as he starts to fill it with a few flakes of tobacco he takes from a small pouch. "Me grandfeyther's, then me feyther's. It's all I've got left of either of 'em now," he continues, "save this shirt. I'm the same size me feyther were now, though I'm 'ardly fit to wear it."

He tamps the tobacco down in the chamber of the bowl, then shields the match from the night breeze that is now picking up to light it.

" 'E came to visit us once. Edwin. Me grandfeyther. Not long after me feyther 'ad died. He were old then. But I remember 'ow strong 'e were. When 'e shook yer 'and, it felt like you was bein' gripped in a vice."

Jem pauses, remembering, his thoughts drifting up and out of Fogg's Yard with the smoke from his pipe, passed down the generations.

"Handloom weavers," he says again, clamping the stem between his teeth. "Aye... They look down their noses at those of us who work in t' mills. 'Where's the skill in standin' at t' powered loom', Edwin'd say? 'It does all t' work for thee. And not 'alf so well neither'. But we do it quicker, don't we, I'd say? A thousand times quicker. 'Aye, lad, I reckon tha' does, but why dost tha' need to be in such a hurry all t' time?' And cheaper too, I'd say. He'd shake 'is head at that. 'Mebbe,' he'd say. 'Mebbe not. That all depends on how tha' does the sums'. What d'you mean, I'd ask? And 'e'd shake 'is head an' say, 'Machines put folk like me out o' work. You talk about progress an' profit but what 'appens to all t' craft, all t' learnin' that gets passed on from feyther to son, down all t' generations. That's got to count for summat, surely…?' I thought of me feyther then. I wanted to ask 'im, 'Why didst tha' give it all up?' But I never did. I knew the answer any road. Once 'e'd courted me mother, gone against 'is own feyther's wishes, 'e'd crossed a line. There were no goin' back then. So 'e worked where 'e could get it. Bit by bit they made their way from Ramsbottom – first Bury, then Heywood, then Middleton, then Royton, then Oldham, then Chadderton, back over to Radcliffe, through Kearsley, down to Walkden, Worsley, into Swinton, then Pendlebury – before finally crossin' th' Irwell to Manchester, endin' up 'ere, Omega Place, 'is last stop. 'E tried 'is 'and at owt – you name it, 'e did it – fruit pickin', shepherdin', hedge layin', in foundries, tanneries, at t' forge, down t' pit – but nowt 'd suit, not for long any road. 'E'd grow restless, quarrel wi t' bosses, move on. Meanwhile there were always more mouths to feed, so that by t' time we reached 'ere, me mother begged 'im to stop 'is roamin' an' try an' make a go of it…"

Jem pauses, relights the pipe, which has gone out during the telling. He follows the passage of the smoke as it curls above where he and Whelp are sitting. He pulls her closer to him, gently enfolds her bony frame with his right arm. She allows herself to rest her head on his shoulder. She watches a moth dancing briefly in the smoke, fluttering towards some light only it can see.

"An 'e did. 'E were true to 'is word. 'E tried."

He remains quiet for several minutes. Their faces become wreathed in smoke.

"Once," he says at last, "once 'e told me a story about 'is time as a weaver."

Whelp shifts her position, extracts herself from the crook of Jem's arm. She senses this is a story Jem has thought long and hard about before deciding to tell her, and she wants to be sure he knows that she's giving it her full attention. She sits upright, her hands on her lap, studying his face, which is now in perfect profile, outlined against a gibbous moon, so that half of him is in light, the other half in shadow.

"It were 1761. Farmer George'd just become t' new king, and now 'e were gettin' wed. 'E wanted summat special for 'is bride, Queen Charlotte. The fame o' t' Lancashire weavers 'ad spread to t' Court, and me grandfeyther, Edwin, bein' a lifelong member o' t' Worshipful Company o' t' Weavers, somehow or t' other managed to win the order. A piece o' t' finest cotton muslin, so delicately woven tha' could see right through it if tha' held it up to t' light, then o'er worked wi' some lace in a pattern. What it were for, were left up to 'im – a shawl, a veil, a coverlet – an' me grandfeyther, that day 'e come to visit, 'e said, 'It were tha' feyther who gave me th' idea. 'E come runnin' in from outside, sayin' as 'ow I just 'ad to see what 'e'd found.' Edwin laughed as he remembered. 'Tha' must've 'eard 'ow impatient tha' feyther was, Jem, always in a hurry – not like thee, I reckon tha' takes after me – but I followed 'im out t' back an' by God, 'e were right. It were summat I'd never seen t' like of afore, an' never again since. I've never forgot it. If it weren't for tha' feyther, Jem, that piece of cloth would never 'ave been made t' way it were'."

Jem turns now to face Whelp directly. The half moon frames his face exactly.

"I wish I'd seen that piece o' cloth," he says, looking at her.

She nods.

"But I feel as though I have, the way me grandfeyther described it. Moths. Caught in a web of laurel."

Whelp feels a knot tighten in her stomach.

"The day after it were finished, me grandfeyther walked wi' it tucked under 'is arm from Norden to Manchester, to arrange for it to be sent by coach to London. It were while 'e were away that me feyther first saw me mother, makin' 'er way whoam from t' mill. From that moment on, 'e were lost. 'E simply upped an' followed 'er, an' then never went back. It broke me grandfeyther's 'eart…"

Whelp looks down. Jem gently raises her chin with his hand so that he can once again see her face directly.

"Me mother worries that history might repeat itself, that's all."

Whelp half opens her mouth, as if she might actually speak, but before she can do so, Jem takes this as his cue to act. He reaches clumsily for her and presses his own lips against hers. A moth flutters agitatedly around their heads.

She does not pull away, but nor does she respond. She simply waits. Until he has finished and pulls away.

"But she needn't worry," he says bitterly. "I'm nowt like me feyther. I've no special skill I'd be givin' up."

Whelp frowns and shakes her head. She places her fingers against his mouth to quieten him. They remain in that position a long time. Eventually she begins to feel the tension leave his body. He lies exhausted by her side, where she watches him mould his body to the shape of the bricks beneath him, till sleep finally takes him, and his breathing becomes deep and regular.

Above her head the moth continues to dance.

*

Wednesday 9th

Manchester is in festive mood.

She has donned her party frock. She has tied new ribbons in her hair. She has pinched her cheeks so that the colour rises in them, almost to the point of being hectic. She kicks off her shoes and dances in the streets.

The Annual Market Fair in Acresfield has been in full swing for five days now but shows no signs yet of abating. Still the farmers drive their livestock into the square, the cows and horses, pigs and sheep, geese and chickens, and still the crowds follow them, the geese nipping their ankles. In the centre is a tall maypole, its multi-coloured streamers flying on the breeze. Young girls, dressed in white for the Whit Walks, weave them in patterns tightly around the erect pole. Grand Chain, Gypsy's Tent, Spider's Web, Closed Plait. Among the many young girls dancing is Fanny, relishing a rare work-free day in the sunshine.

"*Put spindle, bobbin and spool away*
O joy, the hirelings' holiday…"

The young surveyor, who has spent the last few days scanning the faces of everyone who ventures into Acresfield hoping he might once again see her, can scarcely believe his luck. Here she is, right below him, where he watches her dancing from the prime vantage point of the top of his ladder. This is his last day of measuring the angles, heights and distances for the proposed new houses that are being planned for the north-west corner of the square, diagonally opposite St Ann's Church, whose tower contains the bench mark carved in stone, at the level of which he now perches precariously, leaning vertiginously from his ladder in order to maintain an uninterrupted view of the young woman's face, wreathed in carefree smiles as she dances with her friends, blithely unaware of the effect she is having upon him.

He knows he must act at once, not let this unlooked for opportunity pass him by. What is it his father would say? *Carpe diem?* No. *Occupandi temporis?* No, no. *Prende urticam crescet myrtu?* Grasp the nettle? Almost. *Dum candens ferrum percussurus?* Yes, that's it exactly. Strike while the iron is hot.

In his haste, he over reaches, the ladder falls away from under him, and he lands with a clatter in an undignified heap at her feet.

He instantly gets to *his* feet, dusts himself down, apologising profusely for his clumsiness, requiring immediate reassurances that he has not in any way startled or injured her?

"No," she replies, making no attempt to conceal her amusement, as the young man continues to fluster. He picks up his hessian bag, only for all of his tools to tumble out of it. He stoops to collect these, only for his hat to fall from his head. He reaches to retrieve this, only for his shoes to miss their footing, so that he finds himself once more sprawled out on the ground before her, while she laughs harder than ever.

He looks up, his dignity hurt far more than his elbow, which he now rubs vigorously, and sees that there is no malice in her mirth, just innocent amusement. He finds that he too is now laughing along *with* her, which only succeeds in setting her off once more.

"Here," she says at last, when both of them are eventually calming down, and she holds out his hat. He stretches out a hand to take it, but in an impulse she cannot resist, she pulls it away from him, flips it expertly up her arm and deftly places it on her own head, where its size causes it to slip past her ears and over her face. Immediately he reaches towards her and pulls it down further, but he does so with more force than he intended, so that now neither he nor the young woman is able to wrench it clear. There then ensues a somewhat comical tug of war, as he pulls and she pushes, but to no avail.

By this time quite a crowd has gathered around, joining in the fun, each offering their own particular words of advice as to how to remedy the situation.

"Cut a hole in t' crown," says one.

"Rub goose fat inside t' brim," says a second.

"Form two teams," says a third.

And at once this third suggestion is picked up as several volunteers of either sex make a less than orderly line behind each of the two strugglers, all of them gripping the one in front firmly around the waist. At a signal from the gentleman who first came up with the notion – a butcher in a striped apron – who calls for quiet, before counting them in with a "One, two, three," they all set to with a will and heave with all their collective might until the hat is liberated from the young woman's head, and both she and the young surveyor fall backwards, she into a pile of straw and he into a horse trough.

The company of volunteers retires, many of them to one of the inns in the square to quench the redoubtable thirsts their labours appear to have caused, leaving Fanny and the young man to survey the mischief and mayhem that each has wreaked upon the other. The young surveyor shakes himself like a wet retriever, before removing his jacket, which he then proceeds to wring dry one sleeve after the other, while Fanny vainly tries to remove the straw that has found its way into her hair and clothes blade by blade. She sits surrounded by several piefuls of apples spilled from the stack of wooden crates she fell back into, which now she tries to rescue and take back to the trader who, having restored them neatly into a finely balanced pyramid atop his stall, invites her to choose one as a gift. She looks across at the young surveyor. They each have the same thought. He nods, she winks, then carefully selects one from the base of the pile, so that the whole edifice comes toppling down once more. Laughing, she bites heartily into the apple she now holds and offers it towards the young man, who takes it from her and bites with equal relish.

"I fear we've not been introduced," he jokes afterwards.

"Miss Frances Cox," she replies, bobbing a petite curtsey.

"Cox?" he asks. "Like the apple?"

She produces another two from the pocket on the front of her skirt and proceeds to juggle them with the one the two of them have just sampled. "The very same. And you?"

He produces his card with a flourish, which he holds out towards her between the first and second fingers of his right hand.

She is just about to take it from him with the thumb and forefinger of her own right hand, when she hesitates. "I can't read," she says simply.

He withdraws the card before she can grasp it, but she stretches her hand out further and plucks it from him anyway.

"I'm learning, though."

"Are you?" he says, suddenly serious, all game-playing now suspended. "That's good."

"Yes," she continues. "At Sunday School, straight after Morning Service."

"Where?"

"Oldham Street Wesleyan."

"You're a Methodist?"

"I am, sir. And you?"

He shakes his head. "We're not so very different, though. My family follow the Moravian teachings."

She nods gravely. "I shall show this card to my employer. Mr Oldham."

"The felt maker?"

"Yes. And soon I will be able to read it for myself."

He points to the letters that dance across the card and runs his finger along a row of them. "Zachary Robinson," he says. "That's me." He gives a mock bow.

Fanny smiles. She looks down upon the dancing letters once more and tries to match their shape to those two words. Those two words which so ineffectively capture the sum of this man who stands before her.

"Surveyor," he adds, pointing to a separate word.

"Is that what you do?" she asks.

"Yes," he replies shyly.

"Are you good at it?"

"I hope to be."

"And where do you work? Here in Manchester? Or are you just passing through?" She looks at him closely. He half turns away. "What is it?"

"I live in Shakerley," he says. He sees her puzzled expression. "It's between Wigan and Warrington," he adds, by way of explanation. "My father's a wire worker there. This has been my first job as a surveyor, but I finish today. I am due to go home and discuss with my father what my next step might be. To work with him in his wire works, or try to stride out on my own as a surveyor. Mr Edward Byrom, who has given me my chance this past six-month, is pleased with me, I believe, and I have high hopes he may retain me, but I have my obligation to my father to consider."

"Yes you do," she says, clasping his hands in hers. "You must go to him at once. It's a long way, I imagine…"

"Eleven miles."

"Then you must set off now if you are to be there before nightfall."

"Yes," he says, hastily gathering up his tools and putting them back into his bag.

"Will you come back and let me know what you decide?"

"I promise," he says. He bows once more, formally, which she returns with a careful curtsey.

They look at each other a long time. Then he turns on his heel and hurries away. Fanny watches him until she can no longer make him out among the holiday crowds thronging the square. She shifts her gaze back to his card and studies the unruly hieroglyphs before her. "Zachary Robinson," she says out loud, tracing the letters with her finger.

Three quarters of a mile to the north, behind the newly added Palladian wing of the Jacobean Strangeways Hall, recently acquired by Francis and Mary Reynolds, who reside there with their daughter Arabella, Philip Astley has just set up his

Travelling Circus beside the Fish Pond, in the Hall's Pleasure Gardens. Astley, a renowned equestrian, inspired by the shape of the pond, is experimenting with a circular, instead of his usual linear arena. He seats his audience on a series of tiered benches surrounding an area of grass, over which he has sprinkled several barrel loads of sawdust, where he will perform what he describes as his *'Equine Ballet'*. Crowds flock to see him, trampling down the hedges which block the cut-through to the estate from Long Millgate along Walkers Croft, which greatly pleases John Webster, the Reynolds' closest neighbour, a Unitarian who has long campaigned for this footpath to be made publicly accessible. Francis Reynolds, much to his wife Mary's chagrin, will not contest this dispute any further, for he has racked up large gambling debts and has already had to sell off some outlying lands of the original estate as laid out by Sir John de Strangways some two hundred years before, in Cheetham and Oldham, Rochdale and Spotland, Withington and Ardwick. She sees her horizons shrinking, just as Manchester's are expanding.

Two years before, this same neighbour, John Webster, *de facto* seized a section of their land in lieu of non-payment by Francis of an outstanding debt and placed a Corn Mill there. She hates to see the *hoi polloi* marauding through what remains of her orchards, pasture and woodland to sample the somewhat dubious delights of Astley's Circus, but needs must, she tells herself.

Two years to the day since their daughter Arabella first laid eyes upon it…

Arabella, Arabella…

She is delighted by the day. She has already fallen in love with the rake of colts cantering below her bedroom window. She shows them all to Dulcibella, her doll, who she carries with her everywhere, and to whom she tells everything. Dulcibella – named after the daughter of the first John de Strangways, whose grave Arabella found beneath one of the apple trees, and where she likes to sit sometimes to whisper her deepest secrets, the ones she won't even share with her doll, who cannot be trusted not to spill them sometimes, like when she tried to tell her mother about her Daddy's night time visits. "You're a wicked girl," her mother says, "and God will punish you." Wicked? Is that what she is? Or naughty? That's what her Daddy calls her. "Has my baby girl been naughty?" he asks. "Does she need to be taught a lesson?" She lifts up her doll Dulcibella's skirt and smacks her hard on the bottom. Just as Mr Astley gives the slightest of flicks to the hind quarters of his horse, a piebald Lipizzaner, who at once rises up on its back legs, turning in a tight circle below her window, just like the one she has in her music box, which dances in exactly the same fashion each time she opens the lid.

"Arabella?" A voice like a hot knife slicing through butter. "Arabella, where are you?"

She shuts the lid at once. She turns her back to the window. The music stops playing. The horse stops dancing.

"Arabella – there you are. Did you not hear me calling?"

"No, Mamma, I'm sorry. I didn't."

"What were you doing? No, don't tell me. Daydreaming as usual, I suppose. Away with the fairies, the raggle-taggle gypsies." She glances over her daughter's shoulder and sees the circus owner exercising one of his horses on their front lawn, which he is strictly forbidden to do. She observes that he is staring directly towards the very window she is now standing at. The impudence of the fellow. She must ask Francis to have a word with him. Francis, yes, that is why she is here, in her daughter's bedroom, which she has barely set foot in for almost a year. When she needs to see her daughter it is her custom to send for her, to come down directly and speak to her in the drawing room. She takes in this rarely visited corner of the house in the fleetest, most cursory of glances. Evidently it is time for some redecoration. This is a child's room and Arabella is – what? – twelve, thirteen years old? Certainly not a child any longer. She looks her up and down and is filled with an immediate revulsion. In the blink of an eye she will be a young woman. A husband must be found for her. But who, she thinks, appraising her stick-thin body, will want to take her off her hands?

"What's that you're holding in your hands, child?" she demands.

"Nothing, Mamma. Only my music box. The one Father gave me for my fifth birthday."

"Here, "she commands, thrusting out a hand, "let me see."

Obediently Arabella hands it across.

"I should have thought you would have outgrown this nonsense by now."

Arabella says nothing. She looks down, her cheeks reddening.

Mary flips open the lid of the music box, then slams it shut in an instant. "Your father, you say?"

"Yes, Mamma," whispers Arabella.

"Speak up, child. I can't hear you."

"Yes, Mamma."

"That's better. Now – look at me when I am speaking to you..." She seizes her daughter's face in one of her hands and brings her own face down to the same level. "It is about your father I have come to speak."

Arabella flinches.

"He is going on a business trip, to London, to the Admiralty. He was promised a commission but nothing has come of it, meanwhile we moulder away up here... I'm the daughter of an Earl. He only has his title through me, yet it is you he wishes to accompany him on this trip. Well, I suppose someone has to run the house, manage the estate. He hasn't the first idea."

Arabella swallows hard. Her mother has turned her face away from her. "When does he leave?" she manages at last to say.

Her mother spins back around, her composure regained, her temper now quickened. "Today. At once. You must go down immediately. He waits for you in his study."

"But..."

"Everything is arranged. Do as he bids. Remember – you represent *me* in this trip. Do not let me down."

She turns on her heels and strides out of the room without a word further. Only when she has reached the top of the staircase and is certain that she is not overlooked, does she pause. She clutches her stomach, bends forward and grips the banister rail in her silent distress.

Back in her bedroom Arabella instinctively looks out of her window down towards the front lawn. Mr Astley is still there, sitting upright on the piebald Lipizzaner. She waves fiercely at him, beckoning him to come closer. At once he squeezes the horse's flanks gently with his thighs and arrives directly beneath her window. This is her only chance. If she does not take it now, there will be no other opportunity. She opens the window, leans out as far as she dares and whispers loudly.

"I mean to run away, sir," she says. "Will you take me with you?"

If Mr Astley is surprised by what he hears, he gives no indication. Instead he merely says, "How will you get down?"

A slow smile spreads across her lips. It is not an expression she is accustomed to and her cheeks ache with the effort.

"If I jump," she says, "will you catch me?"

"You will not jump," he says. The smile freezes on her face. "No," he continues, "you will not jump. You will fly."

The smile returns, broadening into a grin like a crater on the moon. She leaps, her arms outstretched. Moments later she is in his arms, then astride the saddle of his piebald Lipizzaner, directly in front of him.

"Take the reins," he says. "Now we shall fly again."

The horse rears up on its hind legs, then gallops out of Strangeways Hall and into the open country.

Just two miles further to the north a parade of many different horses is taking place before a growing crowd of appreciative onlookers on Kersal Moor – Arabian and Spanish, Boulonnais and Brabant, Hanoverian, Haflinger, Percheron and Punch, Jutland and Friesian, Cob and Connemara – ahead of the Whitsuntide Races. The gentry and their ladies commingle in their tented pavilions over glasses of port or brandy, or, the latest sensation, punch, from the Hindi for 'five', denoting the number of ingredients. On this particular May morning a special version has been prepared in honour of the forthcoming balloon ascent by Mr Sadler. It is nicknamed the Celestial Syrup of the Spheres and requires the purveyor to pare as thinly as possible the rinds of two China oranges, one Seville orange and two local lemons grown under glass in the gardens of Sir Oswald Mosley in Ancoats Hall. These are then to be infused in a cold syrup of strong green tea, sweetened with a superior Demarara sugar, enriched with the juice of the fruits, before adding a generous measure each of best Jamaican rum, finest French brandy, followed by a thimbleful of Batavian Arrack (the distilled essence of fermented coconut sap), topped with two bottles of Taittinger Champagne. The final *pièce de resistance* is the addition of two dessert spoons of the juice of a Pine Apple, donated by the 1st Earl of Wilton from his recently constructed Orangery at Heaton Park, designed by Lewis Wyatt, nephew of the renowned Sir James Wyatt, the original architect of Heaton Hall, solely for the purpose of growing exotic and expensive fruits, an example of which now takes pride of place as a rented centrepiece for the duration of the Races. The stirred and cooled concoction is then passed whole through a fine lawn sieve until it is perfectly clear, when it is ready to be served with ice, stored in an ice house dug specially for the occasion.

There is a clear demarcation between the tented pavilions, conveniently situated beside the saddling enclosure and winning post, and the main body of the crowd, who are confined within the centre of the Moor, a riotous assembly of Romany fortune tellers, Neapolitan knife grinders, Venetian glass blowers, Arabian perfumiers, along with Turkish rug makers, blind French hurdy gurdy players, and Dutch distillers, who, to avoid the exigencies of the recent British Gin Act, peddle a toxic mixture of turpentine and sulphuric acid.

The crowds have gathered early for what has become in the years since the Earthquake the traditional prelude to the horse races, has in fact superseded them as the main event – the Kersal Cup – which is open to all men aged sixteen years or over, provided they can stump up the required five shillings entrance fee. In addition to the Cup the winner takes the entire stake to do with whatever he wishes. There are two features to the race which have made it so popular: first, there are no rules to prevent competitors from impeding each other by any physical means throughout the duration of the one mile course, and second, the runners are all stark naked.

Two years before, just as Miss Arabella Reynolds was making her leap to freedom and adventure, the race was won by Major-General Roger Aytoun of The Manchester Volunteers, who won it again the following year, and this year is bidding for an unprecedented hat trick. His first victory was something of a *cause de scandale* and had entered the town's folklore. At six feet and four inches he towered over all his competitors. Whereas the other runners caused the usual hilarity, their tackle swinging loose and free between their thighs, Aytoun's equipment stood immediately to attention, where it stayed for the entire race, thrusting before him like a musket, primed and ready with bayonet fixed, enabling him to win the race by a clear length.

Among the ladies in the saddling enclosure covering their mouths with their gloved hands, while at the same time watching his progress intimately through their latest fashion accessory, the lorgnette, newly arrived from Paris, is the wealthy widow Mistress Barbara Minshull. She declares herself at once besotted, presents the Major-General with both the Cup and a laurel coronet, which he proceeds to place not upon his head, but his still erect member.

Mistress Minshull goes down on one knee and proposes on the spot.

Major Aytoun gallantly kisses her proffered hand. "To the victor the spoils," he announces to the entire enclosure. They are married within the week. She is sixty-five years old. He is not yet thirty. It is rumoured he has many outstanding gambling debts.

But on this particular May morning, in 1785, the Major-General's chances of securing that much-prized hat trick of successes appear to be diminishing. A prolonged bout of drinking the previous night, followed by an equally protracted marathon with a number of those fine ladies, who, lured by the evidence of their lorgnettes, have been curious to test the veracity of its fabled powers of endurance, have left him somewhat the worse for wear. The odds on his winning lengthen in exact proportion to the amount that his famed protuberance is shrinking.

"You have such fortitude, Barbara." Baroness Mosley is at her friend's side.

"Elizabeth."

The two dowagers exchange a formal curtsey.

"The Major humiliates you so publicly."

"Whereas you, I imagine, must suffer your husband's peccadilloes in private?"

Baroness Mosley opens her mouth to reply but then thinks better of it. Her husband, the Baronet Sir John Parker Mosley, is well known for his oft-proclaimed recent spiritual conversion, since when he has frequently, and noisily, denounced all carnal pleasures, yet has sired eight children with the Baroness. A failed hatter, he inherited the manorial estates of Manchester from a second cousin, the Reverend Sir Nicholas Mosley who had never married, preferring instead the company of young boys whom, it was rumoured, he paid to sprinkle cold ashes from his parlour hearth over his pale mushroom-like body, before administering as many lashes as he could bear with a knotted rope. The new Baronet, Sir John Parker, now divides his time between his very public rivalry with the Reverend Cornelius Bayley, who, having been turned down for the living of the Methodist Hall on Oldham Street, where Sir John Parker has been a fierce advocate of further separation from the Anglican Establishment, has turned turtle and purchased for himself and his heirs the new church of St James on the corner of George and Charlotte Streets, its spire as tall as it neighbouring mill chimney, and his more private communion with the pigs who root in his manorial pastures in Colleyhurst, a fifty acre tract of once common grazing, where the farmers of Manchester send their pigs to gorge on windfalls each autumn at a cost of sixpence per pig, a third of which goes to the swineherd and the remaining two thirds to the estate. Sir John Parker, it is rumoured, likes to dress up as the swineherd and lie down with the pigs beneath the apple trees, an act lasciviously decried by Bayley from his pulpit, the bitter rift between the two former friends now widening into a chasm.

"I believe we understand one another perfectly, Elizabeth," remarks Barbara as her fallen warrior lies spreadeagled and unconscious at her feet.

"I believe we do," smirks the Baroness, looking down at the heaving carcass of her friend's libertine husband. "Was it not Dr Johnson who remarked, '*A man is not on oath in lapidary inscriptions*'?"

"I'm sure it was," replies Barbara. "That man is always saying something, especially if there is someone at hand to commit it to paper." With a casual, much practised gesture she lays a cloak, handed to her by a servant surreptitiously for the purpose, dismissively over her husband's nakedness, who continues to snore in smiling oblivion. "These gentlemen of ours," she continues, "whose public reputations we strive to protect, while their private actions do untold ruin to our own, have positions to maintain nevertheless, and it falls on us, whether we like it or no, to support them in this task."

"Admirable sentiments, Barbara, but I believe such a course of action is easier for you than it is for me."

Mistress Minshull, looking down upon her drunken husband, now farting in rhythmic concert with his bellowing snores, each competing with the other as to which can be the louder, raises a rueful eyebrow. "How so?"

"Your husband at least has a catalogue of notable achievements to his name."

"I take it you are referring to his role at the Great Siege of Gibraltar?"

"For which he received Royal acclamation."

"Yet now, like the Rock itself, he lies here immovable."

"At least he does not pretend to be other than he is."

"His maternal grandfather was Robert Rollo, the Jacobite."

"As were many here in Manchester."

"He does not boast of this, however."

"One is not obliged to follow in the footsteps of one's forebears."

"Or repeat their mistakes."

"Yet change still comes."

The two women survey the creep of Manchester marching to meet them even here, on the edge of the moor, as the race for the Kersal Cup is roared home. A new victor is presented with the laurel. Though not yet a changing of the guard.

Barbara and Elizabeth part, Elizabeth to her five daughters silently embroidering in the sequestered shadows of Ancoats Hall, while Barbara escorts her whimpering boy, her spanking

Roger, back to Hough Hall in Moston, which she has gifted to him for his private pleasures, where this great bear can lick his wounds before re-entering the fray.

Which he is ready to do as early as that evening.

He arrives in full military uniform, accompanied by his entourage, seemingly none the worse for wear, the earlier insults to his pride forgotten, outside *The Britons' Protection*, on Great Bridgewater Street, ready to tear up the town and take on all comers.

Already inside, celebrating his victory in this year's Kersal Cup, is Leigh Philips. Now twenty-four years old, he is a young man in a hurry. His tactics for winning the day's race were simple. Not for him the waiting game, picking off his rivals in a kick finish. Nor the role of spoiler, impeding his competitors' progress by fair means or foul. He simply hit the front as soon as the flag was lowered for the race to begin and led from gun to tape, finishing a full fifty yards ahead of the rest. Now he is intent on beating his rivals again in the back room of *The Britons' Protection*, where he raises a yard of ale to his lips. He aims to drink more of them, and more quickly, than anyone else. This particular yard glass holds two and a half pints. He downs the first in a single draught in just eight seconds.

Just as he lowers it, wiping the excess foam from his mouth with the back of his hand, he notices, flailing around in the last few remaining dregs in the rounded bulb at the base of the glass, a drowning fly. He recognises it at once. A common blow fly. *Calliphora vomitoria*. That good old faithful, the bluebottle. Or bottlebee, as Sir Ashton had called it on the night of the Earthquake, when his whole collection had escaped from its *vivarium*. Bottlebee. He prefers that too. As if it contains its own distinctive sting that won't give up without a fight. He tips it out onto the palm of his left hand, then with the thumb and forefinger of his right, he picks it up by its wings and brings it right up close to his face.

"Hello there," he smiles, as if to an old friend, which in a way it is. "Got ourselves a little bit lost, have we?" He grins, looks around at his drinking companions, who are regarding him with puzzlement, then promptly pops it into his mouth and swallows it whole. What better way to go for a fly, he thinks, than in the bed of bile and shit that awaits it deep within his gut?

Leigh no longer has a *vivarium*. His mother had put her foot down and his father had stood by her. "She has a point, you know, Leigh," he had said, sitting on the side of his bed the morning after the Earthquake, while soothing poultices of chamomile, oats and honey were being applied to his sore and swollen face, blistered with the bites and stings he had received from the swarm. "The ladies have more refined sensibilities than we do, my boy, and we must defer to their superiority in this."

Leigh had said nothing, luxuriating instead in the cooling touch of the poultice.

"They only seek to civilise us," his father continued, "by appealing to our better natures, and we must indulge them in this, what?"

"Yes, Father," he just about managed to croak. "But what of my collection?"

"Of course, my boy. You must resume it at once. As soon as you are strong enough. But no living specimens this time. Trap 'em, smoke 'em, make 'em drowsy, then pin 'em to a board."

"Yes, sir. Thank you, sir."

"That's the spirit."

"All neatly labelled in Latin, sir, according to species and *genus*."

"Capital. We might stump up for some mahogany display cases. Even your mother'll consent to look at 'em if they're behind glass."

Leigh's eyes widened, imagining them already. "Thank you," he whispered.

"There's still no better opening gambit for attracting the ladies, you know?"

"Father?"

" 'Would you like to come up and see my collection'?" He roared with laughter, as much at the embarrassment on his son's face that his remark had caused as the actual content of it. "Now you get some rest, my boy, and tomorrow we shall discuss this further."

Whether he meant about the mahogany case for his collection, or other ways of attracting members of the fairer sex to consent to sit alone with him, he never discovered, for his father never appeared to have the time to resume either conversation. It was his mother who had presented him with the first of what now comprised more than a dozen display cases on the morning of his next birthday, although she has never requested to examine their contents, nor has he invited her…

Feeling the *calliphora vomitoria* now wriggling down his oesophagus, he smiles as he remembers once more the ferocity of the swarm as they attacked him out on the Daub Holes on the night of the Earthquake almost eight years ago, the way each individual fly had conjoined in their thousands, bound by a single common purpose, the survival of their species. Instinctively they had latched onto where he was his most vulnerable, his face, and ruthlessly exposed his weakness, crawling up his nose, drilling down his ears, prising past his lips and teeth, amassing in his throat, gorging and choking him, biting into his scalp, until at last the smoke of so many fires overwhelmed them, and they could simply be brushed away, knocked aside, with a casual flick of the fingers, and tumble to the ground, where, no longer a swarm, but a seething mass of disunited, teeming individual entities, floundering in the dark, their wings torn off, their bodies heavy with fatigue, their legs stuck fast in their own secretions, and their five compound eyes, each with their thousands of monitors able to detect the tiniest of vibrations in every direction simultaneously in a near three-sixty sweep, now almost blind, seeing only the dank, infected ground into which they sank and perished. But even in their final moments they sought out one last death throe coupling, each female seeking a male, into whose genital opening, located at the tip of his abdomen, she might insert her ovipositor, a long thin tube which would receive the last of the male's sperm she required to fertilise her eggs. Her final act would see her release up to five hundred fertilised eggs into whatever garbage she had alighted upon to give birth and to die. Three days later, long after the flies' corpses had been feasted on by the wheeling flocks of starlings, the eggs would hatch into maggots and begin to feed on the waste into which they had been born.

And so they had grown to form the start of Leigh's next collection. Trap 'em, smoke 'em, make 'em drowsy, as his father had predicted. Then starve 'em of air, suffocate 'em, pin 'em to a board, before being able, at leisure, to embark on his favourite part of the process, the identifying, categorising, labelling and displaying, each in their correct place and position. He has examples now of more than a hundred different species he has found in Manchester alone, with new ones arriving each month, just waiting to be recognised and assimilated.

"This is all very fine," comments his father over dinner one evening, "in its way, as a hobby, a gentleman's pursuit, but we are not gentlemen, not in the truest sense, are we, Leigh?"

"We live like gentlemen," says Leigh, "finer than many. We have more money."

"Only if one looks at us in a certain light. We are cash rich, but land poor. Whereas gentlemen such as Sir John Parker Mosley, Sir Ashton Lever, and others of their ilk…"

"Lord Stanley, the Earl of Wilton, the Duke of Bridgewater…?"

"Precisely so…"

Leigh pours himself a second glass of port, an action not unnoticed by his father, who continues his train of thought nevertheless. "… they are…"

"Cash poor but land rich," butts in Leigh, downing his port in a single swallow.

"I was going to say," corrects his father, "titled."

"One can buy a title," says Leigh dismissively.

"Indeed one can," replies his father, "but it is not the same as a lineage that stretches back to the time of Elizabeth."

"Which ours does not?"

"Which ours does not."

"Times are changing, Father. The old guard must be swept aside if they continue to prove a drain on the country's resources."

"You should watch your tongue, my lad. Such talk is dangerous. It could be regarded in some quarters as seditious, traitorous even."

"On the contrary, Father. I'm as patriotic as it's possible to be. I simply meant that their position is maintained by heredity alone. They regard their lot as an unquestioned entitlement, no matter how deeply in debt they fall, while we have had to work hard for our position in society – or rather you have. I have yet to make my mark."

"Indeed you have not, and that is what I wished to speak with you about this evening."

Leigh reaches for the port bottle again. His father puts a restraining hand on his arm. "I think you've had quite enough for one evening."

Leigh scowls but acquiesces. He sits back, knowing what is about to follow.

"I don't disagree with you that times are changing. Your uncles and I have managed to secure certain positions of influence over time – Thomas as Chair of Magistrates for Stockport, Nathan as a Justice of the Peace for Lancashire, myself as Deputy Lieutenant for Cheshire – but these are mere sops to the fact that we are in a position to bank roll our so-called betters. The real power – the Lords Lieutenant, the High Sheriffs, the Boroughreeves – these are all Crown appointments, and as such will not be bestowed on the likes of us."

"Not yet."

"And not for some while yet, I fear, but in the meantime we must continue to exert what leverage we can by subtler means."

"The power behind the thrones?"

"That's one way of putting it, yes. And so it is imperative, Leigh, that we find a suitable position for you, one which enables us to continue our ascent of rank and privilege undetected, until such time as Manchester is granted municipal status, with all the necessary new legislative powers which will accompany that, affording us more outwardly visible ways by which our financial contributions to the health and well being of the body politic may be more publicly recognised and prominently rewarded."

"I don't follow."

"Positions with genuine capacity for power and influence."

"Such as?"

"The replacement of the Boroughreeve with an elected Town Council, the creation of Police Commissioners controlled by a Chief Constable, a more modern judicature with judges and magistrates under local civic supervision – all of them areas in which sovereignty might pass into hands better suited to administer it."

"Hands like ours?"

"And others like us, yes. We already control the Exchange. It is simply a matter of logic for such control to pass from the economic to the political. A redistribution of wealth, power and status based on merit rather than on birth."

"Who is the one talking sedition now?"

John Philips smiles. He trims a cigar which he offers to his son. "I'm not talking Non-Conformism here, nor Dissent. I have always maintained that it is better to work for reform from within, rather than agitate from without. We are loyal subjects of His Majesty, firm believers in the Church of England. We are part of the Establishment working patiently and peacefully towards change, rather than Radicals or Revolutionaries."

"Political representation at Westminster would go a long way to achieving many of your goals, Father. Would you have me stand for Parliament?"

"Elsewhere perhaps, but not here in Manchester. Such a position will not occur in our lifetimes. Let us not think of running before we have scarcely begun to walk."

"What then?"

"Traditionally a gentleman would choose between either the military or the church."

"But you have already said, I am not a gentleman."

"Not in their definition of the term, no. Nor in mine yet either."

Leigh looks away, his cheeks reddening.

"That is an honour you must earn."

"How?"

"Through your actions."

Leigh sulks and says nothing.

"You could of course enlist for a soldier – if that is what you wish – but not as an officer. You would be forced to climb the ranks one at a time. I doubt you possess the patience for that."

"Could you not procure me a commission?" asks Leigh, regretting his words almost before he has finished speaking them.

His father throws him a withering look. "Hast tha' heard nowt o' what I've been saying regarding merit?" he snaps, his more humble origins laid bare in this sudden reverting of his language to that of his own father, who had first crossed the threshold from farm labourer to mill owner when he founded the firm of *Philips & Lee, Cotton Supplies*.

"I'm sorry, Father."

"And I think we can both agree that you possess neither the temperament nor the calling required to enter the Church?"

"Yes, Father." He waits. He knows what's coming.

"Therefore I propose that you come to work with me and learn every single aspect of the business…"

"Haberdashery?" says Leigh, rolling the word around his tongue with an incredulity and contempt he is unable to conceal.

"Cotton, inkle and tape," continues his father through thinly pursed lips. "So that one day, perhaps, you may take over from me."

Leigh watches the smoke from his almost finished cigar coil towards the ceiling. He considers the weight of it, this smoke, then transfers his gaze to the small mountains of ash which lie scattered about him. He wonders how long each would take to decompose?

"Well?"

"Thank you, Father. I shall give your most generous proposal a great deal of careful thought and then get back to you in due course."

John Philips stubs out his own cigar butt decisively. "You start tomorrow morning. Be ready to depart at seven. Good night." He stands up and leaves the smoking room without a further word.

Leigh waits until he has heard his father retire upstairs, then heads straight out into the yard. He saddles up his horse and rides directly for the snug of *The Britons' Protection*.

That was three days ago.

Leigh has not been home since. Let his father root him out, if he must. He spits out the remains of the last dregs of the yard of ale, which have been swirling round his mouth. He is filled with a mixture of disdain and disgust. Disdain for the pettiness of the haberdashery trade. Disgust for his own pathetic reliance on the generosity of the allowance bestowed on him by his father derived from the profits of that trade, which Leigh has had no qualms in accepting. Until now. For three nights he has caroused in the company of soldiers, listened with envy to their tales of honour and adventure. The spoils of war, the laurels of victory. One of which he wears now, presented to him after his victory in today's Kersal Cup. He balances it ridiculously on his brow, tilted at what he considers a rakish angle, until he catches sight of his reflection in the smeared mirror behind the bar of the tavern, which appears dissolute and bloated, so that he flings it to the floor, where he treads it into the sawdust.

He hears a voice whisper in his ear.

" '*Uneasy lies the head that wears the crown...?*' "

Leigh wheels round, knocking over a bar stool as he does so. He lurches straight into the barrelled chest of Roger Aytoun. Fully clothed now in his Major-General's uniform, he cuts a towering and impressive figure. Leigh staggers away from him towards the door, which is blocked by two of the Major's subalterns. Leigh veers back into the centre of tavern, where he is intercepted by two more. They each take one of Leigh's arms, which they pin behind him, while the other two flank their Commanding Officer, who now approaches Leigh. He lowers his face until it is almost directly touching Leigh's.

"Looking for a way out?" he sneers.

Leigh ceases struggling. How does he know, he wonders? Has he, or one of his lieutenants, been eavesdropping? Leigh has made no secret these last three days of his desire to join the military.

As if reading his mind, Major-General Aytoun steps back. He studies the figure of Leigh standing before him with a detached curiosity, not unlike the way Leigh would examine a new species of fly. But whereas Leigh would then be content to place the specimen carefully behind glass, Aytoun looks as though he might swat Leigh aside at any moment and squash him against it.

Instead he says, "Be careful what you wish for."

He signals to his lieutenants to release their grip on Leigh, who shrugs them away, as he tries to muster some small thread of dignity and self respect. This is the Major-General's turf. This is his patch. *The Britons' Protection.* Where he seeks out new recruits. But his methods are somewhat unconventional. Not for him the subterfuge of the press. If he spots someone who he thinks he might take a chance on, who has all the makings of a fine young officer, he challenges him there and then to a boxing contest. Leigh has heard these rumours but, until this moment, he has not believed them.

"Take him out back," commands Aytoun, and at once two of the subalterns escort Leigh to the stable yard behind the inn. "See that he is ready for me." They salute him as one, about turn, then march Leigh outside. The other two young officers immediately proceed to assist the Major-General with the removal of his redcoat jacket and shirt. Before he steps outside, Roger Aytoun inspects himself in the same smeared mirror behind the bar. It reveals a man back in his element. A broad grin spreads across the face of his reflection, followed by a wink, before he strides out to join Leigh in the yard, where an expectant crowd has now gathered, many of them keen supporters of Leigh, having cheered him home earlier that day in the Kersal Cup.

"The rules are simple," pronounces Aytoun, marking out a square with the heel of his right boot as he measures the space where the bout will take place. One of his officers stands at each corner, encouraging the crowd to fill in the spaces in between them, ensuring that nobody crosses the line in the dirt marked out by the Major-General. "We shall observe Broughton's Rules. No grasping, grappling, gouging or punching below the waist. Hitting an opponent who is already down is outlawed. Anyone disregarding this will be immediately disqualified. If a contestant is legitimately knocked to the ground, the crowd shall begin a count to thirty. If the person does not rise until after that figure has been reached, he shall be deemed to have been knocked out. The last man standing shall be declared the winner. Understood?"

"Yes, sir."

"If I am the victor, no more will be said about your discourteous behaviour this evening…"

"And if I win…?"

The four young officers bray with laughter but are silenced with a stern rebuking glance from the Major-General.

"I like your spirit already. If you prevail, I shall accept you to join the ranks of my subordinate officers." Aytoun notices at once the fire ignite in Leigh's eyes upon hearing this. He goes closer to him and adds, in a voice only Leigh can hear, "And what's more, I'll make you a Captain."

Leigh nods.

"Agreed?"

"Yes, sir."

"Then may the better man win."

They butt their fists smartly into one another, like two stags ready for the rut, then retreat to opposite corners of the square, while the crowd excitedly counts down from ten to one for the bout to begin.

Leigh realises at once that his only chance will be to keep moving. Aytoun is nearly a head taller than he is, with almost twice the girth. The monarch of the glen to his upstart young buck. The first punch he throws is cuffed contemptuously aside, the force of it knocking him off balance and almost sending him to the ground, which would have been fatal, for Aytoun would have stood over him while he regained his feet, ready to release a combination of blows as ferocious as a twelve-tined set of antlers, a true imperial. He just about manages to stay upright, dancing on the balls of his toes, ducking beneath Aytoun's slower, more lumbering reach. He adopts the tactic of launching a series of lightning raids, darting in and out, landing quick fire blows to the Major's body, before smartly retreating. In themselves these have little impact, but cumulatively they begin to take their toll, winding Aytoun and frustrating him. He lowers his head, his foot pawing the ground, as if to make a direct attack upon Leigh, but Leigh is again too fast for him, flicking out a left and then a right, mere glancing blows, bouncing off the side of Aytoun's hammer head, but bloodying his nose nevertheless. The monarch of the glen throws back his head, emitting a bellowing roar, outraged by Leigh's precociousness. His blood is up now and he wants nothing more than to pin his puny opponent to the ground and pluck off his wings one by one, like a bothersome fly, but Leigh remains a step ahead of him, both in thought and action. He understands that eventually his own stamina will wane, that his feet will slow, and that when they do it is likely that Aytoun will finally catch up with him. It will only take him a single blow to send him crashing to the ground, from which he will not be able to climb back up. Somehow he has to try and defeat Aytoun before his speed, his only advantage, deserts him. He begins to dance backwards, lightly around the square, like a travesty of a gavotte he might attempt in *The Assembly Rooms* on Labrey's Fold, mocking Aytoun, deriding him, goading him with taunts and jibes, claiming that not only was he too fat and slow to keep up with him in the Kersal Cup, but that he would never catch him even in the confined space of the yard behind

The Britons' Protection. How will he protect the nation, sneers Leigh, if he cannot even protect himself? This is too much for Aytoun. He propels himself with all the force he can muster at the mincing, minuetting Leigh, who, at the very last moment, dodges to one side, catches Aytoun a stinging blow to the side of his head, so that this, combined with the Major-General's own unstoppable momentum, sends him crashing to the hard ground, head first, knocking himself out cold. The crowd counts disbelievingly to thirty, a stunned Aytoun is unable to get back to his feet, and Leigh is hoisted on high by his supporters, who parade him jubilantly round the yard, through the tavern and out into the thronging Great Bridgewater Street beyond, where it joins with the Dean's Gate.

After completing a full circuit he is carried back inside *The Britons' Protection*, where he is met by a now revived and dressed Major-General Aytoun. "Welcome to The Manchester Volunteers. You'll find us rough but ready, sir. Let me present you to your fellow junior officers."

One of his Subalterns steps forward.

"This is 1st Lieutenant Joseph Hanson. He will be your brother-in-arms. He will accompany you forthwith to your new quarters at the Barracks in Castlefield. Lieutenant Hanson – Captain Leigh Philips."

"Your servant, sir."

Leigh acknowledges Lieutenant Hanson's welcome with an unpractised salute, noting the involuntary pulse that twitches the side of his temple. He is furious, thinks Leigh. He feels slighted, passed over, that he, Leigh, an untrained soldier, who has been recruited to join on the whim of Spanking Roger, as he is known around the town, for having accepted and won a fair, if unconventional challenge that was laid down, has been promoted ahead of him. Captain outranks Lieutenant.

"If you will follow me, Captain?"

Leigh, delighted at the way the evening has turned out, salutes the Major-General once more and proceeds to accompany Lieutenant Hanson. He has the measure of this man.

Leigh does not return again to the house of his parents on Lever's Row, except on one occasion, a few days later, when he calls round at a time that he knows his father will be absent, to bid farewell to his mother and to arrange for the collection of his display cases. At the end of the week he will hope to ride with his new company south to Portsmouth, under the joint command of Majors-General Roger Aytoun and David Lindsay of the 72nd Foot, from where he will set sail for Gibraltar.

Fifty-Seven Men Are Wanted
to COMPLEAT the
72nd REGIMENT of FOOT
or
Royal Manchester Volunteers

For which SIX GUINEAS will be given to any Man
Five feet Six inches tall
and a Guinea more per Inch thereafter.
The Regiment is to be reviewed by
Major-General **ROGER AYTOUN**
in the presence of Major-General **DAVID LINDSAY**
on Monday 30th March Inst
in **CASTLEFIELD, MANCHESTER**
and is afterwards to be received by **HIS MAJESTY**
on their March to **Portsmouth**
where they are to embark for **GIBRALTAR**
the Best Garrison in His Majesty's Dominion.

At Gibraltar Every Man will, besides his pay, have
the following Weekly Allowance of Provisions,
viz:
3ibs of Beef
2lbs of Pork
7lbs of White Bread
3 Pints of Peas
3 Pints of Oatmeal
10 oz of Butter

All fine, well-built Young Fellows (not more than 57 in number) who wish to serve their Country in the Royal Manchester Volunteers, are desired to apply to the Commanding Officer of the Regimental Rendezvous immediately, as it is expected that the Regiment will be compleat and be ordered to march in a week to ten days.

*

Thursday 10th

Mr Carlton Whiteley, grandson of Mr James Whiteley, founder of The Manchester Company of Actors, more widely known as 'Mr Whiteley's Men', despite the fact that they had employed actresses for almost a century, heard the bell of the Collegiate Church toll the half hour and checked the time against his own pocket watch, also inherited from his grandfather, which he withdrew from his waistcoat. He frowned. The church bell was consistently slow, while his own watch, recently modified by Mr Edward Gadd of Cheadle to incorporate the latest *lever* escapement, a refinement of its former *cylinder* escapement developed by Monsieur Louis Breguet of the Prussian principality of Neuchâtel, which laid claim to keep accurate time to within less than a minute a day, and which was subsequently adopted by all of Europe's leading watchmakers, among whose number Carlton counted Mr Gadd, revealed to him that the true time was now fast approaching twenty before the hour of three o' clock, the appointed hour at which their matinee performance of Shakespeare's *Henry VI, part 2* was scheduled to commence, yet his theatre was still less than half full.

As if Shakespeare was not a sufficient risk to begin with, the Histories were notoriously difficult to sell, except for *Richard III* of course, which was a perennial favourite, but which they had played only last season, yet he had been persuaded, against his better judgement it would now appear, to present these least performed sections of the canon because of the anti-French feelings that were running so high among the people just now. Their patriotic tone struck a chord with the times, he had thought, with its close examination of the nature of kingship, a notion the French seemed all too happy to abandon, if the rumours coming from across the Channel were to be believed, but for once it looked as though his instincts, usually so finely in tune with popular taste, had let him down.

Unless more people arrived in the final quarter hour before curtain up, he was likely to take quite a hit, and he might be forced to consider reviving those lamentable sentimental comedies by Mrs Carroll, for whom the public seemed to have an insatiable appetite – *Love's Contrivance, A Woman Keeps a Secret, A Wife Well Managed, The Artifice*. He thought ruefully of his own wife, Henrietta, who was far from well managed and who would, he was certain, have a word or six to say to him about the failure of his Shakespearean folly. It was the theatre's worst kept secret that it was Mrs Whiteley, not Carlton, for all his outward bombast, who wielded the power backstage, for it was she who contrived the purse strings, not he, and what love there may once have been between them had long been consigned to artifice.

But was not that the very essence of their profession? Artifice? Their entire enterprise was built on *maquillage*, on sleight of hand, and they might yet salvage hope from adversity. Why, did his grandfather not grasp the nettle, when, faced with not one, but two rival companies, from Drury Lane no less, who attempted to trespass on his patch to present Mr Addison's *Cato* to celebrate the coronation of King George III, reputedly His Majesty's favourite play – for it was well known he had appeared in it himself when aged just ten to speak the Prologue, "*What, though a boy, it may with truth be said, a boy in England born and bred*"? – and, when denied permission by the Boroughreeve, to whom his grandfather had had to offer a not inconsiderable remuneration, had not only set their stage within the grounds of Lady Mary Clowes of Broughton Hall, which in those days extended down Water Lane as far as the banks of the Irwell, but in addition, in a bid to enable audiences to patronise them, had also hastily constructed a wooden footbridge across the river? And did he not also offer the hand of friendship across the foaming waters to suggest a union between rivals, an act of both generosity and foresight, resulting in their continued presence in the Riding School, with playgoers still making their way across the same bridge to this day? Except that on this particular day very few of them seemed to be directing the passage of their feet towards them.

There was nothing for it. He would have to hold the curtain a further fifteen minutes, explaining to those members of the public already assembled and waiting, that there had been a slight, unforeseen technical hitch, begging their forbearance and indulgence *et cetera, et cetera*, while he rustled up a few boys to round up the usual scallywags loitering backstage in the hope of catching sight of the actresses' legs and persuade them to take up some of the empty seats in the stalls. It pained him to paper the house in this way, but needs must. Desperate times called for desperate measures, as Erasmus so wisely said. Or was that Hippocrates? What did it matter? Quote with confidence, that had always been his grandfather's watchword, and in this, as in all things, Carlton would strive to follow.

Then, when the later starting time had been reached and he knew he must delay no longer, there was a sudden last minute surge of latecomers – Sir Ashton Lever and his not inconsiderable entourage – who poured noisily into the theatre to discover the papered extras had taken their seats. Arguments ensued, scuffles threatened to break out. It was only the timely intervention of his wife, Mrs Whiteley, a renowned exponent of breeches roles, dressed in her tightly fitting corset and silk knee-length pantaloons for the role of Joan of Arc, *La Pucelle*, who, revived as a Ghost and ready to perform the specially written Prologue for her by Carlton himself in a manner, though modesty might forbid him from saying so directly, was, in his humble opinion, indistinguishable from the iambic pentameters of the Bard himself, in order to acquaint the audience with what they needed to know from Part 1 to be able to pick up the story as it unfolded in Part 2, launched instead into an impromptu version of Justice Shallow's song from another of the Histories, *Henry IV, part 2*, which averted disaster and restored peace and harmony among her ardent admirers.

> *"Do nothing but eat and make good cheer*
> *And praise God for the merry year*
> *When flesh is cheap and females dear*
> *And lusty lads roam there and here*
> *So merrily*
> *And ever among so merrily…"*

Mrs Whiteley saved the day. Not for the first time Carlton was reluctantly forced to thank his good fortune.

The play receives a mixed reaction. The battle scenes, as ever, prove popular, provoking much cheering, while the various executions, which pepper the final act, are mixed with audible gasps of shock that gratify Carlton greatly. It is a pity, therefore, that Mrs Carroll, who plays Queen Margaret of Anjou, Henry's wife, and who carries with her the head of her lover, William de la Pole, the 4th Earl of Suffolk, which has been sent back to her after he has been killed by pirates while on his way to exile in France, should drop it in the final scene, causing much mirth among the audience, just when they should have been experiencing the play's full cathartic force. Carlton wonders if she has been drinking again. He will have to have a word with her afterwards. She really should consider retiring, but he knows she will never agree to any such suggestion. Old actresses never die, he muses, they simply lose the plot. He must try to see if he might persuade Mrs Whiteley to give up her breeches roles in favour of these great tragediennes – not just Margaret of Anjou, but Gertrude, Volumnia, Cleopatra – but he must broach this carefully, or she might accuse him of thinking she no longer has the legs for the Violas, Imogens and Rosalinds.

But at least Sir Ashton Lever showed up and applauded long and loud afterwards. That could have been because he was wallowing in his cups throughout. Frequently he was to be heard haranguing the actors, at one point alerting young Mr Grealish, in his first outing as Alexander Iden, a Gentleman of Kent, as to the whereabouts of Jack Cade, leader of the common people's revolt in favour of Richard, Duke of York, when he is hiding in his garden.

"He's behind you!" he called out helpfully, to which Mr Grealish gallantly returned with his thanks, before dispatching the hapless Cade with his sword, placed with rather too deliberate a show of care and precision beneath Cade's armpit.

Carlton tries to intercept Sir Ashton before he can leave. He needs to press him for some much needed sponsorship. He has a little speech prepared. "My liege," he will say, "would you do this poor player who struts and frets his hour upon the stage the peerless honour of allowing him to name his humble rag-tag of rude mechanicals after Your Lordship? I give you 'Lord Lever's Company'." Then he will remove his hat with a flourish and bow with great ceremony.

"The honour is all mine," he imagines Sir Ashton replying.

"I thank you, Sir. When I say 'give', Your Lordship, you understand that I speak metaphorically?"

"I believe we understand each other perfectly," Sir Ashton will answer. "Name your figure."

Carlton inclines his head modestly. "Perhaps…?" And he presses a piece of paper into the Lord's gloved hand on which is written a sum of money he knows he dare not name out loud.

Sir Ashton waves it away. "No sooner said than done, Mr Whiteley. Come, let us shake hands…"

The scene evaporates before Carlton's eyes, taking place only in his mind, not in reality, for Sir Ashton is in his cups precisely because he has just the hour before learned that his house in London's Leicester Square is to be sold off, his *Holophusicon* to be divided up and scattered to the four corners, his hopes of bringing it back in triumph to Alkrington Hall dashed, and he leaves with no memory of having earlier agreed to speak to the Whiteleys after the performance. Carlton faces his wife crestfallen.

Elsewhere in the auditorium a different reflection is taking place.

The three Thomases from *The Manchester Literary & Philosophical Society* are in great excitement.

"I did not care for the production," declares the first of them – Thomas Perceval.

"Nor I," says the second – Thomas Barnes.

"Too much pandering to populism," affirms the third – Thomas Henry.

"Bombast, bathos and beheadings," pronounces Perceval.

"But the Cade Rebellion..." interjects Barnes, raising an eyebrow.

"Food for thought," agrees Henry.

"Plain fare honestly prepared," adds Perceval.

"With plentiful helpings for all," continues Barnes.

"We must speak with Oldham and Gore about this. It may be just the impetus we need in order to act," completed Henry.

"We have already waited too long," urges Perceval. He pauses, then plucks, as if from the air, the quotation from the play that has so palpably seized their collective imagination, impelling them to act. " '*Ignorance is the curse of God...*' " he begins.

" '*... Knowledge the wing wherewith we fly to heaven*'," the other two answer.

Clapping each other on the back, they make their way at once to the Cross Street Chapel to communicate their thoughts to their like-minded fellow society members, fired with a passion to begin a series of schools around the town – Sunday Schools and Evening Classes, schools for children and schools for their parents, where all will be taught to read, and the Bible will be their primer.

As they hasten through Manchester's unlit streets the five hundred yards between the Actors' Bridge and Cross Street Chapel, it feels as though the pavements beneath their feet become illuminated by their fervour, each of them recalling the angry words of Jack Cade.

"Thou hast appointed justices of peace, to call poor men before them about matters they were not able to answer. Moreover, thou hast put them in prison; and because they could not read, thou hast hanged them; when, indeed, only for that cause they have been most worthy to live…"

*

Jem's mother sits on the grimy step. It is many years since she last donkey stoned it. She has become indistinguishable from it. Feet, the hem of her skirt, apron, hands, face – all a featureless grey.

Some nights she is to be found with a bible on her lap, always open at the same much-thumbed, creased page. Proverbs: 31. It is not that she can read, merely that her eyes recognise the familiar shapes and patterns, which she traces with her finger, not looking, up and down, up and down, rocking back and forth, mumbling the oft-repeated passage over and over.

" *'Who can find a virtuous wife? For her worth is above rubies. The heart of her husband doth safely trust in her, so that he shall have no lack of gain. She does him good, and not evil, all the days of her life. She seeketh wool and flax, and worketh willingly with her hands in true delight. She is like the merchants' ships, for she bringeth food from afar. She riseth while it is yet light and prepareth food for her husband. She considers a field and purchases it. With the fruit of her hands she planteth an orchard. She girds herself with strength and makes her arms strong. She perceiveth that her merchandise is good, and that her lamp will never go out at night. She stretches out her hands to the distaff, and her hands grasp the spindle. She stretches out her hands to the poor and reaches forth unto the needy. She maketh fine linen and doth sell it. She doth deliver garments to the merchants. Dignity and honour are her clothing, and she shall rejoice in the time that is to come. Her children will arise and they will bless her'.*"

*

Friday 11th

The whole of Manchester lies wilting in the last of the summer's dog days. All the inhabitants of Omega Place seek the shelter of the high walls of Commercial Street, scrapping for what bit of shade each might find, bad tempered and hot, palms flapping, tongues lolling. The river is sluggish and ripe. Flies bask drugged in the ditches.

Only Whelp does not seem to mind. All seasons are the same to her. Just as the iron frost will scarcely reach her, nor her spirits droop when her body's drenched with spring rain, so this heat fits her like a second skin. She spreads herself out in its fierce glare. When the sun drops behind the ruin of heaped bricks in Fogg's Yard, she barely moves a muscle. She simply exchanges its last rays for the first of the moon, whose glow now bathes her in a green phosphorescence. She watches the stars rise, not knowing their names, only their shapes – the crab, the fish, the scales. She waits for one in particular, the brightest in the whole night sky. She recalls pointing to it one night, back in her old life, in the Hulks, and Septimus had looked down on her and smiled. Sirius, he had said. The dog star.

She sees it again now and points once more, remembering.

If the others in Omega Place notice her pointing, they do not comment. Mostly their gaze is clouded so they do not see the constellations as clearly as Whelp does. Their heads are filled with different questions. Will they be able to find food the next day? Will the Overseer open the windows in the mill tomorrow, for today the heat inside has been unbearable? One of the older women fainted over her row of spindles so that the machine had to be switched off. Angry voices were raised, until they realised that she had not fainted, she had died. Her body was carried outside where – presumably – it was dumped in the river. Then the machines were switched back on again.

Sleep comes hard and slow. Lovers are listless. Babies grow fractious. When it does come, at last, it does not smooth troubled brows or ease tired limbs. It brings broken dreams filled with bony fingers clutching round gasping throats, rusting chains tightening round shrunken ankles. Rodents scratch in the cellars. Foxes stalk in the shadows. Dogs howl at the moon.

But none of this touches Whelp. She traces the pinprick of light falling from Sirius into the yard, watches the millions of dust motes caught in its beam, dancing like cotton, and places herself directly within its beam. She likes the way it changes the colour of her skin. From grey to blue. She slowly rotates the fingers of her left hand into its penumbra. A moth alights upon the knuckle at its back. She patiently lets it settle. Its wings open, then close; open, then close; until finally they remain open. They are fringed with thousands of tiny, almost invisible hairs. Whelp feels the touch of them on her skin. The separate veins, held between each of the wings' paper thin membranes, stand silhouetted in the light of the star and, to Whelp's eyes, appear to be breathing. She has seen this moth, or ones like it, many times before. It is mostly white, peppered with dark, almost black spots. When basking against the trunk of a tree its markings blend in with the bark or lichen, making a perfect camouflage, but now that more and more trees are being cut down, they stand out that much more clearly. Whelp has seen blackbirds and starlings swoop upon them as they rest unsuspectingly on the walls of buildings. It will need to adapt if it is to survive.

She brushes it gently from the back of her left hand with the fingers of her right and watches it flutter drowsily down between the ruined heap she lies upon. She follows its flight until it disappears, lost among the narrow labyrinthine passages between the delicately balanced bricks, which constantly threaten to tumble and collapse. She feels them slip and slide, scrape and scratch, against one another every night she sleeps upon them, moulding her back to their shape-shifting contours, which hold her lightly, like a nest.

It's then when she sees it.

The bricks have changed position once again, emitting a deep rasping groan, a long exhausted sigh of hard baked clay and dried dust.

There, in one of the newly opened spaces, glinting from the centre of the hive, it winks at her in the last pool of starlight, which reaches down to where it has been waiting to be found, but no further, so that Whelp has to peer closer to make certain that what she has seen is real and not just a trick of the dog star. There – it has winked at her again before disappearing tantalisingly from view once more. Gold. A circle. A ring. Like an eye. The light from Sirius peels back the lid. Gold. The dull sheen of buried years feels the cold glow of a star nearly nine light years away and wakes to its touch.

Curious, Whelp stretches down a thin arm, down, down, down, through the delicate tracery and fretwork of scarcely balanced bricks, infinitesimally slowly lest she brings the whole fragile edifice tumbling down, burying the ring for who knows many more years. She is now so close to it she can almost feel the touch of it as she edges her fingers towards it, inch by inch, agonisingly slowly. At one point she feels it against her nail, almost loses it as it threatens to topple back into the darkness, out of sight and out of reach, but at the last moment she rescues it, manages somehow to lever it upright into a near vertical position, so that now she can see only its rim and the black hole it encompasses, the other side of which is just a void. It begins to teeter, first this then that way, from an outcrop of crushed brick. She stretches her arm as far as it will go, somehow squeezing her narrow shoulder through a gap so tight she fears she may not succeed in bringing it back without the whole pile crashing down upon her. Eventually the ring falls. Towards, not away, from her, and slips awkwardly onto the third finger of her left hand. She extracts her arm from the rubble, inch by painful inch, until at last she emerges free, into the sultry, starlit air of Omega Place, the ring safely enclosed within her fist.

She lifts it to the light, holds it between her thumb and forefinger to examine it more closely. A plain, simple band. A man's ring. She realises at once what it is and who it must have belonged to.

To quell any remaining doubts, she plunges head first, back into the heap of ruin, no longer caring what damage she might cause. As the tower of bricks collapses and falls and reconfigures, she just has time to glimpse what she fears has been lying there all the time. The fleshless bone of a severed hand, picked clean but intact, unmistakeable. Jem's father's. Doubtless the rest of him lies scattered further down.

The sound of the crashing bricks has brought out Jem's mother from inside the sepulchral cottage. She eyes Whelp darkly. Whelp clambers down from where she lies sprawled, walks across the parched flagstones of Fogg's Yard, and stretches out her hand towards her. Jem's mother sees the ring lying in the centre of Whelp's palm. She recognises it at once. Her eyes dart back towards Whelp, like a desperate, cornered animal, then with a lightning fast lunge, she snatches it from her, holds it up to her face, then scurries back inside, from where Whelp hears a howl of pain, a vixen who chances on the decomposed body of her dog.

As summer tips into autumn, and a cold wind begins to blow through Omega Place, sending up armies of dust devils in Fogg's Yard, the children stay outdoors. At night they huddle close to Whelp to catch what sleep they can.

One morning they return to find that the bloated belly of Ada Briggs has burst and maggots are writhing in the entrails. Some of the children cry, she might have been their mother, and now cling tighter than ever to Whelp.

The next day they follow her to the Mill, plunging down beneath the Hanging Ditch as if to Hamelin. Jem hires them all for piecers. Whelp shows them what to do, then returns to the Card Room, where she now works, having been promoted by Jem, to comb the fibres of the cotton, so they are smoothed of any knots or tangles.

Like her hair.

She has never cut it. In the Mill she ties it up, like the other women. When she lets it hang loose, it reaches down to the back of her knees.

Now, when she washes it back at Fogg's Yard, the children clamour around her, taking it in turns to comb it for her and hold the tresses up to the light.

Ada Briggs has not left Omega Place for sixteen years. She has not left the cellar for eight of those. Not since the night of the Manchester Earthquake. There are those who still blame her for its cause. She was gargantuan back then. Too wide for the narrow footpaths of Market Street Lane or even the Dean's Gate, she would walk down the centre of the town's highways and byways. Carts or wagons that found themselves behind her would be forced to wait till she turned into a side street before they could pass her by.

Now she is larger still. She lies prostrate in the cellar in Fogg's Yard, stretched out in her own filth. Her bones and joints have seized up over the years, so that she is no longer able to stand. Even if she wished it, she would not now be able to leave the confines of the cellar. The treacherous steps would not withstand her weight. The flimsy door frame is too narrow for her to pass through. She has become a whale.

She continues to expand, like blubber, like fermenting yeast. Her brood of children climb across her whenever they need to go out or come in. They clamber over her mountainous flesh, slither between her udderous breasts trying to find a safe footing, each puss-filled leaking nipple a precarious hand hold, if they are to avoid that cavernous mouth which threatens to consume whole anything that ventures too close. They wade knee deep through the sweating lagoons of lard and fat, grease and shit until they can reach the upper air.

Nobody knows just how many children there are. Least of all Ada. She lost count after twelve. Though she knows there have been more. Then there have been all the countless others she's been wet nurse to. Sometimes there might have been as many as six at a time rooting to latch on to her. She does not know what has become of any of them, only that after a while they are taken from her. A few might linger, suckling till they are four, or even five years old, but then someone will come and snatch these away too, flinging them on to a different midden .

But it was not always so. In the dark, permanent twilight of the Omega Cellars she sometimes transports herself back to a time before. When she was just a child herself.

Her father's huge hand enfolds her tiny one. They are walking along the banks of the Irk, an old Saxon word, her father tells her, named after the herds of roebuck that grazed close by. They still see them now, though not in such large numbers, more often small family groups, a child protected by a parent, as Ada feels this bright Sunday morning. The sun is behind them. Their two shadows stretch ahead of them as they walk, Ada's skittish and small beside her father's looming giant.

"Where are we going?" she asks. "To Chapel?"

Her father says nothing. He merely squeezes her hand a little harder.

Her mother has not come with them. She has stayed behind to look after the baby, who is sick and always grizzling. Her brother. She doesn't know his name, is not sure he has one even, for he is not expected to survive. None of her other siblings have. This one was born outside, in the lean-to shelter of branches fashioned by her father against a small hedge close to Angel Meadow. They have been living out in the open for several months now. Just as they begin to settle in one spot, gamekeepers from the manorial lands owned all around by the Mosley family intervene to move them on. They know her father, for he used to work with them on the Estate, and they are mostly sympathetic, but they have their orders to obey. Her father understands this, so he always complies. He has no wish to put his former colleagues in an awkward situation. He had been one of the blacksmiths for the Earl, looking after the horses who worked the outlying farms, and he had been granted a rough dwelling place for himself and his family alongside the forge in lieu of payment. Little more than a wooden shack it had at least kept them warm and relatively dry. It was the only home Ada had known. But there was no money, so for food they had to scrape by on what they could forage and find, a few eggs from the hen house, a rabbit or two, sometimes a pheasant if the Earl was feeling particularly generous after a good day's shoot. Fish were still plentiful then in the Irk – trout and tench, perch and chub – and eels by the bucketful. But these were off limits to all but the Earl. They all of them fished, though, usually at night, or when the Earl was away. But on the night in question Ada's father was caught by one of the Earl's cousins. A constable was summoned, an arrest was made, a trial was held. The facts of the case were clear cut. Ada's father made no attempt to deny that he had broken the law. How could he? He had been apprehended in the very act of lifting an eel, fat and wriggling, from the waters of the Irk in plain sight. A verdict of guilty was pronounced and the Magistrate duly passed without emotion or qualm the prescribed sentence: removal by axe of the offending hand.

Shorn of one hand, he was deemed no longer able to carry out his former duties as a blacksmith and was dismissed forthwith from service. As a direct consequence of this he lost the right to live in the dwelling adjoining the forge, since when he, his wife, Ada and the new baby had been forced to live where they could. This morning their latest lean-to was removed by a gang of farm labourers, under the watchful eye of the Estate Bailiff, and so now Ada finds herself walking along the lane towards the back of Mr Robert Tinker's *Grape & Compass Coffee House*, at the entrance to the recently opened Pleasure Gardens on Angel Meadow, grandly named *The Elysian Fields*, but universally known as Tinker's Hollow, after the nearby quarry.

"Where are we going?" Ada asks her father a second time.

Again, her father says nothing by way of reply, merely grips her hand tighter in his one remaining hand.

Behind the Coffee House a young gentleman is waiting. He leans nonchalantly against a fence, twirling a freshly picked buttercup between the thumb and forefinger of his left hand. He wears a blue Bath coat with wide lapels, a buff waistcoat, an off-white linen frilled shirt tied with a pale saffron silk cravat, a pair of buckskin trousers tucked into nut brown leather riding boots, topped with a black shellac opera hat, which he removes with a flourish with his right hand, which also sports a honey-coloured Malacca cane embossed in tortoise-shell overlaid with silver.

"*À votre service, Mademoiselle,*" he says, bowing before Ada, who bobs a neat curtsey back to him, as she has seen the fine ladies do in *The Elysian Fields*.

"*Enchanté*," he replies. He then proceeds to circle her, appraising her up and down, in the way she has observed other gentlemen eyeing up a prize filly in the blacksmith's yard when they lived at the Forge. He prods her lightly with his cane, behind her knees, beneath her elbow, across her back. He gently pokes the side of her waist. He lightly raises the hem of her skirt. Finally he stops directly in front of her. He tips up her chin, then places the buttercup against her throat.

"Does she like butter?" he croons. "Let us see, shall we?" He inspects the shadow of the flower against her skin, caresses her neck with its stem. "*Mais oui*," he exclaims, "I think she does."

He stands as close to her side as he can without actually touching her. "Do you know how old you are?" he asks. His voice slips into her ear like curdled cream.

"Yes, sir," she says. "I'll be twelve next Lammas."

He glances sharply back to her father, who nods briefly, once, then look away.

"*Parfaite*," he declares, tapping her behind smartly with his cane, before striding back towards her father.

Ada watches as the gentleman deposits a number of silver coins into her father's sole remaining palm. Her father involuntarily bites each one to test their true worth. The gentleman peels back his mouth's upper lip in a dismissive sneer, turns on his heel and walks back towards her.

"Up there," he commands, pointing to a narrow staircase at the back of the Coffee House, all pretence at flattery now gone. Above the door is a wooden sign with the name spelled out in tarnished gold paint, peeling away from its blistered blood-red background. *The Grape & Compass*.

Ada looks back towards her father, but he has already begun walking away from her. A cold chill passes through her. She suddenly knows what is about to happen. The gentleman will pluck his grape and she will lose her compass.

The scene is played out several times over the next few weeks. The actions are more or less the same. Her father walks her towards the rendezvous spot, her sparrow hand crushed in his huge ham fist, but now all curiosity is gone. She no longer asks where they are going. She does not need to be told. The locations may change. The upstairs room in *The Grape & Compass* is replaced by different rooms in different buildings. But the action which takes place in each is always the same. Ada no longer bothers to take in the details of her surroundings, or the appearance of the gentlemen. Their features may change but the look in their eyes when they are first presented with her – the prized filly, the dish of grapes – remains the same. One time she sees there is a mirror in the room in which she catches sight of herself. She is holding something in her hand which wriggles in her fingers like a fat, slippery eel, and she wishes it were *her* hand that was cut off instead of her father's.

Her father.

He no longer speaks to her. If, when she is returned to him afterwards, she should cry, he hits her, hard across her face, so she decides never to cry again. Instead she expectorates a gob of spit onto the back of his hand clenched tightly around the coins clamped in his fist. The money she has procured for him has found them a roof over their heads – of sorts. A cellar beneath a hastily thrown up cluster of mean dwellings below the level of the river. Omega Place. The last place. A damp, foul-smelling enclave of the desperate. The money also buys them food. Ada demands that she eats before he does. He acquiesces. She greedily devours this one piece of power she possesses. It is precious to her.

But her value is becoming less precious each time she is purchased. She is beginning to lose some of her lustre. The gentlemen prefer their fruit unpicked and she is becoming bruised. The clothes they now wear reflect a gradual descent down the rungs of the social and property ladder. None of them now twirls a buttercup under her chin to see if she likes butter. Instead her body more closely begins to resemble a tub of lard.

One morning she wakes to find her mother and baby brother lying dead beside her. Her mother had withdrawn deeper and deeper inside herself, no longer recognising either of her children any more. When Ada's father discovers the two cold lifeless bodies, picked out by a hard pitiless shaft of light from the low early sun, the only time its rays penetrated their dark underground lair, he drags them clasped around each other like limpets up the slimy cellar steps, then rolls them into the stinking, sluggish ditch the Irk has now become. Ada hears the distant, pathetic, small splash their bodies make as they are sucked below.

Her father does not return. She never sees him again. She leaves the shade of the cellar less and less, preferring not to be looked upon. But the gentlemen know where to find her, and still they come. No longer gentlemen. Now she is a hitching post for anyone who might need to scratch an itch.

Soon after that the babies come. So many she loses count. A brood, a litter, they swarm all over her, blindly nosing into every orifice, tugging at her, hanging from her, sucking, biting, swallowing. The strong survive, the runts perish, yet still they come, more and more of them, until, it seems, the whole town is overrun with all the new arrivals clamouring for work and sustenance, things she cannot give them.

And so she lies there, a bloated eel, seeking a dark corner to spawn, where her eggs might hatch.

And there she stays, until the week of the Whitsuntide Fair, when finally she has swelled to such a gargantuan size that were she to be tethered out in an open field, instead of wallowing within the confines of the sunless cellar, whose extremities she fills like fermenting yeast in a dark oven, and were those tethers to be cut loose, she might rise unstoppably and fly higher even than Mr Sadler's Balloon threatens to do, greater than any loaf of bread the former pastry cook may have ever baked in his former life, so that if she were pricked with a pin, she would simply burst and spiral out of control, the tattered, broken shreds of her covering the whole of the town with their offal and bile.

Instead she merely splits and cracks where she lies, creating yet another minor convulsion of the earth, so that the whole of Omega Place shifts and tilts, then reforms around her festering, spent and misused carcass.

*

And so, on a Friday evening in May, during the week of the Pentecost Fair in 1785, almost two years to the day since Whelp began working at Arkwright's Mill, she is making her usual way back along Long Millgate towards Omega Place, via the Apple Market. It is the end of the day and she hopes there will be the usual crop of thrown-away fruit lining the cobbles, underneath the carts, that she might avail herself of. Being the week of the Whitsun Fair, the streets are more crowded than customary. But it is all one to her. She can squeeze between the tightly packed stalls, weave through the press of already drunken crowds reeling unsteadily from one corner to the next, avoid being stepped on by the huge heavy horses, their harnesses jingling in the low evening sun, or leap aside for the unstoppable, trundling wagons, sometimes ducking beneath them as they pass her by. She emerges, as she always does, unscathed. Nobody sees her. Nobody touches her. She has perfected the art of being invisible.

She comes at last to the Apple Market. The barrow boys and traders are packing up for the end of the day. Rotting leaves and vegetation, mixed in with core and pith, peel and pip, lie ankle deep beneath her bare feet. She walks through them as easily as the rats that nose between each step she takes. Sometimes, in their snufflings, they unearth something shiny, which Whelp's eyes are always on the look-out for. She will pounce on them with an unerring aim. Sometimes her fingers plunge directly in and among a knot of rats, but they do not bother her. Each intent on their own scavenging, they ignore one other, for they recognise a rival when they encounter one, and neither threatens the other. They inhabit parallel worlds within the same universe.

In the far corner pigs are already rooting in the midden. Mostly they are ignored. Occasionally someone will walk into one of them unwarily and aim a resolute kick in its direction to clear a pathway through. The pig, once kicked, will grunt, reluctantly yield its ground, but only for a yard or so, possibly backing into another, so that a domino effect will ensue, the odd brief skirmish breaking out, before they each resume their purposeful foraging.

In amongst the drove Whelp catches sight of another small mound protruding from the rubbish. Immobile, partly covered in burlap, it resembles just one more spilled sack, but then, when someone empties a bucket of slops all over it, it moves. Whelp watches. It's a small boy. Something about him seems familiar, so she decides to take a closer look. Before she can reach him, he picks himself up and stumbles backwards over one of the pigs into where several others are noisily squabbling over scraps of bone and offal. Immediately the squabble intensifies and the boy is bitten and trampled on before finally managing to extricate himself from the heart of their rummage.

Whelp continues to watch. The boy's head has been recently shaved. There are cuts and scrapes along the scalp. He rubs his arm where one of the pigs has chomped him. Luckily the skin appears not to have been broken, but it is sore and tender to the touch. He briefly looks over his shoulder. Whelp sees his face. It is pale and trembling. Its cheeks are gaunt and hollow, streaked with dirt and tears, the eyes dark-ringed and sunk in their sockets. She sees it for less than a second, but that is all she needs to be certain. This is Mattie's lost twin. Alive. Though only just.

He does not see her. He does not appear to see anything. His eyes fix on the largest of the pigs in the square, hunkered against a low stone wall, an enormous sow that has barely an hour ago farrowed a litter of nine not yet weaned shoats, which blindly butt and bump each other in a frenzy to latch onto her teats. The boy regards this. A thought, as sudden and smart as a bullwhip, cracks inside his brain. He launches himself into the heart of the febrile shuntings of the litter and sucks hard on one of the sow's udders that suddenly presents itself, kicking aside the runt he has replaced. The sow shifts and squirms but allows him to feed.

Whelp watches.

A cold sweat prickles her skin.

A long buried memory tries to claw its way to the surface. It scrabbles for traction against the mud, slithering and sliding for a firm hand hold. A bloated leviathan of a body. A beached, barnacle-encrusted whaleskin of grease and blubber. But it slips from her. She feels the bile begin to rise from the pit of her stomach. She hears her throat widen and gag, a dry, empty retch. A taste she thought she had forgotten, sickly and sweet, fills her mouth. Prising up a rusty nail from a rotting plank in a stable door on the edge of the square, she scores it down her arm, a gridded thread of crimson that at once dispels the acid reflux from her mouth and forces her back into the present. She runs straight towards the heaving, writhing sow and pulls the boy sharply away, roughly dragging him towards Commercial Street before he has time to take in what is happening and try to resist. Even if he wanted to, he finds he cannot. The benefits of the sow's reviving milk are already leaving him. He hangs limply from this wild girl's vice-like grip around his arm and simply allows himself to be dragged behind her.

She drops down into Omega Place and from there worms her way through the low ginnel that leads into Fogg's Yard, where she deposits the boy beside the leaking water pump. Over the next half hour she proceeds to scrub every inch of him, not unlike the way, almost two years ago, Jem had done for her. Except that where Jem was tender and gentle, she is rough and hard. The boy makes no attempt to stop her. All the fight has seemingly left him. He lets her scrape and scour him until all her rage has left her and they can neither of them move another muscle.

A long time later, as the sun begins to leave the yard and a cool wind picks up from the river, someone hands her a piece of cloth. She looks up. It is Jem, back from his shift. He is staring down at her with an expression on his face she cannot interpret. It is something like love. She picks up the cloth and, as gently as she can, begins to dry and warm the shivering boy beside her.

Early the next day she takes him with her on her way to the Mill, shows him where he might find bread or fruit for later, if he's hungry, and instructs him to wait for her by the iron staircase after her shift ends.

When the bell rings at five o'clock, she runs down the stairs and finds him in exactly the same spot as where she left him some twelve hours before. She wonders if perhaps he has stayed there not moving all day, or whether he has dared to venture further afield in search of food and scraps. Looking at him, loyal and silent like a rescued puppy, she thinks the former. As they walk away from the Mill, without saying a word, he slips his hand into hers. Astonished, she finds she has allowed him to, and smiles.

They repeat this pattern for nearly a week. Then, on their way back to Fogg's Yard, a route that is now as familiar to him as the pattern of lines on the palm of his hand, he stops on the corner of Long Millgate. Pasted on a warehouse wall is a poster of a man waving as he ascends to the skies in a balloon. He tugs Whelp's sleeve and points.

Whelp looks at the poster also. Above her head a mustering of starlings is preparing to take flight, screeching with impatient excitement, waiting for the signal to lift off as one, shaking free of whatever constraints tether them to rooftops and towers, ledges and casements.

A well-dressed couple pass by. Whelp and Amos disappear into the warehouse wall. Over their heads, the couple pause to read what is written on the poster.

"In Haworth Gardens tomorrow, Mr James Sadler, the Celebrated Balloonist and Aeronaut, will attempt to sweep the cobwebs from the skies…"

Sweep the cobwebs from the skies. Whelp likes the sound of that.

She points back towards the poster and raises her eyebrows questioningly.

Amos jumps up and down in the same excited way as the starlings clamouring above him.

Whelp smiles and nods her head.

Amos skips away from her in a dance of unmitigated delight. At the same moment twenty thousand starlings take to the sky to wheel above the Manchester roofscape.

*

Saturday 12th

It is the Saturday of Whitsun Week, the final day of the Pentecost Fair, the day when Mr James Sadler will at last take to the skies in his famous hot air balloon, which has been much sung about and heralded throughout the preceding days.

> "*In Manchester toon a fine air balloon*
> *They say will ascend about noon*
> *Twill fly in the air, large crowds will be there*
> *To see it rise up to the moon…*"

The stage is now set and, as soon as it is light, eager, excited crowds begin to swarm through the town's narrow streets, converging from all directions towards the appointed place for the ascent in Haworth Gardens. By ten o'clock the place is already overrun. When a low-lying brick wall by the entrance collapses under the weight of so many thousands of pressing people, the decision is hastily taken to switch the event to the wider expanses of Angel Meadow. This will mean foregoing the intended entrance fee that Mr Jonathan Haworth had been hoping to charge, for there would be no safe way of patrolling the perimeter of the Meadow to prevent people arriving from all corners without paying. Mr Sadler offers to forego his fee if that will help deflect some of his host's now almost certain losses on the day, but Mr Haworth will hear none of it.

"A splendid gesture, my fine fellow," he declares, clapping the aeronaut on the shoulder, "damned generous of you. But never let it be said that Jonathan Haworth should welch on an agreement. We shook hands on it, sir, and you have my word as a gentleman that you shall be paid in full. This is an historic occasion, Mr Sadler, a glimpse into the future, and Manchester, as she is increasingly, is once again at the forefront of technical and scientific innovation and adventure. Without risk there can be no gain. I play the long game, sir. I speculate. If, as it seems I may do today, I lose my opening stake, I merely shrug my shoulders. Am I downhearted? Pah! I scoff in the face of such minor setbacks. I look on my likely loss today merely as an investment, which will repay me a thousand times o'er when the race is finally run. Look at the crowds, Mr Sadler, clamouring to see you here today. Look at the hope shining in their faces. They all of them want to be able to say to their children and later to their grandchildren that they were here, in this place, on this day, to witness a moment in time when the eyes of the world were fixed upon Manchester. Whereas I... I, Mr Sadler, look upon them all as potential future customers, what?" He emits an irrepressible bark of laughter and offers his guest a finely rolled Virginia cigar, which the balloonist thanks him for, then stows inside his waistcoat pocket, to save for later. He will not tempt fate until his flight is completed.

The crowd continues to swarm, buzzing into every available nook and cranny, trying to ensure the best possible view for when the ascent will take place in just under two hours' time.

Meanwhile, the roads leading into the town from all corners of the compass become clogged with traffic, wheeled and walking, as word has spread of the historic event. Long queues form at tolls along each of the turnpike roads leading into Manchester – at Kersal Bar, at Moses Gate near Barton, at Rixton, Altrincham, Wilmslow and Withington, at Mather Fold and Hardmans, Saltersbrook and Austerlands, Gilda Brook and Adlington, Bury Bridge and Edenfield, and Irlam's-o'-th'-Heights.

There are two sets of travellers whose reasons for their journey this morning have quite separate purposes, in no way whatsoever appertaining to the dubious delights promised by the first Englishman ever to fly in a hot air balloon. Neither party has in fact heard of either Mr Sadler or his proposed ascent into the heavens, though if they had, they might have been tempted to exchange their current modes of travel – walking alongside heavily loaded wagons – for the flying gondola whose maiden flight was causing such commotion, if it meant that they might reach their destinations more quickly, for both have important appointments to make, and both, now caught like eels trapped in baskets in the seemingly endless queues of human traffic at the toll gates, are growing increasingly anxious that they will fail to meet them, and that their migratory journeys to their promised lands will be thwarted at the last.

Brother John Lees of Dukinfield has been on a personal mission since he first attended the supper given by Brother Joseph Saxon at his home in Spring Gardens on the night of the Earthquake almost eight years before. No – more than a mission, nothing less than a crusade, which has seen him touring the South Lancashire coalfields with which he has been associated all his life. He owns two outright, both in Dukinfield, and these he sells within a year of the quake, which he took as a sign to rouse him into action, since when he has been tireless in securing the money required to establish the new Moravian Settlement in Fairfield.

A sum of six thousand pounds is needed to begin the work – four thousand for the Chapel and the two houses for the Single Brethren and Single Sisters, plus a further two thousand for the remaining buildings. He persuades his congregation in Dukinfield to give two hundred and thirty-seven pounds. The Conference of Unity Elders sends another hundred pounds. A further one hundred and fifty pounds are pledged by various Moravian congregations – thirty-nine from Germany, fifty-four from Fulneck in Yorkshire, twelve from London, thirty-two from Bath, and thirteen from America. A loan from the College in Herrnhut raises another three hundred and eighty-seven pounds, leaving a shortfall of exactly five thousand pounds.

This becomes Brother Lees' mission.

Having sold the Birch Lane and Lakes pits at Dukinfield, he takes himself on a kind of royal progress around the rest of the South Lancashire Coalfields to visit each pit he part owns in turn, to try and find buyers for his shares. He sells off the family home and takes his wife and children with him, together with what few essential goods they deem they need, loaded onto the back of a wagon, not mendicants exactly, for they have something to sell, but supplicants, on their own version of a medieval pilgrimage, stopping off at collieries instead of shrines, their final destination the new Moravian Chapel at Fairfield, which he will build with the proceeds of his sales.

His first stop is in Oldham, the Royley Mine, above a bed of millstone grit, interspersed with layers of sandstones, mudstones, shales and fireclay. Next he proceeds to Lennardyne, by Chadderton, which Daniel Defoe had visited not sixty years before, while undertaking his 'tour through the whole island of Great Britain', in which he described seeing 'coals piled upon the tops of the highest hills around'. Then to the adits of Crompton Moor, Owdham Edge and Werneth Top, mines whose entrances are by more or less horizontal shafts, extracting coal from outcrops on the sides of the hills. Lastly to the pits of the Chamber Company, originally sunk by Brother John's father, James, in 1750, more recently augmented by one of Watt's steam-powered Newcomen engines. Known locally as the Fairbottom Bobs, Brother John has no shortage of buyers here for his part of the mine.

From Oldham he moves in a wide arc from east to west around the northern tip of the Manchester Coal Measures, following the line of the Pendlebury Fault along the course of the Irwell and the Rossendale Anticline. He sells shares at The Delph in Worsley, at The Brassey in Tyldesley, The Rams in Walkden and The Doe at Clifton, The Trencherbone at Bag Lane in Atherton, The Three Quarters at Chew Moor in Farnworth, where the shafts are less than two feet in height, and where he sees children younger and smaller than his daughter, Agnes, who is nine, and his son, James, named for John's father, who is just seven, hauling out the coal.

He makes his way along the Irwell Valley, to the pits of Stoneclough in Kearsley, Ladyshore at Little Lever, Red Moss at Blackrod, finally dropping down to Daubhill in Bolton and Dogshaw in Bury.

The entire odyssey takes him five years until, in 1782, the farmland in the possession of a Mrs Greaves, together with the adjoining land belonging to a Mr Kirkenhead, combining a total of five acres in the hamlet of Fairfield on the edge of Droylsden, each become available on the market and Brother

John has raised sufficient capital to buy them on behalf of the Settlement, with leases agreed for nine hundred and ninety-nine years. By year's end Brother Saxon and his family remove to the farm house on the estate, and Brother John is appointed by the Elders as Site Manager and Paymaster. At once he begins the arduous task of levelling the land and providing the brick kilns for the materials that will be needed for the building of the Chapel and other houses.

But while this great work is being undertaken, there is no room for his family to be with him in Fairfield. Instead his wife, Caroline, named in an outpouring of patriotic fervour by her father after the then Queen of England, the consort to George II, and his daughter, Agnes, must stay in the cramped weaver's cottage of one of his cousins, in the village of Elton, one and a half miles to the west of Bury.

The cottage belongs to Silas, who has lived there all his life. He was born there, grew up there, and now he works there, as a handloom weaver, undertaking work as part of the 'putting out' system, preparing the raw cotton into lengths of spun cloth for Sir Robert Peel's water-powered fulling works and recently opened calico printing mill at Brooksbottom in Summerseat, three miles further north along the Irwell. There are rumours of new steam-powered mills opening up close by – in Ramsbottom, Stubbins, even Bury itself – which will carry out all the different processes – from carding, spinning, bleaching and dyeing – so that one-man operations like his will soon be a thing of the past. This is what Silas's sons, Ham and Shem, tell him – they have already become so in their opinion – and there are dark mutterings in *The Two Tubs* on the Brandlesholme Road, with talk of night time raids to Summerseat and machine wrecking at Brooksbottom.

"And what good will that do us?" remarks Silas, bent over his loom late one evening, after Ham and Shem come home, puffed with ale and bravado. "If tha' shuts *them* down, who else'll gi' thee work round 'ere?"

"We've got to stand up an' fight for what's ours," says Ham.

"We've always been weavers in this family," says Shem.

"Ay, lad," says Silas, "that we 'ave, but all good things come to an end. Sooner or later. That's life, lad. That's the way of it. Things change, an' there's nowt tha' can do about it. I reckon tha' can no more halt it than tha' can hold back th' Elton Brook in full spate."

"But we can't just let the bastards take our livin' away from us, Feyther," urges Ham.

"Not wi'out a fight," adds Shem.

" *'Behold,' sayeth the Lord, 'I shall do a new thing'*," answers Silas, holding up the Family Bible from where it always sits on a shelf by the chimney. " *'Now it shall spring forth. Shall ye not know it? I shall even make a way in the wilderness and rivers in the desert'*. Isaiah 43, verse 19."

"Mebbe, Feyther," says Ham gloomily, "but them rivers tek a thousand year or more to form. Sir Robert's opening up t' new mill next month."

"I know, lad," says Silas, putting a hand on his son's shoulder. "But smashin' t' machines is no answer. We must bear it somehow."

"But how?" asks Meg, Silas's wife, serving up their supper. "We've three extra mouths to feed now Cousin John's decided to park Caroline an' their two childer wi' us."

"Hush now, Meg, they might 'ear thee."

"I don't care if they do."

"John'll see us right…"

And so Caroline and Agnes find themselves sharing the one-up, one-down cottage with Silas, Meg, Ham and Shem, while John labours away in Fairfield, visiting when he can, which is not often, perhaps less than once every couple of months. The loom takes up most of the one room downstairs. Meg and Caroline take it in turns to cook their meagre meals over the hearth, and there's an old church pew against the opposite wall on which Silas and Meg half-sit, half-lie each night. In the one room upstairs Agnes and Caroline share one narrow cot, while James sleeps top to toe sandwiched between Ham and Shem in the other. An earth privy is dug out of a bank at the back of the cottage outside.

Caroline especially finds it hard. She herself grew up in conditions far worse in her childhood home in Ashton, which was riddled with damp and even more overcrowded. She had had to share a bed made of only a piece of sacking on the cellar floor with seven brothers and sisters and at least as many rats each night. Her father was a miner in the nearby Snipe Mine at Ashton Moss, and all the children followed him down the pit to work, including the girls. She'd been a trapper. She'd sat all day squashed up in a dark hole underground. Her job was to open and close a small shutter, to let air in and out of the entrance to the shaft, with just a candle for company. Frequently it would putter and go out. Then she would have to spend the rest of her shift, hours and hours, alone in the dark, until someone came to fetch her. She hated it. But when she got bigger she was set for a pit brow girl, working the tubs once they reached the surface, sorting the coal from the other rubbish brought up from below. This was hard, heavy work. At the end of each shift she ached in every bone and muscle, and trying to sleep on the same old piece of sacking on the cellar floor at night did not bring her body much rest, but at least she was working above ground now, out in the open, with the other girls and women for company.

Five years passed. It was her sixteenth birthday. There was much teasing.

"Time tha' got tha'self a sweet'eart," chorused the girls.

"Leave 'er be," warned her mother, who worked alongside her in the yard. "Plenty o' time for that."

But as the two of them were walking back home afterwards, someone was standing at the cross roads waiting for her with a bunch of wild flowers. John.

"For you, Miss," he stammered, his cheeks reddening as he offered her up the posy.

Her mother smiled and went on ahead. Caroline was perplexed. She'd expected her to have given this young man short shrift. But it did not take her long to work it out.

John Lees.

His reputation went before him.

Here was a man on the up. Going places. Everyone said so. He came from no better stock than she did, but he was already being marked out for advancement. A natural leader, with a calm authority, which the other men took to. He quickly rose. From pitman to gang master. From gang master to site foreman. He displayed a flair for problem solving, particularly for engineering. When the four-foot mine flooded and collapsed the previous year, it had been John who had come up with an ingenious new solution for pumping out the water and shoring up the seam afterwards, which had saved the owners hundreds of pounds.

This did not go unnoticed. Nor was it unvalued.

John was now brought into management, who recognised a good investment when it was presented to them on a plate. Their faith in him was repaid many times. Through his innovations, coupled with the respect he garnered from the work force, who still regarded him as 'one of us', despite his move upstairs, output increased dramatically year on year. His achievements did not go unrewarded. After three years he was offered a seat on the board. That same night he proposed to Caroline.

She accepted without hesitation. She genuinely loved him. That he also offered her a way out of the bone-wearying poverty she and the rest of her family inhabited was remarked upon at once by her mother, an observation which Caroline did not contradict.

They were married within six months.

Six months after that the mine owners purchased the lease to open up new seams at nearby Dukinfield, and John was invited to be the Manager. He agreed but with a condition – that he was offered in addition a ten percent share in the new company. The Board offered him five percent. He accepted, and immediately he and Caroline moved into a new house on fashionable King Street, not five minutes walk from the new Lakes Colliery he was to manage. Walking around the gracious, airy mid-terraced Georgian dwelling, Caroline could scarcely believe her eyes. Modest as it was, to her it seemed like a palace. The whole of the damp, run down cottage she had grown up in could fit into her new home's kitchen with room to spare.

"There's space for your family to join us here too if you would like," offered John with typical generosity.

"I'd like that very much," replied Caroline, "but I'm not sure *they* would. They'd regard it as charity."

John nodded. He understood. Brought up a Methodist, he knew well the virtues of self-reliance. He thought for a moment, then added, "What if we suggested that your next two oldest brothers and sisters came here? I could find each of them a job at the pit, they could pay a small rent, so they wouldn't feel quite so beholden, and they could stay here until they got married themselves, when we could ask the next two oldest to take their places? How would your parents respond to that?"

"They might not say very much," she answered, smiling, "but I think they'd be delighted with such an arrangement."

And so it was agreed. Over the next several years a succession of Caroline's siblings stayed with them in the mid-terraced house on King Street. John not only prospered, but he was frugal. He quickly saved sufficient capital to increase his five percent share in the Lakes Pit first to ten, then to twenty, finally to the controlling figure of fifty-one. The seams underground were rich, the quality of the coal excellent, but when he suggested to the rest of the board that they might consider sinking a second pit in Dukinfield, at Birch Lane, they havered. Predisposed to caution, they began to regard John as an unwelcome cuckoo in their nest, who, the more he flexed his muscles and tried to spread his wings, the less room he left for them. Sensing their reluctance, he decided to act alone. In one respect his fellow trustees had been correct. He *had* outgrown their nest and he was now ready to leave it. He bought the lease on Birch Lane, then immediately offered forty-nine percent of it for sale as shares. There was no shortage of takers, and soon the Ashton Moss trustees came knocking at his door, cap in hand, hoping that there might still be a few shares left for them to invest in. Smiling, John assured them that there were, that he had always intended to save some for his former friends and associates, had anticipated this moment in fact, but that the price of the shares had risen in the time they had been prevaricating. He was certain, he said, that they would not wish him to contravene what was customary by selling his last remaining fifteen percent at prices that were less than what they were fetching on the open market. While not exactly illegal, such insider trading was hardly the conduct of gentlemen. Quite so, they assured him, with much huffing and puffing on cigars, and so hands were shaken and a deal was done.

Now John effectively owned both mines. Caroline enjoyed the status being the wife of such a man brought her. She received invitations from other ladies of a rank that just a few years before she might only have come into contact with as a scullery maid, but who now she sat with drinking tea and sharing the local gossip. The only blight on her happiness was that she had not, in six years of marriage, been able to bear a child. She had on five occasions become pregnant but had lost each one in turn before the end of her first trimester. Her doctor, an elderly, rather irascible gentleman, clearly ill at ease with his inability fully to control the female reproductive body, would peer at her severely over his rimless spectacles as if to imply that her conduct and behaviour during each pregnancy had somehow been negligent and had contributed to the miscarriage – a word she resented, for did it not carry with it connotations of *mis*conduct, *mis*behaviour, *mis*take – as if the fault lay entirely with *her*? He would quote Nicholas Culpeper to her, the 17th century physician, who, in his manual, *A Dictionary for Midwives*, had described miscarriages as 'Nature rejecting a body for not being fit for the nourishment of the child,' before prescribing an infusion of Chaste Tree berries.

John reassured her every time that this was not the case. A much more likely explanation, he would tell her, was that his sperm must be too weak to sustain a child until full term, and that he would speak to a different doctor about supplementing his diet with more strength-giving iron, before urging her to keep trying the infusion, whose vivid violet colour would induce feelings of nausea before she had even tasted it.

The different doctor he consulted was Dr Charles White, of the newly opened Manchester Infirmary near the Daub Holes by Lever's Row.

Just five years before, Dr White had published his *Treatise on the Management of Pregnant and Lying-In Women*, but its recommendations were taking time to become widely accepted. The vast majority of births still took place in the home, frequently in unclean conditions, whereas he believed in the notion of a specialist hospital, catering only for pregnant women and their needs, before, during and after delivery, regardless of their marital status. In the period since, he had embarked upon an experimental version of these ideas, with the aid of his protégée, the midwife Elizabeth Raffald. Word of his methods gradually spread. More and more women began to avail themselves of his services. There were now ambitions for the founding of an actual hospital on the site of where he currently practised, in the vacated premises of *The Bath Inn* on

Stanley Street, just off Old Bridge Street across the Irwell in Salford, which, although it had proved ideal for these early trials, could no longer cope with the increased demands now being placed upon it. As a consequence Dr White was actively seeking new donors from among Manchester's growing mercantile classes to fund his dream.

When John learned that Caroline was pregnant for a sixth time, he requested Dr White to treat her. As a man who had embraced innovation in his own working practice, he openly welcomed the Doctor's radical methods. White accepted with enthusiasm, provided he could oversee the entire pregnancy. He was eager to put more of his theories into practice and confident of a successful outcome. Both men shook hands.

He prescribed a daily diet of five servings of fresh fruits and vegetables, including at least one serving of a dark orange vegetable, two servings of dark green leafy vegetables and one bitter Seville orange, a portion of boiled pork, two eggs, at least three beakers of milk and a half pint of ale. He encouraged her to take plenty of fresh air, windows open at all times, whatever the weather, combined with daily walks, and insisted that the house be kept spotlessly clean at all times – not an easy state of affairs to maintain with the windows flung wide and a husband who worked at a colliery.

But they stuck to every last detail of the doctor's strict regimen and, with the aid of Mrs Raffald, Caroline gave birth to a daughter in the autumn of 1776.

It was at this time also that John had begun visiting the congregation of the Moravians in Dukinfield. He was greatly impressed by their notion of Quietism. The idea that the soul must surrender to God by means of an act of pure faith resonated with him strongly. To make this surrender it was necessary to be modest and quiet before God and make no conscious effort to save oneself. By all means do good and meritorious works, but never as a means to try and earn salvation. That came through faith alone. Faith and love. At a time of rationalism and a growing reliance upon science, with all the accompanying doubts and uncertainties such questioning inevitably brought with it, John found great comfort in the simplicity of the Moravians' motto, *'The Lamb has conquered, let us follow Him'*, recalling the words of John the Baptist, *'Behold the Lamb of God, who takes away the sin of the world'*, together with their emblem, the lamb carrying a flag with the cross of Jesus depicted on it. He was a man of substance, of not insignificant wealth and assets. He employed many hundreds of men, women and children. He worked tirelessly to bring about technical improvements to the machines that turned the great wheels of industry. He served on Committees, had been invited to serve as a Justice of the Peace, his opinion was sought and listened to on a great variety of issues of the day, he lived in a fine house in the centre of a thriving and prosperous town. But what would any of this count for when he came to meet his maker at the end of his days? What kind of society was he helping to build whose only measurement of happiness lay in the amount of wealth one accrued? What was needed, he began to perceive with increasing certainty, was to step away from it all, to renounce all worldly aims and possessions, and to create an alternative vision, build a new community where everyone who lived and worked there did so for the common good of all, pursuing the same vision in harmony together. The Moravians, he learned, had proved that this was possible. They had done so already, with their Settlements in Germany and Fulneck. What was needed now was a new Settlement for Manchester, itself a new town offering new ideas for new ways of living, not to step away from the world entirely, but to live apart, as an example of how a life imbued with the spirit of God may thrive in this new modern age and be offered up as an example, a beacon, that others may follow. The truthfulness of this idea hit him with such force that he fell to his knees.

He looked down on his quiet, sleeping daughter, nestling in her mother's arms, turned to his wife and said, "Let us call her Agnes. After the Lamb."

Caroline was too overjoyed to care one way or another.

And so Agnes it was.

Was. Is. And ever shall be.

Agnes.

Agnes lies sleeping on a piece of sacking on the earth floor of the single downstairs room of Cousin Silas's weaver's cottage, beneath the old chapel pew on which Caroline does not sleep. Instead she frets away the hours of night until the first rags of light, pale and damp, leak through the thin strips of cotton soaked in linseed oil, which serve for glass in the tiny open wind-eyes.

Caroline has come full circle, it seems. Looking down on Agnes just beginning to stir, as she does now, she feels she is looking through the wrong end of a telescope, back to her own childhood days, when she too slept on sacking laid upon the bare earth.

When John has his Damascene moment and decides to follow the Moravians, to sell all of the shares in his mines across the county, so that he can help his new brethren to purchase land for a new settlement, she does not imagine that he will also sell their house on King Street in Dukinfield, that he will force his wife and daughter to become homeless, to adopt the life of vagabonds, travelling by cart from colliery to colliery, taking only those things he deems essential, wandering the highways and byways, depending upon the kindness of strangers, like here, with his Cousin Silas and the already exhausted Meg, who are stretched thinly enough without having to find space for three more, but that is exactly what he does mean.

" *'It is harder for a rich man to enter the Kingdom of Heaven than for a camel to pass through the eye of a needle'*," he reminds her cheerfully, when he leaves them on the doorstep of his cousin, before returning to Fairfield, where he spends all his days now, working in the brick kilns the sale of their house has paid for, making bricks by hand to build the houses for the new Settlement.

Each morning, as she rises stiffly from the hard, unyielding narrow pew, she asks herself how she could have allowed such a situation to develop. Why was she not firmer with her husband? Yes, she should have said, I honour your conversion. I respect your decision to sell off the mines to help raise the money that is needed to enable you to realise your vision. I understand that this means we may *in time* have to leave this house, where we have been so happy and blessed at last with a daughter, but why the hurry? Why not let Agnes and me stay here until all is ready, when you may summon us and we shall join you? But she spoke none of this – only now does she say these things in the bitter watches of the night – and she wonders why she allowed the situation to unravel as it did. Then she looks down on Agnes, awake now, who smiles up at her. "Good morning, Mamma," she whispers, before trotting happily outside to the privy. She was simply too taken with her joy at the birth at last of a child, after so many disappointments, that she simply thought of nothing else. Her entire universe was contained in the tiny orbit of her arms holding her baby to her, yet it was world enough and time.

When she next looks up, she is on the back of a wagon trundling along the turnpike between Ashton and Oldham. Agnes has just turned one and Caroline, although she does not know it yet, is pregnant again, with James...

A week here, a month there, sometimes John manages to arrange for them to stay in a single place a whole season, while he goes over the *minutiae* of a sale, or if he has to be away for any length of time, back in Dukinfield, where the financial transactions prove most complex, or in Fairfield, where the land is being surveyed and initial plans are drawn up for the lay-out of the Settlement. While he is thus engaged, John prefers to picture his growing family safe in one place, rather than unprotected on the road, but this cannot always be arranged, and sometimes Caroline and the children must move on without him, until such times as he can rejoin them again.

His family.

He rolls that simple word around his tongue with amazement. For years it was just the two of them, Caroline and he, with pairs of her younger siblings staying with them in the house on King Street in strict rotation, and he grew content with that. He accepted their childlessness as God's will, though at times the rawness of Caroline's grief, when she lost yet another pregnancy, was almost too much for him to bear. Yet he continued to hope. When Dr White arrived, with his unbending rules on hygiene and ventilation, John embraced them without reservation. Then, when Agnes was born, safely and healthily, his gratitude knew no limits. By this time he and the doctor – Charles, as he now quite freely called him – had become firm friends. What might he do, he asked of this new friend one evening after a chance encounter outside The Corn Exchange on the corner of Fennel Street and Hanging Ditch, to show his appreciation in a more lasting and tangible way? Charles outlined more of his plans for the Lying-In Hospital following his early successes in *The Bath Inn*. With additional funds, Charles argued, they would be able to expand, house more beds, train more midwives, undertake more home visits, initiate an education programme across both Salford and Manchester in the importance of the new hospital's underlying principles of cleanliness, fresh air and diet. John agreed to a second meeting, to discuss the idea in more detail, and an appointment was made for Charles to call on him at King Street the following week.

"Excellent," replied the doctor. "It will also give me an opportunity to check on the progress of mother and daughter."

The two men shook hands and went their separate ways.

The next week Dr White presented himself punctually at the appointed hour. The door was opened by Mercy, a maid who had recently begun working for John and Caroline, since shortly after Agnes was born. Mercy was newly arrived in Manchester from Jamaica, a runaway slave from one of George Hibbert's sugar plantations in the Agualta Vale district of Jamaica. Mr Hibbert, born in Stockfield Hall just outside Chadderton, was the *bête noir* of the Manchester Anti-Slavery campaign, of which John was a strong supporter, having signed his name along with more than ten thousand others on a petition raised by local Quakers, following an impassioned speech delivered by Mr Thomas Clarkson in the Collegiate Church, gaining further support from attenders at the Unitarian Chapel on Cross Street, ashamed that George Hibbert's parents and grandparents had formerly been members of their flock, before they so enthusiastically adopted such a voluble proslavery stance, stridently claiming that Manchester's manufacturing industries would crumble to dust without the benefits of the Slave Trade, as well as many prominent members of *The Manchester Literary & Philosophical Society*, including the doctors Thomas Perceval and John Ferriar, both of whom were fierce rivals of Charles White, a fact of which John was unaware.

Mercy was a welcome addition to the household. Adored by all, she instantly proved a boon to Caroline in particular, while her focus was so entirely taken up with the welfare of Agnes. But when she opened the door, Dr White found himself involuntarily freezing on the threshold before stepping across it, an action not unnoticed by John, who was waiting in the hallway.

Charles said nothing while his hat and cane were being taken from him by Mercy. He waited until he was alone with John in the drawing room before he spoke.

"I must confess I am surprised, John."

"Pleasantly so, I trust?"

"Most emphatically *un*pleasantly so."

"Oh? And why is that?"

"My views are well known. I make no secret of them."

"And what views are those?"

"I have crossed swords on numerous occasions with those who disagree with me at *The Lit & Phil*. I was certain you must have heard."

"I've only recently joined, Charles. I know nowt about past disputes."

"They mean to force me from my position at The Infirmary."

"Who?"

"Why, Perceval and Ferriar of course."

"Those are good men, Charles. They have done great work to better understand the causes of typhus fever."

"Yes, yes."

"They have fine proposals for the creation of a Board of Health for Manchester."

"They mean to oust me, John."

"And why dost tha' say that?"

"Their quarrel with me is political as much as it is scientific. They're Whigs."

"And tha's a Tory."

"And proud to say so."

"And why shouldn't tha' be? We may not always agree wi' one another, but we can respect the sincerity of opinions which may differ from our own. That's what makes for civilised debate, Charles."

"Quite. They're also Dissenters and Non-Conformists."

"As am I, Charles."

"It clouds their judgements. It makes them reluctant to accept the truth, John."

"The truth, Charles? It's a brave man who claims he is the sole custodian o' t' truth."

"But I am not alone. There are others who think as I do, great men, like Pieter Camper, Voltaire even. I have evidence."

"Of what?"

"The regular gradation of men."

"I don't follow."

"Polygenism."

John frowned and shook his head.

"That the different human races are irreversibly divided and ordered in a static and unmovable hierarchy."

"A hierarchy?"

"That is what I said, yes."

"But are we not all sons of Adam?"

"In that case how do you account for the different races?"

"If not Adam, then Noah perhaps? Did not his children travel to t' four corners of th' earth after t' flood subsided?"

"It is of no consequence whether they did or they didn't. The fact is, there are three distinct racial types – European, Mongolian and Ethiopian – and a clear gradation must exist between them."

"We're all equal under God, Charles."

"The biological evidence would appear to contradict you, John."

"How so, Charles?" asked John, sounding calmer and more patient than he felt inside, fearing what was coming next. He wondered if Mercy might be listening outside the door. He dearly hoped not.

"All organisms," explained the doctor, as if speaking to a child, "are arranged in a static chain of being, rising through small degrees from plants to animals to humans."

"Is that so?"

"And in humans the non-white races are inferior and closer to the more primitive species due to the colour of their skin."

John turned away. He could feel himself seething with rage.

"Surely you would concede," continued Dr White, "that women are inferior to men?"

John opened his mouth to rebut this remark, but before he could speak, his erstwhile friend ploughed on. "And the reason for this is simple. Women's bodies resemble the non-white races in the way their bodies reveal areas of darker pigmentation than we men."

"I don't know what tha' means."

"The aureola around the nipple, the pudenda, the verge of the anus, especially as seen in pregnant women."

A silence fell in the room like that which follows a gunshot after a firing squad has dispatched its victim.

John rose slowly.

"I think," he said, "tha' should leave. Now. Before I too say summat I might regret."

"Regret? I regret nothing. I speak as a man of science."

"A science born of prejudice in place of proof."

"But…?"

"Go." He strode briskly towards the drawing room which he flung open. "Mercy? Dr White is just leaving. Will you be so good as to fetch his hat and cane?"

Mercy hurried off, returning in an instance, keeping her eyes cast down as she handed the doctor back his things.

Standing by the open door, Charles whispered urgently into John's ear. "You're not letting her near your daughter, I trust?"

John ushered the doctor out without another word.

Closing the door behind him, he leaned against it, allowing himself to breathe out as much of the tension he had been holding in his body.

"I hope tha' didn't hear anything of what Dr White had to say?"

"No. I was upstairs with Mrs Lees and the baby. You should go up and see her. She just gave her first smile. It was like the sun coming out."

TRANSCRIPT OF THE SPEECH DELIVERED BY MR THOMAS CLARKSON ON THE OCCASION OF THE INAUGURAL MEETING OF THE MANCHESTER ANTI-SLAVERY CAMPAIGN

Mr Thomas Clarkson ascends to the pulpit of the Collegiate Church of St Mary, St Denys and St George. A hush falls on the congregation, almost a thousand strong, who lean forward as one from their wooden benches, anxious not to miss a word of the celebrated abolitionist's address.

"Friends," *he begins*, "I stand before you here in this magnificent House of God a humble supplicant, who hopes you may find something of interest in what I have to say to you today. My interest in our chosen topic can be traced back to an essay I was asked to write while still an undergraduate at Cambridge, which was to set a course for me to follow ever since. The question was this: *anne liceat invitos in servitutem dare?* Is it unlawful to enslave the unconsenting? This led me to consider for the first time in my life the matter of the Slave Trade.

"Perhaps many of you here are not acquainted with the subject of slavery. I will therefore endeavour to explain to you what it is. First, let us imagine a child to have been born of slave parents – poor unfortunate child! From that very day, his birth day, he is considered and classed as no more than a brute. From that very day he becomes property, the property of a master, who may sell him, and do with him what he pleases.

"Let us now look at him as a grown man at his labour in the field. He works there, but he is not paid for his labour. He works hard, but not freely or willingly, as our labourers do, but he is followed by a driver, whose whip leaves the marks of its severity on his back during the remainder of his life, but if he is found to be what is brutally called 'sulky' or 'obstinate', there is yet in store for him worse horrors – the Chain, the Iron Neck, the Collar with its frightful spikes, the Dungeon, and other modes of punishment.

"But let us now look at him in another situation. Weary of his life he flies from oppression and he runs away from the estate. He is almost sure of being brought back and returned to an enraged master, and who can imagine, but they who live in slave countries, what further punishment awaits him? Perhaps he dies in consequence of the cruelties then inflicted upon him? But the Murderer escapes. The matter is hushed up. Who on the Estate dares to reveal it? But suppose the fact, by some accident, does indeed become known and a jury is summoned to sit on the matter, still the Murderer may escape, for who constitute the jury? They are all of them Slave Owners, all interested in favouring one another in support of their arbitrary power.

"A friend of mine was lately in one of the Carolinas, near to the place where a jury had been assembled on account of the murder of a slave. The poor man had been flogged to death. In his agonies he called for a little water, which was brought him. The jury availed themselves of this circumstance and, though they saw before them his body mangled and cut into pieces by the Whip, they yet returned a verdict that it must have been the administration of this cold water in the then excited state of his body which occasioned his death.

"But there are other evils belonging to slavery and to slavery alone. Perhaps a slave has a wife and family? So much the worse, for he may be sold at any moment to go to a plantation perhaps a hundred miles farther off, never to see them more. The wife may be severed from her husband and children in like manner, and the children may be severed from their parents, one after another, or all together, as it suits the purchaser. This is not a unique case, but an everyday occurrence.

"These are some of the evils which you are called upon this day to try to put an end to. I do not doubt your humanity. I do not doubt your willingness to pity and befriend the oppressed at home. Can you therefore overlook these monstrous outrages upon human nature, which have been brought before you, because they take place in a foreign land? Christianity, true Christianity, does not confine her sympathy to country or colour, but feels for all who are persecuted wherever they may live. May I hope then that the Society, which is to be formed after this gathering, may meet with your encouragement and support?"

The congregation rises as one to applaud Mr Clarkson. The sound of it fills the nave, the widest of any church in England, and rises up through the clerestory to the richly timbered roof, supported by fourteen life-sized carved minstrel angels whose faces, looking down the length of the dark brown Colleyhurst sandstone walls to the limestone floors below, containing a number of crinoid fossils of starfish and sea urchins, brittle survivors of the Palaeozoic period, upon which John now stands, waiting to be introduced to the great man and sign his petition to abolish the slave trade, wear an expression of impassive inscrutability.

The night that John expels Dr White from his house, he and Caroline make love for the first time since the birth of Agnes. Their son, James, is conceived in anger and joy.

The following week John attends a second inaugural meeting, at the home of Brother Saxon in Spring Gardens in Manchester, to discuss the idea of a new Moravian Settlement on a piece of ground in Fairfield. He listens in wonder to the words of Brother Swertner, describing a prodigious labour he has undertaken, the drawing of a Great Vine, depicting the spread of their followers around the globe. He pictures himself and Caroline, Agnes and any other children they may, with God's grace, have in the future, as a new cluster of grapes hanging from its branches.

It is then when the Earthquake strikes.

He has put this off long enough.

He hurries home through the night, while the ground buckles and heaves beneath him. The next morning he puts the house on King Street in Dukinfield up for sale, on condition that any would-be buyer will retain the last and latest pair of

Caroline's siblings as sitting tenants and Mercy as the live-in maid.

Within a week the house is sold. John, Caroline and Agnes begin their five year odyssey of the Manchester Coal Measures.

Sometimes he travels with them, mostly he doesn't. He lodges with business associates in each of the small towns their wanderings take them to, while he arranges temporary way stations for Caroline and Agnes.

When they are on the road, to keep up their spirits, they sing hymns, or sometimes, to amuse Agnes, John raps a series of rhythms with forks and spoons against the sides of the wagon, against which they sing a simple nursery rhyme that they make up between them, marking off each colliery they visit, each mine that they sell, like stations of the Cross.

As the years pass, and Agnes begins to acquire the beginnings of speech, she takes such delight in trying to join in that it almost breaks John's will to continue with his quest, except that he knows, in the end, that it is for Agnes, for her future, that he is making this sacrifice. At such times he catches Caroline's eye and is sometimes rewarded with the attempt by her of a shy, awkward smile. She has never once criticised him for the decision he has taken, for which he is eternally grateful, but he knows how hurt and disappointed she must feel, to have given up their former pleasant life for the hardship of the road. He tells himself that once they are all together again, in Fairfield, once the Settlement has been built, she will see and understand the reasons for his irrevocable *volte face*.

> "*From Owdham Edge to Royley Mine*
> *Here we come*
> *Past Chadderton to Lennardyne*
> *Beat the drum*

*By Werneth Top and Crompton Moor
Clap our hands
Red Moss, Blackrod, Ladyshore
Sing and dance*

*Through wind and hail and rain and snow
We beat the bounds
The Rams, The Brassey, The Delph, The Doe
The wheels go round*

*Hew the Measures of Coal and Stone
Through all our days
Daubhill, Dogshaw, Trencherbone
The Lord be praised…"*

Somewhere over Werneth Top Caroline feels her unborn baby's first kick. Her monthlies have never been regular, so that when she starts missing again, she thinks little of it. When she feels queasy at the beginning of each day, she puts this down to the juddering motion of the cart over rutted, unmade roads. When her mouth is filled with sharp metallic bile, she equates it with the silent rage that boils inside her, that her husband can subject their hard won, one-year-old daughter to this degrading state of homelessness, of becoming little more than beggars, of depending upon the kindness of strangers.

And they *are* kind. Again and again they are offered shelter, food, a place to rest their heads, and she is grateful, more than she can find words to express, but this only makes her feel worse. So that when she begins to experience those first faint flutterings of a new life quickening inside her, she dismisses them as merely the physical symptoms of her emotional unease. But when she feels that first kick, the unmistakeable jab of foot, or knee, or elbow, against the inner wall of her belly, there can be no further doubt.

She tells John the next time he joins them. He shakes his head, reluctant to accept that what she is saying can possibly be true, but when she grabs his hand and places it flat upon her stomach, holding it there, despite his efforts to pull away, until she receives another kick, his eyes widen, his face growing visibly pale before her.

"I'm so sorry," he says.

"So am I," she replies bitterly. "Not because I'm pregnant, but because we should be happy about it, and now we can't be."

"I will make sure you are looked after," he says bleakly.

She looks at him squarely. "How?" she says.

He doesn't answer.

"At least I shall have all the fresh air Dr White could possibly ask for," she adds scornfully.

John winces. "Please," he says, "don't even mention that man's name."

But Caroline is no longer listening. Agnes has just woken and needs her full attention.

In the end the pregnancy proceeds without alarm. It is as if having successfully carried one baby to full term, her body has prepared itself to do so again.

She gives birth by candlelight, in the straw of a stable behind *The Seven Stars*, a coaching tavern in Heywood, half way between Rochdale and Bury, quite literally because there's no room at the inn, an irony that does not escape her as she cries out for John, who is not there. He is out at Captain Fold, a small pit near Hooley Clough, leased, illegally as it later transpires, in a deal which in no way involves John, from Lord William Byron, uncle of the poet, Baron of Rochdale, but Heywood is mainly a cotton town, not a mining one, and a hard scrabble life there at that, which Caroline has seen in the gaunt and pinched faces of the people, their thin bodies hunched into the wind as they make their way past St Luke's Church along Wrigley's Brook towards the town's first industrialised spinning mill, Makin Mill, built by Sir Robert Peel, part of a whole chain of mills marching across the West Pennine Moors, so that now there are less than a hundred handloom weavers, where once there were two thousand. She sees this in every village and town they pass through on their great wandering, but John sees none of it, his eyes seeing only the Lamb and the Flag, whose emblem he has tied to the front of their cart, to lead them, to guide them, so that they should not be lost. John, who only arrives with the local midwife after it is all over, and Caroline is lying there, drenched and exhausted, her newborn latching on to her, furious for life.

A son.

John falls to his knees and gives joyful thanks.

"We must call him James," he declares. "After my father."

Caroline, slipping into sleep, turns this over in her mind. James. One who follows. Supplanter. James. John. The sons of Zebedee, the sons of thunder. A hard rain begins to fall. It rattles on the stable roof. The two year old Agnes crawls towards her new brother. Her milky eyes, which have now begun to distinguish different colours, pore over every detail of him, the scrunched up knot of dark hair, the blueish blotch of mottled skin upon his bruised forehead, the cotton cheeks, the crimson bud of his mouth, as she tries to learn the map of him.

Now they are four. Though mostly they are three.

John leaves them for days at a stretch.

He will ensconce them in the house of a friend for a week, two, maybe even three, while he conducts his business in the vicinity beyond. They will just be starting to establish a new routine, beginning to get their bearings, before he will return, a complicated expression on his face, happy to have concluded yet another sale, but guilty that this means yet another move to somewhere else.

"Think of it as a ladder," he says, "like Jacob's, climbing towards the light at its summit, our eventual journey's end, rung by rung."

Caroline says nothing. "Or like crossing off another week, month or year from a prison term," she thinks, "scraping each mark in the stone with your bare fingernails, with no knowing when the sentence will end."

The miles grind by.

Nuttall, Stubbins, Red Lumb, Gigg.

Slattocks, Sudden, Starling, Syke.

Top o' th' Brow, Back o' th' Bank, Side o' th' Moor, Hall i' th' Wood.

Duffcocker, Trub, Jericho, Heap.

The years turn. The children grow. Agnes seven, James five.

The money is raised. John is able to complete the purchase of the farmlands in Fairfield. The building of the New Jerusalem can now begin. The Great Vine can put down a fresh root.

John must now be away for longer periods, overseeing the construction of the brick kilns, producing the raw materials from which the Settlement can rise.

But at last the odyssey can pause. Caroline, Agnes and James can stay with Cousin Silas and his wife Meg – "short for Margaret, but only the Minister calls me that" – and John will visit as often as he's spared.

But that is not often. The work at Fairfield occupies him completely.

Caroline adjusts. At least they are no longer on the move, though at nights, when she lies down on the hard, narrow pew, she can still feel the sensation of the cart moving beneath her.

But she is grateful for the kindness of Silas and Meg, especially Meg, who must not have welcomed another woman invading her territory.

"Tha' must tek us as tha' finds us," she says bluntly. "We must all muck in together. I reckon we'll find a way of joggin' along."

And they do.

Quite soon a pattern establishes itself, and Caroline and Meg become friends. Meg likes having two young children around again, while Caroline delights in the way Meg's older boys, Ham and Shem, are happy to take James under their wing, showing him what's what, allowing him to help them in their daily chores – that is when Agnes will let them, she's a tigress where her brother's concerned and protects him fiercely, but she's also something of a tomboy, who likes to join in with all the boys' rougher games, climbing trees, playing soldiers, sharpening sticks with which to try and spear fish in Elton Brook.

But mostly their days are taken up with work.

The older boys' talk in *The Two Tubbs* is nothing more than that. Cap in hand they make their way to Brooksbottom Mill each day before it gets light, creeping home after dark by way of Burrs and Brandlesholme, tipping out their meagre wages to their mother every Friday.

"It's not much," she says, "but it's better than nowt."

"And it's regular," says Silas, who still weaves the fustian for the calico mill at Heap Bridge and the bleaching works at Hollins, which Caroline takes each day in the cart, James sitting happily alongside her – sometimes, if he's good, she lets him take the reins – while Agnes helps Silas.

"Me own little piecer," he says, as she mends the broken ends, or threads up the loom.

He tells her stories of Bury's past, how the Roman general, Julius Agricola, pushed through a road from the camp at Manchester to the fort at Ribchester, Watling Street, traces of which he takes Agnes to see one Sunday a mile to the southwest of them, at Seddons Farm over by Daisyfield, where they find a broken urn, smashed into hundreds of tiny fragments at the base of a wall and, behind it, four bronze coins, which are so very old they have worn smooth and thin, but when they clean all the muck off them they see that they are Roman, one for each of you, says Silas, solemnly handing them out individually to Ham and Shem, Agnes and James; how a castle once used to stand on an outcrop of high ground, where Bury has its Market Place, The Rock, but was razed to the ground after the Battle of Bosworth, as punishment for the Lord of the Manor, Sir Thomas Pilkington, fighting on the side of Richard III; how Sir Thomas was executed and the remains of the castle were buried beneath the Armoury, outside which Agnes sometimes sees soldiers parading on horseback.

"They reckon," says Silas, "that some of t' stone from t' castle were used to build all t' weavers cottages in Elton."

"Even this one?"

"So they say. An' all t' dry stone walls on t' moors."

Agnes's eyes widen and her jaw drops.

"Ay, lass, but I'd tek that wi' a pinch o' salt, if I were thee. If every claim that's made were true, then that castle must o' stretched more 'n 'alfway to t' sky."

Agnes laughs. She loves her Cousin Silas and will do anything for him. She loves Cousin Meg too, in spite of her sharp tongue sometimes. Deep down she knows she's kind. Agnes may be only nine years old, but she understands enough to appreciate that it must be difficult for them to let her and James and their mother stay with them. She knows her mother is unhappy. She hears her crying in the night sometimes, but pretends not to. Agnes supposes her mother misses where she used to live, but Agnes thinks the weaver's cottage is just perfect. It's the only home she's ever known and she can't think of anywhere better to live. She likes helping Cousin Silas, getting lost in his stories. She likes listening to the way Ham and Shem talk after work, the jokes they tell and the swear words they use when they think she can't hear them, and she likes looking out for James, taking such pride and pleasure in each new thing he learns to do. She likes the sound of the loom as it rattles nosily through most of every day. Sometimes Silas sings a song to match its rhythm and Agnes likes to join in.

> *"Clatterin' loom an' whirrin' wheel*
> *Flyin' shuttle, a steady reel*
> *This is the work to make a mon feel*
> *There's worse jobs nor weaving in time o' need..."*

She likes the way the wind blows through the glassless windows in a storm, the sound of the rain dancing on the roof. When the sun comes out again, she likes running through the fields at the back of the cottage. Most of all she likes going down to the Elton Brook with her brother James to try and catch a fish which they can afterwards gut and roast over the fire to eat for supper, together with Cousin Meg's speciality – black pudding, a thick sausage of pork blood and fat mixed with oats and spiced with pennyroyal.

> *"Tiny skip runnin' o'er wi' t' web*
> *Snowy clob windin' round the beam*
> *Tek a good sniff at t' flyin' drip*
> *It's clay an' dust an' we're nobbut t' same..."*

October, 1784. Sunday.

Autumn has come late to Elton. An Indian summer prevails. Wildflowers carpet the land below the dry stone walls.

Walking back from Chapel over at Bagslate, Agnes gathers as many of them as she can hold in a large bouquet. When she arrives at the cottage she begins to sort them into three mixed bunches, one for her mother, who has recently found work in the mill at Heap Bridge, one for Cousin Meg, who has been troubled with rheumatism of late, and one for herself, because she likes the colours so much. She arranges them on the earthen floor, wondering how she can then transfer them into the single family vase, while at the same time keeping them separate. She indicates to anyone who cares to listen whose is which, her brow creased in concentration.

"Hawkbit, Meadowsweet, Birdsfoot and Ribwort for Mamma. Herb Robert, Campion, Devil's Bit and Selfheal for Cousin Meg." She pauses to frown once more. "Which leaves Oxeye Diasies and Yellow Rattle for me." She blows a loose strand of hair away from her face.

"What about me, then?" asks Silas with a wink. "Don't I get one?"

"Don't be silly," laughs Agnes. "Tha' dun't give flowers to boys. They'd only pull th' 'eads off."

"But I'm not a boy, am I? I'm a foolish, fond old man."

"Tha's that alreet, but tha's not old."

"Mebbe not. I've still got a tooth in me 'ead."

"Here you are, Cousin," she says, giving Silas a mock curtsey as she hands him a single flower.

"Why, thank you, young Miss," he replies, returning her curtsey with a bow. "And what about tha' feyther? Hast tha' got one for 'im an' all? He's due for 'is visit this after'."

Agnes pauses in her fiddling with the flowers. "Very well," she says, suddenly serious. "I'll save one for 'im too – *if* 'e gets 'ere, that is."

Her mother looks up from the corner where she sits sewing.

"Tha' means *when*, child, surely?" says Silas, noting Caroline stiffening, head bent in the shadow.

Agnes shrugs. "I'm off to Elton Brook," she says. "Can I take James wi' me?"

Caroline nods. "Keep an eye on 'im, mind. Don't let 'im stray."

"I won't," she replies, then skips off outside, down across the fields, towards the brook, James whooping and hollering after her.

"Be back before it's dark," her mother calls out to her daughter's retreating back.

Caroline, Silas and Meg look at one another and smile. It's unusually quiet in the cottage. The loom lies silent. There's no fire lit. The only sound is of a mouse scratching somewhere out of sight.

"I'll just step outside a while," says Caroline after a moment or two. She lays aside her sewing, stands wearily and puts both hands in the small of her back. "And keep an eye out for John. Just in case…"

Silas and Meg watch her leave, then sigh, before going back to their quiet Sunday. Silas fetches down the family bible, while Meg picks up Caroline's sewing and tries to make sense of it. "Her mind's not been on this," she says.

Silas opens the bible at Luke.

" *'Consider the lilies of the field'*," he reads, " *'how they grow'*." He looks at the wildflowers gathered from the wayside by Agnes before carrying on. " *'They toil not. They spin not. And yet I say unto thee that Solomon in all his glory was not arrayed like one of these'*." He closes the book, breathes deeply, then continues from memory. " *'If then God so clothe the grass, which is today in the field and tomorrow is cast into the oven…'* " But he finds he cannot complete the verse.

Agnes and James have headed straight for the Elton Brook. It's their favourite haunt. Especially in October, when the salmon run the river. They each of them carry a sharpened stick. With luck they might be able to bring one down in mid-leap.

"That'll make a fine treat for Feyther," says James excitedly.

"Ay. If 'e comes."

They follow the course of the stream, jumping from rock to rock along the bank, almost like salmon themselves, until they reach the weir. This is where the Elton Brook joins the Irwell – the current flows faster here, white water tumbling over jagged stones – and this is where the salmon leap. If they're lucky.

This time last year they came here with Ham and Shem. They threw an old branch across the head of the weir, like a bridge, and then walked along it, precariously, one step at a time, until they reached the centre of it, from where they waited for the salmon to come. They'd not let Agnes or James join them back then.

"You're too young," they'd said. "Mebbe next year…"

Now it *is* next year, and they're both of them older and bigger. Agnes feels confident they can do it this time. Ham and Shem are not with them, but Agnes reckons they can manage just fine without them. She looks around in the grass beside the brook. After a few moments she spots it, the same branch as the one Ham and Shem used last year. Or, if not the same, one very much like it. She pulls it out of the long grass. Yes, she thinks, this will be perfect.

She carries it back towards the weir. It's heavier than she thought it would be, but she'll not let on to James, he might get nervous, and that's the last thing she wants. She heaves it to the edge, steadies herself, takes aim and then, with every ounce of strength she has, she flings it across to the other side. It doesn't quite reach, but it wedges between two of the rocks and feels secure enough. She sidles out along it, slowly testing that it won't dislodge – it doesn't – and that it will take her weight – it does.

She reaches the centre, where she can perch comfortably, squatting down low, her sharpened spear raised above her head, as she waits for the salmon to arrive.

"Come along," she calls back to her brother. "Come and join me. This is the perfect spot. We're sure to catch t' salmon from 'ere."

James shakes his head. "I don't want to," he says.

"Come on," she says. "It's easy."

"I don't want to," he says again. His bottom lip starts to quiver.

"Don't be a scaredy cat," she wheedles. "If *I* can do it, and I'm only a girl, it'll be easy for a big boy like thee."

"I'm not a big boy," he says. "Not really."

"Course you are. Just think how proud Feyther'll be o' thee when 'e 'ears what tha's done."

James wipes the side of his face with the back of his hand where a few tears have already begun to fall.

"Tha'll catch me if I slip, won't thee?"

"Course I will. But tha' won't slip. Tha'll be fine. There's nowt to it."

James takes a deep breath, then begins to edge his way towards his sister, who stretches out her hand for him to reach. The branch shakes. He wobbles, almost losing his footing, but he corrects himself at the last moment and regains his balance.

Agnes sees him gulp. His tiny Adam's apple bobs up and down. "Now tha's just showin' off," she says, and he smiles. "Come on," she says again. "Not much farther now."

He inches his way towards her with careful, painful slowness.

Close, closer, closer.

At last he is within touching distance of her. She can hear the breath rattling in his chest. He reaches out his hand as far as it can go towards hers until their fingers are agonisingly close to each other, almost touching, but not quite. Then, with a final desperate effort, he lunges towards her. But at the last moment he slips. His feet kick empty space. She thrusts out an arm. Her hand grabs hold of the back of his shirt. For one heart-stopping second he dangles over the weir, until she manages to yank him back to the makeshift bridge, where he clings to her so tightly round her neck he almost chokes her. She slowly loosens his grip and his breathing eventually calms.

"That were a close call, our kid," she says, forcing a smile.

He nods, his eyes bulging, his mouth gaping. She tucks her hand under his chin.

"I think tha's tryin' to be a fish tha'self, the way tha's goin'."

James tries to laugh, but he just continues to shake.

"It's alreet," she says. "Tha's safe now, 'ere wi' me. Let's just stay still an' wait till t' salmon come along, shall we?"

He nods as bravely as he can. She hands him her sharpened stick.

"Hold this," she says. "When they start to jump, tha' can spear 'em wi' it. Then tha' can tek it 'ome for Feyther. I'll tell 'im what a brave boy tha's been."

He smiles sheepishly. He's starting to recover now. The two of them perch side by side, shielding their eyes with one hand as they scan the water below, straining to get their first sighting of the salmon run.

"Will they come?" he says anxiously, after they have been waiting in silence for several minutes.

Agnes sees that he is shivering. His teeth are chattering, and it's true, it *is* beginning to get colder. The sun starts to dip lower in the sky behind Red Lumb, which stands proud of the moor like an ancient burial mound.

"Let's gi' it five more minutes," she says, taking back the stick from him. "Then we'll go."

He seems to accept this and readjusts his position, squatting down even lower on his hunkers, eyes peeled on the darkening weir.

"Look," he cries, tugging at her elbow and pointing. "There – dost tha' see?"

She scans the rocks below, where the Elton Brook cascades down to join the Irwell. At first she can't make anything out, but then she sees it – a flash of silver caught in the last of the light.

"Ay," she says excitedly. "There – and there – and there too!"

And suddenly they are everywhere.

The whole world is alive with them. The river teems with their leaping. The thrash and churn and boil of them. The slap of scale and muscle on stone. The cold eyes glinting, the pairs of fins juddering. Dorsal, pectoral, adipose, pelvic. The caudal tail fin a fan of tissue and bone, a wing propelling them through the air.

James and Agnes are mesmerised by them, as if it is they who've been caught by the fish, rather than the other way round. They join in with their dance, turning and twisting, trying to pluck them out of the air, but compared to the salmons' grace their efforts are clumsy, a flailing flap and flounder. Their hearts race to keep pace with them, the irresistible urge to run against the tide, to race the current, to spawn and die, to lay their eggs and live again.

Agnes sees her brother's face, silver with joy in the light of the leaping rainbows. It is how she will remember him ever afterwards, this last sight of him.

Later she will struggle to remember exactly what happened next, the precise sequence of events, first this, then that, then... nothing.

Later, when Ham and Shem find her, crouching catatonic beneath the wild laurel trees on the banks of the brook, she is unreachable. She is like one of the stone carvings of angels in the Church of St Mary the Virgin on The Rock, cold, impassive.

They ask her where James is. She points. They follow the direction of her finger. At first they do not see him. But then Ham spots him, floating face down in one of the shallow pools beyond the weir. His hair floats like river weed. Shem drags him onto the bank. But there's nothing anyone can do. He must've been dead for more than an hour.

Earlier, when she did not come back for supper, Silas sends the boys to look for her.

"Don't say owt to Caroline," he says. "Not yet. They've probably just lost track o' t' time."

Caroline is still out the front, watching for a sign of John's arrival. As the sun drops out of sight behind Red Lumb, she sighs and heads indoors.

"It's very quiet," she says. "Where are the children?"

She sees the look exchanged between Silas and Meg.

"What's happened?" she says.

"We don't know if owt has. Ham an' Shem'll find out."

An hour later they hear them calling out from the back of the cottage. Shem is steering a still not-speaking Agnes gently by the hand. Ahead of them Ham is carrying the body of James in his arms.

They lie him on the floor inside, just beside the loom, which casts its gridded shadow across him. He looks like he could just be sleeping, but they know at once that he's not. Caroline falls upon him, distraught.

Perhaps it is the sound of her mother wailing, gasping for air between painful, gulping sobs, or perhaps it is the shuttle, clattering across the loom, when Silas stumbles into it in his haste to reach Caroline, who is threatening to tear out her hair in her wildness, or perhaps it is the sound of her father's voice, calling from outside, telling them that he's here, sorry to be so late, that wrenches Agnes from the darkness she has fled to, but suddenly she starts to speak, faster and faster, louder and louder, until it is only her voice which hangs upon the wind blowing through the open doors, fanning the flames in the hearth, shaking the roof and walls.

Once she begins, she finds she cannot stop.

"It were my fault, one minute 'e were there, the next 'e were gone, 'e were so 'appy, all t' fish flyin' around 'is face, tumblin' one o'er t'other, an' 'e's snatchin' at 'em, tryin' to catch one for us tea, laughin' cos 'e just can't 'old onto any of 'em, they slip an' they slither, an' 'e says gi' us yer stick again, but I don't cos 'e's too young really, so I put it at t' back o' me, where 'e can't reach it, but 'e lunges for it, gi' us it 'e yells, but I still don't, an' 'e loses 'is balance an' topples on t' edge o' t' bridge we'd made, first this way then that, an' for a minute I think 'e's going to right 'isself but 'e dun't, 'e falls, right into t' weir, an' 'e must o' banged 'is 'ead or summat cos 'e dun't move, 'e just lies there, floatin', an I see t'water go all red like, an' I know I 'ave to jump in an' try to save 'im, pull 'im out, but I don't, I'm too frit, I just stand there, an' 'e starts to drift away from me, out o' reach, till 'e gets snagged up in some reeds near t' bank, an' I start to shout, but there's nobbut me about, so I edges me way to t'other side, jump off t'bridge, t' branch, like, tha' knows, an' run round to t' reeds where 'e's still stuck fast, an' I reach out me stick, to try an' push 'im clear, but I'm scared I might 'urt 'im even more, so I stop, I do nowt, I just stay there, by t' laurel bushes, 'idin', pretendin', wishin' I could turn t' clock back, but I can't, it were my fault, all of it, I should o' tried to pull 'im out, but I... if tha' could o' seen 'em, all them flyin' fish, it were like summat out of a story, 'e were so 'appy, I should've... it were my fault... one minute 'e were there, the next 'e weren't... it were my fault... my fault... my fault..."

Caroline holds her tightly to her, lets her bury herself against her. The room goes quiet at last.

She notices John for the first time, standing in the doorway, bereft, appalled.

They look at each other a long time.

Then, in an explosion of fury, she hurls herself at him, pummelling his chest with her flailing fists.

"You should've been here," she yells. "You should've been here."

She repeats this over and over, hitting him with every syllable, until her strength wanes and she slides to the floor at his feet.

He reaches down to try and comfort her, to lift her back up towards him, but she swats him away with the back of her hand and crawls back towards the body of her son, lying beneath the now silent loom. A pale shard of light from the sickle moon outside falls upon his face, from which Agnes is removing the last few strands of wet hair, stroking his cheek and forehead, before lying down beside him.

Two angels now, their skin cold as stone.

They bury James in the meadow behind the cottage. They place his Roman coin inside the tiny closed fist of one of his hands. When nobody is watching, Agnes puts hers into his other hand. She visits the grave every day. Inside the cottage Silas works at his loom.

> *"Down in t' shed on a winter's day*
> *Wi'out sun shinin' on whitewashed tops*
> *Brids on t' slates are chirpin' away*
> *They whistle a tune to every copse*
> *Clattering loom and whirring wheel*
> *Flyin' shuttle, a steady reel*
> *This is the work to make a mon feel*
> *There's worse jobs nor weavin' in time o' need…"*

But Agnes no longer sits beneath him, tying the loose ends of thread together, his little piecer. She no longer asks him to tell her stories from ages past. Cousin Meg has to force her to eat, but she barely manages more than a morsel.

At night, neither she nor her mother sleep, each in their own separate space, Caroline atop the old chapel pew, Agnes beneath, their breathing as shallow as a mouse. Caroline will lower down her hand towards her daughter's. Some nights Agnes will ignore it. Some nights she will take it in her own, but say nothing. Some nights she will climb up onto the pew and try and squeeze in alongside her mother. Some nights they will wrap their thin, bony arms around each other. Some nights they will lie alone.

Six months pass.

John continues to work away at Fairfield. One evening he returns to say that the Settlement, though not yet complete, is ready for them to move into. The Chapel is finished, as are the houses for the Single Brethren and Single Sisters, as well as one or two other dwellings, including one for them.

"It is large and spacious," he says, "light and airy." He says this privately to Caroline, away from Silas and Meg, lest it should sound like he is in any way complaining, which he is not. He will be eternally grateful to them, more than any words of his can say, especially since James died.

Caroline says nothing. She simply nods her head, then starts to go back inside. She's mostly drifting these days, like thistledown, a dandelion clock on which she tries to blow away time. Just as she reaches the front step she turns back to her husband. "When?" she says. "When do you mean for us to leave?"

"Soon," he replies. "Next week."

She nods again. "I'll go and tell Agnes," she says, then steps through the door.

Agnes does not want to leave. Even if the accident hadn't happened, she would still not have wanted to. This is the only home she can remember. She's been happy here. Until James. Now, her desire to stay is even fiercer. She cannot imagine leaving her brother's grave, which she visits every day, where she whispers to him, secrets she shares with no one else.

When the day comes for them to leave, they have to prise her away, finger by finger, from every crevice, the pew, the loom, the hearth. She has no words of thanks or farewell for Cousin Silas and Meg, or for Ham and Shem, and her father chastises her for this.

"Nay, John," says Silas. "Leave the lass be. We know how she feels," he adds, stepping right up to close to Agnes, so that he can gently tilt her chin. "Don't we, love?"

She sits on the back of the cart, which is loaded up with everything they own. Caroline sits at the front, holding the reins of the old nag who pulls them along, John walks alongside. Agnes resolutely refuses to sit with them, or look in the direction of where they are going. Instead she is determined to keep looking backwards, to Silas and Meg waving to her from the front of the cottage, whose every corner she knows like the palms of her own hand, into which she now digs her fingernails as hard as she can, wanting to make them bleed.

At the last moment she sees Shem running towards her as fast as he can. By the time he catches up with her he is completely out of breath.

"I've brung you this," he pants, and thrusts out his hand. In it is one of the Roman coins they had found the first summer she was there, which Cousin Silas had doled out to each of them. "Summat to remember us by."

She takes it from him. Something catches in her throat and she can't speak, but she doesn't need to. Shem understands this.

"Thank you," she manages to croak, barely audible above the noise of the wheels grinding over the cart track, and watches the figure of Shem recede from her. His brother Ham joins him and puts an arm around his shoulder. They both wave.

She keeps watching them until they are just dots.

And then they are gone.

She opens her hand, where she has been clenching the sharpened edge of the coin. A line of blood scores her palm. A bead of crimson.

She holds this keepsake closely to her as the course of the Irwell deepens and swells on its way towards Manchester, who spreads out her skirts to greet her, and all new arrivals, who she will gather unseen into her thickening, darkening folds.

*

Zachary Robinson arrives at his family's home in Shakerley just as a large moon is rising over the wire works built by his father. The last few miles of his long walk from Manchester have been along the old Roman road from Keeper Delph in Boothstown, crossing Mort Lane to the west of Chaddock Hall, close by Hindson Brook, before skirting the edge of Chat Moss just to the north of Tyldesley Banks, or *Tilsley Bongs*, as the locals call it.

He reaches Factory Street just as the pit men and women are leaving Hope Pit, where wire made by Zachary's father hauls the coal carts up the narrow single shaft from the Rams Mine down below. Many of them greet him, muttering "How do?" without breaking stride. Time was, he would have known everyone, but the township is growing so fast now there are faces he does not recognise.

Shakerley is expanding. It won't be long, he thinks, before it has joined up with Tyldesley in one direction and Atherton in the other. Ten years ago there were only two farmhouses and just eight cottages, everyone working the land in the meadow and pastures, for milk, butter and the famous Leigh cheese, including his father, when he was a small boy, working to help his own father, a nailer, who set up an anvil, a hearth and a set of bellows in an old cowshed in a field at the back of one of these eight cottages. Zachary's father, just six years old, would carry the coal dug out of the ground back to the shed, where his mother would work the bellows, while his father would make a thousand nails a day. That was forty-two thousand strikes of his heavy hammer every single day, year in, year out.

"He who buys a house gets planks an' nails for nowt," he'd say to Zachary's father, ruffling his hair at the end of each day. Or, if he ever dropped a nail, "He who heeds not the lost nail," he'd add, picking up every spilled iron shaving from the ground, "risks losing the horse." Then, a few years later, when he was dying and Zachary's father was promising he would carry on the work of a nailer, he shook his head, hauled himself up from his bed and grasped his son's wrist hard. His breath came in short, painful rasps. "Don't waste good iron for nails," he coughed, "or good men for soldiers…"

Those were his last words and Zachary's father took them to heart. His dead father had been a thrifty man – the medieval word for a penny, *a pending*, was the equivalent to one hundred nails – and, with the coins he'd saved, stored in a metal chest at the back of the cowshed, Zachary's father was able to open the wire works, only small at first, but it quickly grew, so that in less than a triennium it provided work for thirty men and boys.

Now, when Zachary last counted, there were one hundred and sixty-two houses in Shakerley. His father tells him there are nearly a thousand people living there or thereabouts. There is always a queue of people wanting to get into the Chapel, built on the site where John Wesley himself preached, almost two decades before. He came four times in as many years. The first three times he came he spent the evening with them.

Zachary remembers being frightened of him. When he was indoors he seemed unable to quieten his loud voice, so used as he was to reaching out to tens of thousands of people in the open air, so that he boomed when he spoke and all the crockery rattled. But the last time he came his father had by then taken up with the Moravians and so Mr Wesley stayed somewhere else. The Chapel now has to hold several services each Sunday to accommodate all who want to worship there, while just a dozen or so of the Moravian flock meet to pray and partake of the Lovefeast in Zachary's house.

There have been other changes too.

Where Tyldesley was cotton and coal, Shakerley was nails and wire.

But now Shakerley is spinning and carding too. One in three of the cottages has its loom inside. The first steam-driven mill has been built by a Mr Johnson alongside Hindson Brook. Inside, a mighty engine, known as The Great Leviathan, powers the machines. Zachary wonders how long it will be before all of man's labours will be replaced by machines. What will they do then with all that sudden idleness?

But he doubts whether there will ever be such a time, for though the weavers may seek to wreck the mules and jennies and steam looms that threaten to take away their livelihoods, Zachary knows that thousands more of these men, women and children will be needed to work those machines. He has already seen it in Arkwright's Mill in Manchester, and this glimpse he has had into the future has reminded him of the Israelites, when they were bound in servitude to the Egyptians.

'But the more they were afflicted, the more they multiplied and grew.'

Zachary wonders if these multitudes who labour for the profit of their masters truly know the power they possess, for there is strength in numbers. The Egyptians recognised this and they feared it.

'And the King said unto his people, "Behold the Children of Israel; they are more and mightier than we".'

Zachary remembers that the Pharaoh's response to this threat was to heap yet more suffering and indignities upon the masses.

'They did set over them taskmasters to afflict them with burdens, and they made their lives bitter with hard bondage, in mortar and in brick, and in all manner of service. And the Israelites did build for the Pharaohs their Treasure Cities.'

Zachary has witnessed such a treasure city at first hand, as he has surveyed for his Master Architect, Mr Edward Byrom, new sites for the building of great palaces and warehouses, while the indentured labourers who build these grand edifices must squat in their Hulks and bones, or dwell in damp, dark cellars beneath the level of the increasingly foul and pestilential rivers that encircle the town, so different from the fast flowing, crystalline, fresh waters of the streams in and around Tyldesley, the Hindson Brook, which hurries towards the Glaze, which merges with the Croal, which in turn feeds into the Irwell, at Nob End, in Kearsley, where just a few hours before Zachary has passed by, noticing the discolouration of the water already beginning to infect these tributaries, as bleach and dye works being built here in Shakerley empty their waste directly into them. Yet even this is not enough to satisfy the ever-widening Manchester maw.

'Therefore the Egyptians did make the Children of Israel to serve them with more rigour.'

Zachary sees this in the pale, worn faces of those who greet him as he arrives back home from his sojourn in the metropolis, especially those faces he does not recognise, but who appear cheek by jowl with those he does, more and more of them rising up in wave after wave.

'But the more they afflicted them, the more the Children of Israel grew.'

Who will be their Moses, he wonders, as he steps across the threshold of the only home he has ever known? Not him, that's for sure. All he is looking for is a quiet revolution of his own, a modest life with a woman he has barely met but who he feels certain could be his fellow traveller along this road, towards a better life for themselves and their children, and his father's blessing to go back to Manchester and take the first step.

But he hopes he will live to see and recognise this Moses when he does arrive, to lead the people out of the wilderness towards their promised land.

"Well," says his father, after Zachary has told him, "I'll not stand in tha' way. I can see tha' mind's made up and tha' art set on mekkin' a go o' things wi' this lass tha's just met. If she's as good as tha' says she is…"

"She is, Father. I know it."

"… then just make sure tha' dost all tha' can to deserve 'er." He takes his wife's hand into his own before continuing. " *'She brings him good, not harm, all the days of her life'.*"

Proverbs.

The next morning, at dawn, just as he is about to set off on his journey back to Manchester and to Fanny, his mother intercepts him.

"Take this," she says. She presses into his palm a crudely worked point of iron, a nail so old and worn it had become shiny and thin.

Zachary looks up at her.

"This was t' first nail tha' feyther ever made. Back when 'e were a lad. I know 'e'd want thee to tek it. Summat to remember 'im by. Pass it on," she says, closing his fist over the nail. "Pass it on."

He strides quickly away from his house, back towards the old Roman road he walked down the day before, retracing his footsteps, in search of his own promised land. He marches in time with the rhythm of the old nursery rhyme he first learned as a child from his mother.

"For want of a nail the shoe was lost.
For want of a shoe the horse was lost.
For want of a horse the rider was lost.
For want of a rider the message was lost.
For want of a message the battle was lost.
For want of a battle the kingdom was lost.
And all for the want of a horseshoe nail..."

He feels the pull of Manchester like a magnet on the old iron nail his father made as a boy drawing him ever closer, stretched along a single taut wire humming in the air around him.

*

At the same time as John Lees, Caroline and Agnes are following the course of the Irwell into Manchester from the north, and Zachary Robinson is retracing his steps along the Roman road from the west, another group of pilgrims is making its way from the south, a large caravan of handcarts, ox-drawn wagons, mules and people of all ages, so heavily laden some of them, that they are forced to stoop down low to the ground. Babes in arms, small children, young men and girls, expectant mothers, anxious fathers, ailing grandparents, who sit on board the wagons. Fourteen Jewish families, who follow the recently turnpiked road from Chester.

They pass through Altrincham during the Samjam Fair, named for St James, with its malthouses and drying kilns, its burgage plots and warehouses along the banks of the Bridgewater Canal, where they are doubly taxed at the local court of Pye Powder, named from the French for dusty feet, presided over by the Mayor, who seizes the chance for a backhander. From Altrincham they walk to Timperley, the 'timber lea', where night soil is unloaded from the canal to fertilise the vegetables grown in the recently felled clearings. Thence to Sale, site of the sallow tree, with its rows of cottages manufacturing garthweb for saddles, where they are forced to unload their carts and wagons and proceed in single file on foot over the Mersey via the Crossford Bridge, which had been torn down forty years before by order of the Government to slow the advance of the Jacobite army of Bonnie Prince Charlie, who hastily rebuilt it and crossed it anyway on his long march to Derby. The temporary replacement has remained there ever since but is not to be tested by too much weight, so they carry everything singly in relays, which takes them the best part of a day. Early the next morning they navigate their way through Stretford, with its more than three hundred handlooms operating in low roofed cottages along the river, weaving between the scores of wild pigs roaming free. Porkington, they hear the locals describing their town, where they are tempted to try some Stretford Beef, which turns out to be stewed rhubarb from plants growing wild. Just before noon they climb the gently sloping Clepper Hill, which drops them down into Hulme, originally a Norse settlement, an island of marsh and bog within the triangle formed by the Irwell, the Medlock and the Corn Brook. Here, everywhere is chaos and confusion, with the sound of sawing and hammering, the cutting of stone and the hauling of bricks, as wharves, mills, factories and warehouses appear to be rising up by the hour. In ten years the population of Hulme will increase fifty fold and on this bright May morning the traffic is intensified further by the ceaseless press of goods and people entering Manchester, where the Roman road meets the Castlefield Basin, for the Friday of the Annual Whitsun Fair Week, to which thousands more visitors are flocking, seduced by the prospect of Mr James Sadler's imminent Balloon Flight scheduled for later this day, but about which the fourteen families know nothing.

They come to a complete standstill, a bottleneck of people, carts, wagons and animals, all being slowly funnelled towards the Toll at the foot of the Dean's Gate. Tempers fray, scuffles break out, carts are tipped up. The air chokes with dust and fibre.

"Patience," says Lemon Nathan, the leader of them. "We've come this far. Let's not risk being turned back at the very last."

"Remember Joshua at the walls of Jericho," says Aaron Jacob.

"I'd rather not," says Aaron's wife, Rebecca. "Didn't he have to walk around them every day for six days...?"

"Carrying the Ark of the Covenant," throws in Lemon's wife, Sarah, for extra emphasis.

"I don't see any walls," says Benjamin, the eleven year old son of Reuben Halsinger, frowning.

Lemon and Sarah's daughter, Rachel, giggles. Benjamin blushes.

"*Baruch Hashem*," agrees Sarah. "Thank the Lord."

"Patience," says Lemon once again. He mops his forehead in the fierce heat and leans back against the lead wagon.

They have been on the road for more than four years.

Four long, hard years.

That was when they were forced to leave their home in Vienna. Under the strict regime of Maria Theresa, Holy Roman Empress, Sovereign of Austria, Hungary, Croatia, Bohemia, Transylvania, Mantua, Milan, the Austrian Netherlands and Galicia, the only female ruler of the Hapsburg Dynasty, a title she inherited from her father Charles VI, in no short measure due to the Pragmatic Sanction of 1713 he spent most of his reign trying to secure, which established the line of succession regardless of gender, life had become much harsher for Jews.

There were strict quotas enforced on how many families were permitted to reside in any single community, how many children might attend schools and universities, how many might become merchants and in what particular capacity. They could learn a trade but were prohibited from rising to the status of master craftsman. They had to wear gold stars on their clothing, pay a tax only levied on Jews and cattle. Written Hebrew and spoken Yiddish were forbidden. When Maria Theresa died and was succeeded by her eldest son, Joseph, in 1780, they knew of his reputation as an Enlightened Reformer and hopes were raised that a relaxation of these restrictions would be imminent, but such hopes were dashed by the Patent of Toleration, less than a year after Joseph assumed his position as Emperor, which, although it granted certain religious freedoms to Lutherans, Calvinists and members of the Serbian Orthodox Church, did not immediately extend these to Jews. Even those more favoured religions could not build churches until they began attracting congregations of a hundred people or more in private homes, and only then if the church had no direct entrance from the street and had no visible appearance of being a place of worship.

This, for the Nathans and the Jacobs, was the final straw. "We shall skulk in the shadows of shame no longer," they decided. "We shall go where we are made more welcome."

And so their long exodus had begun.

From Vienna they went to Eisenstadt, which had long been an oasis of acceptance and assimilation for Jews, where they briefly stayed with the grandsons of Samson Wertheimer, the former Chief Rabbi of this Iron City, who had risen to prominence through his association with Prince Eugene of Savoy, whose forces he had financed, first in the Spanish War of Succession and subsequently in the Turkish Wars, receiving several concessions for Jews in the city in recompense, but by the time the fourteen families reached there, they found the situation much altered. Wertheimer's descendants were embroiled in a bitter dispute over unpaid debts which they had called in, and which had in turn caused further reprisals to be heaped upon the followers of their faith.

From Eisenstadt they headed west, to Worms, then Mainz, then north to Frankfurt, where, in order to be allowed to stay and set themselves up in work, they would first have to swear the Jewish Oath. This required them to appear before a public court, wear a girdle of thorns around their loins, stand upon a sow's skin atop the five books of the Pentateuch and deliver the following:

"And may that sulphur and pitch flow down upon my neck that flowed over Sodom and Gomorrah, and the same pitch that flowed over Babylon flow over me, but two hundred times more, and may the earth envelop and swallow me up as it did Dathan and Abiram when they rebelled against Moses in the wilderness. And may my dust never join other dust, and my earth never join other earth in the bosom of Master Abraham if what I say or do is not true and right. If not, may I become as leprous as Naaman and Gehazi, and may the calamity strike me that struck the Israelite people who escaped as they journeyed forth from Egypt. And may a bleeding and a flowing come forth from me and never cease, as my people wished upon themselves when they condemned God, Jesus Christ, among themselves, and tortured Him and said, 'His blood be upon us and on our children.' So help me God who appeared in a burning bush which yet remained unconsumed. Amen."

Sarah urges her husband, Lemon, to swear this oath. Others have done it before him, she argues, and then have stayed here to prosper. Frankfurt is a free city, not subject to the same laws and taxes as the rest of the Empire. Our people have thrived here, she says. It is well situated, by the river, with clean streets and fine houses. One of these, marked with the sign of a red shield on the door, is the family home of Herr Mayer Amschell Rothschild, whom they meet one evening when he is back on a visit from Hanover, where he now works as a partner with the banker Simon Wolf Oppenheimer.

"Do not take this oath," he advises, "if you feel it is too shaming. I did not take it myself and I shall see to it that my son never feels compelled to do so either."

"But you have had to leave your home," says Sarah, who is beside herself with anxiety.

"As have you. As have we all. Generation after generation."

"I know, but I am becoming exhausted. I just want it to stop, to find somewhere safe to settle with my children and my grandchildren."

"But somewhere with opportunities, where a man, if he works hard, may find success," adds Lemon, "and then also, perhaps, in time, status and respect."

Herr Rothschild pauses, strokes the beard on his chin thoughtfully for a while, then turns to the Jacobs. "England," he pronounces. "Oh, there are laws and edicts prohibiting us there too, but they are not so rigidly enforced, and there is no humiliating swearing of public oaths to be endured."

The Jacobs look at each other with a fearful hope.

"Try Manchester," continues Rothschild. "I have plans to send my son there when he is older. I am looking to expand my interests in textiles and they have the beginnings of a growing cotton industry there. If you go, you might find some interesting openings. It is always an advantage to be in at the start of things, don't you find?"

Lemon nods in eager agreement.

"Excellent," says Rothschild, rising to his feet. "I have an associate there, a Mr Samuel Solomon. Here is his card. I shall write to him to expect you. Contact him as soon as you arrive in London."

Over the next year and a half they migrate from Frankfurt to Koblenz, Koblenz to Cologne, crossing into the Austrian Netherlands at Aachen. From Aachen they proceed to Antwerp. There then follows a brief stay with Abraham Benjamin, the only Jewish citizen with legal status in the whole of the city, even though it acted as a safe haven for those, like the Jacobs, fleeing persecution elsewhere in Europe. Abraham, being an active trader still with London, where he had lived until the failure of the Jewish Naturalisation Act, repealed after just a year in 1754, furnishes them with some contacts he has maintained there, notably that of Tevele Schiff, the Chief Rabbi at The Great Synagogue in Aldgate. Encouraged, they next follow the course of the River Scheldt to Ghent and from there to Vlissingen on the Zwin estuary, where they take a ferry across the North Sea to Sheerness on the Isle of Sheppey. From here it is a fifty mile walk through Rochester and Dartford before they finally reach London, where Chief Rabbi Schiff introduces them to the city's Jewish community.

They stay in London for six months, totally dependent upon the hospitality of these contacts, a situation all are grateful for, but which none like. During that enforced period of waiting, while contacts are arranged for resting stations *en route* to Manchester, from where Samuel Solomon has written to inform them that yes, he has heard from Herr Rothschild, and that yes their arrival in Cottonopolis is eagerly anticipated, one of their number, Leah Halsinger, wife of Reuben, discovers she is pregnant, and so they decide to wait until she has given birth before setting off on the final leg of their journey.

Abner is born during Hannukah at the end of 1784. The Festival of Lights. When he is born, they all remark on his pale, translucent skin, which they praise God for, how fitting that at the darkest time of the year, this new born baby is so fair that when they hold up a candle to see his face more closely, it appears to shine right through him. He's special, they say. It's a sign that God has rewarded our suffering, is bringing our wanderings in the wilderness to an end. But Leah says nothing. Yes, of course, she thinks, her son is special, but there is something more to the paleness of his skin than a sign of good fortune for their journey. It is a condition she remembers her grandfather having, back in the old country, from when she was just a girl herself, which appears to have skipped a couple of generations and now come back. Abner, she croons to her sleeping angel. Giver of light. Her albino boy.

Three months later, on the Day of Purim, after the Fast of Esther, they say farewell to Tevele Schiff and begin the long walk along Watling Street, which will take them through St Albans, Lichfield, Wroxeter and Chester, before it will at last bring them to their long awaited destination. If they had taken the newly instituted Flying Coach, set up by the Philips family in Manchester, they could have covered the two hundred miles in less than five days, but that would have meant separating both from each other and from their caravan of belongings, which they have carted halfway across Europe, and so now they will take as long as they need, stopping where they can, resting when they must.

Now they have arrived.

Lemon and Sarah Nathan. Their daughter Rachel. Aaron and Rebecca Jacob and their son Philip. Reuben and Leah Halsinger, their son Benjamin and baby Abner. Abraham Cohen. Henry Isaacs and his two boys, Jairus and Uriah. Isaac Franks. These fourteen form the nucleus of them.

"Patience," repeats Lemon, as the crowds queuing to pass through the tollbooth at the foot of the Dean's Gate grow ever more fractious. "We've come this far," he adds. "More than four years since we first set out on our journey. What matter a few more minutes…?"

A scrap of paper swirls in the air above them, tossed there by someone in the press of people, their bodies jostling first this then that way, their feet kicking up the dust. It appears to have a life of its own almost, the way it settles near the ground, only to catch another current and rise up high above them again, buffeted by a breeze, which comes and goes and gathers in pockets, evading the reach of hands and fingers, until finally it comes to rest, a tired, somewhat forlorn figure who, having danced the whole day has decided she will sit this next one out, her crumpled dress, creased and frayed, and settles on the sleeping face of baby Abner. Reuben delicately picks it off and carefully smoothes away its folds and creases.

A frown clouds his face as he reads what is written upon it. He holds it away from him, between finger and thumb, distastefully, as if turning away from a bad smell. Lemon takes it from him and sighs.

"It's nothing we haven't seen before."

"I know that," says Reuben, "but still…"

"What is it?" asks Isaac Franks, always the quickest of them to lose his temper.

"Ignore it," says Lemon, but Isaac snatches it from him anyway.

The blood rises to his cheeks, but Aaron has seen this and is at once by the younger man's side, whispering in his ear, trying to calm him.

"Remember what we promised each other," he says.

Isaac scowls darkly.

"If we want to succeed here, we must assimilate. Do nothing to draw undue attention to ourselves," Aaron continues.

"Even if that means denying who we are?"

"Of course not. But let's not make any kind of public show. We can give vent to our feelings when we are in private, when we're somewhere safe, less exposed."

"I don't see any sign of a synagogue here, do you?"

"Not yet, no. And we won't if we allow ourselves to get arrested as soon as we've arrived."

"And we know already, from what Solomon Simon has written to us, that there are friendly lodging-houses here, where we can arrange a temporary *minyanim*, a quorum of ten, that's all we need, to celebrate *Shabbat*."

"I know," sighs Isaac heavily.

"Give it to me," says Lemon. "I'll keep it safe till we get through this bottleneck, so at least no one around us can read it and direct their feelings towards us while they are hot and cross and impatient to be let in."

PRESCOTT'S MANCHESTER JOURNAL

"...several JEWS and OTHER FOREIGNERS have for some months past frequented the town under various pretences and some of them have procured spinning machines, looms, dressing machines, cutting knives and other tools used in the manufactures of fustians, velveteens and other Manchester goods. And frequent attempts have been made to entice, persuade and seduce artificers to go to foreign parts out of His Majesty's dominions. This will be the destruction of the trade of this country, unless timely prevented..."

Lemon pockets the offending broadsheet just as, a few yards up ahead of them, a sudden commotion erupts, the sounds of horses' hooves skittering on the cobbles and panicked voices shouting.

Trying to force their way through the log jam of people, carts and wagons is a small *esquade* of soldiers on horseback from The Manchester Volunteers, who have been charged with clearing away the crowds and restoring order to the streets.

"Just open the gates," orders Major-General Aytoun. "It's the Whitsun Fair, for Heaven's sake. People are arriving to enjoy themselves and spend some money. Why would we be trying to prevent that?"

He sends Captain Leigh Philips and Lieutenant Joseph Hanson on ahead to take down the barriers at the toll gate and hurry the people through. After the initial surge a more manageable flow establishes itself and the queues begin to filter through more smoothly. All continues calmly until Leigh spots the caravan of Jews approaching the crossing point.

"Hey," he shouts loudly above the general noise of the crowd, "you there! Yes, you – Jews! Halt!"

He forces a way through on his horse, swatting any stragglers not quick enough to leap aside, until he places himself directly in front of Lemon, Aaron and Isaac, thereby obstructing all the others from proceeding further. Reuben hurries back to join Leah and Abner, standing protectively in front of them. This sudden halting of the flow of arrivals causes an immediate domino effect further back as more and more people are squeezed together. The fourteen families are now surrounded on all sides by angry baying voices, faces twisted with fear and hate.

"Arrest them!"

"Turn them back!"

"We don't want them here!"

These taunts are at once countered by others more sympathetic to their cause.

"Leave them be!"

"They've done no harm"

"Everyone's welcome here!"

Minor scuffles start to break out between the different factions, while Lemon and Aaron urge their families to remain calm and stand firm.

Captain Philips fires his rifle into the air above the crowds to silence them, but only succeeds in creating more panic.

"You have no legal status here," he calls out to Lemon. "Not here, nor anywhere in England."

"We are respectable traders," answers Lemon. "Jewellers, engravers, watchmakers."

"Pawnbrokers," sneers Leigh.

"Some of us, yes. We see it as a service."

"Forgers, lockpickers, fencers of stolen goods, miscreants all."

"Are you accusing us, sir? If so, where is your evidence?"

"Your religion is all the evidence I require."

This last remark is met by a chorus of boos and cheers in equal measure. Someone from the crowd throws a volley of potatoes, which knocks Leigh's hat from off his head, causing considerable merriment from all sides. He wheels around angrily, rearing up on his horse, scattering those nearest to him, which in turn produces more panic among the people.

At that moment Lieutenant Hanson gallops through the crowds.

"Don't be such an ass, Philips," he hisses to the red-faced Captain, before immediately assuming command. In a matter of seconds he restores order, quells the panic, calms the crowds.

"Let them through," he says of the fourteen families, and a harassed but relieved Toll Keeper ushers the fourteen families past the gate.

Lemon makes a point of seeking Hanson out and thanking him.

Hanson then retrieves the Captain's hat and tosses it to him. Leigh is red-faced and furious.

"You'd turn a blind eye to the law, would you?" he says, the words spat out with venom.

"If it means averting a full scale riot, yes."

"You undermined my authority."

"You'd already done that yourself without any help from me."

Leigh can barely contain himself. He is on the point of challenging Hanson there and then, to meet him that evening on Kersal Moor, where they might settle the matter like gentlemen, when Major-General Aytoun arrives.

"Good work, Lieutenant," he says.

"Sir," replies Hanson with a firm salute.

"A word in your ear, Philips," says the Major after Hanson has ridden away. "Sometimes it's expedient to look the other way."

"But the law is the law, sir."

"Is it? The law can be quite elastic, I've discovered, if you allow yourself to stretch it a little. Our job is to keep the peace, Captain. Nip situations in the bud. Stop things turning nasty. Sometimes it's wiser to apply a modicum of common sense than adhere to the strict letter of the law. Do you understand me?"

"Yes, sir."

"Good. Now, I don't like these Jew boys any more than you do. But where would we be without 'em, eh, lad? We've all of us had occasion to call on their services from time to time, haven't we? Take your father for instance. How do you think he secures his loans for all his business enterprises?"

The Major is standing very close to Leigh, their eyes locked, their noses almost touching. He steps back, slaps the side of the green young Captain's face lightly a couple of times, then leaves with a low chuckle.

The fourteen families pass through the toll at the entrance to the Dean's Gate, shaken but relieved to be on the move once more. They have barely covered fifty yards when a young man approaches them. He wears a *rekel*, the traditional long black coat, and on his head a black fur *shtreimel* over a white *yarmulke*, beneath which on either side of his head protrude the long *payot*.

"Lemon Nathan?" he calls, placing himself between Nathan and the road ahead.

"Yes?"

"*Geloybt Gat*. We've been expecting you daily."

"Solomon Simon?"

The young man shakes his head. "No, but I'm to take you to him. I am Wolf Polack. If you would all follow me please, I know an easier route, away from these crowds."

"Well, Wolf Polack, you're a sight for sore eyes. Lead on."

Without further delay he guides them away from the still thronging Dean's Gate into the narrower but quieter Lad Lane, which takes them directly into Windmill Street and from there into St Peter's Field, where a Great Fair is taking place. The fourteen families visibly relax. In addition to the myriad of stalls selling pies and puddings, sausages and sweetmeats, bread and potatoes, their eyes hone in at once on the hawkers and traders from Spain peddling leather goods, from Portugal selling wines, from Turkey grinding coffee. They see Venetian glass blowers, Moors and Ottomans, Negroes and Chinamen, and here and there they see others like themselves, openly making a living.

Wolf suggests they leave their carts and wagons on the edge of the Field with a dozen of them to guard their possessions, while he leads the rest past the fire eaters, acrobats, jugglers and ballad singers, towards a row of mountebanks, each vying with the next to entice the people gathered round to try their latest miracle cure.

"On a fine evening fair in the old month of May
O'er the hill came the people a-comin' this way
And the folks they were throngin' the roads everywhere
All makin' haste for the Manchester Fair...

There are lads for the lasses, with favours and charms
There are jugglers and tumblers and folks with no arms
There's a balancing act here and a fiddler there
There are nut-men and spice-men at Manchester Fair...

There are peddlers and potters and gingerbread stands
There are peepshows and poppin-darts and the green caravans
There's fruit from all nations exhibited there
For Punch and for Judy at Manchester Fair..."

Reuben takes Abner from Leah's arms and lifts him high above his head.

"Look around you," he says, his face wreathed equally in smiles and tears. "Our new home. We've walked across half of Europe to get here, and it seems as though half the world has come to greet us."

Wolf points in the direction of the farthest booth, where a large crowd has gathered to listen to the last of the mountebanks. "That is Solomon Simon," he announces with a broad grin.

"Ladies and Gentlemen, may I draw your attention to this tiny bottle I hold in my hand, which contains the latest Wonder of the Age – Solomon's Drops. This bottle may only be small but the few precious drops of the tincture it contains are priceless beyond worth. Made from the Balm of Gilead, the sacred tree of the Holy Land, just one drop a day, mixed and stirred in a mug of ale, can restore the vigours of your youth. Rinse your face in it and all imperfections of the skin will vanish in a moment. Rub it into your scalp and all incipient hair loss will be halted. Not only that, it will be reversed. Feeling under the weather, Solomon's Drops will act as the perfect tonic and pick-me-up. Do you have an irritating cough that you just can't seem to shift? Place a towel over your head and inhale the vapours from just two of Solomon's Drops dissolved in boiling water. Do this every day for a week and your chest will clear completely, your cough a distant memory. Solomon's Drops, Ladies and Gentlemen, is the cure-all you've been waiting for, the answer to your prayers, and today I am selling these last few bottles, not for a crown, not for a florin, not even for a shilling, but for just sixpence. Hurry now, form an orderly queue, and if we run out before you reach the front, do not despair. You can buy my Solomon's Drops, made from the Balm of Gilead, at my shop on the Long Mealgate, next to my good friend Hamilton Levi's Flower Stall."

When he has sold his last bottle, Wolf Polack catches his eye and he leaps down from his booth.

"Lemon Nathan," he says, opening his bear-like arms to embrace the new arrival. "*Ir zent dokh bagrisund*!"

"*Mir danken ir mit ale aundzer harts!*"

Solomon turns to address all those of the fourteen families standing before him. He spies baby Abner and cradles him, no bigger than a toy in his giant hand.

"Now we have *minyanim*. Tomorrow we can celebrate *Shavuot* together, which coincides with the Christian Pentecost. Come, follow me. I take you to your lodgings in Shude Hill. It is all arranged. Your days of wandering in the wilderness are over."

The caravan makes its way down Peter Street, then turns into Mosley Street. Solomon informs them that they are crossing the junction known as Labreys Fold where, more than four hundred years before, the Flemish Weavers had first arrived in Manchester and, two hundred years after that, the Huguenots, both communities now firmly established.

"There's comfort in that, I think, don't you?"

*

Lemon and Sarah's ten year old daughter Rachel stands in the centre of Labreys Fold. She is tossing a ball up and down, from one hand to the other. Each time she throws it up higher and higher, and each time she manages to catch it. Until one time, she throws it up so high that she loses sight of it against the sun, which is now beating down upon the crowds almost directly overhead. She shields her eyes from its fierce glare, holding out her hands, fingers upturned more in hope than expectation, waiting for the ball to fall into them. But still it is lost to her, and she only catches sight of it at the last second. Too late. The ball spills away from her into the oncoming crowds. The ball was a present from Count Rothschild, when they stayed with his family in Vienna, and Rachel's mother has warned her not to lose it. "It is special," she has said, "a souvenir from our old home, which you are carrying with you into your new one. Take care not to lose it."

And so Rachel stoops to the ground, peers between the legs of people, horses and oxen to try and watch where it goes, sees it roll beneath carts laden with bolts of cloth, spies it through the spokes of slowly turning cart wheels as it continues to roll away from her. She crawls after it, heedless of her mother's cries, scurrying against the flow of traffic in pursuit of it.

Her mother spins around but loses sight of her. Desperate, she calls out her name, as do all the rest of the fourteen families. They have come so close, travelled so far, to lose one of the children right at the last.

They separate in all directions, scanning the four corners of Labreys Fold in search of her, but she eludes them. She hears them not, so intent is she on recapturing her prize, the ball, which continues to roll away from her, gathering pace as it tips over the edge of a slope and, for a moment, disappears.

Rachel wipes a sticky hand across her brow, puffs out her cheeks and blows a few wayward strands of hair from off her forehead before hitching up her skirts and chasing after it once more. She descends into Hill Street, where the crowds have thinned.

A few yards in front of her she sees a girl, roughly the same age as herself, she supposes, but with red hair instead of black like her own, wearing a yellow skirted doublet, over which there is a green velvet dress with a crucifix bib and white stockings. Rachel has only seen clothes like these in the paintings she saw in Count Rothschild's lavish home. She stops in her tracks and regards her with wide eyes.

The girl picks up Rachel's ball and examines it carefully. Then, seeing Rachel standing a few yards away from her, and recognising that the ball must be hers, she stretches out the hand holding it towards her. Rachel approaches her curiously.

"*Est-ce que c'est à toi?*" asks the girl.

Not understanding, Rachel replies, "*Sheli*," – mine – and holds out her own hand.

The two girls are now standing very close, face to face. They examine each other minutely. They delicately pick at the other's sleeves. They roll the ball slowly between the palms of their opposing hands. They very slowly toss it up into the air for the other to catch. The crowds slip away from them, until it seems to them that they are quite alone, only the two of them, and the ball passing between them, which now they each hold, circling one another, like twin stars in orbit, first one, then the other, passing from sunlight into shadow and back again...

A voice reaches across space towards them. It is the red-haired girl's mother.

"Rachelle! *Viens ici!*"

Rachelle, thinks Rachel, turning the strange but familiar-sounding name over in her mouth, trying it out on her tongue.

"R-a-ch-e-l-l-e..."

Then a second voice, one she recognises, her own mother, Sarah, calling her unseen.

"Rachel! *Bohena*. Come here."

The red-haired girl releases her fingers from the ball, letting it fall unimpeded into Rachel's waiting hand.

"R-a-ch-e-l..."

Rachel nods. Rachelle smiles. "*J'arrive, Maman.*"

The two girls slip away from one another, their orbits receding back over the opposite horizons. Rachel just has time to see Rachelle rejoin her French Huguenot family before she herself is swept up into the wide embrace of her own fourteen families, each of them treading the same ground, two hundred years apart, in the shimmering heat haze of the noonday sun.

The two children wave at each other until they are each lost from sight. Rachel turns the ball over in her tiny hand. When she looks up again, the Huguenots have disappeared.

"Don't ever do that again," says Sarah, clasping Rachel tightly to her. "I thought I'd lost you."

"I'm sorry, *Maman*," she says, before skipping off to join Benjamin, Reuben's son, who lets her jump up and ride upon his back into St Peter's Field.

"*Maman?*" echoes a puzzled Sarah. "Whatever can she mean?"

"She's a dreamer, that one," laughs Lemon, taking his wife's arm.

"A good thing too," says Reuben, watching the two children gallop away from them into St Peter's Field. "Isn't that what we've all of us been doing these past four years? Come – let's follow where our young ones lead us…"

Treading the same ground, two hundred years before, another caravan of refugees makes its way towards Manchester and a new beginning. Each offer up prayers of thanksgiving for their safe passage.

"*Bénis cette maison, que ta Providence a préparée pour nos affligés. Fais nous y trouver les secours et les consolations qui nous sont necessaires…*"

"Bless this habitation, which thy good providence hath prepared for those among us who are in distress. May we here find that help and comfort of which we stand in need…"

*

"*In Manchester toon, a fine Air Balloon
They say will go off about noon
It will fly in the air, huge crowds will be there
To witness this fine Air Balloon…*"

A marching band, comprising fifes and drums, sackbuts and trombones, viols and crumhorns, leads the procession, at the heart of which is a freshly painted hay wagon, decorated with wild flowers woven in and out of laurel leaves, on which stands Mr James Sadler, Balloonist Extraordinaire, alongside his host and sponsor, Mr Jonathan Haworth, who hoists Sadler's arm aloft, while both gentlemen raise their beaver top hats with their other arm to acknowledge the cheers of the enormous crowds who have gathered to witness this daring ascent into the heavens, which have blessed the good folk of Manchester this fine May morning with cloudless skies of a cerulean blue.

So many people have turned up to watch the display that, at the last moment, it has been decided to transfer the much anticipated launch from the relatively small confines of Haworth Gardens to the much larger open ground of Angel Meadow close by to accommodate what conservative estimates will later declare to be a crowd of in excess of ten thousand souls, drawn from far and near to be able to say afterwards that they "were there" at this historic event, the second flight of a manned hot air balloon anywhere in Great Britain to be undertaken by an Englishman, that same Englishman who had carried out the first such flight, Mr James Sadler of the county of Oxfordshire, but now and for ever more an adopted son of Manchester.

Sadler likes Manchester. He feels at home there from the very first moment he arrives. It's rough, but it's ready. He likes its *'can do'* spirit, its burgeoning self-confidence, its sense of adventure, its refusal to *kowtow* to its so-called London masters. Everywhere he looks there are new buildings being thrown up – mills and factories, along with a great many fine mansions to house the new rising mercantile classes who are reaping the rewards for the risks they have taken. Here, he notes, people make money on merit, as well as through title and deed, and have established their own private fiefdoms. Oh, no doubt there are inequalities, and no doubt there is corruption – the exigencies of the bribe and the back hander are plainly in evidence – but Sadler has no problem with that. He likes the raw honesty of looking your opponent directly in the eye, taking his measure, the spit in the palm, the firm grasp of a hand shake to confirm a new deal. I'll scratch your back, if you'll scratch mine. No doubt too there are genuine grievances brought about by a town whose population is growing by ten thousand a month, whose boundaries are bursting at the seams, yet at the same time does not possess its own Member of Parliament to speak up for it in Westminster, while the vainglorious rotten boroughs, such as Old Sarum, which, with a population of precisely zero inhabitants, nevertheless returns *two* MPs to the House of Commons, but there is something to be said, thinks Sadler, for the frontier mentality that comes with such non-representation. He recalls a conversation over dinner the night before, hosted in Haworth Gardens and attended by several of the town's most successful self-made entrepreneurs. One remark in particular fired his imagination. It was delivered over port and cigars after an especially tasty woodcock pie by Mr John Philips, a textile manufacturer who could trace his lineage back to the Flemish weavers arriving in Manchester more than two centuries before and who had made a considerable fortune since...

"We're rather like the East India Company," he ventured to suggest, "an independent enclave, largely ignored by Parliament, so long as we pay the minimum of taxes, keep our noses clean, cause no trouble, make sure we clamp down hard on any whiff of sedition, and generally draw no unwelcome attention towards us. That way a man with a new idea, a good head for business, not afraid to work hard and take the occasional risk, will do well for himself."

"Hear, hear," responded the rest of the company gathered together in the smoking room. Sadler found himself joining in enthusiastically.

"And like the East India Company," added their most genial host, Mr Haworth, we maintain our own private militia. The Manchester Volunteers."

The expression on the face of Mr John Philips darkened. Rumours had now reached him that his son, Leigh, had, against his most strongly worded objections, recently allowed himself to be recruited to Spanking Roger's reprobates, but his frown was not observed within the clouds of cigar smoke in the candlelit room.

"And another thing," interjected John's brother, Thomas, "there's trouble coming with the French. Mark my words. We'll be at war before the decade's out. Then watch the prices tumble as those less far-sighted than we are here in Manchester speculate on uncertain new markets. There'll be financial ruin in the country at large, but not here. We've already begun to diversify. We're investing in the latest Jacquard looms to enable us to produce even higher quality cloth – there'll always be demand for what's top of the range – silk, fine linens and the rest of it – and we've begun to develop new customers in New York and Boston."

"Provided you can raise sufficient capital to launch your little venture," warned Haworth teasingly, playfully rubbing the middle finger and thumb of his right hand together in a circular motion whose meaning was unambiguous.

"Quite so, Haworth. But don't worry about that. We have certain sums already guaranteed."

"In the form of loans, no doubt, from our Askenazi friends."

Philips narrowed his eyes. "Actually, this is where I thought you might use some of your influence, Haworth."

Haworth regarded him closely.

"The loss of our American colonies may hang heavy on His Majesty's heart," continued Philips, "but it has been a source of new opportunity for the likes of us here in Manchester. Perhaps you might spread the word among your cronies at The Exchange? We could always use more investors."

"Quite so, old man," boomed Haworth, basking in the general *bonhomie*, "Manchester is on the up!"

"W-w-which is w-w-why your being here today, M-M-Mr Sadler," attempted Nathaniel Philips gamely, "is such p-p-perfect t-t-timing. M-M-Manchester's on the up, and s-s-so will you be!"

"Well said, sir!" rejoined Haworth. "A toast, gentlemen. To our most esteemed and honoured guest, the Talk of the Town, the Wonder of the Age, Mr James Sadler!"

"Mr James Sadler," the assembled guests all echoed before draining their glasses in a single draught.

"What is it they are saying on the streets, Sadler?" said Haworth, clapping his new friend on the back. "Tomorrow you shall sweep the cobwebs from the skies…"

And so, the next day, parading through the cheering, thronging crowds into Angel Meadow, where his balloon awaits him, not yet fully inflated, surrounded by a posse of local Constables, who stand on guard for him in readiness to light the fires for his ascent, James Sadler remembers with deep pleasure the journey which has taken him to that spot as the sun beats down upon him from directly overhead. Not just his journey that morning, from Haworth Gardens into Angel Meadow, but from his early days as a pastry chef, when he was mocked for not being able to read the instructions left to him by his master baker, relying instead on his innate understanding of the combustion of certain gases when they are exposed to the air, the way dough rises in the oven in a less than certain way, each occasion dependent upon the degree to which it has been kneaded beforehand, behaving not entirely predictably, but measurably, through a close observation of the way the particles of each individual loaf might separate or come together, knowing what he must do to rescue the seemingly unsalvageable, so that when the loaves finally emerge, fully baked, they would never be an exact copy of any that had gone before, but uniquely themselves, individual, prized, yet recognisably belonging to a known, extended family. He looks around him now and sees the way he is being so warmly welcomed into a new family, of innovators, explorers and pioneers.

The marching band continues to play. The song, which has been pasted up on warehouse walls around the town for the whole of the Pentecost Fair Week, and which has been sung every day in the squares and taverns of the town, is now taken up by the entire crowd, who know every word of it and embrace each one to their hearts.

> "*A man and a hog, sir, a sheep and a dog, sir*
> *It will carry aloft very soon*
> *You may view all the nations' particular stations*
> *If you ride in the hot air balloon…*"

*

Amos and Matthew have been up for hours.

Separated by less than a quarter of a mile in distance, but a world away in experience and expectation, they wake at exactly the same moment, when the upper limb of the sun is tangent with the horizon, and the sky begins to lighten. Their excitement reveals itself physically in both of them. Matthew throws back the covers, leaps from his bed and flings open the curtains. The sky is cloudless, luminescent. Already he is imagining the balloon rising up into it and he can scarcely contain himself. He hears a miaow below him. Smokey, his grey shorthair cat, is winding himself in and out between his legs. Matthew picks him up and holds him towards the window, so that the two of them are looking out together.

"Do you want to see the balloon too? Shall I take you with me?"

Smokey miaows obligingly.

"Perhaps. If you're a good boy."

Smokey miaows again.

"I know. That's what everyone says, isn't it? If you're a good boy. But you're always a good boy, aren't you? Just like I am."

Smokey miaows his agreement.

Matthew rubs his nose affectionately against Smokey's, who is more than happy to tolerate such close attention, provided the gesture is followed by some food, which it invariably is. Matthew loves Smokey. More than his mother and father. More than Fanny even. He knows it is wrong to think this but he cannot help it. It's their secret. There's nothing he likes more than when Smokey curls up alongside him on the pillow next to him at night. He can tell him anything. He knows his innermost thoughts will always be safe with him.

Over in Fogg's Yard Amos has slept lightly, if at all, his senses on high alert, as they have been ever since his escape from the House of Correction, still less than twenty-four hours ago. His first taste of freedom has been a mixed one, elation tinged with fear, which has left a sour sweet taste in his mouth and a gnawing gripe in his stomach. He has all but banished the memory of the gargantuan pig in the Apple Market and he shudders, not so much from the cold in the morning twilight, but the growing realisation that he has only himself to rely on, and he doesn't feel prepared to face the outside world alone. Not just yet. After the enclosed confines of the House of Correction, Manchester feels too loud, too close, too big, while he feels too quiet, too distant, too small. This strange girl who rescued him, who brought him back to this Yard, where he has been invited to sleep on a nest of broken bricks, has watched over him all night. Each time he has opened his eyes, startled by an unfamiliar sound, a nearby scrabbling of something unseen but insistent, she has been there to calm him. She asks nothing of him, in fact she never speaks at all, but she is always there, her green eyes huge in her hollow-cheeked face. At nights in the House of Correction he has often dreamed of being rescued by someone claiming to be his mother. She lost him, she explains, in the night of the Earthquake, and she has been looking for him ever since. Now that she's found him she will take him away from here. Her face is always in shadow, and just when she says these things, she leans forward, into the light, and that is when he always wakes up, so that he never sees her face. It is not *this* face, the face of the girl who has brought him here, that he has imagined in his dreams. He doesn't think that she can be his mother. She's too young. No. Instead she reminds him of a stray cat, of the kind they would sometimes see in the yard behind the House, scrawny, mangy, digging out mice and rats with her paws, before the Overseer would throw a bucket of water over her.

Amos opens his eyes fully as the light grows stronger. The girl is at once beside him. He smiles. He thinks he sees her smile back, he can't be sure, but something about the way her cat's eyes dilate makes him sure she has.

She points up towards the sky.

He remembers.

"Yes," he says. "The balloon. Will you take me to see it?"

She nods, then holds out her hand, gesturing him to follow.

He gets up, slips his hand in hers, and the two of them step out of Fogg's Yard, into the world.

An hour later Catherine Oldham is watering plants in the drawing room. It is a task she always enjoys. She pricks a stem here, a leaf there, talking to them all the while, but the tranquillity of the moment is disturbed by a commotion coming from the morning room close by. In exasperation she bursts through the connecting doors, a pair of pruning shears still in her gloved hands.

"What on earth's the matter?" she demands, on discovering the most unpleasant scene displayed before her. Fanny and

Matthew are engaged in the most undignified tug of war over Smokey, who is resisting noisily. Evidence of his protests is clearly visible in the many scratches scored along Fanny's forearms.

"It's Matthew, Mrs Oldham," complains Fanny, disentangling herself from both the boy and the cat, whereupon Matthew promptly picks Smokey up and makes a dash for the back stairs. "He's refusing to get ready to go out to the Balloon Flight this morning unless he's allowed to take Smokey with him."

"Is this true, Matthew?" asks Mrs Oldham, following her son out of the room.

"Yes!" Matthew is red in the face and hot with indignation. "*She* says," he shouts, pointing towards Fanny, "that it's bound to be crowded in Angel Meadow and that we might lose Smokey."

"That sounds perfectly reasonable to me, Matthew."

"Thank you, Mrs Oldham," says a flustered Fanny, her arm still smarting.

"It's not fair," shouts Matthew again. "You grown-ups always gang up together. I'm a big boy now, you're always saying so…"

"Then act like one," snaps Fanny before she can prevent herself, a remark which provokes an immediate sharp, reproving look from Mrs Oldham. "Beg pardon, ma'am," she adds.

"But Smokey wants to go too," wails Matthew. "I know he does. And I could look after him. We could tie a leash to the collar round his neck, which I would hold very tight and never let go. Please, Mother…"

"Well," says Mrs Oldham, softening, "it's true. You have been a very good boy lately, but I'm still not sure. Just imagine if Smokey got away and you lost him…?"

"But he won't Mother. I promise."

Catherine looks back towards Fanny, who looks down. She knows when she's being invited to contribute, and this is not one of those occasions.

"Let's see what your father says," decides Catherine eventually.

"And what is it I am to pronounce upon?" asks Mr Oldham, entering the morning room with a copy of *The Manchester Courier* tucked under his arm. He taps the barometer by the door. " '*Expect fair weather*'. That augurs well for our visit to Haworth Gardens, does it not, Matthew?"

"Yes, Father."

"Come, come. Why the glum expression?"

Then everyone begins to speak at once. Matthew complains again about the unfairness of it all, Catherine rebukes Fanny for speaking out of place, Fanny apologises but says she was only trying to be sensible, Smokey leaps out of Matthews arms and bolts behind the sofa, Fanny proclaims triumphantly, "There – what did I tell you?", and Catherine laments that her nerves are quite shattered. Andrew waits until they have all three talked themselves out.

"Well," he says at last, picking up a quivering Smokey, who at once purrs contentedly as he is handed back to Matthew, "I take it you understand the consequences of your wish?"

"Yes, Father."

"That Smokey is to be your responsibility the whole time we are out at the Fair?"

"Yes, Father."

"And that if somehow he gets lost, it will be down to you and nobody else?"

Matthew's bottom lip threatens to quiver, but he takes a deep breath and answers, "Yes, Father."

"Then on your own head be it."

"Thank you, Father."

The adults watch the boy leave the room with a degree of self-importance that is somehow not lessened by the sound of the cat miaowing.

The oak long case clock made by Mr James Sandiford of King Street chimes the half hour. Andrew checks it against his own pocket watch, also made by Mr Sandiford, and nods.

"We leave in twenty minutes," he says decisively, flipping shut the glass cover of his watch.

The two women sigh, each for different reasons, while crouching halfway up the stairs, Matthew strokes an ecstatic Smokey under the chin and smiles.

Amos and Matthew converge upon the Angel Meadow from different directions, Amos from the south-west up Shude Hill, Matthew from the south-east along Newton Lane, mingling with the crowds arrayed in their holiday attire, everyone clamouring for a glimpse of this marvel, this wonder of the age, this first ever ascent by a manned hot air balloon in Manchester.

The day is hot and, with the press of the people, feels even hotter.

The hawkers peddling fruit along the banks of the Irk by the entrance to the Meadow do a roaring trade, as does the latest arrival from Italy – cream ice. "Take a tin pot," they cry. "Fill it with any sort of cream you like, either plain or sweetened. Put fruit in, or not, as the fancy takes you. Lay a good deal of ice on the top. Cover with straw and set it in a cellar where no sun or light comes. It will freeze in four hours. But if tha's not prepared to wait that long, stop me and buy one."

"May I try one please, Father?" asks Matthew.

"You may," says Mr Oldham, "but if you do, who's going to look after Smokey?"

Matthew frowns. This is a dilemma he has not considered and he decides he must think about it.

"*Gelati!*" cries an Italian vendor. "*Ecco un poco! O che poco!*"

Few can understand him – "try just a little, oh how cheap!" – but they soon catch on, and 'Hokey Pokey' quickly becomes the order of the day.

"Hokey Pokey, Hokey Pokey, Hokey Pokey!" chants Matthew in delight. "Yes, Father. I think I can manage. If I hold onto Smokey's lead with one hand and the Cream Ice with the other…"

"Very well," says Andrew benignly, "but don't say I didn't warn you."

Amos clings tightly to Whelp's hand. He's never seen such crowds and, if they were to get separated from each other, he fears he would never find her again.

When they step out of Omega Place, she leads him quickly down Long Millgate, where many of the traders are busy loading their stalls for what promises to be a bumper day for them. They are so busy that she has no difficulty in filching a handful of oysters hauled from the Irk earlier that morning, of which she gives the larger share to Amos. He has seen nothing like them. After eight years of little more than gruel in the House of Correction, this is a feast beyond his imagining. He watches her prise open the shells, then slurp down the wriggling fish in a single swallow. He copies her every move and he soon gets the hang of it, relishing the slippery, tangy saltiness of their taste.

Arriving at the same time from the north, having hugged the west bank of the Irwell all the way from Bury, are John Lees, Caroline and Agnes. At Walkers Croft they cross the wooden cattle bridge from Salford into Manchester, coming into Toad

Lane, which follows the waters of the Irk towards Angel Meadow.

John has no idea of the Balloon Flight and the enormous crowds it has attracted. Otherwise he would have taken a different route. But such is the sheer volume of people and horses, pigs and cattle, carts and wagons, that the lane is clogged and they are forced to stop and wait until their way becomes clear once more.

Agnes is still sitting at the back of the cart, for ever looking back the way they have come, still mourning her lost brother and the life she has unwillingly left behind in Elton. She has barely registered the crowds, the music, the excitement, but now that they are forced to stop she begins to take in the scene.

She is facing the river. She can see the different types of craft plying the waters, the flat bottomed skiffs, the barges and row boats. She watches them being loaded and unloaded with different goods – barrels of fish, bales of raw cotton, tablets of salt – and hears the shouts of the men and women working there, some in languages she does not recognise. She sees sacks being hoisted onto various backs, which sink under their weight. She watches these bent figures scurrying between the knot and tangle of all this human traffic undeterred. Nothing is allowed to stand in their way or block their path, climbing over, ducking under every conceivable obstacle, as if following some predestined path, and she wonders: how does she connect with all of this, how does her father, her mother, her brother asleep in the earth, how do any of them fit into all this seeming chaos and confusion, this patternless disorder? A fat bumble bee alights alongside her on the cart, a single still point within all this maelstrom, and Agnes wonders if it might be a queen, taking a moment's rest while searching for a new home, where she might establish a new colony. I don't understand any of this, thinks Agnes, this teeming, restless rabble seething all around me. But for the first time in her life she knows that she wants to be a part of it, and that was what James would have wanted too, and so she decides, at that exact moment, that she will grasp at life again from now on, not retreat from it.

Her mother hands her an apple. She takes it from her and bites into it till the juice runs down the sides of her mouth.

Amos wipes the liquid that has dripped from the oyster shells from off his chin with his fingers and licks them clean. It is so delicious his stomach hurts.

So delicious is the Cream Ice that Matthew does not want to lose a mouthful of it. He inserts his tongue deep inside the licking glass to try and extract every last drop. He is so determined that he forgets for a moment that he is meant to be holding Smokey's lead and he raises both hands to the glass to tip it even higher.

Immediately Smokey is off, diving into the hurly burly of the crowds. In less than a second Matthew has lost sight of him.

Agnes finishes the apple except for a small amount of flesh around the core, which she gingerly places beside her on the cart, where the bumble bee is still drowsily basking. She holds her breath as she watches it crawl inside the core and start to feed. It pushes its thin straw-like proboscis into the tiny piece of apple and slowly sucks out the juice.

The fragile stillness of the moment is suddenly overturned when a grey cat leaps into the cart, in blind pursuit of something Agnes cannot see. A bundle precariously balanced above her falls into her lap, knocking the remains of the apple to the ground, at once disturbing the bee, who buzzes angrily about her head so that she has to swat it hastily away before it gets caught up in her hair.

At the same instant a gap in the traffic opens up in front of them and her father clicks his tongue, jinks the reins on the old horse, who reluctantly heaves to pull the cart once more, which lumbers unsteadily across the uneven ground. The horse's hooves skitter and slip on the dry shiny cobbles, one of the wheels becomes temporarily stuck fast on a large misplaced stone, so that when the horse regains its footing and the wheel breaks free of the recalcitrant rock, the cart suddenly lurches forward, and Agnes is almost thrown off the back.

Amos, too, is distracted by all of this commotion. So unused is he to being out in the town among so many people that every sound, every movement, seems magnified a hundred fold. He hears the horse whinny at the same moment he sees heavy sacks of grain being winched ashore from a barge, so that the horse's scream sounds like the cranking of rusty chains.

He sees a grey cat leap over his shoulder towards a jackdaw strutting along the jetty leading down to the Irk below. It's as if time slows down for him. The cat seems suspended in mid-air for a second above his head. Then all is blur and speed once more, a clash of fur and feathers, beak and claw, the cat and bird a continuous whirl of slash and stab. The jackdaw somehow shrugs itself clear and lifts into the air beyond the flailing reach of the cat, which drops back to the ground with a disgruntled yowl.

The sound draws the attention of Matthew, several yards away, who spots Smokey and shouts his name. One of the bargemen, hearing the cry, tries to grab the cat, who evades his big, clumsy hands and darts back up to the road, right in the path of the spooked horse, which rears up frightened on its hind legs.

Amos, seeing this, hurls himself without thinking in front of the horse, picks up the cat, looks around to see where the voice is coming from that is still screaming out the cat's name. As he turns this way, then that, struggling to keep hold of the cat who is scratching his face and arms in a desperate effort to get away, Amos loses his balance. He falls to one side just as the horse's hooves come crashing back to the earth, missing him by a hair's breadth, but he is not able to prevent himself from falling into the river, releasing the cat from his arms just before he plunges into the water.

It is at this moment that Agnes acts.

She has watched this whole drama play out just a few feet in front of her. As the boy hits the water, her mind immediately flashes back to when her brother James fell from the weir in another tributary of the Irwell as he tried to catch one of the leaping salmon. But this time she does not hesitate until it is too late. Without a second's thought, she leaps in after him, grabs him just as he is starting to go under, and tries to pull him back towards the bank. But he is heavy and his weight is threatening to drag her under too. The bargeman who had tried to rescue the cat sees what is happening and thrusts out a long pole towards her. With her last ounce of strength she lunges for it, clasps her hand around it, still clutching Amos with her other hand for all she is worth, while the bargeman pulls them both to the jetty, where there are several more hands to heave them both ashore.

John and Caroline have rushed down to the water's edge, screaming to be let through. When they finally make it, they arrive just in time to see Agnes coughing and spluttering. Her hair is plastered to the sides of her face and her clothes are wringing wet but she is safe, alive. Her only concern, though, is not to be reunited with her parents, but to check on the boy she has rescued. He lies on the gravel and mud beside the Irk, eyes closed, not moving. There are gasps of concern from the crowd standing round.

"Make way!" shouts a voice. "Make way!"

"It's Dr Perceval," someone says.

Thomas quickly assesses the situation, kneels beside the boy's body and at once turns the head to one side so that water can drain from his mouth and nose. Then he places his hands across the boy's sternum and presses down firmly twice, before turning him back on his side. More water empties from his mouth and he begins to cough. His eyes open and Dr Perceval sits him up. A great cheer rises up from the crowd.

"Who is responsible for this boy?" demands the Doctor.

Agnes looks sharply at her father.

"We are," says John. "How can we ever thank you?"

"It's not me you need to thank, sir, but this young lady here," he says. "Without her prompt action, we would have been too late."

"Our daughter, sir," says Caroline, wrapping both Agnes and Amos in blankets she has fetched down from the cart. "Come, John, we must get these childer home."

They lift Amos onto the back of the cart, where Agnes insists on sitting next to him, and John leads the horse, who has quietened now, slowly through the milling crowds, away from the river towards Swan Street and the road to Fairfield.

Whelp runs after them but cannot keep up. She watches the cart slowly disappear from view. Amos, she wants to cry out, but her throat is too tight and no sound escapes. She has lost him a second time.

Matthew, Fanny, Mr and Mrs Oldham have seen none of what has happened. Once Smokey had evaded the despairing dive of the bargeman, Fanny spotted him heading in the direction of the Angel Meadow, and so they have followed him there, but there are just too many people for them to see where he is. They edge towards the place where Mr James Sadler is about to launch his balloon.

"What's your name?" whispers Agnes to the boy still shivering in shock beside her.

He finally manages to speak. "Amos," he says.

"Amos," repeats Agnes, savouring the sound of it on her tongue.

"He who has been carried," says her father, smiling.

Agnes smiles back.

John and Caroline exchange a look. It is the first smile to have passed her lips since James died.

Agnes looks down at Amos, who is nearly asleep. "Amos," she says again fiercely, "I'll look after you."

*

The basket strains against the ropes tethering it to the ground. It is desperate to let slip its shackles and rise unfettered into the air, but until the knots are loosened, it will not be possible. Like a dog straining at the leash, or a child trying to wrench clear from a parent's restraining hand, it longs to be set free, to test itself as an independent being, born at last into life, its umbilical cord with gravity cut.

Equally eager for the ascent, Sadler saws through one of the ropes himself with a knife, causing the basket to tilt alarmingly to one side, which he manages to right by the release of a little more hydrogen from a canister installed there for the purpose than he intends. This action lurches him violently in the opposite direction. There is a distinct possibility that the balloon will drag him sideways, carving a wide swathe through the crowds pressing in on all sides, desperate to get as close to the aeronaut as they can. A sudden panic ensues as those spectators directly in the path of the balloon careering its way towards them try to push their way back against the surge of thousands more still flowing towards them, like waves in an estuary being swept along by different currents simultaneously eddying back and forth.

Finally the basket slips its noose and rises swiftly into the air, but not before, at the very last moment, Smokey, seeing a blackbird perching precariously on the basket's rim, wriggles free from Matthew's grasp, who has only just that second recaptured him, having pursued him madly between the legs of so many confused members of the jostling crowds, and launches himself after it. The bird flies off just as the cat's claws embed themselves between the woven wicker threads and scramble their way inside. A flustered but triumphant James Sadler lifts up the cat to the resounding cheers of the crowd as the balloon rights itself to the vertical and soars rapidly upwards, witnessed at the last moment by a wailing Matthew.

The band strike up a final stirring rendition of the song.

"From Calais to Dover and all the world over
Mr Sadler now plays a new tune
Our old Gallic neighbours' scientific labours
Are no match for his Hot Air Balloon…"

The crowds cheer and throw their hats into the air which all, unlike the balloon, fall back to the ground close to the spot from where they were first thrown, and watch as first, to their great consternation and alarm, he begins to descend to within a dozen yards of the ground, converse gaily for some time with the astonished spectators, before ascending once more with exceeding rapidity, thereby ensuring that the curious are satisfied, the doubtful convinced, and the unbelievers obliged to subscribe to what they had previously regarded as a jest, but which now their ocular organs compel them to accept, till Mr Sadler decreases and diminishes until he is just a dot, before he disappears from view altogether.

Looking down Sadler is greatly heartened and excited by the sight of more than ten thousand faces all looking up at him. He watches their assortment of hats rising up into the air beneath him, before cascading back to the ground. He gives a series of frantic waves, long after he knows they can no longer possibly be observed from earth, then turns his attention to the cat.

"Well," he says delightedly to his new unexpected companion, "I reckon it's just you and me and God above."

Smokey miaows uncertainly and climbs down to the floor of the basket, as far away from the gas carrier as he can, where he hopes it might be safest. He does not like this sensation of flying one bit.

Having checked the controls and the state of the guide lines connecting the basket up to the balloon, and having ascertained that all is as it should be, Sadler begins to enjoy himself. The silence, after the noise of the crowds, is suddenly immense. He floats free and boundless over the earth, truly lord of all he surveys.

Now that he has reached a height of several hundred feet the whole of Manchester lies spread below him, as if someone has tossed a many-coloured, irregularly-patterned cotton sheet upon the land. He can clearly discern the three main rivers – the Irwell, the Irk and the Medlock, along with their many tributaries – as they converge close to the Collegiate Church of St Mary, St Denys and St George, and the Bridgwater Canal, the Duke's Cut, where it carves its way through the Castlefield Basin. He can still make out the flotillas of different vessels peppering their surface – the sail boats, barges and Mersey flats – bringing in goods from Liverpool and the world. He can see the columns of smoke rising thick and black from the scores of mills and factories now sprouting everywhere in the town, a choking bramble of brick and stone, whose many-tentacled roots spread underground to poke up wherever they find a space, squeezing out all light and air within their rough grasp. He can still make out horses and carriages, wagons and carts, pouring *pell mell* over the bridges of Ducie, New Bailey and Blackfriars, and the people weaving their way in between, the whole town resembling a giant loom, the warp of roads intersecting with the weft of waterways, the people a shuttle being shot through by a force greater than them.

But the higher he rises, the more he sees of Manchester's less recent past, the great ring of Tudor Halls and Manorial Estates, which parcel the land between them – Ordsall Hall, where Guy Fawkes and Robert Catesby secretly conspired to blow up the Houses of Parliament; Clayton Hall, with its still intact medieval moat; Ancoats Hall, seat of the Mosley family, still Lords of Manchester, with its terraced gardens sloping gracefully down to the banks of the Medlock; Strangeways Hall, to the north of Red Bank, once the old reed bank, still surrounded by orchards and duck ponds, from where Miss Arabella Reynolds made her daring escape; Hulme Hall, lately purchased by the Earl of Egerton so that he might develop its land for further expansion of his Bridgewater Canal, abandoning the house to be squatted in by local poor tenant farmers, and Withingreave Hall, now almost swallowed up by bleach and dye works emptying their slurry into the Irk.

Beyond this ring the land is a green checkerboard of fields and hedges, streams and orchards, much as it has been for centuries. But change is coming. Sadler can see this as he circles his thumb and forefinger into a size no larger than a milled half crown. He is now so high he can fit all of present day Manchester within its orbit. But if he were to come back here in another six months time, it will be, he knows, not so easily contained. Even now, as he looks down upon it, it appears to pulse and swell. He is reminded of how he had once looked through his father's microscope to observe the infinitesimal spread of otherwise invisible microbial life, those single-celled organisms such as bacteria and spermatozoa, first noted by his father's hero, Antonie van Leeuwenhoek in Holland, divide and reproduce to form unstoppable colonies.

Or in his own kitchen, during his time as a pastry chef, the way sometimes a bread dough would rise too fast, taking on a life force of its own, before overflowing its tin and spilling uncontrollably from the oven – so Manchester seems to him now.

James Sadler is not a great reader. In truth he can barely read at all. But he likes to pick up books and browse their contents, particularly if they have illustrations. It had been in one such book of his father's that he had first come across the different designs for early *aeronautica* by a Portuguese Jesuit priest, Bartolomeu de Gusmão, who had envisioned an aerial apparatus he called the *Passarola*, which had been the forerunner to the Montgolfier brothers' designs, which Sadler has incorporated into the balloon which now transports him above Manchester, even down to the dimensions of the wicker gondola, at the foot of which his feline companion still cowers.

But the book which has perhaps made an even greater impression on him than *The Aeronautica* has been *The Matter, Power, Form of a Commonwealth Ecclesiastical and Civil*, better known as *Leviathan* by Thomas Hobbes. Not that he has read it, but the illustration on the frontispiece has haunted him. An etching by Abraham Bosse of Paris, it depicts a giant human figure emerging from the land as though created from it, a monster in clay, wearing a crown, brandishing a sword, beneath a quote from the Book of Job.

'*Non est potestas super terram quae comparetur.*' There is no power on earth can be compared to him.

When he looks at the image more closely, he realises that the torso and arms of the figure are composed of more than three hundred flailing, writhing souls in torment. He tries to count them all, but he cannot finish, for these tormented bodies swim before his eyes. He asks his father what it means. His father tells him that this Leviathan is the great Commonwealth of the book's title, and that its power lies in the might of one ruler acting in the interests of all. But to James it looks more as though this ruler is a cruel dictator, who acquires his strength by swallowing whole the common people and draining their life-blood from them.

Now, when he looks down upon the microbial sprawl of Manchester oozing across the land below him, it no longer reminds him of bread dough that has risen and overflowed and cannot be contained. Instead its shape is that of a sleeping giant, its limbs breaking free of the earth just as his balloon strained to be cut loose from the ropes that tethered it, and that its pulsating mass comprises all those swallowed tiny figures desperately trying to claw themselves free, to cut their way through from the hidden darkness of the giant's bowels, erupt into the upper air, just as he has learned to do, rising above the scorn and derision he has had to endure.

The balloon climbs higher. Soon Sadler can no longer make out any sign of human habitation anywhere in this northern landscape. Not a farm, not a church, not a road, not a town. Just rivers and trees, bare rock and grass. He turns his gaze instead towards the cloudless blue of the sky above him. So great is the height to which he has ascended that he sees nothing further of the earth for a full three quarters of an hour.

When the time at last comes for him to begin his descent, he has reached the vicinity of Warrington, from where he can plainly see the Port of Liverpool and the sea stretching out before him. An air current takes him inland, following the course of the River Mersey. Beneath him, striding out from Shakerley, midway between Wigan and Warrington, is Zachary Robinson, who has just received his father's blessing to continue his courtship of Miss Frances Cox. He does not believe it is possible to feel any happier, but the sight of Mr Sadler's balloon lifts his spirits even higher. He imagines himself soaring on that same air current that is bearing the balloon aloft before him, so that it will transport him to his beloved more swiftly.

Once the balloon begins to pass from sight, the crowds disperse. There are more delights to sample in different parts of the town, with all tastes catered for.

Zachary, arriving just at this moment, battles his way against the tide of people now departing. Miraculously he catches sight of Fanny, trying to mollify her still distraught charge, Matthew, who is inconsolable over the loss of Smokey. Fanny sees Zachary over the top of Matthew's head, which is buried into her midriff, and her face immediately breaks out into the serenest of smiles.

He makes to approach her but at once her expression alters.

She points downwards to the sobbing boy and shakes her head. "Later," she mouths. Then, looking around to make sure she is not being observed by either Mr or Mrs Oldham, she adds, "Follow," and indicates to mean that she requires him to do so at a distance.

He nods that he understands and then, as surreptitiously as he can, feeling faintly ridiculous nevertheless, he proceeds to dog her footsteps some twenty yards behind her all the way from Angel Meadow to Newton Lane. Once she reaches the Oldhams' house, she ushers Matthew in through the front door ahead of her, turns back to check that Zachary is still there, holds up the four fingers and thumb of one hand and three fingers of the other, which Zachary takes to signify eight o'clock, and points towards the Methodists' Central Hall across the way from where she stands. Zachary just has time to nod in agreement as she hurries indoors, but not before he is rewarded once again with another of her heart-stopping smiles.

Sadler proceeds to follow the course of the Mersey, where, if he had travelled this same way a few hours before, he may well have seen the caravan of carts and wagons conveying the fourteen Jewish families towards Manchester, which passed this exact same spot. The current blows him north, leaving the Mersey to pursue instead its tributary, the Irwell, towards Bury, along whose banks earlier that day the Lees family had made their slow, conflicted, bitter-sweet progress along its course all the way to Angel Meadow, where they arrived just in time to see the balloon released from the tethers that were holding it earthbound.

A sudden drop in pressure sees the balloon plunge rapidly, landing briefly and somewhat painfully for its two occupants, Mr Sadler and the cat, on the fringes of the small market town of Radcliffe, then bouncing erratically along the ground for more than half a mile, before lifting into the air once more, continuing to follow the Irwell past Bury, over the villages of Elton, Tottington and Summerseat, until it finally comes to earth on the slopes of Holcombe Hill, which overlook the Stygian gloom of Ramsbottom, lost in the steep valley below, obscured from sight by the ceaseless plumes of smoke that rise up from the mills, factories, tanneries and brickyards lining the river and hang in a thick funereal pall over the town.

Just before touching down, the gondola lightly brushes across the canopy of stunted, choking sycamores, which struggle to scratch their roots in the thin, stony soil. Perched on the top of one of these is a grimy, soot-stained blackbird, a distant relation perhaps of the bird whom Smokey had so recklessly pursued some six hours before, from whose defiant beak pours forth a torrent of song. Smokey, aroused by the sound, leaps from the basket ruthlessly towards it, like a guided missile catapulted from a trebuchet in medieval warfare. The bird, disorientated by the unexpected direction of the attack, flies head first into the cat's widening maw.

The first known casualty as an indirect result of human flight.

The remaining words of the song sung by the balladeers back in Angel Meadow are already proving prophetic.

"This noble machine most people have seen
Perhaps as a very great boon
But our wide gaping isle, sir, may expect in a while, sir
The French in their own Air Balloon

Should warfare break out, as it is not a doubt –
To some it might happen quite soon –
The French will invade us, their troops all parade us
Brought o'er in their Hot Air Balloon

Oh I can't believe that, says Michael to Pat
Tis the tale of some humbugging loon
So I say botheration to the frog-eating nation
And success to James Sadler's Balloon…"

Eight o'clock arrives.

The time between when Fanny disappeared behind the Oldhams' front door and when she now emerges quietly from the back has, for Zachary, crawled as slow as minor friars on sacred errands go. He has rehearsed what he will say to her a thousand times, but when she finally appears, lifting up her skirts so that she can run across the road to meet him, the words slip away from him like water through his fingers, so that it is she who speaks first.

"Have you spoken to Mr Byrom?" she asks, wasting no words on unnecessary pleasantries.

"I have," he says, taking her hands in his.

"And?"

"He's agreed to keep me on," he answers. " 'Look around you,' he said. 'There are buildings sprouting up everywhere. Business is booming.' Then he offered me another year's contract."

"And your father?"

"I have his blessing."

Fanny exhales deeply. She has not realised just how much tension she has been holding these past twenty-four hours, and, with that single breath, it all leaves her in an instant.

"Now it is my turn to ask *you* a question," asks Zachary, dropping to his knees.

"Yes," she says, before he can even ask it, lifting him back to his feet. "But not immediately."

"When?"

"I cannot leave Mattie just yet. It's May now. He's enrolled for a Bluecoat at Chetham's in September. Some time after then. He will not need me so much once he's started there."

"Holy Cross then?"

He watches her face go through a series of mental calculations.

"Yes," she says at length. "That will give me enough time to prepare Mrs Oldham too. Holy Cross."

He clasps her to him and she allows him to kiss her, responding with warmth and passion.

"I must go back now," she says, "or questions will be asked."

"Must you?" he asks.

She regards him mischievously. "Why? Do you have something in mind?"

"I do actually."

"Oh?"

"This." He produces two tickets from his inside jacket pocket with a flourish.

Although Fanny is not able to read what the words say on them, she recognises at once the illustration next to them.

"The circus?" she says, her eyes widening.

He smiles broadly, delighted by her unmasked joy.

She pauses by the back step. "Give me five minutes," she says quickly. "I'll check with Mrs Oldham first, to make sure I'm not needed."

He watches her departing back in silent wonderment. She will always be needed. Of this he is certain.

A few moments later, Sadler lands unscathed. He tumbles out of the gondola, rolls down the slope of a fairly steep hill a dozen or so yards away from where the prostrate envelope of the balloon impotently thrashes and gyrates, a beached whale wheezing as it fights in vain for the air that is slowly but inevitably escaping from it.

> "*Though miracles cease, yet wonders increase*
> *Mr Sadler he plays a new tune*
> *Now people have seen this noble machine*
> *They regard it perhaps as a boon…*"

*

Mr Samuel Oldknow nervously paces the Upstairs Function Room at *The Bull's Head*. He has just arrived, having missed the balloon flight, but is evidently early for his meeting, for there is no one but he in the long, dark, low-ceilinged room. He prays all the others are late. Which is a distinct possibility. Jonathan Haworth, who has arranged this assignation, is renowned for the poverty of his time-keeping, but also, happily, for the generosity of his purse.

Samuel sits down. He stands up. Then he sits down again. He is perspiring and endeavours to loosen the white cravat around his neck. He takes out his silver snuff box, a bequest from his late father, who died when Samuel was only three, but who, as his mother, Margery, never tires of reminding him, was a thrifty man.

'Tha' could do far worse than to emulate him,' is the oft-repeated mantra of his stepfather, Mr John Clayton, yeoman of Roscoe Lane Farm, where he and his mother now reside, on the edge of the estate owned by Mr Peter Drinkwater, the esteemed associate of Mr Richard Arkwright and Samuel's own benefactor – until recently, that is. Hence the reason for this hastily arranged interview.

He lays out a line of snuff along the back of his left hand. The pinch of pulverised tobacco leaves looks distinctly unappetising, but as soon as he raises them closer to his nostrils he detects the familiar aroma of camphor, cinnamon, tobacco and spearmint – his own personalised blend, made up for him specially by Mr Aulay Macauley of Acresfield – and inhales it rapidly. The swift, sharp hit of nicotine has the immediate desired effect of calming him, enabling him to carry out a rapid mental inventory of his current impecunious circumstances, so that he might be better prepared for when Haworth and his cronies eventually get here. He finds he is glad to have arrived early after all, to have this time alone, to reflect upon what his strategy might be.

He has not done at all badly, all things considered. He has come a long way from his frugal beginnings on the farm at Rivington with its pervasive Unitarian strictures. His mother's final words to him, when he informed her of this proposed visit to Manchester, were to make him promise to look in on Reverend Gore at Cross Street. He acquiesced to her wishes, for this was the easier option, but he doubts whether he will in fact stop by. He will claim that there simply wasn't time, if pressed, which will probably be true, for this is a complicated venture he is about to propose – if Haworth ever deigns to put in an appearance, that is.

The landlord pops his head round the door once more, asking if he would like a drink yet, or whether he would prefer to wait for the other gentlemen. Samuel informs him, rather curtly, it must be said, that he would rather wait. He immediately regrets his brusqueness and has half a mind to call the fellow back, but then he hesitates. Why should he? What has he to apologise for? It's not as if he isn't bringing him plenty of business as the evening unfolds, which surely it must do eventually.

He settles himself once more to a further bout of self-evaluation. He reminds himself of the old Joseph Addison maxim. '*He who hesitates is lost.*' From his play, *Cato*. Samuel allows himself a second pinch of snuff. Prevarication has ever been his undoing. He thinks back to that lamentable episode with Jenny, Peter Drinkwater's daughter. Everyone had been so delighted when their engagement was first announced. His mother, especially, had been thrilled. "This is just what your father would have wanted," she had said. "You've made me so proud." And of course it had made such perfect business sense. Peter Drinkwater, along with his partner Richard Arkwright, was the most successful manufacturer of the age. Born in Whalley, which, less than eighteen miles away, was close enough to Rivington to have made their two families practically neighbours, he had opened his first mill on the River Weaver in Northwich. In addition, like Arkwright, he successfully adopted the domestic 'putting out' system, farming out fustian work to literally scores of handloom weavers based in their own cottages, before branching out as a merchant and mill owner. His Piccadilly Mill had been the first to use steam power directly to drive the looms and he had made a fortune from it, so much so that he had been able to secure for himself the estate at Prestwich, where he played the role of landed gentry as if quite literally to the manor born. It was there where Samuel had been introduced to him and where he had first met Jenny.

He had managed to obtain a number of Crompton's spinning mules. These particular ones were known as Hall i' th' Wood wheels, which he used to great effect in the mass production of muslin, which enabled him to make his first fortune. It was this which had brought him to the attention of Peter Drinkwater, who invited him to dinner one night at the Manor, a dinner hosted by Jenny, both his daughter and heiress. Drinkwater introduced him to another Crompton – not the inventor of the spinning jenny – but *Abraham* Crompton of Chorley, an investor who loaned Samuel the princely sum of a thousand pounds. With this he moved his operations to Stockport, where Arkwright was already revolutionising the methods of production. Samuel managed to secure an additional loan of three thousand pounds from the great man.

Combining the putting out system, through which he employed three hundred skilled weavers using five hundred looms, together with a series of larger mills and warehouses he constructed in the Tame Valley, he became the foremost manufacturer of muslin in Britain, making a profit of more than seventeen thousand pounds in each of the first two years of his operation there.

He was the toast of the town, and he and Jenny were the golden couple. Unfortunately, Samuel found the rewards of Mammon more tempting than the charms of Jenny. Or any woman, when it came to it. He much preferred to spend his evenings poring over accounts than dancing or attending concerts. And while he understood that business matters often went hand in glove with social obligations, he quickly came to realise that the deals were more likely to be struck over gambling in the Gentlemen's Clubs than dancing in The Assembly Rooms. He found the company of other men more agreeable, if truth be told, than time spent with ladies in general, or Jenny in particular. And so he neglected his duties as a fiancé. Jenny grew fretful. Then she grew angry. Finally she lost patience and broke off the engagement. Although this brought with it a certain public humiliation, privately he felt nothing but relief. But relations with Peter Drinkwater inevitably cooled.

First, he called in his loan – with interest – persuading Abraham Crompton to do likewise. Next came the scandal of the Grand Patent, in which Richard Arkwright aroused public hostility by attempting to bring together all the separate licences he held for various technical innovations to different elements within the production of cotton – carding machines, spinning frames and steam engines – under one all-encompassing umbrella, but the country at large was against so many patents being held simultaneously by a single person. Arkwright took the matter to court to assert what he regarded as his legal rights, but the case went against him, especially when it was alleged that he had stolen several of his ideas from others who had developed them before him, such as John Kay, a clock maker from Warrington, who claimed *he* had refined the spinning frame, shortly after his invention of the flying shuttle, and Thomas Highs, a reed maker from Leigh, whose throstle, a device which enabled the continuous twisting and winding of wool, was, he argued, the precursor to Arkwright's carding machine.

This loss proved costly to Arkwright, but even more so to Samuel, who had invested heavily in his partner's expanding activities in Cromford, Bakewell and Wirksworth, as well as here in Manchester, and so Samuel now found himself in debt to the tune of eleven thousand pounds.

It is this 'anticipation of income', as his creditors have so euphemistically put it, which has so drastically forced his hand, and which sees him now, pacing the floor of the Upstairs Function Room of *The Bull's Head Inn*, waiting for the arrival of Jonathan Haworth, and whoever else he might deign to bring with him.

Samuel is anxious, yes, but he is not desperate. He has raised capital before and he is confident he will do so again, particularly with regard to the proposition he plans to put to the potential investors he hopes Jonathan Haworth has managed to persuade to attend this evening.

He recalls once again the advice of Joseph Addison from his play, *Cato*.

'*Swift and resolute action leads to success*', and '*Self doubt is the prelude to disaster*'.

He stands decisively, strides resolutely across the wooden floor to the oak door, from where he calls down the stairs in a tone that brooks no dissent.

"Landlord," he halloos, "bring me a quart of brandy. My guests will be here directly."

Observing unseen with approval, not so much at the success of the balloon's landing, but rather at the fearful symmetry of the missile cat, is a young boy.

"Here, Puss," he croons as the feline weaves its way between his legs. He picks it up, cradles it in his arms as it continues to crunch the fragile bones of its victim, before finishing with a contented purr.

Mattie remains inconsolable. He refuses to eat supper, and, when Fanny tiptoes into his room to look in on him, he is instantly alert.

"Tell me, Fanny," he says, clutching her hand, "do you think Smokey will come home?"

"Well," she says doubtfully, "I know they say that cats have a homing instinct, but he must've travelled ever so far in that balloon…"

Mattie is crestfallen.

Fanny watches him furiously thinking, his brows knitted together with the effort.

"But do you think he'll be all right?" he asks.

Fanny smiles. "I expect he will, yes. They say cats have nine lives, don't they?"

Mattie nods, blinking back the tears.

"And," she continues, "they always land on their feet."

Mattie swallows hard.

"I wouldn't be surprised, Mattie, if Smokey isn't bedded down somewhere comfortable right this minute."

"Do you think so?"

"I'm sure. Now – you try and get some sleep. It's been quite a day."

He turns on to his side and Fanny creeps away. Just as she reaches the door, he sits upright again and asks, "You won't leave me too, will you, Fanny?"

She sighs, her face in darkness, so that he cannot see its expression. "Good night, Matthew."

When Haworth finally arrives at *The Bull's Head*, lurching up the stairs to the Function Room, he is almost an hour late and already well oiled. Accompanying him are Mr Robert Tinker, owner of *The Grape & Compass* and *Elysian Fields Pleasure Gardens* on Angel Meadow, together with Messrs Roger Bradshaw and John Smith, wealthy merchants residing in palatial houses overlooking the Meadow, and Haworth's neighbours. It has been an excellent day for them already, having made in excess of a thousand pounds from the takings for James Sadler's Balloon Flight, an event which they had promoted, having at the last minute discovered a way of extracting an entrance fee from almost three quarters of those who attended, by means of the employment of some stout, persuasive gentlemen sporting heavy cudgels accompanied by ferocious-looking dogs. By the time they shake Samuel Oldknow's hand, availing themselves of a generous measure from the quart of brandy he has "so thoughtfully provided" for them, they are in an expansive mood. In addition they are joined by Mr Thomas Philips, "representing my brother, John, who regrets he cannot meet with us this evening, for family matters of an important nature prohibit him", and Sir Ashton Lever, who says nothing beyond a somewhat curt "Good evening", and who sits a little apart from the rest of the company.

"Come, Samuel," says Haworth, raising his glass, "time and tide wait for no man. Proceed with your proposal."

Samuel suppresses the urge to deliver the obvious response to this remark. He merely inclines his head and gets to his feet.

"Gentlemen, Mr Haworth speaks with more perspicacity than he intends, for time is indeed of the essence, and it is the need for haste, to adopt the motto of our age, by which I mean speed, gentlemen, which is my theme for this evening, and about which I mean to expound more to you directly."

"Come, man, to the point," interrupts an impatient Sir Ashton, pouring himself a second brandy. "We've not got all night."

"Indeed not, sir. I thank you," replies Samuel, feeling the colour rise to his cheeks. "Mr Arkwright and Mr Drinkwater have, between them, revolutionised the manufacture of cotton. With their steam-powered mills, bringing all elements of production under a single roof, they can now control every process required, from roving, carding, spinning, weaving, bleaching and dyeing. Raw cotton comes in at one door and the finished product leaves by another. Then factor in our current mania for canals – the Duke's Cut has brought Manchester within easy reach of the port of Liverpool and the trading capitals of the world, while the Bolton & Bury Canal is being connected to the Irwell Navigation, the Ashton Canal to the Rochdale Canal, which even as I speak is being extended to Castlefield and west across the Pennines – all of which opens up newer and bigger markets, and enables us to deliver our goods more quickly to all of our customers, wherever they may be."

"Please, Mr Oldknow," says an irascible Thomas Philips, "tell us something we *don't* know."

"At present there are just two of these giant factories – Mr Arkwright's on Miller Street and Mr Drinkwater's on Windmill Street – but it will not be long before there are many more of them. We are all witnesses to the unstoppable rise of building and development along our waterways. I predict, gentlemen, that in less than ten years from now, there will be a hundred such mills in Manchester."

"Ten years is a long time, Mr Oldknow," says Sir Ashton with an icy stare.

"Precisely so, Sir Ashton, and as our host, Mr Haworth, has so wisely pointed out, time and tide wait for no man."

Samuel allows himself a short pause to let the implication of this remark sink in a little further and pours himself a glass of water.

"As some of you will be aware, I am no stranger to the cotton business myself. I have mills in Stockport – one at Hillgate, another at Carrs, a bleaching plant at Heaton Mersey and a finishing works at Bullocky Smith near Disley. The factory in Hillgate alone produces a hundred-and-twenty-count muslin."

"Yes indeed, Mr Oldknow, your reputation for quantity is well known," remarks Thomas Philips, "but it's quality *we're* more interested in. That is why we're investing in the latest water-powered Jacquard looms."

"Different products for different markets, Mr Philips," counters Samuel, "but one thing that unites us is the desire to reach those markets more quickly than our competitors."

"I concede you that," says Philips.

"Now – what you gentlemen may not know is that I have another mill, newly built, at Mellor, a brick structure, six storeys high, four hundred feet in length. As part of its construction I have diverted the River Goyt to create three large mill ponds, a system of tunnels, channels and wheel pits. We refer to them as the Roman Lakes, for we believe the original ponds may well date from antiquity. But there is nothing of antiquity inside the Mill, everything is state-of-the-art modern, including..." And here he again pauses for the maximum effect. "Including the proposed installation of the first ever Boulton & Watt steam engine in the Manchester area."

A murmur of renewed interest ripples around the room.

"This steam engine, gentlemen, is an eight horse-power machine, which can turn more spindles, more quickly, than anything currently envisaged by Mr Arkwright or Mr Drinkwater. Though it is only a matter of time, gentlemen, before any number of them is installed in those new mills being planned alongside our waterways. But – and here's the nub of what I am proposing, gentlemen – my mill at Mellor is already built. All it needs is the addition of this steam engine to bring it up to full capacity within a matter of weeks. What I am asking you for, therefore, is to consider an investment into the purchase of just such an engine – I have placed a temporary order with Mr James Watt himself, pending the outcome of this meeting – for which you will steal an undoubted march on all your rivals. In return I would pledge to this consortium a forty percent share of the profits, which would not, I feel emboldened to predict, be anything less than considerable."

He now pours himself a stiff brandy to reward himself for having delivered what he hopes will prove an irresistible pitch, which he drains in a single draught, and then sits down to receive their response.

He does not have long to wait.

"Fine words, Samuel," declares Haworth genially...

"... butter no parsnips," concludes Sir Ashton.

"Quite," continues Haworth. "Figures, Samuel. We need figures."

"The bottom line," adds Philips. "The final entry in your accounts, the numerical amount which indicates the profit..."

"... or loss," interjects Sir Ashton.

"... of your financial statement."

"Profit, I assure you, gentlemen." Samuel does some quick mental calculations to confirm the numbers he has spent several days going over repeatedly. "The figure I am asking from you is only ten thousand pounds."

There is a sharp, collective intake of breath in the Upstairs Function Room. Immediately the gentlemen divide into smaller splinter groups, discussing the implications in hushed whispers behind the backs of raised hands.

Samuel waits. Actually, the amount he needs to raise is closer to twenty thousand, but he reckons he can sell the works at Bullocky Smith for eight, and he's sure he could raise another two – *if* the gentlemen around this table can summon up the ten he has asked them for.

"You will recoup your investment twice over within the first two years of production," he adds, realising he may risk sounding too desperate. But damn it, he *is* desperate. "Whereas who knows how long you might have to wait before you could see that kind of return on the mills yet to be built here?"

The whispering continues.

Eventually it subsides and the different groups rejoin as one. They turn to face Samuel.

"An interesting proposition, Oldknow," declares Philips, "but not for us, I'm afraid. We Philipses are a conservative bunch, I'm afraid. Oh, we don't doubt the impact Mr Watt and Mr Boulton's steam engine will have on the speed and efficiency of production, but we'd like to wait and see first. We're already fully committed to our new Jacquard looms for the present."

Samuel inclines his head.

"Not for us either, old chap," says Haworth, with a sweeping shrug that takes in Bradshaw and Smith. "We've fingers in far too many pies already."

Samuel feels the back of his neck flushing and he once again is forced to loosen his cravat a little further.

"I might be interested," says Sir Ashton suddenly.

All the eyes in the room turn upon him.

"Unlike the rest of the assembled company here, I am not a man of business. I am a scientist and a gentleman. As some of you may be aware, I have a collection of natural curiosities that some consider to be of unparalleled importance. I speak of my *Holophusicon*."

Haworth, Bradshaw, Smith and Philips exchange silent but meaningful glances.

"At present this *Holophusicon* is housed in a number of houses in London, on Leicester Square. There is talk of the collection being split up, scattered to the four corners. This is something which would cause me great pain. It has been a life's work, and it is now my hope to see it restored and brought back to Manchester, to my home at Alkrington Hall. Therefore, I should be prepared to put in... let's say eight thousand five hundred pounds."

A sober silence descends upon the Upstairs Function Room, which is finally broken by Haworth.

"That's most generous of you, Sir Ashton. What say you, Samuel?"

"Yes indeed, Sir Ashton. Most generous." He walks across to shake his new benefactor by the hand, while at the same time working out just where else he might try to raise the shortfall.

"Well," says Haworth, "I think that concludes our business. I am sure we all have other appointments for the evening. I know I have," he adds with a wink to his companions, as he, Bradshaw and Smith pick up the jug with the remains of the brandy and head downstairs.

Mr Philips rises to his feet, bows somewhat formally and awkwardly, then addresses Sir Ashton from the doorway. "I wish you luck with your collection, Sir," he says. "Some years ago you dined in my brother's house on Lever's Row. You may not remember the occasion, but it was the night of the Earthquake."

"Ah, yes. Indeed. An unforgettable night."

"You inspired my nephew that evening."

"Did I? I don't recall. Wait a minute – was *he* the young man with the *vivarium*, whose flies all escaped?" He laughs mirthlessly at the memory.

"The same, Sir."

"Did he recover?"

"Indeed he did, Sir. He has built up a most impressive collection himself now. *Lepidoptera*, mostly. We look forward to when Manchester has her own museum."

Sir Ashton raises a rueful eyebrow. He has, on several occasions, approached members of the *Literary &*

Philosophical Society about just such a proposition, but has always been rebuffed.

"Quite so," he says simply. "But I believe no building that is suitable can be found."

"Not yet, Sir Ashton," replies Thomas, "but in time perhaps? A tide of opinion is swelling in favour…"

"But time," sneers Sir Ashton, "and tide…"

"Wait for no man. Good night."

Sir Ashton watches Philips depart then turns to Samuel.

"You would like my payment when, Mr Oldknow?"

"As soon as is convenient, Sir Ashton."

"Very well," he replies, a look of distaste passing across his lips. "I shall have my bank draw up an agreement before the end of the month."

"Thank you, Sir Ashton."

"With a schedule for your repayments."

"Naturally."

"Including the forty percent share of your profits quarterly."

"Of course."

Samuel waits until Sir Ashton has left before sitting down with an audible sigh. He is not at the finishing line yet, but he has at least left the starting gate. He takes out a handkerchief and mops his perspiring brow, loosens his cravat still further, then lines up some more snuff on the back of his hand, which he inhales in a single snort.

From below snippets of conversation drift up to him.

"Very wise, Thomas," says Haworth. "I wouldn't go near that Oldknow fellow if I were you."

"I don't intend to."

"He knows how to turn a profit, I'll give him that, but he's always in hock to someone, so there's always the risk his debts will be called in, and any backers will be left with egg on their faces."

"Not me. I prefer the long game."

"In that case, I'd recommend a little flutter on these Boulton & Watt engines Oldknow wants to buy. If they're as good as he says they are – and I don't doubt him on that score – you could do a lot worse than to invest in that company as a whole, rather than merely help a gambler like Oldknow to buy one just for himself. My hunch is that if more and more mills and factories want to convert to steam – and I reckon they're going to be more or less forced to if they want to keep pace – then there are going to be a whole lot of orders for them."

"Hmm. A most interesting proposition. I might take you up on that. Let me come back to you."

"Well don't take too long, old chap. You don't want to try and board that ship once it's already put to sea, if you know what I mean?"

"Ay, ay, Captain."

"That's the spirit – talking of which, mine's a rum…"

Their voices trail away. Samuel is left pondering their words at the top of the staircase. He is about to descend into the main part of the inn when he is intercepted by the landlord, Mr John Raffald.

"I couldn't help overhearing some of what tha's been sayin' to t'other gentlemen, sir…"

"Yes?" says Samuel sharply.

"Only I were wonderin' if tha' were still on t' look-out for investors, like?"

"Possibly. Why? Do you have someone in mind?"

"Tha's lookin' at 'im, sir," says the landlord, smiling crookedly.

Samuel eyes him narrowly. "How much are you talking about, Mr Raffald?"

The landlord furtively looks over his shoulder to make sure he is not being overheard and draws nearer to Samuel, who has to prevent himself from gagging on the publican's sour breath.

"I reckon I can lay me 'ands on about twelve hundred pounds."

Samuel widens his eyes in surprise. "Really? Are you certain?"

"Oh yes, sir. This place does pretty well, all things considered, and my good lady 'as quite a bit put by from the sale of 'er recipe books."

Samuel now forgets all about the landlord's sour breath and looks him directly in the eye. "How quickly can you get this?"

"How quickly dost tha' need it?"

The two men smile.

"I think we understand one another," says Samuel.

"I think we do, sir," says Raffald, who spits into the palm of his hand, which he offers to Samuel, who, after the briefest of hesitations, clasps it firmly in his own.

"Well," he thinks, after Raffald has left the room, "maybe I'm approaching the final furlong."

He tips the last remaining dregs of brandy into his mouth, then takes the stairs leading down to the inn two and three steps at a time.

*

Sadler rights the gondola, makes sure the fire is completely extinguished and then begins the laborious task of hauling back the envelope, removing its wire struts, and folding it in such a way as it can be fitted inside the wicker basket. He hates doing this. The landings, he now realises, after having successfully negotiated three of them, are by definition something of an anti-climax. For one thing he is invariably alone. Not knowing precisely where one is going to land means of course that there can never be the same cheering crowds who see one take off. He corrects himself. That is not strictly true. With his first flight he had simply gone straight up and down a matter of fifty feet or so, landing more or less in the exact same spot from where he had taken off. Which was a matter of such humiliation that he had dearly wished he *had* been alone. The second time he was dragged into a stream with only a handful of Jersey cows for company, who had panicked when they heard the jets of flame sparking in the sky above their heads, and who, as the gondola made contact with the ground, had been so terrified that they ran in several directions at once, some of them getting caught up in the guy ropes and tangled in the envelope, while he was tipped head first into the ditch. Fortunately for him, it had been such a dry summer that the water level was very low, or who knows what might have happened? He might have drowned, for he couldn't swim.

Ideally he needs at least one person to be present, who has witnessed him actually coming down, preferably two, who can be relied upon to verify the exact position, so that he is then able to determine just how far he has travelled.

He looks around. Nobody. Wait a minute – who was that coming over the brow of the hill? Oh. Only a boy. Still – beggars can't be choosers.

"I say," he calls, "you there, I don't suppose you can tell me where I am?"

The boy eyes him suspiciously. He has high, narrow, pointed shoulders. He wears a royal blue velvet jacket, fawn brocaded knee breeches over white stockings, a pair of brown leather shoes with a brass buckle, and in his arms he is carrying the cat. The pair of them blink synchronously.

"You're trespassing, that's where you are," says the boy.

"Oh?"

"Yes. All the land around, as far as the eye can see, belongs to my father."

"Oh, I'm sure I'm begging his pardon, but I believe he'll be forgiving me once he realises who I am."

The bony boy raises a sceptical eyebrow. The cat appears to do likewise.

"I'm James Sadler, the Celebrated Aeronaut, and I've just flown here all the way from Manchester."

"Well be a good fellow and take yourself back there. Or my father might clap you in irons."

Sadler attempts a chuckle. He has to admire the boy's pluck, his audacity and self assurance. But he finds that no such chuckle appears able to present itself. There is something unnerving about the boy, his lofty demeanour of utter self-possession, his unshakeable sense of sheer entitlement.

"Yes, well – if you could just be telling me who you are and the name of this place, then I'll be on my way before you can say 'Jack Robinson'."

"And why would I say that? I don't know a Jack Robinson. Unless he's one of the workers at my father's factory, but then I don't know any of their names. There's no reason for me to."

"No, young master. I can see that. So…?"

"Yes. What is it?"

Sadler somewhat helplessly and apologetically spreads out his hands. "This place…?"

"Holcombe Hill and it's part of my father's estate."

"Your father?"

"Mr Robert Peel, known as Robert Parsley Peel, the largest textile manufacturer in all of Great Britain, owner of twenty-eight different mills and factories, father of *Sir* Robert, 1st Baronet of Bury, in the County Palatine of Lancaster, soon to be Member of Parliament for Tamworth, and *my* older brother." He omits to mention that this is a seat that his brother has recently purchased, along with the rest of Lord Bath's estates in the surrounding area, and is currently in the process of 'buying' the votes of the twenty-four only residents who will consequently 'elect' him.

"Indeed?" says Sadler, a smile beginning to form across his lips. "And *your* name, young master?"

"I am his son – Laurence."

"I'm pleased to make your acquaintance, Laurence."

"The pleasure is all yours, Mr Sadler, I do assure you. Now – do you intend to vacate yourself from this private property, or shall I be forced to call in my father's Bailiff to have you escorted forthwith?" He strokes the back of the cat's neck, who closes his eyes in orgasmic contentment.

"Peel, you say? Now that wouldn't be the Peel of Haworth, Yates and Peel, would it? Textile Manufacturers to the Crown?"

For the first time the boy falters. "Yes. What business is it of yours?"

"Only that your father's business partner, Mr Jonathan Haworth, is a very great friend of mine. Did he not sponsor my balloon flight? Was the ascent not scheduled to take place in the fine Gardens adjoining his most splendid new house by the Angel Meadow? Is not the envelope of my balloon made of several pieces stitched together of a cotton silk fibre provided by your father's business?"

The boy opens his mouth as if to speak, then closes it. He tries a second time, with the same wordless result. He feels he is in danger of resembling one of the carp in the ornamental pond behind his father's house. The cat begins to squirm uncomfortably in his arms. He lets it fall to the ground, where it stakes out the narrowing gap between the boy and the balloonist. The boy hastily collects himself. It is an art that will later serve him well in his own political and commercial career. He recognises where he has been wrong-footed, when he must learn not to dig himself into a corner, but to change his step and dance to the more prevailing tune.

"Why didn't you say so before, sir? You must accompany me at once to meet my father. He will be delighted to hear of your adventures in the heavens, sir. As would I. They say you might touch the face of God."

"Hardly that, Laurence. But the face of the future, certainly."

"Leave your balloon," says the boy, regaining his former confidence. "I'll have someone sent round to collect it for you."

"Thank you. I shall be glad of the assistance. But I should prefer to remain and supervise the procedure, if you don't mind, young master, and perhaps join you and your father later?"

"Of course." And he picks up the cat, tucks it under one arm, and walks back down the slope of the hill. The cat, staring backwards, continues to eye Mr Sadler with an air of supercilious disdain.

As the boy and the cat disappear from view, James decides that this might be the perfect moment to partake of the fine Virginia cigar Jonathan Haworth had furnished him with earlier that day, but a sudden wind picks up from the east, gusting the silk envelope of the balloon, which billows around him. James becomes aware of a torn scrap of paper dancing on the air towards him, before fastening around his ankle. He stoops to pick it up. It appears to be the front page of a newspaper, but not one that he recognises, with a date upon it which does not make sense. Beneath its banner headline is an image of another balloon tethered to the earth, waiting to be released, but one which bears no resemblance to anything he has seen before. Whereas his was an ellipse, this looks more like the still unlit cigar he now holds in his other hand. The words on the page shimmer in and out of focus as James attempts to read them...

*

The Ramsbottom Observer

27th September 1916

ZEPPELIN DROPS BOMBS ON VILLAGE SCHOOL

Two nights ago German Airship LZ21, under the command of Oberleutnant Kurt Frankenburg, rained terror and destruction down on the tiny remote village of Holcombe midway between the cotton towns of Bury and Ramsbottom.

The Post Office, local pub *The Shoulder of Mutton*, and the Village School between them took the full force of the attack, with all three buildings suffering direct hits, resulting in their windows and doors being blown off.

Mercifully there were no casualties – except for one. In an eerie echo of another balloon's unexpected descent upon Holcombe, when Mr James Sadler's gondola touched down 130 years ago, the only known victim of the outrage was a poor thrush, who lost its life through the force of the blast. Perfectly preserved and found by Miss Julie Carter (aged 8 years) of Lumb Carr Farm, who had a miraculous escape. Let her father Mr Adrian Carter explain:

"My wife, baby and I were asleep in the front bedroom. Some time after midnight I heard a startling boom from a field nearby. I rushed to the window, but before I had properly grasped what was happening, there was another terrific report, much nearer and much more terrifying. There were flames issuing from the room in which our two daughters were sleeping – Julie and Angela. I can't really remember what happened after that. All I can think is that somehow I must have dashed in there, scooped them up in my arms and run downstairs, for the next thing I knew I was standing outside, all scorched and stifled, with one of them on each side. The eldest asked me what it was had made the room catch fire…"

That was Julie. The following day she found the poor thrush lying on its side just outside the school gate.

"Our teacher said we must preserve it," the plucky eight-year-old told our reporter, "as a reminder of our lucky escape."

Not so lucky was the town of Bolton, which suffered several direct hits on its factories and houses, with at least 40 people so far reported to have lost their lives.

We now know a little more of what happened that fateful Monday night as thousands of innocent Lancastrians lay safely asleep in their beds. Or so they thought.

The Zeppelin first entered these shores when it crossed the Lincolnshire coast at Sutton-on-Sea at around 9.45pm. At 10.30pm it had reached Lincoln itself, having first by-passed Bawtrey. It then headed north to avoid the searchlights and anti-aircraft guns at Sheffield. An hour later it was spotted above the Derwent Reservoir. It appeared to be following the course of a Milk Train bound for

Manchester via Todmorden, before veering away to Bacup, where it failed to drop any of its bombs on the obvious targets of two highly important shell factories at the Irwell and Height Barn Mills.

It was a clear sky. Stars shone brightly above the graceful airship, this elegant dealer of death, as it stealthily made its way across the moors. The quiet stillness of the night, normally the haunt only of the occasional screech owl, was on this night punctuated by the distant humming of LZ21's engines as it passed overhead.

A Police Constable at Rawtenstall reported sighting it to the north of Waterfoot and Cloughfold, where it appeared to hover menacingly in a stationary position, before releasing the first of its cargo of bombs. He described a light descending from it like "a monstrous bull's eye", illuminating the countryside beneath.

Mr J.H. Whipp, manager at Grime Bridge Colliery, recorded in his diary that "the only damage received was the blowing out of several windows at the nearby Field Top Farm."

Another bomb fell close to His Majesties' White Cotton Mills at Cross Lane Works, which had just started firing up its boilers for the day's production to come. Fortunately it missed the 'Rag Shop', as it is affectionately known, averting what otherwise would have been a catastrophe. It landed instead in the back garden of one Colonel Craven Hoyle, detonating tons of top soil, which were thrown in excess of 200 feet into the air, but harming no one.

Nearby Whinberry Naze also escaped unscathed. On Helmshore Road large crowds gathered to watch the stately progress of the Zeppelin, apparently heedless of the danger, until a waitress from the neighbouring *Bridge End Hotel* joined them, still wearing her apron, the whiteness of which alarmed those who had assembled there, who feared that its brightness might attract the attention of the raider overhead.

Everywhere people behaved with remarkable calmness. Our sister paper, *The Haslingden Gazette*, has described the unperturbed stillness of the crowds who came out, some of them still in their night clothes, to witness the passing of "the cigar-shaped murder craft up in the sky."

At nearby Cockham a farmer and his wife were discovered to have slept on a mattress dragged into a field, which they considered a safer place, out in the open instead of indoors.

Another witness reported seeing several small boys carrying what looked like a heavy black cylindrical object, later learned to be an unexploded bomb, to be deposited for safe keeping at the local Police Station.

The LZ21 then steered a course for Ramsbottom and Stubbins. Two bombs fell on The Rake, another on Dundee Lane, a fourth on the Giles Taylor Mineral Water Works on Regent Street, and a fifth onto a luckily uninhabited cottage over at Pot Green.

An 11 year-old butcher's boy in Callendar Street was awakened by what he thought was the sound of the honey-pot men with their horse and cart collecting the night soil from the cobbled alley at the back of his house, only to discover later that what he had heard had been the dropping of more bombs, which were falling close by in Holcombe, the site of the raid's first casualty, that unfortunate thrush, in the shadow of Peel Tower, the 128 feet monolith erected in honour of Ramsbottom's most famous son, Sir Robert Peel, the father of British policing, whose grandfather, Robert Parsley Peel, had established the first cotton mills in the area.

It is possible that Oberleutnant Frankenburg, who was piloting the Zeppelin, believed he was still following the course of the railway line that led to Manchester. But at a height of more than 5000 feet, despite the clear skies above him, his vision of what lay below was sorely impeded by the plumes of smoke rising from the chimneys of thousands of houses and factories across South-East Lancashire. We may well have been spared further casualties than those so tragically visited upon Bolton by the notorious Manchester smog. What is routinely cursed as our enemy, last night became our friend.

130 years ago, when Mr James Sadler first took to the skies over Manchester in his hot air balloon, there were fears that the new age his heroic achievements so boldly proclaimed might usher in a new kind of warfare, one waged with flying machines, where our enemies might seek to invade us from the skies. Last night's attacks by not just the LZ21 but other airships across the country would appear to have confirmed the warnings of those prophets of doom. But fear not, readers, the skill and bravery of our own pilots, combined with the ingenuity and innovation of the engineers of Manchester's industries will always remain that one step ahead. Oberleutnant Frankenburg's Zeppelin was eventually shot down over the North Sea as it attempted to make its way back to Germany. There were no survivors. The successful attack was carried out by our heroic aviators at the helm of our glorious Royal Flying Corps, spearheaded by the

Avro bi-planes manufactured right here in Manchester. Let us take heart from their new motto, which has just received the royal seal of approval from His Majesty King George V.
Per ardua ad astra.
Through adversity to the stars.

Per ardua ad astra.
Another sharp gust of wind wrenches the newspaper from Sadler's grasp. He watches it sail up towards the darkening sky, where already a few stars are beginning to show. It is as if a great tower looms at his back. Its shadow lengthens ahead of him, like a giant arm outstretched, its crenellated fingers pointing towards a new imagined future.

*

It is the night of the balloon flight.

Many of the crowds who flocked earlier in the day to witness Mr Sadler rise up towards the heavens have remained in Angel Meadow to sample some of the many delights still on offer. Not the formal setting of the Meadow's inner sanctum, however, Mr Tinker's *Elysium Pleasure Garden*, which is for ticket holders and their guests only, who gasp in wonder at the Chinese lanterns, those earliest forms of hot air balloons, which hang in the trees, Pentecostal tongues of flame, lending the scene a magical, fairy-tale luminescence, where a small bewigged orchestra plays a selection of Handel's *Chamber Suite in D*, followed by Herschel's *Oboe Concerto*, featuring the composer himself conducting and playing. Having until recently been the principal organist of Halifax Minster, he has walked the twenty-six miles via Sowerby Bridge, across the high, open moors of Rishworth, Ripponden and Saddleworth, calling in on friends at Denshaw, Delph, Diggle and Dobcross, bringing with him three prized possessions, two of which he carries in a leather satchel – his Newtonian reflector telescope 'with a most capital speculum of my own manufacture' and a recently acquired copy of one of Joseph Haydn's trios for viola, cello and baryton – and the third in its own purpose-made case, an actual baryton itself, a bowed stringed instrument similar to the *viola de gamba*, but with an additional set of sympathetic wire strings, which vibrate in harmony with the seven upper gut strings, or which can be plucked additionally with the thumb. The particular instrument being carried by William Herschel, as he prepares to play the Haydn trio, is claimed to be a copy of the one originally used by Papa Jo's Hungarian patron, Prince Nikolaus of Esterhazy, to whom the piece was first dedicated, the Prince being an accomplished baryton player himself. Rumours have even reached the supposed cultural desert that is Manchester, so far removed as it is from the concert halls of London, a misconception that Mr Tinker is keen to overturn with events such as this, that Haydn is relocating to England. Maybe he might even persuade the great man to perform there himself one day. But for now there is a frisson of anticipation at the prospect of this national première of one of his trios, played on the very instrument for which it was first composed.

But Herr Herschel's interests are inexorably shifting away from the musical towards the astronomical. It is his Newtonian telescope, rather than the Esterhazy baryton, which occupies his thoughts more these days, and he is already thinking beyond the concert this evening to the following day, when he will be a guest of Sir Thomas Egerton, 1st Earl of Wilton, some four miles distant in Heaton Park, where he has been invited to inspect designs by the architect James Wyatt for a new observatory the Earl intends to install on a hill purporting to be the highest point in all of Manchester, recently measured at three hundred and fifty-four feet above sea level. Herschel is impatient to set up his telescope there and further explore the heavens in a far more precise way than can ever be possible from one of James Sadler's balloons, he believes, which he espied earlier in the day while traversing the Saddleworth Moor. Although the day was warm and the air comparatively still, a few hundred feet up in the air the currents were clearly much stronger than down on *terra firma*, even on so exposed a stretch of ground as the open moorland, and so Herschel had difficulty tracking the erratic progress of the aeronaut. In addition the telescope was not designed for use in broad daylight and he frequently found himself looking directly into the sun, causing a temporary, though painful onset of blindness, so that black spots would dance before his eyes, causing him to see double. There were two suns, not one, and two balloonists. He was keenly reminded of his current preoccupation – the investigation of binary star systems, or optical doubles, as he preferred to describe them. Where previously it had been thought that a distant star, especially when viewed through the naked eye unaided, was a single point of light, in fact, when examined more closely through his Newtonian reflector telescope, specifically when taking advantage of the various refinements he had personally incorporated, it became immediately apparent that there were frequently two, sometimes multiple stars which were the source of these far away beams. By observing their true and proper motions he has been able to identify no fewer than two hundred and sixty-nine such systems, and he has made it his mission to catalogue them all through a well-ordered, methodical search of the entire known universe. This has enabled him to calculate more precisely their distance from the Earth by means of the parallax shifts in their separation.

Parallax.

Herschel rolls the word several times over his tongue. The displacement or difference in the apparent position of an object when viewed along two different lines of sight. He places one foot steadily in front of the other, measuring the distance between himself and his intended destination. Things are no longer where we once thought they were, he muses. They shift, they replicate. Double vision. Like looking at the world through a tear in your eye. The more he explores the heavens through his telescope, the more he comes to realise just how little he knows. The more binary stars he identifies and catalogues and pins down with a name, a number and a location, the more he begins to discern there are even vaster tracts of impenetrable darkness in the night skies, from where no light emanates for him to observe their passage earthwards. His good friend and fellow astronomer, the Reverend John Mitchell of Thornhill, in the parish of Dewsbury, has posited the theory of what he calls 'dark stars', which may lie tantalisingly beyond the reach of even the most powerful of telescopes.

In Angel Meadow a few hours later, as he prepares to play the Haydn baryton trio for the first time anywhere in England, the expectant audience of Manchester textile manufacturers and their wives sit beneath ribbons of Chinese lanterns hanging in the trees, winking in imitation of those far-off, distant points of light he now knows to be binary, offering a multiplicity of choices and directions.

Many hundreds more than that privileged elite, who sit in rapt wonder listening to the sound of Herr Herschel's exotic baryton, resonating through them with its deep, celestial music of the spheres, are sitting in equal amazement as they are transported to the furthest edges of human possibility by the performers, human and equine, in Philip Astley's Travelling Circus on nearby St George's Fields.

Among them are Fanny and Zachary.

Having walked to Shakerley and back in less than twenty-four hours in order to receive his father's blessing to pursue both a career and a wife, Zachary has to keep pinching himself to make sure that this night is really happening. But it is. Fanny sits transported beside him. Thrilled by the fire eaters, fascinated and repelled in equal measure by the sword swallowers, excited by the knife throwers, especially when she is chosen to be a volunteer target. She loves her time in the dipped candlelight, trained upon her from a specially lowered iron coronet containing several sconces, each dappling the centre of the sawdust ring with their eerie luminescence, as Signor Farinelli, the celebrated knife-thrower from Naples (though in reality from Wigan), sends a succession of stiletto-sharp daggers whistling past her ears without so much as disturbing a single lock of her hair. She is entranced by the dancing Lipizzaner horses, all that power so finely balanced upon each pair of delicately poised hooves. Zachary will keep throwing her sidelong, covert glances, thinking that she does not notice, but she senses his eyes upon her, desperately trying to read her emotions as they are translated into different expressions, and is secretly delighted at the attention he bestows upon her, causing yet another layer of feeling to pass across her lips, her cheeks, her brow, which surely he can interpret. He has no cause for worry. Her face is a map, with every feature clearly signposted. No hidden lime pit, or unmarked hollows, where he might tumble, slip or lose his way. No blackthorn brake with scratching thorns or briars. There is no hint of obfuscation. Only happiness. She turns towards him, so that he might see her fully, and smiles without reservation. See, her eyes are saying, how happy I am, and he is utterly floored by her. He, who is used to viewing the world through the tools of his trade, his transit and theodolite, his level and his compass, can find no benchmark against which to measure her. She is a *nonpareille*.

The circus is reaching its climax. After all of the acrobats and clowns, jugglers and magicians, Mr Astley has entered the arena to announce what will be the final act, whose reputation for her death-defying deeds precede her. She has added danger and daring, lustre and lucre to the circus as it travels the north country fairs, ever since she first joined them just two years before.

"My Lords, Ladies and Gentlemen," he announces, revolving slowly in the centre of the ring, taking in each member of the audience as he does so, who lean forward in their seats, their faces expectant with excitement, "we now come to the evening's Grand Finale. Will you please welcome the one, the only, the incomparable *Dulcibella, La Funambola, Principessa of the Tightrope*, who will tonight, before your very eyes, walk the high wire!"

He cracks his whip, which sets off a prolonged and tense drum roll, as Arabella Reynolds enters the ring, where she is greeted with thunderous applause. She walks around the perimeter with her arms raised as a string quartet plays Handel's *Entrance of the Queen of Sheba*. After she has completed a single circuit, she lets the cloak she has been wearing – a deep black velvet, which, *"with glitt'ring oes and spangles o'er-run that in her motion such reflection gave, as filled the heavens with silver stars"*, seems to be the very mirror of the night sky above – to reveal a costume so white, so diaphanous, it shimmers in the circlet of candles flickering from the roof of the tent. A tightly fitted bodice, encrusted with sequins, gives way to a many layered tulle skirt, delicate as gossamer, daringly exposing her legs from thigh to toe, clad in silk hose which hug her like a second skin.

She climbs the ladder towards the tightrope, which spans the entire width of the arena, passing directly above the audience's heads more than thirty feet up in the air. When she reaches the top she gestures with each arm towards the sea of upturned faces below, gazing up at her in wide-eyed, open-mouthed admiration. She now appears so tiny but still her costume twinkles, catching the light of the countless candles, so that she appears as the brightest star in all the firmament. The music finishes. Mr Astley calls for silence, which is then followed by another low drum roll.

Arabella looks down from behind the silver, sparkling mask she always wears when she performs anywhere close to Manchester, for fear of being recognised. Her worst nightmare is that one or both her parents might be hidden in the audience, that they will stand up, point directly to her, call her by her name and command her to climb back down. She knows of course that this will never happen. The very idea of either of them mixing with the *hoi polloi* who attend a circus is preposterous – although the thought of her father loitering at the side of the retiring tent outside in order to catch a glimpse of the girls undressing is not so far-fetched – but even if they did, she is certain that they would no longer know her. In the two years since she leapt out of her window into the waiting arms of Mr Astley and galloped away on his piebald Lipizzaner, she has grown several inches in height, while her figure has taken on more shapely curves, a fact accentuated by her close-fitting costume and the appreciative wolf whistles this unfailingly produces from many of the male members of the audience. When she first received such a reaction, it embarrassed her and she confided in Philip that she did not feel she was temperamentally suited to the role of circus performer. It was his suggestion then to wear the mask. "Play a character," he crooned. "Adopt a different persona. Become somebody else. Reinvent yourself." And so she had. *Dulcibella, La Funambola, Principessa of the High Wire.*

But some nights the feeling is so strong that she is certain she will be unmasked and she will fall.

Tonight has been one of those nights.

She stands alone on the small platform at the top of the ladder and looks out along the razor's edge that is the tightrope she must walk along. She visualises herself placing one foot in front of the other, slowly, one step at a time, until she reaches the other side. The secret is, she knows, not to rush, but to feel the lightness of her being, floating in the air, like thistledown, which her tulle skirt always reminds her of. She picks up the thin bamboo cane that is waiting for her by the platform, which she uses to give her extra balance, and prepares to begin.

The drum roll ceases.

All around her is silence, save for the rush of air she feels inside her head.

She lifts one foot out into space, delicately points the toe, then gently places it onto the start of the tightrope. She tentatively tests the torque. There is some give, but it remains taut. Next she raises the other foot, repeating the whole process, so that now she is balanced, a ballet dancer on *demi-pointe*. Then, seemingly without a moment's thought, she skips her way to the centre of the wire. The audience holds its collective breath. Now she pauses. She swivels one hundred and eighty degrees to face the way she has just come, then swivels another hundred and eighty degrees back in the direction she was initially heading. The audience gasps. Arabella waits.

She waits for what seems an eternity. The world is changing, she feels. The earth tilts on its axis. This afternoon a man flew higher than she in a hot air balloon. In this new age a person can reinvent herself. As she has done. She closes her eyes. She raises her front foot high in the air. She allows it to feel its way forward, blindly seeking somewhere safe on which it can land, trusting to instinct, to self-preservation. Sometimes, she thinks, she dreams she is falling. It is not something she fears. Before she hits the ground, she may rise up again and fly. She allows her foot to test the emptiness of space. She feels her centre shift its balance to compensate. She has not yet decided where, or if, she will place her next step.

Zachary and Fanny cling to one another as if to a raft.

Amos is trying to stay awake. But the motion of the cart, the continuous turning of the wheels, is lulling him towards sleep. They are following the course of the Medlock, east of the town, as they make their way the last few miles to Fairfield. Amos remembers the nights in the House of Correction, when he would lie awake listening to the lap of the waters of a different river, the Irwell, against the thick stone walls, imagining himself drifting away upon them. Or when, during the day he might climb up on top of one of the vats where they would tread the wool hour after hour to peep out of the narrow barred window near the ceiling. He would marvel at all the boats and barges plying the river, bringing in goods and people to Manchester from north and south, and wish he were on board one of them, only sailing in the opposite direction, away from the town, to some kind of freedom, no matter where.

"If wishes were horses, beggars would ride..." That's what he heard the old folk say in the House of Correction if ever he spoke aloud his dreams.

Now those dreams are real. He may still be a beggar but he's riding in a cart pulled by a horse with a proper family who have taken him in.

He tries to conjure up the face of the girl who rescued him the night before, who washed him and watched over him, who took him with her to see the great balloon, but already she is slipping from him.

"When can I see you again?" asks Zachary to Fanny's departing back when they reach where Mr and Mrs Oldham's house sits on the corner of Newton Lane and Lever's Row.

"Whit Sunday," she says softly, placing her finger to his lips. "Come to the Pentecost Communion at the Chapel. Let me introduce you after the service."

She hurries indoors, leaving him as though the Holy Spirit itself had descended on him, with tongues of fire blazing in the sky with all the different words in the world for how he is feeling.

Whelp feels a pain inside her unlike any she has ever felt before. It's not hunger, it's not cold. These she recognises and knows what to do when they strike. She also knows that both will pass. But this? It fills her completely. It tightens her throat, stabs her eyes, hammers her chest. Her skin itches, her joints ache, her stomach cramps. She tries to keep up with the cart that carries Amos away but her legs feel heavy and numb. She feels nauseous, feverish. The top of her head is hot to the touch. Her tongue swells up against the roof of her mouth. She hears a sound rising up from deep inside her, parting her lips, so that it might escape.

It is language.

A word. A name.

It reverberates through and around her.

Amos.

She utters it again.

Amos.

He who has been carried.

Away from her. The sound leaves her, like a pebble she must expel, this hard knot in the centre of her, this misbegotten whelp that issues from her throat.

*

Sunday 13th

Zachary arrives early at the Central Methodist Hall on Newton Lane. He finds himself an unobtrusive seat at the back, from where he can see everyone arrive. It has been some years since he last attended a Wesleyan service or sat in a Chapel, although as a child he spent the better part of every Sunday inside the one in Shakerley, assisting his father who was a lay preacher there until he converted to the Moravians, and so he finds the scene reassuringly familiar. A plain cotton cloth covers the altar, red for Pentecost, with a white dove embroidered upon it. There are other splashes of red, too, in the otherwise plain, unadorned Hall, signifying the pillars of fire descending upon the apostles.

Behind him, on a long wooden refectory table, where those members of the congregation who can read and who might wish to follow the service as it unfolds can pick up a hymnal or the Methodist Book of Common Prayer, he notices a different cloth – white, stitched with a pattern of moths caught in leaves of laurel – and wonders who might have made such a delicately worked piece. It feels almost too ornamental for its surroundings, although he appreciates the beauty and skill of the craftsmanship that went into fashioning it. It will be a long time, he thinks, before machines will be able to reproduce the quality of something so obviously and exquisitely hand made.

The Hall is beginning to fill up. Soon there will not be a seat anywhere to be had and people will be forced to stand. He has heard that the Chapel can accommodate upwards of three thousand people and he reckons there must be nearly that number there already, yet still there is no sign of Fanny.

Just when he has resigned himself for having to somehow try and find her among the crowds afterwards when the service is over, he sees her. She is walking behind an elegantly dressed, middle-aged couple, who are evidently well liked and respected. They nod in acknowledgement to people on either side of them as they walk up the central aisle towards a set of chairs that have clearly been saved for them. This must be Andrew and Catherine Oldham. They appear rather old to be the parents of such a young boy. Matthew walks behind, holding Fanny's hand. He looks cross and red-eyed, just as Zachary remembers from the day before, when he had first caught sight of Fanny in the crowds attending Mr Sadler's Balloon Flight. He wonders what has caused him to be so unshakeably angry, or whether this is his natural temperament. Perhaps he was a late child, thinks Zachary, and has been indulged, is used to getting his own way, and so is not so easily diverted, as other children are, if faced with disappointment. He sees him kick Fanny on the ankle as they sit down, which makes her wince involuntarily, the gasp she emits causing Mrs Oldham to turn round sharply to look at Matthew, who shakes his head in wide-eyed innocence, only to sneer slyly back at Fanny as soon as his mother has turned away. Even from this distance he can see Fanny bite her lower lip, not able to say what she really feels, the back of her neck colouring with embarrassment.

She adjusts her shawl, pulling it up higher, and turns around to stop it from slipping further. As she does so, she catches sight of Zachary and waves fleetingly. It is the slightest of gestures but one which is immediately noticed by her mistress, who enquires as to whom she is waving at. Fanny demurely bows her head. He imagines her neck to be flushed once more but the retrieved shawl now hides this.

Zachary is prevented from further speculation by the arrival of the Minister, who greets everyone with a loud "Good morning," before leading the congregation in the Lord's Prayer.

"Give us this day our daily bread, and forgive us our trespasses, as we forgive those who trespass against us…"

After everyone has climbed back up off their knees and settled themselves once more, the Minister makes his way to the modest pulpit at one side of the altar and opens the plain bible that lies upon it.

"Today's reading," he says, "for our traditional service this Whit Sunday morning, comes from the Acts of the Apostles, Chapter one, verses one to four:

" *'And when the day of Pentecost was fully come, they were all with one accord in one place. And suddenly there came a sound from heaven as of a rushing mighty wind, and it filled all the house where they were sitting. And there appeared unto them cloven tongues like as of fire, and it sat upon each of them. And they were all filled with the Holy Ghost, and began to speak with other tongues, as the Spirit gave them utterance'.*"

Sarah, Rachel and Leah assist with the lighting of the candles in readiness for celebrating *Shavuot*. Solomon accepts from Wolf the gift of wheat and barley – the *bikkurim* – which he binds tightly with grasses, declaring them "the first fruits".

"We should have dates and olives, grapes, figs and pomegranates too, but they are not so readily available here in Manchester," he laughs. Then he invites Lemon to read the special passage from the *Tanakh*.

" *'It will be, when you come into the land which the Lord, your God, gives you for an inheritance',"* reads Lemon, " *'and you possess it and settle in it, that you shall take of the first of all the fruit of the ground which you will bring from your land which the Lord, your God, is giving you. You shall put them into a basket, and go to the place which the Lord, your God, will choose to have His Name dwell there. You shall come to the kohen, the priest, who will be serving in those days, who will take the basket from your hand, laying it before the altar'.*"

Solomon smiles. He places the *bikkurim* on a table in the centre of the room between some of the candles lit by the women, then indicates to Reuben to take up the reading from Lemon.

Reuben looks across to Leah, holding Abner, who gazes solemnly back with his large, pale eyes.

" *'The Lord brought us out from Egypt with a strong hand and with an outstretched arm',"* reads Reuben, " *'with great awe, and with signs and wonders. And He brought us to this place, and He gave us this land, a land flowing with milk and honey. So now, behold, I have brought the first of the fruit of the ground which You, O Lord, have given to me'.*"

John Lees, Caroline, Agnes and Amos finally arrived at Fairfield the previous evening, just as the sun was dipping behind the newly completed cupola adorning the Chapel roof, at the same time that Zachary and Fanny held each other enthralled by the feats of *La Funambola* as she walked the tightrope, and Whelp watched from the end of Swan Street long after Amos had disappeared.

Now, in this first morning in their new home, there is an outdoor Lovefeast and service of thanksgiving to commemorate their safe passage, conducted by Brother Swertner, followed by the breaking of new ground for what will eventually be their own home in the Settlement.

" *'And the whole earth was of one language, and of one speech'*," reads John. " *'And it came to pass, as they journeyed from the east, that they found a plain in the land of Shinar, and they dwelt there'.*"

He looks up at his family, but they are paying him no attention. Amos has fallen asleep again, even though it is still only ten of the clock, for the exertions of the previous two days have exhausted him. Agnes lays his head upon her lap, stroking his hair, while Caroline watches this infant *pieta* in silent wonder. She feels a kind of life returning to her, which has nothing to do with the reasons why her husband has brought them to this new Settlement, but which she can see might yet bring them a kind of unhoped-for salvation. John risks a half smile towards her and is rewarded by a look of peace and serenity in her face he has not seen since they left Dukinfield more than five years before. The creaking bones in his back begin to crack as he tries to unstiffen them one by one and stand tall once more, his eyes no longer fixed on the ground, as they have been since he forced his family to leave their comfortable house on King Street. They have found their new home at last.

" *'And they said one to another, "Go to, let us make brick, and burn them thoroughly." And they had brick for stone, and slime had they for mortar. And they said, "Go to, let us build us a city and a tower, whose top may reach unto heaven; and let us make us a name, lest we be scattered abroad upon the face of the whole earth." And the Lord came down to see the city and the tower, which the children of men builded. And the Lord said, "Behold, the people are one, and they have all one language; and this they begin to do: and now nothing will be restrained from them, which, now they have imagined it, they will labour to complete it".' "*

Inside the Central Methodist Hall the Minister exhorts the people to lift up their hearts and voices in *O For a Thousand Tongues to Sing*, one of Charles Wesley's favourites.

*"O for a thousand tongues to sing
My great Redeemer's praise,
The glories of my God and King,
The triumphs of his grace!*

*See how great a flame aspires,
Kindled by a spark of grace.
Jesus' love the nations fires,
Sets the kingdoms on a blaze..."*

A few, like Zachary, follow the words from their hymn books, but most know them by heart. Their faces shine as though bathed in the Pentecostal light of fire, a blind faith that Zachary finds he almost envies, but shrinks back from, in case his fingers get too close and are burned. He prefers the certainty of trigonometry, the measured calculations of sines and cosines to give him the accuracy of distances and angles. He looks around the vast Central Hall through his surveyor's eyes, marvels at the precision of compass and theodolite which has made this building possible. But then he sees the way the light streams through the windows, creating new isosceles triangles of its own, which no amount of measuring could have predicted, the way it falls upon the hair and face of Fanny in front of him, almost as if the building had been designed specifically to capture her in this way, at this moment, as if she is the living embodiment of one of those stained glass angels that the Non-Conformists and Dissenters so denounce, banishing them from their places of worship. Zachary likes to think of himself as a man of his times, rational, pursuing the muse of Enlightenment, but moments such as this can still confound him. He turns his face back to the words dancing before him in the hymnal and tries to match his voice to those more certain ones surrounding him.

> *"To bring fire on earth He came;*
> *Kindled in some hearts it is;*
> *O that all might catch the flame,*
> *All partake the glorious bliss!*
>
> *Saw ye not the cloud arise,*
> *Little as a human hand?*
> *Now it spreads along the skies,*
> *Hangs o'er all the thirsty land..."*

Reuben picks up the *bikkurim* and carries it across to his son, gently swaying it from side to side in front of his face, before returning it to the table.

"Wolf," says Solomon, "read the passage from Ezekiel."

Wolf inclines his head. "I don't need to read it," he says. "I know it by heart."

"As do we all," says Aaron.

Together the men all chant. " '*Then a spirit carried me away and behind me I heard a great roaring sound. Blessed is the presence of God in this place*'."

Lemon thanks Solomon for his kindness.

"Does not the *Tanakh* tell us that the farmer must allow the stranger, the widow and the orphan to gather from his crop?" replies Solomon. "And then does not Ruth say to Naomi, '*wherever you go, I will go, and wherever you lodge, I will lodge. Your people shall be my people and your God my God*'?"

After a day of so many new arrivals, this Whit Sunday morning sees its departures too.

Assembling for reveille, shortly after first light, the company of The Manchester Volunteers lines up bleary-eyed for inspection, hung over after a night of drinking and whoring. Major-General Aytoun, whose own behaviour had been more intemperate than most, stands before them now, as fresh as a daisy, seemingly untroubled by his debauched excesses.

"As you all know," he declares, "this company was formed specifically to go to the aid of His Majesty's forces overseas during the Siege of Gibraltar, a campaign I had the honour of commanding, in which The Manchester Volunteers played a significant role in the defence of our Mediterranean outpost, so that the world may point to us with some justification to say that we contributed in no small measure to that most valiant and successful campaign. The phrase 'as safe as the Rock of Gibraltar' was hard won by the courage of this company. But victory brings with it responsibility. And so it now falls once again upon us to return to the scene of our triumph to relieve the Garrison there and do our stint at keeping the Rock secure from any would-be incursions by the Spanish or the French. Henceforth, we ride today to do our duty once again, true to our motto, *Omnia Audax*, all of us bold. I leave a small platoon here in Manchester, under the capable command of my deputy, Colonel Daulby, to ensure that peace and order is maintained in our growing community here at home. I myself shall return in two years. Till then I wish you all God speed and I now commend you to our Company Chaplain to deliver his blessing upon us."

Captain Leigh Philips and Lieutenant Joseph Hanson eye one another warily across the parade ground. Leigh has not been selected to accompany Spanking Roger on his latest vainglorious mission, after all, whereas Hanson has. Leigh is disappointed. More than that, he is furious – he had been hoping to put as great a distance between himself and his father as quickly as he could – and resentful that Hanson has been chosen in his stead. Hanson is cautiously pleased. He cares little for the Major-General's waywardness. He regards himself as a career soldier, with an eye for advancement, his stint with The Manchester Volunteers as but a stepping stone to more senior positions. A posting overseas, especially somewhere as prestigious as Gibraltar, will do his future prospects no harm, while Colonel Daulby is of a similar bent and disposition to himself. He will have little truck with Aytoun's favourites, such as the upstart Philips, and he senses an opportunity for further advantage upon his return, while his rival impotently fumes. He looks across at Philips now and smiles. Leigh is caught off balance by the expression and frowns back, unnerved. Excellent, thinks Hanson. Score one for me.

The Company Chaplain now addresses the men.

"The lesson this morning is taken from John, chapter fourteen. '*Believe me that I am in the Father, and the Father in me: or else believe me for the very works' sake. Verily, verily, I say unto you, He that believeth in me, the works that I do shall he do also; and greater works than these shall he do; because I go unto my Father. And whatsoever ye shall ask in my name, that will I do, that the Father may be glorified in the Son. If ye shall ask any thing in my name, I will do it. Even the Spirit of truth; whom the world cannot receive, because it seeth him not, neither knoweth him: but ye know him; for he dwelleth with you, and shall be in you*'."

"Amen."

Leigh watches those of his company bound for Gibraltar ride from the town, then wheels his horse around and gallops the length of a near deserted Dean's Gate towards Penniless

Hill, from where he will turn into Market Street Lane towards his family home on Lever's Row. The son must face his father.

The Whitsun service in the Central Methodist Hall is coming to an end. The Minister delivers the final reading to a congregation who lift up their still shining faces towards him.

"Let me leave you this fine spring morning," he says, "with the words of Psalm 104. *'O Lord, how manifold are thy works! In wisdom hast thou made them all: the earth is full of thy riches. So is this great and wide sea, wherein are things creeping innumerable, both small and great beasts. There go the ships: there is that leviathan, whom thou hast made to play therein. These wait all upon thee; that thou mayest give them their meat in due season. That thou givest them they gather: thou openest thine hand, they are filled with good. Thou hidest thy face, they are troubled: thou takest away their breath, they die, and return to their dust. Thou sendest forth thy spirit, they are created: and thou renewest the face of the earth. The glory of the Lord shall endure for ever: the Lord shall rejoice in his works. He looketh on the earth, and it trembleth: he toucheth the hills, and they smoke'*. The Lord bless you and keep you. The Lord make his face to shine upon you. The Lord lift up his countenance upon you. Now and for ever. Amen."

"Amen."

Whelp had stood at the junction of Swan Lane with New Cross long after the cart carrying Amos had disappeared from view. But still she kept her vigil, not quite comprehending that she would probably never see him again. That she had found him after nearly eight years while he had mouldered away in the House of Correction on a chance encounter in the Apple Market, that she had been able to rescue him from a place even lower than any she herself had ever inhabited, to take him back with her to Omega Place and watch over him through the night, then lead him by the hand back among the multitude, to Angel Meadow and Mr Sadler's Balloon Flight, only for him to slip away on an impulse, in pursuit of a stray cat of all things, to startle a horse and be knocked from the highway into the Irwell, from where a girl no bigger than herself had pulled him out, and for her family to haul him onto their cart, seemingly to adopt him, to take him away with them to who knows where, strikes her heart with its sheer improbability, to have him snatched from her within less than a day of having found him.

And so she had stood, long after he had slipped from her sight, until the sky darkened and the moon rose, and still she waited, until sleep at last crept up on her. She lay herself down a few yards away from where she stood, beneath a scraggy laurel bush, where she merged with the midnight monochrome. A nocturnal rat scratched about her ankles for a while but quickly lost interest when its nose picked out the smell of an abandoned crate of broken eggs close by, which it sucked greedily with its tongue, one by one, shell, yolk, albumen all.

Now, as the day breaks, she sleeps on. The sun does not pierce the shadow she inhabits beneath the laurel bush. The early bird parishioners, on their way to Whit Sunday services in church or chapel, pass her by, not seeing her, their faces lifted up to catch the morning sun.

Captain Leigh Philips misses her too. His appointment with his father has not gone well, has not taken place in fact, for at the last second his nerve has failed him. Having reached the house on Lever's Row and dismounted from his horse, he has marched purposefully up to the front door, only for him to pause, his hand barely an inch away from the knocker.

Why has he come, he asks himself? What can be gained from such a meeting? He has taken a path from which there is no turning back. He has gone against his father's wishes, quite wilfully, and now his father wants nothing more to do with him. Had the Major-General requested him to accompany him to Gibraltar, he may, with a better grace, have been able to bid his family a more honourable adieu, paving the way for his return, two years from now, as something of a prodigal, but now that he has been overlooked, he feels humiliated. If he were to knock on the door this morning and seek an audience with his father, it might be misinterpreted, that he was admitting a wrong somehow, or, worse, that he was apologising, seeking his father's forgiveness, when nothing could be further from the truth. No, he will not call on him. He will endure this two year exile within the shadow of where he was born and use the time to rise to a position of prominence in the town, one garnered by dint of his own decisions and subsequent actions. Yes, he will, in short, become his own man.

He withdraws his hand from the knocker, walks back to his horse, remounts it, kicks his heels hard into its flanks and rides away. But not before a curtain at an upstairs window has twitched to reveal his mother wiping away a tear, as she watches him depart, unseen.

Now, he has reached the meeting of New Cross with Swan Lane, when a sudden movement catches his attention. It is a moth. A white peppered moth if he is not mistaken, and he doubts that he is. He watches its lazy, erratic flight until it settles on something dark underneath a laurel bush by the junction. He gets down from his horse to investigate further, taking from the inside pocket of his company redcoat the small apothecary's glass jar he carries with him always, just in case of moments like this. He quickly but stealthily approaches the laurel bush and is delighted to behold such a perfect specimen. He quickly swoops upon it, expertly trapping it in the glass jar, then steps away from the bush to hold it up to the daylight, the better to examine it. He has, in his excited pursuit of it, not noticed the recumbent form of Whelp, asleep beneath the laurel, on whom the moth had alighted.

Yes, it is the peppered moth – the *biston betularia*, to give its true binomial nomenclature, as first ratified by Linnaeus, of the family *geometridae*, of the order *lepidoptera*, in the class of *insecta*, within the phylum of *euarthropoda* – but, now that he can look at it more closely, of a type he has never seen before. In Britain there is only a single form, the white, known as *typica*, but this specimen he holds up before him has a darker pigment, though identical to the *typica* in every other aspect. He finds he has to lean against a wall to steady himself. His breathing has become shallow, his pulse has quickened. Could it be that he has stumbled upon a new variant, one that has hitherto been undetected? Or – and he dares not contemplate even the possibility of this – is what he is holding here before him an example of one species actually evolving into another? If that is so, it would contradict not only the Laws of Nature but of Scripture too, the consequences of which do not even bear considering.

He pops the cork onto the top of the jar, which he then places back inside his redcoat pocket, remounts his horse and trots away, completely oblivious of his immediate surroundings. It must be a new previously undiscovered variant of the already known species, he decides, and he shall name it *insularia* to distinguish it from the *typica*, then add it to his collection.

Whelp's eyes flutter open, blinking in the light.

On the steps outside the Central Methodist Hall Zachary waits for Fanny to appear.

After several minutes she is there. She spots him at once and beckons him across.

"Mr and Mrs Oldham," she says, "please may I introduce you to Mr Zachary Robinson?"

Zachary gives a small bow, which is returned by Mrs Oldham, while Andrew raises his top hat, which he has been carrying under his arm, before replacing it on his head.

"Robinson?" he says. "You're not Caleb's son from Shakerley by any chance?"

"The same, sir."

"Well, well, well – Mrs Oldham and I knew Caleb very well. Back in the old days. We both hosted Mr Wesley, I believe."

"Yes, sir."

"Is he still a Master Nailer?"

"Yes, sir, but he now manages his own Wire Works."

"Does he now? Good man. There's going to be more of a call on his services than ever, I believe, with all the new machines being installed in the mills and factories just now."

"Yes, sir."

"And do you follow him into the business too, Zachary?"

"No, sir," interrupts Fanny proudly. "He's training to be a surveyor. Apprenticed to Mr Byrom."

"Indeed? Mr Edward Byrom?"

"Yes, sir," replies Zachary.

"If you want my advice, hang on to his coat tails. That man's going far."

"Thank you, sir. I intend to."

"Well – good day to you. I dare say we'll meet you again," he adds, with a smile at Fanny, who blushes and looks down. "Now then, Matthew," continues Andrew, turning to his son, who has been staring at Zachary darkly throughout this exchange, "will you not shake hands with our new acquaintance, Mr Robinson?"

Zachary offers out his hand to the boy, but Matthew immediately turns away and buries his face in his mother's side.

"Come now, Matthew. This isn't like you," says his father. "You're not usually shy."

"I expect he's missing his cat," says Catherine by way of explanation. "He'll be more his usual self the next time you meet him," she apologises. "Come to lunch with us next week, Zachary. After service on Trinity Sunday."

Fanny turns round to beam at him as the Oldhams make their way down Newton Lane towards their house.

"Till next week," she mouths.

"Next week," he mouths back.

Jem searches for Whelp all day. He has no idea where she might be, so he systematically trawls each street in turn between the Hanging Ditch and the Daub Holes, concentrating wherever he comes across one of the Hulks, but no one has seen her. Hardly anyone in fact knows who he's talking about when he describes her. It's as though the space she occupies is a void which people simply look through.

Eventually it is she who finds him. He hears the slap of bare feet running on the cobbles behind him on Toad Lane. He stops and looks around. She looks stricken, even paler than usual. She clutches her skirt in both hands just below the level of her stomach and lowers herself to the ground. Her face is scrunched up in pain. The wave passes and she straightens herself once more.

He notices the red stain at once and looks away.

He stands to one side and waits, saying nothing. After a few moments, he feels her slip her hand into his. It feels like a small bird, so fragile that he fears the bones might break beneath his touch. But she has surprised him with her strength before, and he expects she may well do so again.

He says nothing, but allows her to lead him where her feet take her, which is to one of the lime pits on the edge of the Daub Holes. When they reach it, she stops. With her free hand she points downwards. Her eyes are desperate.

"What?" he asks. "What are you trying to show me..?"

6

1761 – 1777

Edwin Stone, Master Weaver, stowed his finished piece of woven cloth safely on board the early morning mail coach at *The Boar's Head* on London Road. He waited until all of the passengers, together with their luggage, had finally boarded, the driver had issued the command for the post horn to be blown by the young boy sitting aloft, and the team of six horses had sped off along the first leg of its journey, the wheels of the coach throwing up mud on all those waving it on its way. But Edwin could not care less about that. He could not have been happier. His cup quite simply runneth over.

It was Tuesday 1st September 1761.

In exactly three weeks time King George was to be crowned in Westminster Abbey, the third English monarch so named, and the piece of cloth which Edwin had just now waved off on its journey to London was a gift for the new Queen-to-be, Sophia Charlotte of Mecklenberg-Strelitz, a tiny duchy tucked away in the north-eastern corner of the Holy Roman Empire. Charlotte, as she was known, was a great admirer of Lancashire textiles and the delicate piece of cloth woven by Edwin had been as a result of a commission he had won to create something special and memorable for the coronation, which also happened to coincide with the new Queen's birthday.

As the mail coach slowly disappeared from view along the London Road, Edwin could not help imagine the pleasure in Charlotte's eyes as she unwrapped the tissue paper and they alighted upon the fine table runner he had created for her. He pictured her delight as she held it up close to examine the workmanship and, in so doing, discovered the pattern of moths caught among laurel leaves, almost as if she could feel their wings fluttering beneath her fingers. He wondered where she might use it. On her dressing table perhaps, in front of a graceful oval mirror, before which she might carry out her daily toilet, the cloth supporting her various tins and boxes of powders, ointments and lotions. Or perhaps she would not wish to use so fine a textile, preferring instead to exhibit it, behind glass, in a cabinet for all of her specially commissioned coronation gifts.

But what he dreamed about most, as he began the twelve mile walk back to his cottage and workshop in Norden, was the prospect of Queen Charlotte being so delighted by the cloth that she would place another order with him. Who knows? In five years time he might be Textile Manufacturer to Her Majesty and be able to place the soubriquet 'By Royal Appointment' beneath all of his future work. What a legacy to be able to pass on to his son Henry.

Henry.

Henry was not yet eighteen but full of impatience. Edwin smiled. He too had been just like that when he was the same age, always champing at the bit, not wanting to do things the same way his own father had always done.

But Henry was a good lad at heart. And this order would see to it that his future was bright and filled with promise.

Such pleasant daydreams kept him fully occupied right until his cottage in the lee of Fenny Hill hove into sight. His wife, Joan, was busily laying out bolts of dyed and bleached lengths of cotton over the hedges to dry. Edwin waved. Joan caught sight of him and waved back. Once again Edwin had recourse to bask in the glow of his contentment. His cup runneth over.

But Joan's wave was swiftly followed by an anxious expression passing across her face. She hastily left the last length of cotton she was laying unfinished and creased, roughly trailing on the ground. She hitched up her skirts and ran down the lane towards him. Without any preliminaries she grabbed the lapels of his jacket and cried out.

"It's Henry," she said. "He's gone."

*

There was equal agitation on board the Mail Coach. It would take five days to reach its final destination of London, by way of four staging posts, where horses would be changed and the passengers fed and watered at various inns established for the purpose. *The Feathers* awaited them in Chester, *The Swan* in Ironbridge, *The Lygon Arms* in Worcester and *The Lamb & Flag* in Oxford, before parcels, packages and people alike were deposited in Lombard Street in the heart of the City of London, a stone's throw from the Bank of England, where the Royal Mail had its headquarters close by the church of St Mary Woolnoth, designed by Nicholas Hawksmoor during the reign of Queen Anne.

Six passengers were squeezed inside the coach, with a further four on top, where they would have to jostle for space with the trunks and boxes and sacks of mail, exposed to the elements. As well there were two drivers, each taking turn to steer the team of six horses or blow the thirty-two inch cylindrical brass post horn to alert the towns and villages of their imminent arrival, and, wedged in between them, was eleven year old Will Yardley, whose job it was to help load and unload the coach at each place they stopped, assist the passengers with any of their needs, and generally do whatever it was the two drivers told him to. This was his first trip and he was as excited and frightened as it was possible to be. He had never been out of Manchester until this day and he was, if he understood correctly, to travel as far as Chester from where, the following day, he would join the team of another coach on the last leg of the return journey. It was an adventure, the start of what he hoped would see him one day blowing the post horn himself, or, even, taking the reins of these fiery steeds, who were now galloping so fast that they might out run Apollo's sun chariot. One of the drivers, whose name Will did not yet know, passed him the post horn once they had begun to leave the last of the buildings behind them on the London Road and invited him to try and blow it. Will puffed out his cheeks and blew with all his might, but succeeded only in extracting a yelp so tiny from it that it would not even rival the squeak of a mouse. The driver laughed, tousled Will's hair and handed him an apple. Will thought he had died and gone to heaven.

The six passengers inside the coach comprised a large red-faced gentlemen with straw-coloured hair protruding from both beneath his wig and from inside each ear and his equally large wife with a basket on her lap, from which she began to produce all manner of delights no sooner had they set off – legs of pork, pigeon breasts, rook pies – of which there appeared to be an endless supply, and which they proceeded to share with the greatest affability. Squashed between them was their son, who was as thin as they were fat, who had constantly to bob himself up and down in order to avoid the side of his head making violent and repeated contact with his parents' large, rounded and ceaselessly jabbing elbows.

Opposite them sat a widow dressed from head to toe in black, a veil covering her face, which she had to keep lifting in order to take dainty but frequent morsels of the pigeon breast she had reluctantly accepted from the red-faced gentleman's wife, but which she found she enjoyed almost in spite of herself. She was accompanied by a young woman of just one and twenty, who, it transpired, was the widow's niece, on her way to take up an appointment as a governess to a wealthy London family, the patriarch of whom had once been an associate of the widow's late husband. The niece had chestnut ringlets which framed her pale face perfectly. She was extremely pretty – at least that was the opinion of the sixth and final passenger inside the coach, a young man of independent means, dressed in what to the niece's eyes were clothes of the highest fashion, which, to the widow, made him appear more like a dissolute rake, whom she had spotted the second the Mail Coach invited passengers to board, so that she had made sure she had placed herself firmly between him and her charge. The thought of their two bodies jostling together in such close, touching proximity all the way to London made her shudder and squirm. Nevertheless her immovable presence so firmly and decidedly positioned between them seemed to have not the slightest effect in deterring him from making the most ludicrous small talk, in finding any excuse he could to lean across towards her niece to point out some trivial thing he happened to have seen outside the window. Her niece would titter and smile and look demurely down, fluttering her eyelashes like the heroine of some silly sentimental novel, which only seemed to encourage the young blade further. He found himself particularly taken by the niece's dimples when she smiled, the way her cheeks blushed when he complimented her upon the necklace of white pearls and black jet, which hung about her delicate neck.

"You want to be careful of that," remarked the red-faced gentleman in between mouthfuls of his leg of pork.

"What do you mean?" she asked, her fingers clutching the sparkling stones.

"We're about to enter the domain of Squire Ned." He amiably tugged at a recalcitrant strand of straw-coloured hair from within his left ear.

"Squire Ned?"

"Take no notice of him, dear," intervened the red-faced gentleman's wife. "It's all stuff and nonsense. Rumours, that's all. Pay them no heed."

"Pay what no heed?" asked the young rake, his interest now piqued.

"There's no smoke without fire," said the red-faced gentleman.

"But who is Squire Ned?" demanded the young rake.

He did not have to wait long for an answer.

No sooner had the words left his lips than the Mail Coach screeched to a juddering halt. The horses reared and bucked, whinnied and neighed in panic and alarm. The driver was forced to steer them off the road and into a ditch, causing a wheel to fall away from the front of the coach, throwing the passengers up top roughly to the ground and those inside into an unwelcome heap across each other's laps, an opportunity the young rake took immediate advantage of to grasp the niece's hand and enquire as to whether she was quite safe. "Oh yes," she said somewhat breathlessly, not removing her hand.

From outside the coach they heard a new voice, loud and clear, commanding their attention.

"Stand and deliver!"

"What did I tell you?" hissed the red-faced gentleman. "Squire Ned."

"A highwayman?" piped the son, the first words he had uttered. "How thrilling."

This was a view not shared by his mother, who proceeded to scream at the top of her voice, a sound which, within the confines of the overturned carriage they now all found themselves in, felt even more frightening than the prospect of what Squire Ned might do next.

They did not have long to wait before they found out.

The door to the coach swung open and in peered the rather dashing form of Squire Ned himself, his body leaning at a forty-five degree angle, the top half of his face covered by a black eye-mask.

"Well," he said with a twinkling smile, "isn't this cosy? My apologies, Ladies and Gentlemen, if I have in any way discommoded you, but we all of us have our livings to make, do we not? Allow me to introduce myself. Squire Ned, at your service. Delighted to make your acquaintance," he added with a flourish. "Now then, if I might trouble you to lighten yourselves of any unnecessary coins or trinkets you might currently be weighed down with, then we can all of us be on our merry way once more."

The red-faced gentleman was the first to speak up. "You're a scoundrel and a blackguard, sir. Here – take this for your pains." He handed over a sovereign to the highwayman. "I have taken it upon myself always to carry such a coin as an insurance, just in case such an incident as this should occur."

"That's very sensible of you, sir," replied Squire Ned, making sure to bite the coin first to test its veracity, before then availing himself of a slice of rook pie from the red-faced gentleman's wife, which he proceeded to eat with relish. "Mmm. My compliments, madam. A most delicious and unlooked-for repast."

The red-faced gentleman's wife, who had now ceased her screaming, giggled and covered her mouth.

"Ah," said Squire Ned, his eyes alighting at once upon the gold wedding ring the lady wore upon her finger, "I shall relieve you of that troublesome burden if you please."

He wrenched the ring from her finger as her giggles turned to sobs. "Come, come," said the Squire consolingly, "you are now a free woman once more."

"I will trouble you, sir," said the red-faced gentleman, "to give me that back, or..."

"Or what? You shall be forced to challenge me to a duel?" He brandished his silver-topped pistol with a flourish. "I do not think so. But I might be persuaded to *sell* it back to you. A gentleman who tries to fob me off with a sovereign usually has more stashed away somewhere. How much are you prepared to part with to win back your good wife's honour?"

"This is preposterous."

"Tut, tut, sir, surely no price is too high for that prize? Empty your pockets."

As the red-faced gentleman proceeded to do as he had been bid, Squire Ned turned his attention to the rest of the company. "My," he said, noticing the pretty young niece for the first time. "I've been somewhat remiss. Never let it be said that Squire Ned did not have a soft spot for a pretty face, especially when that face is a pretty as yours." He leant in closer towards her, stroking her face lightly with his gloved hand, which he allowed to linger longingly upon her neck, where his fingers expertly sought the clasp to her pearl and jet necklace, which he deftly unfastened. "Why," he said, holding up the jewels to the light, "these sparkle almost as brightly as your eyes, my sweet, though not quite. It is most generous of you to bestow them upon me, ever your humble servant. Let me place a kiss upon those ruby lips of yours before I take my leave." He inclined lasciviously towards her, only for the young rake to try and intervene, but before he could move so much as a muscle, Squire Ned had his pistol firmly pressed to the side of his head. "Do you have something you wish to say?" he asked, smiling broadly. When the young rake said nothing by way of reply, Squire Ned allowed himself a quiet chuckle, uncocked the pistol, placed a chaste kiss upon the niece's hand instead of her lips, then withdrew from the carriage. "I bid you all a pleasant onward journey," he said, doffing his cockade hat.

Outside all was chaos and confusion. The drivers and passengers who had been riding up top lay strewn about the ground beneath the ruin of overturned, ransacked chests and trunks and slashed and searched mail sacks. Squire Ned's accomplices had rifled through the lot in search of money and jewels and anything of value that might fetch a price with one of the few fences they still did business with, following the near extinction of the species as a result of the *Transportation Act of 1718*, which had harried the receivers even more vigorously than the actual thieves.

The whole attack had lasted less than five minutes. Squire Ned and his band rode off in a cloud of dust as those who he had robbed and left behind picked themselves up and surveyed the mess and devastation surrounding them. As well as what remained of the spilled contents of the luggage, which lay scattered around them, clothes mostly, different garments adorning the hedges and bushes close by, as though a band of rag-tag gypsies had chanced by to watch the robbery like it was some kind of play upon a stage, the coach lay overturned, one of the horses had bolted, while another lay hobbled and bleeding in a ditch, and an errant wheel lay propped on its side spinning forlornly in the summer breeze.

It took the best part of an hour before everything had been put to rights again, the coach returned to its upright position, the wheel repaired and re-attached, the luggage all gathered and stowed aboard, the passengers rested and recovered, the injured horse put out of its misery. One of the drivers defiantly blew a blast upon the post horn as the re-assembled coach and now four set off for Chester once more.

"Well," said the wielder of the post horn, "this'll be something to tell the folk at *The Feathers*. Worth a quart of ale at least, I'd reckon."

"Ay," returned the driver, "held up by Squire Ned but lived to tell the tale."

Squire Ned had not, in fact, ever taken another's life, but he did not object to the songs that told tales to the contrary. They all added to the mystery and the legend. Unlike many of the other celebrated Gentlemen of the Road, he did not hold up mail coaches for the money. He really *was* a Squire – Edward Higgins of Knutsford – who found the country life rather too slow and uneventful for his liking, his only task of note being to collect the local rents, and so he had decided to pursue a more adventurous life, collecting rents of an altogether different order, before returning unrecognised to his quiet pastoral life in Cheshire. Six years from now he would have strayed further afield, to collecting rents in Bristol, where eventually he was apprehended and marched to the scaffold. But, ever the faithful family man at heart, he had provided for his wife and children by selling his body to the surgeon Andrew Cruikshank to dissect for scientific and medical purposes. His body was thereby cut down quickly as soon as he had been hanged and whisked away for autopsy, where he was discovered still to be alive. It fell to one of Cruikshank's students to mercifully complete the sentence.

But that lay all in the future. Now he rode back to his hideout in Knutsford, a barn on the outskirts of his estate, from where he changed and returned to his home, to be greeted by his wife, with her perennial question, "Had a good day, dear?" to which he answered with his customary, "Oh you know, the usual…"

As the Mail Coach approached the outskirts of Chester, following the course of the River Dee, glimpsing the Cathedral and then driving between the elevated rows of two-tiered streets, before pulling into the yard at the back of *The Feathers*, the driver turned to his second and asked, "What happened to the young boy who was with us this morning?"

The other driver widened his eyes, his face turning momentarily pale. "We must have left him behind," he said.

"Not to worry," said the first. "I expect he'll find help from someone."

"Yes," said the second, "I expect he will," before lifting the post horn to his lips to announce their arrival.

Young Will Yardley had, in fact, seen nothing of what had transpired after Squire Ned had first appeared before them, rising up with his accomplices like the Four Horsemen of the Apocalypse. When the coach was forced into the ditch and turned over, Will had been flung to the ground, where he had hit his head on a stone and immediately lost consciousness. When he came to, everyone had gone. He was completely alone. At first he thought he must have been dreaming, but gradually he realised that somehow or other he had been left behind. Perhaps they had seen his body lying there and mistakenly thought he was dead. Or perhaps – more likely, he supposed – they had simply forgotten all about him in the confusion.

His head hurt badly. He lifted his hands gingerly up to it. It was bleeding. A lot. The thought of it frightened him. He looked about him for something he might use to at least temporarily staunch the flow. A few yards away one of the chests that he remembered helping to pack up on top of the coach before they departed from the London Road lay upturned, its contents scattered where they had fallen. The others must have missed this when they packed up and left. He tried to get up, but his legs gave way beneath him. His head was swimming. Blood was trickling down his forehead and into his eyes, which he instinctively tried to blink away. He crawled painfully towards the chest. Once he reached it, he allowed himself a few more seconds while his vision settled itself again and then turned it over. Still inside it, lying undisturbed at the bottom, was a small package bound in tissue paper. He carefully unwrapped it to reveal a piece of white cloth. It appeared to have some sort of repeating pattern on it, moths possibly, on leaves, but he paid it little heed. He picked it up and began to wind it round and round his head, as many times as it would go, binding it as tightly as he could.

It was in this attitude, in the act of winding the cloth around him, that an extremely tall middle-aged man, walking alone beside the road, came upon him and, stooping low, asked him what was the matter and whether he might be of any assistance. Will was so relieved that he promptly passed out again.

The tall middle-aged man was a Mr Mark Collier, Curate of the Church of St Michael, Flixton, a small village lying in the meadows of the flood plains between the Mersey and the Irwell, some seven miles to the south-west of Manchester. It was a damp place, and the church even damper, so that Mark's joints were for ever creaking and complaining. As he bent down over the prostrate body of this young boy who had just fainted at his feet, he felt, as well as heard, every bone in his body cracking in turn. He quickly took in the boy's plight. He unwrapped the cotton cloth which the boy had tried unsuccessfully to tie around his head, slowly and carefully, so as not to disturb him. The wound that was revealed was, Mark could see at once, only superficial, but it was bleeding still quite freely. Head wounds always do, he thought, remembering his own many scrapes when he had banged his tall head on the numerous beams and door jambs of the low buildings he had to enter in his role as a curate, often visiting the homes and families of the poor and sick and dying. But this boy was not dying. He had just had a shock, that was all, but he needed to be cleaned and patched up nevertheless – and quickly. He looked about him. He was on the Chester Road, in Stretford, between the settlements of Firswood and Gorse Hill. The boy had been particularly unlucky in the stone that his head had happened to collide with. It was something of a local landmark. Known as the Great Stone, some said that it had been left there after the Ice Age. Five feet wide and seven feet tall, others claimed it had been a milestone on the Roman Road to Northwich, while there were those who contested it to be the remains of some sort of Saxon cross. The more prominent view, however, held by locals, was that it was gradually sinking into the earth, an inch a year, and, when it finally disappeared underground, that would be the end of the world. Mark smiled inwardly at the way such superstitions still had the power to prevail, even in these modern times of science and invention, when each month, it seemed, brought a new wonder, yet less than a century before, people were still filling the holes gouged by the action of ice in ages past that lay in the top of the Great Stone with vinegar and holy water in the belief that this would stem the flow of plague. Those same holes now held fresher evidence of where the boy's head had struck it, speckling the millstone grit surface with pin pricks of blood.

  Mark slowly and painfully uncurled his long, rail-thin body, each bone along his spine beating out a military tattoo, and looked around him. He was certain there was an inn nearby. He was not from these parts. He had been visiting his younger brother, Luke, who was following in the family tradition of becoming a curate, as he, Mark, had done, like their father, Matthew, before them, though not so the youngest brother of them all, John, the black sheep, who had pursued an entirely different path, as a poet and artist, one which had taken him far away from these South Manchester villages, to the Pennine towns of Rochdale and Milnrow, so that they rarely heard from him now. Their father refused to allow his name to be mentioned at all, but both Mark and Luke missed their errant younger brother, and would meet on neutral ground to exchange news of him. That had become easier now that Luke had found himself a position at St Peter's in Stretford, where the two brothers could meet and speak freely, away from the disapproving ears of their father, who, even though he had now grown quite deaf, remained as acute as ever if either of them dared to mention John's name. Consequently Mark would visit his brother on the first Tuesday of each month, walking the five miles each way whatever the weather, during which time his bones and joints would slowly loosen, so that by the time he reached each destination he was almost pain-free, only for the stiffness to descend upon him once more, no sooner had he sat down upon arrival. On these monthly peregrinations Mark paid little heed to his surroundings, his mind more naturally turning inwards to focus upon a text he would select for himself before setting off – today's had been the Collect for the 11th Sunday after Trinity, which he had led his flock in contemplation of just two days before and whose contents had been troubling him since – but he seemed to recall dimly that, during his journeys, he had passed an inn. Yes. There it was. *The Angel*. How fortuitously named. They would be sure to help the boy and attend to his wounds more effectively than his own ministrations had been able to thus far, when he had simply unwound the cloth from the poor boy's head and dabbed at the open wound rather squeamishly.

"Come," he said. "Lean against me. Let us make our way to what we pray might be your Angel of Mercy. It is not far."

The boy, whose body was trembling, said nothing, but did as he was instructed, and the two of them limped towards the coaching house. They made a strange pair, the one so tall, the other so small, both of them hobbling curiously in step. To give them courage, Mark recited the same Collect whose meaning had been so difficult to tease, but which now appeared to have found a new significance.

"God of Glory,
Who art the end of our searching,
Help us to lay aside
All that prevents us from seeking Thy Kingdom
And to give all that we have
To gain the pearl beyond all price,
Through our Saviour, Jesus Christ.
Amen."

"Amen," mumbled the boy automatically.

An hour later Mark was on the road again, creaking his way back to Flixton. Will had been patched up and given a bed of straw to rest in overnight in the stable, with the possibility of a job as a pot boy when he recovered, and Mark carried the stained cotton cloth like a scarf tied around his neck.

He made his rickety way down Gammershaw Lane, skirting the moat around Newcroft Hall, to the junction with Church Lane, which marked the entrance to Urmston, where he knocked on the door of Ivy Cottage to beg a beaker of water. He passed Barnfield, the west and south gates of Shaw Hall, the Roebuck Inn, before tackling the long, slow haul of Boat Lane, passing from Urmston into Flixton, up towards St Michael's Church. As he neared The Parsonage, he paused to rest a moment and took off the cloth from around his neck to wipe his forehead, which had grown sticky with the exertion of the walk. He had not really looked at it before, but now that he examined it more closely, he could see that this was excellent workmanship, finely wrought. His mother had been a lace maker before she died and so Mark knew something of what must have been involved to produce so delicate and fine a piece of cotton. The over-stitching, the repeated pattern of the moths alighting upon the leaves of laurel, was quite exquisite.

An idea began to form in his mind as he leant against the church wall. Moths. The altar cloth in St Michael's had been ravaged by them, so that now what had once been a good quality linen – simple, plain and unadorned, but perfectly serviceable – was now full of holes. Embarrassingly, whenever the vicar, the Reverend Humphrey Owen, placed the chalice upon it before dispensing Communion, whole clouds of them would fly up, caught in the dust, and he would be overcome with a fit of the coughing as he tried to administer the sacrament.

Mark looked again at the cloth he now held in his hands. It would need to be washed of course, but a long steeping in cold water, mixed with salt, white vinegar and a few drops of lemon juice, should soon put paid to young Will Yardley's blood stains. He would present it to Mr Owen the following Sunday, freshly laundered and pressed. He was already imagining the look of grateful relief on the Reverend's face.

A dozen years passed.

Mark's father, Matthew, died a long and painful death, his face twisted with rage and fury. There had been no reconciliation with John – in spite of all the combined efforts of the brothers – and so now the four gospels, as Mark's mother had ruefully called them, were only three.

Mark recalled the rhymes John had made up about them when he was just a child, encouraged by the prayer their mother had made them all say every night before going to sleep.

"Matthew, Mark, Luke and John
The bed be blessed that I lie on…"

The bed in question was indeed just one, which they all three shared till first John, then Luke, left for pastures new. Mark, even when he had this same bed all to himself, never quite got used to the fact and would continue to take up as little space in it as he could, his pale, bony feet protruding beyond the end like mushrooms in the dark, a dark that continued to frighten him even after he had left his childhood behind. It was, he believed, a hangover from the final lines of that evening prayer.

"Four corners to my bed
Four angels round my head
One to watch and one to pray
And two to bear my soul away…"

The thought of these two dark angels just waiting for him to fall asleep always filled him with dread. He remembered his father's dire warnings in the sermons he delivered. "Lucifer was an angel once…"

And so John would make up new rhymes to lighten his brothers' spirits.

"Matthew, Luke, John and Mark
Don't be frightened of the dark
Imagine that instead you are
Bathed in light from yonder star…"

And Mark would fix his eye upon the brightest star and feel safe. But this would only work if the sky was clear. All too often a cloud would cover the moon and Mark would feel those dark angels hovering over him, itching to cart him with them to Hell.

"Mark, Luke, John and Matthew
Turn those devils into statues
Not ghost, nor phantom, wraith or spook
Will frighten Matthew, Mark or Luke
For first they'll have to vanquish John
Who'll simply whisper, 'Boo! Be Gone'…"

And by and large they *had* disappeared. With the years went the fears. But still their father punished them. Nothing they did would ever be good enough, not even when he and Luke followed in his footsteps to become curates. Instead their appointments were greeted with grim dismissal.

"Father's gone a-flailing
Brother's gone a-nailing
A second's gone a-leasing
A third will not be pleasing
Mother's gone to Flixton Fair
She and baby will ne'er go there…"

And so in the end John had upped and left. "There's nowt for me here," he'd said.

"Matthew, Mark, Luke and John
Hold my horse till I leap on
Hold him steady, hold him sure
And I'll ride over the misty moor…"

And ride away he did. Across the misty moor, over the hills and far away.

Now, in the year of our Lord 1773, a week before his father had died, John had found success at last. For years he had eked out a living odd-jobbing, while supplementing his meagre income with cartoons he sketched of various local characters who frequented the inns and taverns of Rochdale, Milnrow and Oldham, with witty rhymes to accompany them.

"I charge by the head," he had written to Mark. "If there be five folk leaning against the bar, I charge five shillings," he said. And so his pictures were peopled with all types. "The more, the merrier," he laughed. "They call me the Lancashire Hogarth."

But now he had written an entire book in verse, in a true local dialect, under the pseudonym of Tim Bobbin. "In memory of our mother," he'd said, "the lacemaker." It was a charming love story. A dairyman wooed a milkmaid. At first she turned him down, but he would not be put off. Doggedly he continued until gradually he wore down her resistance. "Perseverance pays," wrote a triumphant John to his father. "Tummus wins his Mary." But his father would have none of it. He flung the book away from him, without reading a word of it. As if in expectation of this unyielding rejection 'Tim Bobbin' had given *The Ballad of Tummus & Mary* a grander, more ambitious title. *Human Passions Delineated*, he called it. "All of life is here…"

And so it was, thought Mark as he read with pride his younger brother's wry observations, a life that had largely passed Mark by, a feeling shared by John another dozen years later when, twenty minutes before he passed away, he hastily wrote his own epitaph.

'Jack of all trades – left to lie in t' dark…'

Mark shuddered when he learned of this, for he too had been Master of None, but neither had he been a Jack of any trade. The truth of this fact hit home most forcibly two years before his father died, two years before Tummus and Mary were first ushered into the light. St Michael's had a new vicar. The genial Humphrey Owen gave way to the somewhat nervous Timothy Lowton, who desired not a thing to be changed from how things had been arranged by his predecessor. This meant for a quiet life as far as Mark was concerned and each week he dutifully washed and ironed the piece of white cotton, which now served most agreeably as the Church altar cloth. Many of the parishioners commented upon the pattern of moths alighting upon laurel leaves most favourably, so that the Reverend Lowton took to patting one of the moths, for luck, before every Holy Communion, just to make sure that they had not flown off, for if they did, he began to feel convinced that they would take away some of the contentment he had felt ever since he had arrived in Flixton.

But the vicar's resistance to change meant that the fabric of the building itself was neglected and began to suffer. When perusing the accounts one day, before they were to be presented by the Church Warden for approval by the Diocese, Mark noted with concern the growing number of purchases there had been, against none of which was there any indication of their having been paid.

Bread and wine for Christmas	5s 4d
Bread and wine for Michaelmas	5s 9d
Bread and wine for Palm Sunday also	5s 9d
Bread and wine for Whitsun yet another	5s 9d

not to mention:

Glazing Repairs	6s 8d
Bell Ringing for 5th November	6s 6d
Bell Ringing for Advent Sunday	7s 6d
Three hundred laths	8s 6d

Replacement Bell Ropes	5s 0d
Lime and hair	1s 4d

as well as small sundry items, such as:

a pound of candles	0s 6d
hooks and nails	0s 4d
wire for clock	0s 6d
parchment for writing lists of births	0s 9d
mending the church gates	0s 4d

and finally:

washing of surplices and altar cloth	2s 0d
new besom	0s 6d, 3 farthings

Shortly after these figures came to light, Timothy Lowton shrivelled before their brightness, locked himself in a darkened room, from which he never emerged until the time came for him to be carried out in a coffin.

"A coffin," declared his successor, the Reverend Thomas Beeley MA, "the parish can scarcely afford."

Mr Beeley was a sharp and angular man, with a sharp, pointed nose and long, thin fingers with sharp, curled nails, which, to Mark's mind, resembled more closely the talons of a peregrine. Once they became fastened upon their prey, they would not loosen it from their grip until every ounce of it had been picked clean.

"That new besom which was so recently ordered," he continued, "may well prove a most sound investment. I intend to make every inch of St Michael's feel its probing presence. A new broom," he pronounced darkly, "sweeps clean."

"Yes," thought Mark, "but an old one knows all the corners."

Mr Beeley turned upon him just then the coldest of cold stares and Mark wondered if he might have voiced this thought aloud. It was a habit he found himself falling into more and more recently, but Mr Beeley made no further comment.

He was, however, as good as his word.

"What... is... *this*?" he demanded with considerable distaste, holding up the altar cloth between the thumb and forefinger of one hand and keeping it as far away from him as he possibly could.

"An altar cloth, Your Reverence."

"Not in *my* church."

"Your Reverence?"

"It is positively pagan. These are laurel leaves, I take it?"

Mark nodded that he supposed they were.

"More in keeping with Daphne and Apollo, who you will *not* find in the Bible. They have no place here." And he tossed it contemptuously to the floor, almost as if he were banishing an unpleasant smell.

Mark stooped to pick it up. "I shall take it away at once," he said, thinking how much he would miss it. A thought struck him. Perhaps he might keep it for himself, a welcome adornment to the narrow, frugal cell-like room he occupied in one of the attics in The Parsonage. But Mr Beeley was ahead of him.

"Do not think to take it for yourself, Collier. It is already spoken for. Sir William Allen of Davyhulme Hall has kindly consented to take it off our hands. He has also most generously donated a most splendid alms dish. His mother, he says, knows of just the setting for this pagan outrage. I hear of all manner of devilry going on at Davyhulme Hall, and so I am not in the least surprised, but the family remain the most generous of benefactors. We must pray for the recovery of their mortal souls."

Mark looked at the altar cloth a final time. In Greek Mythology the soul of a man was represented by a butterfly or moth. He recalled a sculpture he once saw, in a book belonging to the late Mr Owen, of just such a moth flying out of the mouth of a dead man.

"Oh – Collier. One more thing. You've seen the Church Warden's accounts. You don't need me to tell you therefore that there are savings to be made here, and I will start as I mean to carry on. Henceforward we shall no longer be requiring your services. We shall manage without a Curate for the interim, while I decide to redefine more exactly just what our need of one amounts to, and what his duties should accordingly comprise. You may collect your belongings from The Parsonage. But be sure to have vacated the premises by first light. Good day to you. The saint whose name this ancient church bears shall be my guide. St Michael the Archangel. I intend to wield his sword of truth to sweep away the cobwebs and let in the light."

With that, he swept along the nave and out through the double doors, his black vestments silhouetted against the bright glare of the sun outside like a winged apocalypse.

Mark instinctively sought the comfort of shadows, where he might linger unseen and unremarked upon. He had lain in that dark ever since. He had been to Manchester just the once. To see his brother John at some midway, neutral point. They had met on Lever's Row. Beside what were called the Daub Holes. A stray dog had got stuck in one of them. It sucked the poor beast slowly and painfully under. Mark had to shut his ears to its incessant howling. The darkness that now pervaded him felt very much like what he had imagined drowning in the Daub Holes must have been like for that dog. He wanted to howl too, but he knew no one would hear him, so he kept silent.

*

Phoebe was a sweet-natured child. Even as a baby she rarely cried. It was just as well, for her mother died shortly after she was born and her father, Joel Rowe, was a busy man, working as many did in those parts at two occupations – farming and weaving. He was a tenant at Graydle Farm, on the estate of Davyhulme Hall, tending cattle, sheep, goats and pigs, as well as growing oats and barley on the medieval strip fields that still prevailed alongside Carr's Ditch by day, and weaving from the flax and hemp grown closer to home near Crofts Bank by night. Joel simply carried Phoebe with him wherever he went. Then, when she first began to crawl and later to walk, she toddled after him quite happily, keeping up a constant chatter as she did so. As she grew, she took delight in all things – a butterfly opening and closing its wings on a buddleia leaf, an ash key spinning as it descended to earth, a dandelion clock drifting on the breeze – but especially the animals on the farm. It was a surprise to nobody when, having just turned thirteen, she started out as a milkmaid.

Joel was delighted. He could trace his family back through several generations. There'd been Rowes as tenants at Davyhulme Hall since it had first been built. That was in 1180, when Albert Gredle, who inherited the land from Roger de Poitou shortly after the Norman Conquest, had given one carucate of land to Orme Fitz-Seward on the occasion of his marriage to his daughter Emma for a single peppercorn rent of just ten shillings. A carucate was the amount of acreage a team of oxen might plough in a day and this particular plot was thereafter known as Orme's *tun*, later becoming Orme Eston, until finally shortening to Urmston, one of the three villages that formed this secluded enclave at the confluence of the Mersey and Irwell rivers, along with Flixton – originally Fleece Town, or possibly Flikke's *tun*, after an earlier Danish settler – and Davyhulme – Dewey's Holme – the three conjoining at Croft's Bank, where Joel and Phoebe contentedly passed the hours. Croft's Bank, which marked the end of the Nico Ditch, rumoured to have been built to keep out the Danes such as Flikke, unsuccessfully as it turned out, which snaked its way for more than seven miles from Denton – Dane's *tun* – through Levenshulme – Leofwyn's Holme – and Stretford – the street across the water – to where it petered out here, serving as a natural field boundary inside which Joel kept the cows that Phoebe now milked twice each day.

Spring came early in 1775. Aprill with his shoures soote had indeed the droughte of Marche piercèd to the roote. When Captain John Parker led his minutemen to fire their first shot against the British at Lexington, it was not at first heard round the world – they did not hear it in Davyhulme – though later its echo would come to reverberate around Graydle Farm. Phoebe turned fifteen. She was as sunny in both her appearance and her disposition as her name, a name given to her by her father both to honour the king's well known fascination with astronomy, his ascendance to the throne earning him the nickname of Phoebus Apollo, the New Sun King, and to remind Joel that his daughter would at all times be the light of his life. In the sleepy hollow that was Orme's *tun*, Fliike's *tun* and Dewcy's *holme*, no thoughts as yet turned towards the Thirteen Colonies across the Atlantic. Instead all attention was focused on the Annual Rushbearing that was to take place the following week on Rogation Sunday.

The original carucate of land gifted by Albert Gredle had multiplied a hundred fold over the centuries and the estates now numbered several farms in addition to the Home Farm where Phoebe was a milkmaid. There was Day's Farm and Guy's Farm, Sticking Farm and Whitegate Farm, Gorse Hill Farm and Chassen Farm, Willows Farm and Tanhouse Farm, Rudyard Farm, Fold Farm, Broomhurst Farm and Moss Farm. Hands from all these farms helped to build and decorate the Rush Cart, with stooks of reeds and grasses formed into a tall pyramid, interwoven with spring flowers – beech and bilberry, broom and bugloss, stork's bill and cow parsley, mouse ear and fiddleneck, hedge mustard, herb Robert, honesty and hawthorn, lords and ladies, lousewort, saxifrage and sorrel, purslane, pearlwort, candytuft and cornflower.

Seated atop the pyramid were a lad and lass from among the farm workers, selected at random by the pulling of straws. This year Phoebe was chosen and her king for the day was the aptly named Roy, a young cowman of seventeen summers from Brook House Farm on Old Crofts Bank, on land between Carr's Ditch and Bent Brook. The pair blushingly held hands as the cart was carried around the parish – down Moorside, along Flash Lane to Calder Bank and Wood's End, from there past Calamanco and through the Town Gate, down Miller's Lane to White Lake, stopping off at *The Roebuck Inn* for a slice of seasonal snig pie, made from eels caught in the meadows by the Mersey, before the final push up Shawe Lane to St Michael's, where the Reverend Thomas Beeley insisted they remained firmly on the Green, outside the Church, where it was made abundantly clear such pagan outrages were not to be allowed to enter inside, although he did permit the strewing of grasses on the hard-packed earthen floor of the nave, where their newly picked fragrance was, he reluctantly conceded, a most welcome balm to the senses.

Outside there were games and music, singing and dancing. In keeping with the traditions of the day Phoebe and Roy, as King and Queen of the Rush Cart, exchanged a kiss and everyone declared that theirs was a match made in heaven. It seemed as though they agreed with this assessment for, before the day was over and everyone began to make their drunken, cheery ways home, the two of them shared several more lingering kisses as they lay among the rushes.

Throughout the long hot summer that followed the dairyman wooed his milkmaid just like Tim Bobbin's Tummus pursued his Mary. They were the perfect couple, and come Christmas, Joel was expecting to announce their engagement, with the wedding to take place the following spring when

Phoebe would turn sixteen. Why, they may decide to tie the knot on Rogation Sunday itself. That would be fitting, he thought, and his face was wreathed in smiles.

A smile crossed the lips of someone else that Christmas. Sir William Allen's son – Courtenay – who had just returned from the Americas, where his father had assets – in tobacco, cotton and slaves – which were now under a credible threat since the so-called Patriots' unexpected victories at Lexington and Concord. Unlike his grander, more established neighbours, the De Traffords and Egertons, Sir William was something of an upstart. He could rival them in terms of wealth, but not in terms of land, nor in their centuries-old names, which were mentioned in the Domesday Book, as they never tired of telling him if ever their paths should cross, as they did more frequently now since the Duke's Cut, the Bridgewater Canal, skirted the northern edge of Sir William's estate. He could never compete with them in terms of rank or lineage, but he could perhaps match them in land, and so in recent years he had been busily buying up as much of it that lay between those twin outposts of the Mersey and the Canal as he could. Currently he found himself in possession of all of Davyhulme, Flixton and Urmston as far as Newcroft Hall, whose woods and orchards he next had in his sights, but to do this he required rapid and regular access to the more liquid asset of money. Where his rivals had a steady, uninterrupted flow of income each year from their hundreds of tenants, apart from any of their other enterprises, Sir William had to rely on the hearth tax from the paltry figure of less than a hundred eligible households. To boost and maintain his ambitions therefore he had had to turn to trade, principally in the Thirteen Colonies. Where land was a constant, trade was a variable, dependent upon the vagaries of a market which became even more volatile during a time of war. The uncertainty of the situation in America was threatening to bankrupt him – a worry he kept entirely to himself, for he had other more immediate concerns, principally concerning his son, Courtenay. Naturally he loved Courtenay – he was his heir, his flesh and blood – but he did not trust him with the long term future of what had hitherto seemed an unstoppably expanding empire. Courtenay gambled. He caroused. He womanised. Fair enough. He was young. He needed to sow his wild oats. But last year he had turned twenty-one. He had come into the possession of a trust fund which he had, in just a few short reckless months, emptied entirely. He needed to grow up, put away childish things, especially now, when the future was less certain, and so Sir William had sent him packing to carry out a detailed inventory of the family business holdings in the Colonies, hoping that the responsibility might inspire him towards a greater sense of maturity. In this he had been badly disappointed. Courtenay had shown no interest whatsoever in anything other than gambling dens and whore houses and had returned, not with his tail between his legs, but his hands outstretched for yet more hand-outs to pay off his growing list of creditors on both sides of the Atlantic. Sir William was at his wit's end and confided as much in his wife, Agatha.

"He's still young," she had merely said. "He'll grow into himself in time. Just be patient."

"We may not have much more time for patience," he had replied crossly. "You have always spoiled him," he added, involuntarily lifting his finger to massage the tick on the side of his temple, which always pulsed whenever he became anxious, "right from when he was a child. Anything he wanted, you saw to it that he got. That has got to stop. From now on he must learn to curb his excesses. To be blunt, my dear, he shall have to keep himself from now on. He can have a roof over his head, a modest allowance, but nothing more. From Twelfth Night he must follow me into the business."

"I shall have a word with him, darling," she oozed, gently removing her husband's fingers from the side of his head, then kissing them "but not tonight. Tonight is Christmas Eve. Let him enjoy the Yuletide celebrations."

Sir William held his wife's hand tightly, gratefully kissing the fingers one by one. He sighed. "I expect you are in the right of it."

"That's more like it. Now – let us take ourselves to the barn outside, where the tenants and their families are gathered, and give them their Christmas bonuses. They will be waiting for us."

"And they will be disappointed when they see how much those bonuses have shrunk this year."

"No, my pet, they will be grateful that you have remembered them, even in times as frugal and unpredictable as these. We all of us will have to tighten our belts, make sacrifices."

"Even Courtenay?"

"Especially Courtenay. I shall see to it."

"Very well, my dear. Let us once more unto the breach. I don't know what I'd do without you."

Happily ensconced in the Tithe Barn already, where the tenants are noisily gathered, is Courtenay. He has been partaking freely of the wassail cup and his cheeks are flushed a deep crimson. A great fire is roaring in one corner. Long sets of trestle tables are ranged along the far end, upon which a number of dishes of hams and pies are ranged, together with trays of apples and cake. As well as the wassail bowl there are also barrels of ale and cider, all of which are flowing freely. A group of fiddlers are keeping up a merry succession of jigs and reels. There is a space in the middle that has been cleared for dancing, which is filled with *Shepherd's Heys*, *Sweet Kates* and *Sellenger's Rounds*, *At The Beginning of the World*, in which couples join hands and dance the length of the barn. *Gathering Peascods, Rufty Tufty, Hit and Miss*.

Courtenay has positioned himself quite deliberately beneath a sprig of mistletoe hanging from one of the beams, which he eyes quite blatantly in between shooting out glances to all of the pretty girls there, of whom there are many, who giggle and squeal as they take it in turns to be kissed by the master's good-looking son. All except Phoebe, that is, who glowers darkly in a corner. Roy is nowhere to be seen. They have had their first ever falling out, and more than just a lovers' tiff to judge from their current demeanours, she alone with folded arms and stamping feet, he outside drinking more tankards of ale than are good for him. Helping him achieve this feat is the cause of their quarrel: a Recruiting Sergeant from the Cheshires, who has been doing the rounds of all the villages and hamlets in the vicinity trying to drum up new volunteers to help His Majesty fight these troublesome American Renegades. In a fit of patriotic pique Roy has enlisted. Phoebe, when he tells her what he has done, is furious. He had expected her to be proud. Her girl friends try to reassure her with claims of how handsome he will look in the red coat of the uniform. But she is not to be assuaged. "We were meant to be married next Spring," she rails and runs in search of her father, who finds himself caught between a rock and a hard place. He is sorry for his daughter but has some sympathy for his would-be son-in-law. "It's every man's duty to serve his King," he says. "He'll be back before you know it, you'll see. These Yankees need bringing down a peg or two, and I reckon young Roy's just the man to do it."

"Oh Father," cries Phoebe. "You're just as bad as he is."

And she has stormed off, back to the Barn, where now she has caught the attention of Courtenay, who has cut himself a bunch of mistletoe and carried it over to her. He places it beguilingly over his head and waits. When she refuses to respond, has not even appeared to notice him in fact, his desire for her grows stronger.

"Well," he says, somewhat peevishly, "aren't you going to wish the son of your Lord and Master a Merry Christmas?"

"No," she cries. And then, when he has tried to pull her towards him anyway to snatch that kiss from her, she has slapped his face. The musicians stop playing and everyone looks in the direction of Courtenay and Phoebe to see what might happen next. They do not have long to wait. Phoebe simply turns on her heels and storms back outside. The smile that has formed across Courtenay's lips grows even wider. He has to have her.

In that quiet no-time between Christmas and New Year – quiet for those who were not obliged to work – Courtenay was lounging listlessly in front of a warm fire in the library of Davyhulme Hall, having polished off the best part of a bottle of claret. He had spent much of his waking hours since the Christmas Eve party dreaming about the young vixen who had slapped his face, causing so many emotions simultaneously to ripple around the Barn, chased by the shadows thrown upon the walls by the flames of the fire – shock, amusement, consternation, excitement, curiosity. By rights he should have had her dismissed instantly, but he found her spirit alluring. and now, before a different fire, one which, unless he stirred himself to throw on another log, was in danger of slowly going out, he tried to hatch a plan by which he might see her more readily, without putting himself at risk of further rejection or humiliation. Several times he thought he had it, only for it to slip away from him like the smoke rising up the chimney. The closer he got, the further it eluded him. He frowned. He rolled a sovereign over the back of his hand, flipping it expertly between his fingers. It was a characteristic gesture he had, one which he repeated so often he was quite unaware when he did it. He was roused from his reverie by a quiet knocking on the library door. This was followed by the swift entrance of his mother, who, before he had barely registered her presence, had sat herself down beside him and begun to address him in that tone she had, of honey dripping slowly from a jar, when she needed him to do something he would rather not. Invariably she would get her way, but not before he had managed to extract some form of concession from her in return. Today was no exception.

"What is it?" he asked wearily.

"Your father," she said at once.

"Oh God," moaned Courtenay, melodramatically putting his head in his hands.

"Don't be like that," she said, at once placing her hand upon her languorous son's petulantly turned away face in an effort to moderate the extremity of his response. "He has a lot of worries. Please don't add to them by behaving so childishly."

"Why shouldn't I?" he sighed theatrically. "That's all I am to him – a child – so why bother to shatter the illusion?"

"You could surprise him for once."

"Really? How?"

"By acting your age."

Lady Agatha spoke this more forcibly than she had intended and its effect was to shock her wayward son into a rare moment of sobriety. It was in this moment, just as he struck this attitude of penitence, that the idea he had been searching for all afternoon, which had been proving so maddeningly elusive, came to him in a flash. He flipped the coin several times back and forth between his fingers.

"You're looking tired, Mama," he said, suddenly and genuinely solicitous.

"Is it any wonder?" she replied, leaning her head against his.

"What you need is a companion," he said, "a personal maid, who can fetch and carry for you, do all those innumerable errands that take up so much of your time, so that you can devote more of it to doing those more important things, things that you have to keep putting off, and focus your energies on what you do best."

"Such as what?" she said, an amused smile creeping across her lips.

"Looking after me for a start, making sure that I always act on my best intentions instead of my worst."

"Like now?"

"Exactly, yes. Like now."

"I see," she said, smiling more broadly now at her son's irrepressible transparency. "And who would this paragon happen to be? That feisty young milkmaid who so very sensibly resisted your unwanted attentions on Christmas Eve?"

Courtenay's jaw dropped, but, recovering himself quickly, he added, "Great minds think alike. She has an energy and spirit that I am certain will prove infectious and enable you to conquer your lethargy and recover your vigour." He tossed the coin high into the air, catching it on the back of one hand with the palm of the other, and grinned.

"It is *your* lethargy I'd rather see banished," she laughed, "and *your* energy recovered. And more than that – put to some purpose that is not merely pandering to your own idle excesses."

"Mama, you cut me to the quick!"

"I'm glad to hear it."

Mother and son smiled at each other warmly.

"Very well," she added after a pause. "I shall agree to your proposal."

"Good."

"On one condition."

"Oh – not so good."

"That you travel with your father to London next week for some important meetings with his bank."

"Oh Lord, that sounds dull. But if that is your condition, then I agree to it. And I shall be back as soon as I am spared to see how your young charge is progressing."

"Really?" said Agatha, her eyes sparkling with mischief. "How refreshing to hear you volunteer to take on the responsibility for the needs of somebody other than your own."

"I don't know what you mean?" he quipped, opening a fresh bottle of claret and pouring them each a generous glass.

As he did so, in his haste, he knocked over the bottle, spilling the remains of its contents onto the white cotton cloth on the table in front of them.

Shaking her head with fond indulgence, Agatha swept up the cloth, strode back to the door that opened out from the library into the connecting hallway, from which all the other rooms in the house led off, and called for someone to come. A nervous and harassed young maid scurried towards her mistress, wiping her wet hands on the apron in front of her.

"Yes, Miss," she said, bobbing an automatic curtsey.

"Remove the stain from this cloth, would you?"

"Yes, Miss." She bobbed a second curtsey before scuttling back into the shadows below stairs. The moths were bleeding into the laurel leaves.

The next day three people made separate journeys. The day was icy and grey. A thick mist rose up from the meadow where the Irwell emptied into the Mersey and curled around the bare branches of trees. It crept under the doors of barns and cottages, wrapping its cold fingers around everything it touched. Courtenay, Phoebe and Roy walked in isolation, cut off from each other and from the world, which they passed through seeing none of it, each lost in a single shared thought: when if ever would they return to the place they had left behind?

One question, three different answers.

His father's affairs kept Courtenay in London far longer than he had anticipated. Sir William decided that perhaps what his son needed to propel him towards manhood was a short, sharp shock – the shock of the truth. He spared him nothing in revealing the depths to which their finances had sunk. Even Courtenay could see just what a tightrope his father had been treading. But what was he meant to do? All he could do was watch and try to take it in, which for the most part he did. There were times of course when he needed distractions, and he found these in his usual haunts, with the usual suspects, but even when he woke to find himself somewhere he did not recognise, his thoughts would return to the memory of that last Christmas Eve, when Phoebe had slapped his face. Each time he remembered, he felt the slap more keenly. That was his true wake-up call.

Phoebe was under no illusions as to what might lie in store for her when she made her way across the fields from Home Farm to Davyhulme Hall. Sir William's son – she did not then know his name – would be persistent. Of that she was certain, and she would have to make sure she never lingered if she found herself alone in a room with him. To slap someone in front of a crowd is quite a different proposition from trying to repeat the action when alone. There was safety in numbers – she recited that to herself as her creed. And so it was a great relief to arrive at the Big House and find him not there. And an even greater one when he did not return for several months. In that time she adapted herself to the rhythms of domestic service far more comfortably than she had imagined. She did not miss being a milkmaid, although she did miss the company of the other girls. She got on well with her mistress and Lady Agatha surprised herself by just how much she enjoyed Phoebe's company, her sunny disposition, her common sense approach to life. She was respectful but not servile – a fine distinction but one worth noting. Phoebe particularly liked looking after the nice things she found in every room – the china ornaments, the leather bound books, the cut glass vases, the matching place settings. Most of all she liked the white cotton tablecloth, from which the moths seemed always to be just on the point of abandoning in a cascade of flight, which never quite happened, but remained a constant possibility and hope.

Roy regretted his decision to enlist from the very beginning. The iron mist of the day he departed to join up with the rest of the new recruits in Chester instantly sobered him up. He realised the folly of his actions but it was too late to go back. He must somehow survive these three years he had signed up for and return to claim his Phoebe, hoping that in the meantime she would forgive him and wait for him patiently. He tried to picture her as she was on the day of the Rush Cart, but all he kept seeing was the look of fury on her face on Christmas Eve the moment that he told her what he'd done.

From Chester, under the command of Lieutenant-Colonel James Abercrombie, the entire regiment marched with full colours the seventeen miles to Liverpool, from where they set sail for Boston the very next day. If he had regrets before, then these multiplied a thousand-fold once their ship met the full force of a mid-Atlantic swell in winter. He was more sick than he thought it was possible to be, emptying his insides until there was nothing of them left, only for him then to empty them all over again, as the ship pitched and rolled. Following the somewhat Pyrrhic victory for the British at Bunker Hill, the 22nd Cheshire Regiment of Foot, of which Roy was now a part, had been sent as necessary reinforcements to make up for the losses inflicted in that particularly bruising battle. He had hoped for some respite once they reached dry land, but in this, as with his entire experience in the New World, he was disappointed. They set off almost immediately on a long, slow, arduous route march to join up with the rest of the British forces under the overall command of General Sir William Howe, to begin the drearily endless New York and New Jersey Campaigns, where they were bogged down for months, it seemed, in mosquito-ridden swamps, pursuing a course of action so cautious that they constantly kept driving George

Washington's rag-tag army almost to the point of destruction, only to pause at the vital moment, allowing them time and time again to recoup, while Roy and his fellow troops developed malaria, or scurvy, or both.

It would be several months before Courtenay returned for more than just a flying visit. Now, just as the summer of 1776 was tipping over into autumn, he stepped off the Mail Coach at *The Nag's Head* on Croft's Bank and walked the final mile to Davyhulme Hall along Cockedge Lane, before entering the drive from the southern tip of the estate. He heard Phoebe before he saw her. She was singing as she dusted in the library.

"Good morning to you, wither said I?
Good morning to you now
The maid replied, Kind sir, she cried
I've lost my spotted cow…"

The sun slanted in through the open French windows, dappling her face and hair, almost as if she were indeed in some shady grove searching for her lost cow. Courtenay hung back, revelling in the Arcadian image she presented before him as she, quite unaware of his presence, continued to sing.

"No longer weep, no longer mourn
Your cow's not lost, my dear
I saw her down in yonder grove
Come, love, and I'll show you where…"

He was tempted to join in with her song but instead he took advantage of her being so lost in the pleasure of it to creep up on her from behind.

*"I must confess you're very kind
I thank you, sir, said she
We will be sure her there to find
Come, sweetheart, go with me…"*

Just as she was about to repeat the final line he darted towards her. In one movement he placed a hand over her mouth and with the other encircled her waist, pulling her tightly towards her. Whispering in her ear he completed the song for her.

"Come, sweetheart, go with me…"

He buried his face in her neck and Phoebe found that she was not inclined to slap his face on this occasion.

Over the next few weeks he sought her out whenever and wherever he could – in the pantry, on the landing, in the garden, as well as in the library, which always caught the last of the afternoon sun – and every time she allowed him to go a little further, his fingers and tongue exploring every inch of her. But she always stopped short of what he desired most. Eventually he could bear it no longer. It was the week before Christmas, almost a year exactly since he had first seen her glowering with fury in the Tithe Barn, and she had slapped his face for trying to kiss her beneath a sprig of mistletoe. That now seemed a lifetime ago.

"When?" he asked her.
"Soon," she promised.
"Tonight?" he urged.
"Perhaps," she conceded, "but first…"
"Yes?"
"You must do something for me."
"Name it."

"Tis but a small thing."

"What? I'll do anything."

"Tell me you love me."

"You know I do."

"Then say it. Say it and mean it."

"Actions speak more eloquently than a thousand words," he said, pulling her towards him.

"No," she said, placing her fingers between their lips. "Not in a situation like this. You must say it."

He took a step back from her, held her face in his hands, and said with great tenderness, "Very well. I love you."

"There," she said, smiling, feeling some of the tension leaving her body. "That wasn't so hard, was it?"

Courtenay smiled in return.

"Now," she said, more seriously, "you must promise me. If I consent, you will not then abandon me."

"I promise," he said.

They kissed for a very long time.

"Tonight then," she said.

"Where?"

"You choose. But not some corner or cupboard, mind."

"The library," he said. "Where I first saw you after I came home. I'll light a fire."

She nodded, then turned and skipped away from him.

He was as good as his word. When she was sure that the household was all a-bed, she tiptoed barefoot down the stairs to the library where he was waiting for her. A fire was burning in the hearth. There was no other light, just the amber glow of the flames. The sound of the logs splitting and cracking as the fire took hold seemed to match the pounding of her heart as she approached him.

He undressed her with deliberate slowness, taking in every atom of her body as the shadows of the flames licked against her skin. He spread the white cloth below them and laid her down upon it. The moths danced towards the sparks of light as they jumped out of the fire.

Some time later, when the fire had all but burnt itself out, when just the last few dying embers glowed dimly in the dark, Phoebe woke. She felt cold. She wrapped the cloth around her. The leaves attached themselves to her like a second skin. Like bark closing over her. She looked around. Courtenay was nowhere to be seen.

When he had first entered her, it had hurt, but he was gentler than she expected him to be and soon the pain gave way to more pleasurable sensations. She experienced a fluttering of intense rhythmic contractions, her pulse quickened, her heart rate soared, her breathing became shorter, faster, louder, until she came in a series of rapid, juddering bursts. Afterwards they made love twice more, with more care, more attention, but even more passion, until eventually sleep took her.

Now that she was awake, her senses began to retune themselves. Every sight, sound and smell was heightened. Where *was* he? When had he left her? And why?

She thought she heard a whispering outside the door, two voices, low and intense, hissing at one another, just as the last of the fire went out. She recognised them instantly. It was Courtenay and his mother. Phoebe began to make out individual words.

"This has to stop," said Lady Agatha.

"It has barely started," said Courtenay.

"Then end it now," said Lady Agatha.

What Courtenay said next by way of reply Phoebe could not make out. Then she heard footsteps walking away. One set of them. She wondered which of them had left and which had stayed. She did not have long to wait to discover the answer.

The door was flung open and it was Lady Agatha who burst in. She made no attempt to be quiet or kind. She drew back the curtains and a light of cold steel knifed its way into the room. Phoebe made a hopeless, futile gesture to cover herself with the cloth. Agatha regarded her pitilessly.

"I want you gone from this house within the hour," she said. Nothing more. Then she looked her up and down a final time, her lips parting back from her teeth in a slight sneer, shook her head dismissively twice, and left the room.

A few minutes later, having hastily dressed, Phoebe stepped out of Davyhulme Hall and walked along its gravel drive in the grey morning. She carried a small bundle of her few pathetic belongings under her arm, among which was the white cotton cloth she had decided she must wash before it could be returned, although even as she thought this, she knew she would not be coming back. She fancied she caught sight of Courtenay, his face at an upstairs window, but she couldn't be sure. It might just have been the way the wind was tugging at a leafless branch of the wisteria tree that climbed the outside wall of the house, or blowing a wisp of hair across her eyes. She took hold of the recalcitrant strand and tucked it firmly behind her ear. It was not sadness she felt, but anger, at herself, mostly, for being so gullible, for thinking that any of this could have turned out differently.

She placed one foot resolutely in front of the other with no idea where they might take her.

She is walking along the Nico Ditch. She is not sure how she got there. Night is starting to fall. Though in truth the day has been one of those in which it has barely become light. She takes the white cotton cloth out of the bundle she still carries and wraps it round her shoulders. The feeling she had earlier, before Lady Agatha burst in to banish her, of it forming a kind of bark around her, returns. Her arms and legs feel heavy.

Almost as if her feet were sinking into the earth and taking root there. She sits on a stone that juts out from the raised embankment she feels she has been walking along ever since she first left her father behind in Graydle Farm almost a year ago, taking her away from who she was with each weary step.

It is a lonely and desolate spot along the Nico Ditch. Only the occasional farm building peppers the otherwise empty landscape. The ground just below her is wet and marshy, held fast in the grip of a hard frost. She becomes aware of a slight movement in the taller grasses close beside her. It is a heron clumsily taking off for one last wide-winged forage of the moss. Phoebe watches its slow, heavy glide until it lands again, awkwardly, about twenty yards away from her, where it settles, perching on one stilt-like leg. From this distance it appears to be looking directly at her. What is it seeing, she wonders? Suddenly it jerks its head to one side. Phoebe follows the direction of its gaze. In the distance she sees, or thinks she sees, a shape running towards her. The figure runs without once appearing to look where she is going. Either she is sure-footed or frightened. Probably the latter, thinks Phoebe, as the figure comes closer. She can make out the form and shape of her more distinctly. It appears to be a girl, about the same height as Phoebe, and a similar age. Possibly a little younger. But not by much. She is running straight for her. If she is not careful she will collide with where Phoebe is sitting, so she stands up, steps back, to allow her to pass unimpeded. She feels the rush of air as the figure runs past and almost directly through her. She is aware of her carrying a small bundle too, tied with string, under her arm, not unlike the size of the one that she carries. It appears to be all that she possesses and she clings to it as if to life itself. As she passes, she is aware too of a slight discolouration on the side of her face. A strawberry mark. But she cannot be sure. It all happens too fast. Phoebe tries to call out to her but she can no longer see her. She appears to have become absorbed into the body of the Nico Ditch itself. She looks back across towards where the heron was standing, but it too is no longer to be seen.

Phoebe picks herself up, wraps the cloth more tightly round her heavy limbs and slowly continues to walk.

Nine months later Phoebe is in Manchester. How she got there she can't remember. Nor how long she has been there. The days become a blur. She is aware of the swelling in her stomach, a hard knot that heaves and writhes behind its wall. Sometimes it kicks so hard she's sure it will burst right out of her, furiously demanding to be fed, and that she knows she will never have enough to satisfy it. Or them. Sometimes she feels there must be two alien creatures inside her, fighting both her and each other for survival. Which of them will win, she wonders? She knows it shan't be her.

She sees fires burning within the Hulks of roofless, windowless buildings and heads towards their promise of light and warmth. Perhaps there'll be some food there too. She hasn't eaten for days. She can't remember the last time. As she gets closer she begins to make out shapes, darker than the darkness, huddled or separate, staking out their territory. There are as many rats as there are people, tumbling over each other trying to get closer to the fires. The only difference she can discern is that the rats seem to be doing marginally better than the people. Better than she is.

She hears a cough behind her. She turns. An older man is shuffling towards her. He gives the appearance of once enjoying a better station in life, as if he has recently fallen on hard times, but is bearing it with dignity and acceptance.

"Does the young lady wish a lodging for the night?"

Lodging. A curious term for a patch of cold earth beside a puttering fire. She nods. The old gentleman takes in her appearance and sighs. A sad sigh, as if from a father discovering too late the plight that has befallen his daughter and can now do little to rescue her, except to offer her a spot closest to one of the fires. Which he does. She thanks him and settles down for what she feels will be a long night.

A strange wind is picking up. It fans the flames. The other human shapes look around them anxiously.

The old gentleman coughs again. "I'm sorry to have to mention this, my dear, but it is the custom for guests to offer payment for their lodging. As a sign of respect, you understand, nothing more. On account of my most venerable age. That is why they call me what they do. The Old Retainer. For I was here first, you see? But you may call me Septimus if you prefer. My given name."

Phoebe nods. The old gentleman, she sees now, is holding out the palm of one of his hands, surreptitiously, almost as if he were embarrassed to be seen doing so, looking the other way.

"I don't have anything," she says.

Septimus turns back towards her. A pained expression crosses his face. "It's distasteful, I know, but there's no credit available here in the Hulks."

Phoebe spreads her hands helplessly. Just then she feels a rumble rising up from the earth beneath her. They all do. They look around them with increasing anxiety and fear. Only Septimus is unperturbed – and another figure, who Phoebe is gradually becoming aware of, a scrawny runt of a child with matted hair hovering close by, watching her every move. At first Phoebe had thought she was one of the rats, but now she sees the figure is human, though quite feral, her tiny, ungrown body bristling and alert, whose fingers suddenly dart towards her and pluck the piece of now not-so-white cloth from around her shoulders.

"Ah, yes – thank you, Whelp," says Septimus, examining the cotton closely. "Exquisite workmanship," he says, more to himself, then turns back to Phoebe. "This will do nicely."

She looks at him with a puzzled frown.

"In lieu of any coin, my dear."

Another louder rumble shakes the ground. Phoebe feels a sharp pain in her belly and a rush of liquid coursing down her thighs.

Septimus helps her to lie down. He considers whether to lay the cloth over her, like a sheet, but decides against it. As he is thus deliberating, he holds it closer to one of the fires, the better to examine its details. The moths flutter and dance.

Another man, squatting close by, catches sight of it and drops the empty enamel mug he has been clutching. His cup, having once runneth over so freely, is now stubbornly and resolutely dry. He recognises the cloth at once and begins to laugh, mirthlessly and loud.

"Me father made that cloth," he calls out to anyone who might care to listen. "It were meant to make 'is fortune. 'E made it for t' Queen's Coronation but 'e never received a penny for it. They never received it, 'e were told. But is that *my* fault? No," he rails, as he has been known to this many a long year. "Handloom weaving's dead," he mutters. "Gone to hell in a handcart."

He lurches off into the night, bellowing like an animal in pain. The earth bucks beneath him. Phoebe yells. Who are these men shouting at her?

"Run and fetch Mrs Raffald," the Old Retainer orders the feral child.

Phoebe feels the shadow of the young girl on the Nico Ditch ripping through her. What rough beast whose hour must come at last? She feels a pair of hands pulling something from her. She hears the mewling angry cry of the thing that's been torn out of her, its fingers sharp and clawing like a heron's bill. Then nothing.

Time passes – slowly like a dandelion clock being blown on the wind, never quite alighting. She feels she is being carried along with it, as if on a rush cart. But this time she is alone.

The earth tilts once more. She wakes as another stab of pain rips through her. A second creature is fighting to be born. She sees the feral child pluck it from her, hold it high above her as the thunder cracks and lightning strikes, then wrap its bruised and bloodied form in the piece of white cloth. The skin of laurel leaves slides from Phoebe and enfolds the second twin instead. She feels a moth escaping from her mouth and knows she is dying.

A juddering breath empties her, not unlike the sound she made when Courtenay came inside her.

In the silence that follows she hears the far-off, distant sound of church bells ringing by themselves in the chill air. In between each peal she hears the Reverend Mr Thomas Beeley sonorously pronounce, "Whom God hath joined together, let no man put asunder," as Courtenay ties the knot with Miss Emily Gregory of Newcroft Hall. He has already forgotten Phoebe. The ceremony is watched over in relief by both his parents. Emily is biddable and Lady Agatha already has her measure, while Sir William can delay his inevitable bankruptcy another dozen years, hanging on to the red coat-tails of the British Army as they skirmish the length and breadth of the Brandywine River. The final peal of the bell resounds with the single gunshot at Chadd's Ford, which fells the exhausted Private Roy. In his last moments he reaches for the lock of Phoebe's hair he has carried with him from Boston to Baltimore, but he can no longer remember clearly what she looks like.

But even if he did, if he saw her now, he would not recognise her.

The feral child looks down at her drained body, just a husk now, an empty shell, and tugs at the sleeves of Septimus Swain, the Old Retainer. He looks at her, knows what she needs him to do, nods that he understands, and between them they carry Phoebe towards one of the Daub Holes. She is as light as air...

*

Eight years later Jem looks at Whelp, whose finger still point down towards the Daub Hole.

"What," he asks again, "are you trying to show me...?"

Her eyes, which are usually never still, but darting everywhere, like a cornered, feral cat, hold his gaze with a fervour that is unrelenting. Jem looks into them. They appear to him to contain nothing less than the history of the world inside them, all human passions delineated.

7

17th October, 1785: Holy Cross

"I now pronounce you man and wife…"

Zachary and Fanny turn to face a packed congregation in the Central Methodist Hall, smiling, with eyes only for each other.

They walk together down the aisle towards the double doors, which have been flung open to let in the light from outside.

As they stand on the steps, blinking in the sunshine, they are showered with petals and leaves.

"Mrs Robinson," says a tearful Catherine, embracing Fanny. "There – I wanted to be the first to say it."

"It's going to take me a while to get used to it," laughs Fanny.

"Not too long, I hope," warns Zachary with a grin.

Mattie, standing between both his parents, says nothing.

In the back room of the lodging house on Ainsworth Court behind the Long Mealgate, Solomon recites in Hebrew.

"Arise, Benjamin, son of Reuben!"

Upon hearing his name, Benjamin stands, takes a deep breath, looks quickly at his father, then walks purposefully towards the *bimah*, the reading platform. He takes the shortest route possible in order to express his willingness to approach the *Torah*. When he reaches it, he stands to the right of Solomon, facing the scroll. He touches as instructed the beginning and ending of the reading with the *Torah*'s sash and kisses it. He grips both handles of it, then recites the blessing.

"*Bar'chu et Adonai ham'vorach*. Bless the Lord who is blessed."

The fourteen families respond together. "*Baruch Adonai ham'vorach l'olam va'ed.* Blessed be the Lord who is blessed for all eternity."

He reads the designated text from the *Torah*, which he has been practising for weeks. He tries to remember his father's exhortation not to rush it.

"Moses said to God, *'You told me to bring these people to the Promised Land, but You did not tell me whom You would send with me. You also said that You know me by name and that You are pleased with me'*."

He blows the fringe that has fallen across his forehead with relief at having got through it more or less unscathed. Everybody beams. Leah has been distributing apples dipped in honey around the room. At the end of the second blessing they all throw them high into the air, showering Benjamin with them as he walks back to his place, this time taking the longest route possible.

"*Mazal tov!*" they sing. "Good fortune! May a constellation of bright stars light your way to a sweet destiny."

"May the blessings of the Lord God Almighty shine down upon you all on this most auspicious day. In the name of the Father, the Son, and the Holy Ghost. Amen."

"Amen."

The musicians at Fairfield, gathered together beneath the domed cupola on the roof of the barely finished Chapel, begin to play *Hagen*, or *Morning Star*, to mark the official opening of their new Moravian Settlement. Trumpets, trombones, violins, a drum.

A crowd of more than fifteen hundred people have gathered outside in the square to join the celebrations. Among them stand John Lees, Caroline, Agnes and Amos. Fairfield has been their home for four months now. They none of them now look backwards, watching the lives they have left unspooling behind them like a reel of cotton that would eventually snag and break. Instead they have each of them wound in their own personal thread, plus one for James, braided together in a five-count muslin, and are now looking forwards.

"Who giveth this woman today to be married?" asks the Minister in the Central Methodist Hall.
　Andrew Oldham steps forward. "I do."

When the date is first fixed for the wedding, Fanny approaches Andrew just before he retires for the evening.
　"Might I have a word with you please, sir?"
　"Certainly, Fanny. What is it?"
　"Well, sir, you and Mrs Oldham have both been so very kind to me, ever since you first took me in after my poor mother died of the phthisis…"
　"She was extremely brave in her final years, Fanny. We were glad to be able to offer you a position here."
　"Yes, sir, and I've always been extremely grateful. I never knew my father, and so… I was wondering… whether you might possibly stand in for him, sir, on the day of the wedding?" Fanny lowers her head, aware that she is in danger of betraying her feelings too much. Mr and Mrs Oldham are at all times the models of temperateness, rarely displaying any outward signs of emotion.
　Andrew approaches her gently. He places a hand on each of her shoulders, then speaks in a very quiet, very still voice. "My dear, I would consider it an honour."

The Minister beams broadly, first upon Andrew only, then back towards Fanny, and finally taking in the entire congregation.

"This is a most happy day indeed. Fanny is well known to all of us here, and we extend the warmest of welcomes to Zachary, whose father, some of you may recall, so ably assisted our Great Founder, John Wesley, on his visits to Leigh, Atherton and Tyldesley." The Minister diplomatically makes no reference to Zachary's father defection to the Moravians, on whom in any case the Methodist have always looked with tolerance. "Not only are we gathered here this morning to witness their nuptials, but also to celebrate the Feast of the Holy Cross, on which day they have elected to declare their vows. Let us begin therefore with a passage from Psalm Number 95, which is traditional for this day, and which Andrew has kindly agreed to read for us."

Andrew steps up to the lectern. He places his half moon spectacles upon the end of his nose, glances over them briefly for a moment, seeking out his wife, who smiles back reassuringly, then commences to read.

" '*O Come, let us sing unto the Lord. Let us make a joyful noise to the Rock of our Salvation. Let us come before his presence with Thanksgiving…*' "

Less than four miles away in Fairfield, Brother La Trobe is exhorting his own Moravian flock from the same Psalm at almost exactly the same time.

" '*In His hand are the deep places of the Earth. The strength of the hills is with Him also. The Sea is His, and He made it. And His hands made the dry land. O Come, let us worship and bow down, for He is our God, and we are the people of His pasture, the sheep of His hand…*' "

At the commencement of the *Aliyah*, Reuben, as the father of Benjamin, reads from the *Torah* before his son is summoned.

" *'And the Lord brought down the Waters of the Sea, but the Children of Israel walked upon dry land...'* "

He looks over to the place in the room where the women are seated, where he seeks out Leah, her head covered, but her eyes shining warmly upon him.

" *'And Miriam, the Prophetess',*" he continues, " *'the sister of Aaron, took a timbrel in her hand, all the women went after her, with timbrels of their own, and with dances. And Miriam sang unto them, "Sing ye to the Lord, for He is highly exalted. The rider and the horse He hath thrown into the sea"...'* "

Brother La Trobe looks around the filled Chapel benignly. The Settlement is rapidly being expanded. Soon, he thinks, it will be complete. On this day of thanksgiving he praises everyone assembled there for all their efforts, but offers up a special mention for John in the Lovefeast, for bringing them to this particular plot of land, for raising such a large part of the funds required, and for his tireless labours on the site helping to construct the various buildings already erected.

John, sitting in the pews designated for men and boys, looks down modestly. Amos, sitting beside him, proudly squeezes his hand. Caroline and Agnes, sitting among the women and the girls, similarly look down, feeling the gaze of approbation all around them.

On this day there are already one hundred and ten members established within the Settlement. Of this number twenty-two young men occupy the Single Brethren's House and forty-five young women occupy the Single Sisters' House. John, Caroline, Agnes and Amos live in The Manse, one of the first family dwellings to be constructed in the square.

Brother La Trobe reads from Matthew. Chapter 28, verse 18.

" '*Go ye, therefore, and teach all nations, baptising them in the name of the Father, and of the Son, and of the Holy Ghost*'."

He lays down the Bible and speaks directly to the people. "For although this day marks the end of one chapter in our wanderings, it marks the beginning of another. Did not our esteemed Bishop Spangenberg, successor to Count Zinzendorf himself, instruct us in the doctrine of *Unitas Fratrum* to go out into the world and bring others to our fold…?"

When Reuben has finished reading from the *Torah*, he sits down, next to Benjamin. Wolf Polack picks up a ram's horn and proclaims with a delighted smile upon his face.

"Benjamin's *Aliyah* today coincides with the second day of *Rosh Hashanah*, when we are instructed to 'make a noise', specifically by the blowing of the *shofar*." He indicates the ram's horn in his hand, which he then raises to his lips and, after much effort and a number of false starts of squeaks and splutters, he at last manages to produce the required sound, vibrating through the upstairs room of Solomon's lodging house, rattling the windows and doors, summoning up *The Days of Awe* from the beginnings of time, commemorated with holy trumpets and with fire.

On the roof of the Chapel in Fairfield the trumpets blare. The trombones boom and the drum pounds. The fifteen hundred people follow the Sisters and Brethren in a great procession around the boundary of the Settlement.

The service lasts deep into the night, when the grounds are lit with the flames from a hundred fires, and the sounds of more than a thousand voices rise high into the night sky, lifted on the sparks and embers.

"Come Jesus, Lord, with Holy Fire
Come, my quickened heart inspire..."

"Benjamin," says Solomon in a serious tone, looking down on the thirteen-year-old who, although he is now a *bar mitzvah* boy, suddenly appears very young, "from this day on you are a fully-fledged member of your people. Up until now your parents have been responsible for you, and as such they have been able to take the credit for your accomplishments, but they have also had to answer for your mistakes. Today's blessing has marked a change. It has relieved them of that responsibility. Now that passes to you. Use it wisely."

Reuben watches this exchange from across the room. They have done well since they all arrived in Manchester, exactly four months ago to the day. They have begun to prosper. His skills as a jeweller and engraver are already in high demand. His reputation for quality is growing. Benjamin could easily follow him into the trade. But he has other plans. A tiny seed was planted during their meeting with Herr Rothschild back in Frankfurt. He had been right in his assessment. Manchester is a city on fire. Every day Reuben witnesses the changes that are taking place. More and more people arrive each week. Every day, it seems, a new building is taking to the air – a mill, a factory, a warehouse – as well as new homes to accommodate all these new arrivals. And all of these grand schemes and speculations require capital, need financing. Reuben sees in this need a gap that he – and Benjamin after him – might just be able to fill.

The right place at the right time. Isn't that what Lemon has been saying all along, all through their four year odyssey, that the right place would present itself, and that when it did, they would recognise it and know? That right time is now, he realises. He understands this the moment he reads from the *Torah* about Miriam playing the timbrel and dancing, and he catches Leah's eye. Leah. He searches for her now among the guests gathered together in this airy upstairs room above where the Irk flows into the Irwell. There she is. Holding Abner in her arms, soothing him. Abner, who is so frequently fretful, and who is the one cloud in an otherwise clear sky. Reuben loves this second son fiercely. Having arrived more than twelve years after Benjamin, after so many miscarriages in between, he has been an unlooked-for blessing, his pale eyes and translucent skin a sure sign of his specialness. But Reuben worries that Abner may not grow to be strong and that it will be up to him – and now Benjamin – to look after him and provide for him. This plan that is unfolding in his mind about their new future might be just what is needed to secure it. Without him, the idea may never have come to him.

Abner. The bringer of light.

John has shaken hands with so many people this day, thanking him for all that he has done to transform the dream of the Settlement into something real, something tangible, that he has to nurse it with his other hand, for it has become quite sore. He tells everyone that he is just one among many who have laboured to make this day happen. This is not false modesty, but a true reflection of the facts, yet still they seek him out.

Now, as the crowds thin and the visitors leave, it is he who is doing the seeking out. It has been more than an hour since he last saw Caroline, or the children, and he is anxious, as he is most of the time these days, that she does not feel he has abandoned her again. But no. He sees her now, walking back towards their home, The Manse as it is somewhat grandly called, though not by them, with Brother La Trobe at her side. He is to be their guest for the night, a suggestion she made herself quite voluntarily, without having to be asked. He calls to her, and she turns and waves. She is smiling. She looks almost happy again, he thinks, though now that James is lost, he knows that this is an illusion. But Amos has been such a blessing to them, thanks be to God, and to Agnes, who so courageously flung herself into the Irk to rescue him, and who now cannot bear to be parted from him.

"Where are the children?" John asks Caroline, and she points to a low wall near to the Burying Ground.

John nods and goes off to fetch them. When he reaches them they are quite oblivious of his approach, so wrapped up are they in a simple game of Cat's Cradle, in which, heads close together and bent over the length of twine they pass to each other from hand to hand, they are completely immersed.

Their faces, upwardly lit by one of the many open fires burning close by, are solemn and grave, in thrall-like devotion to the shifting patterns they make. Cradle to Diamonds. Diamonds to Candles. Candles to Six-Pointed Star. Six-Pointed Star to Bird's Nest. Bird's nest to Long-Case Clock. Long-Case Clock to Soldier's Bed. Soldier's Bed to Moth.

Zachary and Fanny undress shyly in the darkness of their bedroom in the house on Bridge Street where Zachary has found lodgings for them. There are no curtains at the upstairs window so their bodies are bathed in a silver blue moonlight.

"To have and to hold," whispers Zachary.

"From this day forward," replies Fanny.

"For better, for worse."

"For richer, for poorer."

"In sickness and in health."

"For as long as we both shall live."

"Till death…" Fanny places her fingers gently on Zachary's lips to prevent him completing this last line, and wraps her arms around him.

Some time later, after they have finished, Fanny, out of modesty, has partly covered herself with the cotton shawl she has worn for the wedding. Zachary lies across her. He is almost asleep. She tries to match her breathing to his and thinks back over the rest of the day...

At its start, just as she is finishing getting dressed, Mrs Oldham knocks on her door. It is so tentative, no more than the beating of a lark's wing, that Fanny almost misses it.

"Yes?" she says.

Mrs Oldham hovers on the threshold. "May I come in?" she asks nervously.

Fanny sees that she is carrying something, wrapped in tissue paper, which she holds almost as if it were a baby.

"Oh," she exclaims. "Don't you look a picture? And I've just the thing here," she adds, tapping the parcel, "to finish it off." She pauses, then perches tentatively on the edge of the bed. "I've always liked this room," she says. "When we first built this house, you could see all the way to Ardwick Green from this window."

"Not any more," laughs Fanny. "Every time I look out of it now, there's another new building gone up."

"Yes, dear. I know what you mean. Things change so fast these days you can hardly catch your breath." She shifts awkwardly, then lifts her eyes from the tissue paper on her lap back up to Fanny. "It seems like only yesterday when you found Mattie on the doorstep."

"The night of the Earthquake."

Mrs Oldham nods.

"Wrapped in this," she says, opening the parcel to reveal the delicate muslin shawl. She holds it up to the light. "Moths caught in laurel."

"I thought that were in t' Chapel," says Fanny, puzzled. "On t' refectory table where th' hymn books are kept?"

"It was. But I know how much you've always liked it, the way you washed and ironed it so carefully after we'd taken Mattie in."

Fanny has a mental picture of herself hanging it to dry on the line at the back of the house, the way the wind would take it, and the moths would dance in the sunlight.

"And so," continues Catherine, "I thought you might wear it today, for a veil."

Fanny finds that she is speechless. Her throat feels dry and tight. Tears prick the back of her eyes.

Catherine sees this and smiles. "Here," she says, "let me put it on for you."

She arranges it so that it hangs loose and light over her shoulders.

"I'll give it straight back after," says Fanny.

"No," says Catherine. "Keep it. You found it. It's yours now."

The two women embrace each other warmly.

"We'll miss you," says Catherine. "Especially Mattie."

"How is he?"

"Oh – he'll come round, don't worry. Your going has just been a shock to him, that's all."

"I'll come and visit."

"Of course. But you'll have a husband to attend to now."

Fanny blushes and looks down.

"He's a good man," says Catherine. Then, laying her hands lightly once more across the shawl, she adds, "And a lucky one…"

Now, in their bedroom on Bridge Street, Zachary delicately lifts the shawl from Fanny's body and holds it up towards the moonlight.

"Moths," he whispers, "caught in laurel. Which is which, I wonder?"

"I suppose you think that I'm the moth," teases Fanny, "and that somehow you've set me free?"

"For which I get the laurel as a victory garland," smiles Zachary.

"Which means you get both," laughs Fanny. "That doesn't sound fair." She wraps it round the back of his neck and pulls him towards her. "Now you're the moth," she says, "and it's my turn to capture you."

"Good," he says. "That way I get the laurel twice."

The moon searches out the shawl within which Fanny and Zachary are now completely intertwined, their limbs a blur, as the moths dance among the leaves towards the light.

THREE

The Lot

1798

*in which a lecture is given on aspects of colour
wherein not everything is black and white –
a kaleidoscope is made – a game of cat's cradle is played
– some places and people are given new names –
a lot is cast – three young men come of age –
one discovers his calling, one resists his fate,
one experiences an epiphany –
and a new use is found for some old bricks*

8

1798

29th September

EXTRAORDINARY FACTS

relating to the

Vision of Colours:

WITH OBSERVATIONS
BY MR JOHN DALTON

FIRST READ FOR
THE MANCHESTER LITERARY & PHILOSOPHICAL SOCIETY

31st OCTOBER 1794

READ AGAIN with Revisions
29th SEPTEMBER 1798

"It has been observed, that our ideas of colours, sounds and tastes & co, excited by the same object, may be very different in themselves, without our being aware of it; and that we may nevertheless converse intelligibly concerning such objects, as if we were certain the impressions made by them on our minds were exactly similar. All, indeed, that is required for this purpose, is, that the same object should uniformly make the same impression on each mind; and that objects which appear different to one should be equally so to others.

"It will, however, scarcely be supposed, that

any two objects, which are every day before us, should appear hardly distinguishable to one person, and very different to another, without the circumstance immediately suggesting a difference in their faculties of vision; yet such is the fact, not only with regard to myself, but to many others also, as will appear in the following account..."

Matthew listened with growing unease as Mr Dalton expounded his theory concerning colour blindness, how what was blue to one person may appear pink to another, while he himself admitted readily to being unable to perceive a difference between red and green. Matthew experienced no such difficulties in differentiating between one colour and another, but the fact that some people did, particularly one so eminent as the esteemed Mr Dalton, troubled him, for Matthew liked to deal in certainties. The thought that there may also be contrasting shades of opinion, about any subject one might care to mention, caused him even greater concern.

There were three things he *was* certain of: his parents had both died (within a month of each other), his father had left the felt factory for him to run, he was twenty-one years old.

He remembered his father enthusing about Mr Dalton's lecture four years before, when he had fist heard it, saying that the lecture explained exactly his own condition. He too had thought that everybody experienced the world as *he* did, but now it turned out that only some did, those with colour blindness, or Daltonism, as some academics were already beginning to call it. There were three basic anomalous conditions which Dalton had identified – protanomaly, which is a reduced sensitivity to red light; deuteranomaly, which is a reduced sensitivity to green light, and tritanomaly, which is a reduced sensitivity to blue light and extremely rare. Matthew's father had, it seemed, deuteranomaly, the commonest of the three.

"It's an inherited characteristic," he said. "My father had it too."

"Then why don't I?" asked Matthew bluntly.

Andrew could have replied by saying that it was not an affliction routinely passed down, although incidences were frequent, but he chose not to. Quite deliberately. Instead he decided that this might be the moment to explain the circumstances of Matthew's birth, or, to be more accurate, of his discovery.

And so this was a fourth fact now of which Matthew was certain: that the man and woman he had thought were his parents were not in fact; that, although they had raised him as their own, loved him and protected him, they had actually found him, or rather Fanny had, on their doorstep.

Fanny. The muscle in the side of his face gave an infinitesimal twitch as he thought of her, a minuscule nervous tic, which betrayed an emotion that Matthew did not like to investigate too closely, and so, as he always did if thoughts of her might surface unbidden at any time, he suppressed them. He had not spoken to her since the day she had married that surveyor thirteen years before. If ever she had called upon his parents – his *adoptive* parents, he decided he should from now onwards refer to them as, his adoptive, *dead* parents – hoping for an opportunity to see him too, he always refused and would not come down the stairs. If he ever accidentally encountered her on a street somewhere in Manchester, he would cut her. She was dead to him. As dead to him as his false parents were, who had died so closely on the heels of each other, Andrew quite suddenly of a heart attack, Catherine four weeks later, having fallen into an immediate decline, refusing all offers of medicine or even food.

He was an orphan, he supposed. He wondered, weighing up what evidence he had, whether this counted as a fifth fact.

Possibly. To all intents and purposes he was, and that was a situation he found he liked – alone, independent, neither beholden nor answerable to anyone. But it was still conceivable – he smiled to himself at the aptness of the adjective – that one or other, or both, of his natural parents were alive and out there somewhere. He had to concede that, but *natural*? What on earth was natural about abandoning a baby on the doorstep of a complete stranger? He would rather not think too much about that, and, since the likelihood of him ever knowingly coming across either of them was extremely remote, he wasted little if any effort in giving over idle thoughts to any kind of consideration of them or their whereabouts. He devoted significantly more time to an exploration of what the motives of his surrogate parents might have been in taking him in, offering him shelter, deciding to keep him, when they could so easily, he supposed, have handed him over to the authorities, to a hospital, or the Workhouse even. Love, he imagined. Or need perhaps – they had no children of their own after all. Or simply living true to their Christian creed – being the Good Samaritan, doing unto others, give and it will be given unto you. No. That is unkind. They would not have acted in any way out of expectation of reward. They were good people, he knew this, even if their actions baffled him, the reasons behind them. One of his father's favourite passages was from Matthew, his namesake, which he was very fond of quoting to him, so that he knew it by heart.

'*Beware of exercising thy righteousness before others in order for this to be seen by them, for then thou wilt have no reward from thy Father who is in heaven. Thus, when thou givest to the needy, sound no trumpet before thyself, as the hypocrites do in the synagogues and in the streets, that they may be praised by others.*'

The man who said he was his father lived by this self-denying creed, but Matthew doubted its wisdom. Surely there was a certain *kudos* to be earned to be seen to be doing good works? It was just as hypocritical to claim the moral high ground of altruism by denying this simple fact. Better to be honest in admitting that, if by doing so-called charitable works one gained entry onto various influential boards, other more worldly, more immediate benefits were accrued. As a consequence, Matthew found he was inclined to dismiss altogether the final verse of his father's creed.

'But when thou givest to the needy, do not let thy left hand know what thy right hand is doing, so that thy giving may be in secret, and thy Father, who seest in secret, will reward thee.'

No. Matthew leant toward that other, simpler maxim: '*God helps those who help themselves.*' And that is what he intended to do.

He had attended the lecture by Mr Dalton, therefore, for three reasons: first because, having turned twenty-one, he could; second because he recognised among the members of *The Manchester Literary & Philosophical Society* gentlemen of property and influence, and third because he was genuinely interested in the topic. He was drawn towards a greater understanding of all the latest technical innovations being discovered by the new gods of science and engineering. They were the twin pillars of his faith and he looked to them for clarity, even when, as had been the case with Mr Dalton's lecture, they created more questions than answers, such as the matter of his parentage. How much of his own personality, he wondered privately to himself, was the result of his upbringing, as opposed to what he might have inherited from his own unknown parents? And how much was down to what was inherent within him? Matthew's own thinking tended towards the theory expounded by John Locke in his *Essay Concerning Human Understanding* – the *tabula rasa*, or blank slate, which, to Matthew's mind, allowed for the total possibility of the self-made man, which was how he liked to picture himself, rising on his own merit, towards limitless horizons, dependent entirely on his own efforts, beholden to nobody. He applauded

Locke's confident dismissal of Descartes' notion of an innate idea of God, with which all humans are born, at the same time deriding the Earl of Shaftesbury's assertion that Locke's emphasis on empiricism ejected virtue and order from the world, resulting in a moral relativism which would inevitably lead to rebellion and sedition.

Matthew had thought about this a lot. He was 'inherently' a staunch advocate of the rule of law, firmly established upon principles of precedence, yet at the same time he was a fervent proponent of the view that change was the natural order of things, and that it was down to him, or those like him, whose 'innate' destiny it was to steer that change. Let Proverbs be his guide. '*The churning of milk bringeth forth butter.*' Or, as the woman who called herself his mother expressed it more succinctly, "Cream rises." He intended to start churning the milk.

He was just on the point of leaving the *Lit & Phil's* newly acquired handsome premises on George Street, tucked between Mosley and Portland Streets, in one of the recently built fine houses there, when he was accosted by Dr Thomas Perceval, co-founder of the society and a former close friend of the man who referred to himself as Matthew's father.

"Matthew Oldham, isn't it? Yes, I thought so. Your first visit here? Not here, specifically, to George Street, that has been a first for all of us here this evening, but to the *Lit & Phil*, I mean?"

"Yes, sir. I turned twenty-one earlier this month."

"Splendid. Such a pity you could not have attended with your late father. He would have taken great pleasure in this evening's lecture, I've no doubt."

"Indeed, sir, for he was afflicted with the same version of the condition as Mr Dalton himself."

"Deuteranomaly."

"The same. Yet…" He paused. He had not intended to continue, but that 'yet' had escaped his lips before his brain could intervene. His desire to impress his peers and ingratiate himself with his so-called elders and betters was a trait he had cultivated as a pupil at The Bluecoat School, at some personal cost to his reputation at times, for his need for approval had in the past led him to utter pronouncements of injudicious haste, and he had resolved, especially now that the man he had formerly thought of as his father, whose good opinion he had once sought above all others, had died, to speak only when he was spoken to, not venturing a position until he was certain of his ground first. Irritated, he bit his lip, but it was too late.

"And yet...?" repeated Perceval. "You were about to add a *caveat*, I believe."

"Am I that transparent?"

"Come, come. Be not so harsh upon yourself. It is always better to speak one's mind."

"Well," said Matthew, taking a breath before he continued, "I was about to add that it is a condition which I myself do not appear to have inherited."

"A comforting thought, is it not?"

"Sir?"

"That one is not necessarily preordained to follow a certain path laid out for us by those who have gone before."

"But does not the Bible tell us...?"

" '*I the Lord thy God am a jealous God, visiting the iniquity of the fathers upon the children, even unto the third and fourth generation*'?"

"Yes." Matthew found himself smiling despite himself.

"But have the walls of our most commodious new building come crashing about us for saying such... What is the word?"

"Blasphemy?"

Now it was Perceval's turn to smile. "I've always regarded the Good Book in a metaphoric rather than a literal sense. And who's to say this Daltonism is an iniquity? It does not appear to have prevented him from carrying out his experiments or realising his discoveries, does it?"

"No, indeed."

"And though you may not have inherited your father's colour blindness, you are not blind to the possibility that you may well have inherited from him some of his finer qualities?"

"I hope I do, sir." Matthew inclined his head, feeling the colour rise to his cheeks, a not unpleasant sensation. In public at least he would continue with the charade that Mr Andrew Oldham, friend and associate to so many of the successful and influential gentlemen retiring to the Club's lounge at this moment, was indeed his natural father.

"Come," continued Dr Perceval, perceiving the young man's reticence and misinterpreting it for modesty, "let me introduce you to some of the other members, many of them well acquainted with your father and admirers of him."

He gestured around the room and Matthew recognised several of the gentlemen assembled there – factory owners and scholars, clerics and doctors, men of faith and men of science, all of them men of substance and influence. Yes, he thought, he had done well to visit here, and he recalled another maxim from the Book of Proverbs.

'He that walketh with wise men shall be wise himself, but a companion of fools shall be destroyed.'

He looked about him. Many of Manchester's richest and most successful entrepreneurs were gathered here, most of them highly prosperous merchants in the textile trades, to which he now was affiliated. There was John Philips and his brothers, Thomas and Nathaniel, the latter related by marriage to the family who sat on the topmost branches of the Cotton Tree, the Hibberts, who owned a number of plantations in Virginia and Jamaica, one of whom, Sir Robert Hibbert III, Chair of the West India Merchants Association in Manchester, stood before him now, as Dr Perceval introduced them.

"Oldham?" he said, his thick eyebrows knitting together furiously. "Don't tell me – er... hats!" he declared triumphantly, as if plucking a rabbit from his voluminous waistcoat, into which he was now delving to retrieve a silk handkerchief with which he proceeded to blow his noise noisily and copiously, thereafter subjecting the cloth to a most thorough and scrupulous examination of the contents now to be found there. "Never forget a name," he said. "It's faces I have difficulties with. Causes no end of problems with the ladies," he added with a leer. "All the fillies look the same to me. Pale and unfinished. Prefer my candy black personally. Perhaps I suffer from this colour blindness old Dalton droned on about for so long this evening." He laughed once more, but mirthlessly this time. He was carrying a lorgnette, through which he now began a closer inspection of Matthew. "Take yours, for instance. A perfectly respectable face, but one which I fear I will forget the instant we part this evening. So you'd better say something, preferably something witty, that I might remember you for that, should circumstance ever bring us into the same orbit again."

"I'm afraid I must disappoint you then," replied Matthew. "I'm a rather dull, plain-speaking fellow. At least that's what my teachers said at school."

"Pah!" boomed Sir Robert. "I've always thought education over-rated. I was a complete booby at school. Simply drank and whored my way through Cambridge. But look at me now. It's not what you know, but who you know that counts. That and an eye for the main chance. *Carpe diem* – the only Latin I can remember, but it's served me well enough. Seize the day – that's my motto."

"I intend to," said Matthew, looking Hibbert squarely in the eye.

"Good man."

Sir Robert waved his lorgnette in the direction of a cluster of gentlemen adjusting ill-fitting wigs over a rash of bald pates. "The Philipses and the Hibberts," he gestured. "We're so closely inter-related that even I don't know whether I'm addressing a cousin, an uncle or a nephew. They might possibly be all three. Take old N-N-Nathaniel over there. He's John Philips's younger brother. His wife, Elizabeth, is a Hibbert, the sister of my Great Uncle Thomas, whose daughter Sarah-Anne is married to Nathaniel's cousin George, who's also my brother."

Matthew laughed. "I've neither brothers nor sisters. At least as far as I know."

"Meaning?"

"We none of us know what our fathers might have got up to, do we?"

"From what I hear, your father was a saint, but as far as my own lineage is concerned, it would appear to be not just a family tree we're talking about, but practically a whole forest, with different woods grafted onto each, if you know what I mean?" He nudged Matthew's elbow as he said this, winking suggestively. "Between us we control more than half the export trade between here and West Africa, where the demand for our cloth shows no sign of abating. If anything, it increases year on year. The merchants there buy it from us with the money they earn from selling slaves to the Colonies, who work on the plantations there to produce the raw cotton we import here to make the finished goods the African merchants just can't get enough of. And so it goes on. The Golden Triangle…"

"Otherwise known as the *Sublime* Triangle, where the square on the hypotenuse is equal to the sum of the other two sides."

"Someone was paying attention in school that day, I see," remarked Sir Robert, giving Matthew a sidelong glance. "And yet, look at them," he continued, directing Matthew's attention back to the assembled Philips clan across the room, "earnestly falling over themselves to see which of them can utter the most pious anti-slavery sentiments, while still making an excellent living sliding down one side of that isosceles triangle in pursuit of their Golden Mean."

"I don't follow. That must have been a day I *wasn't* paying attention at school."

"The Golden Mean," explained Sir Robert, "the ideal moderate position between two outstretched extremes. Just listen to them…"

Matthew shook his head. "They're too far away."

"You don't have to be able to hear them," sneered Sir Robert, "just read their lips, look at the expressions in their eyes. 'Of course I'm anti-slavery', they bleat, 'it's a cruel, barbarous trade, but what are we to do? Manchester depends upon it so. I've my workers to think of. I couldn't guarantee to keep them all on if we no longer sold our goods to Africa'. 'And who would grow the cotton in the colonies?' 'There'd have to be some sort of compensation scheme'." Sir Robert turned his back upon them.

"My father signed Thomas Clarkson's petition."

"I'm sure he did, my boy, and quite right too." He patted the young man's head almost affectionately. "I prefer my brother George's position. An appalling man, but at least he doesn't pretend towards piety."

"George?"

"He owns a number of plantations in Jamaica. Senior partner at West India House. If slavery ever does come to an end, he'll make a killing – you mark my words."

Matthew stood and watched as Sir Robert Hibbert III walked across the room to join the other members of his family, full of *bonhomie*, with seeming scant regard to anything he had just been saying to Matthew. His mind went back to something Mr Dalton had said during his lecture, "that the same object should uniformly make the same impression on each mind; and that objects which appear different to one should be equally so to others." Yet in fact this was not the case, Matthew realised. The same object may indeed be perceived quite differently by two people standing in immediate proximity one to the other. Deuteranomaly…

He became aware of Dr Perceval standing once more at his side.

"You're making acquaintances, I see?"

"Hardly, sir. He was just being polite."

"I doubt that very much. The Hibberts never do anything unless they see some gain in it for themselves."

"What possible gain could he hope to get from me?"

"Perhaps he perceived possible hidden depths."

Matthew turned towards his host with a puzzled frown. "What do you mean?"

"You have a steelier complexion than did your father."

Matthew returned his gaze.

"You do not deny it, I see? At least you are honest, and that is an admirable quality, although sometimes you may find it necessary to bite your tongue."

"I hope not too often, sir. A fact is either true, or it is not."

"I have no desire to patronise, Mr Oldham, but it does often seem so to the young. I, too, when I was your age, liked to see things in black and white. A thing was either right, or it was wrong. But as I have grown older, I find I have become less certain. There are shades of colour between those two edges of the spectrum. You may find your opinions may change over time."

"But what of the law? The law is unchanging, surely?"

"Possibly. But not unyielding, I hope. The world is moving at such a pace these days. Change assails us on all sides. If the times change, why not the law, why not our understanding of what is true or false, right or wrong? We must accommodate the times as we live them. To adapt is to survive…"

Matthew pondered these words but did not reply. He was saved from doing so by the arrival of two other gentlemen, brothers, who looked so completely alike they might almost have been taken for twins, except that one, the older, had salt and pepper side whiskers, while the younger's were ginger. In every other respect their appearance was identical. They wore royal blue tail-coats with polished brass buttons, white muslin shirts, with ruffles at the neck and cuffs, tucked into tan calfskin breeches with a tie and buttons at the knee and a fall front. Their waistcoats were double-breasted and orange, to match their cravats. Their boots were a dark brown leather and their hats, which they each carried under their left arms, were tall and conical and, a fact Matthew could not help but recognise at once, made in the Felt Works he had now inherited from the man he must still officially recognise as his father.

Seeing the direction of his gaze, the elder of the two beamed. "Purchased from Oldham & Son."

"And you, I take it, sir," added the younger, "are 'Son'?"

"Indeed. But you have the advantage of me, I'm afraid."

"Forgive me," said Dr Perceval. "Allow me to introduce you. The brothers Grant, Messrs William and Daniel, from Ramsbottom. Mr Matthew Oldham from Manchester."

"Delighted to make your acquaintance," they chorused, accompanying their words with a slight, identical bow.

"I shall leave you now, gentlemen, if you don't mind," said Perceval, "for I have Club matters to attend to. Mr Dalton, I see, is standing quite by himself in the doorway. He doesn't smoke, he doesn't drink, he doesn't gamble, he is steadfastly unmarried. No wonder he's been forsaken by our disreputable members here this evening."

"Does he work?"

"Indeed he does. Indefatigably. At Manchester's so-called 'New' University."

"He has colleagues then perhaps?"

"That I couldn't say. But if he does, he will not have for much longer."

"Oh? And why is that?"

"The word from the rumour mill is that it teeters on the brink of bankruptcy. Good evening."

The Brothers Grant, who had been hovering nearby, now took their opportunity to alight, like a pair of amiable geese, employing their broad, flat feet to bring themselves to a rather less than graceful landing, as they each accidentally nudged the other's elbow, causing both of them to spill a measure of the contents of their generously filled sherry glasses.

"Our card," said Mr William, producing one from the top of his waistcoat, from which he wiped the recalcitrant drops with his brightly spotted handkerchief.

"At your service," echoed Mr Daniel, producing his own card at exactly the same moment, whilst similarly mopping away the evidence of his libationary misfortune.

Matthew held them, one in each hand. He looked from one to the other, then back up to the beaming brothers, and swapped them from hand to hand.

"William? Daniel?" he laughed. "How do I tell you apart?"

"You don't need to," they both replied.

"Just say either of our names..." said one.

"... and one of is sure to answer you," said the other.

"What brings you to Manchester?" asked Matthew.

The brothers looked at one another.

"Actually," began William.

"To see *you*," completed Daniel.

An hour later Matthew walked the less than quarter of a mile from George Street to his home, which he now lived in entirely alone. There was a housekeeper of course, Mrs Crinkle, an older lady from the Chapel who had been a friend of the woman who had duped him into calling his mother, but she did not live in. Sometimes other people came round to do specific jobs, but he did not concern himself with them. He left all that to Mrs Crinkle. Otherwise he had the house to himself, which was how he liked it. There had never been another cat, not since Smokey had leapt aboard Mr Sadler's balloon. Occasionally he would dream of that day and imagine himself rescuing Smokey, of leaping in after him, floating high above the town, looking down on its writhing, heaving, many-tentacled sprawl, trying to pick out where he lived, a feat that was becoming harder and harder to achieve as more and more buildings hemmed his in from all sides. He could still, in these night-time imaginings, discern the factory chimney of Oldham's Felt Works, but with all the dozens of mills that were sprouting up around it, soon even that too would disappear. He did not like that thought. For if his house and the factory disappeared, where would that leave him?

As he made his way along Charlotte Street, emerging onto the still open ground alongside the Royal Infirmary, past the Lunatic Asylum, beside the Daub Holes, he almost stepped on a nest of rats. They were fastidiously stripping the carcass of a blackbird and paid him no heed whatsoever. They were far too numerous to count and within less than a minute all that remained of the bird were its bones, its beak and its feet, so efficiently had they disposed of the skin and feathers. Matthew watched all this with a cool detachment. He was not squeamish about rats. Not like some people. They had their place in the scheme of things. They had a job to do and they did it well.

He mulled over again the proposal the Grant brothers had put to him. It intrigued and excited him.

"Take advantage of this building boom," they had said. "Find your own particular niche. Fill in the gaps before someone else does. Then expand."

"And what do you think my niche might be?" he had asked them. "Not just felt, surely? Not the manufacturing of more and more beaver hats?"

They smiled. "Oh, there'll always be a steady supply of customers for beaver hats," they had said, "but you haven't the space on your factory floor to produce many more than you already do. No," they continued, "we could do that for you. We've got space and room a-plenty in Ramsbottom."

"What are you suggesting? A partnership?"

"No, no, no," they beamed in chorus, spreading their hands out wide, "nothing so formal or fixed as that. We live in rapidly changing times, do we not, Matthew, so we all of us need to be... What is the word, Brother Daniel?"

"Nimble, Brother William."

"Flexible, Brother Daniel."

"Fleet of foot, Brother William."

"Precisely so," they concluded together.

"No – what we are proposing is a modest speculation," said Mr William.

"Speculation?" echoed Matthew, raising an amused eyebrow.

"Are you a gambling man, Matthew?" asked Mr Daniel.

"Do you like a little flutter?" continued Mr William.

"On the horses?"

"At the table?"

"Hardly," laughed Matthew. "My parents were strict Methodists."

"Come, come. You are your own man, are you not?"

"I like to think so."

"A man of business?"

"I hope to be."

"Then what is business if it does not involve a little gambling?" urged Mr William.

"Nothing ventured, nothing gained," pressed Mr Daniel.

"I'm averse to risk," replied Matthew.

"Without risk there is no advancement," pronounced Mr William.

"Prometheus would not have discovered fire," declared Mr Daniel.

"Columbus would not have crossed the ocean," added Mr William.

"Mr Arkwright would not have opened his Mill," they both concluded together, shaking each other by the hand and patting Matthew on the back simultaneously with the other.

"Then the risk must be low," conceded Matthew.

"It cannot lose," said Mr William, offering Matthew a cigar.

"What the gentlemen of the turf…" continued Mr Daniel.

"The grooms at Tattersall's…" interrupted Mr William.

"… refer to in racing parlance as," concluded Mr Daniel, lighting the cigar which his brother had so helpfully placed in Matthew's mouth, "a dead cert."

"Indeed?" said Matthew, removing the cigar and handing it back to Mr Daniel.

"*You* supply the patterns," said Mr William.

"*We'll* provide the raw materials," added Mr Daniel.

"And the machines to produce them," said Mr William.

"And the men to work the machines," concluded Mr Daniel.

"Then we'll divide the profits," said Mr William.

"Forty for you…" offered Mr Daniel.

"Sixty for us," accepted Mr William.

The two brothers shook hands, as if somehow they were completing the deal exclusively between themselves.

Matthew could not resist a smile.

"That's a very generous arrangement," he said, "if all I'm providing is the pattern for the design."

"All?" they exclaimed, immediately taking out their silk handkerchiefs from their waistcoats and mopping their brows simultaneously. "All?"

"I don't understand," said Matthew, genuinely perplexed.

"Your name!" they chorused. "Your father's reputation is without equal."

"A *nonpareil*," squeaked Mr William.

"*Incomparabilis*," chirruped Mr Daniel.

Matthew nodded, beginning to understand. "So you would take over all hat production from me while retaining the name 'Oldham's' for the brand, in return for which you give me forty percent of all sales?"

"All *profits*," corrected Mr William.

"We will have our own expenses, you understand..." explained Mr Daniel.

"Production costs," added Mr William.

"The initial outlay..."

"The additional work force..."

"Packaging..."

"Distribution..."

"Advertising..."

"You know the sort of thing...?"

"Indeed I do, gentlemen, and I appreciate your candour, as well as your generosity."

The two brothers shifted uncomfortably from foot to foot, anticipating what might be coming next.

"But as you have so rightly said, my father's name is..."

"Beyond compare," ventured Mr William.

"Beyond price was what I had been going to say."

The brothers William and Daniel looked at one another, sighed, then shrugged their shoulders rather helplessly.

"You're not telling me that that is your best offer, surely?" asked Matthew, regarding the two men incredulously.

"Do you have a suggestion of your own?" pouted Mr William somewhat sulkily.

"Fifty percent," smiled Matthew.

"Forty-five," offered Mr Daniel gloomily.

"Of sales?" asked Matthew.

The brothers looked at each other once more, both tapping their fingers in front of their stout stomachs straining at their waistcoats, then nodded as one and turned back to Matthew.

"Agreed!" they chimed, all smiles at once restored.

Hands were shaken, cigars were lit, and Matthew bade them farewell.

He realised that they had not answered his question to them about what they thought his own niche might be, but he reckoned he had discovered it for himself. He had a head for business and could drive a hard bargain. He recognised when he held the high value cards and he knew how to play them. No point keeping them close to his chest when it was clear what the outcome would be. That only wasted time, and time, he knew without a shred of doubt, was of the essence if you wanted to keep ahead of the game. Time was money.

He also recognised a good idea when he saw one, even if it was not his own in the first place, especially if it was not his own, in fact. There was no price at all on just an idea, not until it was patented, and then, if it was a good idea, once it had been tested and proved, then no price was too high for it. Like the value of a good name.

In their conversation they had let slip the idea they had for a scheme they were planning to implement in their factories back in Ramsbottom. Tokens. Instead of paying their workers' wages entirely in money, they were toying with the idea of paying them partly in tokens, tokens which could be redeemed for food and drink, but only in the shop and the public house owned and run by themselves. This got Matthew thinking. Why limit the tokens just to those two establishments? Why not also build workers' houses, the rent for which could also only be paid for in tokens? Matthew smiled. He began to envisage an entire colony, where the workers who toiled in his factories also lived in his houses and purchased all of their essential goods from his shops.

He looked down at the rats foraging around the Daub Holes. How far would they roam in search of their next meal? As far as they had to, he calculated. But what if that meal was provided for them right here where they now dwelt? They would stay in the same spot. He was sure of it. What other incentive would they need? A place to lay their head? A guaranteed daily supply of nourishment? And in return for what? Loyalty. Nothing more would be required of them. Merely the actions of a grateful child to secure the approval of his surrogate parents.

He opened the front door of his house and stepped across its threshold into the soothing silence on the other side, where he could be just whoever he wanted.

Here he could dream big plans, ambitions to implement significant changes to Oldham's Felt Works, and, gathered around him this evening, had been the men who could help him to achieve them – not just the Grant Brothers, but the Philipses, the Hibberts, even the Percevals and the Daltons. He would maintain the name – Oldham's – for that undoubtedly had value, especially now that, following the death of the man he would continue to refer to as his father when in company such as these, Newton Lane had been changed by a binding decision of the Court Leet to Oldham Street. That afforded him a certain weight and standing among these men of influence and substance, and he would use it to his advantage.

'I have set before thee an open door…'

For now, he closed the door behind him, content in the knowledge that he possessed the key to open it whenever he needed to.

9

15th October

"My husband was not a wicked man," said Lady Ashton, removing an olive green glove and placing it on the table in front of her. "I want you to understand that before we proceed any further."

Facing her across the polished mahogany table Reuben Halsinger spread his hands with practised acknowledgement. Of course, his gesture appeared to imply. He inclined his head politely at the same time but as yet spoke no words. He would let Her Ladyship finish what she needed to say first. He recognised in her a woman of forceful opinions, of great clarity of mind, somebody, in short, it would be unwise to underestimate.

"He was a foolish man," she continued, "to the point of recklessness in fact. The consequences of which I know only too well," she added, removing the second glove. "At times, a selfish man. One could call his behaviour obsessive – his mania for collecting was an illness, an addiction, from which he could retreat for long periods, sometimes for months, but it would always come to reclaim him in the end. As it did so catastrophically last year."

Reuben sensed that this was an opportunity for him to speak. "I am most sorry for your loss, Your Ladyship."

"Thank you," she said, somewhat curtly, batting back his words with a cursory flap of her ungloved hand, turning her face away from him at the same time, quite expertly, so that it lay in shadow a moment, thereby concealing the considerable effort she was exerting to ensure that no outward sign of any distress she might be feeling could be visibly detected by him.

Reuben admired her self-control and waited patiently for her to recover and so resume her theme.

"He came to see you himself, I believe, not long before he...?"

"He did, Your Ladyship. Though not here. I did not have these offices then."

"No. I see. I imagine it was in an upstairs room above *The Boar's Head*?"

"*The Bull's*," corrected Reuben, as delicately as he could.

"Yes, I suppose it would have had to be one of them. He was for ever visiting such establishments in the hope of securing some deal or other."

"It is where such deals are usually done," offered Reuben kindly.

"Yes. He was already at the Infirmary by the time I reached him. They told me nothing of the circumstances surrounding his attack. At first I refused to believe them. Sir Ashton had the heart of an ox. Or one of those great beasts he used to keep in our grounds at Alkrington. But when I saw him lying there, his face grey, his mouth slack, I knew they were right. This was not the husband I knew, merely a shadow of him."

She paused once more to recover her composure.

Reuben thought her magnificent.

In the silence that ensued he had time to reflect upon the changes that had taken place so rapidly since he and the rest of the fourteen families had first arrived here, merely thirteen years before. There were more of them now of course and some who had left them. Old Lemon Nathan, who had led them out of Vienna and guided them across Europe, had passed on and was now at rest in the new burial ground at Brindle Heath in Pendleton. Samuel Solomon, who had been the first to welcome them into his home here, had found such success with the selling of his Balm of Gilead that he had moved back to his family in Liverpool, where he had built himself a fine house in the Kensington district there, as well as purchasing land on Mossley Hill as a plot for a mausoleum. But his brother Simon had stayed to grow his jewellery business. They had moved the synagogue from the rented room in Ainsworth Court to an airier upper chamber on Garden Street behind The Withengreave, which everyone now called Withy Grove, where Lemon's brother Jacob was the Overseer and Aaron Jacob served as Reader, and also as *shochet*, slaughterer of birds and animals for food, according to their dietary laws of *kashrut*. It was rumoured that already Manchester was the fourth largest settled Jewish community in England and rising fast. It would not be long before they were second only to London. Their cause had been much helped by news of the imminent arrival of the millionaire banker and financier Nathan Meyer Rothschild, who had first encouraged them to head for Manchester when they had met him while resting from their wanderings in Frankfurt. He was having brand new offices constructed in Brown Street, plus a house on Mosley Street, within easy reach of a vast warehouse he was constructing on Back Mosley Street, as well as a country mansion on Downing Street in fashionable Ardwick, less than a mile and a half away from the centre of Manchester but still a rural retreat clustered around a green and a pond and some outlying orchards. He would arrive as soon as these buildings were completed and had indicated he would invest heavily in the basic raw materials of dyes and untreated cotton, which he would sell on to the manufacturers and merchants, the likes of the Philipses, to whom, Reuben knew, the late Sir Ashton had gone to try and secure loans to service his rapidly escalating debts before trying his luck with *him*, in that rather shabby meeting in the upstairs room above *The Bull's Head*, to which his stoically composed widow had so recently alluded, for he, Reuben Halsinger, had taken Herr Rothschild's advice to them in Frankfurt all those years before quite literally to heart. As soon as he felt his family were settled in their new surroundings and immediately after his son Benjamin's *bar mitzvah*, he had taken steps to expand his traditional practice of pawnbroking and focus instead on banking and financing. He quickly found that his services were in steady demand, first as so many merchants attempted to hang on to the coat tails of Messrs Arkwright and Drinkwater by opening up more and more cotton mills along the banks of the Irwell and Irk, and second as the blockade imposed by the French across the Channel following the resumption of hostilities between the two countries after the execution of Louis XVI began to bite, and the price of cotton began to tumble in the Exchange, so that those same merchants suddenly found the liquidity of their assets to be drying up faster than they could replenish them. Reuben's business grew ever more lucrative, so that when it came to settling on the rates for the repayment of loans, it was generally he who called the tune. As a result he had moved his family from their cramped lodgings on Shude Hill to more spacious apartments on desirable Brazenose Street, where his wife Leah could be accepted as an equal among the wives of the likes of Herr Franklin, the silversmith on St Ann's Square, Herr Mendelson, the watchmaker on Cross Street, Herr Gumpel, the surgeon on Princess Street, and Herr Freeman, the renowned miniature painter who had installed a studio just a few doors down from them on Brazenose Street, all the best addresses, and walk tall beside them. His son, Benjamin, now twenty-six years old and fully coming into his own as a man, had secured a position as a teller in Heywood's Bank on King Street, through links the Rothschilds had with the Sephardic Finance Houses in Amsterdam, where he was already being singled out as a person with prospects.

All of this flitted through Reuben's mind as he waited for Lady Ashton to come round to what he knew was her reason for seeking this appointment with him. It was what everyone came to see him about. A loan. And now he could receive them in his office here on Jackson's Row, barely a furlong from his home on Brazenose Street, where clients were reassured by the evident prosperity of the mahogany furnishings, any accompanying qualms they might be experiencing at once assuaged by the lack of unnecessary ostentation or adornment. Here was a space without extraneous embellishment, where the matter was money, presented not in coinage but in the far more valuable commodities of contracts and bonds, the most prominent features in the room being the inkwell, the quill pen, the finest linen paper, all the essential items required to produce that holy grail of Reuben's business – the promissory signature.

"My husband," began Lady Ashton once more, "was, for all his faults, an honourable man. His word was his bond."

Reuben nodded politely in acknowledgement.

"It was this, I believe," she continued, "which must have contributed to his untimely, premature death."

Correct on all three counts, mused Reuben, though he did not say so out loud. The untimely and premature nature of Sir Ashton's death had created a shortfall for Reuben that was not insignificant. He had accepted this meeting with his widow on the assumption that it would be the first of these three points which would now be causing her a certain agitation, a feeling that somehow a way might be found to restore her husband's honour but not leave her destitute by so doing.

Reuben spread his hands once more, this time accompanied with a shrug. "Debts must be repaid, Your Ladyship."

"Quite," she replied, with an iciness whose audacity only served to impress Reuben even more. She would not give him an inch. Very well. Let her play her part. He could accept that, for he knew, when at last they came to it, she would agree to pay him what he was owed. Now it was his turn to play his.

"When your husband came to see me, Your Ladyship, it was about the business with Mr Oldknow."

Lady Ashton flared her nostrils and exhaled bitterly. "A foolish enterprise. I warned Sir Ashton from the outset, but did he listen? Of course not. Once he got the bit between his teeth he had to ride the nag to the end of the race, even if it fell at the first obstacle. And that Oldknow fellow, anyone could see he was not to be trusted. It's not as if he hadn't duped investors before. He had form. I told Sir Ashton time and time again."

"I cannot speak for Mr Oldknow, Your Ladyship, or his scheme…"

"Well *I* can…"

"Of course. But I *can* speak for your husband, who, when he came to see me, had lost a considerable sum of money on the venture. Eight and a half thousand pounds, to be exact."

A hiss of air escaped from between Lady Ashton's teeth, rather like a kettle coming to the boil.

"Although the investment was unwise, it was not illegal. Mr Oldknow had merely presented his scheme to an assembled company of gentlemen, requesting them to consider supporting him in the purchase of a number of new steam engines to power a cotton mill he was converting. The other gentlemen declined, your husband agreed. The fact that Mr Oldknow's scheme did not then succeed meant that your husband did not recoup any of his initial investment, nor any of the anticipated profits he had no doubt counted on collecting, and so he lost all of it."

A second hiss of air from Lady Ashton, even louder than the first, followed this exposition.

"A further difficulty for your husband was that he had been banking on using the returns he hoped to make through Mr Oldknow's scheme to pay off other debts he had accrued previously against other gentlemen both here and in London."

At this point the kettle that had been simmering within Lady Ashton now boiled over with emissions of expletives Reuben would not have expected such a fine-born lady to have known, let alone used. It only made his admiration for her grow even more. She was quite remarkable. An image of a prize mare haughtily rearing up on her hind legs if anyone was foolish enough to try and put their hand upon her black mane rose in his mind.

"And there was, I assume," she said after she had once more collected herself, "some collateral set against these loans and these losses?"

At last, thought Reuben. Now we have come to it.

"Perhaps Your Ladyship might care for a glass of water?" he said, rising from his chair.

"I think I might be better with something stronger, don't you?" She looked him directly in the eye when she spoke this. Once again she impressed him with her refusal to be coy, to pretend the situation was anything other than it was.

Reuben gave only the slightest of pauses as he made his way from behind his desk to a sideboard where a crystal decanter stood with two matching glasses by its side, from which he poured, into one glass only, a generous measure of the port wine it contained, which he quietly placed in front of her. She raised it to her lips, caught the fragrance of it, smiled infinitesimally, before draining the contents in a single draught. How Reuben wished he knew what that smile had meant. Was it confirmation of something she had suspected all along? That, when it came to the finer things in life, like a good wine for example, his taste was somehow lacking? Or was it – he hoped it was – that she recognised someone of rare cultural qualities which told her that there was more to this man than simply a usurer?

"I see no point in beating about the bush," he said. "The collateral your husband offered was…" Here he found himself involuntarily pausing, even though he had meant not to. "… Alkrington Hall."

The gasp which fell from Lady Ashton's lips then was so spontaneous, so unforced, that Reuben could tell that this was a complete – and unpleasant – shock to her, as unexpected as it was unwelcome.

"Then where am I to live?" she asked, her face suddenly devoid of all artifice.

Reuben took out a handkerchief from the drawer in his desk, which he always kept there for just such emergencies and proffered it to her, which she took without apology or embarrassment.

"I think," he said at last, "I think... there may be a solution."

Lady Ashton looked up sharply from the handkerchief that she had been holding to her mouth.

"Then enlighten me immediately," she urged, leaning forward in her seat and looking directly at Reuben, the expression on her face now one of absolute and unguarded openness.

Reuben took a deep breath and began.

"Everything your husband did was predicated on him being able to preserve his *Holophusicon* entire and complete."

Lady Ashton rolled her eyes and sat back in her chair.

"That damned collection of his has been the bane of my life," she said.

"And most likely the cause of his death," added Reuben. "I hope you will forgive me saying so but I think you know this already."

Lady Ashton rested her chin on one hand and nodded.

"At first I did not understand this, fully appreciate, I mean, the extent to which it was the ruling passion of his life..." He stopped abruptly, putting a hand to his chest. "I'm sorry," he added hastily. "That was clumsily put."

"Not at all," she said. "I knew very early on in our marriage that I came second in his affections to his 'curiosities', as he would so fondly refer to them. Please continue."

"At our one – and only – meeting, when he presented me with the full extent of his debts, which were – *are* – prodigious, I saw at once that he could clear these quite readily..."

Lady Ashton leant forward. "How?"

"If... if..." Reuben paused to take a sip of water.

"... he would be prepared to split up the collection," declared Lady Ashton, taking advantage of Reuben's hesitation.

"Exactly so," he replied, putting down the glass. "But..." He spread his hands out wide once more, a gesture with which Lady Ashton was becoming familiar.

"He wouldn't."

"No," echoed Reuben. "He wouldn't."

Lady Ashton stood up and walked towards a window to one side of the desk. The office was on the first floor of the building on Jackson's Row. She folded her arms across her chest and looked down to the street below. A child was crouching by a low wall playing with a spinning top. It was a simple wooden affair onto which the child had drawn a series of concentric circles with differently coloured chalks around it. Each time she tried to spin it, using her thumb and forefinger, she hoped it would pick up sufficient speed so that all the colours would merge into a single blur of white, before separating back into their separate hues when it finally came to rest, whereupon the child would pick it up and start the process all over again. Spin, watch. Spin, watch. No colours, all colours. No colours, all colours. The whole spectrum of possibility contained in a single object. A teeming metropolis, bursting with curiosities.

"Do you have children?" she asked, turning back into the room.

"Why, yes..." replied Reuben, somewhat surprised by the unusual turn the conversation was now taking. "Two sons," he added, sensing that more information was required.

"I do not," she said. "I didn't mind. Not at first. Later I did." She sat down at the desk again, flicking one of her olive green gloves idly with one hand against the other. "But my husband said quite emphatically that he didn't want them. They'd be a distraction, he'd say. At first I thought he was saying this to make me feel better, but then I realised that he meant it. Literally. His animals were his children and anything else would indeed have distracted him from them. At times I felt that *I* did too…" She trailed off and turned her face away so that Reuben could no longer see its expression, although he could imagine how clouded it had become. He took this pause as his cue to return to his proposal.

"Your husband, recognising that his *Holophusicon* was his prize asset, did indeed try to sell it after the collapse of the Oldknow affair, but only if it could be guaranteed to be kept intact, with his name attached to it."

"His name, yes. That I can understand."

"But there were simply no takers. It was simply too large."

"And too expensive no doubt?"

"He even tried to tempt *The Manchester Literary & Philosophical Society* to take it, at a knocked-down price, and use it to create a Museum for the town, but…"

"They turned him down."

"Actually they did not. But they asked for more time to explore in more detail just what the full implications would be – a building, or buildings, to house the items would need to be found in addition to the cost of the collection – and whether they could raise the necessary funds. This they could not do at the drop of a hat. They needed time."

"And time was something he did not have?"

Reuben shrugged. "His creditors were growing impatient."

"So that was when he suggested using Alkrington Hall as a guarantee against any further loan you might be able to arrange for him?"

Reuben nodded. "But I refused to accept it."

Lady Ashton raised her eyebrows in astonishment.

"And that was when he suffered his seizure."

A silence hung between them, Lady Ashton picturing the moment, Reuben remembering it. After what he felt was a respectful pause, he resumed.

"But now, Your Ladyship, if I am understanding the situation correctly, there is no longer an imperative to keep the collection intact?"

"None whatsoever."

"In which case I can state with a certain confidence that buyers can be found for all the items, which can be sold at auction in a mixture of single and multiple lots. I have contacts in London, where the collection is still housed on Leicester Square, who can act as your agents if you so desire it…"

"I do."

"Very well. If you would place your signature against these instructions, which I took the liberty of preparing for you in case we reached such an agreement this morning… here, here… and here…"

Lady Ashton signed where Reuben indicated. Her signature was bold, as he would have expected, culminating in a characteristic flourish.

"How long will this now take?" she asked.

"Not long," Reuben replied. "There is pressure from the proprietors to remove the *Holophusicon* as speedily as possible. I shall instruct Bonham's to proceed immediately."

"And…?" Lady Ashton faltered before continuing, as if what she was about to ask pained her, which Reuben anticipated at once, interrupting her to save any further embarrassment.

"I can assure you that the auction will raise sufficient funds to clear all of your husband's debts."

"Including that to you, I hope?"

Reuben spread his hands once more, saying nothing.

"And you will not omit to take a fee for your services in arranging matters so adroitly this morning, I trust?"

"Your Ladyship is most kind."

She rose from her chair and sighed deeply. "Thank you, Mr Halsinger. A great weight has been lifted from me. I have an annuity from my late father, which is more than ample to meet my needs, especially now that you have reassured me that I will not have to give up Alkrington after all. It would have been my children's, if I'd had any, but now I intend to use a wing of the Hall as a refuge for orphans and foundlings."

"A most generous act, Your Ladyship."

"I'd far rather see children running around the estate than wild animals roaming there."

"Although sometimes there can be little difference between the two."

He permitted himself a small smile, which was returned with great warmth by Her Ladyship.

"I cannot imagine for one minute that either of your two boys are to be found running wild, Mr Halsinger."

"Oh – they have their moments, but no, they are well behaved, most of the time."

"Tell me about them," she asked, picking up her olive green gloves and placing them back on her hands while she listened.

"Well... Benjamin, my eldest, he works as a teller at Heywood's Bank on King's Street."

"Inheriting his father's skills in finance?"

"I believe these new banks may well put an end to the likes of me and my profession," he chuckled. "But that is a good thing. Our chief hope when we came here was to assimilate, to be accepted, to be able to pass in the streets unnoticed and untroubled."

"There has been *some* trouble then since you arrived?"

Reuben shrugged. "A little. But less than we expected. People are by nature suspicious of things they do not understand, of difference. Things became hard for a time when the Government passed the Aliens Act, when the War with France began."

"Yes. I expect they did."

"One of our number was forced to leave us. Wolf Polack. A good man. He was deported."

"Why?"

"Some of the newspapers here urged their readers to inform on us."

"Mr Wheeler's *Manchester Chronicle*, I imagine?"

"We have no official status here. Wolf was a pawnbroker. A necessary trade but he had doubtless accumulated enemies who had harboured resentment. Mr Wheeler merely gave them the chance to express it."

"This town needs a newspaper that is more in keeping with the times."

Reuben shrugged. "Perhaps. But mostly Manchester has welcomed us."

" '*Be not forgetful to entertain strangers*'..." said Lady Ashton, surprising herself almost.

Reuben gave a puzzled frown.

"From our Bible. Paul's Epistle to the Hebrews."

Reuben's frown turned into a smile. "Perhaps I should read it."

"My father used to make me learn great chunks of it by heart. '*For thereby some have entertained angels unawares*'. I hated it at the time. I always wanted to be somewhere else."

"That is what fathers must do sometimes – encourage their children to wish they were elsewhere."

Lady Ashton finished putting on her second glove.

"Tell me about your second son. Does *he* wish he were somewhere else too?"

Reuben's face broke out into a wide smile. "Ah yes. Indeed he does. Abner. His head is in the clouds, that boy."

"Abner? That's an unusual name."

"It means 'filled with light'. It suits him in more ways than one. He was born shortly after we first arrived in England. He is much younger than his brother – exactly half his age – we had thought we could not have more children, then Abner was given to us. He's albino. His hair is white, his skin so paper thin you can almost see the light pass through it..." He paused a moment, collecting himself. "He's a dreamer. He'd spend all his time gazing at the stars if you'd let him. 'You should pay more attention to things down here on Earth, I tell him'. 'Yes, Father', he says, but the next minute, there he is again, looking up to the heavens. 'What do you see up there', I ask him, 'that you can't find down here?' He just smiles. 'What are you looking for?' 'I don't know,' he says. 'That's why I'm looking'…"

Lady Ashton smiled. "He sounds a most interesting boy."

"That's one word for him."

"But I can understand why you're concerned. My husband was a dreamer and it didn't do him much good in the end. What is he going to do, do you think?"

"That's just it. He has no idea. It's his *bar mitzvah* next month. That is when he officially becomes a man," he explained, observing Lady Ashton's querying expression.

"But he's still just a boy."

"That may be so, but he must earn his living somehow in the world."

"A man of science perhaps?"

"You are most kind, Your Ladyship, but I prefer him to have his feet on the ground."

"And I must be on my way back to Alkrington." She extended her gloved hand towards him which, after a moment's hesitation, he took in his own and bowed formally. "Thank you," she said, "for your practicality and reassurance."

"I shall write to you the moment I hear the collection has been sold and all the debts cleared. Good day, Your Ladyship."

"Good day, Mr Halsinger."

Reuben watched her elegantly descend the polished staircase which curved round into the entrance hall, where a porter was on hand to open the front door for her and escort her into the teeming hubbub of the streets of possibilities outside.

He never saw her again.

*

A fortnight later, however, on the afternoon following Abner's *aliyah*, which coincided with the *Rosh Chodesh* of *Cheshvan*, there was much laughter and celebration in the upper chambers of the synagogue on Garden Street, following the reciting of the *V'tein Tal u-Matar* – 'Deliver Dew and Rain' – while outside a typical Manchester downpour was drenching the Withy Grove.

The service had ended. People were standing round with plates of *knish*. The men were coming up to Abner and shaking his hand, while the women were playfully pinching his cheeks. All were indulgent and forgiving of how he had stumbled over his reading from the *Haftarah*, for he had come through what they all knew must have been quite an ordeal for him. "Good boy," cried Aaron Jacob, smiling. "My son Philip did not do half so well at his *bar mitzvah*, and now look at him. Today he concludes the arrangements for opening a new tailor's and dressmaker's shop. What are you going to do now you are a man?"

"Whatever it is, I wish he would tell me," joked Reuben.

"I will, Father, I promise. As soon as I know myself."

The other, older men roared their approval, each proceeding to ruffle Abner's white-gold hair in turn.

"He shall not cry, nor lift up, nor cause his voice to be heard in the street. A bruised reed shall he not break, and the smoking flax shall he not quench. He shall bring forth judgement unto truth, bring out the prisoners from the prison and open the eyes of the blind..."

The mood was joyful. All the guests had just sat down round the Sabbath Table and had begun to sing a version of the traditional *Adon Olam* when they were interrupted by an insistent knocking on the door to the street below. Benjamin was sent down to investigate. He returned a few moments later bearing in his arms a cylindrical package wrapped in cloth addressed to '*Mr Abner Halsinger*', then a simple inscription which read, '*on the occasion of him becoming a man*'. It was unsigned.

Benjamin handed it solemnly to Abner who, aware of everyone's gaze upon him, carefully folded back the cloth to reveal what lay inside. The look in his eyes, as he realised what it was, rendered his face even more translucent.

"Look," he whispered, holding it high above his head.

There was a collective sigh from the assembled company, followed by a burst of applause.

Abner carried it across to his father as if he were holding the key to the kingdom of heaven in his hands.

"A telescope," he said in a tone of hushed awe. "I wonder who could have sent it?"

Reuben placed his hand upon the side of his son's shining face and smiled.

*

Later that same evening, less than a half a mile to the north in Omega Place, Jem was surveying the final death throes of Fogg's Yard.

In the past ten years most of it had been swept away. The cellars had been drained and knocked through to make room for the dozens of new buildings which had filled up most of the space. A garment district had grown up there. Sweat shops where finished cotton from one of the scores of mills which now spread back from the Irk and the Irwell, criss-crossing Ancoats, even encroaching onto Angel Meadow, which was less salubrious than in former days. *The Pleasure Gardens* were still there but now catered for less sophisticated tastes. No Chinese lanterns hung from the trees, no classical music concerts were performed in tented pavilions. The fine mansions that had once lined the Meadow, lived in by the likes of Messrs Haworth, Tinker and Bradshaw, were now decaying lodging houses above tanneries and dyeing works, butchers and cobblers, taverns and brothels.

One by one the tenants of Fogg's Yard had left, or been forced out, as the maggot sprawl of Manchester spread, claiming each available square foot in its relentless march, gobbling up every last inch in its slavering maw, till all that was left was the narrow stone cottage where Jem still lived, along with Whelp whenever her wanderings took her there, and the unruly heap of scattered bricks not yet plundered. The cottage, now shorn of its neighbours, its outer walls pitted and exposed, poked up through the pile like a broken tooth, its jagged nerves vulnerable to every blast of weather and time.

Jem winced in the raw bite of an east wind. He pulled up the collar of his thin jacket and bit down on a lone potato he picked from the ashes of one of the small fires that always smouldered among the Hulks.

He'd lost his way. He still worked at Arkwright's Mill but had not made the hoped-for advancement he had anticipated when he first began there, passed over in favour of younger, more well-connected men, the new overseers, who strutted like peacocks along each of the factory floors.

Whelp still worked there too, but none of it seemed to touch her, the noise, the dust, the windowless sheds, the lascivious looks from some of the men. It all washed over her, like water off a gander's back, making its convoluted course through the matted locks of her hair. The children who worked there, the little piecers scurrying beneath the looms to tie off the broken snags of loose threads, all adored her, and, in their all too fleeting breaks for lunch, they would scamper all over her, waiting for whatever crumbs of bread and comfort she might throw their way. She always appeared to have plenty for all.

Sometimes she would return with him to Fogg's Yard, or climb into his bed beside him if she had been working a late shift to his early, and he would cling to her like a raft. He had no idea of how she felt about these snatched couplings, for she still barely spoke, but he supposed she did not mind them, for she would keep coming back, even if, sometimes, she would stay away for weeks.

He knew he should leave Omega Place, and Arkwright's Mill, strike out into something new, but what? Cotton was all he knew. And somehow he felt tethered to the Yard. For as long as the ruined heap of shattered bricks and masonry from the long ago explosion in the kiln that once had stood here remained, under which, far below, his father's bones lay broken, a smashed mosaic that could never be put back together again, he knew he would remain, for pieces of *him* lay buried there too. Since his mother had died, shortly after Mr Sadler's balloon flight, when all the air seemed literally to escape from her in a single sigh, he had felt this even more keenly. His brothers and sisters had likewise scattered to the four winds.

As he stood there, ruminating for the thousandth time what, if anything, he might do to salvage just something to which he could put his mark, he became aware of a shadow falling across him.

He turned around and saw a man, perched atop a pair of open step-ladders, from where he trained his eye through astrolabe, diopter and theodolite, before coming down to measure the distance from the pile of bricks to the Hanging Ditch below.

"Here," he said to Jem, handing him one end of the tape, "canst tha' hold this for me a moment please?"

Jem took it automatically.

"Thanks."

Jem watched the man proceed to measure and survey, making meticulous notes of every height, distance and angle. In the end his curiosity got the better of him.

"What's tha' doin'?" he asked.

"This patch of ground's been finally sold," said the man. "T' new owner wants it all cleared."

"Why's that then?"

" 'E wants to build a tailor's an' dressmaker's shop wi' a workshop at t' back."

Jem nodded. "But I live 'ere," he said and pointed to the broken tooth of the cottage teetering next to him.

"I reckon as 'ow that's seen better days," remarked the man not unkindly.

Jem shrugged. "Aye. But it's still 'ome."

The man frowned. "How long hast tha' stayed 'ere?"

Jem shook his head. "I'm not sure. Mebbe twenty years. Mebbe more. Since I were a lad any road."

"Doest tha' pay owt for t' rent?"

"Not since t' factory fell down."

The man approached Jem and held out his hand. "I'm Zachary, by the way. Zachary Robinson. I'm a surveyor."

"Jeremiah Stone," said Jem, shaking him by the hand, "but folk just call me Jem."

"I work for Mr Edward Byrom, Architect," said Zachary, "an' 'e's been commissioned to design t' tailor's an' t' workshop I spoke of afore for a Mr Philip Jacob of Shude Hill."

Jem nodded to indicate that he understood.

"The thing is," continued Zachary, "Mr Jacob reckons 'e's bought up th' whole plot, includin' that cottage o' thine. We're due to start clearin' t' site next week. But wi' what tha's just told me, tha's thrown a dirty great spanner into t'works."

"I don't understand."

"Ever 'eard of 'Adverse Possession'?"

Jem shook his head.

"Squatter's Rights to thee and me, Jem. If a person's been livin' in t' same place continuously, wi'out a break, for twelve years, and the owner's not asked 'im to leave in that time, then that person can claim 'adverse possession', and there's nobbut a soul can turn 'im out."

"I see."

"And has anyone asked thee to leave, or try to collect rent from thee in that time?"

"No."

"And canst tha' prove tha's been livin' 'ere for twelve years?"

"Ask anyone."

In which case," said a different voice, "it would appear you have a cast iron claim to remain."

"Ah," said Zachary, hastily approaching the newcomer, "Mr Jacob, tha's 'eard what we've been saying?"

"Indeed I have, Zachary. Under Common Law, Mr – er…?"

"Stone, sir."

"Mr Stone… the previous owner's right to eject you has lapsed, and so, under the *Limitation Act of 1623*, if my lawyer's advice is to be trusted, which I have no reason to regard otherwise, this… property is yours."

"Thank you, sir."

"Instruct Mr Byrom, Zachary, that he will need to come up with a new set of plans to incorporate Mr Stone's cottage into the overall design for my new commercial property."

"Yes, sir. But…"

"I have no desire to turn a man from his home, Zachary."

"I accept that, sir, but there will be a loss of overall square footage available for your use."

"Understood. I am well used to making compromises. I've done so before, and doubtless shall do so again."

"It's just possible," said Zachary, evidently thinking on the spot, "that we might be able to build right up to, and over t' top of, Mr Stone's cottage, which may still allow us to accommodate all o' tha' needs, sir."

"Whatever. I leave the details to you and Byrom."

"In that case, sir, we can still begin clearing away all t' rest o' t' site tomorrow mornin' as planned."

"Excellent. Some of these abandoned bricks might perhaps be reusable? It would save a little on costs, I am thinking."

"Perhaps, sir, though most of 'em look pretty weather-worn."

"As you think best. Now, if would guide me back to the Hanging Ditch, it has grown so dark here I fear I may miss my footing..."

"Excuse me, Mr Jacob," said Jem, nervously coughing.

"Yes?"

"Dost tha' mean to shift *all* these bricks?"

Mr Jacob looked in turn towards Zachary.

"Aye," said the latter. "We need to level the ground."

"Only, me feyther..." faltered Jem. "'E... 'e's buried somewhere underneath 'em. After th' accident... when t' brick factory exploded... a great sink 'ole opened up... causin' bits o' t' buildin'... an' people... to be sucked in... They've never been recovered..."

A silence fell between the three men. Zachary lowered his head out of respect. Jem looked helplessly towards Mr Jacob who, after he had allowed a sufficient amount of time to elapse, approached him.

"I am most distressed to hear this, Mr Stone. I understand the importance of a proper burying ground. That is why the procurement of land for such a purpose was one of the first things our people did when we first arrived here in Manchester, so that we could lay our loved ones to rest with all due ceremony. That has been denied to you, and for that I am truly sorry." He sighed heavily. "But... I imagine, after all of this time, when the workmen arrive to clear the ground, there is little likelihood of them finding anything that will be in any way..." He paused before continuing as delicately as he could. "... recognisable. Remember your father as he was, Mr Stone, that's my advice, and take comfort from the thought that his bones will add nutrients to the earth, to make new things grow because of him. Good night, gentlemen."

Jem stood alone as the darkness fell across this last remaining corner of Fogg's Yard, while Zachary escorted Mr Jacob back towards the Hanging Ditch, where a few oil lamps protruded from iron sconces, which would light the rest of his way back to his house on Shude Hill. Jem felt as though the stone he had been rolling up that steep hill for the past twenty years, which, every time he neared the top, would roll all the way back down to the bottom, so that he would have to begin the whole Sysyphean task again, was finally coming to a point of balance. One last push might see it teeter over the brow at last, from where it could roll down the other side unaided until it was finally out of sight for ever. Who knew what collateral damage its untrammelled progress would create? Or he would not push it, and it would roll back down again, this time crushing him beneath its weight.

He must do something, he decided, and tonight. It would be a great work, one which might make his father and grandfather proud of him at last. He looked at the pile of bricks patiently waiting for him to begin, bathed in a pale starfall, and took a step towards them.

10

31ˢᵗ October

The Festival of the Reformation. The Solemnity of All Saints. Hallowmas.

The day had many names. At Fairfield they preferred the simpler All Hallows. Although distinct from the Lutherans, for whom this was a highly significant day, commemorating as it did the posting by their founder of the *Ninety-Five Theses* on the door of the Church of All Saints in Wittenberg exactly two hundred and eighty-one years before, itemising specific complaints of corruption, most particularly the sale of indulgences, against the Roman Catholic hierarchy, the Moravians honoured the day with a keen devotion. Partly because they recognised kinship with their fellow Non-Conformists, partly because they too had received shelter and kindness from the Elector of Saxony in their earliest days, but mostly because the words of Martin Luther's hymn *A Mighty Fortress Is Our God*, a paraphrase of Psalm 46, chimed so resonantly with their own vision.

Here at Fairfield they had built their own fortress, which steadfastly protected them from the storms and buffets of the outside world, and so each year they gave a special service of thanksgiving and praise on this particular day, whether it fell on a Sunday or not. This year it fell on a Wednesday.

The Chapel was full to capacity for the evening service. Brother Swertner led the faithful in prayer, exhorting everyone there present to lift up their hearts and voices in a rendition of the Psalm, as they prepared for a night of vigil and fasting ahead of the Lovefeast to be held the following day, All Hallows itself, when they would silently remember all those saints who did not have a special feast day of their own, the countless martyrs and scapegoats who daily carried out a thousand selfless tasks of sacrifice and denial for the good of others, expecting nothing in return.

"Let us light a candle," said Brother Swertner. "For as the Bard so wisely tells us, '*How far this little candle throws its beams. So shines a good deed in a weary world*'."

Brother John Lees strode towards the communion rail in the northern segment of the hall, every joint and bone in his body creaking and unlocking as he did so, set a candle on the table there and lit it, looking first towards Caroline, next to Agnes, seated along the eastern wall with the rest of the Single Sisters, finally towards Amos, who sat opposite along the western wall among the other Single Brethren. They each returned his gaze, breathing deeply as they did so.

"Now," continued Brother Swertner, "by the light of this little candle, let us sing the Psalm, bending the flame, so that its smoke carries the words up towards our Heavenly Father."

Brother Gottfried struck the first chord on the organ and the congregation began as one to sing the verses they all knew by heart.

"God is our refuge and strength, a very present help in trouble
Therefore will not we fear, though the earth be removed, and though the mountains be carried into the midst of the sea
Though the waters thereof roar and be troubled, though the mountains shake with the swelling thereof
Selah

There is a river, the streams whereof shall make glad the city of God, the holy place of the tabernacles of the most High
God is in the midst of her, she shall not be moved: God shall help her, and that right early
The heathen raged, the kingdoms were moved: He uttered his voice, the earth melted

The Lord of hosts is with us, the God of Jacob is our refuge Selah.

Come, behold the works of the Lord, what desolations He hath made in the earth
He maketh wars to cease unto the end of the earth, He breaketh the bow, and cutteth the spear in sunder, He burneth the chariot in the fire
Be still, and know that I am God: I will be exalted among the heathen, I will be exalted in the earth
The Lord of hosts is with us. the God of Jacob is our refuge. Selah..."

As the final notes of the Psalm faded away, their echo remained, an antiphonal *diminuendo* that hung in the air around them. The congregation sat. The tension in the silence that followed was so thick, so palpable, that it seemed like an additional presence in the space, of which everyone was aware. Agnes and Amos stared towards each other across the wide distance of the opposite sides of the Chapel that separated them, he with the Single Brethren, she with the Single Sisters, locked onto each other's eyes as if through the telescopic sights of a surveyor's transit. The rest of the congregation were all too aware of the strength of their attraction, seeing it as the true benchmark for a level of adoration they each separately hoped they might one day attain for themselves, but doubted they ever would.

Brother Swertner, aware of the importance of the moment, addressed them all directly.

"This evening we come not only to celebrate All Hallows Eve, but to put to the Lot the question of whether Brother Amos and Sister Agnes may be joined as one in holy matrimony. The Elders will convene directly our service has ended and the decision relayed at once to those concerned. But such is the interest sparked by this proposed match it has been agreed that all who wish may remain here afterwards to receive news of what the Lot has deemed is right and just before God."

A frisson of anticipation rippled around the Chapel, which Brother Swertner was impelled to quell with a stern word and a look, calling for a minute of silent prayer, during which "each of us may look into our hearts for the wisdom and humility to accept with grace whatever the Lord decides."

The Casting of the Lot held great spiritual significance for all Moravians everywhere, and Fairfield was no exception. The practice had its roots in the Bible, where it was first mentioned in the Acts of the Apostles, shortly after Judas was killed and his replacement sought. It was felt that no human hand should be involved in the choice.

'And they gave forth their Lots; and the Lot fell upon Matthias, and thus was he numbered with the eleven apostles.'

In Fairfield the Lot was used sparingly, for guidance or judgement when faced with a critical decision, such as whether to accept a new member to join them, or with regard to the choosing of a spouse. Such decisions were too important, it was felt, to be left simply to chance or, worse, to a person's own fancy, for human beings were fallible by nature. Only God, the Infallible One, could be trusted to make these decisions, and this was done by the Casting of Lots. If, for example, a new person arrived within their midst, requesting to be received into the Congregation of the Settlement, three pieces of paper would be placed into a wooden box. On one was written 'Aye', on the second was written 'Nay', while the third would be left blank, signifying, 'It is not now the time for such a judgement; let the matter be submitted again at a later date.' Once the question had been put and the pieces of paper folded and placed unseen within the box, the Elders would retire to pray.

The matter for this All Hallows Vigil was whether permission might be granted for Amos and Agnes to be wed.

Although members of the Single Sisters, under the strict supervision of an Elderess, were, if not actually forbidden, at least discouraged from indulging in private discourse with any of the Single Brethren, everyone in the Settlement knew that Amos and Agnes had eyes only for each other. It was a match approved of by John and Caroline and looked on with great fondness by all who dwelt among them. The ratification by the Lot, if so it came, would serve to bestow God's blessings upon the star-struck pair, who had both turned twenty-one earlier in the year, now master and mistress of their desires, if not their destinies.

Who could say with certainty where the spark of love was kindled? Or when? From the moment that Agnes first pulled Amos from the foaming waters of the Irk, she looked down with unbridled affection upon him, her new-found brother, someone to replace James in her heart and release her from the terrible burden of guilt which had weighed so heavily upon her since she had lost him to the salmon-leaping weir at Elton Brook. The first thing that Amos saw when he opened his eyes after being hauled from the river he had tumbled into was the sweet smiling face of Agnes. So serene did it appear, haloed against the sun, that he was certain he had drowned and gone to heaven, and that here was an angel bending over him. Only later, coming up for air, expelling the water and weeds from his mouth, did he truly surface, and the force of the reality, that this vision was no angel but a living, breathing child his own age cradling his head in her lap, was so much stronger than the dream. He had a sister, and her name was Agnes.

Amos and Agnes. He who had been carried and borne aloft by the lamb.

But when did the love of sister for brother first transubstantiate into something more, something altogether different...?

Was it when I saw them sitting on the wall beside the Burying Ground, wonders Caroline, shortly after our arrival here, playing cat's cradle? The gentle, tremulous care they each of them took when passing the string from one pair of hands to the other? The way the light from the torches danced in their eyes? Like a kaleidoscope...?

The kaleidoscope, thinks, John, looking at each of them now. Was it then? Amos must have been – what? Eleven? Twelve? It was difficult to be certain for Amos himself did not exactly know how old he was, or when it was his birthday, and so they had decided to celebrate it each year on the anniversary of when he had first entered their lives, when Agnes had rescued him out of the Irk, on the day of the balloon flight on Angel Meadow. As it had soared into the cloudless skies above them while they made their way to Fairfield that long, hot afternoon, John had strained his neck, trying to follow it for as long as he could, the reds and blues and yellows and greens of its cotton envelope shimmering like shards of coloured glass upon the mirrored surface of the Medlock, beside whose banks they determinedly travelled. It was that which had given him the idea, the remembrance of it, when the boy's birthday next came around.

He took Amos with him, down from the attic in Brother Mallalieu's three-storey building where he had been helping to card the raw cotton, to the ground floor of the adjoining building, where the horses drew the mighty water wheel, round and round, to power the looms above. He pointed to the small window at one end of the shed and showed Amos how to watch the light as it flickered each time one of the wheel's paddles passed it by. His eyes widened with wonder and delight at the way this light would refract into a myriad of colours, changing moment by moment the patterns they made upon the horse's back.

"Would you like to make something that could do the same?" John had asked him.

Amos, who rarely spoke, except to Agnes, when the two of them would incline their heads together as thick as thieves, nodded.

"Come with me then," said John, taking a deep pleasure from the way the boy placed his small hand inside his own cracked fist.

Perhaps he was a thief too, he wondered, stealing these precious moments from the boy's growing up, to hoard away and save for when he would leave them, which he did two years later, when he entered the Single Brethren's House at fourteen, as was the custom in the Settlement, with Agnes taking her place with the Single Sisters just a few short weeks afterwards. They still saw both of them daily, he and Caroline, but in passing only, in between work and meal times, at prayer meetings, choir practice, and in Chapel, for Sunday Worship, or midweek services, like tonight, the Feast of All Hallows Eve, while they awaited the decision of The Lot.

And so he takes out one of these hoarded memories now, picks it up and polishes it, holds it up to the light, turns it slowly round, to savour every moment of it.

The kaleidoscope.

John and Amos had made it together. John found an old glass bottle. With the aid of a sharp knife he made a small scratch no more than one eighth of an inch in length just below the mouth of the bottle, enabling him to make a clean cut by placing his thumbs on either side of the scratch and pushing away from him. Then he smoothed the sharp edges with sandpaper. While he was doing this he instructed Amos to collect as many small fragments of coloured glass he could find anywhere in the Settlement and bring them back to him in half an hour. He returned with a cupped handful, holding them as carefully as if they were a bantam's egg. John took these from him and placed them in a jar for safe keeping. Then he explained to Amos that he needed him to cut a piece of stiffened felt to a length slightly less than that of the now cut and smoothed glass bottle. Once he had done this, John asked him to score two lines equidistantly along the felt, dividing it into three, then fold these over to form a long triangle, which he must glue firmly together. When the glue was dried and the triangle was securely fixed, he slowly slid it inside the glass tube. John asked Amos to cut two circles slightly larger than the mouth of the glass tube with a pair of scissors from a piece of wax paper, then colour one of these black with a short stick of charcoal, while he went in search of a small off-cut of muslin from Brother Mallalieu's attic. With the point of one of the scissor blades Amos then created a pinprick hole in the centre of the now black wax paper, which he fitted to the end of the tube, fastening where it overlapped the rim tightly with a thread of cotton. John returned with the piece of muslin, which he draped loosely across the other side of the glass. Into this he made a small impression with his finger of approximately one and a half inches, and the bowl this formed Amos filled with all of the pieces of coloured glass he had found earlier and which he now took from the jar. The second, uncoloured circle of translucent wax paper was then placed over the shiny shards and securely attached in the same way as the first. Satisfied that the cylinder was now secure, John handed it back ceremonially to Amos.

"Happy birthday," he said.

Amos held it with great reverence. "What is it?" he whispered.

"Hold it up to the light," said John. "Put your eye to the pinprick hole in the black wax paper and tell me what you see."

Amos duly did as he was shown. "Patterns," he gasped, "like when the horse pulls the wheel past the window."

"A kaleidoscope," said John, finding himself drawn within the penumbra of the boy's pleasure. "Turn it very slowly in your hands as you look."

As Amos lost himself in the ever-changing rainbow of colours inside that magic tube, John was no less entranced by the shifting patterns of unalloyed joy passing across the boy's face like feathery clouds on a summer's day.

"Thank you, Brother John," said Amos, spontaneously hugging his adoptive father. "I must show Agnes at once."

John watched Amos run across the cobbled square towards the house he had built for them calling out his daughter's name. She came out at once from whatever chore she might have been helping her mother with, and the two of them sat side by side on the front step, where they took it in turns to share each other's sheer delight in the miracle of pattern and colour, light and glass, they held in their hands and passed between them.

Cradle to Diamonds.

Then, when the time came for them to leave their home and enter the separate houses of Single Brethren and Single Sisters, they took the kaleidoscope with them, taking it in turns to have it by their bed at night, exchanging it with each successive waning Christus, waxing Deus moon...

Now, in the Chapel Hall, as the choir sings from Psalm 46 while they await the outcome of the Elders' deliberation and the Casting of the Lot which will decide the future of Amos and Agnes, John stares intently towards the flame of the candle he earlier carried to place upon the table behind the Communion rail, seeing the different shapes it makes, bending to the movement of the air, and listens again to the words which mould its ever-changing shape.

Cradle to Diamonds.

Diamonds to Candle.

> *"God is our refuge and strength, a very present help in trouble.*
> *Therefore will not we fear, though the earth be removed, and though the mountains be carried into the midst of the sea;*

*Though the waters thereof roar and be troubled, though the mountains shake with the swelling thereof.
Selah..."*

Everyone in the Settlement loved Amos and Agnes. Whenever anyone passed either of them, at work, at prayer, in factory, in field, they always came away feeling lighter of step and heart. Each of them emanated such a brightness of hope that people believed that somehow tomorrow would be better than today because of them.

They were rarely seen together of course. It was not considered proper for Single Brethren and Single Sisters to convene in unchaperoned, intimate discourse. Consequently it was not possible for them ever to be alone, just the two of them, though no doubt they would occasionally find ways, a glance here, a secret note pressed into the palm of a hand there, for that is what lovers have always done.

In Chapel, where Amos would sit along the western wall and Agnes along the east, his head bowed low in modest supplication, her face hidden from view by the Single Sister's bonnet, they somehow managed to radiate their feelings towards one another in a way that was understood and perceived by all, even though no words were spoken or looks exchanged.

At work, where Amos toiled alongside John in the brick kilns and Agnes kneaded flour in the kitchen, neither would see the other throughout all the hours of daylight, yet both would feel connected, each of them engaged in baking, their faces suffused with the heat of ovens, he with clay, she with bread, both their faces enflamed by it.

On Sundays, after the singing of hymns and the offering up of prayers, after the Lovefeast and the Covenant, children, released from the strictures of having to sit still on hard wooden benches, would run to the Burying Ground, pick buttercups, which they would hold under each other's chins to see if they cast a golden shadow there from the sun. "Do I like butter?" they would impatiently clamour to discover. "Mebbe," would come the reply, "but I reckon I know who does."

"Agnes and Amos," they'd all shriek back, and then they would gather daisies from the grass and pretend that *they* were Agnes and Amos as they plucked petals from each flower. "She loves me, she loves me not. She loves me, she loves me not. She loves me…"

The answer always came out, "Aye".

The Lot.

Three pieces of folded paper waiting to be drawn from the box.

Aye. Nay. Blank.

Which will it be?

Another turn of the kaleidoscope.

Caroline redirected her gaze from the candle towards her daughter, hoping to catch her eye, give her an encouraging smile, but there was no reaching her. Her eyes were open but turned inward. Doubtless she was praying, as they all were. There was never a single hour that passed when somebody somewhere in the Settlement was not at prayer. It was something Brother Worthington, their first minister when they all arrived here, had instituted in their first year, and it had been carried on by his successors, first Brother Zander, now Brother Swertner, who continued to labour daily over his painting of the Great Vine. A profound ecstasy would take him when he led the faithful in prayer. The worshippers felt that Christ owned them then, inspiring in them fervent songs of rapture and thanksgiving.

But not this night. This night they fell into silent contemplation. Caroline sensed, looking at Agnes's frozen expression, just how high the stakes were. If the Lot said "Aye", then all would be well. If it returned a blank, then all would not be lost. It would simply be counsel for delay, a prolonged period of waiting during which Agnes and Amos might reflect more deeply on the seriousness of the step they were so eager to take. But if it said "Nay", what then? Such was the certainty of their love for one another, she doubted whether they could be bound by such a refusal. There would be no alternative open to them but to leave the Settlement.

Caroline shuddered at the thought. There had not been a day since she was born that Agnes had not spent some part of it by her side. Even after she went, willingly and of her own volition, to live within the house of the Single Sisters, their paths would cross at some point each day – at breakfast, or supper, at choir practice or at prayer, in the laundry or bakehouse. Since they first arrived, more than thirteen years ago, they had not left Fairfield once.

Not that they were forbidden to do so, it was simply that there was no need. Everything they could wish for was here, their every want, physical or spiritual, was provided for them. And there were frequently problems with those from outside who attempted to break in and trespass on their sequestered serenity within the confines and boundaries of Fairfield.

"The labourers of each congregation are most earnestly entreated," urged Brother Worthington, "to prevent apprentices being sent by their parents or masters to neighbouring towns or villages, or any other place where they might suffer harm."

Another twist of the kaleidoscope.

"We are sorry to see such a great defect in our married people touching the care of their children." Brother Zander this time. "Instead of preserving them from the world, they show an inclination to lead them into it. I must speak to them on this subject, and we must pray together for guidance."

Work was the answer, work and prayer. Order and discipline. Chastity and obedience. Beside weaving at the large looms of Brother Mallalieu, or carding for Brother Radley in the attic above the large three-storey building in the centre of the square, or spinning for Brother Henry Nalty in a room at the back of the Single Brethren's house, or assisting Brother Peter Halley who manufactured nankeen, or being set to one of the two hundred spindles belonging to Brother Ignatius Hindley or Brother Joshua Warren, there was saddlery, farming, a bread round, brickmaking and a dozen other skilled crafts to keep them busy. Agnes excelled at lace work. Some of her tambours and samplers were purchased for the christening of Princess Adelaide in Germany.

But always there was the threat from outside.

A watchman was employed to guard the Settlement against thieves and robbers, packs of wild dogs. "We resolve to have no bitches in this place," proclaimed the Elders, "and those that are must be banished from our midst."

Unwelcome visitors were dealt with equally peremptorily. Seven Brethren, John among them, were appointed by the Elders to "keep careful watch of our place", especially on Sundays and during meetings. "We believe it would not be advisable to assemble in our usual way at the Burying Ground, lest a mob might gather and disturb us." They resolved instead to meet at six, or "just before light", inside the Chapel Hall.

Against such daily threats a round-the-clock regime of work and prayer and sleep was established and never broken.

"Idle hands are the Devil's workshop," Brother Swertner would warn. "Our hard labour makes all sweet when on toil we enter."

How, worried Caroline, would Agnes and Amos survive if cast out into the world if the Lot so decreed. She closed her eyes and prayed even harder for an outcome in the affirmative.

The kaleidoscope resides with Agnes this month. She never tires of holding it up to whatever source of light is at hand to watch the coloured glass shimmer and dance before settling into yet another abstract pattern, a pattern that is as changeable as that of her daily life is invariable. She relishes the certainty of knowing what she will be doing each minute of each hour of each day, unchanging, *'while the earth remaineth, seedtime and harvest, cold and heat, summer and winter, day and night shall not cease.'*

Yet within that unceasing round there is joy in sensing those minute shifts and gradations which render every moment fresh and new. The cast of light when the dawn comes and wakes her each morning is different every day, unique, and it is as if she experiences each task or duty she must carry out like it is the very first time. Washing the feet of her fellow worshippers in the Single Sisters' House with her hair, she traces each separate droplet of water as it arcs in slow motion through the air from each strand, caught in the early morning sun. They startle her just like the kaleidoscope, each time she turns it in her hands.

She stares deep into the candle lit by her father and placed upon the communion table and allows her mind to drift, each twist a different memory. This is her home and she has no desire to leave it behind…

Intoning the daily watchword in a rhythm with every step…

The purity of tone in the nightly *Singstunde*, the singing meetings, each note hovering in the air till the last drop of the Cup of Covenant has been drained…

Listening to the handwritten leaves of *Hernhut* being read to her out loud, hanging on every word of how their brothers and sisters fare in the farthest corners of the world…

The first Sunday in May. The Single Sisters' Festival. Beginning before sun up with musicians ascending into the cupola to play as loudly and as sweetly as they can in song and celebration. *'So the singers, Heman, Asaph, and Ethan, were appointed to sound with cymbals of brass; and Zechariah, and*

Aziel, and Shemiramoth, and Jehiel, and Unni, and Eliab, and Maaseiah, and Benaiah, with psalteries on Alamoth; and Mattithiah, and Elipheleh, and Mikneiah, and Obededom, and Jeiel, and Azaziah, with harps on the Sheminith to excel...'

Attending the Girls' School, the first, she is told, anywhere in England to provide lessons for girls who are not well born, but she hates that term, for are we not all well born in the eyes of the Lord? Did not Jesus say, *'Suffer the little children to come unto Him and forbid them not'*? "We learn reading and writing from Sister Mary Tyrell," she excitedly tells her mother, "who is always kind, she gives us chalks to make our marks upon the slates. We must learn our Catechisms by heart…"

A fire breaking out in the Single Brethren's House at four in the morning, in the first month Amos was there, the whole of the Settlement awakened by the sound of the bell, the timely arrival of the engine which, being so well conducted and well supplied with water, that within two hours, the fire was quite got under. A soaked and exhilarated Amos running towards her, holding out the kaleidoscope in front of him, having saved it from the flames…

Amos…

His eyes, the line of his mouth, which curves upwards always into a smile…

Even when Single Sister Sarah Mellor, sitting down upon a chair, gets a needle caught in the upper part of her thigh, the Elders deeming it so dangerous that they call at once for a surgeon to remove it without recourse to the Lot…

The Lot…

Married Woman Hannah Kenyon, lying on her deathbed, requesting to be received into the Congregation, her being such a good and kind woman that everyone present is convinced of her sincerity, yet the Lot says, 'Nay…'

Sitting on the wall beside the Burying Ground with Amos playing Cat's Cradle. In the midst of life we are in death. I will wear no mourning clothes. If I die today, I live tomorrow. Candle to Six-Pointed Star...

Amos holds in his hand the iron ring he has fashioned at the forge in Brother Joshua Warren's workshop earlier that day. He twists and rotates it between his fingers, round and round, back and forth. He keeps his eyes fixed firmly on the floor. He will not look up until the Elders return. The wait for the Lot to let its will be known seems endless. Why don't they come? Surely the answer must be 'Aye'. Then he will give a prayer of silent thanks as the Congregation applauds. He will look across to where she is sitting, hoping she may turn her head sufficiently so that he might make out just what little of her face will be visible from beyond the outline of her Single Sister's bonnet. He will seek her out immediately, as soon as they step outside the Chapel, so that they might be alone together, however fleetingly, before they must make their separate ways to their respective Single Houses. He will bid her close her eyes, then quietly slip the ring onto her finger. He has not had to measure it. He knows it will fit her perfectly.

The door at the back of the Chapel opens. The Elders walk through it in single file into the centre of the Hall, towards the communion rail. The Choir stops singing. The organ ceases to play. The Elders hand the piece of paper to Brother Swertner, who opens it, reads what is written there, folds it once more, then stands. His face shows no outward sign of any emotion.

"The Lot has answered," he says solemnly. He unfolds the paper and holds it out for all to read. "It has decided, 'Nay'."

There is an audible gasp from the Congregation. Caroline shouts out, "No, it cannot be," before she can prevent herself. Amos and Agnes each feel their skin grow pale and their blood turn to ice.

"The Lord has chosen to speak to us through his instrument," continues Brother Swertner through the whispering. "We know this to be true because Scripture tells us. Ours is not to reason why but to obey. '*My tongue shall speak thy words, for all thy commandments are righteousness*'."

But his words are barely heard. The low murmur of disappointment rises to a rumble of disbelief, spilling out of the Chapel into the square outside, as people leave, incredulous and distressed.

"It makes no sense," comments Brother Mallalieu, shaking his head.

"If ever two young folk were meant for one another, it's Amos and Agnes," says Married Woman Hindley.

"Whatever must they be thinking?" asks Sister Sarah Mellor, rubbing her thigh where the needle had once been stuck, a gesture she does habitually these days, as if trying to exorcise the ghost of a painful memory. "They've done everything by the Book."

"Ay, that's true," agrees Brother Warren, "and now they'll have to abide by its ruling. They're only young yet, they'll get over it, tha'll see."

"Now Joshua," says Married Woman Hindley fiercely, "how can tha' be so heartless?"

"I'm not," he says, "but there's nowt to be gained by cryin' over what can't be helped. What's done's done. The Lot's been cast."

"Where *are* they?" asks Sister Sarah, trying to see if she might see them as they all walk across the square back to their various homes. The gas lamps, which have only recently been installed, throw eerie shadows across the cobbled ground.

"John and Caroline are speakin' to 'em, over by t' Single Sisters' House," calls out Brother Mallalieu, as he turns towards his own front door. "They'll be all reet."

"Though I for one think the Lot got it right," says his wife when she's sure they're out of ear shot. Joseph raises an eyebrow. "Well," she continues, "though they be not blood relatives, they've been raised as brother and sister. T'in't natural," she adds, closing the door behind them.

"Gi' o'er wi' tha' nonsense," says Joseph as soon as they step indoors. "They've lived quite separate in t' Single Brethren an' Single Sisters' Houses these past seven years."

Outside in the square Caroline and John tried to comfort Agnes and Amos, who stood rigid with disbelief. Neither of them cried, neither of them railed against the perceived injustice of it all, they simply stood, looking hard and unflinching at one another, communicating in that practised, wordless way they had, shutting out the noise and distraction, ignoring their parents' well-meant but impotent words of comfort and futile gestures of love. Instead they seethed with a cold, silent fury. The Settlement, which, until this night, had been their entire world, and to which, until the decision of the Lot was announced, they had dedicated their whole lives, had betrayed them.

The Watchman passed them without a word out of respect for their situation as he made his final rounds for the night. The lamps in the square were extinguished.

Amos and Agnes allowed themselves to be separated and led, seemingly acquiescent and compliant, back to their respective Houses, both looking over their shoulders all the way, their eyes like flints of coloured glass in the blackness, till they were each lost from the other's sight.

Afterwards John and Caroline stared at one another exhausted and disconsolate. They slowly walked back to their too large, empty house, which echoed with the sounds of happy children from lost years running from room to room, mocking them.

The next morning, when the Settlement assembled for prayer, Agnes and Amos were nowhere to be found. Their beds had not been slept in. On each of their pillows lay the same identical message, chalked on a slate, followed by the drawing of a six-pointed star.

"The thief cometh not, but for to steal, and to kill, and to destroy: I am come that they might have life, and that they might have it more abundantly."

✡

*

At the precise moment when Amos and Agnes fled from Fairfield, a great meteor shower appeared in the northern sky, the Andromedids, whose radiant lay in the constellation of Cassiopeia, named for the Ethiope queen in Greek mythology, who was claimed to possess unparalleled beauty, a statement with which Abner Halsinger would have challenged the world to dare to dispute, as he explored her in all her glory through the achromatic lenses of his Dollond & Aitcheson telescope, through which he watched from the roof of his father's house on Brazenose Street, transfixed by her ceaseless streams of cosmic debris, which converged onto a single celestial point deep within her heart, from where the meteors appeared to emanate, these Daughters of Cassiopeia, Andromedas chained to a rock in a vast and pitiless universe to assuage the wrath of a vengeful, unseen god.

At the same instant, Jem takes up his great work in the last unclaimed corner of Omega Place. He delves within the abandoned pile of unfired clay bricks, which had remained in their mountainous heap since the explosion which had killed his father, shortly after the great Earthquake more than twenty years before. He had noticed the way Whelp had picked out those which she had placed together to form a kind of a bed when he first brought her to Fogg's Yard, how they had moulded themselves to the contours of her scrawny body, the way she had allowed gravity to let the bricks fall about her as she lay upon them, until they became the shape of her, where they had rested, precariously, on the irregularly balanced jumble of other bricks and joists beneath her.

She no longer sleeps outdoors. Since his mother had died, after withdrawing so completely into herself that she all but disappeared, Whelp has shared Jem's bed inside with him. He studies the geometry of absence she left behind on the bricks, not so very different from the indentation on the sheets where her body has lain through the night, from which he tries to conjure her presence after she has risen from it. The hollow in the pillow where her head has been. The empty spaces around his own body, carved from where she has tucked and folded herself into him. The elbow's crook, the shoulder's crevice. The stomach's pit, the hand's span. How reluctantly he releases himself from each position lest, in so doing, he somehow disturbs the place where she has been, erasing her almost, like smoke coiling up a chimney, or motes of cotton fibres drifting in the engine shed of Arkwright's Mill after all the workers have left, a memory, an imprint, a ghost.

Like his father, whose absence still haunts him, whose deep sense of failure he feels he has inherited, whose bones, he knows, lie buried beneath the mountain of bricks, touched once by Whelp, years before, sliding down and through, then returning with his ring without having dislocated its anatomical edifice, of which his father is a part, now unextractable. He must raise him somehow. Like Lazarus. Pay him the homage he is due. Before it's too late. Before the last of Fogg's Yard is razed to the ground, which he knows will be only a matter of time.

There's only Whelp and him left now. And tonight only him, for Whelp is away somewhere, combing the unlit streets of the town for her waifs and strays, rats who she will lead to the soup kitchens on Cross Street, like the Pied Piper. Pity, the people call her. Pity. For she has so much of it and bestows it wherever she perceives it's needed. Which is everywhere. Pity. He decides it is what he will call her from now on too. She has long outgrown Whelp, the name given to her by others, which has stuck, but which now she must cast off, a sloughed snakeskin.

Just as he must also.

For too long he has toiled in his father's shadow. For too long he has danced to another's tune. When the Factory Overseer speaks, he – Jem – has jumped. The cards he has been dealt have been marked. The dice loaded. The lot already cast. No more. And even if the gesture he will make this night is futile, ephemeral, at least he will have the satisfaction of knowing that, for as long as the meteor showers spark and crack in the sky above his head, he will place his mark upon this ground. He will resurrect his father and he will come into his own.

He scours the pile of bricks with a different gaze. Where before he has viewed them as a scar, a badge of guilt and shame, now he allows the scales to fall from his eyes and trains them upon them for what they are, not what they have hidden or buried, but what they might still build. He tugs at fallen walls, fireplaces, foundation footings, not caring what domino damage he incurs, until he finds what he is looking for. The remains of a low wall, five feet high, three feet wide, two rows thick. Crucially it is free-standing. But for added insurance he manages to drag it and prop it against what is left of the tall round chimney, which had once taken the smoke from the kiln's firing oven when the factory had still been operational, three quarters of which still remains, a jagged finger pointing defiantly up at the sky.

He regards the wall closely. He walks slowly all around it, trying to get a sense of where he might begin. Another meteor flares above him, briefly illuminating the last corner of Omega Place, bringing out the vividness of the red clay from which the bricks had first been fashioned. He has it. The whole image comes to him in that instant. He will carve the figure of a man, emerging in relief from out of the very bricks of which he will be made, a weaver, his body bent over the loom, his head looking up into the sky. In his mind's eye this man is his father, and his grandfather too, bowed but not defeated, heroic, creating something solid, something real, from the very air around him.

Spurred on by this vision, trying to hold onto it before it fades from him, like the showers of meteors streaking across the sky above him, he takes a nail and begins to scratch rapidly without stopping the outline of what he sees into the unfired clay. When he is satisfied he has got the shape and composition right, he lifts his hammer and hits the nail along the scored lines, gently at first, but then more firmly with each ensuing blow, chipping away the extraneous waste, till the figure of the forgotten weaver begins to take three-dimensional shape.

Borne aloft by the Andromedids' rebellious pyrotechnics, Amos and Agnes, using the stars' light as their guide, speed through Lumb Clough, Littlemoss and Cinderland, Bell Wood, Holt End and Lord's Brook, crossing the Medlock via Ash Bridge, past Cutler Hill till they reach the Rochdale Canal, which they cross at Whitegate, then on to Butler Green, past Nimble Nook, Thatch Leach, skirting the lower slopes of Tandle Hill, bordering the grounds of Alkrington Hall where, if they were to glance up briefly from the frost-hard fields they focus on for fear of turning an ankle, they might see a lamp shining in an upstairs window from which Lady Ashton looks towards the night sky, a smile forming across her vermilion lips, to which she applies a delicate gloss of deer tallow, castor oil and beeswax, as she thinks of Reuben's boy, Abner, observing these same phenomena through his prized spyglass, but they do not. Instead, heads bent low to the ground, like a fox and his vixen pursuing a scent, they track towards Rhodes, then Simister. They see no one. From here they turn north, through Back o'th' Moss, past Captain's Cross and Lomax's. They wade through the marshes round Roch Weir, Hollins Brook, and Bealey's Goit, where they disturb a nest of water voles coiled around each other to keep out the worst of the cold. An owl screeches in a roofless barn at Fletcher's Fold. A pair of badgers unswervingly crosses their path at Old Hall Farm, where the Bolton & Bury Canal joins with the eastern banks of the Irwell, whose course they now follow.

The Daughters of Cassiopeia continue to dance defiantly above them, lighting their way with each *grand jeté* and *pirouette*. The sky crackles and sparks like gunfire. They will not be diverted...

At Lower Hinds they hear a leveret's haunting cry, keening like a lost child. At Tentersfield they stumble across a ewe giving birth to a lamb, hunkered low to escape the wind in the lee of a blackthorn hedge, its sloes long since gorged by redwings. She is visibly straining. The first water bag bursts, releasing a thin, pale fluid through the vulva. The ewe continues to strain and a second water bag is pushed through, bringing with it a thicker, slimier mucous, through which they catch a glimpse of the lamb's nose and hooves in the light of the meteor showers still streaming across the sky. The ewe tries with considerable effort to expel the lamb, forefeet first, followed by the head. Amos and Agnes watch transfixed. They have seen lambs being born before, on the farm at Fairfield, but it's a sight that still possesses the power to freeze time. The ewe is having difficulty with the head and the shoulders of the lamb passing through her pelvis. Amos and Agnes recognise the signs. They know what needs to be done. Slowly, silently, they inch their way towards the ewe, who senses they are not a threat and allows them to approach. Amos takes hold of the feet while Agnes slips her hand inside the ewe's vagina, feeling for the head. Once there she manoeuvres her fingers till she can feel the lining of the foetal membranes. It is as she feared. The cord has become entangled around the lamb's head. Gently she loosens it until the head is free. Then, when the ewe is calm once more she synchronises her movements with the renewal of the ewe's straining, ensuring that the cervix is now fully dilated, so that with the next push, the head and shoulders are released. Agnes removes her hand carefully from inside the ewe, and it is not long before the hind legs follow. Amos clears the mucous from the lamb's nostrils, while the ewe begins to lick the rest of her. He leans back and waits for the lamb to struggle to its feet which, after a few false starts, it manages to do and then immediately locks onto the udders, despite its eyes being not yet fully open. Amos breathes a deep, satisfied sigh and stands, as if ready to move on, but a gesture from Agnes halts him. She has gently eased her hand back inside the ewe. After a few moments she slides it out once more and whispers to Amos.

"I thought so. There's another lamb in there waiting to be born."

Amos nods and sets himself back in front of the ewe, stroking her head and calming her. Before long the whole process begins again. Two more water bags burst, fluid is released, and the head and the front legs of the other twin present themselves. This second birth is much easier than the first. There is no need for Agnes to untangle the cord, and in what appears no time at all, Amos is cleaning out this one's nostrils and putting him to nurse alongside his brother.

An hour later the placenta and afterbirths are safely passed, which the ewe begins to eat. Amos stands back, watching. Something flickers in the farthest recesses of his mind, but it remains distant, formless, elusive, and he cannot retrieve it...

"Come on," says Agnes, taking hold of Amos's hand. "We've done our work here."

The Andromedids at last begin to fade. Any streaks of grey that might herald the dawn have yet to carve an opening in the sky.

Agnes is on familiar ground now. Her feet fly across the fields, hauled up from a long-buried muscle memory, through what to Amos is an impenetrable blackness. She could have run this final stretch blindfold.

Six hours, twelve miles and two births after leaving Fairfield she stops at a gate on the edge at last of their journey's end, Elton, and points towards an old stone cottage with strips of sacking pinned across the glassless windows to keep out the first of the winter draughts, the home of Cousin Silas and Meg, and their sons, Ham and Shem, whom she last saw thirteen years ago.

She turns to Amos and says, "We're here."

They have not once looked back.

She sets off towards the cottage but has not gone more than three paces when she realises Amos has not followed her. She turns back to face him.

"What is it?"

He is standing beneath a black poplar tree, looking up through its now leafless branches, at the way the dawn light is falling through it, splintering into tiny filaments.

"Come here," he says softly, holding out his arms towards her.

She joins him, naturally falling within his wide embrace.

"Look up," he says.

The two of them crane their necks upwards, feeling the fragments of light forming a nest around them.

"Six-Pointed Star to Bird's Nest," he says.

"Six-Pointed Star to Bird's Nest," she repeats.

He takes out the iron ring he has soldered in Brother Mallalieu's workshop not twenty-four hours before and holds it up so that it glints in the broken light.

"With this ring I thee wed," he says.

She smiles back at him. "With my body I thee worship."

"And with all my worldly goods I thee endow." He places the ring on to her finger.

"In the name of the Father," she says.

"In the name of the Son," he answers.

"And of the Holy Ghost," she says.

She takes from within the folds of a pocket in her dress the Roman coin that Shem gave her the day she left Elton all those years before, in memory of her brother James.

"I don't have a ring," she says, "but I have this. Accept it as a token." And she places it in Amos's palm and closes his hand over it. "Keep it in remembrance of me."

They kiss deeply beneath the penumbra of the black poplar.

"We don't need the Lot, or a Church, to tell us we can marry."

They kiss again.

"Come," she says. "I want you to meet Cousin Silas."

Jem stands up from the brick sculpture just as the last of the shooting stars fall from view. He has been carving for six hours straight. He places his hands on either side of the small of his back and pushes, tilting up his head at the same time. A smudge of light is slowly spreading across the sky. It falls upon Omega Place like a blessing. Dust floats in the air from where Jem has been chipping away at the wall of bricks throughout the night. It coats his hair and clothes and skin so that, standing there now, not moving, contemplating the results of his labours, he resembles a statue himself, or a ghost.

Slowly he begins to move. First he unrolls the stiffness out of his shoulders. Next he places a hand at the back of his neck, supporting his head while he painfully rotates it, hearing every bone release and crack. Then he circles his elbows and arms, testing them in the morning air as if they could be wings which might one day carry him away from here. Finally he stamps each foot upon the ground, shaking off the pins and needles which have gripped them until, at last, he is ready to propel himself forward.

He makes a complete circle of the finished statue, studying it from every angle, the front, the back, the sides, looking down on it from above, looking up to it from below. He nods. He is satisfied. It is finished.

He stands there now, regarding this figure, this heroic handloom weaver, his grandfather, the man his father could have been but never was, until now, who somehow Jem has released from his prison of bricks. The way his hands, his body, his face, all strain to free themselves from their yoke of clay, yet remain shaped and defined by them, reaching out towards the loom, which will hold him there for ever, chained in the mockery of a lover's embrace. He will never break free completely but nor will he desist from the effort of trying, his eye fixed on something it cannot see but knows is there.

Jem stands beside it now, following the line of its gaze, towards the still dark town, slowly beginning to stir, a chained beast clambering out of the earth.

Suddenly Whelp is at his side, coalescing out of the air as she so often appears to do. She tugs at his sleeve and points towards the statue of bricks.

"Yes," he says, his voice barely a croak, coughing the dust that furs his tongue, coats the roof of his mouth, and clogs the back of his throat. "My father."

Whelp shakes her head. Then she swings her arm slowly round and points it back to Jem.

"Pity," he says, looking at her with a deep and certain longing. "Pity, come to me."

Abner prised his red-rimmed eye from the telescope. He would not see such a display from the Andromedids again for another quarter of a century. There was such purity and perfection in the cold and pitiless way the stars went about their business, the ceaseless orbit of birth and death, dust and debris like afterbirth, to be swallowed up by the future.

He already knew enough of the vastness of the universe to grasp that there was far more of it that he could not see, would never see, than he ever could, but that that would never stop him from revelling in the wonders of what he did see, like tonight, and from trying to see more and more of them. He knew something too of the nature of the speed of light to recognise that the meteor shower he had witnessed so vividly this night, moment by moment, were in all probability celestial events that had taken place thousands, if not millions, of years in the past, yet here they were, resonating so palpably here and now in the present.

The thought then struck him with the suddenness and clarity of one of the Andromedids that he knew exactly what he would do in the future. The purity and perfection of the behaviour of the stars, that cold and pitiless quality he had so admired, could, he now realised, be found in the unplumbed precision and fathomless logic of mathematics. If God resided anywhere, thought Abner, it was in the cold but wondrous heart of numbers. There lay truth, a hard, glittering diamond that could never diminish or be tarnished. It was an unyielding overseer, who might allow you to touch it, briefly, tantalisingly, for the fleetest of moments, to reward the faithful acolyte for his unfailing devotion, but who would never allow you to possess it, not wholly, for it would always slip from your grasp, deflecting its light into as yet unexplored corners of darkness. Number was an elusive God, a slippery taskmaster, who once it had you in its grip would never release you, nor would he, Abner knew, ever wish to be, for he would always be in thrall to its mysteries and the possibility of unravelling at least a few of them. He also knew, for he had heard his father and the other men discuss this endlessly, that it could be manipulated, stretched and twisted into difficult shapes, which might hoodwink the unwary traveller, but for the true devotee there would always be a way of uncovering this concealment.

Yes. His father would be pleased when he told him of his decision, for he knew how his father worried about him, and above all other things, even more than his love of the laws of natural physics, he wanted to please him. He would become a book-keeper, an accountant. He would compile beautiful, unarguable proofs, written in copper-plate columns on linen paper bound within calf-skin boards, perfectly balanced sets of figures, whose bottom line would always be absolute zero.

He put away his Dollond & Aitcheson telescope, back into its leather case, which was indeed the key to the kingdom of heaven, and which he would continue to take out nightly, to cross again those vast, unknowable distances of space and time, to unlock their secrets, to measure and calculate, catalogue and calibrate, probing further and further, deeper and deeper, into the remotest corners of the universe, where the hard glittering diamond of truth twinkled in the heart of the kaleidoscope.

"Wait," said Amos as Agnes strode ahead of him towards the cottage of her cousin.

"What is it?" she said. She scanned his face, flickering across the entire map of him, his eyes the constellations of the whole night sky, each pin-prick of light emanating from the radiant in the centre of his iris.

"Have you brought the kaleidoscope?" he asked.

She smiled. "It's here," she said, patting the calico bag that was slung over her right shoulder. "Come on."

She held out her left hand towards him, the iron ring catching the first of the morning's steel light.

He took it in his own, feeling with his other hand for the Roman coin in his pocket. He gripped it tightly.

Together they ran towards their new home.

FOUR

Weights & Measures

1804

in which an early atomic theory is expounded – a duel is fought – an eminent French ambassador visits Manchester – a person is placed under house arrest – a painting is commissioned – a play is given – a bequest is used to bring light into darkness – and a balancing act is attempted one last time

11

1804

2nd February – Lammas

Manchester Literary & Philosophical Society

ON THE

ABSORPTION OF GASES

BY

Water and other Liquids

By JOHN DALTON

Read first on 21st October 1803

Succeeded by a further Four Essays

Delivered at Quarterly Intervals during 1804

Essay No. 1

"If a quantity of water thus freed from air be agitated in any kind of gas, not chemically uniting with water, it will absorb its bulk of the gas, or otherwise a part of it equal to one of the following fractions, the same gas always being absorbed in the same proportions..."

Here Mr Dalton pauses...

Agitation and absorption.

Mr Carlton Whiteley, Actor Manager Extraordinaire, whose company still ply their precarious trade in the converted Riding School approached via the rickety wooden footbridge across the Irwell, which can still only be accessed by the slippery stone steps from Water Street, weighs these words equally in each hand as he leaves the fine town house on Charlotte Street, which serves as the home of *The Manchester Lit & Phil*, where next month he is to deliver a lecture on his beloved Bard – on Shakespeare's enduring relevance in this first decade of a new century – a rare literary item in the Society's programme, to be set against the overwhelming array of scientific or philosophical topics normally presented, like today's offering from Mr Dalton. He wonders if anyone will turn up – the constant preoccupation of the actor manager.

Agitation and absorption. The members experienced both states in equal measure during Mr Dalton's troubling lecture, the full consequences of which only now appear to be sinking in, as they all disperse north, south, east and west across the town.

If what Mr Dalton has claimed is true, then nothing, it seems, is certain any longer. Not even the points of the compass which direct the path Carlton's feet now take, back to his lodgings above the Riding School. If matter is not fixed, if the fundamental nature of things can be altered, even slightly, by these twin actions of agitation and absorption, what remains on which one can reliably fix one's bearings? Why, the very Chain of Being itself might be called into question, the fabric of the social order, where everyone knows their place, might be tossed aside and overthrown.

What would Shakespeare have had to say on the subject, muses Carlton, as he makes his way down the even slimier stone steps towards the footbridge?

'*That wrens make prey where eagles dare not perch...?*'

Richard Crookback. A favoured role, one which Carlton has not essayed for far too long. Next season perhaps...?

He passes a man pasting up bills and posters on walls and hoardings – an action with which Carlton is intimately familiar – and lingers in order to read what they say. He lives in daily fear of a rival company coming to town, but no – these are advertising yet another Political Meeting, exhorting the public to protest at the food shortages currently ravaging the town, along with calls for greater representation.

"Manchester's population continues to grow year on year. Our citizens now outnumber those of Oxford, Bristol and York, rivalling those of Liverpool and Edinburgh, yet still we have no Member of Parliament, while others, Rotten Boroughs like Tamworth, recently bought by Sir Robert Peel of Ramsbottom, son of Parsley Peel, along with the residue of the late Lord Bath's estates in the area, for a sum rumoured to be less than £400, have only twenty-four inhabitants, each one of whom can be bribed to vote for the sitting incumbent, who, as their landlord, holds their livings in his pocket..."

Carlton draws back from the poster. He understands well the necessity at times to paper the house, offering free tickets to passers-by in order to swell the ranks of what would otherwise be a very thin audience.

Change, he thinks. Change is coming. He can smell it in the air all around him, above and beyond the ubiquitous odour of corruption and decay that hangs above the town and will not shift. The air which, even when covering his muzzle with a protective hand, Carlton is breathing in as he walks. The air which Mr Dalton has demonstrated less than an hour before comprises smaller and smaller particles than were ever previously imagined, those same atoms once defined so neatly by Democritus, now being sliced and cut, interfered with and altered by Mr Dalton, in order to weigh and measure them, even though these infinitesimal particles, will not be seen, will remain undetectable to the naked eye, yet whose effects will nevertheless be felt, probing smaller and smaller, until what...? An overthrow of the state? As has happened so thrillingly yet disturbingly in France?

A verse from Paul's first letter to the Corinthians springs unbidden into his mind.

'For it is written, I will destroy the wisdom of the wise, and will bring to nothingness the understanding of the prudent...'

Carlton is not sure what this means. Is God condemning the pursuit of knowledge, which tests the boundaries of faith, or is He pouring contempt on those who avoid risk, settling instead for what is safe and comfortable, what is familiar, what is known? Carlton has always regarded himself as something of an innovator, a taker of risks, both artistic and occasionally financial. Why then do the consequences of Mr Dalton's lecture cause him such disquiet?

The Bard once more comes soothingly to his rescue. Those lines from near the end of *Measure for Measure* perhaps?

*'Haste still pays haste, and leisure answers leisure,
Like doth quit like, and measure still for measure...'*

Spoken by The Duke when he throws off his disguise. Carlton has played this role once only. He struggled with it in truth. Not for nothing is it referred to as a 'problem play', neither comedy nor tragedy, but harsh and unrepentant. Actors loved it for its complexity, its ambiguity, but audiences didn't warm to it, stayed away in droves, a guaranteed recipe for emptying theatres, so they had not revived it, though it would certainly hold a mirror to the troubles of the times.

He shakes his head. Not *Measure for Measure*, but Shakespeare will remain his salvation. He will come to his aid, as he has always done, in times of direst need.

Perhaps he might present *Coriolanus* this Michaelmas? Manchester has Roman origins after all, is circled by hills, the etymology of its ancient Latin name – Mamucium – referring to the breast-shaped protuberances arising from the confluence of the three rivers... Carlton is distracted here by the image of several pairs of breasts he has had the pleasure of mounting, and it requires not inconsiderable resolve from him to banish those images and return to the matter in hand. Where was he? Yes – circled by seven hills... Well, not seven exactly... Nevertheless, Manchester, like Rome, is building an empire of its own, maintained by armies of, not soldiers, but workers, driving the machines of factory and forge, mine and mill, machines that spin the thread which stretches to every corner of the world, so tightly wound he fears that one day it might snap...

Carlton is enjoying himself hugely now, ratcheting up the rhetoric in his imagination as he crosses the rickety footbridge. *Coriolanus*. Yes. He begins to grow ever more excited at the prospect. The Local Hero. The Mighty Warrior. The Would-Be Emperor. Displaying the scars of war on his body like banners, brought low in the end by his loathing for the common people who worship him so unquestioningly. He pauses briefly to speak out loud.

> *"All the contagion of the south light on you,*
> *You shames of Rome! Boils and plagues*
> *Plaster you o'er..."*

He rubs his hands. This is proving more and more interesting. Perhaps he may come out of retirement and put in a brief cameo appearance as Menenius, Coriolanus's friend, who has that wonderful speech about the body politic. How does it go now? He never forgets a single role he has played, not once he has committed the lines to memory, though dredging it up from the basement of his brain proves more troublesome than he would care to admit. Ah – he has it now.

The starving, disgruntled citizens press for various wrongs to be righted.

"They ne'er cared for us yet, suffer us to famish, and their store-houses crammed with grain, repeal daily any wholesome act established against the rich and provide more piercing statutes daily to chain up and restrain the poor..."

Carlton, now as Menenius, climbs back up the slippery stone steps as if ascending to the Senate, turns to address the populace thus. Carlton pictures the whole scene in his mind's eye, rolls up his sleeves like a toga, declaims to an audience of indifferent rats foraging by the water's edge.

"There was a time when all the Body's members
Rebelled against the Belly, thus accused it:
That only like a gulf it did remain
I' th' midst o' th' body, idle and inactive,
Still cupboarding the viand, never bearing
Like labour with the rest; where th' other instruments
Did see and hear, devise, instruct, walk, feel,
And, mutually participate, did minister
Unto the appetite and affection common
Of the whole body. The Belly answered..."

Here Carlton-Menenius, pauses, looks around to gauge the attentiveness of his audience. The rats scrabble for purchase in the mud, unimpressed. *Sotto voce,* Carlton furnishes them with their line, hissed from behind the back of his hand – *"Well, sir, what answer made the Belly?"*

Carlton wheels around to face his inquisitors, tossing his imagined toga over his shoulder.

> *" 'True it is, my incorporate friends,' quoth he,*
> *'That I receive the general food at first,*
> *Which you do after live upon; and fit it is,*
> *Because I am the storehouse and the shop*
> *Of the whole body. But, if you do remember,*
> *I send it through the rivers of your blood,*
> *Even to the court, the heart, to th' seat o' th' brain;*
> *And, through the cranks and offices of man,*
> *The strongest nerves and small inferior veins*
> *From me receive the natural competency*
> *Whereby they live...' This says the Belly.*
> *You, my good friends, what say you to 't?"*

Carlton-Menenius bows deeply, imagining and savouring the applause which greets his rendition of the speech.

"Your most humble, grateful and obedient servant," he utters sonorously in his best stage whisper, "I thank you."

Yes, yes, yes. The idea grows stronger with each second.

Coriolanus does not see that change is coming. He clings to the old order with obstinacy, pride and contempt. Only faltering when faced by his mother, Volumnia, to whom he is in absolute thrall. Volumnia, who cannot countenance any alternative course of action lies open to her son, even if it must end in his death, who simply refuses to contemplate the possibility of failure or retreat, who cannot – will not – see that hitherto unacknowledged forces are lurking beneath the surface, are agitating for change. Like Mr Dalton's particles. Agitation and absorption.

Yes. He will do this. He will dress Volumnia as Britannia, complete with shield and trident. He will cover her breasts – oh, that word again – with plated armour. Coriolanus will appear as an over-reaching tyrant, a Dandy, a Narcissus, with shades of Bonaparte, while the populace will be dressed as Manchester Weavers.

It will be a Night to Remember. *Une cause celebre. Un succès de scandale.* They will be the Toast of the Town. He takes the thirteen steps back down to the wooden footbridge in a single bound. He then performs a neat *cabriole*, first to the right, next to the left. He executes an elegant *sauté*. He even contemplates *un grand jeté* to complete his exit from the bridge, but quickly changes his mind, he's too old – and too fat – to risk incurring lasting damage to his knee, or ankle, or both, which he would later regret. Instead he manages a less than graceful vault over the side rail, checking over his shoulder to make sure that no one has witnessed his less than perfect landing. The rats continue to disregard him completely.

But then he stops.

At the height of his imagined success, after taking his umpteenth curtain call, with flowers raining down upon the stage, one of which, a rose, he picks up, lifts to his nose to savour, eyes closed, its delicious fragrance, he perceives a problem. A flaw in the iris. Something he had not at first foreseen. That no matter how deeply one probes, or how greatly one magnifies the lens, there will always be something more, something further, something smaller, always tantalisingly just beyond reach. There is no final piece in the puzzle.

Mrs Whiteley will expect to play Volumnia. She will insist upon it. She will clasp him to her bosom, her extremely ample bosom, a thought not wholly unpleasant to him, but one not so pleasant as once it was. She will supervise the costume fittings. She will interfere with every aspect of his production, disrupt the purity of his vision, so that it will become blousy, overblown, obscuring the heart of what he is trying to convey. Instead she will want the play to be a vehicle, a backdrop, for her, and her alone. She will demand the final word on casting. She will suggest young Mr Ponsonby for Coriolanus, who is altogether too young, too lightweight, too insubstantial, for such a role. And besides, he has a lisp. Perfectly fine for Benvolio, or one of the gay blades in Mr Sheridan's or Mr Congreve's comedies of manners, but a Coriolanus? A tragic warrior hero? Why, the very thought of it makes Carlton go pale. He shudders at the mere idea of such a travesty. But Mrs Whiteley will not be thwarted. She will intend to place herself at the play's centre, a true matriarch coming to the rescue of her poor deluded Rome, a voracious queen bee, who must be fed and fed again, until she becomes bloated like a hot air balloon – not a difficult transformation, for she appears to swell before his eyes by the minute – no, he scolds himself, that is unkind – but even as he remonstrates with himself for this unnecessary cruelty, he pictures her floating above the audience's head, threatening to encompass all the world, all the stage, within her ever-expanding, unstoppable girth. Carlton imagines taking one of her hat pins, creeping up on her from behind while she is too busy primping and preening with her powders and puffs to notice his stealthy approach. He will stick the pin into her wide, voluminous arse and watch with delicious fascination as she farts and fizzes into the air, spinning like an out-of-control top, until all that is left of her, the burst and tattered shreds, fall at his feet like a used pig-bladder condom.

A slow smile spreads across his face but then, as quickly as it rises, it falls. Like so much else these days. He will not enact his fantasy. He will not do any of these things. He is nothing more than a eunuch. A gelding, a jennet, a *castrato*. It is Mrs Whiteley who controls the purse strings, not he. Without her the theatre cannot function. It would be bankrupted in a heartbeat. Carlton knows this, and Mrs Whiteley knows that he does. But at the same time he cannot stomach the thought of his glorious vision being so compromised. Long gone are the days when Mrs Whiteley could hold the stage with one of her breeches roles on which she built her reputation. Her Viola was a *nonpareille*, her Rosalind a *tour de force*. Her Imogen was unsurpassed, her *La Pucelle* a paragon. But those performances, which had seen her star ascend to the same dizzying firmament of a Sarah Siddons or a Mrs Jordan, which had first so driven him wild with desire for her – there is something so ineffably arousing in the sight of a young woman sporting close-fitting men's breeches and squeezed into tightly-strung corsets – are a thing of the past. Now she resolutely gives her Gertrude, her Queen Margaret, and yes, her Volumnia.

No. He will not allow it and so he must suppress any urge to mention it to her. Better not to do it at all than see it so sullied. They will play *The Rivals* again. She will give her Mrs Malaprop once more, a much-loved crowd pleaser, and he his Anthony Absolute.

His agitation not yet fully absorbed, he enters the theatre.

*

Whelp – or Pity, as she has now learned to answer to – has never been to a theatre. But she's seen enough comedies and tragedies for a lifetime already. She's thirty-five years old. Or thereabouts. She herself does not know. Nor does it concern her. She has one of those faces that it's hard to place. When she was a child she looked old beyond her years. Now she is a woman, she looks more like a child.

Entrances and exits – she's even been pursued by a bear once, at the Michalemas Fair in Acresfield – near misses and last minute rescues.

She has only been asked to supply her age once – by Jem, when she started work as a piecer at Arkwright' Mill. Fifteen, she'd told him at the time, and he'd accepted it. More than half a lifetime ago. She's been with Jem ever since. Off and on.

Jem.

Pity can't imagine a life without him. She loves him. Though this is not a word she uses. She still hardly speaks. Only when no other alternative presents itself does she hear herself forming those strange guttural sounds which bubble up from the back of her throat. She hears language all around her every day, is assailed by it, so that she finds she understands it instinctively, whatever tongue it comes in, but mostly she finds words unnecessary and inadequate. The love she feels for Jem is the kind of bond displayed by animals that survive in packs, the wild dogs she sees roaming Manchester's streets after dark, foraging for scraps to take back to their lairs.

This is not the kind of love, though, that Jem feels for her, which is of an altogether different order. Pity knows this but she cannot change the way she feels. Though she can change the way she acts. She knows what it is that Jem wants from her and she has no problem providing him with what he needs. Back in his lair.

Jem's lair is the small brick cottage his father had built, the one his mother died in, now subsumed by Jacob's Tailor's, where she, Pity, now works. Her fingers are as quick and nimble as ever they were. They dance with needle and thread to stitch the clothes in the airless, windowless sweat-room at the back of the smart shop, the part the customers don't see when they come to order. Sometimes one of the girls will be asked to model these clothes at the front, so the customers might see what the finished garment will look like. The girls get an extra sixpence for it. Pity is never asked to do this. She doesn't mind. She wouldn't want to anyway and she doesn't need the money. Jem earns enough for both of them, now that he's a mason. Zachary found him a position the day after Jem finished the brick statue of his father at the loom, which still stands in the yard at the back. Mr Jacob has installed a new water pump next to it, the old one having disintegrated into rust, which draws water from the Irk, near to where it flows into the Irwell.

Flows. No. It doesn't so much flow as ooze these days. Sometimes Pity will remember when she saw Amos fall into the river at this very spot, when the young girl dived in to rescue him, when he was driven away on the back of the girl's family's cart, since when she has never seen him. If he fell into that spot today, she thinks, he would not be so easily rescued. He would be sucked down into the sludge and slime that chokes it.

Several times she has thought she has seen him. A face in the crowd on Market Street Lane, or a figure bolting between the wheels of a wagon, or hunched asleep in one of the Hulks. But it never has been. She wonders now if she would recognise him, for it's been – what? Almost twenty years. It was the day of the Balloon Flight that she saw him last. Up, up and away...

But she thinks she would. For she sees Matthew often, striding out of the Exchange, standing on the doorstep of his fine house on Oldham Street, polishing an apple on the velvet lapel of his jacket, before biting into it, then tossing a chunk of it away, which, after he has gone back indoors, she will be unable to resist retrieving. The same doorstep she had laid him on, barely a scrap, clinging to life on the night of the Earthquake...

She has seen him in the Court Leet too. Where he is a Magistrate now. He did not know *her* of course. But why would he? She had stood before him, having been picked up by a Special Constable one night and charged with vagrancy. She'd been careless. She'd followed him home one time, during one of her nightly foragings, a habit she cannot ever fully shake off, having been born into it, marking out her old territories, like a cat who must spray, and had watched him from across the street, at the corner of Lever's Row. He had not drawn the curtains in his front room. A housekeeper had brought in his supper. She had lit a lamp, which she had then placed in the window. He had begun to pick at his food, half-hearted and distracted, and she had approached him then, drawn by the expression on his face, which seemed momentarily absent, or elsewhere, as if he had lost something, was missing it, but could not now quite remember what it was. She found herself walking towards the window. He looked out. He saw her then, she was sure he did, for it seemed like their eyes fused for an instant between the glass. Then she felt a hand upon her shoulder. A Constable was speaking to her and pulling her roughly away. Matthew rose. For a moment she thought he might intervene, but all that he did was to draw the curtain between them.

When she saw him next, it was in the Court Leet, standing before him. He was the Magistrate who would try her case. He looked at her then, not seeing her at all, seeing only an unkempt child-woman, who had spent three not unfamiliar nights in an overcrowded cell of the New Bailey Prison, of the sort he must have witnessed a hundred times before. But when he heard her name – Pity – he seemed to look at her properly for the first time. And when he heard Jem, then Mr Jacob, vouch for her character and confirm that no, she was not a vagrant, and yes, she had an address on the Hanging Ditch, those cold features in his face flushed slightly, and he rapped his gavel on the bench before him and said, "Case dismissed", and she was ushered out, back into the morning air.

"Time to take somebody home," Jem had said. "Time to give somebody a wash," he had added, then grinned. "Like we had to do once before."

They looked at each other a long time then, remembering.

"I thought I'd lost you," he said.

She put her hand in his.

"Come on," he said, "my sister-wife."

Is that what she is to him, she thinks? When asked in the Court Leet, Jem had said that she was his sister, a fact that Mr Jacob had confirmed. And that is how they present themselves to the world. Jeremiah Stone, mason, bricklayer, known to all as Jem, with his unmarried sister, Pity.

But when the door is closed on the outside world and he lights a candle to guide their way upstairs to the one bedroom, she follows after him not unwillingly as his wife.

12

1st August – Lammas

> Essay No. 2
>
> *Mr Dalton resumes....*
>
> "If a quantity of pure water be boiled rapidly for a short time in a vessel with a narrow aperture, or if it be subjected to an air-pump, the air exhausted from the receiver containing the water, and then be briskly agitated for some time, very nearly the whole of any gas the water may contain, will be extricated from it..."

*

Leigh Philips arrives at the grove of black poplars just before sunrise. He walked the four miles from Castlefield to Kersal Moor while it was still dark, for the most part following the course of the Irwell, whose surface was a dark mirror reflecting the last torn threads of starlight as a cold dawn rose. From time to time he was aware of rustlings in the grass beside him, the occasional slithering, then a faint splash. An eel most probably, waking a long buried instinct to make its journey back to the place where things had first started.

Kersal Moor.

Leigh has barely been back since that day almost twenty years ago when he had outrun Major-General Roger Aytoun to win The Kersal Cup, then defeated him again a few days later in a drunken brawl behind *The Britons' Protection*, and by so doing secured his commission. Aytoun is still alive as far as Leigh knows. Five years before, after his wife Barbara

Minshull had died, having lived far longer than anyone could have predicted, Aytoun was, to everyone's astonishment, quite devastated. For all his serial infidelities he was, it seemed, devoted to her. Though he did not remain so for long. He retired to his maternal grandfather's family seat in Scotland, the notorious Jacobin, the 4th Lord Rollo, where he married, so the rumours said, his cousin, Jean Sinclair, another older woman.

Leigh was promoted to Major and appointed Commander of the Manchester & Salford Volunteer Corps, as Aytoun's hotchpotch militia was now known, but it was a hollow victory, awarded only on the grounds of seniority and length of service, rather than as a result of any glorious deeds in the field.

Now, as he crosses the Kersal Moor towards the grove of black poplars, he reflects rather bitterly at the uneventful way his life has spooled. No laurels of victory for him – not since he was garlanded somewhat unceremoniously after nakedly breasting the tape in The Kersal Cup all those years before.

Unlike his nemesis, Lieutenant-Colonel Joseph Hanson, for whom he now waits as a pale sun begins to rise…

Sir,

If you consider yourself a man of honour, I request the presence of your company at your earliest convenience, so that this matter between us may be settled once and for all. Please state the day, the time and the place.

As befits a soldier and a gentleman, sir, I expect your reply within the hour.

Respectfully yours etc

Leigh Philips, Major
1st Regiment Manchester & Salford Volunteer Militia

Sir,

It gives me no pleasure but to accede to your most ignominious request, but as a man of honour you leave me no choice.

My second will await the presence of your second at the following appointed hour – six of the clock – on Lammas morning, August 1st, at the Kersal Moor, within the grove of black poplars in the centre of the racecourse.

You may choose your weapon, sir. Pistol, sword – it is of no consequence to me.

Should you decide, even at this late hour, not to proceed further with this matter, but accept the ruling of His Excellency the Lord Lieutenant of the County Palatine, I shall not deem you to have foregone your obligations as a gentleman.

Yours & co

Joseph Hanson, Lieutenant-Colonel
Salford & Stockport Independent Rifles
Manchester Home Guard

Sir,

You're a damned impudent rascal not worthy of the Regiment whose name you besmirch and whose reputation you sully with the disrespect you persistently bestow upon it with your actions. Honour must be satisfied!

Six of the clock – 1st August – Kersal Moor – by the grove of the black poplars – pistols!

I shall arrange for a surgeon to be present to attend to what are certain to be most grievous wounds inflicted upon you thereafter.

Your de facto Commanding Officer

Leigh Philips, Major
Combined Manchester Forces upon His Majesty's Declaration of Home Rule during hostilities overseas with the French

As he waits, Leigh reflects once more upon the train of events that have led him to this point, standing in the shadows cast by the black poplars, as the sun continues to climb the sky, while the minutes tick by. He considers again the actions of his rival...

Mr Dalton resumes.

> "If a quantity of water free from air be agitated with a mixture of two or more gases (such as atmospheric air), the water will absorb portions of each gas the same as if they were presented to it separately in their proper density..."

It was Hanson who had challenged his authority when Leigh had wanted to enforce the Aliens Act most forcibly, when crowds flocking to see James Sadler's Balloon Flight had threatened to get out of control, and arrest and deport the influx of several Jewish families into the town.

It was Hanson, not he, who had been chosen by Aytoun to accompany him back to Gibraltar – scene of the General's greatest triumph – at the outbreak of the French wars. At the time Leigh's disappointment at not being selected to go himself was partially mitigated by a promotion closer to home. He had been flattered to have been installed as Aytoun's deputy in charge of the Castlefield Garrison for the duration of the Major-General's absence, that he had been entrusted the role of such a prestigious stewardship, but over time he came to realise that this was because the Major-General regarded the position of civic custodian of law and order in Manchester far less highly than the chance of further glory overseas.

It was Hanson therefore, not he, who had been at the Major-General's side when he had relieved the Rock for a second time. It was Hanson, not he, who had assisted in the daring rescue and subsequent sheltering of the *Duc d'Angoulême*, Count of Artois and uncle to the uncrowned King Louis XVII, from Robespierre's Terror. Copies of the famous painting by John Kay, depicting the Major-General standing next to the Count, the former's gigantic stature of six feet four inches dwarfing the latter's five feet six inches – cruelly the same height as Leigh – were widely circulated in all the newspapers. Titled *The Great And The Small Are There*, it portrayed the two men on the field of one of the many battles the Major-General had fought in Spain and in France.

But it was Hanson, not he, who had stood shoulder to shoulder with Aytoun, for which he had been rewarded with the Command of the Salford & Stockport Independent Rifles, a much older regiment than Leigh's Manchester Volunteer Corps, with a greater lineage and tradition. And now it was Hanson, not he, who had seized the initiative and declared himself as Lieutenant-Colonel in overall supreme command of all the Manchester Regiments, a combination of resources being currently proposed by His Majesty's Government as a way of strengthening the town's Home Guard, should any invasion be launched by Napoleon Bonaparte, a possibility the entire country was hourly anticipating.

Leigh, always a stickler for the finer points of protocol, was outraged. He outranked Hanson in terms of seniority. He had been commanding a regiment for far longer than him, despite not having seen action abroad. It was he, not Hanson, therefore, who should by rights have received this posting. He had written letters. He had demanded satisfaction. But none had been forthcoming. And so there had been only one course of action left possible for him, and this was what had brought him to this secluded spot at dawn on this, a Thursday morning in August, the Feast of Lammas, the traditional time for cutting the wheat.

A mist rises from the river. Dew sparkles in the grass. Cobwebs garland the black poplars in the centre of the Moor, hanging in thin rags. His second approaches with his batman from the south-east. His second, a loyal Subaltern whose name he cannot bring to mind, salutes upon reaching him. His batman, whose name he *can* remember – young William Robinson, Billy, the son of a surveyor, only recently joined up, but who had caught Leigh's eye in a race around the Parade Ground he had witnessed only last week, which Billy had won, laughing throughout, reminding him of himself when he had outrun the Major-General to win The Kersal Cup – is not laughing this morning. He looks white and terrified, as well he might, thinks Leigh, for this is not what he imagined the role of a batman might be, to be carrying a set of duelling pistols on a fine summer's morning. Shaking, he hands them to the Subaltern – Francis, that's his name, he remembers it now, 1st Lieutenant Francis Wainwright – who in turn passes them to Leigh for his inspection. He lifts one, checks that it is not yet loaded, peers down the single bore, nods curtly, then hands it back to the 1st Lieutenant. Billy, he notices, looks as if he might be sick at any moment.

"Have you eaten?" he asks him.

Billy nods. "A little bread, sir."

Leigh turns to Wainwright. "Give the boy some rum," he says quietly. "Just a tot. He looks scared to death."

"Yes, sir."

Billy manages a small swallow, but it is enough for Leigh to register some colour returning to the boy's cheeks.

"Perhaps he'll not come, sir," says Wainwright.

"Oh, he'll come," says Leigh, turning away to scan the Moor. "You can be certain of that. Lieutenant-Colonel Hanson, as he now insists we must call him, will most definitely come."

"Yes, sir. But..." Wainwright falters.

"But what?"

"If he's late, sir, even by five minutes, we would be within our rights to refuse to face him when he comes. It would be he who would be the dishonoured one, Sir, not you."

Leigh looks at the Subaltern. He's trying to protect me. He's worried I'm going to lose, he thinks with a wry smile.

"We'll wait fifteen minutes," he says.

"Yes, sir."

Leigh turns away. His attention is caught by a peppered moth alighting upon the bark of one of the black poplars. The Manchester tree, as some people call it, for it survives the thick black plumes of smoke belching from the many mill chimneys in the town better than most. The moth is another of that rare hybrid Leigh has perhaps seen five times since he sighted his first one, on the evening of Mr Sadler's balloon flight, not white, though not yet black either, but something in between, a new species evolving. It's what he too must perhaps learn to do if he is to survive these rapid changes.

> "If water impregnated with any one gas (eg: hydrogenous) be agitated with another gas equally absorbable (eg: azotic) there will apparently be no absorption of the latter gas, just as much gas being found after agitation as was first introduced to the water, but upon further examination the residuary gas will be found to contain a mixture of the two, and the

parts of each, in the water, will be exactly proportional to those out of the water."

To:
Mr Zachary Robinson
14 Bridge Street
Manchester

Dear Feyther,

I'm not sure I like t' life of a soldier. I thowt it'd be all marchin' an' playin' t' drums but it's not like that at all. I've been made 'batman' to Major Philips. 'E's a real stickler, let me tell thee. 'E likes to see 'is reflection in 'is boots, which I 'ave to polish every day. But that's the easy bit. I reckon as how thee and Mother 'ave trained me well enough how to do that. But lately 'e's got a reet bee in 'is bonnet about summat. 'E's allus shoutin' an' wantin' to gi' us a thug in t' lug. 'E's got me traipsin' up an' down everywhere deliverin' what 'e calls "urgent missives" – that's 'letters' to thee an' me. 'E slams t' seal down that 'ard on each one afore 'e gives it to us I think 'e'll smash reet through t' desk wi' 'is fist. Then I 'ave to run across to t' other side o' town to deliver it there an' then in person an' not go back till I'm given a reply – or I mun get meself to t' Boar's Head on t' London Road to make sure they catch t' Mail Coach.

'E don't believe in t' Tuppenny Post neither. Instead 'e 'as me runnin' all over t' show. I've told 'im, 'e should be reet proud, for 'ere in Manchester we 'ad t' first Penny Post in t'

world, an' now that Prinny's passed a law sayin' we mun pay tuppence for postin' a letter anywhere in t' same town, we've got t' best postal service in all England. But the Major don't seem to want to 'old wi' it. So – while I'm wearin' out me shoe leather criss-crossin' 'ere, there an' everywhere for 'im, I see t' other Post Boys, all dressed up in their fine uniforms wi' brass buttons an' a reet nice cap, wi' a sack on their backs, all orderly-like, postin' letters through one door then another, wi' none o' this runnin' pell mell, helter skelter. I reckon as 'ow I'd change places wi' 'em at t' drop of a 'at – if I 'ad a 'at to drop, that is, an' if I 'adn't signed up for t' Volunteers for t' next three years!

Oh well, mustn't grumble, as tha' would say. There's plenty o' folk worse off nor me an' no mistake. I've made me bed, I'll just 'ave to lie in it. So – any road up, I've sent you this letter by t' Tuppenny Post just so you know what I'm talkin' about.

I do 'ope Mother's feeling less poorly now. Mebbe she'll be well enough soon to read this for 'erself, but till then please will tha' read it to 'er for us? Ta.

Now I shall go off to t' wash house to soak me blisters before t' Major sends me off on another "urgent missive". 'E's 'oppin' mad about summat. Earlier today 'e 'ad me mekkin' sure the bore of 'is Wogden & Barton flintlock pistol is all smoothed an' primed an' ready for use, checkin' that there are no voids in t' moulding o' t' lead bullets that might affect their accuracy. Whatever next?

Your son,

Billy

A blood red sun climbs the sky, which shifts from its pre-dawn monochrome through various shades of blue as if an unseen painter is mixing different hues on his palette, spreading them boldly with his knife – cobalt, turquoise, phthalo; manganese, indanthrene, Prussian – before settling on a fierce cerulean, into which the sun prepares to bleed.

The different birds have woken up and call to each other across Kersal Moor. Larks rise and fall, catching the early morning currents, swooping and dipping, as though on the look-out for signs of Hanson's imminent arrival, so that they may signal his approach.

Leigh watches them now, skimming across the hummocky grass beyond the rim of the black poplars, from whose topmost branches a quarrelsome parliament of rooks berate each other raucously, as if sitting on opposite sides of the House, some for Leigh, some for Hanson. A woodpecker darts into the grove and immediately begins a rapid staccato drilling into the deep striated fissures of the bark of one of the trees. Its beak strikes at the tree more than twenty times a second. Its repeated hammered attacks sound to Leigh like gun shots, jolting him from his reverie, at the same time disturbing the peppered moth from its basking. It flutters reluctantly into the air, where it is at once seized upon by a thrush. It must evolve more quickly if it is to learn to survive, thinks Leigh somewhat ruefully. In the distance, striding across the moor with the sun at his back, Hanson appears. To Leigh he resembles no less a figure than the archangel Michael from the Book of Revelation, ready to do battle for the War of Heaven, and he, Leigh, for the first time in his life, experiences doubt. Overhead the mocking of the rooks grows louder, a baying mob in full cry.

My Dear Leigh,

It grieves me to have to write to inform you that your father is gravely ill. Dr Perceval does not believe he has very much time remaining to him. He grows weaker by the day, and he would, I know, face death with calmer equanimity if he were at the last able to be reconciled with you.

I urge you, as a Christian and as a dutiful son, to put aside your quarrels and your differences and pay one last visit to a man who loves you, who has always loved you, as a father should, with kindness and pride.

Your most loving and anxious Mother

Dearest Mother,
Does he ask for me directly by name?

Yours most sincerely,

Your loving and obedient son,
Leigh

My Dear Son,
Your father has all but lost the power of speech, so that I cannot before God truthfully say to you that he has requested your presence directly, but believe me when I tell you that he most urgently desires it.

Many has been the time, in the months and years past, when he has heard a horse ride past our house and he has risen from his chair in the hope that it might have been you, come to pay your parents a visit, only to have those hopes dashed as the rider passed by.

Or whenever a letter has arrived from our newly installed penny post, he has all but skipped up to the mat to pick up what lay there, eagerly skimming through the stamped envelopes, hoping his eyes would light upon your familiar hand, only to deposit them upon the hall table in disappointment, when no such envelope presented itself.

If ever reports appeared in the newspapers describing your various exploits, he would call in the entire household to the drawing room, from where he would insist on reading the entire report to one and all, after which there would be warm applause and a shilling's bonus for all. He would bask in the glow of such news for days and weeks.

Whenever you and I met, Leigh, in secret in town, or here at home when your father was away on business, I would always tell him, for he would want to know how you looked, what you said and, of course, whether you might have asked after him. You must not blame me for telling him these things, for I may be your mother, but I am also your father's wife, and I have a duty to you both.

Please, then, for my sake if not your father's, come and visit him before it is too late. Make your peace with him, I beg you.

*Yours pleadingly,
Your Mother*

*Dear Mother,
Unless my father calls for me by name I shall not come. He knows where my quarters are at the Castlefield Barracks when not on His Majesty's duty elsewhere. He knows where my club is in King Street. He knows where I keep my collection in rooms on Mount Street. He could, if he had so wished it, visited me at any one of these establishments, but*

he chose not to.

He made his position abundantly clear to me when I decided not to follow him into the textile business, to pursue instead a career in the military, which I hope I have executed with honour at all times. He professed his disappointment in my decision and told me that he thought I would come to regret it, and that I would indeed be always welcome to return to the family fold once I had purged myself of those childish soldierly ambitions.

But such a time – until very recently, that is – has not materialised. I have been proud to serve my King and my country, and I hoped that my father would come to share that pride. I am touched by your descriptions of him reading aloud any accounts of my military prowess he came across, but he never elected to follow up such actions by seeking me out. Given that his last words to me when I left the house on Lever's Row, that I was only to return there should I decide I no longer wished to remain a soldier, I felt I possessed neither the right nor the permission to do so. The decision was his, Mother, not mine.

I mention above a brief caveat – 'until recently' – which is troubling but, I pray, temporary. You may have read that a new Manchester Volunteer Militia is to be formed to provide the most efficacious Home Guard for the town while hostilities between Great Britain and France continue, which will bring all the current companies under a single command. I was promised that command, but – most wickedly and dishonourably – it is threatened with being taken from me and given to that upstart Hanson. Naturally I have written letters demanding my reinstatement – to the Earl of Derby and Lord Hawkesbury, no less, from whom I am hourly expecting replies.

I repeat, therefore, dearest Mother, that if my father calls for me directly by name, then I shall fly to his side.

Yours obediently,

Your son
Leigh

"If a quantity of water in a phial, having a ground stopper very accurately adapted, be agitated with any gas, or mixture of gases, till the due share has entered the water; then, if the stopper be secured, the phial may be exposed to any variation of temperature without disturbing the equilibrium: that is, the quantity of water will remain the same whether it be exposed to heat or cold, if the stopper be air-tight."

To the Most Honourable the Earl of Derby
Lord Lieutenant of the County Palatine of Lancaster

My Lord Derby,

Please forgive this letter from your most loyal and humble servant. I hope that, when you have read its contents, you will pardon me for so intruding upon your person in the form of this most urgent supplication.

It may have come to your notice that, late last year, I had the great honour to be granted command of the 1st Regiment of the Manchester & Salford Corps, a volunteer militia with a proud record born out of its distinguished achievements during the Great Siege of Gibraltar, to serve as part of

Britain's Home Guard during the current French Revolutionary Wars His Majesty has so wisely seen fit to engage us in. It came as a great shock and insult to us, therefore, when one Joseph Hanson, a former Subaltern within the Manchester Regiment, having deserted us for the Salford & Stockport Independent Rifles, unilaterally declared himself Lieutenant-Colonel Commander over all local volunteer forces. He did so, in the face of my own appointment, with the spurious claim that the Independent Rifles is the oldest corps in the district, in spite of it not having seen a fraction of the active service in the field boasted by my own Regiment.

I entreat you, my Lord, to act with the utmost expedience to quash this upstart Hanson's unjust claim and officially bestow primacy to the Manchester & Salford Corps the better to serve the needs of His Majesty during these unpredictable days.

I remain, my Lord,

Your most humble and obedient servant,

Major Philips. Commander:
1st Regiment Manchester & Salford Volunteer Corps

Sir,
His Lordship, the Most Honourable Earl of Derby, has instructed me to acknowledge receipt of your recent communication concerning the dispute over the Command of the proposed Combined Forces of the various Manchester militias.

His Lordship obliges me to point out that he does not

intervene personally with such appointments and would refer you instead to the Secretary of State, the Right Honourable Lord Hawkesworth, under whose jurisdiction this matter more properly falls. However, he urges me to point out that, in so advising you, he is in no way implying that he supports your claim. On the contrary, His Lordship recognises the historic primacy of the Salford & Stockport Independent Rifles. Furthermore he praises the selfless and devoted service of Lieutenant-Colonel Hanson who, while under the command of Major-General Aytoun, acted with courage and distinction during his posting in Gibraltar.

His Lordship would like it to be known that, while he has always held your father, Mr John Philips, in the highest esteem, especially with regard to his time when he served as His Lordship's Deputy in the County Palatine, this admiration and gratitude do not extend themselves into any action or decision on the part of His Lordship that could in any way be misconstrued as showing undue grace or favour to any members of his family.

We understand that Mr Philips is currently gravely ill. His Lordship conveys his deepest sorrow on learning this and promises that he will write to Mrs Philips separately. Her husband – your father – has done much for the town of Manchester, its inhabitants and its environs, helping it to grow into the major Cottonopolis it has now become, with an unsurpassed reputation for its progressive industry and enterprise.

We remain
Yours etc

Richard Challoner, Sir
Equerry-in-Waiting to His Lordship the Most Honourable

Earl of Derby, Lord Lieutenant of the County Palatine of Lancaster

Sir,
I have neither time nor inclination to reply to your most injudicious letter of the 17th inst. But reply I must in my position as Secretary of State since your communiqué was delivered complete with the regimental seal, which I deemed most inappropriate since the matter you raise is, in my view, personally rather than professionally motivated.

Lieutenant-Colonel Hanson has behaved quite properly in accordance with due process and has my full confidence to assume his position as Commander of all Manchester's Volunteer Corps, as deemed necessary by the recent order of His Royal Highness the Prince Regent, acting with the Royal Prerogative while his father the King is currently indisposed, to establish a fully professional Home Guard to protect the interests of our towns and cities throughout the land while our country is at war with the French.

Please understand that we shall accept no further correspondence on this matter, which we now regard as closed.

Yours etc

Lord Hawkesworth
Secretary of State
His Majesty's Government

"If water be impregnated with one gas (eg: oxygenous), and another gas, having an affinity for the former, (eg: nitrous), be agitated along with it, the absorption of the latter gas will be greater, by the quantity necessary to saturate the former, than it would have been if the water had been free from gas."

Dear Major Philips,

It is with the deepest regret that I write to you this day to inform you of the untimely passing of your father, Mr John Philips, who departed this world for a better place earlier this morning.

Your mother, as you must imagine, is too distressed to write to you herself. She has instead bestowed that unfortunate honour upon me, your father's secretary these past eleven years. She asks whether your duties with the Manchester Militia will spare you to attend the funeral, which will take place a week today at the Collegiate Church of St Mary, St Denys and St George at 11 o'clock on Thursday 1st August in the Year of our Lord 1804.

If you would be so good as to direct any communication or reply to me rather than your mother, who has been advised by Dr Perceval to rest completely. I am sure you will understand.

Your most obedient servant,

Christopher Hopwell Esq.
Private Secretary
J&N Philips, Textile Manufacturers

Mr Hopwell,
I thank you for your recent correspondence. It is never easy to be the bearer of ill tidings.

Please assure my mother that I will of course do everything in my power to attend the service at the Collegiate Church. I have another most pressing engagement earlier the same morning, which my honour as an officer and a gentleman precludes me from foregoing, but I shall do all in my power to make sure that I am there.

If it so please my mother, I can arrange for a Guard of Honour from my regiment to be present along the route of the procession both outside and inside the Church in true recognition of the high esteem in which my father was held throughout the town. Please let me know by return if this is something she would wish.

Yours etc

Major Philips
1st Regiment Manchester & Salford Volunteer Corps

Dear Leigh,
Please – I beg you – under no circumstances arrange for the Guard of Honour, which you proposed in your letter to the estimable and kind Mr Hopwell, to be present during your father's funeral. It is a most grotesque suggestion, which is abhorrent both to me and to the memory of your father, who was the quietest and plainest of gentlemen, who never in his life desired to draw attention to himself, preferring instead his deeds and actions to speak for him.

Your presence alone, as a grieving son and individual,

rather than some representative of a larger body with which your father had no connection other than that you were a part of it, is all that is required – if you can be spared from your other "pressing engagement", that is.

*Yours, in haste
Mother*

Time for Leigh grinds to a standstill. He remains motionless in the centre of the grove of black poplars, while all around him is motion. The choreography of clicked heels and curt, formal bows. The ceremonial opening and closing of lids. The smooth, polished surfaces of mahogany. The glinting of brass fitments on the pistols. The gloved hands of the seconds. The aloof separateness of Hanson. The early morning mist rising from the ground enveloping him in what appears to Leigh a cloud of seething fury, while the inside of his own head swarms. He is suddenly reminded of the night of the Earthquake – almost thirty years ago, when he was still a boy, on the cusp of becoming a man, and the flies from his *vivarium* escaped. They are back now. In his hair, on his eyelids, invading every orifice. But mostly they are inside his head. The noise of their incessant buzzing threatens to overwhelm him. He swats wildly at the invisible host. Hanson regards him with cold contempt.

"Are you quite yourself, sir?" hisses Wainwright.

Leigh regards him uncertainly. It takes him a moment to register who he is. Yes. Of course. The Subaltern, his second, who is noticeably perspiring in the full dress uniform the occasion demands.

"You may still withdraw," Wainwright continues. "It is not too late. All you have to do is suggest a joint command, a parity of status between the two regiments. If he declines, there is no loss of honour, sir, if you then relieve him of any obligation to proceed further this morning, for you will have captured the moral high ground."

"Captured?" snaps Leigh. A flame rekindles in the sunken sockets of each eye. For an instant he is jolted back into himself.

"I beg your pardon, sir – retained. That position has always been yours."

"Quite so."

"Given that technically he arrived late, such a conciliatory gesture on your part would be magnanimous and statesmanlike."

Leigh considers this for a moment. There is merit in what the Subaltern has said, but the flies inside his head resume their insurrection.

"He will reject the notion," he says, "and I will not give him that satisfaction. Come, Wainwright. Let us waste no more time. Ask Billy to attend on me. Tell him he is needed now to carry my coat and my hat."

"Sir."

The Subaltern salutes and strides across the grove, first towards Billy, into whose ear he relays the Major's request, next towards his opposing second to check that he and Lieutenant-Colonel Hanson are quite ready. Billy, who normally runs everywhere – the quality which first brought him to the Major's attention – on this occasion walks with inordinate slowness towards his master. He takes large, ungainly paces, as if he is pretending to be wearing seven league boots, his arms held stiffly by his sides, all the while his head glancing this way, then that.

Leigh does not notice. His thoughts have turned inwards again. As he removes the bright red jacket of his uniform to reveal the plain white shirt underneath, he feels himself become less visible, merging with the paleness of the mist which continues to leach from the ground and circle around him. He is thinking of the way the peppered moth is gradually learning to camouflage itself more successfully and wonders if he might do the same. Does he really want this wretched command? The flies rise up as one inside his brain. Furiously they swarm and bite. Yes, they cry! Yes! Your father would require nothing less of you!

And in that moment they are gone. He sees them soaring high above him, until they are just a single dot against the sun, like the transit of Venus. He watches their slow but certain progress for a full minute, while Billy folds and re-folds his jacket, again and again, as if trying to slow the hands of a clock. Wainwright places the pistol into the Major's open palm, and then is forced to close his fingers round the handle for him.

"Gentlemen," he calls in a voice that booms like a far-off bittern, "please take your positions in the centre of the grove."

Hanson and Leigh stand back to back.

"We don't have to do this," whispers Hanson. "You can retain control of your regiment, as a battalion under my command, fully autonomous."

But Leigh is not listening. He is noticing how even the rooks in the poplars have ceased their raucous racket.

"On my count," continues Wainwright, "you will take ten paces away from each other, then turn and fire. Are you ready, gentlemen?"

"Don't be an ass, Philips," hisses Hanson.

The words jolt Leigh back into the present.

"Ready," he calls.

"Colonel Hanson?" asks Wainwright.

"Ready," he replies, expelling the tension he has been holding in a single reluctant breath.

"One – two – three..." begins Wainwright.

Billy accompanies each number with a heavy beat on the drum, still straining his head in all directions.

"Four – five – six..."

Just at that moment, cresting the brow of Kersal Moor a small indeterminate dot appears, a speck of grit in the eye, a cloud crossing the sun. The dot grows and separates, clusters and re-forms.

"Seven – eight – nine…"

Billy stops beating the drum. The number ten falters on Wainwright's lips before it can be spoken. Leigh feels the flies descend in a sudden rush all about him, he flails wildly with his arms. The cluster is now clearly several dots, Constables racing into the centre of the grove, blowing whistles and issuing commands. The rooks shriek from the treetops. Leigh fires his pistol, the bullet embeds itself into the bark of one of the black poplars, in the exact spot where he had glimpsed the peppered moth. Billy covers his ears and ducks to the ground. Hanson whirls around in the chaos and mayhem, raising his arms, letting his pistol swing harmlessly from one finger.

"Stop!" cries one of the Constables. "By the authority of the Court Leet I do hereby arrest all present here for an unlawful breach of the peace and for gathering at this hour to carry out an action prohibited under common law."

"Wait," replies Hanson. "The Major and I will accompany you willingly, but let the rest here go. They assembled but on our bidding and have no answer to make before the law."

The Constable nods. The seconds each look to their officers, who separately signal their permission for them to leave the ground. Leigh is vaguely aware of Billy speaking to the Constable before he goes. The Constable appears to be thanking Billy. Leigh dimly understands. It must have been Billy who somehow raised the alarm. By rights he should have him clapped in irons, or flogged, or both, for such gross insubordination. But he doubts now he will do either. The flies have deserted him. Venus has completed her transit across the sun.

The Manchester Courier

2ⁿᵈ August 1804

MANCHESTER SAYS FAREWELL TO KING COTTON

Thousands of mourners lined Manchester's streets yesterday to say a poignant farewell to John Philips, known affectionately to all as King Cotton.

Warden of the Collegiate Church of St Mary, St Denys and St George, the Reverend Henry Sudlow, paid the illustrious textile manufacturer a glowing tribute in his eulogy, and the coffin was carried between a Guard of Honour comprising officers and men of the Manchester Volunteer Corps, under the command of the deceased's son, Major Leigh Philips, who was visibly grief-stricken, and who ordered a 21 gun salute to be fired after the ceremony in nearby St George's Fields.

The Manchester Herald

3ʳᵈ August 1804

COTTON MAGNATE'S SON ARRAIGNED

In a bizarre twist of fate, on the day immediately following the funeral of his father, the late, lamented John Philips, the eminent Cotton Magnate, Major Leigh Philips, Commanding Officer of the Manchester Volunteer Corps, was this day arraigned to appear before Magistrates at the Court Leet, together with Lieutenant-Colonel Joseph Hanson of the Salford & Stockport Independent

Rifles, for allegedly engaging in an unlawful duel on Kersal Moor on the morning of Thursday 1st August.

But for the vigilant civic duty of a passer-by, who alerted the local Constabulary, who in turn arrived promptly at the scene to break up proceedings, this newspaper might well have been reporting lamentable loss of life, rather than the potential loss of liberty.

Presiding over the case will be Mr Matthew Oldham, Justice of the Peace.

The Manchester Chronicle

6th August 1804

DEMISE OF A ONCE PROUD INSTITUTION

Following what was to some the surprisingly lenient sentence passed by the Court Leet on the two Officers who attempted to engage in mischief last week on Kersal Moor which, though claimed by the would-be duellists to be born out of their mutual desire to protect their honour as gentlemen, in fact served to bring nought but dishonour, to their families, themselves and their regiments.

Lieutenant-Colonel Joseph Hanson has been publicly cleared of all charges, being guilty, if we are to believe the verdict of Mr Matthew Oldham JP, of nothing more than responding in kind to threats made against his person and his standing. Major Philips, on the other hand, has been forced to suffer the additional public disgrace of having his attempt to wrestle command of the newly formed Combined Volunteer Militia Corps for Manchester, Salford and Stockport thwarted not once, not twice, but thrice.

Already lampooned in some of our rival organs of the press in the town, Major Philips has now been ignominiously driven to resigning his commission.

In an act of unparalleled loyalty, a further 53 of his fellow officers have resigned in sympathy – an action this paper believes does them far more credit than the cause which they have so espoused.

As a consequence the Manchester Volunteer Militia, formerly under the command of the eccentric but much-loved Major-General 'Spanking Roger' Aytoun, has been disbanded with immediate effect, a great loss to the safety and prestige of the town.

Lieutenant-Colonel Joseph Hanson, however, has extended the hand of friendship to all former members of the now defunct Manchester Regiment, saying there will always be a welcome for them in the new Combined Corps under his now uncontested command.

Dear Feyther,

I remember tha' sayin' when I were a nipper, "Beggars can't be choosers". Well – if wishes were horses, then beggars would ride.

I expect tha's heard t' news about Major Philips resignin' 'is commission? As a result, th' whole Regiment's been disbanded. We've been told we can either go over to t' Salford & Stockport Rifles, or we can be let go wi'out 'avin' to finish what we signed up for, an' collect a shillin' for our trouble.

So – I've took the shillin' and left. No more soldierin' for me. I've joined the Tuppenny Post. I start tomorrow. But it means I shall be coming back 'ome to thee an' Mother. I'll be wantin' me old bed back an' all, so tell that kid brother o' mine, 'e'll 'ave to get used to sharin' again!

Happy days!

Your son,
Billy

*

My Dear Sir,

I am instructed to write to you this day as Financial Executor of your late father's will, which we have been holding in trust here at Heywood's Bank.

We have been in possession of the original, safely deposited in our vault these past ten years, in addition to a codicil, which your father enjoined us to insert a few weeks before his most untimely death. Copies of both the original will, plus the codicil, were also kept in a locked drawer of your father's desk in his house on Lever's Row. Your mother has compared both the originals and their copies and declared them to be an accurate description of what she understood to be your father's last wishes in terms of the final disposal of his assets. Consequently I am writing to you today to confirm the details of these documents in so much as they appertain to you.

In summary, your father left the house on Lever's Row to your mother, plus a most generous annuity. The business – J&N Philips – has been left to your father's brother Nathaniel and subsequently his heirs on the sole condition that its name remains unchanged. In addition your father left instructions for a series of small bequests to various local charitable institutions.

The residue – amounting to the not inconsiderable sum of £20,000 – has been left in a trust bearing your name. The terms of this trust are further explained in the codicil, which states:

'To be left in full to my son, John Leigh Philips, who may dispose of it as he deems fit and proper. He may draw from it an annual allowance or take possession of it in its entirety. It is all one to me...'

The codicil then goes on to state:

'If my son elects to pursue the folly of seeking outright command of a combined new regiment of all previous Volunteer Corps within the Hundred of Salford, then this offer is null and void. If, however, he renounces this claim, or if he resigns his Commission and thereby leaves the military, then this will be sufficient to trigger the aforementioned clause...'

Now that it is public knowledge that you have resigned your position within the Manchester Volunteer Corps, and that the said regiment has been further disbanded, you are accordingly eligible to receive this bequest from your father's estate. All that remains is for you to advise us on whether you wish to withdraw the full amount, or arrange for us to put in place the necessary annuity.

We await your instructions.

Yours most diligently,
Benjamin Halsinger
Financial Executor
Heywood's Bank, King Street

Leigh declines the bequest.

To begin with, he merely writes a courteous reply to Mr Halsinger, thanking him for his pains and informing him, briefly, that he has no intention of claiming his inheritance. His army pension, coupled with his existing allowance, is more than sufficient for his modest needs. But when he learns that if he does not agree to accept the money, it must remain tied up and unavailable for use by anyone else, he relents. That would be a waste, he understands this, and so he agrees, reluctantly, to meet his mother to discuss the options, with Mr Halsinger as mediator between them, on the neutral territory that is Heywood's Bank.

"Think of it not as filial duty," she argues, "though that is reason enough. Regard it instead as an opportunity for you to contribute to your father's legacy."

"And how would I do that, Mother?" he responds. "We did not see each other these twenty years. I have been nothing but a source of disappointment to him."

"That is not true, Leigh. He always knew that one day you would..."

"What? Come to my senses?"

"That is not what I was going to say and well you know it."

"What then?"

"That one day you would..." She pauses over her next choice of words. "... leave the army."

"On a matter of principle, Mother. Not so that I could carry on Father's work in the factory."

"Of course not, dear. Nathaniel has all of that in hand. Besides, you never had the aptitude for it. Nor the interest."

"Thank you, Mother. At least we are being honest with one another."

"I see no point in being otherwise."

"Well," said Leigh, standing up and walking towards the window, "we seem to have reached some kind of impasse."

Benjamin's office was on the first floor. Leigh looked out onto the scene below him. It was past nine o'clock. The evening was already beginning to grow dark. A lamplighter was making his way down King Street with a long pole, the end of which was wrapped in sacking soaked in oil, pulsing with an amber flame. He reached up to ignite the various torches in their sconces one after the other, but even after every one of them had been lit, there was still barely enough light to see by, and what little there was danced and flickered, making more shadow than light, as the flames puttered and died. Little wonder so few people ventured out after dark unless they had to. Little wonder the streets felt so unsafe. The unwary pedestrian risked life and limb just by being abroad. If he wasn't assailed by footpads, he might just as easily step into a pot-hole and break his ankle, or, worse, fall headlong into an unguarded cellar where who knows what awaited him. He might even find himself tossed into one of Manchester's three rivers or one of their many tributaries, a bourn from which no traveller returns. And if *he* happened to be *she*, then the risks were even more hazardous and the consequences more dire. Under his command The Manchester Volunteers had frequently been asked to operate a Night Watch, but they could not be everywhere at once, and they too faced the same dangers as civilians. He had on more than one occasion urged the Court Leet to install proper street lighting.

"Gas," he would say. "There lies your solution. Manchester is a modern town and should adopt modern ways."

But the Court Leet would wring its collective hands. "Yes, yes, yes, Major. This is all very fine, but who is going to pay for it?"

Leigh is not normally a man to seize upon a business opportunity. His complete disinterest in such matters is well known. But this is something perhaps that might in some way mitigate the sense of failure which he wears now like a hair shirt. Shorn of his uniform he feels grey and anonymous. He can slip between the crowds in Manchester's teeming streets and squares and almost disappear completely. Gone are the days when he would enter such places on horseback like a bird of prey and clear them in a matter of minutes. Woe betide any stragglers who failed to get out of his path, for his sabre would flash in the sunlight, a razor-sharp beak impaling them as if they were no more than an unwary moth. Like Hezekiah, praying to the Lord in the temple, he would hear his voice ringing loudly in his head, proclaiming, "I will defend the city, to save it, for mine own sake, and for thee, my servant's..." Now he hears no such voices. He is becoming one of the stragglers, uncertain and confused. But perhaps, too, he is mutating, like the peppered moth. Soon he will blend into his surroundings so completely that he will become invisible.

But danger still lurks in these unlit streets, he knows, when night falls, which it is doing even as Leigh continues to look down upon them from the first floor window of Benjamin's office in Heywood's Bank. He becomes aware that he has been silent for several minutes. His mother and Mr Halsinger are watching him with concern. He must say something.

"Gas," he repeats. "Let us bring light into the darkness."

"Leigh," says his mother fearfully, "are you quite well?"

"No," he replies, wheeling round to face her. "I am not."

Mr Halsinger looks away from this sudden intimate encounter.

"My father was a successful man," says Leigh.

"He was," says his mother.

"He made a lot of money," continues Leigh. "He built a fine house. He employed thousands of labourers. He paid them the going rate, he didn't mistreat them, he arranged for them to be seen by a doctor if any suffered an injury, he was not against them attending evening classes at one of the town's many Chapels, even though he was not a chapelgoer himself, he was not against them forming Combinations or joining Benevolent Societies, as many of his fellow mill owners were and still are. But he did not walk among them. He did not visit the cellars and hovels where many of them are forced to live because it is all they can afford."

"He gave most generously to the Church," his mother retorts, beginning to bristle with indignation. "How can you say such things, Leigh? You did not know him. You took yourself away as soon as you turned twenty-one. Had you stayed you would have seen with your own eyes the good he did for people. But no – you were rash, impetuous, hot-headed. As you remain to this day. But your father kept faith in you, hoped right up until his dying breath that you would return to him, that the two of you might become reconciled."

"Yes. I see that now."

He turns back to the window. The street below is now completely fallen into shadow. Through the glass the darkness seems quite impenetrable. Benjamin lights the oil lamps in his office, then proceeds to pour his two guests a glass each of red wine.

"But none of this matters," says Leigh, "if we don't leave something behind us."

"Yes," says his mother, joining him at the window. "A legacy." She takes his arm and steers him back towards the desk, behind which Mr Halsinger is seated once more. "Sit down," she says. "Tell us what you mean."

He looks at them blankly.

"Gas," prompts Benjamin.

"My father was always interested in innovation, in installing the latest technical advances into his factories, to make them more efficient." He pauses, takes a sip of wine, looks back towards the darkness beyond the blindless window.

"Yes?" says his mother, trying to keep her son from becoming distracted again.

"I was in Preston last month," says Leigh, returning his gaze back to the room, "for the raising of a new regiment there, the Prince Regent's Own, the Lancashire Loyals. I'd been invited as a guest of their Colonel, representing the Manchester

Volunteers, before…" He swallows hard. "Before recent events came to a head as they did." He takes another sip of wine to compose himself. "I stayed for supper. Afterwards I was taken on a tour of the town. It was night. But all the streets were ablaze. Illuminated by gas. The first town anywhere in England outside of London to have such lighting. And I'm thinking, if they can do this in Preston, surely we can do the same here in Manchester?"

Benjamin leans forward eagerly in his chair.

"This bequest," says Leigh.

"Twenty thousand pounds," reiterates Benjamin, elucidating each syllable slowly and precisely.

"There's a patch of recently cleared ground on St Mary's Gate," continues Leigh.

"I know it," nods Benjamin.

"Extensive enough to accommodate a Gas Works, wouldn't you say?" asks Leigh.

"I would," agrees Benjamin.

"One that could supply the town's lighting needs well into the future?"

"If properly managed."

"I want nothing to do with any of that," adds Leigh hastily. "I am simply suggesting that this sum of money might be used to build and equip such a factory. I leave others to sort out the details."

"The bank could certainly help with those arrangements, put together a consortium, appoint a Board of Trustees, implement a Memorandum of Articles…"

"Yes, yes. Whatever you think necessary. All I would wish to do is provide you with the initial investment, then withdraw completely."

"I understand, sir."

"May I interpose something here?" said Mrs Philips.

Benjamin and Leigh both turn their attention towards her.

"The bequest is yours, Leigh, to dispose of as you see fit. I'm relieved that you are now proposing something so beneficial to the general safety and well-being of the whole town, rather than refusing to accept it, which was your position less than half an hour ago. I think it's a splendid idea, one which your father would doubtless have approved. Might I be so bold as to request that his name – the family name, Philips – may be attached to this new Gas Works, whoever may eventually end up running it..." She takes this opportunity to throw a less than gracious glance in the direction of Benjamin before adding, "... and reaping the financial rewards?"

Benjamin silently spreads his hands, a gesture he has inherited from his father, Reuben.

"A legacy," says Leigh, rising. Now that a decision has been made he is anxious to leave. The office feels suddenly airless and overheated.

"A legacy," echoes his mother. "We all of us desire to leave something behind, after we've gone."

How true, thinks Benjamin, escorting Leigh and Mrs Philips out of his office and down the marble staircase to the bank's now locked front door, to which he is entrusted with a satisfyingly heavy key, and which he now opens for them.

"Good night," he calls, closing and locking the door behind them. An unexpectedly excellent outcome, he reflects. He had feared the worst on seeing the former Major Philips's somewhat surly demeanour when he arrived, but now – a most promising investment opportunity. He decides he will stay longer to prepare the necessary documents. Strike while the iron is hot, as his grandfather might have said, back in the old country, where he was a blacksmith in a village in Austria, who, when he smote the molten metal with his hammer and watched the sparks fly up towards the sky, would dream of unimagined futures for his children after he had gone. Benjamin never knew his grandfather, but he has grown up hearing stories of him from Reuben, who will quote this proverb back to him, when he later relates the passage of events which have unfolded this evening.

Outside a carriage is waiting for Mrs Philips.

"Can we drop you?" she says to her son. "The streets feel so unsafe at nights. Once I could have walked them all blindfold. When I was a girl. But now every week brings new buildings. I no longer recognise where I am. These gas lights of yours will be such a boon."

"No, thank you, Mother. I prefer to walk."

"As you wish." She takes the cabman's hand as he helps her into the carriage. "Thank you," she adds, leaning out towards her son. "Your father would have been so proud."

Leigh finds he can barely speak in reply. His throat constricts. He manages a quick "Good night", then turns on his heels and strides away, the darkness swallowing him up almost at once.

He has done this for himself more than his father. He realises the truth of this with some bitterness as he makes his way through the labyrinth of unlit streets and alleyways of York Street, through Spring Gardens to Pall Mall, on towards Cross Street, skirting Acresfield to the newly cleared ground by St Mary's Gate, where he stops. It gapes, raw and open, bearing the scars of its recent ravaging, sore and bleeding, an empty mouth from whom all the teeth have been yanked and pulled, just a few charred and blackened stumps remaining. Already what few corners and holes and ruined piles of broken bricks that are left have been occupied by those in need of shelter. Another new, albeit temporary Hulk. But then all the Hulks are temporary, thinks Leigh. That is the nature of them.

He looks around him at this vast space, where a few small fires are now burning, and imagines the Gas Works which will soon begin to grow here, pushing up from the earth from the tuber he has just planted. He looks up at the night sky, a great tract of it revealed by the land clearance. He can see the wide upturned bowl of it, as opposed to the narrow rectangles afforded between closely pressed buildings elsewhere in the town, shutting off the light within their constricted sunless canyons, all of which will be illuminated in all their filth and feculence, once his lamps have been fitted and fed, budded and bloomed. Perhaps then the streets will be cleaned as well as lit. But he doubts this. The planets arch overhead. Saturn, Mars and Jupiter to the south. Mercury and Venus to the east. Will he still be able to see these too, once the gas lights flicker? Or will they diffuse the stark clarity of the night skies and turn his eyes earthwards, seeking instead some sequestered shadow that the new illumination cannot reach, a place he recognises that everybody needs at times. As *he* does. Especially tonight.

Leigh makes his way south along the Dean's Gate, passing Bridge Street and Brazenose Street, where in the bedroom at the top of the house he shares with his brother Benjamin, the now nineteen-year old Abner Halsinger trains his Dollond & Aitcheson telescope on the moons of Jupiter – Io, Callista, Gannymede and Europa – as Leigh walks, unseeing, beneath them, back to his rooms in Byrom Street.

He closes the door behind him, savouring the silence. He does not light a lamp or candle. Instead he lets his eyes adjust to the accustomed, familiar dark. It is like re-entering the safety of the womb.

He climbs the stairs, where the comfort of his collection awaits him.

> "Pure distilled water, rain, or spring water usually contain their due share of atmospheric air; if not, they acquire that share by agitation in it, and lose any other gas they may be impregnated with. It is remarkable, however, that water by stagnation, in certain circumstances, loses part or all of its oxygen, notwithstanding its constant exposure to the atmosphere. This I

have universally found to be the case in my large wooden pneumatic trough, containing roughly eight gallons, or one and one third cubic feet of water. Whenever this is replenished with tolerably pure rain water, it retains its share of atmospheric air, but in the process of time it becomes deficient of oxygen. In three months the whole surface has been covered with a pellicle, and no oxygenous gases whatever were found in the water. It was grown offensive..."

Here Mr Dalton removes his glasses and looks up from his papers towards his audience, who are all leaning as one forward in their seats.

"Though not extremely so." *He smiles kindly.*

*

Over the next ten years Leigh walked abroad in Manchester, if not invisible exactly, alone and unobserved. He watched the town continue to strive upwards and outwards towards the light, a light to which his decision had in part contributed, but which he carefully shunned, preferring instead to seek those corners which still lay in the shadows, where he might find hitherto undiscovered species of fly or moth or caterpillar, things which crawled among the filth and waste, where winged creatures might alight to lay their eggs, from which other forms might flutter up towards these blooms of light and there perish.

Except that they did not perish. They flourished. Each month brought him new discoveries, new variants, new hybrids. Manchester widened its long-armed embrace to gather in them all, swallowing then excreting them when it had sucked their nutrients dry. Angel Meadow had been consumed whole. No more Pleasure Gardens, no more balls or banquets, concerts or circuses. Now, more than a thousand warehouses, mills and factories squatted toad-like on what formerly were fields and orchards, slithering across them like the fat, bloated eels which the Irk had once been famous for. Now, Eugène Buret, the celebrated French philosopher in exile from his native land, along with various other fellow Jacobins and Huguenots, who had made their way towards this haven of non-conformity as inevitably as migrating birds seeking out a new habitat when their own familiar breeding grounds had been drained or swamped, ravaged or torched, described the river as 'the most disgusting it is possible to imagine, with houses rotting in humidity, hanging precariously over the water. I had always thought none could surpass the Bièvre, a tributary of the Seine, for filth and depravity, but that is a stream in Arcadia when compared to the stagnant waters of the Irk'.

But Leigh saw none of this. His own flight path was much narrower, following the same familiar trails each day, so that anyone paying close attention might have set their watch by him, his feet making a well-worn groove between his rooms in Byrom Street, along the Dean's Gate, past the mushrooming Gas Works that bore his family's name on St Mary's Gate, towards the now grassless Angel Meadow.

It was at the Gas Works where he first saw the brick sculptures. One morning, as was his custom, he was walking, head down in search of what new discovery he might make among the gutters and drains, when a shower of brick dust fell upon his head and shoulders like a russet snowfall. He looked up. Through the motes and particles descending all around him he discerned a man high up atop the factory roof. He was barechested, a hammer in one hand, a chisel in the other, and he was carving something. It took Leigh quite some while to work out what it was until finally he realised, the abstract, geometric shapes coalescing to form a scholarly-looking man, with spectacles, a long thin pipette held to his lips, through which he was drawing gas from a marsh below him...

Now that he had seen one, he began to notice other similar sculptures, carved into the faiences of several of the forest of new buildings sprouting everywhere across the town – not just mills or factories, but banks, shops, houses. He saw a pair of compasses over a surveyor's office, scales balanced with coins at a money lender's, a shoe stretched over a last at a cobbler's, a pair of shears and a tape measure at a tailor's. He saw weavers, miners, coopers and wheelwrights, farriers, foundrymen, lacemakers and lamplighters. Lights were being lit all across the town.

One afternoon, while returning from one of his forays in search of new specimens, he found himself face to face with a young man in the smart new uniform of a postal worker, who stopped dead in his tracks and saluted him. The buried instinct surfaced immediately.

"At ease, soldier," he said without even thinking. Then, when the young man still did not move, he added, "Do I know you?"

"Yes, sir," said the man. "At least I hope so, sir. I'm Billy, sir. Billy Robinson. I was your batman, sir."

"Billy – yes... I remember you now. You're doing well, I see."

"Thank you, sir. I just changed one uniform for another, sir."

"So I observe. And very smart you look too."

Leigh made to pass the boy by when Billy stepped once more in front of him. He opened his mouth to speak but found he could barely stammer.

"I'm sorry, sir."

"Sorry? What for?"

"It were me, sir," said Billy. Then it all tumbled out in a rush. "I told t' Constables, about you an' Colonel Hanson, that you were meeting for a duel. I couldn't bear t' thought of one or both o' you getting' killed. It were wrong of me, sir. I know that now. I never meant for thee to leave t' regiment, sir. There – I've said it."

Leigh looked at the frightened young boy trembling before him. "You did the right thing," he said at last. "I see that now. Though at the time I saw only betrayal. I don't mean from you, Billy, but everyone. I've had plenty of time to reflect on that since." He held up the glass jar he had been carrying, in which the specimens he had collected that day – the flies and moths and beetles – still buzzed and fluttered and crawled, searching for a way out. "Now," he continued, "I prefer solitude."

"Yes, sir."

"Good afternoon, Billy. You've done well for yourself. Your father must be proud."

"Yes, sir. Thank you, sir."

Billy watched the former Major Philips stride away in the direction of the Dean's Gate, until he almost disappeared completely from view. On an impulse he decided to follow him. He remained far enough behind him so that he would not be observed until he saw the Major turn off into Byrom Street. He waited on the corner, noted the number on the door of the house he had entered, and promised himself to keep an eye out for him whenever he could. Something about the retired soldier's demeanour had troubled him.

In fact that proved easier than Billy could have imagined. Over the next few months Leigh embarked upon a regular correspondence with William Roscoe, a fellow entomologist in Liverpool. He would take these letters to the newly opened Post Office in Spring Gardens, where he would deliver them by hand to Billy, entrusting him to make sure they caught the earliest Mail Coach to Liverpool, while Billy, whenever he could, would personally post the replies through Leigh's front door on Byrom Street.

Sir,

It is some years since I was an occasional attender at meetings of the celebrated Roscoe Circle with you and your associates (Messrs Carey, Currie and Daulby) in Liverpool. My military duties prevented me from participating in your discussions as frequently as I would have preferred. Recent circumstances, however, have rendered it possible for me to return to the fold, if that is something that you and your members would welcome.

I have, I believe, stumbled upon a fascinating discovery – a new species of moth, which appears to be altering its form, mutating from its customary, known manifestation into something quite other. I refer to the white peppered moth.

I would welcome an invitation to present my findings to your members at the earliest opportunity.

I remain, Sir,

Your most humble and obedient servant,
Leigh Philips Esq.

My Dear Mr Philips,
I thank you for your recent communication, which I duly read out to our meeting of the Circle last month.

I am bound to report that its contents produced something of a furore here among our members. What you appear to be suggesting – that one distinct species might somehow evolve into another – goes against all known science. What is worse, it goes against the immutable laws of the universe, as set down in the Great Chain of Being, whereby all living things have their allotted space in the hierarchy, with God and the Angels at the top and dirt at the bottom. Just as rocks never turn into flowers, nor worms into lions, so one type of moth may not transform into another.

I refer you to Professor Carl Linnaeus's 'Systema Naturae', in which the celebrated taxonomist divides the physical components of the world into three kingdoms of plants, minerals and animals. Here at the Circle we had the gross misfortune to be forced to undergo the heretical ravings of one Jean-Baptiste Lamarck, a self-appointed French Radical, who attempted to set forth the preposterous notion of life consisting of a progression *of forms, striving from the simplest of creatures towards greater complexity. He cited the work of his countryman Henri Mari Ducrotay de Blainville, an apparently eminent, though to my mind discredited, anatomist and zoologist as further proof of his thesis for a so-called transmutation of species, not unlike what you appear to be suggesting.*

We soon sent him packing, let me tell you. Why, such an idea is little more than alchemy, a way of thinking that has long been dismissed as belonging in the realms of fantasy, whose followers mistakenly hold the belief that, since all beings are linked into the Great Chain, so that there is a fundamental unity of all matter, then it somehow must follow that transformation from one link in the chain to another might also be possible. That way madness lies, the doomed search for that fabled philosopher's stone, which might enable its discoverer to turn base metal into gold. The reason that nobody has ever achieved such a feat is for the simple reason that it is not scientifically possible and goes against all known Laws of Nature.

No, Mr Philips. I regret to inform you that, if you persist in clinging to this assertion that you have identified a species of moth which is contradicting these inviolable laws, then you will not be welcome here at the Circle which bears my name as its soubriquet. I suggest to you, Sir, that what you have stumbled across, as you so aptly have stated, is in fact merely a pre-existing species you yourself have not previously encountered. If you would like to bring one along to our monthly meetings for the purpose merely of identification, then I am certain one of our members may well be able to assist you.

Respectfully yours, Sir

William Roscoe
Roscoe Circle
Croxteth Hall
Liverpool

Billy delivers letters to his old Major for almost a decade. As regularly as clockwork, week after week, month after month, year after year. So that when one week the Major does not appear at the counter in Spring Gardens, Billy is surprised, but not especially concerned. But when that week transforms into a month, he begins to grow anxious. He has in the interim continued to post Leigh's daily correspondence through his door in Byrom Street. The following day, therefore, he resolves to investigate further.

Upon arrival at the address, instead of merely depositing the mail through the letter box, he decides to knock. No answer. He knocks again. Still no answer. He lowers himself down to peep through. He lifts the flap. He espies a near mountain of uncollected, unopened mail piled against the door. He looks around. He sees a Constable at the corner of the street. He halloos him. Each recognises the status bestowed upon them by the wearing of their respective uniforms and greets the other with an unspoken acknowledgement of this fact. Billy explains his predicament. The Constable frowns. He strokes his chin.

"A regular customer?" he says.

"As clockwork," replies Billy.

"Hmm…" The Constable deliberates further.

"He may be ill," suggests Billy.

"Indeed he may," concurs the Constable. "Right," he says at last, after another prolonged pause. "We'll have to break in. There's nothing else for it."

The Constable is a burly fellow. The contrast between him and Billy, who is as thin as a rail, could not be more pronounced. With a few concerted shoulder charges, the door gives way and the two of them tumble into the hallway, wading through the drift of unopened envelopes as if plunging through mud in the marshes of an estuary.

They realise at once that something is amiss. It is Billy who notices it first. A faint and distant drone which, once they have heard it, grows ever louder and increasingly more insistent. It emanates from upstairs and, with it, the unmistakable, sickly-sweet smell of death.

"Fetch a Doctor," says Billy, suddenly taking charge.

The Constable, despite his normally ruddy complexion, has grown visibly pale. He is only too happy to oblige. He holds a hand to his mouth and lurches back outside into the street, where he gulps a lungful of the less-contaminated air there, then runs off in search of medical assistance.

Billy ventures up the stairs slowly and deliberately, two steps at a time, until he reaches the door of what he presumes is his former Major's study. Carefully he turns the polished brass handle. The noise grows louder. The smell intensifies. He inches open the door and is at once engulfed in a nightmare of fly. A thick, impenetrable cloud of them fills the room. Lowering his head, covering his face with his sleeve, he battles his way towards the sealed window at the far side of the room. In order to open it, he must lower the arm that is protecting his face. At once the flies are everywhere. In his eyes, his nostrils, his mouth, his hair. The window is stiff and at first will not budge. Eventually, after what seems like minutes, Billy manages to force it open. Immediately the flies begin to surge through it, dispersing in their thousands across Manchester. Billy flaps at them wildly, until only a smaller, more manageable number remain. These, for the most part, home in on the prostrate body of Leigh, who lies on his back in the centre of the room. His body stiff, his limbs splayed awkwardly. His face, what is left of it, still wears the rictus of the seizure which must have struck him first.

Billy forces the remaining flies from the body until finally all have departed and the only sound to break the silence that has descended like a pall upon the scene is that of his own laboured breathing, which gradually he is able to bring under control. He looks about the wreckage of the room. It would appear that Leigh had set up a *vivarium* once more. Billy observes the glass cabinets, with their doors ajar by only a crack, but evidently enough. There are display cases everywhere, strewn across the floor, but their contents still intact. Three large mahogany cupboards line one wall, inside which are drawer upon drawer of further specimens, thousands of them, each meticulously labelled and pinned to a board. On Leigh's desk is an unfinished letter. A pen still lies, diagonally straddling a piece of paper, where Leigh must have dropped it before he fell, a spider trail of ink threading down the page.

"I hereby leave my Cabinets of Curiosities to the People of Manchester..."

Nothing else is written. No signature, no seal, no mark.

Billy hopes that an undertaker may be found, to clean Leigh's broken body, to embalm the skin, drain the excess fluid, dress him in his old army uniform of redcoat jacket and white trousers, which he is sure must be hanging in a wardrobe somewhere, place him in a coffin and lay him to rest, where members of his old regiment may come to view him, pay their last respects, then bury him deep in the earth, place a headstone to mark his grave, chiselled by some skilful stonemason, the man who carves the brick sculptures perhaps, which Leigh so admired, stating his name, his family, his profession, just as if he too were a specimen in his Cabinet of Curiosities.

Just before he turns to leave, Billy notices one case that is placed apart, separate from the rest. In it is what appears to be a collection of the same moth, row upon row of them, the only thing distinguishing them, one from another, being the minute gradations of colour, from black through grey to white. Beneath each one is a label, handwritten in immaculate copper plate, bearing the identical classification:

"Biston betularia carbonaria – the black-bodied peppered moth."

13

29th September – Michaelmas

Essay No. 3

Mr Dalton continues.

"It must be understood that quantities of gas are to be measured at the pressure and temperature with which the impregnation is effected…"

*

In all but one aspect of his life Matthew was content with his lot.

He had successfully expanded his business. His partnership with the Grant Brothers had flourished to the mutual advantage and benefit of all, though trade between them was mostly conducted these days through Mr Laurence Peel, Sir Robert Parsley's nephew, who had been present on Holcombe Hill when Mr Sadler's balloon had concluded its unseen and unceremonious final landing. He was just three years older than Matthew and they discovered they had much in common.

When they first met, it was in the front office of his family's mill in Ramsbottom. Laurence was sitting behind a desk, a large grey cat purring noisily on his lap, who regarded Matthew with a certain disdainful reproach.

"You must be Oldham," enquired Laurence, not getting up. He stretched out his own paw above that of the cat, which Matthew took in his own. It had long nails, Matthew noted, which, unlike the cat's, could not be retracted by their owner, so that they dug sharply into his palm.

"If we're to do business with each other, I think we might dispense with the formalities," he said. "Please – call me Matthew."

"As you wish," said Laurence, tipping the cat from off his lap, then brushing away some of the fine grey hairs that lingered on his maroon-coloured trousers. "The Brothers Grant said you might call."

"Which one?"

"Does it matter?" asked Laurence. "Personally I can never tell them apart, the way they finish each other's sentences."

Matthew smiled at the memory.

"Still, they have their uses. They expand the business nicely, which leaves the rest of the family more time for what really matters."

Which is?"

"Politics, my dear boy. Politics. It's Westminster wields the power."

"If one is lucky enough to live somewhere that has an MP," remarked Matthew, wondering how his new acquaintance might reply to such a potentially provoking response.

Laurence turned his most winning cat-like smile upon Matthew. "Yes, of course. I was forgetting. Manchester does not have the same advantages that we enjoy here in Lancashire. Thomas Stanley..." He pauses, observing the fleeting frown creasing Matthew's brow. "Our present incumbent. A Whig, but not a bad old stick for all that. He knows which side his bread is buttered, and he has proven a good friend to the Mill Owners. It pays to have a tame poodle in the House."

"So I have heard. Don't get me wrong. I don't think Manchester's ready yet for its own representation. Not in my personal opinion at any rate. If all those thousands of men received a vote, the Lord alone knows what damage they might do by trying to impose all manner of so-called reforms. No, I believe we are much better off being completely unregulated, allowing men of vision like..."

"Like you, Matthew?" smiled Laurence, arching one eyebrow.

"People like us, I was going to say, who see an opportunity, then seize it."

"Bravo."

"All I meant was, it must be – what is the word? – advantageous to have access to a seat at the top table?"

Laurence nodded briskly. "The rest of the country must satisfy itself with the scraps." He then bent down to pick up the cat once more, who had begun to wind itself insinuatingly between his legs. "Like you, Smokey, my sweet."

"Smokey?" asked Matthew.

"For his colour. Isn't it obvious?"

"Yes, of course. It's just that..."

"What?"

"I had a cat called Smokey once."

"Indeed? It seems we have more in common by the minute."

"He leapt into a hot air balloon which was taking off from Haworth's Gardens almost twenty years ago."

"Curiouser and curiouser. I found your cat. He leapt straight into my arms when the balloon landed on my father's estate and never left my side from that day on. This," he said, holding out the cat for Matthew to take, "must be your Smokey's great-great-grandson."

Matthew took hold of the cat and allowed it time to wriggle and settle and accustom himself to being carried by a complete stranger. It took less than a few seconds.

"Somebody's a natural," sneered Laurence. "You'll be making me jealous."

Memories from when he lost his cat flooded through him, a pain in truth he had not felt quite so keenly since. Except perhaps when Fanny left to marry Zachary. But that was more about jealousy too.

"No, no, no," he said, in a lame attempt to pacify, "he's yours." And he handed the cat back to Laurence. Smokey watched with what could only be interpreted as an amused grin, as the two young men continued to spar guardedly with one another, bearing allegiance only to the one who would feed him next.

"Come," said Laurence, now adopting a more businesslike tone, "let me show you around. There's much to see."

"I've no doubt."

From the sanctuary of the office they made their way towards the factory floor. First on the agenda was the Peele Coat of Arms, which Laurence languidly pointed out.

"Commissioned by my father. A lion holding a shuttle. Over an insignia of just a single word – *Industria* – with his personal motto inscribed underneath: '*A man, barring accidents, might be whoever he choose'*."

"What happened to the last 'e'?" asked Matthew. "You spell your name without it now."

"That was my father's decision too." Laurence placed his thumbs behind the lapels of his jacket and struck up a pose which Matthew assumed was meant to be an imitation of the *pater familias*. "Ay, lad," he said, at once adopting a broader Lancashire accent, "I see no use for owt as 'as no use. It adds nowt to 'ow tha' speaks it, so best get rid."

The two young men laughed together at this joke at the older man's expense. But if Laurence was expecting a reciprocal confidence to be shared with Matthew offering a similarly droll impersonation of Mr Oldham Snr, he was to be disappointed. Instead Matthew's attention was caught by a set of old wooden printing blocks mounted in a glass case on the wall below the coat of arms.

"What are these?" he asked.

"Yes. Interesting that they should catch your eye," replied Laurence. "I suppose you might say that this is where the Peel Empire began. Back in Oswaldtwistle, where my father was born, in a house on Fish Lane. He started experimenting with them, using them to print directly onto wool. My wife's brother, William Haworth – Uncle Willy – was just returning from an apprenticeship to a calico printer in London, and the pair decided to set up in business together. They borrowed money from another William – Yates – the landlord of the local public house and formed Haworth, Peel & Yates. That was back in 1750. They had a factory in Blackburn and a warehouse in Manchester. And so it began. From tiny acorns do mighty oaks grow, as they say. Now we have twenty-three factories and more than a dozen warehouses." He waved a hand expansively. "But are you sure you want to hear all this? It's ancient history."

Matthew assured him that he did. His own lineage went back just as far, with his father beginning from nothing in a way not dissimilar to Laurence's father, the difference between them now being that, whereas Haworth, Peel & Yates had grown into a mighty empire, Oldham & Son remained quite small, specialising in a single product – felt – and its various uses. But Matthew was keen to change that and he saw this meeting with Laurence as another step along that road, the first having been the association he had already formed with the Brothers Grant, who had paved the way for this meeting today. Oiling the cogs. Smoothing the wheels. He took a coin from out of his trouser pocket and unthinkingly began to turn it over rapidly between his fingers along the back of his hand. His new acquaintance observed this with an amused detachment. Back and forth, back and forth.

"Very well," continued Laurence. "If you're sure. In which case, no tour would be complete without you seeing this." He led Matthew a little way along the corridor from the wooden blocks to a separate glass case, behind which sat a sprig of dried parsley flanked either side by a pewter plate and a blue apothecary's bottle containing Goulard's Powder, an acetate of lead used as an early mordant to fix dyes in Laurence's father's early experiments.

"Rumour has it," explained Laurence in a rather bored voice, as if this was something he had had to repeat many times, "that my older sister Nancy, when she was a girl, brought in some parsley she had picked and begged my father to use it as a pattern. To please her – for she's always been such a Daddy's girl, still is actually – he etched it onto a pewter plate, which he then transferred to a piece of cloth, and which was then finished with an iron by Mrs Milton, our cook. My father then produced a run of it on calico, using those same wooden blocks in the display case there, and it became an instant success with customers, who loved it. It's still one of our most popular designs today."

"And hence your father came by his nickname of Parsley Peel?" quipped Matthew.

"Quite. Though I think that might have been Mr Yates's idea. Being a publican he always had a knack for novel ways to attract new customers."

"So the story about your sister rushing in from the fields with that sprig of fresh parsley might all be a fabrication?"

Laurence shrugged. "Who knows? And frankly, who cares? What people want is something they can relate to."

"And aspire to, surely?"

"Meaning?"

"The happy family gathered around the hearth. The homespun cottage industry. Isn't that why there are still so many handloom weavers around today?"

"Whom my father used almost exclusively to begin with."

"The Domestic System."

"Putting out material to rural producers who chiefly work from home."

"And in some cases put out to others in turn."

"It certainly reduces overheads – "

"– specifically labour costs…"

"But in the end it remains just that – a cottage industry. If you want to expand, spin more and more finished bolts of cloth, distribute those to wider and bigger markets, you have to mechanise."

"To meet the growing demand…"

"A demand you help to create…"

"… by flooding the market with ever increasing supplies…"

"Reducing the price…"

"But growing the profits…"

"Increasing production…"

"At the same time reducing wages…"

"Thereby making handloom weaving no longer viable."

"The economics of scale…"

The two men regarded each other with growing respect and admiration, though still through the prism of mutual suspicion.

"But how did your father avoid trouble?" asked Matthew after a brief pause.

"Trouble?" replied Laurence, eyeing his visitor closely once more.

"Strikes? Machine-wreckers?"

Laurence waved away the remark dismissively.

"Follow me," he said, and led Matthew through a set of double doors, which led directly onto the factory floor.

The noise was deafening. The rumbling of the powered looms and other machines that dealt with all the different processes necessary for the production of finished cloth thundered through the shed, which made the entire building shake, a vibration Matthew was aware of instantly. It was nothing he had not witnessed or experienced before, though admittedly in a much smaller way in his own felt factory in Manchester, but here the scale was enormous. It quite literally took his breath away. It reminded him of nothing less than a cathedral, with huge timbers supporting a magnificently vaulted ceiling. Motes of dust and cotton fibres floated in the air, caught in hard-edged shafts of light which poured in through the factory's windows, stained with smoke and grime, rather than angels or saints. Matthew watched the familiar pantomime of workers communicating through signs and gestures, mouthing their words with exaggerated slowness, their voices redundant beneath the machines' mighty roar. It was a vision which never failed to fill him with awe. Some, he knew, had compared the scene to Dante's inferno, but for him the rhythmical push and pull of the looms, the unstoppable sliding of the shuttles, the tightening warp and weft of it all, resembled more closely Michaelangelo's painting in the Sistine Chapel, which of course Matthew had never visited, but copies of which he had seen in the library of the *Lit & Phil*. The way it depicted the New Covenant through Christ, with all of humanity labouring under one roof towards salvation, a single cause shared by all, through a lineage of ancestors, towards a common good. The whole enterprise seemed to Matthew to be one harmonious dance, performed to the music of, if not the spheres, then a chorus of Leibnitz Wheels, stepped cylinders with sets of teeth of incremental lengths, turning to the relentless beat of hundreds of mechanical counting machines, each of them calculating the unstoppable flow of pounds, shillings and pence, which seemed, as Matthew looked about him now, to be transmuting those motes of dust and cotton fibres falling all around him into swirling coins of silver and gold, like benisons.

"We've had our teething problems, I'll admit," said Laurence, trying to make himself heard above the din.

"Such as?"

"My father has always liked tinkering. He worked with his neighbour James Hargreaves to come up with a carding machine but decided against it, urging instead for something altogether more radical. Hargreaves came up with the Spinning Jenny. My father saw at once that this had the chance to change everything. He installed them in his Stubbins factory, where they were blamed for job losses. The mill became a target for riots. Machines were broken. My father, far from being put off by such attacks, saw them as fortuitous. People have always been fearful of progress, of change. If these new innovations sparked so much hostility and rage, it could only mean one thing. They represented the face of the future. And so it proved. My father left Stubbins and set up here instead."

Matthew nodded. "My own father held a similar view. 'You can't turn back the clock,' he'd say, and he'd hold his pocket watch up to my ear. 'Tick, tock. Tick, tock. On and on it goes, never stopping.' 'But don't you have to wind it up?' I'd ask him. 'Someone has to, Matthew,' he'd answer, 'you're right, and that will fall to you in time. Make sure then that you don't over wind it.' 'Why not?' I'd ask again. 'Because,' he'd reply, 'you might break the watch, and then what would we do? We wouldn't know where we were – yesterday, today, tomorrow – they'd all merge into one, and we'd all become lost. People like to know where they are – it's eight o'clock on a Monday morning and I should be at work – everyone where they should be at exactly the time they are meant, like now. That's what gives us purpose, that's what gives us hope.' 'Hope? Like Pandora's Box?' 'Yes, Matthew, exactly like that. I have always felt ambivalent about that story. When the Gods presented Epimetheus with a gift in the form of a beautiful maiden, Pandora, they did so as an act of revenge, to get back at his brother, Prometheus, for stealing fire from them. Epimetheus had a jar, which he kept sealed at all times, for it contained all the sicknesses and evils of the world. He trusted Pandora with keeping it safe, making her promise never, under any circumstances, to open it. I've always thought it wrong that we should criticise Pandora for breaking her word, for who among us could resist such a temptation? Curiosity kills the cat, they say. But a cat has nine lives and curiosity is what enables us to make new discoveries. That is why I like the ending of the story so much more. Realising what she's done, Pandora shuts the jar as quickly as she can, though not before all the evils it contained have escaped, but she manages to keep one small thing inside, scratching at the underside of the lid. Hope. Always there, waiting to be released, when we have need of her most... Now, where should *you* be today?' 'School,' I'd answer gloomily. 'Quite right,' he'd say again, 'so hurry up and get ready. You don't want to be late.' 'What about early?' 'Ah well, now that's another matter entirely. The early bird catches the worm, Matthew. He who is up with the lark will see the sunrise'."

"My father's sentiments exactly," interrupted Laurence, who had neither time nor patience for such wistful reminiscing. "Get up early to steal the march. But I like your Pandora story nevertheless. That's how my father has managed to steal that march on all his competitors. Create a sense of loyalty and belonging. We all of us like to feel we belong somewhere. That's why my father came up with the idea of the factory as family, the mill as model village."

"The Tally System."

"Precisely. If you work for my father, you must live in one of the houses he provides for you, for which the rent is deducted from your wages at source, so in effect you feel like you are paying no rent at all."

"Your wages then come in the form of tallies..."

"... which you can use in the shop and pub that my father has also provided."

"Yes. The Grant Brothers explained this to me. I've already begun implementing it."

"I'm delighted to hear it. The Body is less likely to try and chop off the Head if it knows it needs it to provide it with sustenance."

Matthew recognised the allusion – not its original source – but in how it applied to him also. "And so I will continue to provide you with more felt..."

"... for which we will continue to pay you a more than fair price..."

"... and which you will continue to turn into all manner of products..."

"... from which we will continue to sell at a profit..."

"... which in turn will continue to reward us both for our initial investments."

"So indeed we hope."

"Hope? I believe we shall continue to keep *her* tightly sealed in her jar until the time when she is needed. No – I prefer the word 'trust'."

"Quite. Hope is for fools. Let us keep that jar not only sealed but locked away in a deep, dark place. Wise men have no need of her."

"Nor her sisters Faith and Charity?"

"On the contrary, they continue to serve our noble enterprise. It is to them we may entrust the key to where Hope must languish."

The two men shook hands. Their business was concluded. They each knew they would not meet again. There would be no need. For they would each see the shadow of the other, lurking beside them when they looked in the mirror each morning."

Smokey's descendant reappeared to wind itself between them, waiting to see which of them would acknowledge him first.

At that moment they were interrupted by a small boy careering headlong towards them. He butted Laurence in the stomach, then lunged for the cat, who rewarded him with a hiss and a scratch.

"Who's this?" asked an amused Matthew.

"My nephew," replied Laurence, looking distinctly displeased. "My older brother Robert's boy. Also called Robert. My father's first grandchild, on whom he dotes."

"Naturally."

"Possibly. But he's disgustingly spoiled, aren't you, Bobby?"

"I don't know what you mean, Uncle." He turned abruptly towards Matthew. "Who are you?"

"Don't be so impertinent, Bobby. This is Mr Oldham, a business associate of mine."

"How do you do? I suppose you're in textiles too?"

"I am, yes."

"How boring."

"It can be, but it has its rewards. What would *you* like to be when you're older?"

"Prime Minister."

"Indeed?" chuckled Matthew, as the young boy glowered back at him. "And why is that?"

"Then I wouldn't always have to do what I'm told. I could tell everyone else what to do instead."

He then kicked the shins of both gentlemen, picked up the protesting cat and ran back outside.

*

Matthew, following the example suggested to him by the Grant Brothers, had rapidly built more than a hundred houses along the banks of the River Irk, each floor of which had been converted into single roomed apartments to accommodate his employees, which now numbered in excess of two thousand souls. They paid him the going rate for these basic, somewhat less-than-salubrious dwellings, several of which lay below the level of the river, which flooded frequently. The lodgings may have been cheap, but labour was cheaper, and, if anyone thought to complain, there was always a steady stream of replacements to be found, as more and more people flowed into Manchester to provide human fodder for the always hungry factories. More than a hundred new cotton mills had sprouted across Angel Meadow and Ancoats in the last five years. The trees and orchards which had flourished there for centuries had been swept away, to be replaced by a forest of brick chimneys, every one of which belched out black smoke night and day. Even where he resided himself, on Newton Lane, now renamed Oldham Street in honour of his late father, Matthew could not escape the intrusion of their constant exhumations – cleaning their grime from the more than twelve tall windows of his grand house proved the bane of his housekeeper Mrs Crinkle's life, so much so that only last week she had handed in her notice and left in high dudgeon – but Matthew paid such inconveniences no heed. He could, as so many of his associates did, have easily removed himself to the outer, greener pastures of Ardwick, Hulme or Chorlton-on-Medlock, but he preferred the hustle and bustle of life in Manchester's centre. More than eighteen hundred warehouses for the storage of the thousands of tons of textiles the town produced each year now mushroomed into the air, each of them jostling its neighbour in the rough and tumble of trade. Matthew had sharp elbows and he liked to be at the heart of things, and so he preferred to stay right where he was.

He was not therefore an entirely absent landlord. Cellars were emptied annually. Sackcloth was supplied where glass was broken. Rat catchers were deployed when the yards became overrun. A shop sold basic provisions at which workers and their families could purchase goods with the tallies which formed part of the wages, the proceeds of which contributed nicely towards the erection of more rows of tenements as and when Matthew's continuing expansion required. Additionally, taking his lead from Laurence's elder brother Sir Robert, now Baronet of Drayton, who had introduced the *Health & Morals of Apprentices Act* just two years before, which limited the number of hours children could work in a single day to just twelve and obliged mill owners to provide some form of schooling, he arranged for a classroom to be built adjoining the recently opened brick church of St Michael's & All Angels, where employees from his felt factory might attend on their evenings off and Sundays in order to learn to read and write. He considered himself a fair-minded, enlightened and philanthropic employer.

The town was like one enormous hive, he realised, with his labourers the worker bees, toiling ceaselessly to produce his honey. But hives needed a queen, and this was the aspect of his life which would surface to torment Matthew in the darker reaches of the night, when sleep would elude him. He had no queen.

He was still only twenty-seven, young still, but old enough to recognise that most men his age had already tasted of that fruit, some were married already, many more engaged. No longer having parents, he had become a magnet for several of the wives of his older colleagues in the Exchange, or the Court Leet, who had taken it upon themselves to introduce him to various eligible unmarried daughters of the wealthier merchant families, seating him next to a seemingly endless parade of Penelopes, Emmas, Janes or Elizabeths, until they had all merged into one. He was a poor conversationalist when the topic strayed from business, he could not dance, speak prettily, sing or play a musical instrument. He pursued no hobbies, read no books, did not attend the theatre. Neither did he shoot, hunt, fish or ride. He did not drink – in that he had inherited his parents' Methodist temperance – he did not gamble, nor – crucially – did he womanise. It would not be long, therefore, before the latest Penelope, Emma, Jane or Elizabeth would grow bored and begin to look elsewhere around the room, after which it would not be long either before other eager drones began to buzz around her, and Matthew could breathe a sigh of relief. He would turn his attention back to the more fascinating topic of balance sheets, over which he liked to pore, adding ever more items to the column marked 'profit', barely troubling himself with entering anything into that marked 'loss'.

And yet he was aware that, in the fullness of time, this was something he would need to address. He recalled overhearing one of the mothers of yet another Penelope he had failed to impress whispering behind her gloved hands to her other female confidantes, who all observed him with puzzled curiosity over their fans that, "It is a truth universally acknowledged, that a single man in possession of a good fortune, must be in want of a wife", each of them tutting and shaking their heads. He assumed this was from something they had all recently read.

The more concerning aspect for Matthew lay in the knowledge he had gleaned of the hierarchies of the hive from a talk given only the previous month at the *Lit & Phil*, where he had learned of the somewhat precarious existence of the male drones. When a virgin queen flies to a site where male drones may be waiting, she will mate with several while in flight. The male will mount the queen, insert his *endophallus* and ejaculate his sperm. Immediately after ejaculation, the male will pull away from the queen, his *endophallus* ripped from his body, tearing open his abdomen, after which death is instantaneous.

Matthew tried to suppress such violent thoughts, but the sight of a new potential queen fluttering beside him at a supper party would reawaken them, and once again he would become tongue-tied until she had flown off in search of more attentive company.

Three years before, Matthew was appointed as a Justice of the Peace, by no means the youngest in Manchester's history, but the youngest currently, a position secured for him through the influence of Sir Robert Hibbert III who, since they had spoken after Mr Dalton's lecture on colour blindness, had rather taken him under his wing.

"Damn it, man," he had said when Matthew suggested he might not be ready for such a responsibility at just twenty-four years. "If you're good enough, you're old enough. Pitt was Prime Minister at your age, my boy. Time and tide, what?"

And so it proved. In less than three years he had tried dozens of cases – minor felonies and misdemeanours in the main – and he had quickly established a reputation for a rigorous application of the finer points of the law. He did not shy away from administering harsh sentences when the seriousness of the offence merited it – he had on five occasions issued the death penalty, not one of these causing him to lose a moment's sleep – but he would also acquit those accused if he felt circumstances had prevailed against them. As such, those who found themselves standing before him knew what to expect. He was tough but fair and always sober.

It is the first day of the Michaelmas Sessions at the Court Leet, 1802. Matthew presides at the Bench.

After the customary parade of waifs and strays, rogues and vagabonds, thieves and footpads, molls and mendicants, jilts and jays, tricksters and toms, all of whom Matthew has dealt with in his usual brisk manner, scrupulously issuing sentences neither too lenient nor too excessive, each according to the strictures imposed upon by him by the guidelines appertaining to each respective offence, it comes as something of a surprise to find standing before him a gentleman of middle years, both well-spoken and well-dressed, though in respect of the latter there is irrefutable evidence of someone who had once known better times, but who has recently embarked upon a somewhat rapid fall from grace. The cuffs and collar of his shirt are frayed, his jacket is now patched and threadbare at the elbows, his trousers creased, his boots worn, and his cravat unfashionable.

"Name?" demands Matthew, addressing the Court Leet's Clerk, rather than the gentleman directly.

"Allen," replies the Clerk, checking against a list. "Courtenay."

"*Sir* Courtenay," corrects the gentleman with a certain put-upon fastidiousness.

Matthew looks up from where he has been writing the details on the papers before him on the desk. The accused is staring directly at him. Matthew sets down his quill and stares back. He observes a face that bears all too clearly the signs of a dissolute life. A red pigment suffuses the skin, which is bloated and sweating. Broken veins score his cheeks and nose. His eyes are bloodshot. His hands cannot betray a slight tremor, no matter how tightly they grip the rail behind which he now stands. Yet despite all of these failings he remains resolutely intransigent and unapologetic in his bearing, an attitude which Matthew finds himself forced to admire. This man knows his number is up but he refuses to yield. He will not be cowed. Not even when Matthew proceeds to interrogate him. Would *he*, he wonders, be so defiant in the face of such public humiliation? But he dismisses such thoughts at once as idle, wasteful speculation. He would never allow himself to fall so low.

"An inherited title," he asks, "or one awarded on individual merit?"

"Inherited," replies Courtenay tersely.

"From your father?"

"And his before him."

"Indeed?"

"We can trace our lineage back to the Domesday Book."

Matthew reacts inwardly to this. The sense of entitlement displayed in such sentiments appals him. As if the gift of a six hundred-year-old name releases people from any form of moral responsibility. Purchases should be paid for. If they are not, debts accrue, and who suffers then? Why, the creditors of course, those without the benefit of land or title, who seem to regard everyone else as merely expendable to their own desires, which must always be gratified whatever the cost. He tries not to show what he is feeling, to keep his expression as impassive as he can, but he fails. A tell-tale pulse flickers at the side of his temple, as it always does when he tries to suppress how he truly feels, and he involuntarily raises a finger to still the recalcitrant nerve.

Courtenay notices this and is at once taken aback. It is a reaction and gesture he remembers from his late father, whenever he was angry with him, which was increasingly the case in his final years., but one which he himself has not inherited. Nothing has ever bothered him that much, he supposes. He always felt that eventually he would be bailed out, whatever he did, until recently, that is, after his father had died and all those hares he had set running came scurrying back, with more and more angry wolf hounds baying at their heels.

"Charge?" asks Matthew, still not taking his eyes from the accused, who is damned if he will look away first. Matthew smiles thinly, as if to say, "Very well, I shall grant you this little victory, albeit a Pyrrhic one," and directs his gaze back towards the Clerk.

"Bankruptcy," the latter replies.

The word is like a gunshot. Matthew can sense its power as it appears almost physically to penetrate the armour of pride and denial in which Sir Courtenay has encased himself.

"With outstanding debts no doubt?" A second firing of the pistol.

The Clerk hands Matthew a long list, which he quickly scrolls through, accompanied by a long, low whistle.

"Are there any creditors here present?" he asks, looking around the Court.

A dozen hands are raised. Matthew nods in acknowledgement, before returning his attention back to the accused, who is starting to breathe noticeably heavier. If he had his way, he would like to crush Sir Courtenay Allen beneath his heel and grind him into the earth, but the law, not emotion, will as ever be his guide.

"Bankruptcy," he sneers. "From the Latin for two separate words, which we have since joined together. *Bancus*, meaning bench. And *ruptus*, meaning broken. When a trader who conducted his transactions from a bench in a public place and was then, for whatever reason, no longer able to meet his obligations, the bench was broken, in a symbolic show of failure." Matthew smoothes his hands along the polished surface of his own bench in front of him and leans towards the accused. "Not many years ago," he continues, "you would have been pilloried. Quite literally. You would have been chained to a series of hinged wooden boards – the pillory – which had holes placed within it, through which your head and various limbs would be inserted, from where you might be publicly mocked and humiliated. In addition, one ear would have been nailed to it, which would then be cut off once you had been deemed to have paid your debt and served your penance."

Courtenay blinks rapidly. Otherwise his face betrays nothing.

"Alternatively, I might have ordered you to bare your backside before a jeering crowd and strike it three times with a rock, declaring, 'I am a bankrupt'."

Several in the Court Leet's Public Gallery guffaw loudly, but all that Matthew requires to silence them is a stern look accompanied by a single, sharp rap of his gavel. He turns back to the accused.

"But now we live in what some are pleased to call more enlightened times. I have no such exotic practices to pronounce. The Law could not be clearer in its instruction. But before I pass sentence, do you have anything you wish to say by way of mitigation?"

Courtenay says nothing, lowering his head at last.

"I'm glad to hear it," says Matthew. "But in such cases as these, it is frequently not just he who has declared himself bankrupt who suffers. His family also must share his burden and his shame. Are you married?"

"Widowed," he replies.

"Children?"

Courtenay turns away.

"For the purposes of the Court, you will answer," demands Matthew.

"None," replies Courtenay, louder than he intended, then adds, almost in a whisper, "as far as I am aware."

Matthew regards him with repugnance.

Courtenay returns the look with equal disdain. His wife, Emily, did not survive the birth of her first child. Nor did the child. He was not present at the time. He cannot now remember just where he was. Probably some gaming house or other.

As if reading Courtenay's mind, Matthew declares, " *'There hath no temptation taken you but such as is common to man'*."

Courtenay supposes this to be from the Bible. That is what pious men always fall back on when they sit in judgement upon him – his late father, his father-in-law, and now this upstart of a Magistrate, young enough to be his son – but he recognises the truth in it nevertheless and takes comfort from the thought that his transgressions are to be found in all men. Though he could not imagine this bloodless individual about to pass sentence on him has ever indulged in any kind of flutter. He is not the type, thinks Courtenay. He will risk nothing. Instead he will calculate his chances, not acting until he is as sure of success as he can be, the kind of man, in short, who Courtenay's father would have preferred for a son instead of him. But Courtenay has never been able to resist betting on anything. His whole life has been played out upon the roll of a dice, the turn of a card. Why – he recalls placing fifty pounds once on which of two flies crawling up a window would reach the top first. They were identical in every visible way, yet something must have been different in one of them for it to have prevailed over its twin. Naturally, Courtenay backed the wrong fly. Even now he begins to speculate on what the length of his sentence might be and begins to work out imaginary odds against which he might place a wager – if he had anything left to wager with, that is, but he hasn't, not even a farthing, only the clothes he stands up in. What if he were to wager his boots on it? Instinctively he begins to roll an imaginary coin across the back of his right hand, flipping it expertly from finger to finger, a long-held, habitual action of his, one which he remembers his mother teasing him about the day he came up with his scheme to bring – what was that milkmaid's name again? Daphne? Phoebe? Something to do with Apollo. Phoebe, yes, that was it – over to Davyhulme Hall, as a companion for her, a ruse she saw through immediately... He pauses. His mother died more than ten years ago and there's not a day goes by when he doesn't miss her. He smiles, remembering that occasion when his desire for Phoebe had been so strong, he simply had to have her, and his mother had guessed it at once. Now he can scarcely remember a single thing about her. The colour of her hair perhaps, like rushes, not so dissimilar from that of his accuser... Has he always been so transparent? Probably, he thinks. But at least he has never pretended to be otherwise. Unlike the rest of the hypocrites he sees around him, like this Magistrate, who...

Courtenay's thoughts stop in their tracks. He looks back towards Matthew, who, he sees, is doing the exact same gesture that he has just completed in his imagination, rolling a coin back and forth between his fingers as he weighs up his options. He watches in astonishment as he flips the coin up into the air, then catches it on the back of one hand, concealing it with the palm of the other, which he then raises, as if the side on which it has landed – heads or tails – will determine what choice he will make.

Matthew pockets the coin.

"I hereby sentence you to a period of hard labour of an as yet indeterminate length to be carried out in the New Bailey

Prison, where the produce of your labour will be sold to pay off the debts you have accrued. Once all of these debts have been honoured, you will then be released back into society, where you might serve as a warning and deterrent to any others who may be tempted to follow the same path that you have done. Take him down." He raps his gavel once more, then looks down, his attention now given to the business of affixing his signature to the appropriate papers.

The father passes within just a few feet of the son, each continuing on their separate paths in ignorance.

Another year passed. In all that time Matthew had not given Sir Courtenay Allen a moment's thought. Once he had passed judgement on a case and pronounced sentence, he dismissed it from his mind. He never involved himself with what happened to any of those who appeared before him once they had been escorted from the Court. He made few prison visits – he left the welfare of its inmates to the Governor, or to those charities that made it their business to agitate for Reform – unless he was called in to question a felon accused of some misdemeanour while still serving sentence within its walls. It was not that he held a particularly strong view about the state of the conditions inside the domain of the New Bailey's dungeons either way. It was simply that he did not want the distraction. The Law was the Law and should, he believed, be administered solely on the merits of each particular case, regardless of any extraneous clutter. Matthew loved it with all the fervour of a zealot. The logic and clarity of statute and precedent exercised a particular pull upon him. He was utterly in thrall to its implacable will, its pitiless purity.

If he had a weakness, it was a surprising one. Sometimes a name might stop him in his tracks. A Faith, or Hope, or Charity. He would look at such defendants with a keen appraising eye and ask himself if they warranted clemency on account of the impulses that had driven their parents so to christen them.

The other week a wretch called Pity was brought before him. She was filthy, bedraggled, undernourished, though these were attributes he generally paid little heed to, since time spent in the New Bailey Prison would render even the most respectable of gentlewomen to look similarly disadvantaged, but this one – Pity – did not apologise for her appearance. In fact she said nothing at all. Not a single word. Not even her name, which he learned only from the array of witnesses who appeared so surprisingly to testify to the goodness of her character, when the charge of vagrancy was read out to her. But she was not, if these witnesses were to be believed, a vagrant at all. She had an address, which she shared with her brother, a respectable stone and brick mason, and an occupation of her own, as a seamstress for Mr Jacob's thriving establishment on the Hanging Ditch. And so he found himself once again taking note of a defendant's name, and had indeed pitied her, and found her not guilty. She had said nothing to him then either. Not even a thank you. No. Instead she had looked at him, seemingly without blinking, unflinchingly, with eyes that felt too large for her head, boring into him, as if trying to reach the very core of him. It was an expression that appeared to convey that it was *she* who was pitying *him*, rather than the other way round, almost as if she knew somehow that deep down he was lacking something, and that she wished him to find something that would fill that emptiness.

Her face stayed with him. It would rise before him unbidden, so that, sometimes, he had to be brought back to the present moment and whatever matter was in hand by a puzzled insistence from whomever he happened to be with at the time, repeating the same question to him, and then asking him if perhaps he was ill, with an expression of bemused concern. The prevailing consensus was that he must have finally succumbed to the charms of one of the fairer sex and they would withdraw from him with an amused smile they made no attempt to conceal, which Matthew found quite maddening.

That was two years ago.

Then, one year later, as he took his position in the Court Leet for the start of the Michaelmas Sessions of 1803, her face rose up before him again, those same questioning, unblinking eyes drilling into his chest. He blinked his own eyes three times in rapid succession. When he opened them again, the vision had disappeared. Standing in their place was the latest defendant, the customary rags for clothes, the unwashed skin, the shuffling gait, the chained wrists, the bowed head.

"Name?"

"Chant, Mercy."

"Mercy?" He turns away from the Clerk of the Court, who has been reading the details of the charges, and addresses the defendant directly. "Is that your given name? Mercy?"

The woman nods.

Mercy. He feels his skin prickle and tingle. Pity's eyes hover and dance above him.

"What is the charge?"

"Theft," replies the Clerk. "Theft and soliciting. It is alleged that on the night of…"

The Clerk continues to read the bare facts of the case from the paper in front of him, but Matthew has ceased to listen. He knows it well enough without hearing the specific details. It follows the familiar pattern. Loss of occupation, loss of dwelling, hunger, theft, lack of shelter, lack of money, prostitution. Instead he watches the woman while the charges are read. She doesn't react. She neither protests her innocence, nor sinks to her knees desperately pleading for a second chance. She neither seeks nor expects, it seems, pity or mercy, to say nothing of justice. She merely stands there, not moving, not speaking, not once lifting her head to offer an imploring, beseeching look. She reminds Matthew of the painting of *Daphne and Apollo* by Paulo Veronese. He is not a particular lover of art, but a reproduction of this hangs in the library of the *Lit & Phil*, along with various other Renaissance copies, and so its composition is familiar to him. The way Daphne just stands there, not moving a muscle, waiting with agonising patience for her limbs to be encased in the bark and branches of a laurel tree, while Apollo, her pursuer, mad with desire for her, is frustrated at the last, unable to have the thing that he most wants.

Matthew looks at her a long time. Long after the Clerk has finished reading the charges. He is conscious of the eyes of the Court upon him, waiting for him to begin his cross-examination of the woman, who still has not moved.

"Mercy," he says at last, "Mercy, do you have anything to say to us that in any way might mitigate the sentence that otherwise the Court must pass?"

Something in the tone of his voice reaches through to the woman, more than the actual words themselves. They are formal, but they are not unkind. They are tinged with sorrow. She had not expected this. Instinctively she looks up, curious to know who has spoken thus, roused to inspect the visage of the speaker, to see if his expression might match the tone in which his question has been couched.

When she lifts her head, she takes a half step forward, inching into the light that falls through the Court Room window at this particular time in the morning. It is only then that Matthew realises that the dark, unwashed skin he had barely registered when she was first brought before him, is in fact the lustrous patina of skin which shines as black as polished coal. She must be one of the growing category of freed plantation slaves from the Caribbean who have been arriving in Manchester in ever greater numbers during the past decade. Matthew has been aware of them, but he has never been in such close proximity with one before. His eyes pore over every inch of her. They feast upon her. They cannot get enough of her.

Mercy recognises that look. She has seen it many times before. Although more than five thousand black people now live in Manchester, about a third of whom are female, they are still regarded as a novelty. She has become so used to being openly stared out that she no longer pays it any heed. Mostly it is curiosity that drives these stares, innocent and child-like. Only rarely is it nakedly hostile. While there is much talk in the churches, the gentlemen's clubs and societies, the Exchange, in the newspapers and on the streets about Abolition, the various arguments for and against; while Dr White and his followers debate matters of race and polygenism from a supposedly scientific perspective, and while Anglicans and Dissenters alike scour the Bible for verses to prove one hypothesis or another, citing great immutable Chains of Being on the one hand, or the belief that all are equal before God on the other, Mercy finds that such positions, however entrenched, fall away when it comes to dealing with people on a face to face basis, that they are literally only skin deep.

Since circumstances prevailed which have made it necessary for her to embark upon a series of financial arrangements regarding the temporary possession of her body, she has quickly come to realise that, for the most part, such trade is conducted like any other. One person has something to sell that another person desires. That other person suggests what he considers is a fair price, she disagrees. They proceed amicably enough to the next stage. They barter. They enter into a brisk exchange of offer and counter offer. The predictable rules of engagement are deployed until eventually an agreement is reached, confirmed with a shake of the hand, or, in Mercy's case, a tug of the sleeve to an alleyway round the corner, where the business is transacted. Then the two of them will part company, he temporarily gratified that an itch has been scratched, she relieved that she now has the means to pay for a roof over her head for one night more, the two of them in all probability unlikely to do business with one another again. Only rarely do her customers get past that threshold, of fully taking in her appearance, the colour of her skin, the inky blackness in which they might lose themselves. Only once has someone ventured further, dived deeper, and begun to discover the whole spectrum of colour that is to be found within her. But he is gone, long gone, and she knows it profits her nothing to waste time in idle speculation on when he might return. He won't. He could not have been clearer about this the last time she saw him, nearly two years before...

Now, when she sees the Magistrate quite literally thunderstruck at the sight of her before him, she is reminded, if only for a moment, of the look that other gentleman would give her every time she stood before him. Here, she thinks, is the chance for a reprieve, an escape from the downward spiral she has fallen into since he left the last time. She adopts her most pleading, penitent face and turns its full force to work on Matthew.

Matthew, normally so swift in grasping the particularities of a given case, so sure in dispensing the necessary judgement, finds himself at a loss for words. He decides he must play for time until he has recovered his equilibrium. He begins by reciting to her from the notorious Bloody Code, through which sentencing practices are normally carried out.

"In 1688," he states, addressing the court as a whole, "there were fifty offences on the statute book punishable by death. By 1776 that number had risen to over two hundred. Theft, for example." Here he pauses and wills himself to look directly at the defendant, whose eyes meet his with such force that he is once more immediately thrown from his course, so that he must look away again. "If what is stolen amounts to more than twelve pence worth of goods, then the death penalty is justly warranted. If, either through theft or procurement..." He finds himself inexorably drawn back towards a contemplation of Mercy's face which, on the mention of the word 'procurement', has modestly cast down its eyes, so that he cannot bring himself to believe this young woman to be capable of such an act. "If, through that act of procurement," he repeats, collecting himself once more, "the amount received exceeds one twentieth of the aggrieved party's weekly wage, then that too permits this court to sentence you to death."

He hears a shudder in his voice. The Clerk of the Court regards him with concern. "Do you require some water, sir?" he whispers *sotto voce*.

Matthew shakes his head. It is not as if he has not pronounced the death penalty before. He is not known for harshness or cruelty *per se* when administering justice, but nor is he wont to be squeamish when the case requires it. On the contrary, he has a reputation for rigorous fairness. He will apply the spirit rather than the letter of the law at times, but neither is he one to show clemency or mercy without due mitigation or cause. Mercy. He looks down upon her once more.

"It is a melancholy truth that, among the variety of actions which men and women are daily liable to commit, no less than a hundred and sixty have been declared by Act of Parliament to be felonious without benefit of clergy; or, in other words, to be worthy of instant death."

The Clerk of the Court, who, despite the shake of the head produced by Matthew when answering his former question, has nevertheless fetched a glass of water, which Matthew now avails himself of.

"Alternatively, *The Transportation Act of 1717* permits me to refer you to a period of penal servitude with a term of indenture in Van Diemen's Land, or one of His Majesty's other overseas realms. But I am minded that such deportation, although it may rid these shores of undesirable criminal elements, at the same time deprives the kingdom of many subjects whose labour might be deemed useful to the community, and who, by proper care and correction, might be reclaimed from their current evil course. I am inclined to the opinion that you would benefit from such a course of correction, and I hereby sentence you to six months' hard labour at the New Bailey Prison."

He is on the point of bringing down his gavel to confirm his decision when he halts, the gavel less than an inch away from the bench.

"But before I do so, I wish to see the Defendant in my Chambers before she is taken down."

He now completes the action of bringing the gavel down upon the bench and stands, quitting the Court before the Clerk has had time to order all present to rise.

A few minutes later Mercy is brought before him in his Chambers. She is still wearing irons on her wrists and ankles and is accompanied by a Prison Officer.

"You may remove the chains," says Matthew curtly, "then you may go."

"Yes, sir." If the officer is surprised, he does not show it. It is not his place. He unlocks the padlocks on each of the chains, which he wraps around his closed fists before taking his leave.

Mercy rubs the soreness around her chafed wrists.

"Thank you, sir," she says. These are the first words Matthew has heard her speak. How appropriate, he thinks, that they should be expressing gratitude, directly to him.

He suppresses the urge he has to rise from behind his desk and walk round to her, to take her in his arms, to insist upon her giving him access to those charms she has been on trial for illegally putting up for sale in a public place. But this is not a public place. Not strictly. It is on the grounds of the Court Leet, true, but his own inner sanctum, within which all transactions are conducted as matters of the utmost privacy. It is what he imagines that upstart of a Prison Officer is thinking he will be doing. No doubt he is at this very moment standing outside the door, supposedly on the pretext of remaining on guard, awaiting further instructions, but in reality straining to listen for any tell tale sounds of carnal desires being satisfied from behind the key hole.

No, he will not give him, or anyone, the slightest pretext for thinking that what goes on inside his Chambers is anything that might in any way besmirch his spotless and unimpeachable reputation for moral scrupulousness at all times.

Therefore he remains where he is, seated behind his desk, considering this woman before him.

"I imagine," he says, "that you are not sorry to be relieved of those heavy bracelets." He indicates her wrists, which she is continuing to massage gently. "You would doubtless appreciate a more delicate variety? Silver, perhaps?"

She looks up at him sharply. "Sir?"

He has moved too quickly. He realises this now. She regards him as a startled deer. He must draw back. Yes, he can do that. He understands the need at times to play a slow hand.

"I have a proposition to put to you," he says, his tone reverting to its more customary judicial coldness.

She says nothing. She simply stands, waiting to see what he will say, or do, next.

"I have sentenced you to six months' hard labour," he continues. "It lies within my gift to modify that somewhat."

Still she says nothing, holding his gaze. She senses an opportunity here.

Something about the boldness of her expression unsettles him, and it is he who is forced to look away first. Her eyes are like tunnels. With no light at the end of them. He could lose himself too easily there.

"I could commute the hard labour element to a more palatable domestic servitude, but increase the term to a year, in keeping with the severity of your offence."

He pauses, allowing her the chance to respond, but still she waits, holding her ground, waiting until he has finished.

"M-my housekeeper," he adds, barely overcoming a tremor in his voice, "M-Mrs Crinkle, has left my employ – retired, I should add, after m-many years of loyal s-service. I am seeking a replacement."

He spreads his hands wide, as if to indicate that he has completed what he had to say and is now awaiting her response.

Now we come to it, thinks Mercy. Housekeeper. She understands a euphemism when she hears one. But the lack of certainty in his voice – that sudden, scarcely concealed stammer – suggests to her that he is stepping into unknown territory. She has grown finely tuned to the intonations in men's voices, especially when they are entering uncharted waters, waters with which she is much more intimately familiar.

"Housekeeper?" she repeats.

"Yes. The duties would be relatively light," he explains, "when compared to breaking rocks or picking oakum, but no less onerous for all that, for I maintain exceedingly high standards."

"I see," she says. And she does. Only too clearly. The ghost of a smile forms upon her lips. "A year, you say?"

"I do."

"After which I would be free to go?"

"Or stay. The choice would then be yours."

"Then?"

"Naturally. Till then you would be kept under lock and key, confined to the house. This is a custodial sentence after all."

"And if I need provisions?"

"I shall make arrangements for them to be delivered."

She nods, briefly, once, indicating that she has understood the terms and conditions, the weights and measures of the arrangement, but not that she has yet accepted them. A choice still exists for her, hanging in the air between them. She rapidly considers the options. A year's loss of liberty in exchange for what might turn out to be something of a pampered existence. She recalls that off-the-cuff remark he made about a silver bracelet. He's a distinctly odd fish, there's no doubting it, and a cold one too, but not a dangerous one, she feels. She's had men put a knife to her throat while they carry out their business in an unlit alley, or up against the rough wall at the back of a church, but she does not believe this Magistrate is such a man. She may not have her freedom in this arrangement he is proposing, but she may well retain the power.

"Very well," she says. "I accept."

He sighs. She watches the tension leave him as he expels the air in that long, sustained outward breath.

"Anything else?" he asks, recovering his composure.

Now she sees what it is that he wants. "No," she says. "Thank you."

"Good. I believe we understand one another." He strides towards the door. "Constable," he calls, to the officer still standing outside, "I should like you to escort the prisoner to this address at precisely six o'clock this evening." He hands the officer his card who, if he experiences surprise, does not register it. After he has gone, and taken the young woman with him, Matthew completes the entry in his log book.

"Chant, Mercy. Charged with theft and soliciting. Guilty. Committed to one year's domestic servitude. Matthew Oldham, Justice of the Peace."

He closes the book. He feels a surge of energy course through his veins. He has a whole year in which to woo her. He must be careful not to rush things. He springs to his feet, takes the stairs leading from his Chambers down to the front door of the Leet three at a time. The air outside, when it hits him, feels unusually fresh and bracing. He will hurry home at once, purchase some flowers perhaps, make his house ready for her arrival.

But first he takes himself to Jacob's Dress Shop on Hanging Ditch. There he arranges for Mr Jacob himself, together with a female assistant, to be in attendance the next morning at his home in Oldham Street to measure Mercy for whatever garments she will need for the coming year.

Next he hastens down Tib Street, passing the Animal Market, where his eye is caught by a stall selling caged song birds. In one of them is a lone yellow-coloured bird, which sings a complicated melody of chirrups and trills. He enquires of the stallholder as to its details. It's a canary, he's informed, from the Azores. The perfect companion for a lady. Matthew's knowledge of geography is hazy. He knows that the Azores are somewhere out in the Atlantic. Isn't that where the Caribbean Islands are also situated? Perhaps this bird will remind Mercy of her home and make her more predisposed to warm towards him.

As the bell in the clock tower of the Collegiate Church of St Mary, St George and St Denys tolls the hour of six, at exactly the same moment as the sixth chime is rung, Matthew hears a knock on his front door. When he opens it, Mercy is standing there meekly, head bowed, once more back in chains, the same prison officer accompanying her as before. She has been washed, Matthew notices. Her hair has been combed and all traces of straw from the cells in the New Bailey Prison have been brushed from her threadbare clothes.

"You may release her, Constable," he says in as formal and neutral a tone as he can muster. He stands and watches as the restraints are removed, then unobtrusively proffers the officer a sovereign for his trouble. The Constable tries not to register either pleasure or amazement, but merely touches his hat before turning on his heels and returning back to the New Bailey.

"Come inside," says Matthew gently.

Mercy steps across the threshold as the door is closed and locked behind her.

She quickly takes in her surroundings – not in detail, for there will be plenty of time for subsequent exploration – but sufficiently to note that here is a once comfortably, if modestly furnished home that has grown cold over time. It lacks a woman's touch. It is apparent that the Magistrate lives frugally and alone within what might otherwise be a very fine house.

Matthew ushers her into the drawing room and directs her attention towards the canary. It swings on a perch inside its cage, which hangs in the window, with a direct view of the world outside, beyond its bars. Mercy approaches it enchanted. At once it starts to sing and, for the duration of its song, she forgets the immediate details of her present circumstances. When the song comes to an end, she turns to face Matthew directly, remembering the rule he implied at the end of their last encounter.

"Thank you," she says and smiles. Her face is transformed and Matthew cannot help but advance closer towards her. Instinctively she takes a step back, placing herself directly next to the canary.

If Matthew feels any disappointment, he does not show it. Instead he says merely, "I'm glad the bird pleases you."

"Yes, sir. Very much."

The two regard one another in silence, wondering just how the drama will unfold, this yet-to-be written play that will be performed to no other audience but themselves.

"Might I be allowed to open the cage," she says at last, "so that it may fly more freely?"

Matthew smiles. He slowly shakes his head. "It must accustom itself to its new surroundings first."

Mercy acquiesces. So this is the game, is it? His meaning cannot be clearer.

"I'm tired," she says.

"Of course," he says emolliently. "It's been a long day. You must be exhausted. Let me show you to your room. I can explain your duties tomorrow."

"Thank you," she says again, accompanying the words with a deep curtsey, which fills Matthew with immense gratification.

This first evening could not have gone better.

He leads Mercy up the central staircase from the hall. Mercy allows her hand to caress the finely carved mahogany banister. It reminds her of the home of John and Caroline Lees, where she worked so happily as a maid when she first arrived in Manchester, who were both so kind towards her, but whom she has not seen for fifteen years, when they sold the house and left her in the care of the new owners, which marked the beginning of her subsequent troubles.

Matthew opens a door on the landing which leads into what had been Fanny's bedroom, before she broke her promise and left to marry Zachary – when was that, he wonders? Fifteen years ago, he realises. No one has slept there since.

After Matthew has shown her in, then bid her good night and shut the door behind him as he left, she hears him turn a key in the lock. She lies back on the bed. Just another prison, she thinks. Pampered and perfumed perhaps, but still a prison for all that. Locked inside this bedroom and in turn locked within the house. She ponders how she might be able to alter the arrangement, a problem which occupies her throughout most of the night, yet even on such heightened alert, sleep eventually overtakes her.

The next morning she is woken early. She fancies she can hear the canary singing in its cage downstairs. She goes to the curtains, which she pulls back. But the window too is locked. The room feels stuffy and airless. He has forgotten to provide her with a jug or basin. She has only the clothes she arrived and slept in, the same clothes she has been wearing for weeks. This will not do, she thinks. She knows she possesses a certain power in this scenario, but as yet she is uncertain as to how she might exercise it.

Below, the bird stops singing.

She knows at once what she will do.

She reaches back, to when she was a child. Unbidden, one of the old slave songs pours from her lips, like a bird in a cage.

"Me know no law, me know no sin
Me's just what ever dem make me
Dis is de way dey bring me in
So God nor Devil take me..."

Within a heartbeat she hears the key turn in the lock. Matthew stands there, waiting.

"I reckon you must've been spying on me through the key hole," she says.

He blushes. "I just happened to be passing," he says, "when I heard you singing."

"Did you like it, the song, I mean?"

"Very much."

"I shan't sing again unless you promise not to lock me in here at night. I'm not going to run away. Besides, you lock the front and, I expect, the back doors downstairs anyway."

"Very well," he says, after a pause.

"Thank you," she says again. "Now, might I have a jug and some water and some clean clothes?"

He hesitates.

"You can stay and watch if you like."

He hurriedly shuts the door. She hears him scurrying along the hallway and down the stairs. Soon he returns. He knocks nervously. "I'll leave everything just here," he says. The water sloshes in the bowl. He does not come in. As he retreats back down the stairs, he calls out over his shoulder. "I'll be in the kitchen when you're ready. To explain your duties."

She smiles.

And so it begins.

Soon a pattern establishes itself.

The next day Mr Jacob and his assistant arrive to measure Mercy for new clothes, which are all made up and ready and sent round the next day, a different outfit for each day of the week. Matthew arranges for all deliveries to be left in a porch at the back of the house. Mercy can enter the porch from the kitchen, but she cannot go outside into the small back garden from there, for the porch door is locked and the key is left in a place outside that only the delivery boys know about. Mercy is instructed to keep the kitchen door locked at all times, thereby preventing the possibility of any of these delivery boys being able to enter the house. After they have gone, she is to unlock the kitchen door from the inside, step into the porch, carry the groceries back inside the house, then lock the door behind her.

In the mornings she must clean the house from top to bottom. Matthew is most particular about this. He appears to harbour something of a phobia where cleanliness is concerned. Mercy observes him obsessively washing and re-washing his hands on numerous occasions when he is at home. He has scrupulously clipped fingernails. It was one of the first things she noticed about him. She wonders how he manages outside, in the dust and dirt and crowds of Manchester's narrow streets. The one exception is his bedroom, which she is strictly forbidden to enter and which he keeps locked at all times. "I have private papers in there", he tells her. Otherwise everywhere must be scrubbed and polished daily. Each evening, when he returns home, he makes a rapid tour and inspection of the house, checking up on her, she supposes, that she is carrying out his instructions. So far he has had no cause for complaint.

In the afternoons she must prepare his supper for when he gets home, an unvaryingly sparse plate of cold meat, or fish, and a modest portion of two seasonal vegetables, all washed down with water. Never wine or ale. Sometimes he prefers soup, made with the bones from the previous day's meat as stock, mopped up with bread, but never butter. Occasionally he permits himself a piece of fruit afterwards, especially if he has had a good day in the factory or on the bench, as a reward.

During these meals Mercy's role is to serve it to him, then stand to one side until he finishes, so that she may then clear away the plates. She is expected to have eaten before he gets home. He likes her to look her best whenever he is there, so she must put away any apron she might have worn while preparing the food, washed her hands and face, attended to her hair, applied a touch of the make-up he has provided for her.

He likes to spend the evenings alone, in his study, working. When he has finished, and before he requests her to retire for the night, he might ask her to sing for him, or read to him from a book of his choosing. Defoe is a particular favourite – *A Tour Through The Island of Great Britain, A Journal of the Plague Year, Robinson Crusoe, Colonel Jack* – but not, Mercy notes with some amusement, *Moll Flanders*.

Afterwards they go to bed. Separately. He prefers to watch. While she undresses he will affix his eye to the keyhole of her bedroom door, which he no longer locks. Sometimes Mercy will not shut it properly after her, so that he might watch openly instead of peeping through the crack. She makes sure to stand where, if there is a bright moon, its light will fall upon her. Or, if not, she will arrange the candle so that its flame casts flickering shadows along the length of her body. She makes sure to take plenty of time over these nightly preparations. When she has finished, she blows out the candle with a single breath. In the utter darkness that follows, she hears Matthew creep away back to his own room.

He never touches her.

After a few weeks a new ritual is added. He will ask her to punish him. "For the sin of transgression," he explains. By watching her undress he has committed a gross violation, he implies. Fornication in thought, if not in deed, and he must suffer for it. He *does* suffer, he says. He lies sleepless in torment throughout the night, wracked with guilt. But not enough. She apologises, demurely. No, he insists, it is he, not she, who is at fault. "Can a rose be blamed for being what she is? She is as nature made her." Complete with thorns, thinks Mercy. But Matthew is in full self-flagellating flow.

" '*The tempter or the tempted, who sins most? Ha!*
Not she: nor doth she tempt: but it is I
That, lying by the violet in the sun,
Do as the carrion does, not the flower,
Corrupt with virtuous season...' "

Measure for measure.

On these nights Matthew prostrates himself before her, asks her to remove his shirt, then hands her the chains which were used to manacle her wrists when she first arrived and beseeches her to whip him with them.

As in all things, she obeys him.

Now it is he who says thank you, as, chastened but shriven, he retreats to the cell-like sanctuary of his own room.

Six months in to her sentence, he surprises her again.

For five years Matthew has been banking with Heywood's. Encouraged by the arrival of Nathan Rothschild in Manchester, but recognising that such a luminous bank as the Count's might be seen as too ostentatious for a humble felter, he had chosen Heywood's on a recommendation from Sir George Hibbert III, who spoke with customary candour on the subject.

"When it comes to money," he had said, tapping the side of his nose with his forefinger, "a word to the wise. There's a view that somehow it goes against Christian moral principles to make money out of lending other people money, and so over time it's been left to those of a Jewish persuasion to sully their hands with the filthy lucre, but I say, 'Bollocks to that!' The plain truth of the matter is that their rates of literacy and numeracy are higher than ours, and so, quite simply, they're better at applying themselves to those annoying little amounts of shillings and pence that have that nasty habit of proliferating and accumulating. Take a tip from me, Matthew, when it comes to your investments, trust the experts."

And so Matthew had put his financial affairs into the hands of Benjamin Halsinger at Heywood's, a decision he has had not a moment's qualm about since. Benjamin has steered Matthew's money through the vicissitudes of a turbulent economy with unerring success. Caution and conservatism are his watchwords. Play the long game is his motto. No South Sea Bubble or Tulip Mania.

"No," says Benjamin, "the secret lies in never becoming over-reliant on a single stock or bond. Maintain a broad portfolio. Modest returns, but low risk."

These words are all music to Matthew's ears. He pays Benjamin a handsome dividend for studying trends, for forecasting stormy weather before it arrives, and for making safe provision accordingly.

On this particular day, the third Wednesday in the month, which has come to be their regular appointment, Benjamin is urging Matthew to consider moving a little more of his capital into corn.

"Yes, I understand," he says, "that textiles may be booming right now here in Manchester, but mark my words. With the War against France showing no sign of abatement, and their blockade of the French ports still as strong as ever, food prices will continue to rise. Especially bread. It only takes a couple of poor wheat harvests here – and if there's one thing we *can* be certain of in these uncertain times, it is the English weather. Sooner or later, it will rain. The crops will rot and there will be shortages. It is then just a short stride away from the Government stepping in to guarantee the price of corn. It depends heavily on the gentry farmers for its support if it is to maintain power, and so – with your permission of course – I recommend a slight rebalancing of your stocks...?"

Matthew nods. He sees the sense of what Benjamin is suggesting. There have already been food riots in the town. He himself has had to draw up contingencies for restoring order should the situation worsen. The Chapels are setting up soup kitchens.

While he is signing the necessary forms, his attention is caught by a series of portraits – oil paintings – which hang on the wall behind Benjamin's desk. Over the years he has been coming to Heywood's this has become quite a gallery, each of them depicting a member of Benjamin's family and wider community. Matthew has been introduced to each of them as they have arrived – Benjamin's father, Reuben; his mother, Leah; Lemon Nathan, the patriarch; Aaron Jacob, the tailor, and his son, Philip, from whom Matthew had ordered Mercy's wardrobe, and now, he notes, there is a new arrival. The latest portrait depicts a serious-looking young man, standing at a desk on which are strewn various papers filled with meticulously annotated mathematical proofs. A quill pen hangs loosely from the fingers of his right hand, while his left lovingly caresses the outer casing of a telescope on its stand, pointing up towards the star-filled sky, which can be viewed through a skylight window. But what draws Matthew to the painting more than any of these details, arresting as they are, is the expression upon the young man's face, which is one of near beatific ecstasy. He has the fairest hair of almost anyone Matthew can remember seeing. It is practically white, while the paleness of his skin is translucent. Even more compelling are the eyes. The pupils are ice blue, but the iris is subtly infiltrated by the blood vessels from inside the eye showing through, so that they appear to have a reddish tinge.

Benjamin observes Matthew's curiosity.

"Ah," he says. "You have seen my latest addition? My brother. Abner."

"Abner?" says Matthew, momentarily turning away from the painting. "An unusual name."

"It means 'Father of Light'," he explains.

Matthew turns back to the painting, nodding. "I don't believe I've ever seen eyes like these before."

"He has ocular albinism," says Benjamin. "An extremely rare condition. One which is passed down through the male line, though it can skip one, sometimes two, generations."

"So his children may not in fact be born with it?"

"Perhaps, perhaps not. It also depends on whether the mother is a carrier. There's no way of knowing for certain."

"Is it debilitating?"

"You would not say so if you met Abner, but it can be. People tend to point or stare. But that is something we Jews have had to learn to grow used to."

Matthew thinks of Mercy, the colour of her skin.

"I think perhaps that that is changing. Manchester now wears Joseph's coat of many colours, I believe. *'All flesh is grass, and all its beauty like the flowers of the field'*."

"Isaiah."

Matthew raises an eyebrow in surprise.

"Isaiah is to be found in our *Tanakh* as well as your Bible."

Matthew considers the painting once more. "What does he do, your brother?"

Benjamin smiles. "He dreams. He spends half the night peering at the stars through that telescope."

"And during the day?"

"He studies Mathematics at the New College on Jackson's Row…"

"The Dissenting College?" Matthew's preconceptions continue to be confounded.

Benjamin smiles. "The eminent Mr Dalton is his teacher. Hence those equations in the painting. He will soon train to become an accountant."

"And join the bank?"

Benjamin spreads his hands. "*Be'ezrát hashém.*"

Matthew nods.

"But for now," Benjamin continues, laughing, "his head is in the stars."

"It's a very fine painting," says Matthew. "Who is the artist?"

Benjamin looks down. "My wife," he says. "Rachel."

"She has a remarkable gift."

"*Elohim gadol.*"

Matthew pauses. An idea is forming. He wonders if he might be able to articulate it somehow in a way that does not cast suspicion either upon himself or his motives.

"I was wondering…"

"Yes?" says Benjamin, aware of a sudden change in the temperature.

"Might your wife…?" he hesitates, wondering whether to pursue this notion that is growing in his imagination or not. Benjamin says nothing. Yes, thinks, Matthew privately to himself, why not? "Might she consider the possibility of taking on a new commission?"

Benjamin leans forward, sensing the importance of his client's surprising request. "Do you wish a portrait of yourself?" he ventures.

"No," says Matthew quickly. "It is of… someone else." He feels himself redden. Benjamin tactfully looks away. Matthew continues more rapidly. "It is of a prisoner," he says, "a most unusual case. Convicted of theft and… well, let's just say it's someone I have taken rather a special interest in…" His mouth has grown completely dry.

"Not a member of your family then?"

"No. A servant, in fact. But someone with prospects. If given the right opportunity. A most interesting countenance."

"I see."

"I shall pay Mrs Halsinger a fee of course."

Benjamin inclines his head politely. He wants to buy our silence and discretion as well as pay for the finished portrait.

"Do you have a fee in mind?"

"I..." Matthew is floundering. "That depends on the number of sittings, I presume?"

"How many would you wish?"

"Well... I'm not sure. What would be usual? For a painting such as this?" he asks, turning back to the portrait of Abner to steady himself.

"I think three should be sufficient," replies Benjamin. "If she requires more time, she can always complete the commission privately. Would you like my wife to paint the sitter *in situ*, or would you prefer her to come to her studio?"

Her, thinks Matthew sharply? He doesn't recall referring to the subject's gender. Is he so transparent? Clearly he must be.

"No," he replies quickly. "The painting must be done in the drawing room of my home on Oldham Street. By the window, beside a caged bird. The setting is most important."

"I understand. When would you like my wife to start?"

"As soon as she can."

Now that they are discussing the details, like any other matter of trade, Matthew can begin to feel more comfortable.

"Next week?"

"Perfect."

"Shall we say Wednesday? At what time?"

"Early afternoon. The room has the sun then."

"I will instruct my wife to arrive at two o' clock."

"Agreed."

The two men shake hands.

"Will you be present also, sir?" asks Benjamin.

"I will not," replies Matthew.

The mood between them has become noticeably cooler.

"And shall I expect you as usual next month?"

Matthew nods before walking briskly towards the door of Benjamin's office. Just as he reaches it, he pauses, turns back, and says, "Art is a good investment too, is it not?"

"It can be, sir. Are you considering becoming a collector?"

"Let's see how this first experiment goes, shall we?"

Once outside on St Ann's Street, Matthew begins to breathe more freely again. Is that how he regards Mercy, he asks himself? As a piece of Art? A painting or a china vase? To be locked inside a display case to be taken out once in a while to pore over and admire? Or as an investment, an experiment?

1st Sitting

Rachel arrives as arranged the following Wednesday. She finds Mercy standing, as instructed by Matthew, in the French window of the drawing room beside the wire cage, inside which the canary lies silent. She has begun to moult and is feeling cross and sorry for herself.

Rachel wonders at the nature of this unusual relationship which must exist between Mr Oldham and the young woman, whose name she learns is Mercy, that she is not permitted to leave the house under any circumstances, yet who, as she greets her now, appears measured and composed.

She is undeniably beautiful and Rachel can understand why a portrait of her should be so desirable.

Rachel asks her if she might show her the pose that Mr Oldham requires her to adopt for the painting. Mercy at once complies. She turns her face in profile, towards the cage, her hand reaching towards the bird. The way the sun is falling through the window behind throws the shadows from the bars of the cage across her face. Rachel explains the problem. Mercy replies that she is certain that Mr Oldham will be quite satisfied with a different pose, the one that Rachel, the artist, might suggest, with her more practised eye. They experiment with a range of positions. But nothing is quite right. If Mercy stands slightly behind the cage, to avoid those troublesome shadows, it makes her appear that she herself is behind bars. Which in a way she is, of course, though Mercy does not say this out loud. She doesn't need to. She senses that Rachel, who is visibly pregnant, is beginning to guess, at least in part, the purpose behind this commission. Pregnancy, Mercy has noted, often brings with it a certain intuitiveness.

Eventually Rachel says that what she is certain Mr Oldham will want is a painting that captures the full beauty of Mercy's face and figure. She does not say this to flatter, but rather to state an obvious fact. They try a number of other configurations. Mercy opening the door of the cage and reaching her hand inside. But this only serves to alarm the bird, who will not remain still, becoming agitated, even, at one point, pecking Mercy's forearm and drawing blood.

In the end they settle upon a pose inspired by two quite similar paintings by Jean-Honoré Fragonard, an artist much admired by Rachel, *A Young Girl Reading* and *The Love Letter*. She will attempt to capture the absorption of Mercy, as she loses herself in a book, as in the first of Fragonard's portraits, but she will alter the profile of that original to incorporate the full face, looking up in barely concealed agitation, as revealed in the countenance of the sitter shown in *The Love Letter*, whose startled eyes, unguardedly caught in an act of betrayal, convey a deep, unrequited longing and a barely concealed eroticism. Behind her, Rachel will paint the bird in her cage, beak wide open, bursting into song. Whether it is this song, or something that Mercy has stumbled across in the book she is reading, or a combination of both, which has provoked this expression will be left for the viewer to interpret. She plays further with the angle at which Mercy is to be sitting. Should she be looking back towards the singing bird, or away in the opposite direction, listening with suppressed intent? Mercy says that she would prefer to be staring straight ahead, directly at whoever looks upon the finished portrait, almost as if she is challenging them to understand her true motive, and Rachel decides to trust this instinct. All that remains is to choose which book Mercy will have upon her lap.

"What are his tastes?" she asks.

Mercy considers this question.

"He likes me to read Defoe to him," she says.

Rachel wrinkles her nose. "*Nein*. Too modern. What we need is one of the classics. Something timeless. More universal."

"How about this?" asks Mercy, and she pulls a copy of Ovid's *Metamorphoses* from the library shelf.

"*Ja*. Perfect," says Rachel. "Choose a passage you like, then, when I paint you looking up from it, I shall reveal the book lying open on that page. The astute spectator may be interested to learn what lies upon it."

Mercy scans quickly through the leather bound volume.

"How about this?" she says, smiling.

Rachel reads out loud.

" '*A heavy numbness seizes Daphne's limbs*
Her soft breasts are girded by the creeping bark
Her hair grows into foliage, her arms to boughs
Her foot, just now so swift, clings to sluggish roots
Her face the top of the tree, her lone remaining splendour…

" '*Apollo, with his right hand placed upon the trunk,*
Feels her heart still trembling in the rind
Embraces her branches as limbs with his arms
Till the wood shrinks from his kisses…

" '*The Laurel nods her new-made crown; the canopy,*
As if it were her head, shakes her hair of leaves'."

She looks back towards Mercy, who is still smiling impassively. She reminds Rachel of those plaster saints whose faces are a mask of inscrutability, whose eyes reveal nothing of what they've seen. Rachel would like to close the book – it describes a world beyond her comprehending – yet this woman standing before her, who is clearly intimate with such experiences, bears not the slightest trace of being in any way a victim. How has she managed this, she wonders? How has she maintained her separateness within this life of servitude? She would like to find out if she can.

She hands the open book back to her and says, "Why don't you tell me something about yourself while I set up my easel and prepare the canvas and the paints? That way the time will pass more quickly, and you will not feel you are having to strain, to hold the same position for hours."

I was born in Jamaica, in 1772. My father was rumoured to be John Hibbert, the younger brother of Thomas, the plantation owner in Kingston. But, looking at the colour of my skin, I don't think he could have been. I'd have been much lighter. My mother, Abigail, was married to another slave, by the name of Henry Chant, but when a white master wanted a taste of black candy, there was nothing he could do to prevent it, and so that was what must have happened. My mother would go with John Hibbert some nights, but in between times she would return to Henry, who was most probably my father. In any case John died of malaria the same year I was born, and soon afterwards Henry died too. "Lord, grant me mercy that I might live long enough to raise my daughter." That's what my mother is meant to have said the day her husband died, and that's how I got my name. Or so I was always told. "Lord, grant me Mercy", and that's just what He went and did.

Mr Hibbert's brother, Thomas, then took me in. He never married, but against all convention he lived with another African slave, Miss Charity Harry, who he freed and treated as his wife, taking her to balls and parties and state dinners, and the like. They had three daughters – Jane, Margaret and Helen – but Helen died when just a few days old. I think I came to replace her in their minds, and they looked after me as if I were their own. My mother was more than happy with this arrangement, for it meant I would never have to live the life she had done. And mostly I haven't. I came to look upon Jane and Margaret as my sisters and playmates. We went to school together. I received a proper English education, first in Kingston, and then back here in England, after Mr Thomas died, when we were shipped over to Liverpool. Jane took ill during the crossing and never fully recovered. She died within a month of arriving here.

Thomas's sister-in-law, Anne, arranged for Margaret and me to live in the Rectory of St Mary's Church, Reddish, not far from Stockport, where she knew the vicar, the Reverend Charles Westcott and his wife. She paid for a governess to teach us, a Miss Thrynne, whom I did not like, and who did not like me. She would tell me that I must be a great sinner if God had seen fit to give me such black skin, and she used to make me scrub myself with a rough soap made from animal fat and ashes until my body was so sore it would bleed. Then she would cry out, "Again, again! You must keep on till your skin turns white."

This would have been 1781. I was nine years old.

Margaret was nearly fifteen. She used to try and look out for me, but when she turned sixteen, it was decided she no longer needed further schooling. By then she could speak French, play the piano, sing, recite poetry, do fine needlework, all the accomplishments a young lady needed in order to attract a husband. Anne took Margaret completely under her wing *from then on, and I was left to the tender mercies of Miss Thrynne unshielded.*

Without the restraining presence of Margaret, who might have reported her cruelties to uncomprehending ears, Miss Thrynne was now able to give full rein to the wilder, more fanciful realms of her imagination and let loose, unfettered and unshackled, the more inventive brands of punishment she had doubtless been waiting so long to unleash. I shall not go into details. Suffice it to say that from that day on, my life was a torment. It was nothing, I knew, compared to what my mother, Abigail, had had to endure as a child and a young woman, but this was not what she had anticipated when she handed me over to the care of Mr Thomas after my father died.

Months passed. I had three choices. Either I meekly submitted, which I knew I could not do; or I went to see the Reverend and told him what I was being made to endure, but would I have been believed? At ten years of age, I very much doubted I would. Or, I could take matters into my own hands. This third option seemed my only possible choice.

I thought about what I, a mere child of just ten years, could possibly do to exact revenge upon a grown and respected adult, a woman with a reputation, a pillar of the church. And then it struck me. That was exactly where she was most vulnerable, the place where she considered herself unassailable. I came up with several ideas but rejected them all at once. They were either too fanciful, or too complicated, or depended too much on coincidence and good fortune. What I needed was a foolproof plan, something doable and direct, something that would utterly devastate her, so that she would feel she could never hold up her head in civilised society again.

I had it. The idea delighted me. It was perfect in its simplicity yet had the potential for inflicting maximum damage.

Every Sunday morning she would supervise my getting ready for church. This ritual humiliation seemed to be the highlight of her week. The amount of pain she accorded me being in exact proportion with the pleasure it afforded her. First she would make me stand naked and shivering in the cellar, where she would pour icy cold water over me, standing beside me while she forced me to rub my skin raw with the rough soap she still insisted I used, despite the scratches and the bleeding, in her missionary zeal to wash me white. Then, when this refused to yield the desired result, she would plunge my hands into scaldingly hot water to see if that might produce the hoped-for effect.

Lately she had taken to smearing my face with a mixture of white lead and vinegar in order to create the temporary illusion that I was gradually becoming lighter-skinned under her proselytising influence. She would also apply the same pigment to her own skin to give it additional lustre. I wonder now if this might partly explain her viciousness of temper, for she perhaps was already suffering from lead poisoning, but I think not. The impulse in her to hurt was too ingrained.

You will probably not be surprised to learn that she eschewed all mirrors. They were the Devil's instrument, she would say, and sought to make us vain, encouraging us to waste away the hours we could have been spending more profitably in the service of God by worshipping our own reflections. "Thou shalt not make unto thyself any graven image," she would say. "Pride is the first and greatest of the Seven Deadly Sins." Consequently, she relied on her years of experience to know just how much of the pigment to apply to her own face. Then, as we made our way the few yards from the Rectory cellar to St Mary's Church, she would walk with both gloved hands raised in front of her face, so that not even the slightest movement of the air might spoil her handiwork. Only when she had sat down in her allotted pew, from where she could see and be seen, would she lower her hands into her lap. When the Rector requested us to say together the Lord's Prayer, she would thrust me down hard onto my unprotected knees directly upon the cold stone floor, while she would barely lower herself more than a few graceful inches onto her own personal raised kneeler, so that she could look around at the assembled congregation and see who might rival her for piety and fervour. With a grim satisfaction she believed there were none.

I made my plans for the First Sunday in Lent, which was always the high point of Miss Thrynne's liturgical year, with its strict and severe emphasis on the mortification of the body. I prepared a special concoction of black lead, used by the housekeeper for polishing the grate, to replace the white lead and vinegar she always used. I pretended to be frightened by a rat in the cellar – there were always rats scurrying in the shadows – and she, as I predicted she would, scolded me for my childishness, but beat them away with a broom handle, as I prayed that she might. While she was thus occupied, I made the switch. "All this fuss over nothing," she said. "We must hurry now or we shall be late for Church." Then she looked me disapprovingly up and down, while she administered the pigment to her face deftly and expertly, after which she put on her gloves without once needing to look down at her hands, for she was so intent on looking for blemishes in my own appearance.

We then walked to Church as we always did, marching in step, our gloved hands held high in front of our faces. When we reached our pew, she lowered her hands as usual, but instead of the polite and deferential acknowledgements which normally greeted her arrival, she was met with gasps. These gasps grew, in number and in volume. Then they turned to laughter. The Reverend Westcott hurried over to her, bearing the small hand mirror that the organist used so that he might receive signals from him during the service to lengthen or shorten whatever he was playing. He held it up before Miss Thrynne's face. She shrieked, then she screamed, then she wailed, then she aimed a blow at the side of my head, causing the congregation to gasp once more, then she fled. In that instant, wearing her black face like a badge of shame, she appeared to me for the first time more of a real person, than some story book ogre. Frailty, thy name is not woman, but human.

I never saw her again.

That same night, I collected what few belongings I possessed and tied them up in a cotton shawl I found, which I carried on the end of the broom handle Miss Thrynne had used to chase away the recalcitrant rat. At first light the next morning, I slipped out of the back door of the Rectory and began to walk. I had no idea where I was going. Leaving the village of Reddish, I came to a cross roads, with a fingerpost pointing out four different directions I might take: north-east to Dukinfield, north-west to Droylsden, south-east to Stockport, south-west to Cheadle. For no other reason than I liked the sound of its name, I chose the Dukinfield road.

On such random choices are futures found and destinies forged...

2nd Sitting

I walked all morning. All these years later I can still recall it vividly. The fear. The not knowing where I was going, where I might end up. The road, little more than a lane, passed through fields and orchards mostly, the occasional farm or cottage, the odd hamlet or two. Bredbury, Woodley, Haughton Green. I crossed the River Tame at Arden Bridge. There were laurel bushes growing along its banks, I remember. I passed grand manor houses on the edge of Hyde. Bayley Hall in Hyde Park. Oakfield Hall, spied through the trees of Newton Wood. And then finally Dukinfield itself, where the landscape changed. There were coal mines and iron works. The air was thick with black smoke. Then it began to rain, thick globules of water that bounced off the road. Within seconds I was soaked to the skin. I needed to take shelter. I looked around for the first thing I could find. It was a covered verandah at the back of a fine house on what I later learned was called King Street. I huddled into a corner and within seconds I was asleep.

It was Caroline who found me. Mrs Lees. She was delighted. I learned later she was trying for a child, so it was as if the stork had delivered me. I was showered with love. I couldn't have been happier. Caroline's husband – John – owned the coal mines I had passed on my long walk to Dukinfield. He knew the Hibberts through his business with them. They had mills in and around Stockport and he supplied them with coal. He told me that Anne – Mrs Hibbert – had reportedly been out of her mind with worry when I was discovered to have gone. She was so relieved I'd come to no harm. So grateful. But not so much that she asked to have me brought back. Not that I would have wanted to go. I'd've only run away again. But with John and Caroline, I felt safe. No one was going to try and wash me white there. Or ever again, I vowed to myself.

They arranged for me to go to the local Sunday School. Set up by the Methodists, of which John was a member. Although he was already wrestling with himself about that. Not that I understood it at the time. I'd come across him down on his knees in different rooms of the house, praying for enlightenment. I just assumed he was very devout. For he did not display the fanaticism of Miss Thrynne in any aspect of his behaviour. Nor did Caroline. They couldn't have been kinder to me.

As well as Sunday School, I went to another school in the week. It was run by a group of people who called themselves Moravians. They had no special church, they met in each other's houses, sometimes in John and Caroline's. They were wanting to build their own community, with houses, and places to work, and a farm, as well as a church and a school. So John set aside a building in one of his collieries for the children to go to. It used to be a canteen for the miners, but that had been replaced, by a bigger one, because more and more people were coming to work there. Sometimes I would be teased. They'd look at my face and ask me if I'd been down the pit digging for coal. But they didn't mean it unkindly.

Our teacher was a Miss Farley, the daughter of a Unitarian minister, who sometimes would let us call her Emily. She was as kind as Miss Thrynne was cruel. She had brown curly hair, which framed her lightly freckled face. She always had rosy cheeks, whatever the weather. She used to make me think of the apples that grew in the orchard at the back of John and Caroline's house. She was especially fond of books and, in addition to the Bible, she would encourage us to read fiction. There are lessons in life to be learned from their stories, she'd say. And so she introduced us to Fanny Burney, Samuel Richardson, Oliver Goldsmith.

Years passed.

When I was thirteen, it was decided I should help out more in the house. Caroline was pregnant, and she had the sickness right through her time. She'd previously suffered many miscarriages and was desperate not to lose this one. Caroline's younger sister, who had been living with us for two years, had just left to get married, and she had been replaced by her even younger brother, who was going to work with John in the Mine Office. And so I was asked if I might like to be Caroline's personal maid and housekeeper. "You are such a capable little Miss," she said.

I was happy to be able to do something to repay them for all their kindness. They gave me a maid's uniform to put on, which I enjoyed wearing. It made me feel important. I now had to remember to refer to John and Caroline as "Sir" and "Madam" and learn to say things like, "If you'll just come this way, Miss", or "I shall just enquire if Mr Lees can see you now, Sir."

But it was about this time, just after Caroline had given birth to Miss Agnes, and we were all so very busy, that John had his Damascene moment. "I have seen the light," he said. "God has shown me the way. I now know what I must do."

What he must do turned out to be far more drastic than Caroline could possibly have imagined, and it was to have far reaching consequences for me too.

He had decided he would devote his life completely to the establishment of that Moravian Community I had heard him discussing this with others some years before. It seemed that some land had become available in nearby Fairfield. He would sell his mines, along with several other enterprises he owned around Manchester, together with their beautiful house on King Street. The proceeds from all of these he would donate entirely to purchase the land and the leasehold and to build everything that was going to be needed there. Even more drastically, he would live on site in makeshift tents or barns, while Caroline and Agnes would travel by cart from place to place, like circus folk, only without the circus, living where they could, with various family members and friends, until Fairfield was ready for them to move into.

Caroline was appalled at the prospect but she would not argue with her husband. She saw what this meant to him, and she knew that, in the long run, it was what they had all been dreaming of and striving towards for so many years. "It's important to have dreams," she said to me the night before they left.

They were the last words she spoke to me, and I never saw her again…

She pauses. Rachel has been watching all the minuscule movements of her mouth and eyes while she has been speaking, trying to capture something of their essence in her portrait of her. She reminds her more and more of the canary in the cage beside her. From a distance she appears so finely etched in her markings, such beauty and poise. But the closer Rachel gets to her, the more she becomes aware of the way the fine hairs on the back of her neck, along each arm, tremble and quiver.

"I know something of the travelling life," she said after a moment. "We roamed over half of Europe before we alighted here."

"Was it worth it, in the end?"

"*Ja*, I think so. We all of us want somewhere to call home, don't we? *Heimat*, we call it in German."

"*Heimat*?"

"*Ja*. It means more than just the house you live in. Home*land* is a better translation. Somewhere you feel you can belong. A sense of history. Roots."

"But what if those roots get torn up?"

"You must wrap them up, keep them safe, till you can replant them, then you must water them and watch them grow again."

"I hope that Caroline felt that. She thought she'd found her home on King Street."

"*Ja. Ich verstehe*. But sometimes circumstances change."

Mercy nods.

"You did not accompany your Mistress?"

"No. John did not think it fair to ask that of me. Though I would have gone, if he *had* asked me. He arranged for me to stay on in the house as maid to the new owners. It was a condition of the sale."

"Ah. I see. That might have been a problem, I think?"

"Actually, it wasn't. The family who moved in couldn't have been nicer. *Très charmants, en fait.*"

"They were French?"

"Huguenots. Lacemakers. They were younger than John and Caroline. They'd just sold their business in Newton Heath and moved out to Dukinfield, which they regarded as the country. Though the mines and the mills were spreading along the Ashton Canal even then. In time it will join with Manchester in an unbroken chain."

"And children?"

Mercy shakes her head. "But they had books – Rousseau, Voltaire, Diderot – and they would hold *soirées*, full of talk and music. I'd be allowed to sit in and listen sometimes."

Rachel regards her. "Do you," she asks, as delicately as she can, "have children of your own?"

Mercy looks away.

"I thought perhaps you didn't."

"Not yet," adds Mercy, jutting out her chin defiantly.

"*Natürlich*," says Rachel. "*Du bist nach junge.*"

Mercy frowns.

"You're still young," repeats Rachel. She places her hand upon her belly and massages it abstractedly. She pauses for a moment and closes her eyes.

"Is everything all right?" asks Mercy.

Rachel smiles and nods. "*Ja*," she says. "She is moving a little, that's all."

"She?"

"I think it may be a girl, *ja*? Come." She stretches out her hand towards Mercy. "Would you like to feel it?"

Mercy moves across to her, allows Rachel to place her hand gently upon the swollen bulge, feels the movement beneath the stomach wall, like the fluttering of wings against a cage.

3rd Sitting

The Huguenots – Monsieur et Madame Robidoux – belonged to a widening circle of French émigrés and their supporters. This was 1791. Two years after the Revolution. The start of the Terror. Many who had supported the original aim to bring an end to the ancien régime now suddenly found themselves on the wrong side. Their desire for change was considered to lack the necessary zeal. They were labelled traitors and they had fled to England. Nevertheless they remained staunch Republicans. In

Manchester they found several allies sympathetic to the Jacobin cause. Some of these even formed a splinter group of the venerable Lit & Phil, the society having found itself almost equally split between those who declared themselves loyal subjects of King George – and by extension of King Louis also – and those who favoured the overthrow of the latter – and were thus at once assumed to be plotting the removal of the former. With England now at war with France it was a dangerous time to be seen speaking out in praise of Reform, however moderately. Meetings were held in secret, therefore, never in the same place twice, but the house on King Street, such an ironic name given the febrile climate of the times, remained at the heart of it, producing pamphlets, distributing broadsheets, inviting poets to address them. Southey and Shelley came one night. They argued fiercely and passionately, I remember. Southey left the next morning for the Lake District, where his wife owned a property, and where he was to meet with Wordsworth, with whom he would also quarrel, while I found Shelley in bed with my Mistress when I entered her chamber with coffee as was my custom. Neither seemed in the least perturbed.

I was now twenty years old. This was an education of an altogether different order.

A few weeks later there was a great hullaballoo in the house. A rumour had reached them that "a most important personage" had arrived in Manchester and was residing nearby. I did not hear his name at the time. All I knew was that once he had had the ear of Marie-Antoinette, then Robespierre, and now Le Petit Corsicain. Some said that he was over here in hiding, others that he had been trying to broker a treaty with Parliament between England and France. But whatever the truth – and this was something I was later to learn was never wholly possible to ascertain, to my own very great personal cost – his whereabouts were to be kept a secret. He was in need of a maid. It was the Robidoux's honour to have been tasked with finding him one. I should consider it my moral duty to volunteer.

Well – of course, that is what I did. Caught up in the revolutionary fervour of the moment, I packed my bags at once. A barouche was waiting for me outside – my first, and so far only journey in such a conveyance – and I was whisked away at daybreak to a remote farmhouse to the east of Levenshulme – Brook House, close by the Cringle Brook.

So instilled was I with a youthful passion to the cause espoused by my Mistress and Master and their circle of friends, that as the barouche sped on its way, I imagined myself being transported in a tumbrel along the streets of Paris, toward victory or death. And if I was to die, then let it be for a cause worth the sacrifice. I heard myself singing La Marseillaise loudly in my head.

Allons enfants de la patrie
Le jour de gloire est arrivé…

"Stop," commands Rachel. "Hold it right there please, that expression on your face if you can. That is what I must try to capture."

Mercy tries to remain as still as she can, freezing time as she relives the excitement of that first meeting with him.

"Tell me about him," asks Rachel. "I will try to paint as quickly as I can."

Charles Maurice, Duc de Talleyrand-Perigord, 1st Prince of Benevento.

Talleyrand.

He had a terrible reputation. You can't trust him, people said. You never know whose side he is on. Except his own. No secret is safe with him. He lies, he cheats, he deceives. He dissembles, he entraps, he betrays. He seduces.

Oh yes, I knew all about him long before I met him. Beware, they said. He's a terrible womaniser. He has more than a dozen mistresses, in every country in Europe, yet remains devoted to his wife. He has scores of illegitimate children, whom he adores but then deserts.

I knew all of this, yet still I was beguiled.

When I arrived at the farmhouse in Levenshulme, I was shown into a sitting room. He was not there at first and I was instructed to wait. I did not have to wait long. He burst into the room like a meteorite. He was accompanied by his secretary, a scholarly young Subaltern who had been seconded to him for the duration of his stay in England, and who was trying to write down as many of the words that Talleyrand unleashed in the comet's tail of fire that raged around him.

It was like that every time he entered a room. He flooded it with light and I was dazzled by him. As were all who came within his orbit.

It took him a while before he noticed me. But when he did, he was the epitome of gallantry and courtesy, treating me to many bows and flourishes. He took my hand and kissed it. The Subaltern was dismissed. He sat beside me on a chaise longue. He asked me my name. He bade me tell him all about myself. I was in thrall to him.

It was not long before I joined him in his bed, another notch upon his belt. But it did not feel like that at the time. He had the knack of appearing to give whoever he was with his complete and full attention. When he was with me, he told me he loved me, and in those moments I believed him, even though I knew deep down that when he was not with me, he would be hard put even to remember my name.

But I was young. Not yet twenty-one. Naïve enough to hope that perhaps I would be the one to stop him straying elsewhere. He was a most attentive lover. Passionate but gentle. He liked to make sure that I derived as much pleasure from it as he did. He was my first, but having had so many since, I can also say he was my best. He is the yardstick, the benchmark, against whom everyone else must be measured. Afterwards he would be so tender, so solicitous. He would speak to me then almost like a child, artlessly, concealing nothing. Or so it seemed to me then. I realise now that he never told me anything that might in any way have compromised his more important mission – the treaty he was trying to broker between the two warring sides. He was indiscreet in the names he mentioned – princes, prime ministers, ambassadors – but never in what any of them might have said. He revealed nothing of that. No state secrets passed between us in spite of everything else that did.

"Keep your friends close," he would say, "but your enemies closer."

"And which am I?"

He would put his hand across my mouth then and whisper, "I do not say this. These are the words of another..." And then he would proceed to kiss every part of me, and we would begin again.

But in the morning, when I awoke, he would always be gone. I would never hear him leave.

And then the time came when he left the farm house, left Levenshulme, left England and returned to France. He did not say adieu, but he left word with his subaltern, who handed me a sealed letter one morning, in which he expressed the hope that I would not forget him, "ton pauvre Talleyrand qui désire à te baiser une mille fois."

I was asked by the Robidoux to stay on, in case he should return, which, they said, remained a distinct possibility. And he did. Several times over the next few years. But he never stayed for long. "La guerre," he would say. "La politique." Then he would get that look in his eye, and he would carry me upstairs like a trophy. It was all a game to him. The Art of War. The Art of Changing Sides.

One time he was away for more than a year. It was rumoured he had been in America, where he allegedly got his fingers badly burned over an arms deal. But when he returned, apart from a few more grey hairs, which I caught him once trying to conceal with pomade, he was just the same.

"Ah," he sighed, "my secret is discovered. I am not the man you thought I was."

But he was.

"It's all a game," he would say, "a conjuring act performed with a sleight of hand, a trick of the light."

But is it? I wonder. Another thing he said, which I have always remembered, one time after we had made love, and he was beginning to feel a little sleepy, was this. 'In Paris, during the height of the Terror, when Madame La Guillotine's thirst for blood was insatiable, no one was safe, not me, not Napoleon, not Danton, not Robespierre. The situation was out of control. The people ran through the streets like frightened chickens. And even when their heads were cut off, still they ran, trampling on one another until they all collapsed in a mountain of twitching corpses. And then more chickens came, climbing and scrabbling up that rotting heap of dead bodies, screeching and squawking, until their heads were chopped off too, and they ran screaming through the streets, flapping their clipped wings in rage and fury.'

When I asked him what he meant, he said only this. "There has to be a better way."

"He was right," says Rachel, mixing a new colour with her palette knife.

"The next morning he was gone. That was the last time I saw him. The Robidoux received word that he was in Switzerland. The Treaty of Amiens, which he'd been working on for so long, had failed. England and France resumed hostilities."

"And meanwhile the harvests fail, the cost of bread rises, and there are food riots. I'm not sure I like your Monsieur Talleyrand, but he was right about saying we need to find a better way. We all of us want to make a better life for ourselves and for our children…" Rachel pauses while she looks down on her swollen belly. "That's why we traipsed across half of Europe to get here in the first place. But not if that means stealing the bread out of our neighbours' mouths."

"Something's coming," says Mercy. "I can feel it. It's in the air. It's in the song of this canary." She turns towards the cage suspended above her head. "It's in the turning of the water wheels powering the mills. It's in the rhythm of the looms, the shuttles flying forward and back, faster and faster. Something's got to give."

Rachel says nothing. She applies a few more brushstrokes to the painting.

"What happened?" she says eventually. "After he left?"

"The farmhouse was needed for someone else," says Mercy simply. "I had to leave. I walked west. To Manchester. I had no money. Only the clothes I stood up in. Admittedly very fine clothes. But nothing else. I needed a place to live. I found a room in Ancoats. Above a tavern on Butler Lane. *The Angel*. But they just wanted a skivvy. On call night and day, emptying slops, cleaning up vomit. No pay, just a bare room upstairs, with not a stick of furniture, not even a bed. I thought, this was not what my mother had in mind for me when she waved me away from Jamaica, bound for England and a better life."

"Couldn't you have found work as a maid in one of the nicer houses?" asks Rachel.

"I could have, I suppose. The Robidoux would have given me a reference. But I felt my days as a maid were over."

"Why was that?"

"The essential qualities for a maid are the same as for a child – be neither seen nor heard."

"Not this one," says Rachel, looking down at her belly. "I want her to make as much noise as she can and I intend never to let her out of my sight."

"Well – I wasn't a child any longer, and I never was very good at keeping quiet or invisible. I found a room above a different ale house. *The Crown & Kettle.* On the corner of Oldham Street and Ancoats Lane. Not far from here actually. The victualler was a Mr William Knowles. It was much better there. I was left to fend for myself. I could come and go as I pleased. So long as I paid my rent each week, he didn't much care what I did. I soon learned that the colour of my skin exerted a strange fascination with people. Especially the men. It gave me a kind of power. Something to bargain with. You want something different? Fine. You can have me. But it'll cost you. And no coming inside."

Rachel shudders. The contrast between her own intimate life with Benjamin and what Mercy now describes could not be more extreme.

"Anyway," continues Mercy, "I kept telling myself, it's only temporary. Something better will turn up soon. But then, before I knew it, a year had passed. Then two. I decided I had to stop. And I did. Only then I found I couldn't pay the rent. Mr Knowles was understanding. He let a couple of months go by before he said anything. Even then he gave me another month's notice. In the end I gave him no choice. All the same he wished me luck the day I left. I was on the streets then. I'd bed down in the Hulks. It wasn't so bad really. You'd meet all kinds there. People who'd once been respectable but had fallen on hard times. People who'd been born there and known nothing else. And people just arriving in Manchester from elsewhere, thinking it was the land of milk and honey and that the streets were paved with gold, only to discover that they weren't, not unless you belonged to the privileged élite, or somehow you married into it. This was the largest group by far. There were always new ones arriving, every day of every week, from somewhere or other. Lancashire, Yorkshire, Derbyshire, Cheshire. Or further afield, like Scotland or Ireland. So many from Ireland. And then people like me, from over the sea and far away…"

"Like me also. There are always more of us arriving, seeking refuge here."

"And you give it to them."

"Yes. If we can."

Mercy nods. She realises that she hasn't yet found that *heimat* to which Rachel referred earlier. She has always been on the outside of life, rather than at its centre. Except for a few times. When she was first with Jane and Margaret in Jamaica. Or with Caroline, shortly after Agnes was born. With Talleyrand.

Manchester is a melting pot into which, despite considerable agitation, not all the different elements have been absorbed. It is a rich stew into which many ingredients have been mixed, but which have yet to fully blend. It requires a skilled cook to stir them up sufficiently. Mercy wonders who that might be, and when it might happen. She only knows it needs to, and soon.

"So what happened?" asks Rachel. "To bring you here?"

Mercy looks down.

"I was hungry. I stole some bread. The baker caught me. I couldn't pay him. I said he could have me instead if he liked. A Constable overheard me. I was arrested. I could've been hanged, transported to Australia, at the very least thrown into prison. But Mr Oldham, the Magistrate, took a shine to me. Twelve months domestic servitude. At His Majesty's Pleasure. Or rather, Mr Oldham's. An experiment. So here you find me."

Rachel frowns. She adds a few last delicate brush marks to the canvas.

"And how has it been, this experiment?" she asks.

"Oh," says Mercy, looking around at the elegantly furnished room, smoothing down the folds in her fashionable dress, "it has its compensations."

Rachel nods. "And as you say… It's only temporary."

She puts down the paintbrush.

Mercy waits.

Rachel stands and stretches. She puts her hands into the small of her waist and tilts her head up and back.

"Do you want to see it?" she says. "I think it's done."

The two women stand together before the finished canvas. The portrait is the same, but each of them views it differently.

As does Matthew when he arrives home later that evening.

Rachel has departed leaving him a note stating that she hopes he is satisfied with the painting and requesting he may settle payment of the agreed fee with her husband at his earliest convenience.

Mercy is to be found sitting beside it, on the same chair, arranged beneath the caged bird, as the composition to be found in the painting, which is placed upon the easel next to her, in what is for Matthew an unnerving double vision. Only her expression varies. She is bent over some sewing when he enters the room. She glances up immediately, but the look upon her face could not be in greater contrast with that conveyed in the painting. She regards Matthew anxiously, nervously biting her lower lip. She grasps her stitching so tightly that she inadvertently pricks her thumb with a needle. Almost absent-mindedly she raises it to her mouth and sucks the blood, her eyes never straying from Matthew's face.

Whereas, in the painting, those same eyes are lifted towards the viewer – presumably Matthew also – in a kind of rapturous ecstasy. They burn with a passionate longing. The lips, slightly parted, yearn to be kissed.

Matthew looks first at one, then the other. Before Mercy can say a word, he snatches up the painting and rapidly flees upstairs with it, in his haste knocking the easel to the floor. The startled canary cheeps in alarm.

Matthew stays in his room upstairs a long time. He hangs the portrait in a recess next to the fireplace. Beneath it he affixes a narrow shelf to the wall, on which he places a lit candle on either end. He positions a chair exactly in the centre, from where he can sit and give the finished painting his full and undivided attention. The whole scene resembles a shrine, at which Matthew can worship. The parallel is not lost on him and it fills him with self-loathing. Yet still he sits there. Hour after hour. He cannot tear himself away. He pores over every last sordid detail of it.

Not for him, he knows, did that expression of spontaneous, unbridled joy arise. Yet only he will look upon it. The bitter irony twists inside him like a knife, a knife he knows that *he* has plunged there, no one else. He decides to hang a curtain before it, which, when he can no longer bear to gaze upon the expression on the face a moment longer, he may draw across it.

Until the next time. And there is always a next time.

Each time he draws that curtain back, he part convinces himself that this time he will feel differently. He will see that look of rapture and be persuaded that it is for him and him only, but, within a heartbeat of revealing it, he knows that not to be true.

She will betray him. Over and over. Till the last syllable of recorded time.

This is his future, he realises now, and the future of Manchester. *His* town. Or so he has always thought. He wants to own her, to possess her utterly, and for her to be everlastingly thankful to him for it. He wants to break her, to bend her to his will, to stamp the heel of his shoe into that face of ecstasy and press it down into the mud.

But he does none of this. Instead he gazes in unrequited longing upon her, imagining again that perhaps, after all, those lustrous eyes, those sensual, half-parted lips, are his, and his alone. Since none puts by the curtain that will show them but he.

What, then? What, if not he, causes that spot of joy to rise in her cheeks? Her breasts to heave and swell? He studies the painting minutely for some clue.

Yes. At last. He has it.

The bird.

Her beak open wide, singing with unalloyed pleasure, her gaze fixed at some unseen point beyond the canvas, beyond the confines of her cage.

A rage so fierce roars through his entire body that before he knows it, he is on his feet, knocking over the chair he has been sitting on, the suddenness of his movement snuffing out the candles, and tearing down the stairs to the sitting room.

He will confront her.

The next morning Mercy sleeps late.

For the first time since her captivity began, Matthew has not come to spy on her. She has not heard the landing creak to his shame-faced, barefoot creep towards her door. Last night, when she washed, she knew she was unobserved. No ritual flagellation followed. Instead she was aware of other noises emanating from behind Matthew's own closed door. The hammering of nails into a wall. The scraping of a chair upon the wooden floor. Later she thought she heard a deep-throated cry of pain, the sound of Matthew running down the stairs. Then sleep had taken her.

The three sittings with Rachel for the painting had emptied her and now that it was finished she felt exhausted, as if a kind of exorcism had taken place. And so she had slept more deeply than she had in years, so deeply that she had not heard Matthew leave the house for work that morning.

She splashes cold water on her face, washes the sleep from her eyes. She feels a lightness about her, so that she wanders idly down the stairs, still in her nightdress, trailing a hand upon the curved banister. A clear spring light slants in from outside through the hall window, in which dust motes turn and dance. The air feels warm on her skin.

She walks barefoot into the sitting room to greet the canary, which is how she likes to start each day, stretching out her hand towards the cage to coax her to sing, the notes capturing her own unspoken longings.

But on this particular morning the silence in the sitting room strikes her as soon as she enters. There is a heaviness here, quite distinct from the hope she felt on the stairs and in the hall. The curtains have not been opened. She flings them back. Sunlight scissors the room, cutting it into thin, sharp, bladed stripes, a carved *chiaroscuro* platter, across which Mercy runs, her flailing limbs alternately sliced in shadow and light, until she reaches the cage, its wire door swinging open, the hinges snapped and broken. There, in the centre, the light pools around the bird, her limp and lifeless body, her neck wrung and broken, her beak half open, her eyes dull, no longer shining.

Another month passes.

Barely a word passes between them. Matthew leaves the house early and comes back late. Mercy spends the days perfunctorily cleaning, sewing, mending, occasionally reading. She cooks meals neither of them wants to eat, meals they take separately and alone. Matthew retreats to his room as soon as he gets home each evening. He resists for as long as he can the temptation to draw back the curtain to reveal the painting, but eventually he yields. Then he lights the candles and loses himself utterly in his fruitless nightly attempts to find evidence of himself lurking somewhere, however deeply, in the penumbra of the sitter's gaze.

And then, having failed once more, he will draw the curtain across and blow out the candles.

Mercy waits for him to come to her, almost hoping now that he will, but he never does, hearing his moans of onanism and despair echo along the landing.

Dear Matthew,

There are now only three months remaining on my sentence of servitude here, after which you must, by law, release me. Unless you wish to bring against me a further case to prosecute. But on what grounds might you so act? Have I tried to escape? No. Have I not carried out all of my domestic duties as required? Yes. Have I not at all times been amenable to any other special requests you may from time to time have made of me? Yes. Would you be happy to present yourself as a witness if such a case, however spurious, was brought, exposing yourself to unwelcome public scrutiny? I think not.

And so, Matthew, I am certain that you will want to do the correct and proper thing according to both the spirit and the letter of the law. You have always been most scrupulous and honourable when it comes to such matters, and I trust you will be so again.

In the meantime I believe we must try and reach some kind of modus vivendi. Three months will seem a very long time if this war of attrition between us is allowed to continue to fester.

What I propose therefore is this.

We try at all times to be civil towards each other. The meals I prepare each evening we take together, during which we might exchange news of what we have each been doing in our separate domains. You will have much more of interest to impart than I, for you go abroad out into the world each day. I should take great pleasure from hearing about the people you encounter, the conversations you have with them, the changes you observe taking place around you across the town.

I realise I enjoy far more privileges than I would have, had I been given any of the other sentences you might legitimately have imposed upon me. I could have been transported halfway across the world. I know that my experience is far removed from that of others less fortunate than I who, as I write these words to you, languish in the dungeons of the New Bailey Prison. You took pity on this poor wretch standing before you at the Court Leet when I was at my lowest point, for which I shall always be grateful. But I am still deprived of my freedom in this permanent state of house arrest under which I suffer. I see people passing by the window of your home wherein I am incarcerated and long to be out there with them, adding my own small footprints to the constant flow of human traffic which constantly surges past. And so, hearing news of this tide of events, from your perspective and observations when you return each evening, will partly compensate for what I am daily deprived of, if only vicariously.

It will also, I hope, mark the first step in my rehabilitation. Prison, I believe, fulfils four basic functions: it punishes the offender; it protects society from their illegal activities; it deters others from becoming tempted to transgress the law themselves, and it reforms the criminal so that, after she is released, she will not re-offend, but that she will have learned her lesson and be ready to make a more positive contribution to society once she is returned back to it.

If I am to reap the benefits of your initial compassion in offering me this alternative to what would have been a much more difficult sentence for me to endure, one which I fear may have broken my spirit completely, then perhaps it is now necessary to institute some form of halfway house for me, whereby I might be allowed outside of my prison, under licence, supervised either by yourself, or by someone you trust and appoint for the task, for brief periods of time – possibly half an hour each day – during which I might take the first few tentative steps on the road back to liberty?

I assure you, Matthew, that if you were able to consider such a dispensation, you would find me most appreciative.

*Your obedient servant
in hopeful anticipation*

Mercy

After she has finished the letter, she re-reads it carefully, twice, before folding it in an envelope, which she places on the mantelpiece above the hearth in the dining room, along with all his other correspondence. It will have to do. She hopes it will appeal to that better side of Matthew's nature she has not seen evidence of for many weeks.

He agrees.

While part of him would like to keep her there for ever, a living incarnation of the bird who has not been replaced, another part recognises that her continuing presence would only serve to disquiet him further. He knows he could easily find quite legal ways of extending her sentence there if he so desired, and sometimes he does desire this. He also knows that even if were never to release her, her presence in his house, should he decide to invite guests again at any time – something he has not done once since Mercy came to stay with him – could easily be explained. "She's my maid," he would say. "Yes, she was at one time carrying out a period of domestic servitude here. When her sentence came to an end, I realised I could not manage without her." No. He cannot imagine himself participating in such a conversation. He can all too readily picture the exchange of looks, the knowing raised eyebrows, the whispers behind backs of hands whenever he appeared in so-called polite society, at those suppers and balls and parties, from which he is already beginning to find his name omitted when invitations are distributed.

And yet another part of him cannot now imagine her not remaining there always. But he has her portrait, which enthrals and mocks in equal measure. He tries to see if he can resist its pull for just one night, but finds he cannot. How long before the rage that impelled him to wring that damned canary's neck might tempt him to act with the same violence upon Mercy herself? Then what? The consequences are simply too appalling to contemplate. Everything he has worked for thrown away on the whim of a moment, the weakness of his will. He will take out the chains and punish himself harshly when such weakness threatens to overwhelm him, but the gratification is never so sweet as when Mercy administers those strokes herself.

No. He has to let her go. He understands this. But then he is consumed by the fear of just how much she knows about his private longings. His secrets. His darker desires. She could ruin him. There are many disreputable newspaper editors who would pay handsomely for such gossip. But that is all it is. Gossip. Unsubstantiated tittle-tattle. Who would believe the word of a convicted thief and harlot against that of his, a respected factory owner and magistrate? A Justice of the Peace. The son of his father. He puts his head in his hands at the thought of the shame such an article, were it to be published, would bring not only to himself, but to the legacy of his late father, against whom Matthew will always measure himself, even though he now knows him not have been his father. Except that he did take him in, when he could so easily have not. That he did decide to raise him as his own, instilling into him the values and beliefs he so devoutly held, values which Matthew, by these actions which Mercy could so easily expose to the rest of the world, has so manifestly failed to live up to.

He has no choice. Even were her claims to be discredited, the damage to his reputation could take months, years even, to recover from. He must accept her demands.

And yet, when he re-reads her letter for the umpteenth time, he realises she is making no demands. There are no threats there. Only a request. To be made ready for when the time comes to release her. By allowing her a few brief minutes of walking abroad each day, accompanied and supervised. Does her final remark, expressing just how appreciative she would be should he accede to her request, contain a promise? Or a threat? Unsaid but implicit nevertheless? He has no reason to think so. Nothing about her behaviour thus far has demonstrated any malice aforethought.

He realises he knows nothing about her. Nothing whatsoever.

And so he agrees.

"Yes," he says to her the next day, holding up the letter. "But not every day. Not to begin with. Let us work towards that. What do you say to once a week?"

Mercy has always known her letter would just be the start of a process, the opening round in trade negotiations, before a deal could be struck. Both of them are experienced in the choreography of barter.

"Twice a week," she says.

"Agreed," he replies. "Let us shake hands on it."

He holds on to her hand far longer than he needs to, but she does not object. It is the first time he has ever touched her.

*

Saturday 29th September 1804
GRAND MICHAELMAS FAIR
St Ann's Square, Manchester
(formerly known as Acresfield)

For One Night Only

Philip Astley's Travelling Circus
featuring

The One & Only Dulcibella Principessa of the High Wire

Performing for the Very Last Time
For Your Delectation & Delight

The Incomparable La Funambola

Will Walk The Tightrope

From the Summit of the Cotton Exchange
To The Topmost Tower of St Ann's Church

A splendid time is guaranteed for all

Arabella puts the finishing touches to her make-up and costume in the small tent behind the circus ring, which serves as her dressing room. It's been almost two decades since she last performed in Manchester, on the night of Mr Sadler's Balloon Flight, since when she has toured the whole country, sometimes performing quite close by, at fairs in Bolton and Bury, Rochdale and Oldham, Wigan and Warrington, Stretford and Altrincham, but never in Manchester itself. Several times Philip has urged her to, but always she has refused. The fear that her father, Mr Francis Reynolds, might step forward from the crowd, denounce her as his errant daughter and demand that she be returned to the bosom of her family, has always haunted her. Even though she has long passed the age of consent, and even though she and Philip have been living as common law husband and wife for more than half that time they have spent wandering in exile, awaiting the chance to return to the promised land.

But now that chance has come at last. Word reached them in the spring that her father had died of an apoplexy after being thrown from his horse while hunting, her mother having died several years before, reputedly of a broken heart after she, Arabella, had climbed out of her bedroom window at Strangeways Hall to the waiting arms of Philip, astride his white Lipizzaner stallion, to gallop them away to freedom. While she had lived at home, Arabella had seen little if any evidence to support the claim that her mother possessed any kind of heart at all.

So now here they were, pitching up for the last night of Manchester's Annual Michaelmas Fair, taking place, as it had for half a millennium, in what until only last year had been known as Acresfield, was still called that by everyone, but which had been rechristened as St Ann's Square. A smart, new address for the smart, new houses which now surrounded it on all four sides. Arabella cannot imagine the residents there tolerating the rough and tumble of the Michaelmas Fair taking place there for very much longer.

Arabella has decided to retire. This performance will be her last. In recent weeks her nerve – and her balance – have threatened to desert her. Twice last month she almost fell. The crowd gasped and then applauded all the more when she recovered and completed her walk. They probably thought it was all just part of the act, designed to make it look even more death-defyingly spectacular than it already was. But those near misses had not been planned. They left her shaking and terrified afterwards.

"I can't do it any more," she told Philip. "One of these days I'm going to fall. Then the crowd really will have had their money's worth."

"Don't say such things," said Philip, taking her into his arms.

"But it's true. Isn't that why they come? To see me fall?"

"No, my darling. They come to gaze up at you in awe and admiration. They adore you."

"They come to see me die," she said.

"To *cheat* death, not to die."

"Well I can't do it any more, Philip. I just can't."

Philip held her closely. He could feel her shoulders shaking in his arms. It was true. She had lost her nerve and she could no longer continue.

On the other hand they were booked at fairs across the country right through till the end of the year. To cancel would be unthinkable. For one thing the loss of revenue would be catastrophic.

But he loved Arabella, and the thought of losing her outweighed all other considerations.

"May I suggest a compromise?" he said at last, after she had begun to calm down.

She looked at him through narrowed eyes, her senses immediately back on high alert. "What kind of compromise?"

"Let's make this season your Grand Farewell Tour, with Manchester the final performance. It would be fitting, don't you think, to end where it all began?"

Arabella saw the symmetry of that. She appreciated that Philip was trying to make finishing easier for her. A series of goodbyes to audiences who had watched her down the years, marvelling at her skill and daring, now coming to say a heartfelt thank you for all the thrills and excitement she had given them. And then to finish for good with a performance back in Manchester felt like the perfect way to bring the curtain down on what had been a life spent on the move, travelling the spine of England, along its highways and by-ways, its roads, rivers and canals, observing all its many changes, the growth of its foundries and factories, mines and mills, the shift in power from the rural market towns of the south to the industrial power houses of the north.

Yes. She could manage that. Putting a date to the final show, knowing that afterwards she would no longer have to climb that ladder, up into the sky, feel the rush of air upon her face, then step out on to that humming, swaying wire, has made the prospect of those few remaining dates more bearable.

Since then, she has been fine. There have been mercifully no repeats of those terrifying losses of balance, and now, as the final night approaches, she feels calm, her nerves under control.

"Five minutes," says Philip, popping his head round the flap of the tent. "Let's make this a night to remember."

"A night to remember indeed," says Mr Carlton Whiteley to the rest of his cast of *The Rivals*, which has just completed a week of sell-out performances at their makeshift theatre across The Actors' Bridge. "We've been the Hit of the Season, the Talk of the Town. The critics from London are beginning to take notice. Mark my words, they'll be flocking to our next production in droves, if you'll pardon my mixing of metaphors."

He is still wearing his frock coat and wig for Sir Anthony Absolute, in which role he has, though modesty forbids him from saying so out loud, excelled, while Mrs Whiteley's Mrs Malaprop has been a veritable triumph. The two of them now take the plaudits from their loyal and admiring company before sitting companionably side by side upon the rather moth-eaten chaise longue, which features in as many productions as possible.

"Well, my dear," he continues, beaming, "that's quite enough from me. What did *you* think of my performance?"

The rest of the actors laugh politely at this oft-heard joke.

Mrs Whiteley points her fan at the chandelier above their heads. "How many actors does it require to change a candle?" she asks.

"Ten," chorus the cast, who are well rehearsed in this post-performance repartee.

"Ten?" demands Mrs Whiteley imperiously.

"Yes," they cry. "One to change the candle and nine to say, 'That could have been me up there'."

"You naughty children," scolds Mrs Whiteley, pointing her fan at every one of them. "You'll be the death of me."

If only, thinks Carlton, then hastily looks around to check that he has not spoken this thought aloud, which is something he does increasingly these days. But there appears to be no come-back. The actors are conversing gaily among themselves. 'Zounds, a reprieve! He leans across to plant a kiss upon his wife's rouged and powdered cheek, who reacts as if she has never been kissed before, by him or anyone. She flutters her eyelashes, calls for smelling salts, then furiously fans her ample bosom, far too much of which is revealed for Carlton's liking. "Lud, Sir Anthony," she gushes, "I am all undone!"

We're behaving as if the play is continuing, thinks Carlton. But then, aren't we always? An actor is never off stage. Well, they have got away with it, if truth be told. Despite his public bravado, he knows, at best, that this has been no more than second rate. Ah, if only he could have given them his *Coriolanus*... But that was not to be.

So what *will* be their next offering? He watches with distaste the foppish Mr Ponsonby flirting disgustingly with Mrs Carlton. He kisses her hand, he whispers in her ear, he fetches her wine, he goes down on one knee and offers her one of the paper roses they use as props. "She loves me, she loves me not," he chimes, plucking a petal with each phrase. Mrs Carlton, who is old enough to be the boy's mother, and who really should know better, serves only to encourage him. She simpers, she giggles, she trills, she tra-las. '*Like the poor cat i'th' adage.'* Ugh! The spectacle sickens him. She takes what remains of the paper rose from Ponsonby's reptilian hands and raises it to her nostrils, closing her eyes as if its fragrance has enraptured her. What game are they playing, he wonders? *'Look like th' innocent flower, but be the serpent under 't...?'*

No. Wait. Now he sees it. He has been watching the wrong play. Ponsonby has received favourable notices for his portrayal of the witless buffoon Franklin in Mr Sheridan's play. Hardly an achievement, that. The real genius lies in the casting, as always. Ponsonby merely had to open his mouth and pipe in that effeminate lisp of his to become Franklin incarnate, And even then he had to be dragged through each performance by Miss Appleby as the delightful Julia. Ah, sweet Miss Appleby, thinks Carlton. So tender, so innocent. How apt her name – *Apple*by – her cheeks, her curls, her dainty charms, just waiting to be plucked...

He stops himself from imagining anything further. His hands already, he notices, have formed themselves into upturned cups as if already receiving a bountiful windfall...

Miss Appleby, his protégée, who would have made the perfect Virgilia, had he presented his *Coriolanus* after all. But of course. Juliet. That is the part she was born for. He looks back at Ponsonby, still cavorting ridiculously on his knees. " '*A rose by any other name would smell as sweet*'," he declaims, coming up for air from between Mrs Whiteley's mountainous breasts, casting an eye in Carlton's direction. He is auditioning for Romeo right before his eyes. And his wife is actively encouraging him. "I could give my Nurse again. What think you, husband?" And at once she steps into character, with voice and gait so finely woven, that she is the very cloth of her.

" *'I remember it well.*
Tis since the earthquake now a deal of years,
And she was wean'd, I never shall forget it,
For I had then laid wormwood to my dug,
Sitting in the sun under the dove-house wall...

*For then she could stand alone – nay, by the rood,
She could have run and waddled all about,
For e'en the day before she broke her brow;
And then my husband – God be with his soul,
He was a merry man – took up the child:
'Yea,' quoth he, 'dost thou fall upon thy face?
Thou wilt fall backward when thou hast more wit,
Wilt thou not, child? And, by my halidom,
The pretty wretch left crying, and did say, 'Aye'.'"*

The entire company bursts into spontaneous applause, which Mrs Whiteley milks for all it is worth.

Ah well, sighs Carlton. Second-guessed again. I suppose this means we shall present the play. Ponsonby will be Romeo, Miss Appleby Juliet. The star-crossed lovers. His wife will give her Nurse, for it is indeed a deal of years since she laid wormwood to her dug, while he... Yes, he might be tempted to pronounce the Prologue – "*where civil blood makes civil hands unclean*" – and then return, perhaps, to deliver judgement as the Prince – "*a glooming peace this morning with it brings; the sun, for sorrow, will not show his head*". Why, he might even revive as well his Apothecary in a cameo – "*my poverty, but not my will consents*," hanging his head in a charade of mock sorrow.

"Come," he commands, "a toast. An end to all rivalries. *Merde!*"

"*Merde!*" they reply in unison.

"Then let us repair to the nearest tavern.

" *'The which if you will patient ears attend
What here shall miss, our toil shall strive to mend'.*"

Dulcibella blows her lover a kiss, wraps the glittering diamante black cloak around the sequined sparkle of her white ballet tutu, then places the silver mask upon her face. This precaution she adopted to disguise her true identity has now become the signature trademark of *La Funambola.*

She takes a deep breath, then signals she is ready.

Outside the orchestra strikes up the opening bars of Handel's *Entrance of The Queen of Sheba.* The enormous crowd bursts into excited applause, clapping along in rhythm, before plunging into a silence so deep it appears to envelop the whole of Manchester, as if the entire town is hovering on the brink of something momentous.

Among the crowds thronging the square are Zachary and Fanny, who were in St George's Fields nearly twenty years ago for Dulcibella's première performance. The night of the Balloon Flight. The night Zachary proposed. Less than six weeks later they were married. Since when they have not spent a single night apart.

Back then their whole futures had seemed to stretch out before them. Like Dulcibella they had placed one foot in front of the other as they walked the precarious high wire. They had not known for certain whether that foot, as it stepped out trustingly into thin air, would find a place that it could step upon, or whether it would miss, and bring them both crashing down to earth.

But that has never happened. They've kept going through all these years, and here they are, still walking together, still trusting that they will not miss their footing. When Zachary had first viewed Fanny, through the sightlines of his compass and theodolite, she had set a benchmark that remained for him the Golden Mean, the yardstick by which every other moment in his life would be measured, and never once has she come up short. In fact she has surpassed it, day after day, year after year. It was from the top of the church tower, while surveying for some of the fine houses which now decorated the square, that he had first seen her, entering from a passageway behind the

Exchange, and now the *Principessa* of the High Wire will walk the tightrope that is stretched directly between those two vantage points, those twin pillars of commerce and religion, the Exchange and the Church.

He looks up. The wire is so narrow he can barely see it, a thin black line carving the sky. It seems impossible that anyone could manage to cross it. Fanny clings to him tightly, as if sharing the same thought. She has always been his *principessa* and he squeezes her back. She coughs, only a little at first, but it is not long before her whole body is wracked with it. He passes her a handkerchief, which she holds to her mouth. After the fit has passed, she quickly puts the handkerchief away in her pocket, but not before he has glimpsed the tell-tale spots of red speckling the white linen. She smiles weakly up at him. He smiles back, then looks away. A breeze has picked up, smarting his eyes and making them water.

Also among the throng are Benjamin and Rachel, who carries their new-born daughter, Naomi, on her arm. These Manchester streets have become so familiar to them over the years since they first arrived, when the town was decked out for another Fair, at Whitsun, their *Shavuot*. Several in the crowd greet them as they pass. The women all want to coo over the baby, nodding and smiling, as they decide which of their parents she most takes after.

"She has her father's eyes," says Rachel.

"But thankfully her mother's sweet nature," adds Benjamin.

On the other side of the square Rachel catches sight of Mercy, walking beside Matthew, her arm linked through his. Her jaw drops – she cannot help it – and she tugs her husband's sleeve and points. Benjamin firmly steers them away in the opposite direction. Matthew is a valued customer but he has no wish to engage with him socially, although he recognises that

Rachel may well have wished to catch up with Mercy. Another time perhaps.

Mercy and Matthew position themselves midway between St Ann's Church and the Exchange, from where they should be able to take in the entire walk. It is Michaelmas Day. Mercy's twelve months' sentence has been completed. She has been released from her servitude but has agreed to accompany Matthew to the Fair. He asked her quite formally and stiffly over breakfast if she would allow him to escort her to the square, where he thought she might like to witness the extraordinary spectacle of *La Funambola*, who has been the only topic of conversation on people's lips for a fortnight. The town will be more than unusually crowded this evening, he had added, and she might value his protection. She had smiled when he said that. But she recognised it too for what it was and thanked him for his thoughtfulness and consideration. Yes, she had said. She would be delighted. His face had lit up. She does not believe she has ever seen him smile before.

Now they stand with the rest of the crowds. The excitement is infectious. The music has finished playing. A tense drum beat accompanies each step Dulcibella takes as she slowly climbs the ladder that has been affixed to the side of the church tower, which will take her to the tiny platform that awaits her. While she climbs, Matthew leans in to Mercy and whispers in her ear.

"I have a proposition to put to you," he says.

Mercy's eyes widen in surprise. Surely not, she thinks?

"No," he adds hastily, seeing the astonished expression on her face. "I merely wonder if you might consider staying on?"

"In what capacity?" she asks.

"A *paid* capacity," he adds.

"As what?" she replies, more bluntly than she intends.

He pauses. Her directness has taken the wind out of his sails. But he is not surprised. She is bound to be suspicious. After all that has happened between them.

"As maid and housekeeper," he says.

"And nothing more?" She holds his gaze. It is he who looks away first.

"No," he says, under his breath. "Nothing more."

Not yet, she thinks, but I know you. You're a patient man. You think to wear me down over time.

"Thank you, Matthew," she says. "That is most kind. But no. I need to strike out on my own."

"Yes. Of course." His tone is less sad, than resigned. "I expected you to say no. But I thought I'd ask anyway. Just in case."

"Just in case what?"

"Our last weeks together might have changed your mind."

"Yes. I see." There is something in what he says. These last few weeks *have* been different. Better. They have found their *modus vivendi*, which she had asked for in her letter to him. She has been allowed to venture out of the house twice a week under the watchful eye of the Clerk of the Court and a Constable, who have followed her respectfully a couple of paces behind her. She quickly got used to their presence. It was as if she had two shadows. Sometimes one would walk ahead of her, the other behind, but neither of them ever spoke to her, or looked her in the eye, except to bid her "Good day" when they arrived to collect her and when they once more deposited her back at the house on Oldham Street. Two shadows. Each guarding different directions, in case she tried to take advantage of her gaoler's dispensation. But she was never once tempted to run. Just to be out in the air was enough. To feel the breeze upon her face.

As she does now, as the evening closes in, and *La Funambola* nears the platform at the summit of the ladder.

"In that case," says Matthew, rousing her from her reverie, "perhaps you will do me the honour of accepting this?" He holds out a purse before her. "As a token." He presses it into her palm. "To tide you over till you find your feet."

"Matthew," she begins, "I can't accept this."

"Why ever not?" he says, seemingly not in the least offended. "I'd say it was a sensible thing to do. You're just starting out again. You haven't a penny to your name. You've turned down my offer of a job. What will you do for food and lodgings?"

"Thank you," she says. "But I'll manage."

"Like you did last time? In less than a month you'd be back before the Bench. I would not be able to be so accommodating next time."

"Accommodating?" She regards him with incredulity.

"There'd be fewer options open to the Court. One would have to take into account the fact that it was a repeat offence."

"A repeat offence?"

"How else will you survive?"

She looks up at *La Funambola*, who is about to take her first step upon the high wire. There is a dramatic drum roll to accompany her.

"Oh," says Mercy, "I shall simply place one foot in front of the other."

"And if you fall?"

"I shan't. But if I do, I'll take my chances. That's the thing about freedom, Matthew. It's like love. It must be unconditional. You can't place restrictions on it. You can't buy it, no matter how much money you have. You can't keep it in a cage or hidden behind a curtain. You've got to let it into the light, let it feel the air on its skin. You've got to trust it, Matthew, however fragile and precarious it may seem."

They both look up.

Arabella is walking the tightrope. She never once looks down. Instead she looks ahead. The rivers and canals radiate away from the town, bringing the raw materials she needs, carrying away her finished goods. The Irwell, the Medlock, the Irk, and all their many tributaries and canals. The Bridgewater, the Rochdale, the Ashton. The Bolton & Bury, the Stockport &

Tame. An intricate spiderweb of veins and arteries, circulating round her body, tightening the warp, stretching the weft, pouring from her outstretched fingers, like constellations. The Plough. The Forge. The Kettle. The Scales. Weighing the losses and gains in their vacillating balance.

Step by step Arabella nears her destination. Just as she is approaching the end of the wire, as it climbs steeply towards the roof of the Exchange, she pauses. She lifts one foot into the air, lets it hover unsupported, suspended in empty space, before placing it down in front of her. Then, instead of completing the climb, she wheels around in a complete one hundred and eighty degree turn, to face once more the direction she has travelled from, sinks low on her knees. The crowd gasps. She raises one leg slowly to the side and executes a perfect *ronde de jambe en l'air*. She has a smile upon her face. She swivels back round and completes her final step towards the other side.

Matthew is entranced. He turns to share his wonder with Mercy, but she has gone. He just has time for one last sight of her until she becomes absorbed among the crowds. Black on black. He feels a slight agitation in the air above his head as a moth gently brushes against his face before she is gone.

Mercy weaves in and out between the milling throngs. She finds that she is singing. The old slave song her mother taught her.

"Me know no law, me know no sin
Me's just what ever dem make me
Dis is de way dey bring me in
So God nor Devil take me..."

14

25th December – Christmas

Essay No. 4

"Why does water not admit its bulk of every kind of gas alike? This question I have duly considered, and though I am not yet able to satisfy myself completely, I am nearly persuaded that the circumstance depends upon the weight and number of the ultimate particles of the several gases, those whose particles are lightest and single being least absorbable and the others more according as they increase in weight and complexity."

My Dear Father,
It is with a sad and heavy heart that I write to you and Mother this cheerless Christmas morning.

We are all confined to quarters here in the Barracks – at my urging – in case there is any repetition of the disorder which swept through Shude Hill three days ago, an event which I am certain you will have read about, but in case news of it has not reached you, I enclose the following cutting from The Manchester Mercury...

The Manchester Mercury

23rd December 1804

Shude Hill Potato Riot

Distressing Scenes in Manchester's Heart

Thousands of starving men, women and children converged on the markets of Shude Hill yesterday in a desperate attempt to procure for themselves the barest necessities in basic foodstuffs.

Following two successive poor harvests, exacerbated by the French blockade of Channel ports, thereby preventing the import of grain from Europe, the food shortage hit a crisis point this month, and prices have rocketed, way beyond the means of the average Manchester labourer and his family.

The spark which ignited yesterday's riot came when a rumour spread around the town of a shipment of potatoes arriving by barge on the Bridgewater Canal. This precious cargo was escorted to the markets under the armed protection of the Manchester Home Guard, commanded by Colonel Joseph Hanson. He and his men had to hold back the clamouring crowds the entire length of the Dean's Gate from the Castlefield Basin to Penniless Hill. But when, within minutes of the potatoes going on sale, the whole paltry amount was sold to merchants at inflated prices, leaving nothing left for the ordinary families so desperate for sustenance, tempers, which were already fraying, finally snapped.

The angry crowds turned into a snarling, unchained beast, which, in its fear and agitation, turned over market stalls, looted nearby shops and threatened to inflict damage upon the persons of the wealthy merchants emerging simultaneously from the Exchange.

Magistrates ordered The Volunteers to turn from escort to peacekeeper, which in swift order progressed into law enforcer with calamitous consequences. Officers, with swords drawn, harried and pursued the crowds through the streets of the town, cornering many scores of them in alleyways and *cul de sacs*. Several of these unfortunate souls who found themselves thus trapped were women and children. The sounds of their screams of terror and panic will long haunt all those who heard them.

Many arrests were made. Their cases will be heard by local Magistrates and Justices of the Peace in the coming weeks. Meanwhile those awaiting trial will be spending their Christmas this year as guests of the wardens of the New Bailey Prison, where at least the meagre fare of bread and water they will receive there will be more than those not arrested might expect to partake of in their bare, mean homes.

The Manchester Mercury, while it cannot condone actions of rioting or looting by members of the public, however desperate their circumstances, at the same time proclaims that the actions of the soldiers in clearing the streets, and the decision by the Court Leet and the Boroughreeve to order them so to proceed, brings shame and dishonour upon a town which rightfully claims to be the world's first truly modern metropolis. An even greater shame is that thousands of its citizens should go hungry when the wealthy few, the manufactory and mill owners, sit down this Christmas to their roast goose with all the trimmings beside roaring coal fires, while the providers of their wealth – the mill workers and miners – shiver and starve.

... In the days since, Father, the men and I have had much to reflect upon, particularly with regard to our own role in these most distressing events. Did our intervention prevent a full scale riot, or were our actions partly to blame, adding further fuel to a fire that might otherwise have sputtered and died? For my own part, Father, I fear it was the latter. And I have been much disquieted in rumination of this possibility.

When I first joined the military, almost two decades ago, I was an idealistic young man with dreams that I was serving my country for the cause of the greater good, to bring peace and harmony at home and abroad, but now I have begun to doubt whether I have achieved any of these things. Rather, it seems as though I might have contributed, albeit unwittingly, to the exact opposite.

Accordingly I have decided to resign my commission. I do so with a heavy heart but I believe I have no alternative if I am to remain true to my original ideals, ideals which you and my dear Mother instilled in me from my birth, and which I have always tried to live by. I hope you will not be too disappointed in me, Father.

I should like, with your permission and blessing, to return home to you in Ardwick. As you know, I am not yet married. I currently have no children or other responsibilities. I am therefore free to assist you in the running of your several textile businesses alongside the many charitable good works among the labourers and their families that I know you undertake. I wish to be of some use to you, Father. I wish to atone for my past and present wrongs. I wish to make a difference.

Your loving and obedient son, who wishes you as merry a Christmas as he can, in these current distressing circumstances.

Joseph
(Hanson, Colonel: Manchester Home Guard Volunteers).

Herewith is affixed my last official use of the Regimental Seal

*

Zachary sits beside Fanny as the first grey streaks of light begin to seep through the thick blanket of dark sky this pale Christmas morning. He has kept watch throughout the night, until sleep finally stole upon him, and he wakes now with a start. The candle next to her bed has burnt out and for a moment he thinks she must no longer be breathing, for the room is heavy with silence. Then, another rasping cough shakes her thin, tired body, and her eyes open. He damps the end of a handkerchief with some drops of water and lays it gently upon her cracked, parched lips.

"Thank you," she croaks, her voice little more than a rustling of dry leaves.

He looks down on her shrunken form, a bare husk beneath the cotton sheet, which, light and threadbare as it is, feels too heavy for her. She's already slipping away from him, disappearing before his eyes, like a wisp of smoke, a ghost of the woman who first swept him up in her wake, when her energy and power was like the Irwell in full spate, but whose force has now been reduced to less than a trickle. He does not know how he will survive without her.

She tries to speak but her words evaporate almost before they leave her lips. He bends his ear towards them and listens again. Her voice now only a whisper, the faintest disturbance in the fabric of the air.

"It's time," she says.

He nods. He knows what she means. She wants him to bring the children to her. He lays his hand as gently as he can upon her arm and nods again. Her skin is paper. He smoothes the damp feathers of her hair away from her forehead.

"Yes," he says. "I'll fetch them now."

He tiptoes softly towards the door. As soon as he opens it, all the children rise as one from the oak settle on the landing around which they have been gathered and waiting all night. One by one they creep into the room, like church mice.

Billy, the eldest, still in his postboy's uniform.

Susannah, the practical one, ushering in Richard and Paul, the twins, who wipe the sleep from their eyes with identical gestures.

Ginny, who has not stopped crying since it became clear that their mother was not going to get better, bites her lower lip in an effort to stop. Susannah whispers in her ear to try and be brave. She nods her head up and down several times, then reaches out her hand for her sister to take.

Lemuel, who has put on a sudden growth spurt over the summer, shooting up several inches, is now almost as tall as his brother, Billy. He is all arms and legs, which he has not yet found a way of keeping under control, so that he practically stumbles into the room.

And last of all Lavinia, the oldest of the girls, who carries baby Jemma in her arms, who is fast asleep at last, having been fractious and fretful for most of the night. Jemma, who is not yet twelve months old, since whose birth Fanny has never fully recovered. Fanny, who did not have a baby for the first three years of her marriage to Zachary, who began to wonder if perhaps she might never have any, who then proceeded to have eight in twelve years.

But it has not been this near permanent state of childbirth which has laid her low, though Lord knows, thinks Zachary guiltily, it can't have helped. But she was always delighted each time she found herself pregnant. Her face would shine as she announced the news to Zachary, and he would shake his head and smile. "We shall need more room," he would say, and when the lower floor of the house on Bridge Street became available, as well as the upper floor they already occupied, Zachary used the modest sum he had raised from the sale of the Wire Works in Shakerley after his father died to purchase it. His mother came to live with them too at that point and was a great help and comfort to them, but she did not survive her husband's passing by more than a couple of years, after which Lavinia, and then Susannah, took on more of the duties of child care, while Fanny devoted herself to the next new baby.

No, it was the phthisis which took Fanny. What began as a dry, ticklish cough gradually progressed to something much worse, a condition which accelerated rapidly after the birth of Jemma, who, unlike all the previous children, had proved a difficult pregnancy and was now a sickly child, who only Lavinia, it seemed, knew how to calm and soothe.

But Lavinia did not live at home. From a very early age she exhibited a cleverness and aptitude for learning that Fanny and Zachary recognised at once and were at a loss how best to encourage and nurture. Then Zachary's father wrote to them about the schools that the Moravians had set up in Fairfield, one for boys and, uniquely, one for girls, the first so created anywhere in England. Zachary's father had remained in close contact with the community in Fairfield, still ran a small meeting house in Shakerley, and said he would write to them there to see if they might take Lavinia. Although Zachary and Fanny were staunch Methodists, first attending the Central Chapel on Oldham Street where they had got married each Sunday, then later the Independent Chapel on Mosley Street, when the Central Hall could no longer guarantee to have sufficient spaces for their rapidly growing family, they soon received word that there was a place for Lavinia at Fairfield, both in the school and in the Single Sisters' boarding house, where she could lodge and receive food as well as learning.

That was five years ago, and there was always much rejoicing each time she came back to Bridge Street for the holidays. This year, when she returned for Lammas, she saw the change in her mother at once. She did not return to Fairfield for Michaelmas, and she had somehow managed to be everywhere at once. Zachary has come to depend on her utterly. He could not have managed a single day without her. Nor can he imagine managing the children alone after her mother has died, which is now a mere matter of minutes away, if Lavinia should return to Fairfield, which Zachary does not in any way wish to prevent.

But more than this, Zachary cannot even begin to conceive of a life without Fanny. Since their wedding there has not been a day when they have not been together, not a night when they have been apart. He feels already, as he and the children gently gather at her bedside, that an essential part of him is beginning to leave his body. He feels that he too is disappearing, mingling with the smoke rising upwards from the candle that Susannah has relit.

When he was a child, Zachary used to visit his grandfather every afternoon when he finished school. He would usually have his tea there, potatoes and pork, before returning home when it grew dark, when his mother and father would be back from their shift at the Wire Works. His grandfather had only one leg. The other was sawn off at the knee. He had lost it, he told Zachary one time, when he was sick of being pestered with questions about it by his chatterbox of a grandson, in an accident at the saw mill. That had put a quietness on Zachary, who never asked about it again, except when his grandfather would complain about how he still felt an ache in it sometimes, years after they had cut it off. Remembered pain, he called it, and now Zachary knows exactly what his grandfather meant. He feels it acutely now, in the centre of his chest, where his heart is now cracked and broken.

Fanny says her final farewells to each of the children in turn. With a look, a smile, the lifting of a hand, sometimes, even, a word. When it comes to Lavinia's turn, she somehow manages to summon one last ounce of strength to hold her to her for longer. She whispers something to her that no one else can hear. Afterwards Lavinia ushers the children downstairs, so that their parents can spend these last few moments together, alone.

Fanny points feebly towards an old trunk at the foot of the bed. Zachary nods. He knows what she wants. He goes towards it, lifts its lid and gently takes out something wrapped in fine white tissue paper. He carries it towards her reverently as if he is one of the three wise men. He lays it by her side, then carefully begins to open it. Inside is the white muslin cloth, with its lacework pattern of moths, caught in the leaves of a laurel. He holds it up for her to examine. Her fingers brush against it. The moths appear to flutter then settle again. It is what she wore to get married, given to her as a gift by Mr and Mrs Oldham, because she had always admired it, ever since her eyes first fell upon it, when she found the baby Matthew folded in it, left on their doorstep on the night of the Earthquake.

Zachary places it upon her head, arranges it so that it falls delicately onto her thin shoulders, tucks her hair inside it, leans her head back against a pillow.

He takes both her hands in his, barely touching their paper skin, translucent and fragile as a moth's wings. She closes her eyes, smiles. One last slow sigh empties her.

Later, when it has become as light as it will get this Christmas morning, he comes downstairs. The children all rise. He looks at Lavinia. He is cradling the cotton shawl in his hands. He walks across to his daughter and places it into her hands. She nods.

"From now on," she says, turning back to her brothers and sisters, "I will be your little mother."

*

Abner sits at his desk in the upstairs room on Brazenose Street. The night sky is too cloudy for him to observe it through his telescope. Instead he is putting the finishing touches to a set of calculations he has been set by Mr Dalton, measuring the exact proportions of different gases in the air, once they have been absorbed after considerable agitation.

The diagram he has drawn to represent the different interactions that occur between each one reminds him of the astronomical charts he has pinned to the walls in this room, as he seeks to unlock their eternal mysteries, probing ever further, ever deeper, into the vast distances of space to find the absolute heart of the tiniest atom, rescued from the daily disturbances in atmospheric pressure.

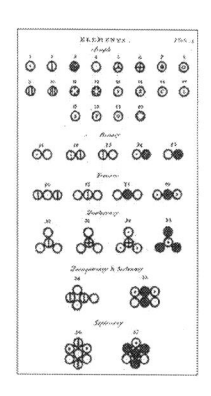

*

Mr Dalton looks up at his audience over the rim of his half moon spectacles.

"An enquiry into the relative weights of the ultimate particles of bodies," *he says*, "is a subject, as far as I know, entirely new and, because of this, naturally disturbing. It is worthy of much greater study."

He picks up his papers, shuffles them together, then steps down from the platform.

Laurel continues in:
Volume 2: Victor
(Ornaments of Grace, Book 7)

Dramatis Personae

(in order of appearance)

CAPITALS = Main Characters; **Bold** = Significant Characters;
Plain = Characters (who appear once or twice only)

Gabriel Locke, a carter
Edwin Stone, a handloom weaver
Joan Stone, Edwin's wife
Henry Stone, Edwin's son
Dr Charles White, Manchester Infirmary
Thomas Barnes, co-founder of Manchester Lit & Phil
Thomas Henry, co-founder of Manchester Lit & Phil
Dr Thomas Perceval, co-founder of Manchester Lit & Phil
Elizabeth Raffald, a midwife
Brother Joseph Saxon, a Moravian
Brother John Swertner, a Moravian
Brother Worthington, a Moravian
JOHN LEES, a miner from Dukinfield, later a Moravian
Brother La Trobe, a Moravian
Sir Ashton Lever, founder of the Holophusicon
LEIGH PHILIPS, son of John Philips, later a soldier
Lady Ashton, Sir Ashton's wife
John Philips, a cotton magnate
Nathaniel Philips, John's brother
Thomas Philips, John's brother
Andrew Oldham, a prominent Methodist and felt maker
John Wesley, the Methodist preacher
Catherine Oldham, Andrew's wife
John Raffald, Elizabeth's husband, a publican
Josephine Philips, John Philips' wife
Septimus Swain, The Old Retainer, the Hulks
PHOEBE, mother of Amos and Matthew
Robert Gore, Unitarian Minister
WHELP, later **PITY**, a street urchin
Tom, Sir Ashton's groom

Mrs Clamp, a drunken wet nurse
The Spaniard
Maud, a wet nurse in New Bailey Prison
Alfred, a Beadle
AMOS, born on the night of the earthquake
Frances 'FANNY' Cox, the Oldhams' maid
MATTHEW, twin brother of Amos
Rev. Beilby Porteus, Bishop of Chester
James Sadler, a Balloonist
ZACHARY ROBINSON, a surveyor
Overseer in House of Correction
Jonathan Haworth, a rich merchant
The Great Usurper, Swain's successor, the Hulks
Jeremiah 'JEM' Stone, Foreman at Arkwright's Mill
Ada Briggs, resident in Fogg's Yard
Mrs Stone, Jem's mother
Francis Reynolds, Strangeways Hall
Mary Reynolds, Francis's wife
Arabella Reynolds, Francis's daughter
Philip Astley, founder of Astley's Circus
Major-General Roger Aytoun, Manchester Volunteers
Barbara Minshull, Aytoun's wife
Baroness Elizabeth Mosley, Lady of the Manor
Lt Joseph Hanson, rival to Leigh Philips
Mr Carlton Whiteley, an Actor Manager
Mrs Henrietta Whiteley, Carlton's wife
Mr Briggs, Ada's father
Gentleman at The Grape & Compass who first 'buys' Ada
CAROLINE LEES, John's wife
AGNES, John & Caroline's daughter
Cousin Silas, a weaver
Cousin Meg, Silas's wife
Ham, Silas's older son
Shem, Silas's younger son
MERCY CHANT, a freed slave
Dr John Ferriar, successor to Dr Charles White
James Lees, Agnes's younger brother

Zachary's Grandfather
Zachary's Mother
Lemon Nathan, patriarch of the 14 families
Aaron Jacob, of the 14 families
Sarah Nathan, Lemon's wife
Benjamin Halsinger, son of Reuben, later works at Heywood's Bank
Reuben Halsinger, a financier
Leah Halsinger, Reuben's wife
Abner Halsinger, Benjamin's younger brother
Rachel Nathan, later Halsinger, Benjamin's wife, a painter
Isaac Franks, of the 14 families
Abraham Cohen, of the 14 families
Rebecca Jacob, Aaron's wife
Philip Jacob, Aaron's son, later a tailor
Henry Isaacs, of the 14 families
Jairus & Uriah, Henry's sons
Wolf Polack, a pawnbroker
Solomon Simon, a pharmacist
Hamilton Levi, a member of Manchester's Jewish community
Rachelle, a Huguenot child
Samuel Oldknow, an entrepreneur
Roger Bradshaw, a cotton merchant
John Smith, a textiles manufacturer
Laurence Peel, son of Sir Robert 'Parsley' Peel
Oberleutnant Kurt Frankenburg, Zeppelin pilot
Julie Carter, 8 years old, witness of the airship
Adrian Carter, Julie's younger brother
Police Constable, Rawtenstall on night of the airship raid
J.H. Whipp, Manager of Grime Bridge Colliery
William Herschel, the astronomer & musician
Will Yardley, stable boy
Red-faced Passenger on Mail Coach
Red-faced Passenger's wife
Red-faced Passenger's son
Widow on Mail Coach
Widow's niece

Fashionable Blade on Mail Coach
Squire Ned, a highwayman
Mark Collier, a curate
Matthew Collier, Mark's father
Luke Collier, Mark's brother
John Collier, aka 'Tim Bobbin', Mark's brother
Rev. Thomas Beeley, St Michael's Church, Flixton
Sir William Allen, Davyhulme Hall
Joel Rowe, Phoebe's father
Roy, Phoebe's sweetheart, later a soldier
Courtenay Allen, son of Sir William
Lady Agatha Allen, Courtenay's mother
Ghostly Figure on Nico Ditch (premonition of Lily Shilling)
John Dalton, the scientist
Sir Robert Hibbert III, Chair of West India Company
William Grant, a factory owner
Daniel Grant, William's twin brother
Brother Gottfried, organist at Fairfield
Brother Mallalieu, Fairfield
Brother Radley, Fairfield
Brother Ignatius Hindley, Fairfield
Brother Joshua Warren, Fairfield
Sister Sarah Mellor, Fairfield
Married Woman Hannah Kenyon, Fairfield
Married Woman Hindley, Fairfield
Mr Ponsonby, an actor
Miss Appleby, an actress
Billy Robinson, Zachary & Fanny's son, a soldier, later a postman
Lt Wainwright, second at duel
Christopher Hopwell, a solicitor
William Roscoe, a botanist
Constable, on Byrom Street
Robert 'Bobby' Peel, Laurence's youngest brother
John Hibbert, plantation owner
Henry Chant, Mercy's father
Abigail Chant, Mercy's mother

Charity Harry, freed slave
Jane Harry, Charity's daughter
Helen Harry, Charity's daughter
Margaret Harry, Mercy's classmate
Anne Hibbert, Thomas Hibbert's sister-in-law
Rev Charles Westcott, Reddish Church
Miss Thrynne, governess
Miss Farley, teacher
Hélène Robidoux, a Huguenot
Monsieur Robidoux, Hélène's husband
Charles Maurice, Duc de Talleyrand-Perigord, an ambassador
Susannah Collins, Zachary & Fanny's daughter
Richard & Paul Collins, the twins
Ginny Collins, Susannah's sister
Lemuel Collins, Zachary & Fanny's second son
Lavinia Collins, Zachary & Fanny's eldest child
Jemma Collins, a baby

The following are mentioned by name:

[Sir Oswald Mosley, Baronet]
[S & N Buck, engravers]
[Old Ned, a horse]
[Thomas Hibbert, Virginia plantation owner]
[Robert Hibbert, Thomas's brother]
[Edwin Stone's children]
[Older Weavers working for Edwin]
[James Hargreaves, inventor]
[Richard Arkwright, inventor]
[Samuel Crompton, inventor]
[John Kay, inventor of fly shuttle]
[Edwin Stone's father]
[Edwin Stone's grandfather]
[King George III]
[Queen Charlotte]

[Sir James Darcy Lever, Sir Ashton's father]
[Joseph Bancroft, industrialist]
[Putrescents, Manchester Infirmary]
[The Inner Circle of Archers Company]
[Captain Cook]
[Henry VIII]
[George II]
[Prince Frederick]
[John Beswick, Dr White's neighbour in Sale]
[Attenders at Beswick's Funeral]
[Hannah Beswick, John's sister]
[Baronet Warburton]
[Bishop Spangenberg, founder of Moravians]
[Charles Wesley]
[George Whitfield, early dissenter]
[Countess of Huntingdon, patroness of non-conformists]
[Moravians in Lightcliffe]
[Moravians in Fulneck]
[Count Zindendorf of Saxony, early protector of Moravians]
[James Taylor, Moravian]
[John Ward, Moravian]
[Mrs Greaves, Droylsden landowner]
[St Paul]
[Alexander Fordyce, a fraudulent banker]
[Squatters in the Hulks]
[Duke of Bridgewater, Earl of Ellesmere]
[Nancy, a kitchen maid, Lever's Row]
[Drunkards in The Bull's Head]
[Daniel Defoe]
[Bedlam Boys]
[Jays, toms, dollymops, molls during earthquake]
[Hellfire preacher]
[Isabella Beck, a philanthropist]
[Mrs H, former inmate of New Bailey Prison]
[Gatekeeper of House of Correction]
[Castor & Pollux, a pair of Cleveland Bays]
[Joiner boarding up windows]
[Nurses in Infirmary]
[William Cullen, Edinburgh physician]
[Young Couple walking]
[Driver of ox cart]

[Church & Chapelgoers on morning after earthquake]
[Priests, vicars, canons, curates]
[Sir Edward Knatchbull MP]
[Balloon Seller]
[Market Traders, Acresfield]
[Shadowy Figures, Ackers Gate]
[Matron, House of Correction]
[Apothecary, House of Correction]
[Boys in House of Correction]
[Board of Governors, House of Correction]
[Crowds on Scotland Bridge]
[Carter on Red Bank]
[Shopkeepers, Market Cross]
[Merchants from the Exchange]
[Pig & piglets, Apple Market]
[Woman emptying slops, The Bull's Head]
[Eve]
[Prometheus]
[Columbus]
[William Harvey]
[James Watt]
[Ballad Singers]
[Overseer's Assistants]
[Cotton Spinners, Mill St]
[Piecers, Arkwright's Mill]
[Dwellers in new Hulks]
[Children in Fogg's Yard]
[Sparks, landlord of Fogg's Yard]
[Maypole Dancers]
[Tug o' War teams]
[Edward Byrom, Master Surveyor]
[John Webster, neighbour of the Reynolds, Strangeways Hall]
[Dulcibella, a doll]
[Crowds at Kersal Moor]
[Lewis Wyatt, architect Heaton Park]
[James Wyatt, Lewis's uncle, architect Heaton Hall]
[Romany fortune tellers]
[Neapolitan knife grinders]
[Venetian glass blowers]
[Arabian perfumiers]
[Turkish rug makers]

[French hurdy gurdy players]
[Dutch gin distillers]
[Ladies with lorgnettes]
[Sir John Parker Mosley]
[Rev. Sir Nicholas Mosley]
[Rev. Cornelius Bayley]
[Dr Johnson]
[Robert Rollo, Jacobite]
[Soldiers in The Britons' Protection]
[Lord Stanley]
[Earl of Wilton]
[Subalterns in Manchester Volunteers]
[Major-General David Lindsay, 72nd Foot]
[William Shakespeare]
[Carlton Whiteley's Grandfather]
[Edward Gadd, Cheadle watchmaker]
[Louis Breguet, watchmaker]
[Mrs Carroll, sentimental playwright]
[Joseph Addison]
[Lady Mary Clowes]
[Erasmus]
[Hippocrates]
[Audiences for Henry VI, part 2]
[Overseer, Arkwright's Mill]
[Mrs Briggs, Ada's mother]
[Ada's baby brother]
[Estate Workers, for Lord Mosley]
[Earl's cousin]
[Constable, who arrests Mr Briggs]
[Robert Tinker, Grape & Compass]
[Blacksmith, Tinker's Hollow]
[Gentlemen who 'buy' Ada]
[Barrow boys, Apple Market]
[Crowds at Haworth Gardens]
[Queues of wagons at Turnpike Tolls]
[James Lees, John's father]
[Sir Robert 'Parsley' Peel]
[Caroline's father]
[Children in Snipe Mine]
[Board of Dukinfield Mine]
[Caroline's brothers & sisters]

[Nicholas Culpepper]
[George Hibbert, pro-slavery campaigner]
[George Hibbert's parents & grandparents]
[Congregation listening to Thomas Clarkson]
[Pieter Camper]
[Voltaire]
[Lord William Byron, uncle of poet]
[Julius Agricola]
[Sir Thomas Pilkington, Lord of Manor of Bury]
[Richard III]
[Single Brethren & Sisters at Fairfield]
[Miners at Hope Pit]
[Crowds at John Wesley's open air service]
[Mr Johnson, early pioneer of steam-powered mills]
[Inhabitants of Shakerley]
[Industrial labourers in Manchester]
[Babes in arms]
[Small children]
[Expectant mothers] – all migrants to Manchester
[Anxious fathers]   at Samjam Fair
[Ailing grandparents]
[Mayor of Altrincham]
[Bonnie Prince Charlie]
[Jacobite Army]
[Wagons on Crossford Bridge]
[Inhabitants of Stretford]
[Maria Theresa, Holy Roman Empress]
[Emperor Charles V]
[Emperor Joseph]
[Samson Wertheimer, Chief Rabbi of Eisenstadt]
[Prince Eugène of Savoy]
[Herr Mayer Amschell Rothschild]
[Simon Wolf Oppenheimer]
[Abraham Benjamin of Antwerp]
[Teveli Schiff, Chief Rabbi of Aldgate]
[Toll Keeper on Dean's Gate]
[Hawkers & traders, St Peter's Field]
[Fire Eaters, acrobats, jugglers, mountebanks]
[Rachelle's Huguenot parents]
[Marching Band at Balloon Flight]
[Smokey, a cat]

[Italian 'hokey-pokey' sellers]
[Bargemen on Irwell]
[Crowds in Haworth Gardens]
[Guy Fawkers]
[Robert Catesby]
[Earl of Egerton]
[Antonie van Leeuwenhoek]
[Bartolomeo de Gusmão, Jesuit priest]
[Thomas Hobbes, author]
[Abraham Bosse, artist]
[John Clayton, Samuel Oldknow's grandfather]
[Peter Drinkwater, Piccadilly Mill]
[Aulay Macauley, tobacconist]
[Jenny Drinkwater, Samuel Oldknow's wife]
[Abraham Crompton, industrialist]
[Thomas Highs, reed maker]
[Lord Bath]
[Angela Carter, friend of Mercy]
[Angela's teacher]
[Colonel Craven Hoyle]
[Staff & guests, Bridge End Hotel]
[Cockham Farmer & wife]
[11 year old butcher's boy, Callendar Street]
[King George V]
[George Frederick Handel]
[Joseph Haydn]
[Audience at music concert, Angel Meadow]
[Crowds at Circus]
[Congregation at Methodists' Central Hall]
[Minister]
[Colonel Daulby, Manchester Volunteers]
[Company Chaplain]
[Driver of Mail Coach]
[Post Horn Blower]
[Crowds at London Road]
[Nicholas Hawksmoor, architect]
[Andrew Cruikshank, surgeon]
[Mrs Higgins, Squire Ned's wife]
[Rev. Humphrey Owen, St Michael's Church]
[Mrs Collier, a lacemaker]
[Church Warden, St Michael's Church]

[Rev. Timothy Lowton, St Michael's Church]
[Albert Gredle, Flixton landowner]
[Roger de Poitou, earliest landowner, Urmston]
[Orme Fitz-Seward, landowner]
[Emma Fitz-Seward, Albert Gredle's wife]
[Capt John Parker, a minute man]
[Rushbearers]
[Exhausted Maid at Davyhulme Hall]
[Patriots at Lexington]
[Christmas Revellers at Davyhulme Hall]
[General Sir William Howe, New England Campaign]
[Lt. Col James Abercrombie, Cheshire Regiment]
[George Washington's rag-tag army]
[Heron, Nico Ditch]
[Courtenay Allen's Bride, Newcroft Hall]
[Wedding Guests for Fanny & Zachary]
[Crowds for opening of Fairfield]
[John Locke]
[René Descartes]
[Earl of Shaftesbury]
[Audience for John Dalton's Lecture]
[Mrs Crinkle, Matthew's housekeeper]
[Herr Franklin, silversmith]
[Herr Mendelson, watchmaker]
[Herr Grumpel, surgeon]
[Herr Freeman, painter of miniatures]
[Girl on Brazenose St with spinning top]
[Bonham's Auctioneers]
[Mr Wheeler, Manchester Chronicle]
[Nightwatchman, Fairfield]
William Congreve]
[Thomas Sheridan]
[Constable at Court Leet]
[Duc d'Angoulême]
[Robespierre]
[Earl of Derby]
[Richard Challoner, Equerry]
[Lord Hawkesworth]
[Special Constables, Kersal Moor]
[Soldiers firing gun salute for John Philips' funeral]
[Eugène Beuret, philosopher]

[Messrs Carey, Currie & Denly, members of Roscoe Circle]
[Workers in Peel's Factory]
[William Yates, landlord]
[William Haworth, Laurence's Uncle]
[Nancy Peel, Laurence's sister]
[Epithemeus]
[Pandora]
[Clerk of the Court Leet]
Prison Officer]
Constable at Court Leet]
[Caged bird]
[Jean-Honoré Fragonard, artist]
[Ovid]
[Mrs Westcott, Reverend Westcott's wife]
[Congregation at Reddish Church]
[Fanny Burney]
[Samuel Richardson]
[Oliver Goldsmith]
[Robert Southey]
[Percy Bysshe Shelley]
[King Louis XVI]
[Marie Antoinette]
[Napoleon Bonaparte]
[Danton]
[Mr William Knowles, victualler, The Crown & Kettle]
[Crowds at Michaelmas Fair]
[Actors in Mr Whiteley's Company]
[Naomi, daughter of Benjamin & Rachel]
[Rioters on Shude Hill]
[Soldiers on Shude Hill]
[Joseph Hanson's father]

Acknowledgements
(for *Ornaments of Grace* as a whole)

Writing is usually considered to be a solitary practice, but I have always found the act of creativity to be a collaborative one, and that has again been true for me in putting together the sequence of novels which comprise *Ornaments of Grace*. I have been fortunate to have been supported by so many people along the way, and I would like to take this opportunity of thanking them all, with apologies for any I may have unwittingly omitted.

First of all I would like to thank Ian Hopkinson, Larysa Bolton, Tony Lees and other staff members of Manchester's Central Reference Library, who could not have been more helpful and encouraging. That is where the original spark for the novels was lit and it has been such a treasure trove of fascinating information ever since. I would like to thank Jane Parry, the Neighbourhood Engagement & Delivery Officer for the Archives & Local History Dept of Manchester Library Services for her support in enabling me to use individual reproductions of the remarkable Manchester Murals by Ford Madox Brown, which can be viewed in the Great Hall of Manchester Town Hall. They are exceptional images and I recommend you going to see them if you are ever in the vicinity. I would also like to thank the staff of other libraries and museums in Manchester, namely the John Rylands Library, Manchester University Library, the Manchester Museum, the People's History Museum and also Salford's Working Class Movement Library, where Lynette Cawthra was especially helpful, as was Aude Nguyen Duc at The Manchester Literary & Philosophical Society, the much-loved Lit& Phil, the first and oldest such society anywhere in the world, 238 years young and still going strong.

In addition to these wonderful institutions, I have many individuals to thank also. Barbara Derbyshire from the Moravian Settlement in Fairfield has been particularly patient and generous with her time in telling me so much of the community's inspiring history. No less inspiring has been Lauren Murphy, founder of the Bradford Pit Project, which is a most moving collection of anecdotes, memories, reminiscences, artefacts and original art works dedicated to the lives of people connected with Bradford Colliery. You can find out more about their work at: www.bradfordpit.com. Martin Gittins freely shared some of his encyclopaedic knowledge of the part the River Irwell has played in Manchester's story, for which I have been especially grateful.

I should also like to thank John and Anne Horne for insights into historical medical practice; their daughter, Ella, for inducting me into the mysteries of chemical titration, which, if I have subsequently got it wrong, is my fault not hers; Tony Smith for his deep first hand understanding of spinning and weaving; Sarah Lawrie for inducting me so enthusiastically into the Manchester music scene of the 1980s, which happened just after I left the city so I missed it; Sylvia Tiffin for her previous research into Manchester's lost theatres, and Brian Hesketh for his specialist knowledge in a range of such diverse topics as hot air balloons, how to make a crystal radio set, old maps, the intricacies of a police constable's notebook and preparing reports for a coroner's inquest.

Throughout this intensive period of writing and research, I have been greatly buoyed up by the keen support and interest of many friends, most notably Theresa Beattie, Laïla Diallo, Viv Gordon, Phil King, Rowena Price, Gavin Stride, Chris Waters, and Irene Willis. Thank you to you all. In addition, Sue & Rob Yockney have been extraordinarily helpful in more ways than I can mention. Their advice on so many matters, both artistic and practical, has been beyond measure.

A number of individuals have very kindly – and bravely – offered to read early drafts of the novels: Bill Bailey, Rachel Burn, Lucy Cash, Chris & Julie Phillips. Their responses have been positive, constructive, illuminating and encouraging, particularly when highlighting those passages which needed closer attention from me, which I have tried my best to address. Thank you.

I would also like to pay a special tribute to my friend Andrew Pastor, who has endured months and months of fortnightly coffee sessions during which he has listened so keenly and with such forbearance to the various difficulties I may have been experiencing at the time. He invariably came up with the perfect comment or idea, which then enabled me to see more clearly a way out of whatever tangle I happened to have found myself in. He also suggested several avenues of further research I might undertake to navigate towards the next bend in one of the three rivers, all of which have been just what were needed. These books could not have finally seen the light of day without his irreplaceable input.

Finally I would like to thank my wife, Amanda, for her endless patience, encouragement and love. These books are dedicated to her and to our son, Tim.

Biography

Chris grew up in Manchester and currently lives in West Dorset, after brief periods in Nottinghamshire, Devon and Brighton. Over the years he has managed to reinvent himself several times – from florist's delivery van driver to Punch & Judy man, drama teacher, theatre director, community arts co-ordinator, creative producer, to his recent role as writer and dramaturg for choreographers and dance companies.

Between 2003 and 2009 Chris was Director of Dance and Theatre for *Take Art*, the arts development agency for Somerset, and between 2009 and 2013 he enjoyed two stints as Creative Producer with South East Dance leading on their Associate Artists programme, followed by a year similarly supporting South Asian dance artists for *Akademi* in London. From 2011 to 2017 he was Creative Producer for the Bonnie Bird Choreography Fund.

Chris has worked for many years as a writer and theatre director, most notably with New Perspectives in Nottinghamshire and Farnham Maltings in Surrey under the artistic direction of Gavin Stride, with whom Chris has been a frequent collaborator.

Directing credits include: three Community Plays for the Colway Theatre Trust – *The Western Women* (co-director with Ann Jellicoe), *Crackling Angels* (co-director with Jon Oram), and *The King's Shilling*; for New Perspectives – *It's A Wonderful Life* (co-director with Gavin Stride), *The Railway Children* (both adapted by Mary Elliott Nelson); for Farnham Maltings – *The Titfield Thunderbolt, Miracle on 34th Street* and *How To Build A Rocket* (all co-directed with Gavin Stride); for Oxfordshire Touring Theatre Company – *Bowled A Googly* by Kevin Dyer; for Flax 303 – *The Rain Has Voices* by Shiona Morton, and for Strike A Light *I Am Joan* and *Prescribed*, both written by Viv Gordon and co-directed with Tom Roden, and *The Book of Jo* as dramaturg.

Theatre writing credits include: *Firestarter, Trying To Get Back Home, Heroes* – a trilogy of plays for young people in partnership with Nottinghamshire & Northamptonshire Fire Services; *You Are Harry Kipper & I Claim My Five Pounds, It's Not Just The Jewels, Bogus* and *One of Us* (the last co-written with Gavin Stride) all for New Perspectives; *The Birdman* for Blunderbus; for Farnham Maltings *How To Build A Rocket* (as assistant to Gavin Stride), and *Time to Remember* (an outdoor commemoration of the centenary of the first ever Two Minutes Silence); *When King Gogo Met The Chameleon* and *Africarmen* for Tavaziva Dance, and most recently *All the Ghosts Walk with Us* (conceived and performed with Laïla Diallo and Phil King) for ICIA, Bath University and Bristol Old Vic Ferment Festival, (2016-17); *Posting to Iraq* (performed by Sarah Lawrie with music by Tom Johnson for the inaugural Women & War Festival in London 2016), and *Tree House* (with music by Sarah Moody, which toured southern England in autumn 2016). In 2018 Chris was commissioned to write the text for *In Our Time*, a film to celebrate the 40th Anniversary of the opening of The Brewhouse Theatre in Taunton, Somerset.

Between 2016 and 2019 Chris collaborated with fellow poet Chris Waters and Jazz saxophonist Rob Yockney to develop two touring programmes of poetry, music, photography and film: *Home Movies* and *Que Pasa?*

Chris regularly works with choreographers and dance artists, offering dramaturgical support and business advice. These have included among others: Alex Whitley, All Play, Ankur Bahl, Antonia Grove, Anusha Subramanyam, Archana Ballal, Ballet Boyz, Ben Duke, Ben Wright, Charlie Morrissey,

Crystal Zillwood, Darkin Ensemble, Divya Kasturi, Dog Kennel Hill, f.a.b. the detonators, Fionn Barr Factory, Heather Walrond, Hetain Patel, Influx, Jane Mason, Joan Clevillé, Kali Chandrasegaram, Kamala Devam, Karla Shacklock, Khavita Kaur, Laïla Diallo, Lîla Dance, Lisa May Thomas, Liz Lea, Lost Dog, Lucy Cash, Luke Brown, Marisa Zanotti, Mark Bruce, Mean Feet Dance, Nicola Conibère, Niki McCretton, Nilima Devi, Pretty Good Girl, Probe, Rachael Mossom, Richard Chappell, Rosemary Lee, Sadhana Dance, Seeta Patel, Shane Shambhu, Shobana Jeyasingh, Showmi Das, State of Emergency, Stop Gap, Subathra Subramaniam, Tavaziva Dance, Tom Sapsford, Theo Clinkard, Urja Desai Thakore, Vidya Thirunarayan, Viv Gordon, Yael Flexer, Yorke Dance Project (including the Cohan Collective) and Zoielogic.

Chris is married to Amanda Fogg, a former dance practitioner working principally with people with Parkinson's.

Printed in Great Britain
by Amazon